James De Mille

An open Question

A Novel

James De Mille

An open Question
A Novel

ISBN/EAN: 9783743356931

Manufactured in Europe, USA, Canada, Australia, Japa

Cover: Foto ©Andreas Hilbeck / pixelio.de

Manufactured and distributed by brebook publishing software (www.brebook.com)

James De Mille

An open Question

A NOVEL.

BY

JAMES DE MILLE,

AUTHOR OF

"THE LADY OF THE ICE," "THE AMERICAN BARON," ETC., ETC.

WITH ILLUSTRATIONS BY ALFRED FREDERICKS.

NEW YORK:
D. APPLETON AND COMPANY,
549 & 551 BROADWAY.
1873.

CONTENTS.

AN OPEN QUESTION.

CHAPTER I.

THE MANUSCRIPT OF THE MONK ALOYSIUS.

DR. BASIL BLAKE had plain but comfortable apartments in Paris, on the third story, overlooking the busy Rue St. Honoré. A balcony ran in front of his windows, upon which he could step out, whenever he felt inclined, to watch the crowds in the street below. On the present occasion, however, the balcony was deserted, the windows were closed, and Dr. Blake was seated in an arm-chair, with a friend opposite in another. It was now midnight, but, late as it was, this friend had only come in a few minutes before ; and, by the attitude, the actions, and the words of both, it was evident that they were intending to make a night of it. Bottles, decanters, glasses, cigars, pipes, and tobacco, lay or stood upon the table; and Dr. Blake was even now offering a glass of Burgundy to his visitor.

Dr. Basil Blake was a young man, with a frank face, clear eyes, open and pleasing expression. His friend was a fellow-physician —Dr. Phelim O'Rourke—with whom Blake had become acquainted in the course of his studies in Paris, and who, in every respect, presented a totally different aspect from his own. He was much older, being apparently between forty and fifty years of age. His frame showed great muscular strength and powers of endurance. His hair was curling and sprinkled with gray. His nose was straight and thin. He wore a heavy beard and mustache, which was not so gray as his hair, but dark, shaggy, and somewhat neg-

lected. His eyes were small, dark, keen, and penetrating.

"I wouldn't have bothered yees at this onsaisonable hour," said O'Rourke, who spoke with a slight Irish accent, "but the disclosures that I have to make require perfect freedom from interruption, and ye see ye're all the time with yer frind Hellmuth through the day, and so I have to contint mysilf with the night, ayvin if I were not busy mysilf all through the day. But the fact is, the matther is one of the most imminse importance, aud so ye'll see yersilf as soon as ye're infarrumed of what I have to tell.' Ye know I've alriddy mintioned, in a casual way, that my secret concerruns money. Yis, money! gold! trisure!—and trisure, too, beyond all calculation. Basil Blake, me boy! d'ye want to be as rich as an imperor ? Do ye want to have a rivinue shuparior to Rothschild's ? Have ye ivir a wish to sittle yersilf for life ? Answer me that, will ye ? "

Saying this, O'Rourke slapped the palm of his hand emphatically upon the table, and fixed his small, piercing black eyes intently upon Blake.

"Oh, by Jove !" said Blake, with a laugh, " you're going too far, you know. Don't exaggerate, old fellow—it isn't necessary, I assure you. Money, by Jove ! I'd like to see the fellow that needs it more than I do. I'm hard up. You know that, don't you ? Don't I owe you five pounds—which, by-the-way, old chap, I shall be able to—"

"Tare an ages !" interrupted O'Rourke, " don't be afther talking about such a paltry matther as five pounds. By the powers, but I ixpict, if I can only injuce ye to give me a lift in my interprise, that before long ye'll look upon five pounds as no more than five pince, so ye will, and there ye have it."

"Go ahead, then, old fellow; for, by Jove! do you know, you make me wild with curiosity by all this mixture of illimitable treasure and impenetrable mystery."

"Mind, me boy," said O'Rourke, "I ask nothing of ye—only yer hilp."

"And that I'll give, you may be sure. As for any thing else, I'm afraid you can't get it —not money, at any rate; blood out of a stone, you know — that's about it with me."

O'Rourke bent his head forward, and once more fixed his keen gaze upon the frank, honest eyes of Blake.

"It's in Rome—that it is," said he.

"Rome?" said Blake.

"Yis—the trisure—"

"Rome? ah! Well—it's very convenient. I was afraid it would involve a voyage to California. Rome—well, that's a good beginning at any rate."

"It is — it's mighty convanient," said O'Rourke. "Well, ye know, I've been in Rome over and over, and know it like me native town. I've been there sometimes on professional jutics, sometimes on archayological interprises, and sometimes on occasion of any shupriminint ayclisiastical ayvint. I may mintion also that I've got a rilative living there—he's dead now—but that's nothing; he was second cousin to me first wife, and, of course, in a forryn country, such a near relationship as that brought us very close togither, and I attindid him profissionally, free of charge, on his dying-bed. It was from this rilative—Malachi McFee, by name—that I obtained the inforrumation that I'm going to convey to you. The poor divvle was a monk in the monastery of San Antonio. I saw a good deal of him, off and on; and one day he had a fall in the vaults of the monastery—he had a very bad conchusion; mortification set in, gangrane, and so forruth—so he died, poor divvle. It was on the death-bed of poor Malachi that I heard that same; and ye'll understand from that what credibility there is in the story, for a man on his death-bed wouldn't be afther speakin' any thing but the truth, unless he could get some real future binifit of some sort out of it, pecuniarily, afther he was dead, or before, but that's neither here nor there."

O'Rourke paused here, and looked sharply at Blake.

"D'ye care to hear it now?" said he.

"Care to hear it? of course. Don't you see that I'm all ears?"

"Very well," said O'Rourke, "so here goes."

As he spoke, the deep toll of a neighboring bell sounded out as it began to strike the hour of midnight. O'Rourke paused again, and listened silently to the solemn sound, as one after the other the twelve strokes rang deeply out upon the still night air, and, even after the full number had sounded, he sat as though listening for more. At length he drew a long breath, which sounded like a deep sigh.

"I don't know how it is," said he, "but there's nothing in all the wide wurruld that affects me like the toll of a bell at midnight. I moind me, it was in such a night as this, and the bell was tolling just this way, when poor Malachi died. Well—well—he's dead and gone. *Requiescat in pace—*

"That same Malachi," continued O'Rourke, "was, as I said, a monk in the monastery of San Antonio, at Rome. Have ye iver been in Rome? No? Thin there's no use for me to tell you the situation of the monastery, as ye wouldn't understand. It's enough to say that Malachi was a monk there. Now, ye must know that San Antonio, like many other monasteries, has a divvle of a lot of old manuscripts in the library—some copies of classics, some thaological, and some original—the work of the monks. This Malachi was one of the most crudite and profound scholars that I iver saw. He had all thim old manuscripts at his fingers' ends—ivery one of thim. Now, what I have to tell you refers to one of those manuscripts, that was hauled forth by poor Malachi out of a forgotten chist, and studied by him till he began to think there was in it the rivilation of some schoopindous secret. It was written in Latin, of course. Ye know Latin, I suppose—a little. Yis—yis. I know what the ordinary iducation amounts to, but could ye read a manuscript written in Latin, in a crabbed hand, full of contractions and corrections? I don't think it. I have that manuscript, and I've read it; and I know that the number of min who could take up that and read it as it stands is not Lagion by any means. I haven't the manuscript here. It's home, with my valuables. It isn't a thing

I'd carry about, but I've got the substance of it in me mind. It's a modern manuscript, bound up like a book, not much larger than what we call juodecimo size, of about a hundred pages of tho writing I've mintioned. Now, tho manuscript purported to have been written in tho year sixteen hundred and tin, and by all appearances had niver been touched by any hand since it lift the author's, till poor Malachi drew it out of tho chist, but lay there among piles of others, neglictid and unknown. It purported to be an account of certain advintures and discoveries of one Aloysius, a monk of San Antonio, some twinty years before, which he had committed to writing, and deposited in the library of tho monastery, so as to transmit to tho future some memorial of things that he did not wish to have altogither forgotten. Me cousin Malachi studied it all over and over, and he gave me tho book on his death-bed, and told me tho whole contints juring my attindince there before I had iver read a line meself. Now I'll just tell you tho story of tho monk Aloysius, fust of all, as it was told me by me cousin Malachi, and as I read it meself, and then ye'll begin to comprehind what I'm driving at.

"Well, now, this Aloysius was a monk of San Antonio, as I said. He was a quiet, sober, religious, contintid soul, according to his own showing; a good, average Christian monk, with all his wants confined to his own cloisthers, and no desires beyant. Now underneath the monastery there were thin, and there are still at this day, vast and ixtinsive vaults, stritching underneath tho whole idifice, and, in some places, they are two stories deep. Here, in these places, they seem cut out of some rocky substratum — tho rock is soft sandstone, and must have been worked easy enough—and, moreover, it was the opinion of me cousin Malachi, who was, poor fellow, as I alriddy said, a divvle of an archayologist, that these double-storied excavations were tho work of the ancient Romans. Now it is with the mintion of these vaults that tho manuscript of Aloysius begins.

"It seems that he was sint down to the lowermost vaults one day, in company with another monk—Onofrio by name—to remove some wine-casks, or overhaul thim, or something, whin, juring tho course of their labors, they reached the rock forming the extreme west end of tho vaults; and here, to the surprise of both, they saw an archway, which had been walled up so as to prevint any passing through. The sight excited both of thim immincely, and they stopped short in their work, and engaged in some prolonged argumintation as to tho probable use of such a passage-way. They differred in their opinions: Aloysius holding that it once was a subterranean passage-way to tho outside of tho city, made in former ages, to bo used in case of need; while Onofrio contindied that it was nothing more than a recess, closed up because it was no longer needed; or because, perhaps, some one may have formerly been buried there. This discussion excited thim both to such a degree that at lingth nothing would satisfy aither of thim but an examination. Onofrio was at first opposed to this, from tho belief that some one had been buried there, and he shrank from the discovery of some possible horror committed in the course of those maydiayval ages, when min were burnt alive, or buried alive, to any ixtint, and all ad majorem Dei gloriam. It was tho way of tho worruld in those ages, and a way that Onofrio did not wish to be reminded of.

"Well, at length they decided to examine it at once. Aloysius was the one who did tho business. They had a bit of a crowbar with thim, which they had brought down to move the bar'ls, and with this he wint at the wall. The stones were small, and were mixed with brick; the mortar had become rotten and disintegrated with the damp of cinterries; and so it was aisy enough work for a brisk young lad, like Aloysius seems to have been thin. They had a couple of good-sized lamps with them all the time, to give light for their work in the vaults, ye know; and so, as there was plinty of oil in thim, they had plinty of leisure for their work. Well, Aloysius says that he worked away, and at last had a hole made big enough to see through. The wall had not been more than six inches thick, and crumbling at that; and, whin this hole was made, the rest followed quick enough, I'll be bound. Well, tho ind of it all was, that tho wall at lingth lay there, a heap of rubbish, at their feet; and there was tho open archway full before thim, inviting thim to inter."

O'Rourke now poured out a glass of wine for himself, and looked inquiringly at Blake, to see how he felt. One look was enough to show him that Blake was deeply interested, and was waiting very anxiously for the remainder of the story. O'Rourke smacked his lips approvingly, set down the empty glass upon the table, and continued:

"Onofrio shrank back. Aloysius sprang through. Thin Onofrio followed, somewhat timidly. Both of thim held their lights before thim, to see the size of the interior. It was a passage-way about four feet wide and six feet high, but the length of it they were unable to see. Walking forward a few paces, they still found no ind visible as yet. Suddenly Aloysius saw something which excited his attintion. It was a slab of marble about six feet long and a foot in width, fustened in the side of the passage-way. There were letters on it. Beyond this he saw others, and, as he stared around in amazement, he saw that these slabs were arranged on both sides, reaching from the floor to the top of the passage, one above another, three deep, and in some places four. Upon this he turned to his companion, and said: 'You're right, Onofrio. This is some ancient burial-place of the monks of San Antonio.' Onofrio said nothing, but, holding his lamp eagerly forward, tried to make out an inscription that was cut on the marble slab. The slab was much discolored, but the lettering was quite visible. These letters, however, were apparently a mixture of different characters; for, though he could make out here and there one, yet others occurred in the midst of them with which he was not familiar. The Latin word IN could be made out, and, on another slab, he made out IN PACE. On all the slabs there was a peculiar monogram which was unintilligible to them.

"'These were all good Christians,' said Onofrio; 'for no others would have "_in pace_" over their graves.'

"'They must have lived long ago,' said Aloysius. 'And they had a fashion of writing that is different from ours.'

"They walked on some distance farther. The graves continued. They were very much amazed, and, in fact, quite schupefied at the imminse number which they passed, all cut in the walls of this vault, all covered over with marble slabs, the same kind of inscriptions. At length, Aloysius, who was going first, uttered a cry; and Onofrio, who had paused to try and make out an inscription, hurried up. He found Aloysius at a place where their passage-way was crossed by another passage-way, which was like it in every respict—the same niches on the walls, the same marble slabs, the same kind of inscriptions. In addition to this they saw that

their own passage-way still ran on, and was lost in the darkness. They both saw that it was far more ixtinsive than they had imagined.

"'You were right,' said Onofrio, 'such a long passage as this must be more than a burial-place.'

"'Be the powers, thin,' cries Aloysius, 'we're both right, for it is a burial-place, and if it don't go all the way out of the city, then I'm a haythen.'

"Well, they walked on some distance farther, and thin they came to three passage-ways—in all respicts the same—no one could have told any differince—and it was this that made thim stop in this fust ixpidition.

"'Sure to glory,' says Onofrio, 'it's lost we'll be, if we go any farther, for sorra the bit of differ I see betune this passage we're in, and the rest of thim; so don't let us go any farther, but get back as quick as we can, while we know our way.'

"At this Aloysius tried to laugh away his fears, but without success. Onofrio was afraid of being lost—moreover, Onofrio was superstitious—and had got it into his head that the place was no other than the general burying-ground of pagan Rome. He didn't know but that the pagans buried their dead like Christians; he wasn't enough of an archayologist to decipher the inscriptions around him; and he was terrified at the spectacle of so many pagan graves. Besides, in addition to what they had seen, the passages leading away seemed to give ividince, or, at least, indications, of an ixtint that was simply schupindous! So, Onofrio was bint on going back, and there was no hilp for it but for Aloysius to follow. But he swore to himsilf all the same, that he'd go again if he had to do it alone.

"So back they wint, and Onofrio wouldn't hear of stopping till they had got back behind the fust crossing, and then he felt out of danger. So here the two of thim, having nothing ilse to do, rayzhumed their ifforts to decipher the inscriptions. At length Onofrio called to Aloysius. Aloysius went to where he was standing. He saw there a slab cut in letters which were all Roman, without any mixture of those strange characters — Greek, no doubt—that had puzzled thim before—ye know the monks in those days often knew a little Latin—Latin being the language of the Church, and widely used for colloquial purposes even outside of the Church, at least in Rome, by foreigners and pilgrims—and so ye see the two of thim put their heads togither, and made it out. I remimber the whole of it. It wasn't long—it was simple enough—and it told its own story. Let me see."

O'Rourke bent his head, and seemed to be recalling the words of which he spoke.

"Fust, there was a monogram which naither of thim understood. It's this—ye know it well enough."

Stooping forward, O'Rourke dipped his finger in his wineglass, and traced on the mahogany table this monogram:

"Ye know that," said he; "it stands for Christus, being the two Greek initial letters 'Ch' and 'R.' It was marked by the early Christians on their tombs. Ye see, also, it makes the sign of the cross. As for the inscription, it ran this way somehow, as near as I can remimber :

"' In Christo. Pax. Antonino Imperatore, Marius miles sanguinem effudit pro Christo. Dormit in pace.'

"So ye see by that," continued O'Rourke, after a pause, during which he looked with his usual searching glance at Blake, "that the place was full of Christian tombs. Ye've heard of the Roman Catacombs. Well, that's the place where these two were, and didn't know it, for the reason that they niver heard of such a place.

"'Sure to glory!' cried Onofrio. 'It's no pagan burying-ground at all, at all. It's Christian, and we're surrounded by the blissed rilics of martyrs and saints. Oh, but won't the abbot be the proud man this day whin we tell him this!'

"'Tare an ages, man!' cried Aloysius, 'ye won't be afther tellin' him yit; wait till we find out more. Let's come again; we'll bring a bit of a string with us, and unrowl it as we go on, so as not to lose our way.'

"Well, with this agreement they left the Catacombs, got back into the vaults of San Antonio, and, as it was vesper-time, they rowled the bar'ls against the opening so as to hide it, and wint away to rezhume their explorations on the following day."

———

CHAPTER II.

THE CATACOMBS.

"So ye see," continued Dr. O'Rourke, "what sort of a place it was they had stumbled upon. It was the most sacred spot on earth. It was the burial-place of the saints and martyrs that had suffered at the hands of the bloody pagans—a holy place—a place of pilgrimage!"

At this, he crossed himself devoutly, and took a glass of wine.

"Well, the next day the two of thim wint once more, and this time Onofrio was as eager as Aloysius. The manuscript doesn't say what aither of them wished or ixpected to find; it simply states that they were eager, and that they took with thim several balls of string, to unwind so as to keep their course. Well, this time they wint on and came to the place which they had reached on the previous day. They unwound the string as they wint; and, thus letting it out, they passed boldly and confidintly beyant the place where they had turruned back before. Going on, they came to passage afther passage, and there was not a pin's difference between any one of thim and any other. Well, at last they came to a place where there was a cross-passage, and here an excavation had been made, circular in shape, and about twelve feet in diameter. This place had a more cheerful aspict than any thing that they had yet seen, if any thing can be called cheerful in such a place. The walls had been covered with stucco, which still remained; though down about a foot from the floor it had crumbled off. Over the walls they saw pictures which had been made ages before, and still kept their colors. These were all pictures of things as familiar to thim as the streets of Rome. There was Adam and Eve plucking the forbidden fruit; Noah and his ark; Abraham offering up Isaac; Jonah and his whale; and iver so many more of a similar chyaracter. Of course, all this only showed still more clearly that the place was a Christian cinotaph, and it was with something like riverince that they gazed upon these pictures, made by the hands of saints. Well, then they started to go on, whin they suddenly discovered, yawning before them, a wide opening in the flure, or pavemint. It was fower feet wide, and six long. Beneath all was darkness. Aloysius tuk his string and lowered his lamp. About twelve or fifteen feet below he saw a flure like the one where he was standing, and a passage-way like those around him. He also saw slabs with inscriptions. By this he knew that there were ranges of passage-ways filled with tombs immejitly beneath, no doubt as ixtinsive as these upper ones. The sight filled him with schupefaction. This was the limit of their second attimpt. The other passages leading away from what he calls the 'painted chamber,' were narrow and uninvitin'; the lower passage-way, however, was broad and high, and gave promise of leading to a place of shuparior importince. By this time Onofrio was as full of eagerness as Aloysius, and it didn't need any persuasin to injuice him to make a further tower through these vaults on another day. This time they brought with thim, in addition to their lamps and string, a couple of bits of ladders that Aloysius had knocked up for the occasion.

"Well, now came the time of their third exploration. They tuk their ladders, and descinded into the lower passage-way. Down here they found ivery thing just as it had been up above. In one or two places they saw, in side-passages, other openings in the flure, which gave ividence of another story beneath this again, containing, no doubt, the same tombs ranged in the same way. Such an apparently indless ixtint almost overwhelmed them. Well, at last, whin they had span out nearly all their string, they saw before them an opening, wide and dark, into which their passage-way ran. They intered this place.

"Now liston," said O'Rourke, impressively. "This place is described in the manuscript of Aloysius in the most minute manner, just as if he was writing it down for the binifit of posterity. It was a vaulted chamber, like the one which they had found before. The walls were stuccoed and covered with painted pictures — the dove with the olive-branch; the mystic fish, the 'Ichthus,' the letters of whose name are so mysteriously symbolical; and the portrayal of sacred scenes drawn from Holy Writ; all these were on the walls. Now, this chamber was fewer times bigger than the other one.

"You remimber that thus far they had found nothing loose or movable. What may have been in the tombs, of course they could

not see. But here all was different. The very first glance they threw around showed them a great heap of things, piled up high in the far corroner. Onofrio hesitated—for he was always superstitious — but Aloysius bounded forward, and at once began to examine the things.

"Now, Blake, me boy, by the powers but it's me that don't know how to begin to tell you this that they found! Whin I read about this in the manuscript—when I saw it there in black and white—tare an ages!—but I fairly lost me breath. What d'ye think it was, man? What? Why, a trisure incalculable, piled up tin feet high from flure to vaulted ceiling; there was gold, and silver, and gims, and golden urruns, and goblits, and perrils, and rubics, and imeralds; there was jools beyond all price, and tripods, and censers, and statuettes; and oh, sure to glory! but it's meself that'll fairly break down in the attimpt to give you the faintest conciption of a trisure so schupindous; candelabras, and snuffer-trays, and lamps, and lavers, and braziers, and crowns, and coronits, and bracelets, and chains—all of them put down in that manuscript, in black and white, as I said—coolly enumerated by that owld gandher of an Aloysius, who missed his chance thin, as I'll tell you. But there they were, as I'm telling ye, and I'd jist requist ye to let yer fancy play around this description; call up before yer mind's eye the trisure there— the trisure that the worruld has niver seen the like of before nor since, saving only once, whin the gowld of Peru was piled up for Pizarro's greedy eyes by the unfortunate Atahualpa; but no wonder, for what he saw there was no less a thing than the *trisure of the Cæsars!*"

At this, O'Rourke stopped and looked at his companion. Blake by this time showed evidence of the most intense and breathless excitement.

"By the Lord!" he exclaimed, "O'Rourke, what do you mean by all this? It is incredible. It sounds like some madman's dream!"

O'Rourke smiled.

"Wait," said he—"wait till ye hear the whole of the story, and then we'll be able to discuss the probabilities. I'm not done just yit—I'll hurry on. I can't stand the thought of the glories of that unparalleled scene.

"Well, Aloysius was already taking up the things one by one in amazement, whin Onofrio came up. Onofrio gave a cry of wonder, and caught up several small statuettes, but, afther a brief examination, ho threw them back with a gesture and a cry of abhorrence.

"'Come away!' says he—'come away!'

"'What do you mean?' says Aloysius, grabbing up a heap of perrils and diamond jools.

"'They're the divvle's own work, sure enough,' says Onofrio, all of a trimble. 'Sure he's put it all here as a bait for our sowls.'

"'Whist then, Onofrio darlint,' says Aloysius. 'What's the harrum of whipping off a bit of a diamond or imerald for San Antonio?'

"'Oh, sure to glory!' cries Onofrio, 'but we'll be lost and kilt intirely, and we'll niver get home again. Down with thim!' says he. 'Fling them back, Aloysius jool,' says he. 'They're the work, and the trap, and the device of Satan,' says he, 'an' nothin' 'll iver come of it but blue roon to both of us.'

"'Sure, an' how could Satan get in here wid the saints and martyrs, ye ould spalpeen?' says Aloysius.

"At this Onofrio declared that this chamber had no tombs, and was thus ungyarded, so that thereby the powers of Darkness were able to inter and lay their snares—

"'But,' says Aloysius—and oh, but it's the clear head that same had on his shoulders—'how,' says he, 'would Satan,' says he, 'be afther laying his snares down here where no mortal iver comes?'

"'Sure, and that's just it,' says Onofrio; 'didn't he see us comin'—didn't he just throw these things in here for us to grab at thim? Oh, come back, Aloysius darlint!—drop ivery thing—back to the protiction of the saints and martyrs, and out of this!'

"Well, just at this moment several of the gowlden braziers and tripods, which had been loosened on the pile by Aloysius pulling away some of the gowlden candelabra and diamond bracelets from under thim, gave a slide, and fell with a great clatter to the flure. At this Onofrio gave a yell, dropped his lamp, and ran. Aloysius was for the moment frightened almost as much, and followed Onofrio, both of thim with not the least doubt in life but that the Owld Boy was after thim. So they ran, an' they didn't stop till they reached the ladder, when they scrambled up, and pulled the ladder up after thim. They now felt safe,

and waited here awhile to take breath. Now, mind you, Aloysius had been frightened, but there was an imirald bracelet that he'd slipped on his arrum, and a diamond ring that he'd stuck on his finger, and these two remained on as he ran, and when he felt himself safe he didn't feel inclined to throw thim away. But he could not keep thim concealed from Onofrio, who detected thim by the flash of the gims that outshone the lamp and dazzled him. Upon this he set up a great outcry that they were lost, and would niver see the wurruld again, and implored Aloysius to tear the Satanic traps off, and throw them behind him. But Aloysius refused.

"'Whist,' says he, 'do ye know where ye are?' says he. 'Arn't these the saints and martyrs? Would they allow any blackgyard imp to show as much as the tip of his tail? Not they. Niver.' But Onofrio wouldn't be consoled at all, at all, and all the way back wint on lamenting that one or the other would have to pay dear for stealing Satan's jools. So at last they got back safe into the vaults of the monastery, and thin—partly to console Onofrio, and partly out of a ginirous filial sintimint and loyal regyard to San Antonio and his monastery—Aloysius towld Onofrio that it would be best to let the abbot know; and this consoled Onofrio, for he saw that he could get the abbot's help against Satan. And so the two of thim, without any more delay, walked off and towld the abbot the whole story.

"And oh, but wasn't the abbot the happy man that day! He quistoned thim over and over. He bound thim by a solemn promise niver to breathe a word of it to another sowl. He thin infarrumed thim that he would visit the place himsilf, and told thim that they both would have to go with him. Well, Aloysius was glad enough, and poor Onofrio was badly scared; but the abbot, the dear man, had his own projicts, and wasn't going to lose the chance of such a trisure as this, ispicially whin, as ye may say, it might be called San Antonio's own gold and jools.

"'Sure to glory!' cried the holy abbot in rapture; 'don't I know all about it? There's been a tradition here for ages. It's the trisure of the Cæsars. Whin Alaric came before Rome, the sinit and people of Rome tried to save something, so they imptied the imperial palace—the *Aurea Domus Neronis*—me boys, of all its trisures—its gold, its gims, its jools, its kyarbuncles, its imiralds, and prieious stones—and where in the wide wurruld they put thim nobody iver knew till this day. Alaric was fairly heart-broke with disappointment. They were niver tuk up, for Rome was no longer safe. Genseric came ravagin', and missed thim. They escaped the grasp of Odoacer, of Theodoric, of Vitiges, of Totila, and of Belisarius; of the Normans, of the robber barons, of Rienzi, and of the Constable Bourbon; and have been kept till this day, through the ispicial protiction and gyardianship of holy Anthony—may glory be with him!—and now he's handin' it over to us, for the honor and glory of his monastery. Look at this,' says he, whippin' on his own arrum the bracelet that Aloysius had found, and putting the diamond ring on his own finger, and howlding arrum and hand up to the light. 'Tare an ages! boys, but did ye iver see any gims like thim?'

"So the holy abbot wint off, iscorted by the two monks; and ye may be sure they kept that same ixpedition a saycret from all the rest of the monks. It was night whin they wint down—as the manuscript says. The prisince of the blissid abbot gave the two boys a since of protiction, and even Onofrio seemed to have lost his fears. He grew bolder, and peered curiously into those darker side-passages which crossed the main pathway. The clew lay along the flure all the way, so that there was no trouble. Well, they wint on an' reached the painted chamber, and found the ladders lying where they had left thim. They wint down. Each one had his own lamp. They walked on for about fifty paces; alriddy Aloysius was reaching forward his hand to show the holy abbot how near the trisure-room was, whin suddenly there was a noise—'a noise,' says the manuscript, ' like rushing footstips.'

"At that moment Onofrio gave a terrible cry. Again, as before, the lamp fell from his hands, and was dashed to pieces. With yell afther yell, and shriek afther shriek, he darted back, and bounded along the passage-ways. The abbot and Aloysius heard the noise, too; but of itself, says the manuscript, that noise might not have driven them away, for the holy abbot was riddy with no ind of exorcisms and spells to lay the biggest imp that might appear. But the yells, and the sudden flight of Onofrio, filled thim with uncontrollable horror. The abbot, in an instant, lost all his

prisince of mind. He turned and ran back at the top of his speed. Aloysius followed, and could scarcely keep up with him. Aloysius declares that, as he ran, he still heard the sound of rushing footsteps behind him, and was filled with the darkest fear. '*Ingens terror,*' he says, '*implebat nos; membra rigebant; cor stupebat; horror ineffabilis undique circumstabat; et a tergo videbantur quasi catervae horribiles ex abysmo, surgentes, sequentes atque fugantes. Nos ita inter mortuos, seminortui; inter fugantes fugientes erepti sumus nescio quomodo ex illo abysmo; et ad cryptum monasteri vix semianimi tandem advenimus.*'

"Well," continued O'Rourke, after pausing, perhaps to take breath after the Latin which he had quoted from the old manuscript, "whin they got to the vaults of the monastery, they recovered from their terror, but only to ixperience a new alarrum. For there, on looking around, they could see nothing of Onofrio. They searched all through the vaults. He was not there. They had locked the monastery door, which led into the vaults, on the inside, and it had not been opened. If he was not in the vaults, he must yit be in that horrible place from which they had fled. But they had seen nothing of him since his first flight. They had not overtaken him. The abbot had a vague remimbrance of a figure before him vanishing in the gloom of the passage-way, but no more.

"They waited for a long time, but Onofrio did not make his appearance. Thin they shouted at the top of their voices, but the sounds died away down the long, vaulted passage without bringing any risponse ixcipt what the manuscript vaguely and mysteriously calls a '*concentus quidam susurrorum levium, ut videbatur, sonorumque obscurorum, quae commixta reverberationibus tristibus ac segnibus, volvebant quasi suspiria de profundis.*'. . .

"At last their anxiety about their companion proved stronger thin the horrors of shuperstition, and they vintured back, growing bowlder as they wint, and they wint as far as the fust passage-way. Thin they called and halloed. But no risponse came. Thin they wint as far as the painted chamber, the holy abbot howlding before him the sacred symbol of the cross, and muttering prayers, while Aloysius did the shouting. And the manuscript says that they remained there for hours. The opening into the regions below lay within sight, but they didn't dare so much as to think of going down there again. They saw the projiction of the ladder above the opening, but dared not go nearer. At last it became ividint that there was no further hope just thin. They wint up and found it daylight above-ground. The abbot was wild with anxicty. He gathered all the monks, got sthrings, and crosses, and torches, and down again he wint with thim. This time, embowldined by the prisince of numbers, he descinded the ladder and stud at the fut. He didn't dare, though, to vinture any further. He didn't tell the monks any thing except that Brother Onofrio was lost. Nothing was said about the trisure. The most awful warrunings were held out to the monks against wandering off. Small need was there for warruning thim, however, for they were all half dead with fear. There they stud and sang chants. They did this three days running. The monk Aloysius distinctly affirrums that nothing kipt away the minacing demons but the sacred chants and the prayers of the holy abbot.

"Well, nothing was ever heard of Onofrio. After three days they gave up. The abbot had the opening walled up, and thin, over-whillumed by grief, he tuk to his bed. The damp of the vaults had also affected his lungs. He died in about sivin weeks. He loft directions for perpetual masses to be said for the repose of the sowl of Brother Onofrio. As for Aloysius, his grief and remorrus were deep and permanint. He niver ceased to reproach himsilf with being the cause of the terrible fate of poor Onofrio. He niver attimpted to get the trisure which he now and ever after-worruds most ferrumly belloved to be all that Onofrio had said. Still there was the secret on his sowl, and so he wrote this story of his, and put his manuscript in the library of the monastery. And there ye have it."

With these words Dr. O'Rourke concluded his story, and, turning toward the table, refreshed himself with another glass of wine.

CHAPTER III.

THE TREASURE OF THE CÆSARS.

Dr. O'Rourke swallowed a glass of wine, and then proceeded to light a cigar with the air of one who felt that he had done enough, and was desirous of resting from his labors, and of leaving to his companion the task of making further remarks. So he lighted his

cigar, leaned back in his chair, and turned his eyes toward the ceiling.

Basil Blake, for his part, had been a listener of the most attentive kind, and O'Rourke could not have wished for any more absorbed, or earnest, or thoughtful hearer. Now that the story was ended, he remained in the same position, and, like our first parents with the affable archangel, "still stood attentive, still stood fixed to hear."

At length he roused himself from his abstraction, and, drawing a long breath, looked fixedly at O'Rourke.

"Well, old chap," said he, "all that I can say is that, for a story, this is the most extraordinary that I have ever actually listened to, and, in order to find a parallel, I have to refer to the story-books of my boyhood—the 'Arabian Nights,' 'Tales from the German,' and 'Fairy Lore.' I see you are expecting me to give an opinion about this, but it is difficult to do so; for, in the first place, I don't know whether I'm to regard it as mere fiction or actual fact."

O'Rourke laid down his cigar upon the table.

"That's the very remark I expected you to make, so it is," said he, "and so, sure enough, there rises before us at the outset the great question of the authenticity of the manuscript and the credibility of the narrative. You see, thin, that this question is twofold, and should be considered as such."

Blake nodded.

"Now, first," said O'Rourke, "as to the authenticity of the manuscript—there can be no doubt about that whativer. Me own cousin, poor Malachi, a dying man, gave it to me with his dying hands. He was a monk in the monastery of San Antonio, and in the library of that same he found the manuscript, written, as the date informs us, cinturies ago. So, you see, the gincalogy is straight and certain. Howandiver, this is only ixternal ividince. What about the internal ividince? The handwriting of itself is sufficient proof that it was written whin it says, together with the faded ink, the peculiar vellum, and the giniral aspict. Internal ividince of a still stronger kind may be found in the sintimints, the exprissions, and the jaynius of the writer; but these all inter into the discussion under the second head—namely, the honesty, the cridibility, the veracity, of the author.

"Now, with rifirinco to this, I will make a few observations:

"First, the writer could have had no motive whativir in writing down any thing but what he believed to bo true. Remimber, he speaks as an eye-witness—nay, more, an actor in the ivints which he narrates. To a man in his position and calling, a work of fiction would have been impossible. He was not a sinsation novelist. He was a man of the sixteenth and seventeenth cinturies—a monk, a recluse, a man near his ind. He had no aujience; no reading public; he wrote his worruk, and consigned it to the oblivion of the library. Under such circumstances, no man could write any thing but what he believed true.

"But, secondly, there are other things which tind to sustain his intire cridibility. These are the circumstances mintioned in the book, the feelings, the words, and the deeds of the actors. First among these things described is the place itself, now famous as the Roman Catacombs. The mintion of this place is enough for mo. In the time when Aloysius lived, the Catacombs were unknown. They had been forgotten for ages. Their very ixistince was not suspicted. The labors and explorations of Bosio, Arringhi, and others, had not yet taken place. Aloysius thus stands alone among his contimporaries in this knowledge of the ixistince and the appearance of the Catacombs. He saw them as they appeared to Bosio, with the slabs untouched, the pictures fresh-colored, the ipitaphs undeciphered, and, I may add, the graves unrifled.

"Now, you must not only appreciate the full force of this most significant fact, but you must also bear in mind that all the descriptions of Aloysius are as vivid and as accurate as possible. I have been in those Catacombs which are now open to visitors, and can answer for the truth of the manuscript. There are the passages, the tiers of graves, the chambers, the walls covered with stucco, with pictures of Scripture scenes, the schupindous multichudo of Christian dead. The arrangement of the ixcavations in different stories, shuperior, and mejium, and inferior; the openings in the paths, the peep down into the abyss of darkness beneath—all these are wonderfully accurate, and are the description of an eye-witniss.

"Again, there are those vivid descriptions of human life and imotion; of exultation, curiosity, triumph, sudden fright, deep horror, succeeded by grief and despair. Recall the horror of Onofrio, the anguish of the abbot. I wish ye could only read that crabbed manuscript for yourself, so as to see with what vivid simplicity these terrible things are told.

"There's not the least doubt in life, thin, that at the beginning of the seventeenth cintury, or the ind of the sixteenth, the man that wrote this was down in the Catacombs, and that his companion perished there, as he narrates. There's not the least doubt in life that those multichudinous minute details are all corrict, and actually happened as set forth.

"Still one fact remains, and this is, after all, the prayiminint fact for us now. It is the assertion of the discovery of a Great Trisure. With regyard to this, we ask ourselves two questions:

"First—Is it possible?

"Secondly—Is it probable?

"Now, the question of its possibility is easily disposed of. Of course, it's possible, and more unlikely things than that have taken place. So the other question remains —is it probable?

"Now let us turrun our attintion to this for a few mominks:

"When you think of it, you must see that nothing is more probable than that, in the course of ages, in the history of a great city like ancient Rome, trisure has been concealed to a vast ixtint. Think of the numerous sieges and sacks that have taken place since the days of Alaric the Goth. The sacks of Rome began with Alaric. The spell of Roman security was broken whin the Goths minaced the Ayterrunal City. In the short space that was left between his arrival and the capture of the city an imminse amount must have been hastily concealed. At that time the ixistince of the Catacombs was known. It had, at what might be terrumed a comparatively recent period, been a hiding-place for persecuted Christians. It was thin a sacred place, as St. Jerome says, and was believed to be hallowed by the bones of the martyrs. 'Deed, St. Jerome himself wint down to inspict their graves, and tells his emotions.

"There is no doubt, thin, I may rezhume, that an incalculable amount of trisure must have been hid away in Rome juring cinturies of warfare and chumult; and it is equally ividint that at certain times the Catacombs must have been foremost in the thoughts of those who wished to hide money—as prayiminintly, if not exclusively, the best place for such concealment. The quistion, therefore, that now comes forth is, which, out of all the cinturies in the life of the Ayterrunal City, is the most likely one in which a great trisure might be hid in the Catacombs?

" In order to answer this, let us cast our eyes over the sackings of Rome. The great sack by the Constable Bourbon was ividintly not the time that'll shoot our purposes, for the reason that the ixistince of the Catacombs was not even suspicted. The same thing may be said of the various sieges or sackings that occurred juring the middle ages—undher the Hohenstaufen imperors, whither Rome was minaced by a Ghibelline arrumy, or capturcd and plundered by the Norramans. So, ye see, we've got to go back still further till we come to the days of Belisarius, and the warrafare of that iminint gineral against the Goths. One answer meets us here, and that is, that in his days there was scarcely enough trisure in Rome to be worth concealmint. We know that fact by the state of Rome at the accission of Grigory the Great, at the ind of that same cintury. Whin that pope ascinded the chair of Saint Peter—glory to his name!—he found Rome a city of paupers. If it hadn't been for him, Rome would not have been in ixistince now. He was a second Romulus—he saved Rome—he created it anew. But, by this simple fact, we see that in his days there was no trisure to conceal.

" It is ividint, therefore, that we are pushed further back.

" Now, the conditions that we have seen both ixist side by side in the greatest degree at the time of the first sack of Rome by Alaric. What do we find then? Wilth incalculable; the accumulated trisures of the ages; the stored-up plunder of cinturies—all piled up in Rome! Not yet had any hand of violince been laid upon the imparial possessions. True it is that the Imperor Constantine had taken away some trisures of art—some rilics, perhaps, and coined money, togither with what things he could conveniently appropriate; but such saquistrations as those were but a flea-bite, and made no perceptible diminution in the hoarded wilth of the cinturies of domination and shuprimacy. It excited no alarrum. Rome stood untroubled. Time

rowled on. The gowld, and the gims, and the jools, and the trisures of the ancient pagan timples were perhaps transferred to Christian idifices; but they still remained in Rome. No one thought as yit of concealmint—at least, not on any grand scale. In those days the House of Nero was yit the Golden—the Palatine stood up one of the wondhers of the wurruld.

" Now at this time—imagine the approach of Alaric—what would be the fust act of the Romans? those let us say who were gyarding the mighty trisures of the imparial palace? Most ividintly their fust impulse would be to hurry away every movable thing of value into a place of concealmint. And into what place of concealmint? In that age there would be nicissarily but one place thought of—the Catacombs. There their Christian fathers had hid from a mightier than Alaric, in the days whin a Roman imperor was at the shuprame zaynith of his power; there, in that same place, it would be easy to hide min or trisure from the grasp of a barbaric raid.

" Now I contind," continued O'Rourke in a calmer tone—" I contind that all this is iminintly probable, and, more than this, I contind that it is also probable that it may be there yit; but we'll see about this prisintly. I may mintion one other theory that has suggisted itsilf to my mind, and that is, that the pagan priests may have concealed their timple trisures from the Christians some time between the reigns of Constantine and Theodosius. This I thought of for the reason that Aloysius says so much about tripods, statuettes, censers, braziers, and so forth. But the answer to this, and the objiction, is this, that pagan priests, even allowing that they might have concealed their timple trisures out of dread of aggrissive Christians, would niver have vintured into a place like the Catacombs—a place in its origin, its use, its associations, prayiminintly Christian. To do so would have been to vinture into inivitible discovery and capture. At the same time," continued O'Rourke, elevating his eyebrows and giving a thoughtful glance at his cigar, now utterly extinguished—" at the same time this opins before us an intiresting field of inquiry, and much may be said on both sides.

" As for Aloysius," continued O'Rourke, " it is ividint from the tone of his writing that he considered the trisure as altogither pagan, and therefore Satanic. Onofrio seems to have ricognized their pagan characters at a glance. He flung down with horror the statuette, and looked with equal horror on the jools that Aloysius had taken. Both of those min were shuperstitious; it was of course the characteristic of their age. Even afther the lapse of twinty years Aloysius still thinks the noises which he heard Satanic; and it niver seems to have intered the dear man's head that the rattle among the gowld and silver vessels may have been the result of the action of the ordinary laws of gravitation; while those terrible sounds—'*as of rushing footstips*'—of which he speaks, he seems incapable, from his nature aud from his age, of attributing to such humble and commonplace agencies as—rats, or bats, or both. Rats—or bats—those were the imps, the demons of the poor monk's fancy—that drove poor Onofrio to a hijeous death in the interminable passages, the endless labyrinths, and the impinitrible gloom of the Catacombs.

"One more thing I may say which has just occurred to me. Ye don't know Rome, and so ye can't understand the position of the monastery of San Antonio. Well, ye can understand me whin I say that it is situated on a street that begins not far from the Corso, and that the Palatine Hill is not an ixtravagant distance off. Now, it is quite within the bounds of possibility that the subterrancan passage led in that direction; and I've made maps according to my own fancy, which shows how those two explorers may have wandered along till they were standing beneath the Palatine. Now, on that Palatine stood the Golden House of Nero—the imparial palace—now a heap of ruins. But that palace was distinguished for the vast depth of its foundations, and the imminse ixtint of vaults beneath. There are some archayologists who have suggisted that there were actual openings or communications with the Catacombs themselves—

"If so, how easy it was for the gyarjians of the imparial trisures to carry them all down below! It was merely going downstairs. This chamber, thin, may have been immejiately beneath the imparial vaults—the cellars or dungeons of the palace—and thus the chamber upon which Aloysius and Onofrio stumbled would be the very chamber where once was concealed the trisure of the Cæsars. Moreover, if it once was concealed there, it is easy to account for the fact of its remain-

ing there. The terror of Gothic arrums; the names of Alaric, Attila, Genseric; the chumulchuous assimblages outside and inside the city; the puppit impirors put up and overthroun by barbarian soldiers—all these things would have injuiced the gyarjians of the imparial trisure to suffer it to be there unremoved. And thin ginerations would pass; and the gyarjians would die out; and the secret, transmitted from father to son, would at last be lost. The gyarjians, or their descindints, would be driven away from the palace; their places would be occupied by Gothic servitors; the palace itself would go to decay, the vaults fall in; the subterranean passages would sink in ruin; and so, at last, even if the secret was known, the path that led to the trisure-chamber would be no longer discoverable."

Dr. O'Rourke had spoken rapidly and vehemently, and in the tone, not merely of one who believed all that he was saying, but of one who was a positive enthusiast in that belief. This enthusiasm, more than even the arguments themselves, produced a strong effect upon Blake, in spite of the utter incredulity which he had felt at first; and he now found himself at length swept onward, by O'Rourke's vehemeuce and enthusiasm, to the conclusion that, after all, the probabilities in favor of the truth of this wild idea were of a highly-respectable character."

"You have said nothing about your cousin —Malachi."

"No," said O'Rourke. "I am not quite through yet; I am coming to him. I confess that, without poor Malachi's own story, I would not have the least idea in life that there was any prospect of doing any thing now—in short, I would have regyarded the story of Aloysius as a species of modified fiction. But me cousin Malachi had his own story to tell, which, though not conclusive, is still important enough to make the story of Aloysius seem like a living fact.

"It seems, thin, that poor Malachi, as I said, stumbled upon this manuscript, and read it through. It prejuiced such an ifflct upon him that he could not have any rist untill he had tested the truth of it to some ixtint, howiver slight. So, what did he do but he determined to make a slight exploration on his own hook! He was afraid, though, to take any companion, for fear that he would meet with the fate of poor Onofrio.

"Well, first of all, he went down into the very same vaults where Aloysius and his frind had gone; and there, sure enough, he found the very opening mintioned in the manuscript, which opening was thin just as it had been walled up after the search for Onofrio had inded. So poor Malachi took a crowbar, and did as Aloysius had done before him. He knocked down the wall without difficulty, and there, sure enough, he saw the passage-way and the tiers of tombs.

"He didn't go far that day, but waited for a time. The next time he brought down a ball of twine and some lanterns; and, ar-rumed with these, he wint in, and wint along, onrowling the twine for a clew.

"Well, all was as the manuscript said. He came to the first crossing, and wint on beyond this.

"He says he niver felt comfortable there. He always felt as if the ghost of poor Onofrio was watching him; but poor Malachi was a very risolute boy, and he kipt at it. He went in several times, and at last vintured as far as the painted chamber.

"Beyond this he saw the opening in the flure. He looked down, and saw all the darkness beneath. He never wint any farther.

"There were two reasons for this: First, he hadn't the nerve to do it; he felt uncomfortable enough where he was, but down below he didn't dare to go, and scarcely dared to look; for there, he fully believed, the ghost of Onofrio was wandering, confined to that lower story, and haunting it. You and I may smile at poor Malachi's shuperstition, but a monk leads a ghostly sort of life, and it was no joke to go alone as he wint, right afther reading such a manuscript as that of Aloysius.

"The other reason why he didn't go any farther was, that he had no motive. He was utterly and sublimely destichute of any desire for money. All his wants were supplied; he was contint. Why should he bother his head?

"Still he thought it his juty, for the sake of the monastery, and out of loyal regyard to San Antonio, to tell the abbot. This he did in the most effective way by reading the manuscript to him. The abbot listened with deep and painful feelings. He was not a strong-minded man, nor was he avaricious. Moreover, he was shuperstitious. He would not have gone below in search of that trisure, as

his predecessor had done, for all the worruld. In fact, he charged me cousin Malachi to wall the passage-way up as he had found it, and niver to mintion the subjict to any of the other monks. This me cousin Malachi did. He walled it up again as he had found it; and, as he didn't wish the monks to get into any trouble through him, he kept his secret till his death, and thin confided it to me."

<hr/>

CHAPTER IV.

A STROKE FOR FORTUNE.

SOME further conversation followed upon the story of Aloysius, and Blake asked sundry questions of a character which showed that he had not lost a single word. Blake conceded the possibility, nay, even the probability, of a treasure having once been concealed in the catacombs; but was inclined to think that, in the course of ages, it must have been discovered. O'Rourke, on the other hand, reminded him of the nature of the Catacombs, the utter ignorance about them which existed through many centuries; their comparatively recent rediscovery, and the small extent that had been explored in comparison with what yet remained to be investigated. He insisted that there were portions or districts of these vast subterranean realms which must have been for ages untrodden by the foot of man; and that any thing once placed there, no matter how long ago, had most probably been unseen and untouched ever since. He laid great stress upon the fact mentioned by Aloysius—that all the slabs were on their tombs; that no grave was open—a circumstance which, in O'Rourke's view, proved beyond a doubt that they had never been profaned by the presence of robbers or plunderers. No graves are sacred from the thief, and the undisturbed condition of these graves proved that their existence had been unknown.

"And no wonder," said he. "Have you any idea of the ixtint of the Roman Catacombs? Did ye iver pay any attintion to the subjict, or begin to farrum any conciption about thim? The Catacombs have an ixtint that I can scarce give any idea of. They ixist beneath all that surface which once forrumed the site of ancient Rome; and not only so, but all that surface which was covered by the suburbs. These suburbs, as we know, were vast, and perhaps contained a population as great as the city itself; for, as was said, one could not tell where the city inded, and the country began. More than this, the Catacombs have been found near Ostia, and passages have been discovered which seem to go under the Tiber, anticecpating the Thames Tunnel by eighteen cinturies. The vulgar idea of the Catacombs is, that they were made for the purpose of obtaining Roman ciment for building-purposes. This is now exploded. The catacombs are excavated in a rock that cannot be used for ciment of any kind. The latest researches have shown that they were undoubtedly made for burial-purposes; and the only question is whether they were originally Christian or not. That they were eventually Christian is ividint. For meself, I have no doubt as to their Christian origin.

"Another misconciption about thim is as to their farrum. There has been a privilent opinion that they ixtinded uninterruptidly in innumerable passages. It is now known, however, that they only exist where there is that peculiar soft sandstone in which they are ixcavated. As this only ixists in certain places, so the Catacombs forrum distinct quarters, or districts. These are all ixcavated in stories, one above the other—sometimes as many as four or five are found—but many are disconnected altogither with any other district. The whole of the ground under Rome is not all honeycombed, therefore, but only certain portions over an imminse ixtint of country. Now, the place which we are considering seems to me to be one of these isolated districts, the very ixistence of which is unsuspicted. No ixplorers have troubled it thus far. Me cousin Malachi found the tombs undisturbed. We may call thim the Palatine Catacombs—since they certainly seem to run under the Palatine—and, if this is so, I can only say that the Palatine Catacombs are worthy of being ixplored—and soon, too—before any of these blackgyard archayologists git wind of their ixistince."

"But allowing that the treasure was once put there," said Blake, "and even allowing that it may be there yet, do you think that there is any possibility of any one getting at it?"

"Do I think that? And, if I didn't think that, what d'ye suppose I'd be talking meself hoarse for? It's not for idle intertainment I'm talking now. It's business I mean. Don't ye see that? Am I not earnest enough to show ye how risolute I am? But as to gitting at it, I can answer that. I believe it to be possible, but I haven't yet actually tested it. Still, I haven't the smallest doubt in life. Listen, now:

"The monastery of San Antonio is in the Via San Antonio, that begins near the Corso, and runs toward the Palatine and the Forum. It is thickly built up with houses. These houses are, without exciption, all very old, and strongly built; they look like houses that have deep vaults beneath. The people living along here belong to the poorer classes. Now what is there to privint any one from rinting one of these houses, or the lower part of one? If I were to rint one, I'll tell ye what I'd do. I'd begin an ixcavation on a small scale, so as to try to feel my way toward the passages of the Palatine Catacombs. I feel confidint that a moderate ixcavation would lead me into some passage. In the Catacombs, or in any of their districts or divisions, the passages are numerous, and lie close togither. I believe, thin, that any one, by digging from the cellar of one of these houses, would reach before long the very passage of Aloysius itsilf. That passage runs in a diriction which ought to make it nearly parallel with the Via di San Antonio; and the only trouble would be to know how to dig, and in what diriction. This is the only trouble, and it is one that would, of course, be rimidied by time and perseverance.

"It's true the vaults of San Antonio must be deeper by at least one story than the cellars of the adjoining houses; but, in that case, the explorer would have to arrange his course with rifirince to that, and aim at a lower livil. One advantage I have is, that I have so accurate a discription from me cousin Malachi of the starting-point of the passage of Aloysius, and of its diriction, that I'm confidint I could hit it without any trouble or disippointmint whativer. Howandiver, I'll find out for meself before long, and know exactly what the probabilities are. Of course, whin once inside the Catacombs, one can find the passage of Aloysius, which must still be recognizable by the ind being walled up. Once find that, and thin all that there is to do is to follow the course mintioned in the manuscript. Any one can do it, provided he has the requisite knowledge, and is distichute of shuperstition, and is not afraid of the ghost of Onofrio, like me poor Cousin Malachi.

"Well, now, me boy, the question is this: do you feel inclined to accompany me on this ixploration? Ye know the whole now. The fact is, one can't do much alone. Things must be taken down—ladders and lamps, and perhaps pickaxes and spades. We must expict some ravages to be made by time. The passage may have fallen in, and may have to be cleared away. All this may be so difficult for one man to do alone, that the obstacles may utterly defeat his attimpt."

"Oh, by Jove!" cried Blake, "as for that, if there's even a ghost of a chance of success, I'd go—like a shot."

"Didn't I know it? Sure I did," exclaimed O'Rourke, with genuine satisfaction in his tone. He thereupon poured out another glass of wine, and slowly quaffed it.

"Any thing that may better my circumstances is welcome to me," said Blake. "I can't lose any money, for I have none to lose. I can only lose time—and, unfortunately, that is a commodity of very little value to me just now, or to anybody else. It may be a wild-goose chase, but I'm willing to try it."

"Sure, and ain't that the true spirit of a man, a Christian, and a hayro?" cried O'Rourke. "Ye're sure to be successful—but it's just as well for ye not to feel sure—if it's only to keep yer head cool, and yer hand stiddy."

"Oh, I'm not at all sanguine," said Blake, with a laugh. "I go in merely for a speculation."

"The fact is," said O'Rourke, "it's now over two years since me cousin Malachi died, and since thin I've been reading the manuscript over and over, and brooding over it, and arranging some plan. But I soon found that I couldn't do any thing till I could get the proper associate. I wanted a man of pluck and honor, of risolution, and nerve, and hardihood. All these qualities it is difficult to find combined in the same man —and in my case I wanted a man whom I could rely on as a frind—one who would stand by me in sickness, and not leave me in the lurch. Now, me boy, I've only known you for a year, but you come nearer to the standard than any man I know, and this is the reason why I've taken you into my confidince, and asked you to come with me into this interprise. If it is successful the half is

yours; if not—why, thin—sure to glory— there's no harrum done—and nothing lost but a few months' time."

"Well, old fellow," said Blake, in a frank and cordial tone, "I thank you for the compliment you pay me, in taking me into your confidence, and, whether we succeed or not, I shall feel just the same sort of—a—gratitude, you know, and all that sort of thing. As to standing by you, I assure you, my dear fellow, you may count on me to any extent, and under any circumstances. I can do a good day's work—if it comes to that—I'm not superstitious—I don't believe in ghosts of any sort or kind; and if there's any gold down there, I tell you what it is, that gold will have to show itself to the light of day, for I'll have it up, or else I'll leave my bones in the Catacombs along with those of our mutual friend Onofrio!"

O'Rourke smiled blandly.

"Sure, and if it comes to leaving your bones—or my bones," said he, "we couldn't find a better, a quieter, or a more respectable and altogither unexceptional place, than thim same Catacombs."

"Well," said Blake, cheerily, "when do you propose to begin?"

"As soon as possible, if you consint," said O'Rourke.

"Of course I consent. I have no choice. I'm a hard-up man. In those few words you may read a melancholy story."

"Sure and the wisest and the best of the human race are in the same fix, as a general thing," responded O'Rourke. "Well—as to our work—I propose, as I said, to begin as soon as possible. Now, my intintion is to set out for Rome to-morrow—since you have decided in favor of this interprise—and thin I intend to indivor to rint one of thim houses along the Via San Antonio, as nigh to the monastery as possible. Sure and there can't be any doubt but I'll be able to rint some one among them; and my opinion is that if I offer rint high enough I'll be able to git the house that stands next door. If I do so, I can hit the passage of Aloysius in one night's work. But, be that as it may, whativer house I git, I mean to go to work at once, alone, and see what I can do. I think it's better for me to attind to the preliminaries alone. It's quieter, safer, and less suspicious. I don't want to indanger the project by ixciting attintion of any kind if I can help it."

"But you surely don't intend to do all that digging yourself?" cried Blake.

"Sure and I do."

"Oh, but I ought to help you to some extent."

"So you may."

"How?" asked Blake.

"Why, by not saying one word about this to any living soul."

"Oh, I'll keep dark."

"Yis, but you mustn't even hint at it—not to any living soul, male or female, man or child, frind or rilitiv. No one must have the least suspicion. If you do, you'll indanger it all. It's so strange and unusual a thing, that the very mintion of it would sit the mind agog, and it would git sprid abroad."

"Oh, well, as to that, it's easy enough for me to keep secret. I've no relative in the world except my poor dear old mother, and I should not feel inclined to bother and worry her by making her the confidante of any such plan as this. She'd be worried out of her life, poor old lady. And then as to friends, I have only one besides yourself—Hellmuth, you know—and he's not a fellow that I should choose to talk to about a thing like this. He'd scorn the whole thing—treasure and all. Oh, no, I value Hellmuth's good opinion too much to say any thing to him about this. So you see the secret is inviolable, from the very nature of the case, and of my circumstances."

"Well, it's just as well to have it so," said O'Rourke, pleasantly. "There's no harrum done by keeping this a secret, but if it is not kept secret, it may lead to all the harrum in the worruld."

"Well," said Blake, "those are the only ones that I should mention any of my affairs to; my other friends are not at all on an intimate footing; they are merely acquaintances, and, in fact, I see very little of anybody here in Paris, except Hellmuth and yourself."

"I've niver had the pleasure," said O'Rourke, "of meeting with your frind Hellmuth."

"No," said Blake. "The fact is, you both keep so much by yourselves that it is next to an impossibility that you should ever stray across one another's paths. Still I wonder that you haven't sometimes stumbled upon one another here. He comes here a good deal—and so do you."

"Yis," said O'Rourke; "but I'm so busy

all day that, whin I do come here, it's generally late—"

"Well, I hope you'll both meet some day; and I'm sure you'd like him—he's a man of no common kind. If you'd known him, you'd not have chosen me—though I don't know, either—for Hellmuth has such a scorn of money that I don't believe even the treasure of the Cæsars could induce him to swerve one hair's-breadth from the line of life that he has marked out for himself."

"Sure, in that case," said O'Rourke, "he'd niver do for me at all, at all. I'm an impecunious man, and I love impecunious min. The man that has no need of money is too prosperous to shuit me. He is an alien to me, and with such I have no sympathy."

"Well," said Blake, "and so you intend to go at once to Rome?"

"Yis."

"And how long may it be before I may hear from you?"

"That depinds upon circumstances of course. I may be through ix a week, and I may be detained longer. On the whole, it is best to fix the outside limit."

"Well, what is that? I intend leaving Paris shortly myself—to recruit for a time—and will not come back, if I can help it, for some weeks."

"Sure, and while yer about it ye can give yerself months if ye choose," said O'Rourke. "The outside limit which I should fix would be at least three months."

"Three months? Oh, that will suit me capitally."

"Ye see, I have to rint the house, and thin work to git to the Catacombs. I'll have to work slowly and cautiously, so as not to be suspictid. But in three months, at the very farthest, I ought to do all that I can ixpict to do, and if I don't do it in that time, it'll be because I can't do it alone, in which case I'll have to git you to hilp me."

"Well, you know, I'd help you at the very first if you'd let me."

"Yis, but I don't want ye—at the first. So we'll say three months."

"Very well."

"Are ye going any distance?"

"No—I don't intend to go out of France. I'm simply going to recruit, and I haven't made up my mind yet where I shall go."

"Well, that's about the best way to recruit. Wander off. Let yerself drift. That's

"But as O'Rourke heard it there came over his face a sudden change."—Page 17.

the way. But ye'll be back here in three months?"

"Oh, yes, and probably in three weeks."

"Very well, thin. I'll know where to find ye—or to write to ye if I can't come mesilf—"

O'Rourke now rose.

"Well," said he, "me boy, it's glad I am to git ye for an assistint, and, still better, a frind. Ye'll allow me to say though, that in this case, as I ferrumly believe, it'll be the very best stroke of work that ye iver turruned yer arrum to. I'll make ivery thing riddy, and, at the shupreme momint I'll call on you to accompany me on a promenade along the passage of Aloysius. Ye may be sanguine or dispondint, whichiver ye choose, only mind ye kcep the secret—that's all—and thin ye'll find yerself—with me—the heir of the *trisure of the Cæsars!*"

"I swear, old fellow," said Blake, suddenly, "you could never guess what an odd idea struck my mind just now."

"An odd idea?" said O'Rourke; "such as what—for instance?"

"Why—this. You've read the 'Arabian Nights?'"

"Sure, and I have, but what of thim?"

"Do you remember the immortal story of 'Aladdin and the Wonderful Lamp?'"

"Mesilf does—of course. But what thin?"

"Nothing—only it was such an absurd fancy. You looked to me just then exactly like the magician who came to Aladdin, and persuaded him to accompany him to the cave where the magic lamp was kept, you know."

Blake said this in a careless and lively tone, with a bright gleam in his clear and pleasant eyes, and a joyous smile on his frank and open face. It was a passing remark, thrown off with the utmost nonchalance; but as O'Rourke heard it there came over his face a sudden change—and a total one. His complexion changed to one of a sickly pallor; his brow was darkened with a frown; his piercing eyes rested gloomily upon the face of his companion; his hands clutched one another behind his back. But this was only for a moment. Blake had not time to notice it. In another moment it had passed away, and O'Rourke's face was as before.

He laughed boisterously.

"Well—well," he said, "I hope it may be so, and for my part I believe—though you don't—that it will be so—so I do; for, as I've

been saying, I believe that in those Palatine Catacombs there is the trisure of the Cæsars, and, if I'm right—why thin, sure—and it's mesilf that'll be the majician that'll put in your hands a wilth in comparison with which even the fabulous riches of Aladdin would be paltry and contimptible. Well, we won't indulge just now in visions like these. We'll defer all this till we find the reality. It's late, and I must be off; and so, Blake, me boy, good-night, and good-by."

He held out his hand. Blake took it, and they shook hands cordially. O'Rourke then took his departure.

CHAPTER V.

VILLENEUVE.

The Lake of Geneva is one of the most attractive places in the world, and to the grace of natural beauty is added the more subtile charm that arises from the closeness with which its scenes have become blended with the great events of history, and the majestic names of men of genius. The memories of Rousseau, Voltaire, Gibbon, Byron, and many more, are inseparably connected with it; but among all it is to the two Englishmen that its fame owes most, for they surely loved it best. The shade of the great historian seems still to haunt the gardens of Lausanne; while all the surrounding scenes still wear those epithets with which the mighty poet endowed them. There is clear, placid Leman; the Alps, the pyramids of Nature; Jura, with her misty shroud; there too under the shadowy mountains rises the Castle of Chillon, sombre and melancholy, once the scene of wrong and cruel oppression, but now a place of pilgrimage:

    .... "For 'twas trod,
Until his very steps have left a trace
  Worn, as if the cold pavement were a sod,
By Bonnivard!—May none those marks efface!
For they appeal from tyranny to God."

It was early morning, and the sun was just rising, when two young ladies left the hotel at Villeneuve, and walked slowly along in the direction of the Castle of Chillon. Both of them were young, and each was beautiful in her way, though they were utterly unlike and dissimilar in features, expression, manner, and tone. One had clear, calm blue eyes; golden hair, which flowed down from a chignon of very moderate dimensions, in a rippling tide of frizzled glory ; dimpled cheeks; and small mouth, the lines of which were of such a nature that they formed the impress of a perpetual smile. Her companion had a delicate and ethereal face, over which there was an air of quiet thoughtfulness ; her eyes were soft, dark, liquid, and lustrous, with a peculiar expression in them that a superficial glance would regard as savoring of melancholy, but which to a closer observer would indicate less of sadness than of earnestness. Her hair also floated behind, after the same fashion as her companion's; but, while the one owed its beauty to the crimping-irons, the dark masses of the other curled lustrously in the graceful negligence of Nature.

They walked slowly, and noticed the successive features of the surrounding scenery, which they spoke of with great animation. At length a turn in the road brought them in sight of the castle.

"O Inez!" said the lady with the golden hair, "what a darling old castle! Look!— did you ever see any thing like it in all your life? and isn't it perfectly lovely ? "

The one called Inez said nothing for some time, but stood looking at the sombre pile in quiet admiration.

" It must be Chillon," said she, at length.

" Chil—what, Inez dear ? " asked the other.

" Chillon," said Inez. " You've read Byron's ' Prisoner of Chillon,' you know, haven't you, Bessie ? "

Bessie shook her head with a doleful expression.

" Well, Inez dear," said she, "really you know poetry is so stupid, but I dare say, after all, I have read it, only I don't remember one word about it ; I never do, you know, dear. You see I always skim it all over. I skim Shakespeare, and Bacon, and Gibbon, and Sir Isaac Newton, and all the rest of those stupid writers. They make my head ache always."

Inez smiled.

" Well, I'm sure, Bessie," said she, " if you try Newton and Bacon, I don't wonder that you find it rather difficult to read them. I should skim them myself."

" Oh, you know it's all very well for you, Inez dear, when you've got so much intellect,

but for poor me! At any rate, what is there about this Chip—Chil—how is it ? "

" Chillon," said Inez.

" Chillon, then. Tell me the story, Inez dear, for you know I'm awfully fond of stories, and you tell them so deliciously. I only wish I was so clever."

" Nonsense, Bessie ! " said Inez ; and, after this disclaimer of Bessie's too open flattery, she proceeded to give her companion the substance of Byron's poem.

" Well now, really, Inez dear," said Bessie, as her companion finished her story, " what was the use of it all ? Why did that poor, silly creature go to prison at all ? Sure its mad he was."

At this, Inez looked at her friend with sad, reproachful eyes. Bessie's intonation and accent were somewhat peculiar ; for, though she was perfectly well bred and ladylike in her tone, there was, however, in her voice a slight Hibernian flavor, originally caught, perhaps, from some Irish nurse, and never altogether lost. There was an oddity about this which was decidedly attractive, and the " laste taste in life av the brogue," which was thus noticeable in Bessie, gave to that young person a wonderful witchery, and suggested infinite possibilities in her of drollery or archness.

" People often have to suffer for their principles, of course," said Inez, gravely.

" But I don't see why he should bother about his principles," persisted Bessie. " No one thanked him for it, at all at all."

" He had to. He believed in them, and of course could not give up his belief."

" But he needn't have gone so far, you know, Inez dear. Why couldn't he have made it up with the count or the juke, or whoever it was ? "

" Why, Bessie, how absurd ! A man can't give up his belief so easily. Some things people must suffer. You and I are Catholics, and if we were ordered to change our religion we couldn't do it. We should have to suffer."

Bessie shook her pretty little head.

" Well, I'm sure I really don't see how I could stand being put in a dungeon with rats and things, and so dark too; and besides it was different with this man. It wasn't his religion, but some absurd bother about politics. I'm sure there's no danger of my ever getting into trouble about politics. But, oh, Inez dear, there he is—I knew it—look ! "

The sudden change in Bessie's remarks was caused by some one whom she happened to see coming up the road behind them as she casually looked back. Whoever it was, however, Inez did not choose to look, as Bessie told her. On the contrary, she seemed to know perfectly well who it was, and to feel some slight embarrassment, for a flush came over her face, and she looked straight before her without saying a word.

"Now, I think it's a great shame," said Bessie, after a moment's pause, in a fretful tone.

"What do you mean?"

"Why, Dr. Blake, since he's joined us, I never see any thing of you."

"Why, Bessie, what perfect nonsense! You are with me all the time."

"Oh, but I mean I never have you to myself now at all. It's nothing but Dr. Blake all the time. He is always with you. Your papa and you are fairly bound up in him. And it's a great shame entirely, so it is. And he is so awfully devoted—why, he worships the ground you tread on!"

At this, the cheeks of Inez blushed like flame.

"I wish you wouldn't be so absurd," said she. "You are talking nothing but the most perfect nonsense. Papa and I, of course, both esteem Dr. Blake, and he is of great use to poor papa in his illness, and I'm sure I don't know what papa would ever have done without him."

"Well, I'm sure," continued Bessie, in a plaintive voice; "of all stupid people, the very worst in the world are two devoted lovers."

"You absurd, silly child!" exclaimed Inez, turning away.

"Why, I'm sure I do not know what else to call you. Doesn't he give you flowers all the time? Doesn't he sit and fasten his eyes on you, and look as though he longed to eat you up? Doesn't he always look at me, whenever he condescends to notice poor me at all, as though he thinks I am always in the way? Don't I have to bear the painful consciousness in my unhappy breast that I am *de trop?*"

"Hush, you silly little goose!" cried Inez, hurriedly, as she heard the sound of footsteps close behind her, fearful that Bessie's words would be overheard. Bessie, however, stopped short, and demurely moved away

from Inez, as though she wished to allow the new-comer every chance with his inamorata —a movement which the other noticed, and tried to baffle by keeping close to her. But this little by-play was now interrupted by a clear, manly voice, which sounded close beside Inez.

"Good-morning, Miss Wyverne. I had no idea that you would be out so early after your fatigues of yesterday."

Inez turned with a smile of pleasure, and the face which met the new-comer's eyes, still wearing the flush which Bessie had called up, seemed to him to be inexpressibly lovely. He was a tall young fellow, with a fine, fresh, frank, open face; short, crisp hair; whiskers of the English cut, and a joyous light in his eyes, that spoke of bounding youth and the bloom of perfect health, and of something more, too, that might have been due to the present meeting. He stood with his hat off, and hand extended. Inez accepted his greeting, and said simply:

"Good-morning, Dr. Blake."

"Miss Mordaunt," continued Dr. Blake, addressing Bessie, who was on the other side of Inez, "good morning. What do you think of Villeneuve now? Will you ever dare to abuse it again? Confess, now, did you ever see such a lovely sight? For my part, I think it's far and away the prettiest place I ever saw, and for invalids it is perfect. But, by-the-way, Miss Wyverne, have you seen your father this morning? How is he?"

"Oh, thanks, he is much better," said Inez. "He was up and dressed before I left. He had slept better than usual, he said, though, of course, he never sleeps much now —poor papa!"

"Oh, well, we must be patient," said Blake. "We cannot expect any very rapid improvement, you know. This is the place where he can find just what he needs. It is so quiet, and so mild and beautiful. And there is the castle. I suppose you intend to visit it as soon as possible?"

"It is not open so early as this, is it?" asked Inez.

"Well, no; this is a little too early," said Blake. "For the present we must content ourselves with an outside view. But the castle itself and its surroundings will be enough for a first visit. There are the battlements from which the sounding-line was cast a thousand feet into tho waters below; and there is tho 'little isle,' which is mentioned in the poem:

> " '. . . . a little isle
> Which in my very face did smile,
> The only one in view—
> A small green isle it seemed no more
> Scarce broader than my dungeon-floor,
> But in it there were three tall trees,
> And o'er it blew the mountain-breeze,
> And by it there were waters flowing,
> And on it there were young flowers growing
> Of gentle breath and hue.' "

Blake was full of the enthusiasm of youth, and inspired by the scene around him, and the companionship which he had. He talked eloquently, and showed so wonderfully intimate an acquaintance with the scene before him, that it seemed as though he must have made Lake Leman a specialty, or at least have read up very lately.

They sauntered along thus, and at length sat down upon a grassy knoll by the roadside, while the whole prospect spread itself magnificently before them.

Bessie's remarks were justified by the present appearance of things. It was as she said. It was the old, old story of two lovers. The doctor had no words or looks or thoughts for any one but Inez; and the joy that was in his face, the animation of his manner, the eloquence of his words, were all due to the intoxication of her presence. However all this may have seemed to Inez, it is not to be expected that it would be altogether pleasant to Bessie; but Miss Bessie was not one who would allow herself to be imposed upon, and so she proceeded to solace herself for the neglect which she supposed to be shown her, by entering upon a deliberate and elaborate system of teasing, which was directed against Inez. After what she had already said, Inez could not allow herself to be absorbed so fully by Blake as she had formerly done; and there was now in her mind a sense of great uneasiness as to what Bessie might do, which feeling was by no means lessened by her friend's actions.

Soon after they had seated themselves, Bessie began to move away from Inez as far as possible, thus ostentatiously showing a desire to leave the lovers by themselves, and kept her face turned away, as though she would on no account be an eye-witness of their proceedings. All this embarrassed Inez greatly, for the relations between herself and Blake were thus far of a purely friendly character, nor had she as yet thought very much of any thing more. Her delicacy was shocked excessively by Bessie's movements, but she did not know how to prevent them. She shifted her seat once or twice, so as to keep near to her friend; but, on every such occasion, Bessie would make such a point of removing again, that it seemed more unpleasant to follow her than to sit still. At length Inez could endure it no longer, but rose, and, calling Bessie, who by that time had taken up her station with her back turned to the lovers about a hundred yards away, she waited for her to join her.

Bessie approached with an air of demurest gravity, which would have made Inez laugh if it had not been so provoking. As she came near she threw at Inez a deprecating glance, and, with an air of childish shyness, walked by her side on a line with the others, but on the other side of the road. Inez gradually drew nearer to her, whereupon Bessie allowed herself to fall behind.

None of this was noticed by Blake, who was too much absorbed by the joy of the moment to detect any thing so covert as Bessie's course of teasing. In fact, he felt quite grateful to her for keeping away, and allowing him thus to have Inez all to himself. This feeling he could not help showing, and this only increased the annoyance and embarrassment of Inez. The position of a young lady in the presence of an ardent lover is never quite free from embarrassment when spectators are by; but, when the spectator is one who has shown herself to be a merciless tease, capable of dragging to the light the most hidden secrets of the young lady aforesaid, why it stands to reason that the embarrassment must become intolerable. So it proved with Inez. Her attention was thus distracted between Blake and Bessie; and, if she noticed any unusual devotion of manner or earnestness of tone, it only served to excite her fears that Bessie would see it also, and treasure it up in her memory for future reference.

When Bessie, therefore, fell behind, Inez slackened her pace also; upon which the former managed to increase the distance between them still farther.

"Bessie," said Inez, stopping short and waiting for her to come up, "I'm afraid you must be fatigued after your journey yesterday."

"Oh, dear, no, Inez dearest," said Bessie, with a smile. "Not at all. I am watching something that is awfully amusing. Go on. I'll join you as soon as—as it is advisable."

Upon this Inez turned away in despair, and walked thus with Blake back to the hotel, while Bessie followed at a little distance.

The hotel stood facing the water. In front of it was a portico. At this portico stood an elderly gentleman, whose appearance had in it much that would arrest the attention of the most casual observer. He was a man of medium height, and might have been about fifty years of age, yet there was an air of decrepitude about him which must have been caused by some other thing than his fifty years. He looked as though he might once have been portly, and that too not very long ago; but now the ample outline of his frame had receded somewhat, and an air of looseness was thus given to his figure. His hair was quite gray; his face was still full, but every trace of color had gone from it. He stood on the portico, leaning heavily against the base of a pillar, and his face was turned toward the water.

It was this face, and this alone, that gave this man his striking appearance. It was no common face. It was pale, ghastly pale, in fact, and the flesh which had once rounded its outlines had shrunk away, and now hung loosely in folds. His eyes were fixed upon vacancy, with a far-off, abstracted look. It was not the lake, or the mountains, or any material scene, that he was looking at. The placid water and the towering heights were reflected on his retina, but had no place in his thoughts. There was trouble in that face, deep, perplexed, and bewildered; and he who had thus come forth to gaze upon the face of Nature, presented his own face to the gaze of his fellow-man, and showed there something so woe-worn, so tragic in its sombre gloom, so full of despair, that it seemed as if the traces of crime, or of a ruined life, were marked upon it.

The ladies and their companion walked toward the hotel, and saw the old man, though they were not yet near enough to see his face.

"Papa is down," said Inez.

"Yes," said Blake. "He seems to be en-joying the view. I feel confident that this place will benefit him."

"Oh, I am so glad to hear you say so!"

As she said this, a footman came up to the portico. He had come from a house not far away. He had a letter in his hand. This letter he handed to the old man. He took it and opened it hastily. As he looked at it a change came over his face. With a quick gesture he crushed the letter together in his hand, and looked in an abstracted way all around. Blake and the ladies were near enough now for him to see them, but he did not notice them at all. The look seemed to have been an instinct blindly obeyed. He then turned his back to the street, and, opening the letter, stood there reading it. As he did so, he staggered slightly, and one hand caught at the pillar for support.

These strange actions, and the singular attitude of the old man, arrested the attention of Inez and Blake. They stopped, and looked, and as they stopped Bessie came up to them.

Suddenly the old man started. He staggered forward, and half turned. They were near enough now to see his face plainly. Upon that face they saw a wild look of terror—a look such as a drowning man may give while seeking for help.

Bessie caught Inez by the arm.

"Look! Oh, do look at your papa, Inez dear!" she cried. "Something's the matter."

There was no need to tell Inez this. She had seen it, but so great was her horror, that she had stood rooted to the spot, mute and motionless. But, as Bessie spoke, Blake started off at a run toward the portico.

If he anticipated what was about to happen, he was too late. Before Blake had gone a half-dozen steps, the old man gave a deep groan, and, suddenly collapsing, sank down senseless. At that moment Blake reached him. The next instant a dozen servants had arrived at the spot. Then Inez came flying up with a pale face, wild with alarm. The sight that met her eyes could not lessen that alarm one whit. That prostrate figure—that head swaying loosely as they raised him up, those nerveless hands, those staring eyes, those venerable hairs soiled with dust—all this only served to intensify her fears. Unaccustomed to scenes like these, she lost all presence of mind, and, clasping her hands in despair, she watched the servants with white lips and staring eyes, as they raised the senseless form and bore it into the house, and up the stairs to his chamber.

Here Blake sent away all the servants except one. He tried to urge Inez to go also, but she refused. Thereupon he devoted himself to the care of his patient, and sought in all possible ways to resuscitate him. An hour passed away, and, at the end of that time, there was little change perceptible. He was breathing, however, and he had closed his eyes. These were encouraging signs, but the stupor yet remained, and it did not seem as though he could be roused out of this.

Several hours more passed, and mid-day came. Blake now made one more effort to induce Inez to leave.

"I assure you, Miss Wyverne," said he, earnestly, " that your father is now doing as well as can be expected under the circumstances. These sudden shocks are very much to be dreaded, but in this case the worst, I hope, is passed. You see him now—he is sleeping. It may, perhaps, benefit him in the end. He has not had much sleep of late."

Blake spoke this as the man, and not as the doctor, because he wished to give Inez some hope, and Inez grasped at this hope which was held out.

" Sleep ? " she said. " Yes, it is—it must be sleep—but, oh, if he had only waked once —just to speak one word ! "

" He will wake in time. But let us be patient. Do not let us wake him now, Miss Wyverne. And now will you not try to get a little rest for yourself ? Let me entreat you as—as—ah—your medical adviser—to—to take care of yourself."

Inez at length allowed herself to be persuaded to retire, and sought her own room. Here Bessie came to her, and held a letter in her hand.

"Inez, darling," said she, "isn't this awful ? You know your poor, dear papa was reading a letter when he fainted. It was on the portico. He let it fall. I saw it and picked it up. This is it. You had better read it, and perhaps you can find out the cause of all this."

With these words she handed to Inez the letter which the old man had been reading.

Inez took it, and read the following:

" PARIS.

" MY DEAR HENNIGAR : I am sorry you are not the man you used to be, for you need all your strength now. The event which we have all along dreaded as barely possible has at last come to pass. B. M. is alive ! Worse —he has come back. I have seen him with my own eyes in Rome. He has not seen me. I have learned that, after he has attended to his ecclesiastical business, he intends to visit you. Fortunately, you are out of England. Would it not be well for you to go into hiding for a time—in Russia, or the East, or, better still—America ?

"I have just arrived here, and leave tonight for London, on important business. I hope soon to see you. You had better send away those girls at once. Above all, you must get rid of that boy. You were mad to encourage him. His mind has been poisoned by his mother. Depend upon it, he will ruin you. At all events send him off at once, and get Inez out of the way. B. M. will hunt you up, and find you, unless you fly out of his reach. It seems to me that it would be advisable, if possible, to get up a well-concocted *death*—so as to throw him off your track. Think of this.

" I hope to see you before a week.

" In great haste,

" Yours,

" KEVIN MAGRATH."

CHAPTER VI.

IS IT DELIRIUM ?

To Inez, this extraordinary letter was utterly unintelligible, and yet terrible on account of the dark and impenetrable mystery in which it was shrouded. She had read it with breathless interest, yet not until she reached the end was she aware of the fact that she was reading that which had never been intended for her eyes, or for any human eyes except those of Hennigar Wyverne himself. The deed was one which she felt to be dishonorable in itself, yet she could not blame herself. She had read it solely out of a pure and generous impulse—a desire to learn the cause of this sudden blow which had fallen upon her father. She had read it without hesitation, because she had never imagined that around that honored father could cling any secret that had to be veiled from her eyes or from any eyes. She had read it, and the deed for good or for evil was done beyond recall, nor could she forget one single word of all that ill-omened and evil-boding letter. As she had read it, Bessie had stood watching her; and now, as Inez looked up, she saw her friend's eyes fixed on her with sharp, eager scrutiny. The moment that Bessie caught the glance of Inez, she turned her eyes away; not so soon, however, but that the latter could read the meaning that was in them. By the expression of Bessie's face, and the look that was in her eyes, Inez saw plainly that she, too, must have read the letter; that she, too, had been startled by its mysterious meaning, and was now waiting to see the effect produced upon her. At this discovery an indignant feeling at once arose, which, however, in a few moments, was checked. For, after all, how could she blame her? She knew Bessie's thoughtless and wayward nature, her inquisitiveness, and her impulsive ways; she could easily understand how she, too, could read it with the same thoughtless haste that had characterized her own perusal. So she checked the sharp words that arose to her lips, and merely remarked:

"It's some business of poor papa's. I don't understand it, and I ought not to have read it."

She then flung herself upon the sofa, and turned her face to the wall. Whereupon Bessie softly left the room.

Left thus to herself, Inez, as she lay on the sofa, became a prey to all the thoughts which that letter was calculated to create. The more she thought about it, the less was she able to understand it; but the secret of the letter, though impenetrable, was something which she could not avoid thinking upon, and, though the full meaning was beyond her conjecture, there were a few plain and very ugly facts which stood forth clearly and unmistakably.

First of all, she saw that there was some one living of whom her father stood in mortal dread, named here as B. M. The dread of this mysterious man was evidently no new thing. He had been absent long, but they had always considered his return possible. They had hoped for his death, but found that he was alive. This B. M. was in Rome. He was on his way to England, to see her father.

Secondly, so great was the terror that attended upon the presence of this B. M. that the correspondent's first suggestion to her father was instant and immediate flight, even to the uttermost ends of the earth—Russia, the East, America.

Thirdly, this correspondent urged him to get rid of *the girls.* The girls! What girls? There could be no doubt that she herself and Bessie were meant, and herself more particularly, since greater emphasis was laid on her name. This dark secret affected her then, but how?

Fourthly, who was "the boy?" About this Inez could have no doubt whatever. "The boy" must be Dr. Blake. To no other could the term "encouragement" apply. He had certainly been "encouraged." Though an acquaintance of no very long standing, her father had manifested for Dr. Blake a regard which was wonderful, and quite unaccountable. This must be the "encouragement" of which the letter spoke. But who was the boy's mother, and how had she "poisoned" his mind? How was it that Dr. Blake could ever be the ruin of her father? Had he any connection with those dark events of the past? Dr. Blake had always seemed the most open, frank, and transparent nature in the world; and she could not understand how in his breast there could lurk the knowledge of any secret that could make him able to ruin her father, even if he were capable of wishing it.

Fifthly, this correspondent hinted that a pretended death might be advisable. Such a hint seemed to Inez the most terrible thing in the whole letter. It revealed an abyss into which she dared not allow her thoughts to venture. What terrors must cling to the past life of her father when there impended over him a danger so great that he could only escape it by instant flight or pretended death! Alas! as her father now was, if death was to be thought of, it might be only too real.

Again, this thing of terror, this mysterious "B. M.," who was he? What was meant by his "ecclesiastical" business? Could he be a priest? It must be so. Who else but a priest could have ecclesiastical business at Rome?

And, finally, who was this correspondent himself? He called himself "Kevin Magrath." Could it be a real name? It was evidently an Irish name. She had never heard of it before in all her life. The sound was utterly unfamiliar. Whoever he was, he seemed to lead a roving life, going from Rome to Paris, and from Paris to London, and promising to come here to Villeneuve. Whoever he was, he must be an old friend of her father's, and an associate in this dark mystery. With him, too, her father must have kept up a constant correspondence, for how else could this Kevin Magrath know his present address to be such an obscure place as Villeneuve?

She thought for a moment of asking Bessie about this man, but the next moment she dismissed the thought. She felt an invincible repugnance to making one like Bessie—or any one, in fact—a confidante of her present feelings. This secret seemed a dishonor to her father; and Bessie's knowledge of the existence of any such secret was of itself most disagreeable to her. Instead, therefore, of saying any thing to her friend about it, she saw that it would be far better to hide her feelings from her, and make it appear, if possible, that she thought nothing of it whatever. By so doing, she might induce Bessie to suppose that it was of no importance. This she hoped, but the recollection of that look which she had encountered from Bessie made her suspect that behind all her friend's apparent volatility and frivolity there were other qualities of a graver character—qualities, too, which might prove formidable in the future if it should ever happen that Bessie's interests should be blended with those of the enemies of her father.

The impenetrable secret thus baffled Inez completely, and there was nothing left but to wait for the disclosures of the future, and bear the intermediate suspense as best she could.

This Inez resolved to do, and her resolution was made easy by the situation of Mr. Wyverne. He lay, as he had been prostrated, without much change, upon the last verge of life, motionless, his breathing short and quick, opening his eyes wildly at times, murmuring incessantly to himself, and all the while his heart throbbing fast and furious He was not senseless now, for he could answer when he was addressed, but he seemed to be the prey of the most agonizing feelings, the torment of which made him unobservant of things around him.

Inez now watched over him incessantly, and the doctor also was equally devoted. He did not seek to conceal the truth from her. The danger was extreme. He knew it, and he could not bring himself to deceive her. She, on her part, being thus forced so constantly into the society of Blake, and with her secret gnawing at her heart, more than once thought of asking him about it; but no sooner had the thought came than it was repelled. Whatever might be her feelings toward him, she saw that this was clearly a case in which he could be of no assistance to her. She could not show that letter to one who, after all, was a stranger in a certain sense. She could not ask his advice in a case where a father's secret and a father's honor were involved.

Day after day passed, and there was no change. One day Inez implored Blake to tell her the worst.

"I can't bear this suspense," said she. "I expect the worst, the very worst, and I try to make up my mind to it; but I should like to know if there may be any ground for hope."

"Miss Wyverne," said the doctor, sadly, "while there's life, there's hope."

"I know—I know," said Inez, "that old formula, used to disguise the worst intelligence."

Blake sighed, and looked at her compassionately.

"Oh, how I wish," said he, "that I could spare you this!"

"You have no hope, then?" wailed forth Inez, looking at him with awful eyes.

Blake returned her glance with a mournful look, and in silence.

Inez had hoped for some faint encouragement, and this silence was almost too much. But, by a strong effort, she controlled herself.

"Tell me all," she said, in a scarce audible voice. "Let me know all."

"Agitation," said Blake, solemnly and slowly, "is fatal. If I could see any hope of saving him from this—if I could only gain control over his thoughts! But there is something on his mind always. He never sleeps. He eats nothing. Opiates have no effect. It is his mind. There is trouble, and it overwhelms him. If he should sleep, his dreams would be worse than his waking thoughts. I cannot 'minister to a mind diseased.'"

At this, Inez went away to her own room and wept.

So Wyverne lay, struggling with the dark secret that was over his soul, murmuring words that were unintelligible to those beside him, with that in his mind which was a horror by night and by day. Thus a week passed, and during this time he grew worse and worse. Of this there was no doubt. The doctor saw it. Inez knew it.

At length one day came when he opened his eyes, and fixed them with a glassy stare upon Inez, who, as usual, was sitting at his bedside.

"Papa, dear," said she, in a choking voice.

"Who—are—you?" were the words that came with a gasp from the sick man on the bed.

Inez shuddered.

She took his hand tenderly in hers, and, bending over him, she said:

"Don't you know me, papa dear—your daughter—your child—your Inez?"

Mr. Wyverne frowned, and snatched his hand away.

"I have no daughter," he gasped. "You are not mine. You are *his*. *He* is coming for you—for you and—for—vengeance! *He* is coming. *He* is coming. *He* is coming—"

A groan ended this, but the sick man went on murmuring, in a sing-song way, like some horrible chant, the words, "*He* is coming! *He* is coming! *He* is coming! *He* is coming!"

A cold shudder passed through Inez. She drew back and buried her face in her hands. Was this real? Did he mean it? What horror was this?

Blake had heard all, and had seen her distress. He bent over her and whispered:

"Don't be distressed at what he says. He don't know you. It's his delirium."

The whisper seemed to attract the attention of the sick man. He turned his eyes till they rested upon Blake's face. His own expression changed. There came a gentle smile upon his wan features; he sighed; and then he reached forth his hand faintly.

Blake saw this, and took his hand wonderingly.

"Basil!" said Mr. Wyverne, in a soft, low voice, full of a strange, indescribable tenderness, "Basil—is your—your mother still alive?"

"Yes," said Blake, full of amazement—Mr. Wyverne had called him by his Christian name!

The sick man closed his eyes. There were tears in them—they trickled slowly down. Inez still sat with her face buried in her hands. Blake wiped those tears away, and waited to hear what might be said, with all his soul full of wonder and awe, and a certain fearful expectation.

"Basil," said Mr. Wyverne, opening his eyes again, and fastening them with the same look upon Blake, speaking faintly and wearily, and with frequent hesitation, "I dare not tell you—ask *her* to tell you—all—all—all."

Once more his thoughts wandered, but he still clung to Blake's hand, and would not let it go.

After an interval, he opened his eyes and looked at Blake.

"Kiss me—Basil," he said.

At this Blake bent down and kissed the forehead of the sick man—damp and cold as with the chill-dew of death.

Not one word of all this had been lost on Inez, and at these last words she raised herself, and saw through her tears what was done. Full of wonder, and deeply wounded also at the neglect with which she was treated, she sat there a prey to the deepest grief. Blake saw this, and, as the sick man again closed his eyes, he murmured in her ear:

"*It's his delirium.*"

The sick man again opened his eyes; they rested upon Blake as before, and then wandered toward Inez, whose pale face was turned toward him, and whose eyes were fixed entreatingly upon him, as though seeking for some look of love.

He looked at her mildly, and then, turning his eyes to Blake, there came over his face a smile of strange sweetness.

"You—love—her—Basil?"

These words came from him faintly. As he said this, the face of Inez flamed up with a sudden and violent flush. Blake said nothing, but pressed his hand. The sick man took Blake's hand in his own left hand, and reached out his right hand feebly, looking at Inez. She took his hand in hers, not knowing what he wished, but still hoping for some word of love. He drew her hand toward him, and joined it to that of Blake's, pressing the two together between his feeble palms. Then he looked at them both, with that same strange, sweet smile on his face.

"My children! my children!" he murmured. "My children!" he continued, after a pause, "you will love one another. You will—love her—Basil—and—make her—yours—promise!" and he looked earnestly at Blake.

To Inez all this was exquisitely painful, and Blake did not know what to say.

"Swear," said the sick man.

"Oh, yes," said Blake, in a low voice.

Mr. Wyverne gave a sigh of satisfaction, and lay for some time exhausted, but still holding their hands. Once more he rallied.

"Basil," said he, "I cannot tell you—what is on—my mind—dare not—you shall know all—your mother—ask her—you will forgive me, Basil—my son."

Son! that word had a strange sound, but it seemed to mean *son-in-law*, and thus they both understood it. But in the mind of Inez this declaration interweaved itself with other thoughts which had been called up by that mysterious letter.

"Your mother," continued the sick man, looking at Blake, "will tell you all—all. Swear that you—forgive me."

"I swear," said Blake, willing to say any thing which might humor the sick man's fancies.

"And you—you," continued Mr. Wyverne, turning his glassy eyes toward Inez with an agonized look, "you—*his* daughter—you will tell all to *him*—that I repent—and die—of—of—remorse!"

At this Inez tore her hand away, and once more flung herself forward in an agony of grief.

"*It's his delirium!*" whispered the doctor again. These words restored Inez. It was all fancy, she thought. It was not—no, it could not be the truth.

But now the sick man seemed utterly exhausted. As Inez raised herself up, and looked at him once more, she saw that a change had come over him, and that change frightened her.

"I'm dying," he gasped, "send a priest—a priest!"

At this Blake at once hurried from the room.

He did not have to go far.

There was a priest in the hotel. He had arrived the night before. He had come from Italy, and was on his way to Paris. The doctor had heard of this, and went at once in search of him. The priest had arrived late, and had slept late. He was just dressed, and thus Blake found him.

He was a man of medium stature, with dark complexion, browned by exposure to the weather. He had piercing black eyes and heavy eyebrows. His jaw was square, massive, and resolute; yet, in spite of all this, the face was one full of mildness and gentleness—showing a strong nature, yet a kindly one—a face where dwelt the signs of a power which might achieve any purpose, and the indications of a nature which was quick to sympathy, and full of human feeling. His frame was erect and vigorous. His hair was black, and sprinkled with gray. He could not be over fifty, and might be much younger. This was the man that Blake found.

The priest at once prepared to comply with Blake's request, and followed him to the sick man's chamber. As he entered, Inez shrank out of sight, and retreated to her room, waiting there, with a heart full of despair, the result of this last interview.

The priest took no notice of her. His eyes, as he entered, were fixed upon the bed where lay the man who had sought his offices at this last hour of life.

There lay Hennigar Wyverne.

A great change had passed over him since the morning when he had received that letter. Feeble though he then was, there still might be seen in him some remnant of his former self, something that might show what he once was; but now not a vestige remained; the week's illness had altered him so greatly that he had passed beyond the power of recognition; he was fearfully emaciated; he was ghastly pale; his cheek-bones protruded; his eyes were deep-sunk; his lips were drawn apart over his teeth; his white hair was tangled about his head, and short, gray bristles covered his once smooth-shaven chin. He lay there muttering to himself unintelligible things, and picking aimlessly at the bedclothes.

The priest approached. Blake stood by the door.

The priest bent over the sick man, and roused him.

Wyverne opened his glassy eyes and fastened them on the priest. As he did so, there came over him an appalling change.

In those dull, glassy eyes there shone the light of a sudden and awful recognition; and, with that recognition, there was a look of ter-

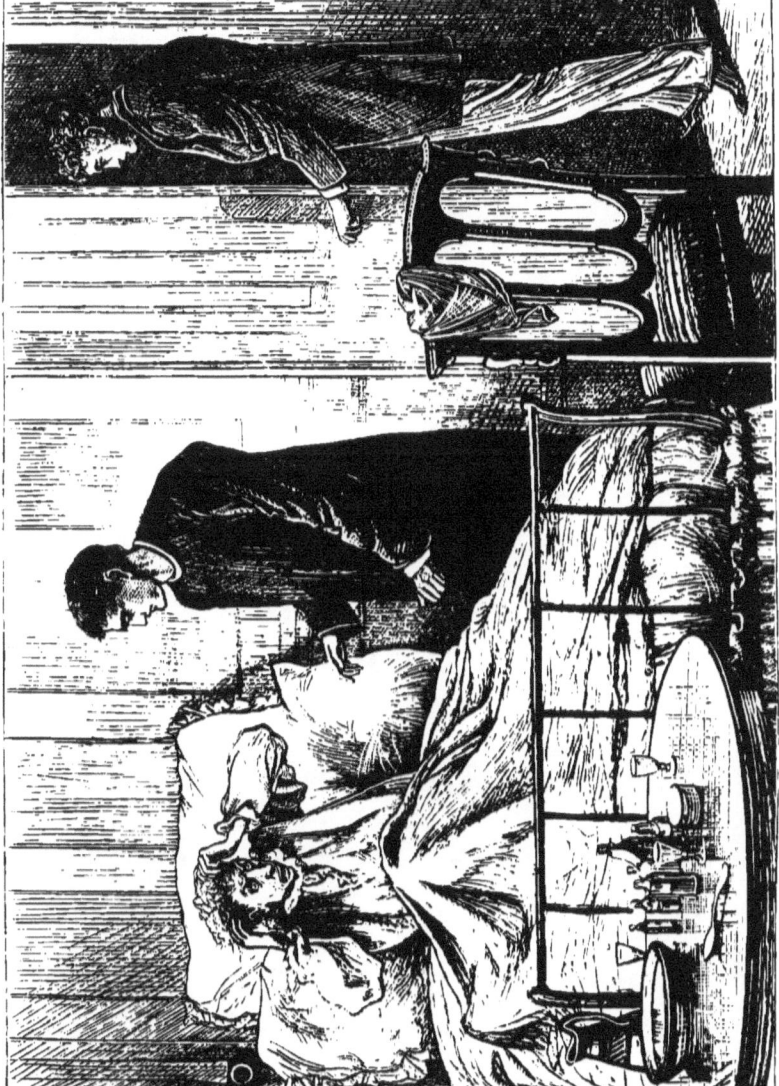

"In those days, grimly dye, there shone the light of a solemn and awful recognition." —Page 36.

ror unspeakable, of horror intolerable. Yet that look seemed fascinated; it could not be withdrawn; it was fastened on the face before him in one fixed gaze. Suddenly, and with a groan, he gave a convulsive start, as though he would fly from that which either his eyes or his wild fancy had thus presented before him. But the effort was too much. His strength was gone. This was its last effort. One movement, and then he fell down.

He lay motionless now.

Blake was just about leaving the room; but he saw this, and waited. As Wyverne fell, he rushed up to the bedside with a pale face. He looked at the form which lay there, and then at the priest. The priest looked with a mournful face at the figure on the bed.

There it lay, the thin, emaciated frame from which the soul had gone! That horror which had been the latest expression of those features still lurked there; the eyes stared at the ceiling; the jaws had fallen.

Blake stooped down and closed, with tender hands, the eyes of the dead.

"I have come too late," said the priest, in a low and mournful voice.

"The delirium has lasted for a week," said Blake. "He has imagined something terrible in you."

CHAPTER VII.

THE GOLD CRUCIFIX.

THUS the blow had fallen at last; and, though Inez had tried to prepare herself for it, she felt crushed by it when it came. For the death itself she might have been ready; it was not the mere fact of bereavement, not merely the sorrow of a loving daughter, that now overwhelmed her. It was something far different which had its origin in the circumstances that had preceded and immediately accompanied his death. Already she had felt sore distressed and perplexed by the terrible possibilities that had been hinted at in that unintelligible letter, and she had tried to turn her thoughts away from so painful a subject. In vain. The circumstances around her had not allowed her to do so. The sick man himself forced them upon her; and, in addition to all that she had already learned, he had uttered words most terrible even to hear as

delirious ravings, but which, if true, told things that could not be endured.

Let us see, now, what the circumstances were that immediately followed Mr. Wyverne's death.

Inez had left the sick man's chamber as the priest entered. She had gone at once to her own room. She had flung herself upon her couch, with her face buried in the pillows, recalling every incident in that terrible scene which she had just witnessed. That her hand should be joined to the hand of Basil Blake might, under different circumstances, have had in it nothing distasteful to her feelings; but, at this time, and under such conditions, it had been simply frightful. For her father had struck her down by the terrors of the revelation that he had made; he had installed another in her place next his heart, and it was only through the medium of this supplanter and usurper of her place that he received her back to his love.

Her father had said that she was not his daughter. This was the one thought that now stood preëminent in her mind. And was this declaration the act of a sane man, or was it the raving of an insane man? Dr. Blake had insisted, over and over again, that it was delirium. Did Dr. Blake really believe so himself, or had he said that merely to console her for the time?

How could she answer such questions as these?

In the midst of these thoughts she suddenly became aware of a certain awful hush—a solemn stillness through all the house. It was as though all in the house had simultaneously stopped breathing.

Something had happened.

There was only one thing, as Inez knew well, which could account for this—the one thing toward which her fearful soul had been looking. But it was doubly terrible now. It was too soon. She expected to see him again. Her last hope would be that he might take back all those words. What if he had left her now forever? What if his last words to her should be nothing more than those appalling ones which she had just heard.

She started to her feet, and stood with her hands clasped together, her limbs rigid, her pallid face turned to the door in awful expectation, her eyes staring wildly, her ears strained to catch the slightest sound. The silence continued for what seemed to her a fearful length of time. At last there were footsteps in the hall. She wished to go and make inquiries, and put an end to her suspense; but she could not move.

Then there came a light knock at the door. Inez tried to speak, but could not. The handle was turned. The door opened slowly.

It was her maid Saunders.

The maid's face was quite pale; she held a corner of her apron to her eyes, and looked furtively and hesitatingly at her mistress.

"Oh, if you please, miss," she began, and then stopped.

Inez tried to speak, and again was unable to utter a word.

"Miss Mordaunt thought I'd best let you know, miss—immejitly, if you please, miss—and, if you please, miss, he—it—your poor papa—it's—it's all over, miss."

"He's dead!" moaned Inez, in a low, tremulous voice; and then, turning away, she flung herself again upon her couch.

Saunders stood looking at her for some time, as though waiting for orders. But no orders came from her mistress. She satisfied herself that she had not fainted, and then quietly left the room. Outside, Miss Mordaunt was waiting, who came in and looked at Inez for a moment. She saw, however, that nothing could be done, and therefore very naturally concluded that for the present the bereaved daughter ought to be left to herself.

Inez now remained motionless for several hours. All the while her mind was filled with the remembrance of those words which formed so strange a legacy from a dying father to a daughter, and with the unparalleled thoughts to which those words gave rise. It was easy to recall them all. Over and over again she reiterated them: "*I have no daughter! You are not mine! You are his! He is coming for you and for vengeance!*" Together with these words she recalled his words to Blake. It was Blake who had kissed him. It was Blake to whom he had shown a father's love. It was also Blake, no doubt, who had closed his eyes when all was over.

It was about an hour before sundown when Inez at length roused herself. She rose, arranged her dress, and called her maid. Saunders came in, as before, cautiously, and watching her mistress furtively.

"I wish to see him," said Inez. "Go and ask if I may see him now."

She spoke in a low voice, but without any tremor that could be detected.

"Oh, yes, miss," said Saunders, "you may. They told me to tell you more'n an hour ago."

Inez said no more, but left the room, followed by Saunders, and went to the apartment around which so many griefs were already gathered. She opened the door. The curtains were drawn.

"Wait here for me," said she to Saunders, and then, entering, she closed the door behind her.

The room was too dark to see any thing, and Inez drew one of the curtains aside and thus let in a dim light. Then she turned toward the bed, whereon she saw the outline of the figure stretched out there. For a moment she hesitated, and then advanced till she reached the head of the bed, where she stood for a few moments in thought. At length, with a steady hand, she drew down the covering from off the face of the dead.

There it lay, all that was mortal of the man whom she had called father, but who had disowned her with his last, dying words, and who, before her very eyes, as she sat crushed and stricken before him, had installed another in her place, and driven her from his heart. Against such treatment her soul rebelled; the dark doubt that he had cast into her mind as to whether he was her father prevented her now from mourning over the dead with a daughter's grief; and, even as she looked at the face of the dead, her chief and uppermost thoughts were about the impenetrable mystery that now surrounded her.

That thin, withered face, cold in death, with its sunken cheeks, and projecting cheekbones, and hollow orbits, where the closed eyes lay sunken, bore no resemblance to the one who in life had been known as Hennigar Wyverne. The lips were drawn back, and the teeth were disclosed, so that there was formed something like a grisly smile. It seemed to Inez that this man was yet mocking her even in death, and that this ghastly smile had been called up by her approach. The thought was too horrible. She drew back the covering, and turned away.

She turned away and stood in the middle of the apartment with her face averted from the dead. Of the manner of his death she had as yet heard nothing. Whether he had said any thing more or not—whether he had retracted or confirmed his declaration about her, she could not know, and this she was eager to learn. This she could find out only from Dr. Blake. To send for him was, however, so repugnant to her delicacy that she hesitated for some time; but finally, seeing that there was no alternative, she went to the door and told the maid to ask him to come.

In a few moments Blake entered. He bowed to her in silence. He did not attempt to console her, or to condole with her. There were reasons which made any such things impossible, for, while the astonishing words of the deceased had disturbed Inez as we have seen, they had produced in the mind of Blake an effect in every respect as perplexing, as confusing, and as agitating. Those dying words lived in his memory as in hers, but she was the last one in all the world with whom he would care to discuss them.

Inez was seated near the window, and Blake took a seat not far away. The silence lasted for some time. Inez had much to ask, but knew not how to begin.

"Dr. Blake," said she, at length, in a low, mournful voice, "it was very unfortunate that I left—him—so soon—but I thought that he would be spared to us a little longer. Was there not time, after his confession, to call me?"

"There was not," said Blake, slowly—and then after a pause he added, "There was no confession."

"No confession!" exclaimed Inez.

The doctor shook his head.

"He was not able to speak when the priest came to him. Before you had been gone ten minutes—all was over."

Inez looked at him earnestly.

"He said nothing, then?"

"Nothing," said Blake.

For this intelligence Inez was not quite prepared, for she had hitherto supposed that a confession had been made to the priest—in which case she hoped that some result might come of it. But he had died and made no sign, and this it was that now seemed most bitter. And now what next was there to inquire—what more should she ask of him? That next question trembled on her lips, yet she feared to ask it. The question would be a final one—a decisive one. It would change her whole future life—it would affect it materially for weal or woe. It would put an end to her suspense on one point, and confirm one dark suspicion or remove it.

"Dr. Blake," said she, at length, after a long delay, fixing her sad eyes earnestly upon him, with a look that showed him that no evasion would be tolerated now; and speaking in a voice whose mournful intonations found an echo in the depths of his soul—"Dr. Blake—you know what his dying words—his last words to me were—and his last acts—you know also what those dying words and acts were to you. You must understand the whole force of their appalling meaning—and you must see that even the death of one whom I have loved as a father, cannot be more terrible than that revelation which he seemed to make. While he was speaking you told me that it was only delirium. I ask you now in the name of that God who sees us both—did you speak the truth? Will you now say to me that it was delirium."

She stopped, and her eyes, which had never withdrawn themselves from his, seemed now to rest on him with a more imperative earnestness, as though they would extort the truth from him. His own eyes fell, and a feeling of something like dismay took possession of him, as he thought of the answer which she was forcing from him.

"You will not answer me," said Inez, mournfully, after a long pause.

Blake drew a long breath.

"It is not always possible to say exactly," said he, in a hesitating manner, "how much of delirium enters into the fancies of a sick man. He was feverish—he had been taking powerful drugs—at that time his mind may have gone altogether astray. It is hardly possible to answer your question positively."

"Have you thought of those words since?"

"I have, and I assure you most solemnly that I cannot attach any intelligible meaning to them."

"In my case," said Inez, thinking of the letter, "circumstances have occurred which give a strange and painful significance to those words, though I cannot understand how they can be true."

Blake said nothing. He, too, had his own reasons for attaching a painful significance to those words. But he did not wish to say one word which might increase the trouble of Inez. He wished, if possible, to say that which might remove her suspicions, yet this very thing he knew not how to say.

"One more question," said Inez. "Do

you now believe, in your own heart, Dr. Blake, that those words were the language of delirium ? "

Blake's heart beat fast. He looked at Inez, and then looked away. He knew not how to answer this direct question. He would have been willing to evade, or even to indulge in a little mild deceit for her sake; but with those clear, sad, earnest eyes fastened upon him, no deceit, however slight, was possible.

" You do not answer," said Inez. " Your silence can have only one meaning. Will you say that you believe those words were delirium ? "

Blake looked at her with a face full of mournful deprecation. It seemed to him at that moment that his inability to give the answer which she wished, was placing between them an eternal barrier, yet that answer was one which he could not give. In his secret soul he knew perfectly well that the words of the dying man were sane and rational.

Silence now followed, and Blake, after waiting some minutes, and finding that Inez had nothing further to say, rose and took his departure, leaving her alone with the dead.

And now an incident occurred which seemed to complicate still more the extraordinary net-work of bewildering circumstances that was interweaving itself about Inez.

She was sitting by the window. Her back was turned toward the bed. In order to put herself in that position, she had moved the chair a short distance from the place where it had been standing. It was a heavy stuffed chair, without castors, and to move it required some effort. As she sat here, her feet rested on the very place where the chair had originally stood.

As Blake retired, she leaned her head forward, and, feeling weary, she looked for some support to it. The window-ledge was at the right height to give this support. Upon this window-ledge she placed her right hand, and then turned herself slightly, so as to rest her forehead on this hand. As she made this movement, her foot struck something that lay upon the floor, and a slight clinking sound arose. Thinking that it might be some ornament which had fallen, she stooped to pick it up.

On lifting it up, she found, however, that it was no ornament, but something of a far different kind.

It was a crucifix, to which was attached a small fragment of chain. Raising it close to the light, the very first glance filled her with astonishment.

The crucifix was about three inches long. It was of solid gold, and of the most exquisite workmanship. The broken chain was also of gold, and it seemed to have been snapped asunder unknown to the wearer, who had gone away, leaving it here behind him.

But who was the owner ?

Not Mr. Wyverne. He had nothing of the kind, nor was he a man who would have carried such an article on his travels.

It seemed to Inez most probable that this golden crucifix belonged to the priest. This priest had come, but his office was not performed. There may have been some agitation in his mind at so sudden a call, followed by so sudden a death; and, as his thoughts were occupied with this unusual event, he may not have noticed the loss of the crucifix. The chain may have broken by catching on some projection, such as the arm of the chair. It had fallen to the floor, and perhaps under the chair, where it had lain unnoticed until she had moved the chair from its usual place.

In this way Inez accounted for the extraordinary presence of the golden crucifix in this chamber. But, while she was thus thinking, she was gazing intently upon the elaborate work, and the exquisite design of the crucifix itself; and, finally, having studied one side, she turned it over with the idea that the name of the owner might possibly be engraved on the reverse, or something else which might give a clew to its ownership. The moment that she turned it over, her attention was arrested by some letters. Looking at them closely, she read the following.

At the intersection of the arms of the cross were these letters :

B. M.

In Memoriam.

I. M.

On the lower part of the cross, and running down its length, were these words:

Pie Jesu Domine,
Dona ei requiem. Amen.

As Inez looked at these letters, she felt utterly confounded, and could scarce believe her own eyes. Yet there were those letters unmistakably, the initials which for a week and more had filled all her thoughts; the mysterious letters, B. M., which all that time had been present in her thoughts by day and night. What did this mean? How came the crucifix here—this crucifix, marked with such signs as these?

That it did not and could not belong to Mr. Wyverne she felt confident, as has been said. She knew that he had brought no such article with him. He was indifferent to all religious matters; and, besides, she had been his nurse for a week, during which time that very chair had been frequently moved. She reverted then more confidently than ever to her former conclusion, that it belonged to the priest; and then at once arose the question, How came this priest by any such thing as this? One wild thought instantly arose that the priest himself was B. M. The letter had stated that he was in Rome, on his way to England. Might not this priest have been the very man? And, if so, what then? What had happened at that interview? Had they spoken together, or had Mr. Wyverne avoided his dreaded enemy in a more efficacious manner than that which the letter had suggested, and fled from him, not by a pretended death, but by one that was real? Could the priest be B. M.? If so, she might see him, and solve all the mystery.

With this thought, she called in her maid. "Is the priest here, Saunders?" asked Inez.

"Oh, no, miss; he left long ago."

"Long ago? How long ago?"

"Not very long, miss, after—after poor master's—after he was took," said Saunders, hesitating in the effort to find some suitable way of mentioning the dread subject of death. This intelligence was to Inez a sad disappointment.

"Do you know where he went?"

"No, miss."

"Do you know his name?"

"No, miss; but, if you please, miss, I'll go for John Thomas. I think he knows, miss."

"Send him to my room," said Inez. "I'm going there." Saying this, Inez rose, wearily, and returned to her own apartment.

In a few minutes John Thomas made his appearance. He was a tall footman, with heavy face and irreproachable calves. He bowed, and said:

"I beg pardin, miss; but wos you a wantin' me?"

After which he stood with the corners of his mouth drawn down, and a lugubrious aspect on his face, which was maintained by an occasional snuffle.

"I want to ask you about that priest," said Inez. "Do you know his name?"

"Me, miss? No, miss; and, wot's more, there's nobody about 'ere as knows it. I allus likes to know wot's goin' on, miss; but this 'ere priest got ahead of me."

"Didn't he give any name?"

"Name, miss? No, miss. He came late last night, and left early this mornin', not long after the—the late mournful bereavemink, miss."

At this, Inez felt utterly disheartened.

"Nobody knows hany think about 'im more'n me; an' wot I knows hain't no more'n the letters of 'is name, which I see 'em on 'is valise, as 'e walked out of the hinn."

"Letters of his name!" exclaimed Inez, catching at these words. "What letters did you see?"

"Why, miss, I felt hinquisitive about 'im, and, has I couldn't find hout 'is name, I watched 'is valise. It 'ad two letters on it, painted quite big—"

"Two letters!" said Inez, breathlessly. "What were they?"

"The letters," said John Thomas, "wos B. M."

At this confirmation of her theory, Inez was too much overcome to make any rejoinder, but sat in silence and perplexity for some time. At last she looked up.

"What did he look like?" she asked, abruptly.

"The priest, miss?—mejium size, miss; dark complected; heyes black, and 'eavy heyebrows; 'is 'air, too, miss, wos a hir'n gray. He looked more like a Hitalian than a Henglishman, miss."

To Inez this information gave no assistance; but she noted in her mind the chief points in this description, in case of future need.

She saw Dr. Blake once more that same evening, and received from him a still more minute description of the personal appearance of the priest "B. M."

CHAPTER VIII.

THE EBONY CASKET, AND ITS STRANGE CON-
TENTS.

THE remains of Hennigar Wyverne were
sent home for burial.

Inez and Bessie, with their servants, left
for home immediately.

Dr. Blake accompanied them as far as
Boulogne. He had no encouragement whatever to do this. Inez was preoccupied, and
so buried in the depths of her own gloomy
thoughts that she seemed to be unconscious
of his presence. At Boulogne, therefore, he
bade her farewell, and stood upon the pier,
gazing with mournful eyes upon the steamer
that bore Inez away from him, until it was
out of sight.

Inez had not chosen—for reasons already
mentioned—to make a confidante of Bessie.
It is to be supposed, therefore, that this young
lady had no idea of the peculiar troubles of
her friend, but attributed them, as was natural, to the pain of bereavement. She showed
the utmost delicacy in her behavior toward
Inez, and never sought to utter any of those
condolences which are so useless to assuage
the true grief of the heart. She refrained
also from intruding upon the solitude of Inez
when she showed that she wished to be alone,
and merely evinced her affection by sundry
little attentions which were directed toward
the bodily comfort of her friend. Whatever
Bessie's own thoughts or feelings were, they
never appeared; nor was it certain at all
whether she felt wounded or slighted by the
reserve of one from whom she might perhaps
have claimed greater confidence. But Inez
was naturally of a reserved temper, and, even
if she had been the most communicative soul
in the world, the secret that she now had was
one which few would care to communicate.

In that great craving and longing to express her secret griefs which Inez felt, as
most people feel, at this time, she had re-
course to a simple plan, which was not without its advantages. She wrote down the chief
facts of her mysterious case in her private
memorandum-book, and over these words her
eyes used often to wander, not merely in the
solitude of her own room, but even in the
greater publicity of rail-cars and steamboats.

What Inez wrote down was as follows:

1. *For some unknown cause, H. W. and
B. M. were mortal enemies.*

2. *It seems as if H. W. was the offender,
and B. M. the injured one.*

3. *For this reason, perhaps, H. W. stood in
mortal terror of B. M.*

4. *A third party in this case is one Kevin
Magrath.*

5. *I have been brought up as the daughter
of H. W.*

6. *H. W., on his death-bed, and with his
last words, has solemnly said that I am not his
daughter.*

7. *H. W. has said, on his death-bed, that I
am the daughter of his mortal enemy, B. M.*

8. *H. W. has said, on his death-bed, that
Basil Blake is his son.*

9. *B. M. is a Roman Catholic priest.*

10. *How can I be the daughter of a R. C.
priest?*

11. *B. M. was present at the death-bed of
H. W., and saw him die.*

12. *If he is my father, why did he not
seek for me? Answer—Because he may have
been told that I am dead.*

13. *B. M. dropped his crucifix. I found it.*

By constantly brooding over these things,
which she had thus summed up that they
might be always present to her eyes, Inez
found herself sinking deeper and deeper into
an abyss of bewilderment from which no out-
let appeared. The great question was, What
shall I do? and this she could not answer.
Her own helplessness was utter. Her position was most false and intolerable. The
name by which she was known was not hers.
Her parentage was thrown in doubt, and that
doubt indicated something intolerable to a
mind like hers. Out of all this confusion and
misery she had one definite purpose only, and
that was, to carry on the search as soon as
she reached home, and take the first opportunity that presented itself of investigating
the papers of Hennigar Wyverne.

To one who was so eager as she was, the
first opportunity would inevitably be seized.
Scarce had Inez set foot within her house, than
she began a search among those effects of the
deceased which had been sent home already.
Here she found nothing; but a greater search
was before her—one, too, which she had held
in view all along, and for which she had prepared herself before leaving Villeneuve. This
was the investigation of the cabinet of Hennigar Wyverne, where she supposed he would

have been most likely to keep any thing relating to the great mystery, if, indeed, any
thing at all had been kept. At Villeneuve
she had thought of this, and had prepared
for it by obtaining then, before the effects of
the deceased were packed up, the keys of that
very cabinet. These he had carried with
him, and she found them in his travelling-
desk.

Inez had no difficulties thrown in her way.
Bessie showed no inclination to interfere
with any of her movements. She still maintained the same delicate consideration which
has already been mentioned. She seemed
rather to wait for Inez to make the first advances toward their old confidence, and ventured upon nothing more than the usual kiss
at meeting in the morning and parting at
night, and an occasional caress when the
mood of Inez seemed to allow it. Bessie had
also cultivated a pathetic expression of face,
which was quite in accordance with her style
of beauty, and made her look so very interesting that Inez once or twice felt inclined to
break her resolution and confide all to her
friend. This, however, was but a momentary
impulse, which a second thought never failed
to destroy.

The city residence of the late Hennigar
Wyverne, Esq., was a large and handsome
edifice in a fashionable quarter of London.
Opposite the morning-room was an apartment
which was called the library, but which had
been used by the deceased as a kind of office.
Books were around on three sides, while on
the fourth were two articles of furniture devoted rather to business than to literature or
learning. One of these was a closet, filled
with papers all neatly labelled and lying in
pigeon-holes. The other was a massive cabinet, which contained the more important books
and papers. It was this last which Inez wished
more particularly to search.

To carry on such a search would require
time, and it would be necessary to be free
from observation. These conditions could
not be obtained by day, and night must be
the time. Among the hours of the night it
would be necessary to choose those when the
household would be certain to be asleep.
Those hours would be, at least, not earlier
than two in the morning. At that time she
might hope to be unnoticed, unsuspected, and
undisturbed. This was the time, then, that
Inez decided upon, and she resolved to carry

her great purpose into execution on the second night after her arrival.

In spite of the great necessity which she
felt pressing her on to this task, it was one
from which Inez recoiled instinctively. It
seemed to be a dishonorable thing. But this
notion was one which she reasoned herself
out of; and by pleading the dictates of duty
she silenced what was perhaps, after all, nothing more than false sensitiveness.

It was not so easy, however, to overcome
that weakness of nerve and natural timidity
which were caused by the nature of her undertaking. Setting out thus on this midnight
errand, it seemed to her as though she were
about to commit some sin; and it was some
time, even after the hour had arrived, before
she felt strong enough to venture down. At
length she rallied her sinking strength, and
stealthily left her room. Pausing there, she
stood listening. All was still. She carried a
wax-candle, but it was not lighted. She had
some matches, and could light the candle
when she reached the library.

Softly and stealthily she descended. There
was no interruption of any kind whatever.
She reached the library and entered, after
which she shut the door as softly as possible,
and locked it on the inside. She then took
her handkerchief and stuffed it into the key-
hole. After this she examined the windows,
and found that the blinds were closed. No
light could now betray her presence here, and
so she lighted her candle and looked around
her.

The dim light of the single flickering candle but feebly illuminated the large and lofty
room. In the distance the walls and shelves
stood enveloped in gloomy shadows. But
Inez had eyes only for that cabinet which she
had come to explore. It was immediately in
front of her, and she held the keys in her
hand.

For a moment she hesitated. It seemed
to her now that the moment had come—the
supreme moment when the secret would be
all revealed. Yet about that revelation what
horrors might not hang! Already one revelation had taken place, and it had been bitter
indeed. Would this be less so? It seemed
to her as though about the secret of her parentage there lurked endless possibilities of
crime, and shame, and dishonor.

But there was no time to lose. Suddenly
mastering her feelings, she put the key in the

lock. The bolt turned back. She opened the door.

Before her lay the ordinary contents of a cabinet. There were account-books standing upright, and papers filed away and labelled, so numerous that the sight discouraged Inez. It would take many days to look over them all. But they were all labelled so carefully that it seemed possible for her to get a general idea of most of them after all. She knelt down in front of the cabinet, and, drawing up a chair, she put the candle upon it. Then she began to look over the papers, beginning at the right-hand corner.

This task soon became very wearisome. Bundle after bundle of papers revealed no name that had any connection with those initials whose meaning she was so eager to discover. Some were receipts, others letters, others documents of a business nature. At length she paused, and her eyes wandered despondently over the whole assemblage of papers, to see if there was any thing there which seemed by its position or appearance to indicate any thing peculiar, any thing different from the monotony of the others.

In the very middle of the cabinet there was a square drawer about a foot in width and depth, and this seemed to Inez to be a place where more important or more private documents might be kept. It seemed best to open this at once. She had the whole bunch of keys with her, which she had obtained possession of at Villeneuve, and felt sure that the key to this drawer would be among them. One by one she tried the keys that were on the bunch, and at last found one, as she had hoped, which would fit. She unlocked the drawer and opened it.

One look inside showed her that at length she had found one thing at least which she desired—something different from the general assemblage of receipts, letters, and business documents.

A casket lay there before her, inside the drawer. It was quite small, not more than six inches in length, and was made of ebony, with silver corners and edges, together with silver feet, and a handle of the same metal. At the sight of this, she felt an uncontrollable impatience to get at the secret of its contents, and snatched it with eager hands out of the drawer. Some letters on the silver plate of the casket, immediately underneath the handle, attracted her attention. She held it close

to the light. The silver here was somewhat tarnished, and the letters were of an antique Gothic character, such as are used for inscriptions over the doors of cathedrals, and at first were not quite intelligible. But Inez rubbed at the silver with her sleeve till the plate grew bright, and then once more held it to the candle.

The letters were now fully revealed. Her heart throbbed wildly at the sight. The letters before her eyes were those same ones which so haunted her—

B. M.

And, now, what should she do? Stay here and examine the casket? No. She was liable to discovery. She had been here long enough. Better, far, to take the little casket away and examine its contents in her own room, at her leisure, without the terror of possible discovery impending over her constantly, and constantly distracting her thoughts. In that casket she felt must lie all that she could hope to find, whatever it might be; and, if this were empty, or if its contents revealed nothing, then she would have to remain in her ignorance. If the casket held any thing, she might keep it; if not, she might return it at some future time; but, meanwhile, it was best for her to take it away.

So she now closed the drawer, locked it, then shut up and locked the cabinet; after which she rose to her feet, and, hiding the casket in the folds of her dress, she took the candle and prepared to leave the room.

Before unlocking the library-door she stood and listened. As she stood, she thought she heard a low, breathing sound close by her. Starting, in terror, she looked hastily around. But the room was all in gloom, and all empty and deserted. It seemed to her that it was merely her fancy. But once more, as she waited listening, she heard it even more plainly. This time it seemed like a suppressed cough. It was on the other side of the door.

In an instant it flashed upon her that she had been watched and followed, and that some one was now outside trying to peep through the keyhole. But who? Could it be some burglar, or could it possibly be one of the servants?

She waited still, and listened. But there was no further sound. The cough had been suppressed, and, if there was any one watching, he gave no sign now. There was something fearful, to this defenceless young girl, in the thought that on the other side of the door might be some lurking enemy, and that the moment she opened it he might spring upon her; and, for a long time, she stood in fear, unable to open it. But beneath this fear there was another fear of too long a delay—the fear of being discovered in this place—of being compelled to give up her casket before she had examined its contents; and this roused her to a sudden pitch of resolution.

She removed her handkerchief from the key-hole, and inserted the key as noiselessly as possible. Then turning it, she opened the door, and peered tremblingly into the darkness. She saw nothing. She put forth her head. Nothing was revealed. Could it have been, after all, a mistake? She tried for the moment to think so. She dared not blow the light out just yet, however, but walked with it up the stairs, and then, reaching the top, she extinguished it.

It was dark all the rest of the way to her room, and she hurried on as quickly and as noiselessly as she could, but there was a terrible sense of being pursued which almost overcame her. When at last she reached her own room, she closed her door hastily, locked it, and then instantly lighted the gas, whose bright flame, illuminating the whole apartment, quickly drove away every vestige of her recent terror.

Had she not found that casket, there is no doubt that the smothered cough which she had heard or imagined would have impressed her much more deeply, and excited within her mind some strange suspicions; but, as it was, the casket filled all her thoughts, and she had an inordinate and irresistible longing to open it at once.

Once more she searched among the keys. One there was, the smallest in the bunch, of very peculiar shape, which seemed exactly adapted to that casket. She tried this one first of all. It was the right one! She turned it. The casket was unlocked.

Her heart was now throbbing most vehemently, and for a moment she delayed before lifting the lid, fearful of the result of this search. At length, however, the momentary hesitation passed; she laid her hand on the lid and raised it.

The casket was there, open before her eyes.

Inside of this there was a parcel. On the outside of this parcel were written these words:

"MY DARLINGS."

Inez opened the parcel, with hands trembling now in this supreme moment of excitement, and the contents soon lay revealed.

What it contained was a locket made of gold, of most exquisite design and finish, around the edges of which was a row of brilliants. This locket was about two inches in length, and somewhat less in width. Its shape was oval. It was constructed so as to open in three places, and on the edge there were three springs. By pressing the spring on the right, the side of the locket flew open; the left spring opened the left side of the locket; and the middle spring opened the locket in the middle.

Each one of these openings disclosed a miniature portrait, exquisitely painted on ivory. One of these represented a lady, the second a girl of about twelve years of age, the third a child. Under each portrait was a tablet, on which was engraved some letters. Under the lady's was the name "Inez;" under the girl's was the name "Clara;" and under the child's was the name "Inez."

As Inez opened these and looked at them one by one, her heart beat so fast and her hands trembled so violently, that she had to lay the locket down. She gasped for breath. She buried her face in her hands and wept. These tears brought relief, and, once more taking up the locket, she looked at the portraits through her tears.

She looked at those portraits, and there arose within her feelings mysterious, unspeakable, unutterable. They seemed like dreams—those faces. Where in her life had she seen the lovely face of that lady who smiled on her there out of that portrait so sweetly? Where had she ever seen the face of that beautiful girl Clara, whose deep, dark eyes were now fixed on her? And who was that child Inez? Who? Could the thought that was in her mind be true? Dare she entertain such a fancy? Had she herself ever been one of those three? Could it be that she herself had ever, in far-off days, been the original of that beautiful child-portrait that now met her eyes—smiling in its innocent happiness? Was that her sister? Was that her mother? Was it possible that this which was in her mind could be any thing else than a feverish, a delirious fancy—a fancy brought

out of the workings of that brain which of
late had been so intensely and so unremit-
tingly active?

No; the faces were not unfamiliar. These
were not the faces of strangers. Inez!
Clara! Inez!

Hitherto her eyes had been fascinated by
the portraits, but now they caught sight of
something else at the bottom of the casket.
It was a piece of paper folded like a letter.
She took it up. It was a letter. It bore
the address:

"HENNIGAR WYVERNE, ESQ.,
"*London.*"

It was a fine, bold hand, and resembled
the same one in which the words were written which Inez had seen on the parcel. On
opening it she read the following:

"MY DEAR HENNIGAR—*Will you have the
kindness to keep this casket for me until I send
for it? It contains their miniatures, which,
after some deliberation, I have concluded not to
take with me. Ever yours,*
"BERNAL MORDAUNT."

Bernal Mordaunt!

Inez read that name over a hundred times.
This was the meaning of the initials, then.
And Mordaunt! Why, that was Bessie's
name. What was the meaning of that?
Did Bessie know, after all? Had she all
along been acquainted with all this? Could
it be possible that Bessie had known that
secret which she tried so hard to conceal
from her? She had been in the habit of
regarding Bessie all along as a sort of human
butterfly, but she began to think that Miss
Mordaunt might have a far deeper nature
than she had ever imagined.

For hours Inez sat up, thinking over this,
without being able to understand it. At last,
however, her exhausted nature gave out, and
she retired to bed.

———————

CHAPTER IX.

A CURIOUS FANCY.

BLAKE watched the steamer until it was
out of sight, and then turned sadly away.
The great change that had come over Inez
disheartened him, for, although he was aware
of the cause, he was not prepared for such a
result. It seemed to him now as though this
separation was an eternal one, and the startling revelation which had been made by the
dying Wyverne, while it filled him with
amazement, seemed also to fix between him
and Inez, for all the future, a deep and impassable gulf. His present residence was
Paris, and he returned there on the following day.

Arriving there, he spent some time in his
rooms, after which he went forth in the direction of the Quartier Latin. Here he entered a house, and, going up to the second
story, knocked at the door of a room in the
rear of the building.

"Come in," said a deep-bass voice.

Blake entered thereupon, saying: "Hellmuth, old fellow, how are you?"

At this, a man started up, letting a pipe
fall from his mouth to the floor, and upset-
ting a chair as he did so.

"Blake!" he cried. "By Heaven, Blake!
Is this really you? Welcome back again!"

And, with these words, he strode over toward his visitor, and wrung his hand heartily.

Dr. Blake's friend was a man of very
peculiar physiognomy. He was a tall man,
broad-shouldered, deep-chested, and large-
limbed. His hair was short, his beard was
cropped quite close, and a heavy though
rather ragged mustache, with long points de-
pending downward, overshadowed his mouth.
Hair and beard were grizzled with plentiful
gray hairs, which gave an air of grimness to
his face. His brow was deeply wrinkled, his
eyes were deep set, and gray and piercing.
His nose was aquiline, and he had a trick of
stroking it with the forefinger of his left hand
whenever he was involved in thoughts of a
graver kind than usual. It was an austere
face, a stern face, yet a sad one, and one, too,
which was not without a certain charm of its
own; and there were many who could bear
testimony to the warm human heart that
throbbed beneath the sombre exterior of Kane
Hellmuth.

The room was a large one, and a bedroom adjoined it, but both were furnished in the most
meagre manner. The floor was of red tiles.
There was a sofa and an arm-chair. A plain
deal table stood in the centre. Upon this
was a tumbler and a bottle, a tobacco-box,
and several pipes.

Blake flung himself on the sofa, and Kane

"No; the faces were not unfamiliar. These were not the faces of strangers." —Page 30.

Hellmuth picked up the chair, and seated himself on it again.

"You've been gone a long time, Blake," said he, stooping to pick up his pipe, and filling it again as he spoke. "I began to think that you had emigrated altogether from the capital of civilization, to saw the bones of outside barbarians."

"Oh, I've been rusticating a little," said Blake, indifferently, "and doing a little in the way of business. I've been last in Switzerland—I'll give an account of myself, some time. And what have you been doing with yourself?"

"Won't you take something?" said Hellmuth, without noticing Blake's last remark. "I've some cognac here."

"Cognac! what! you with cognac?" said Blake, in evident surprise.

"Yes," said Hellmuth. "I've had to come to it."

Saying this, he rose from his chair, and going to a closet he produced a tumbler, which he gravely placed on the table.

"Take some," said he.

Blake poured out a little. Hellmuth poured out half a tumblerful, and gulped it down.

"You'd better smoke," said he.

"I think I shall," said Blake, and, producing a meerschaum from his pocket, he filled and lighted it. Hellmuth lighted his also, and soon the room began to grow somewhat cloudy. Silence now followed for some time, which may have been owing to the occupation afforded by the process of smoking, or may have been caused by preoccupation of mind on the part of both of them.

Kane Hellmuth, however, seemed more absorbed in his own thoughts than Blake. He stretched out his great, long legs, leaned back his head, and, with eyes half closed, puffed forth great volumes of smoke toward the ceiling. Blake lounged on the sofa, occasionally watching the form of the other as it loomed through the gathering smoke-clouds. He seemed on the point of speaking several times, but each time he checked himself.

The silence was at length broken by Kane Hellmuth.

"Blake," said he, suddenly—and, as he said this, he sat upright and rigid, fixing his piercing gray eyes on his friend.

"Well," said Blake, unconsciously rising out of his lounging position, and looking up in some surprise.

"Do you believe in ghosts?"

"Ghosts," repeated Blake—"believe in ghosts? What a question! Why, man, what do you mean?"

"I mean this: do you believe in ghosts?"

"Why—I believe in—apparitions, of course—that is—you know—I believe that in certain abnormal conditions of the optic nerve—"

"Oh, of course—of course," interrupted Kane Hellmuth, with a wave of his hand. "I know all that—every word of it. All jargon—nothing but words. That is the case wherever science deals with the soul. I need not have asked you such a question. You're a materialist, and you believe nothing but what can be proved by experiment. I once had the same belief. But let me tell you, my dear boy, your materialism is only good for the daylight and the sunshine. Wait till it is all dark—outside and inside, for mind and body—and then see what becomes of your materialism. It goes to the dogs."

"Perhaps so," said Blake; "but, at any rate, science can have nothing to do with fancies. It is built up out of actual facts. Science is not poetry or superstition. It is the truth, whether pleasant or unpleasant. For my part, I am a scientific man, and nothing concerns me that cannot be proved."

"Well," said Kane Hellmuth, "we need not argue. I might say that science is in its infancy, and can decide nothing; that there are things as far out of its reach as the heaven is beyond the earth, but what's the use? I come back to myself. I'm glad you're here, Blake. I've got an infernal load on my mind, and I want to tell it to somebody, if it's only for the relief that one feels after a clean confession."

Kane Hellmuth drew a long breath, laid his pipe on the table, and, turning his eyes toward where Blake was sitting, sat for some moments in silence, staring intently before him. It was not at Blake that he was looking, but at vacancy; and his thoughts were far away from the scene immediately before him. Blake did not interrupt him, but sat watching him, waiting for him to speak.

At last Kane Hellmuth broke the silence. His voice was harsh, and he spoke with solemn and impressive emphasis.

"Blake," said he, slowly, "I'm a haunted man!"

At this extraordinary remark Blake's first impulse was to laugh, but there was something in the expression of Kane Hellmuth's face which checked the rising levity.

"The circumstances are so extraordinary," murmured Hellmuth, as though soliloquizing, "and it has been repeated so often that it cannot be explained on the ground of fancy, or of hallucination. You see, an hallucination generally arises out of a surrounding of exciting circumstances, and is always accompanied by some degree of mystery, unless, of course, as you said a little while ago, the optic nerve is immediately affected; but, mind you, my boy, you take a thoroughly healthy man— a man of iron nerve, clear head, practical mind, strong body—put that man in a public street, or in a railway-train, or in the midst of his daily duties, and say would it be possible for such a man to be subject to an hallucination, and to experience it, not once but four several times, and in such a way that the form presented before his eyes was most certainly no mere apparition, but a real existence?"

Kane Hellmuth had been looking at the floor as he spoke, and, on finishing, raised his eyes with earnest and solemn inquiry to Blake.

Blake made no answer. He was not prepared to form any reply.

Kane Hellmuth was putting his case very strongly, but Blake's ignorance of all the circumstances forced him to wait till he should hear more.

"As to the face," continued Hellmuth, once more lowering his eyes, and falling into his soliloquizing tone, "there is no possibility of mistaking it. It can belong to one, and to one only. The features, the eyes, the expression, could by no possibility belong to any other. Yet how this can be, and why it can be, I cannot comprehend."

"What is the form that is commonly assumed by this—this—ah—appearance that you speak of?" asked Blake, as Kane Hellmuth again paused. "Is there only one apparition, with only one shape, or are there several, with something in common?"

"There is only one," said Kane Hellmuth, solemnly. "It is always the same features, form, and dress."

"Would you have any objection to tell what it is like? Is it a man, or a woman, or a child, for instance?"

"It is a woman," said Kane Hellmuth. "She is always dressed as a nun. The face is always the same, and bears one unchanged expression."

"A nun!" said Blake. "That would be a black dress. Pardon me if I allude to spectral illusions, but have you ever investigated the subject of colors with regard to optical delusions, and do you know how black would affect such illusions?"

"I have not."

"Nor have I. I thought, perhaps, that the suggestion might be worth something."

"No," said Kane Hellmuth, "it is worth nothing in this case, for, after all, the dress is the least important part of this visitor of mine. It is the face—the face, the features, the look, above all, the eyes, that fix themselves upon me, and seem to penetrate to my inmost soul."

"Is this face that you speak of at all familiar—that is to say, does it look like any face with which you have formerly been acquainted, or is it some perfectly strange one?"

"Familiar?" exclaimed Kane Hellmuth. "It is only too familiar. It is the face of one who has been associated with the brightest and the darkest moments of my life—one who was more to me than all the world, and whose memory is still dearer to me than all other thoughts. Years ago I lost her, and that loss broke up all my life. I never think it worth while, Blake, to talk about so unimportant a subject as myself; but I may remark that I was once a very different man from what I now am, and occupied a very different position. She was with me in that old life; but, when she died, I died, too. I am virtually a dead man, and it seems that I hold communion with the dead."

To Blake this strange discourse seemed like the ravings of incipient insanity. It was unusual in Kane Hellmuth, who had all along, ever since Blake had known him, been distinguished for his perfect clear-headedness and dry, practical nature. Yet now it seemed as though beneath all this there was some lurking tendency to insanity, and that Kane Hellmuth's strong intellect was giving way. His strange language, and his fancy that the dead had appeared to him, together with his evident liability to spectral illusions, all awakened new feelings in Blake's mind, and he now felt anxious to learn what his friend believed had appeared to him, so as to see the direction which his wandering fancy or his disease might be taking. It was a friendly sympathy with such an affliction, and an earnest desire to be of some service.

"Yes," continued Hellmuth, in the same strain, "I died once. We died together, at the same time. I am now dead, in law, in reality, virtually dead—a dead man! And it is because I am still moving about among living men, I dare say, that she comes to me now to warn me. Last night's appearance showed that things were coming to a climax."

"Last night?" asked Blake. "You saw this as recently as last night, did you?"

"Yes," said Hellmuth, "for that matter I see it now—that is to say, I have so vivid a memory of it that by shutting my eyes now I can reproduce it."

"How many times have you seen it altogether?"

"Four times."

"How long is it since you first saw it?"

"About two years ago."

"Have you any objection to tell me the kind of appearance which presented itself each time, and the circumstances under which you saw it?"

"Objections? certainly not; I am anxious to tell you exactly how it was in each case."

Hellmuth drew a long breath, and was silent for a few moments. He then continued:

"I came to Paris about two years ago. Not long after my arrival here I went to Notre-Dame. I went to hear Père Hyacinthe. I was a great admirer of his. There was an immense crowd there, as usual. I was in the midst of it when it parted to make way for a procession. At that moment I saw, straight in front of me, just across the space made for the procession, not more than six feet away, the figure of a nun! She was clothed in black from head to foot. Her face was turned to me, and her eyes were fixed on mine with a burning intensity of gaze that penetrated to my inmost soul. The face was full of unutterable sadness and mournfulness, and there was also in it a deep and overpowering reproachfulness. I cannot describe it at all. There, however, was this black nun with the pale face of death opposite me, within reach, standing there, motionless as a statue, with her eyes, full of a terrible fascina-

tion, fixed on mine. It was the figure, the face, the look, the eyes, the attitude, and the expression of my dead wife!"

Kane Hellmuth looked at Blake with a gaze that seemed to search out the thoughts of the other, and again paused for a few moments.

"Well," he resumed, "I need not enlarge on my own feelings. Words are useless. I will only say that this figure thus stood, motionless, looking at me, and I stood, motionless, looking at her, across this space that seemed to have opened on purpose to disclose her to me; and the time seemed long, yet it could not have been longer than was necessary to allow the procession to come six feet or so. The procession moved on, and, in the smoke of incense, and the confusion of the crowd, the figure was lost to sight. After the procession had passed, I looked everywhere, but saw nothing more of it.

"I must say that I was very much upset by this; but the habit of scientific thought came to my aid, and I accounted for it in various ways—such ways as you would suggest to explain away what you consider the fancies of a disordered brain. Still, I knew perfectly well that my brain was not in the slightest degree disordered, and so I fell back, or tried to fall back, upon the theory that it was some chance resemblance that had so affected me. Various things affected my belief in this; but, nevertheless, it seemed the only terrible one, but the impression produced on me was deep, and seemed likely to be lasting.

"Well, several months passed away, and at length I had occasion to take a run over to England. It was early morning. The train in which I was had gone about ten miles, and reached a small station, the name of which I forget. Another train was stopping there, and, just as we came in, it was beginning to move out. I was sitting on the side next to the other train, carelessly looking out of the window. I was facing the engine, so that the other train moved toward me, and thus I threw my eyes over the passengers as they passed by. Suddenly my gaze was riveted by a face which was turned toward me. It was on the other train. It was a nun—the same nun—the same face, the same look, the same expression, the same eyes; and they fastened themselves on mine with the same burning intensity of gaze which

I had noticed at Notre-Dame. At this second meeting I felt even more overwhelmed than on the first occasion. Again the time seemed very long in which those eyes held mine in the spell of their terrible fascination ; yet it could not have lasted longer than the brief moment that was requisite for the other train to pass us.

"After this second visitation, I confess I felt more bewildered than ever. I gave up my journey to England, and, quitting the train at Amiens, I came back here. If the first sight of this nun figure had been unaccountable, this second one was even more so. Several months more now passed away, and I can only say that I remained in a state of perfect bewilderment as to the cause of the two appearances which I have described. I began now to think that, since I had seen it twice, I might see it again, and was conscious of an uneasy state of mind, in which I felt myself to be constantly on the lookout. Thus far it had appeared in the midst of crowds, and by daylight ; the next time it came it might appear in solitude, and amid the darkness. The thought was not a pleasant one, and yet I cannot say that I felt exactly afraid. It was more awe than fear, together with a decided reluctance to be subjected to any further visitation.

"At length it came again. It was during the last *fête Napoléon*. It was a little after nine in the evening. I was seated in front of the *café* Vigny, on the Boulevard de la Madeleine. I was smoking, and indolently watching the crowd of people that streamed by, and listening to the confused murmur of idle chat or noisy altercation that rose all around me. The crowd was immense ; and the passing forms, the rolling carriages, the noise, tumult, music, and laughter, all served to draw my mind out of certain thoughts over which it had been brooding somewhat too much.

"It was at this moment, and in this place, then, sitting there smoking, amid the surroundings of every-day life, and the flare of prosaic gas-lights, that I saw it again. It passed along the edge of the sidewalk. I was looking toward the other side of the street when it glided into sight. It moved slowly along with a solemn step ; and, as it moved, it turned its face and fixed its eyes full upon me. It was the same figure—the black nun's dress—and the same look, inexpressibly sad, despairing, and reproachful. It did not stop, but moved along, and was gradually lost in the crowd.

"There was something about its glance that thrilled through me, and seemed to take away all my strength. I felt as before—petrified. I longed to advance toward it, and find out for myself whether this shape was corporeal or incorporeal. I could not. Even after it had passed I felt unable to move for some time. When at length I was able to rise from my seat, I went off after it in the direction which it had taken, but I could not find out any thing whatever about it, or see any figure whatever that bore the slightest resemblance to it."

Kane Hellmuth fixed his eyes more solemnly than ever on Blake, and, after a short silence, continued :

"Last night I saw it once more. But there are certain circumstances connected with this fourth meeting which cannot be entelligible to you without further explanation. I think I shall have to trouble you with an account of my past to some extent, if you care to listen, and don't feel bored already."

"My dear old boy," said Blake, earnestly, "I shall feel only too glad to get the confidence of a man like you."

CHAPTER X.

THE FATAL DRAUGHT.

BLAKE drew himself nearer to his friend, in the intensity of the curiosity that was by this time awakened within him. Kane Hellmuth rose to his feet, poured out a glass of raw cognac, drank it down, and then, resuming his seat, he sat erect, with his eyes fixed on vacancy.

"When I say," began Kane Hellmuth, "that I am at this moment a dead man, and that I died ten years ago, you think, of course, either that I am using figurative language, or else that I am showing signs of insanity. Neither of these is the case, however. When you hear what I have to say, you will perceive that these words are true, and actually describe my present condition.

"It is a little more than ten years ago that I was married. My wife was an English girl. She was at a *pensionnat* in this city. Girls in this country are seldom allowed any

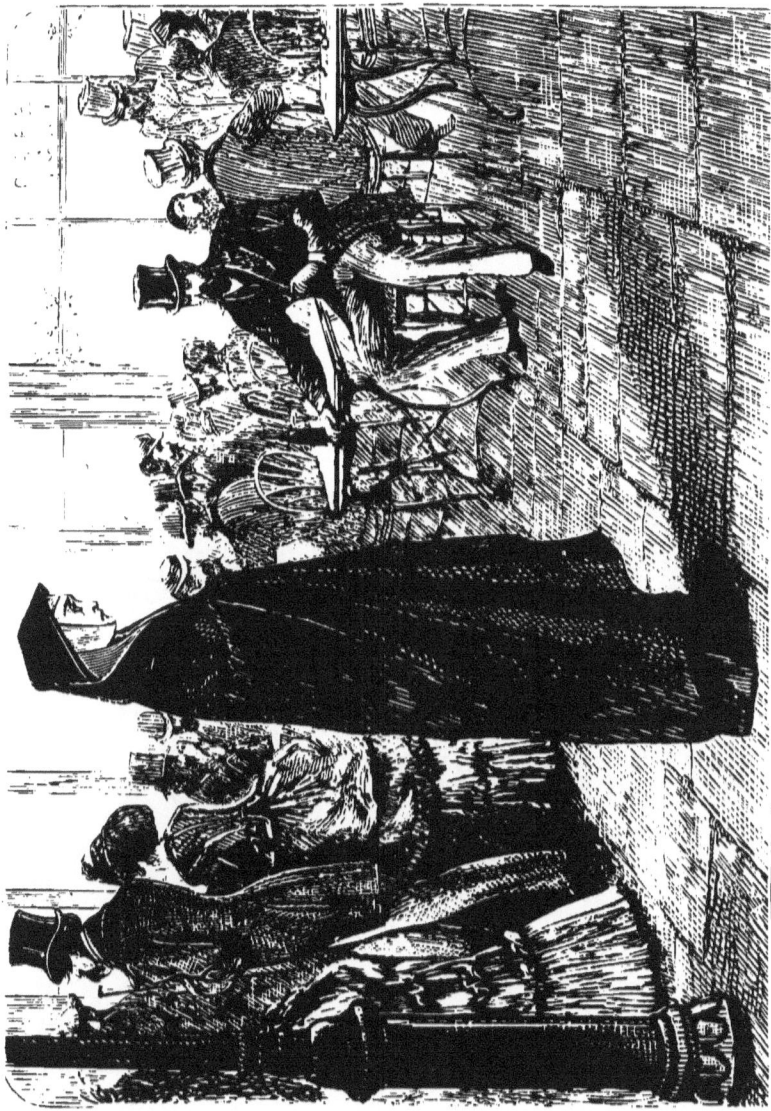

liberty before marriage; but she was an English girl, and for that reason, perhaps, was allowed a far greater degree of freedom than would otherwise have been possible. I became acquainted with her through the medium of an English family—people, by-the-way, whom I thought very singular associates for one like her. She was about seventeen, fair, fragile, innocent as an angel. The first time that I saw her, I loved her most passionately. I was able to see her frequently, and at length induced her to marry me.

"I had nothing whatever to marry on. I was at that time a mad spendthrift; and, though I began life with a handsome allowance as second son, I soon spent it all, and had plunged head over heels in debt. My father paid my debts once, and died soon after. My elder brother would do nothing for me, and so I soon found myself in a desperate position. I had to leave England, and come here. Here my bad habits followed me, and I soon found myself involved as heavily as ever. It was under these circumstances that I had the madness to get married, and drag another down into the abyss in which I was.

"She was an orphan. She had lost her mother four years before. Her father was broken-hearted, and left the country. She heard of his death soon after. She had been at this boarding-school ever since. She had a guardian. There had been a sister in her family, a mere child, who had also died. Thus she was alone in the world, and under the authority of a guardian whom she had never seen but once, and who took not the slightest interest in her. She had no future before her, and loved me as passionately as I loved her, and was therefore quite willing to be mine.

"Well, I had a little money about me, and with this I started on a bridal tour. We went to Italy, and spent three months there —three months of perfect happiness—three months which, in so miserable a life as mine has been, seem now like a heaven of bliss, as I look back. I drove away all thoughts of my circumstances. I gave myself up altogether to the joy of the present. I would not let the cares of the future interfere for one moment with the happiness which I had with her. I knew that there would have to be an end, but waited till the end should come.

"At length, the beginning of the end approached, and I began to see the necessity of exertion of some sort. I had already written to the guardian, acquainting him with the marriage. I now wrote to him a second time. He had taken no notice whatever of the first letter, which excited my suspicions that he was inclined to be severe on us. I had an idea, however, that he might have some property belonging to my wife, and wished to know what there was to rely on.

"Paris was not a very pleasant place for one in my circumstances, nor was it safe for me to go there; but I risked all, and went there, expecting that the guardian would prove amiable, and trusting to the chapter of accidents. While I was about it, I wrote also to my elder brother, telling him that I was married, that I intended to lead a new life, and asking him to use his influence to get me some office.

"I got my brother's answer first. He had always felt a grudge against me, because my father had once paid my debts. It seemed as though so much had been taken from him. I never knew before what an avaricious and cold-hearted nature he had. If I had known it, I would not have written. His letter was perfectly devilish. He sneered at my marriage, and lamented that his circumstances would not allow him to do the same, reminded me of all my shortcomings, threw up the old grudge about my debts, and told me that with my talents I should have won a rich wife. Such was his letter. It prepared me for worse things, and these soon came to pass.

"On my arrival at Paris, my creditors all assailed me, of course. I went to see the chief ones, and gave them to understand that my wife had money, and that, when I could come to terms with her guardian, I would settle every thing. The thing seemed plausible to them, and they consented to wait. It was a lie, of course; but, when a man is in debt, there is no lie which he will not tell to fight off his creditors. The course of a failing merchant, or a gentleman going to ruin, is generally one prolonged lie.

"At length, wearied with waiting, I wrote once more to the guardian, telling him that, if I did not hear from him, I would bring my wife, visit him in person, and force him to render an account of her affairs.

"This time I got an answer; it was not

very long. He said that my wife had no fortune at all for which to render an account, that she had been maintained at his expense thus far, and he had hoped that she would do far better for herself than she had done. Her marriage without his consent, he declared, had destroyed all claims that she might have on his consideration. He cast her off, and thought it but just that the man who had stolen her should support her. In answer to my threat about coming in person, he merely remarked that for one in my position England would hardly be a desirable place to visit.

"Ill news soon spreads. This break-up of my last hope became gradually known. It may have been gathered from my own words or manner; but, whatever the cause was, it was certainly found out, and I soon began to feel the effects of it. The crowd of clamorous and hungry creditors gathered thick around me, and ruin, utter and absolute, was inevitable. I had no more money; I could not even fly, for I was watched, and could not buy my tickets. I owed my landlord, who also was as clamorous as the rest. One day more, and I should be thrown into prison, with no hope of escape. I should be torn from my wife forever. And she—what would become of her? She whom I had guarded so tenderly — she who had never known what it was to struggle for herself, with all her youth and beauty and innocence —what could she do, if I was torn from her, if she was driven from the boarding-house into the streets, alone, penniless, alone in a great city, and that city Paris? There was hell in that thought.

"Such was my position. For me there was ruin—imprisonment perhaps for life—eternal separation from my wife!—for her a fate worse ten thousand times—the hideous fate which awaits the unprotected innocent in a city like Paris. Thus the crisis had come. One day more would decide all. The landlord had threatened me with ejection and arrest. One day more would plunge me into a prison-cell, and throw my wife on the streets. We had no friends. She was alone in the world. So was I. She loved me so passionately that separation from me would be death to her—death? that would be the lightest of the evils that awaited her."

Kane Hellmuth paused. He had spoken thus far in low but vehement tones, and, though he tried to restrain himself, there were visible marks of the intense agitation of feeling that was called up by all these bitter memories. He sat erect and rigid, with his eyes fixed gloomily before him, and his hands clutching the arms of his chair. But the hands that grasped the chair were strained to whiteness by the convulsive energy of that pressure; and his brow lowered into a frown as black as night; while on his face the brown, weather-beaten complexion had changed to a dull, ghastly pallor.

"Death!" he repeated. "Yes, death! If I had been torn from her, and flung into prison, I should have killed some one, and have destroyed myself. Arrest was death. For my wife there was no better fate. For her the best thing that could take place was death. Death was before us in any case, and therefore the question in my mind became reduced to this: How shall this death, which is inevitable, be best encountered?

"These thoughts had been coming to me gradually, and out of these thoughts came this conclusion. It took shape when my brother's letter came, and assumed a final and definite form when I received the answer from the guardian. For myself it was easy to decide—but in this case I had more than myself to consider. My wife. How could she bear the thought? Or how could she receive the communication which I wished to convey when it was one like this?

"Thus far she had known nothing except that I loved her. I had not shared with her a single one of my cares. I had spared her all unnecessary distress. In my own anguish it pleased me to see her innocent happiness, to listen to her bright plans for the future, to watch the expression of her eloquent face as she talked with me. Never was there a man more devotedly loved—more adored than I was by her. The whole wealth of a loving nature she poured forth to me. She had not one single thought apart from me. Her love was like worship in its devotion, but it had the warmth and the glow of human passion.

"But the communication which I longed to make was made at last. It had to be made. It was the day—the last day of our freedom. The next day was to end all. It was early in the morning. I had not slept all night long. In the morning she told me that she had not slept. Then she looked at me with unutterable mournfulness. We were sitting at the breakfast-table at that time. She looked at me as I have said, and then with a sudden impulse she flung her arms about me, and, burying her face on my breast, burst into tears.

"I said nothing. These were her first tears with me. I dared not even soothe her, for fear lest I should be unmanned.

"At length she overcame her feelings. She raised herself, and, looking at me with intense earnestness, she began to speak, in a low, calm voice, in which there was not a trace of emotion.

"'You are keeping from me some terrible secret,' said she, 'and I am miserable. What is it that is on your mind? There is nothing that you need not tell me. There is only one thing that could be a calamity to me—to lose your love. And I have not lost that yet—have I, darling?'

"As she said this, I drew her close to me, and pressed her to my heart. And then I told her all. I told her, looking into her eyes, and watching her face. She listened in silence.

"I told her what was before us. . . . I told her what there was—for her—and for me—prison—death—worse. . . .

"Finally, I told her what I had thought of as an escape for both of us. . . . I tried to lighten the blow, by speaking of our eternal union hereafter—to be secured by leaving this life together.

"She was terribly agitated. So sudden had been this revelation! It was too sudden. In my own excitement at that time I did not notice it so much; but in the years that have elapsed since then, I have recalled every look of hers, every act, every word. Above all, I have been haunted by that first look that was called up on her face—that look of mournfulness inexpressible—of despair—of mute reproach—all of which were in her face—and the burning intensity of gaze with which her sad, earnest eyes fixed themselves on mine. She clung to me. She again hid her face on my breast. She wept there long; and all the time I talked on. I caressed her. I tried to console her as best I could.

"At length she raised herself again, and looked at me with unutterable love and devotion; her voice was calm again. She told me she would do whatever I proposed—that she was mine, body and soul—for this life and the next—that life without me was impossible—that if I were torn from her she would die—that she would rather die with me than

away from me—and to die together would be sweet, since we had to die.

"All these sweet and loving words filled me with delight and enthusiasm. I began to speak about the life to which we were going, and, as I had filled my head with the sentimental ravings of French novelists, I had no lack of assurance as to the immediate bliss that awaited us in spite of such a mode of departure from this life. To all this she listened quietly. She did not share my enthusiasm. Her religious training must have made it seem false to her. But, in her, love triumphed over religion, and she consented to die because I asked her. She did not expect to go to heaven; that is evident to me now; but she only wished to go with me wherever I should go—or wherever I should send her. There was in her heart the stimulus of a glorious purpose—of which I knew nothing, but which had occurred to her then, and animated her to the task."

Kane Hellmuth stopped abruptly, and, closing his eyes, let his head fall forward on his breast. He was overcome by his feelings, and by the throng of dark memories which were gathering around him; and waited for a while to collect his thoughts and his strength before relating the end. Blake watched him in silence, with a face full of a mournful interest. At last Hellmuth raised his head and went on, speaking very rapidly:

"She said that it would be sweet to die for me, and that she would only take the fatal draught from my hand. She said that she would give me my draught. Thus, she said, we would avoid the guilt of suicide. It seemed then like the sweet casuistry of love; but since then I have known that it was an act of divine self-sacrifice, the sudden impulse of devoted love, that threw her own life away in calm self-abnegation; and sought to find a way to save me by the sacrifice of herself. But I suspected nothing then. I let her do as she chose. I put the phial of poison, which I had procured already, in her hand, and she went to the sideboard and poured it out in two glasses. Then she came back and placed them on the table. She handed one to me and I handed the other to her. Then we sat looking at one another for some time. She was now trembling violently. I took her hand and held it, hoping thus to strengthen her. In vain. I began to falter at the sight of her great distress. But at that moment I was roused by a noise at the door. I thought at once of the officers of the law, and the landlord, and hurried there to see who it was. I saw no one. Then I came back—and this last alarm restored my resolution. I took her hand—and we both drank. . . ."

Again Kane Hellmuth paused, and it was now a long time before he went on.

"This is what I mean," he resumed in a hoarse voice, "when I say that I died then, and am a dead man now. Out of that death I revived. I found myself in a hospital, just emerging from a burning fever. I learned that I had been there for months. It was months before I was able to leave. I learned that I had been sent here. And where was she? Who had buried her? How had I escaped?

"For days and weeks there was but one thought on my mind. How had I escaped?

"And gradually there came to me a thought that made life more intolerable than ever. I saw it all at last. I recognized her loving purpose, in her proposal to give me my draught. She had designed to save me. She would die—willingly, since I wished it; gladly, since death would be administered by me. She would die; but, nevertheless, she would save me, and this was her sweet deceit—to give me a draught which should produce senselessness, out of which I might come back to life, while she would go where I sent her.

"I thought also that I could see another reason. She had understood from my words, no doubt, that she had reduced me to this. She saw that my care was for her, and that, were it not for her, I should not die — or think of dying. Alone, I could live; but I could not support her. This, no doubt, she saw, although no such thought ever came to my mind. This she saw, and therefore she died. —Yes, Basil Blake—look on me, and recognize a villain who has done to death the most loving wife that ever gave her heart to man. She died, that I might live; that I might be free from what she supposed was an incumbrance to me in my poverty. Ah, now—how well I understand that look which she gave me when first I communicated to her my fatal plan! Ah, great Heaven! Why did death reject me? What business have I in life?

"The moment that I was able, I fled from Paris. I considered myself dead. I resolved

to begin a new life. You wonder that I didn't kill myself. I wonder too. At any rate, I considered myself a dead man. My name is not Hellmuth; what it used to be is no matter. It is Hellmuth now. Once only did I make use of the old name. It was in a letter which I wrote to the guardian. I found myself cherishing a faint hope that she might have escaped. I wrote to him, telling him briefly what had happened. After some delay, I received an answer. It destroyed my last hope. It informed me that my wife was dead; that she was found dead in the room on that morning; and that she was buried in Père-la-Chaise, through the pity of some one of the creditors who had relented at the sight of the ruin which had resulted from my vicious and guilty extravagance.

"After this, I became a wanderer. I worked with my own hands to get my living. I have been over all the world as a common seaman. I have worked as a laborer. About two years ago I came back to Paris, feeling an uncontrollable desire to visit her grave. It is at Père-la-Chaise. I go there often. It is a simple slab bearing her name, with the date of her death.

"And now," continued Kane Hellmuth, "you will be able to understand the full significance of what I spoke of first. That black nun is the form and face of her who is buried in Père-la-Chaise. The expression on her face is precisely the same which I saw there when I first told her of my purpose. All that despair and mournfulness unutterable; all that mute reproach; and even all that deep, self-sacrificing love—all is there. It is the same face always. Remember this, and bear this in mind, while I tell you what happened last night at Père-la-Chaise."

CHAPTER XI.

DEAD OR ALIVE?

KANE HELLMUTH gulped down another glass of raw cognac.

"She is buried in Père-la-Chaise," said he. "They put a stone over her grave, and I found it without trouble. I went there the moment I reached Paris. No one knew me. All danger for me was over, if I had cared for danger. I came only to weep at her tomb. It's the fashion on the Continent for men to weep, you know." He frowned, and tugged at his tawny, ragged mustache.

"Yes," he added, "and a very convenient fashion it is, too, sometimes—or else —a poor devil's heart might break."

Something like a groan burst from him, and he dashed his brown hand across his eyes.

"It's two years," he continued, "since I came here. You know how I live. I happened, in my wanderings, to be at the Cape of Good Hope the time the diamond excitement broke out. I had nothing else to do, so I went to the diggings, and had moderate luck. That's one reason why I came here. I put my gains in government stock, and got enough francs to keep me in my plain fashion. All I want is to be within walking-distance of Père-la-Chaise—not too near, you know; enough to take up a good day, if necessary, in going, staying there, and coming back. Somehow, during these late years, my religious views have changed. I no longer hold to the gospel of the French novelists. I do not now believe that I should have gone straight to heaven from my lodging-house; and I comfort myself by praying for the soul of my lost Clara. The Church stands between the living and the dead. I feel a strange consolation in the thought that I am not cut off utterly from her whom I have lost. The Church sends up her prayers, and I blend mine with them. By her grave I feel nearest to her, and therefore I go to Père-la-Chaise. Therefore, also, I have adopted the mode of life which you see me following—acting as a sort of lay-brother, going about among the poor devils of fallen humanity whom I see around me, and trying to do something to give them an occasional lift. I would have scorned the African diamonds if they could have given me no more than a living for myself. I took them for Clara's sake; and, since she made me live, and sent me back to life when she went to death, so I study to make my life such that I may meet her hereafter with—with less shame than I might otherwise feel.

"But now, my boy, listen," continued Hellmuth, rousing himself and drawing a long breath, "listen. You know Père-la-Chaise—that is, in a general way. You know the tombs there. The grave is about fifty paces away from the gate, in one of the more obscure parts of the cemetery. Close by it is

a cenotaph, with an iron door, and inside this cenotaph is an altar, as is often the case. On this altar the friends of the dead place *immortelles*, and frequently on Sundays or holidays, or on the anniversary of deaths, they place lighted candles there. Yesterday was one of these occasions, and the candles were burning after dark, throwing out a faint gleam through the iron bars of the door.

"No one is allowed there after dark; but, when one is inside, he may stay, for no one can see him easily among so many monuments. I went there toward evening, and stayed after dark. I had frequently done so before. Amid the darkness, it seemed as though I was drawn nearer to her. By her grave it seemed as though I could hold communion with her departed spirit. At least it was consoling to be so near even to her mortal remains.

"So I remained there, and the gates were shut, and I was alone in that city of the dead. The shadowy monuments rose all around on every side, and looked like a ghostly population. I was by her grave. From the cenotaph nearest me the lights shone forth, and illuminated a small space in the gloom. As I sat there I thought over all the events of the mournful past. I had been praying for the repose of her soul, but what was the meaning of that visitation which I had had three times? Was her spirit not yet at rest after so many years? Was there any thing which she wanted of me? What was there that I could do?

"Then I knelt over her grave and prayed.

"How long I was kneeling I do not know. I haven't the slightest idea, nor is there any way of finding out. There are occasions in a man's life when human measurements are useless, and duration extends itself independently of the limitations of time. It might have been long, or it might have been short; I do not know. I only know this, that, suddenly, in the midst of the deep abstraction of prayer and meditation, I became aware of a presence near. There had been no noise that I was conscious of; there was no footfall, no breathing even—nothing. How the knowledge came I do not know, but it did come, and I was thus aware of some object, some shape, some being, in my neighborhood.

"I had been meditating profoundly and praying earnestly. I had striven to abstract myself from all thoughts of the external world, but thus it was that, through all the solemn gloom of that self-abstraction, and that elevation of soul above the world, there came to me this suggestion of a living thing near me.

"I roused myself, and raised my head, and looked forth into the scene before me.

"The first glance was enough. There was something, as I had been aware, and what it was I saw instantaneously. The feeble light of the wax-candles came glimmering out through the bars of the iron gate of the cenotaph into the gloom, and fell upon an object there, which was standing full before me, not more than half a dozen yards away—standing there erect, a human shape, with black robes—the robes of a nun. The light shone on its face, and the face was full before me, and it was on this face that my eyes rested as I raised them. The eyes of this being also were fixed upon mine, and chained them, and held them with a terrible fascination.

"All that I have said about that face was there now, but to me the whole expression seemed intensified. It was the old, well-remembered look—the look of her face as it had appeared when I saw it last in life. There was that mingled grief and amazement, that sharp anguish, and dark despair. There, too, was still that melancholy reproach, which, on that morning, had conveyed the protest of an innocent young life against the destruction which I had brought upon it; but now the reproach seemed deeper and involved a profounder condemnation. The eyes that chained mine in their gaze seemed to have more of that burning intensity which I had noticed before, and glowed with an awful lustre as they met mine.

"I knelt and looked, but I did not breathe. I could not move. I did not have any impulse to fly away or to spring toward it. It seems to me now as if I was for a short time in a state of perfect mental torpor. My state of mind was not one of horror. It was imbecility, or, rather, vacuity. I thought of nothing. I desired nothing. I feared nothing. I was simply conscious of the presence of this being who thus confronted me.

"At length the figure moved its hands, and then seemed to shrink away into nothingness. The darkness swallowed it up. As I looked, I perceived that it was no longer there. It was gone. It had vanished. I was alone.

"I remained there for some time—I do not know how long—in the same position, and in the same state of mind. At length I gradually regained the use of my faculties. I rose from my knees, and walked forward in the direction where the figure had vanished into the darkness. I found nothing whatever. I waited and walked about for some time longer, and then I went to the gate, roused the keeper, made some explanation of my presence there, and was let out. I then came home."

Such was Kane Hellmuth's story.

After he had ended it, he lighted his pipe and began smoking. Blake said nothing, but imitated his friend's example. The former seemed lost in his own meditations, and the latter found it very difficult to make any comments.

"Well," said Kane Hellmuth, at length, "I should like to hear what you have to say. Say it out. Don't be afraid of offending any prejudices or prepossessions of mine. You're a materialist. I am not. Let me hear what you, as a materialist, have to say."

"Well," said Blake, slowly, "in the first place, I have merely to say this, that I cannot for a moment share your belief. For every thing that I have ever seen in all my life, or learned, or studied, shows this to me with perfect clearness, that the dead can never—never come back to life—never—never."

"You are begging the question," said Kane Hellmuth, quietly.

"Any theory is acceptable rather than yours," said Blake. "The dead are the dead. They come back no more. No fond longings, no prayers, can bring them back. Superstition may call up visions, but these are only projections of the brain, the images wrought by the vivid fancy. With these, science and reason can do nothing. No proof has ever been adduced—no proof can ever be adduced—that the dead can reappear, or can have any existence, that we can comprehend."

"Very well—we differ," said Kane Hellmuth, "and now let me hear what you—rejecting, as you do, my belief—have to propose as a theory of your own."

"I cannot, on the instant, propose a theory which will satisfy every contingency in your case," said Blake. "You yourself say that you have already tried to account for this

"Standing there was a human shape, with black robes—the robes of a nun."—Page 46.

semblance to her to pass off as her at a distance."

"Impossible!" said Kane Hellmuth; "you forgot that this one is in a strange garb; you forget what casual meetings they have been; above all, you forget that this face is identical with that of my lost wife—not in feature only, but in expression—and an expression of a very peculiar nature. For the look that she gives me is not one that can be caught up by some impostor. That is inconceivable. For it is the last look of my dying wife—dying under such circumstances—a look which for years has haunted me, and this is the look which I now see in this presence which has appeared before me. No. The theory of hallucination is preferable to this last one. I will allow that my brother may be anxious to prove my death; I will even concede that he may have emissaries in search of me; but I maintain that this being of whom I speak cannot possibly have any connection with that."

"Very well," said Blake, after a pause; "we will let this pass. I said there were two alternatives. This is one. There is yet another. It is this—do not start when I suggest it; you told me to be frank; I speak it with all respect and sympathy for you and for her—Kane Hellmuth, after all, *your wife may yet be alive!*"

At these words Kane Hellmuth started to his feet, and regarded Blake with an awful face.

"She is dead!" he said, in a harsh voice.

"Who says so? Who has seen it?"

"Did I not get that letter from her guardian?"

"You did—but what of that? He said that some others said so; it is third-hand information. Did you ever go back to that house to ask?"

"Yes."

"When?"

"When I came back."

"What! two years ago? eight years after it occurred! Why, by that time the people had forgotten it all, or else they had gone away."

Kane Hellmuth stared at Blake.

"You are right," he said, hesitatingly; "they had gone; I have never been able to find them."

"Mind now," said Blake, "I am only arguing against your theory of the supernatu-

ral. I am showing you how this may be rationally accounted for on other grounds; and I say this, that you have not yet had reason to feel certain that she died. If *you* escaped, why should not *she?* How do you know that she gave you a weaker draught, and took a fatal one herself? That is only a theory of yours; you have no proof. How do you know that the drug was strong enough? It may have lost its virtue; it may have been badly made up; she, in pouring it out, may have made a mistake. There are a dozen ways of accounting for it other than the way you have fancied. No; she has lived; she has become a nun, thinking that you were dead. You have come across her own self, by chance, on various occasions. Your intense excitement has thrown around her various semi-supernatural adjuncts which have imposed upon your reason. Go and accost her when you see her next. Speak to her. Do not allow yourself to sink into a stupor."

To all this Kane Hellmuth listened with a frown. Gradually, however, the frown passed. The old look came back. He resumed his seat.

"Well," said he, calmly, as Blake ceased, "it is quite right for you to say this. I have thought of all that, however, though I must say it comes with fresh force from another. Still there is no conceivable reason why any human beings should take the trouble to get up such an elaborate piece of deceit. It was no one's interest to do so. No one could gain any thing by it. The people who laid her dear remains in the grave had no motive for acting a farce. The guardian had no motive for keeping it up. Who could have been benefited, or what end could have been gained? There is her grave, and there is the stone with her name. How can it be accounted for if she is not dead?"

"If I were to suggest all that is in my mind to say," remarked Blake, "you would call me visionary. I should think, however, that, until you know more than you seem to have learned—more than even she herself seemed to know about her antecedents, about her father, and her guardian, and the nature of that calamity which so strangely deprived her of all her friends—until then you have no right to say that there was no motive for imposing upon you and the world a false account of her death. But this is a thing which I do not care to speak of. One thing only I should like to ask—if you have no objections—her name, her maiden name."

" Clara Mordaunt," said Kane Hellmuth, in a low voice.

Blake started.

"Mordaunt!" he repeated.

The name was a familiar one, associated with the happiest hours of his life, with the presence of Inez; for, wherever Inez Wyverne was, there too was her friend, Bessie Mordaunt.

Kane Hellmuth, however, was looking away, and did not notice the start which Blake gave.

"I do not like this guardian," said he, after a pause. "You should see that man."

" So I intended to," said Kane Hellmuth, "but unfortunately it is too late — he is dead."

"Dead? Ah! that is bad. Did he die very long ago?"

"Oh, no; only about a week ago. I saw it in the papers."

"Ah!"

" Yes; he died in Switzerland somewhere—Villeneuve, I think—yes, it was Villeneuve. The name is so peculiar a one that it caught my eye at once. I saw it in *Galignani*, a day or two ago. I am old enough now always to look at the deaths and marriages, the first thing."

Blake did not hear more than half of this. He heard only the first words. As he heard them, his heart throbbed wildly, and a feeling of indefinable terror came over him. Died at Villeneuve!—the guardian!—the guardian of a girl named Mordaunt! He had suspected evil on the part of this guardian; he had given utterance to those suspicions. All the wild words of the dying man came back fresher than ever to his memory—all the grief of Inez, and all the horrors of that final death. His face grew ghastly white. He clung to the arm of the sofa for support.

"What was his name?" he gasped.

"His name?" said Kane Hellmuth. "What? the guardian? It's a very odd name. It's—Hennigar Wyverne!"

"Great Heaven!" exclaimed Blake, with so strange a cry that Kane Hellmuth started and looked at him in amazement.

———

CHAPTER XII.

THE amazement of Kane Hellmuth at the sight of Blake's face was unbounded. Thus far he had been the prey to excitement, and Blake had been the sympathizing friend and spectator. The tables were now turned. The emotion had passed to Blake; the *rôle* of sympathizing spectator to Kane Hellmuth. As for Blake, there was every reason, as is evident, why he should be overwhelmed by surprise and agitation. What his feelings were toward Inez have been sufficiently explained; what his feelings were toward Hennigar Wyverne may be conjectured. Mention has already been made of the dying man's declaration—that Blake was his own son, and of Blake's perplexity at such an announcement. He now found that this man who was standing in so peculiar a relation toward himself was identical with the very man whose connection with Kane Hellmuth he had found so suspicious; and against whom he had just been trying to lead up the suspicions of his friend. Would he still maintain those suspicions? Would he now carry out to its ultimate consequences that train of thought which was on his mind just before Kane Hellmuth had mentioned the name of Hennigar Wyverne?

The exclamation of Blake was followed by a long silence and a profound meditation, in which he was evidently in a state of great embarrassment and perplexity.

" Well," said he, at length, " this conversation has certainly taken a turn which is most extraordinary and most unexpected. I will not conceal from you that I feel completely upset, and that the mention of this guardian's name puts me in a most astonishing position with regard to this affair of yours. I have been brought of late into very close connection with this man, and there is a very mysterious prospect of a still closer connection being discovered. I have not mentioned any thing of the events with which I have been connected during the past few weeks, but there is something in my affairs which seems to run very wonderfully into your own. There is something also in them so puzzling, so confounding, that I am unable to grapple with it altogether. Perhaps you can help me. Perhaps we can help one another. Perhaps my affairs can throw some light on yours, or yours may throw light on mine."

"Go ahead by all means, old fellow," said Kane Hellmuth; "at any rate, it will divert my thoughts, and Lord knows I want something to divert them just now, or else I shall go mad."

"Very well," said Blake. "My story begins from the time that I left here six weeks ago. I was worn out by overwork. I had an undertaking of immense importance before me, before entering upon which it was absolutely necessary for me to recruit my strength. A change of air to the sea-side was the most important thing for me, and, accordingly, I went to St. Malo.

"On my arrival here I found an English party, who at once excited my deepest interest. There was an elderly gentleman in feeble health and two young ladies, one of whom was his daughter and the other was his daughter's friend, and perhaps relative. She seemed to look upon the gentleman as in some way her guardian; but perhaps that is my fancy. Now you will begin to understand some of the significance of my story when I tell you that the name of this elderly gentleman was Hennigar Wyverne."

"Hennigar Wyverne!" repeated Kane Hellmuth. "Ah, is that so? Why, then, you must have been with him when he died, if you were in Switzerland—that is, if you got acquainted with him, which I presume you did."

"I did," said Blake. "I will come to that presently. I was saying that there were two ladies—one Miss Wyverne, the other—the one whom I may call the ward—Miss Mordaunt."

Kane Hellmuth started in strongest agitation.

"Miss Mordaunt!" he exclaimed, "a ward of Hennigar Wyverne. Great Heavens! man, what story is this that you have to tell me? Miss Mordaunt! What was her other name?"

"Bessie," said Blake.

"Bessie. Ah, that means Elizabeth—Elizabeth—H'm—Clara had a younger sister who died. Her death may have been a mistake. But, no; that sister's name was not Elizabeth. It was some foreign name—unusual. I don't remember it at all. A similarity of name, probably a relation. Wyverne seems to have had a strong interest in the Mordaunt family.

But what did this Miss Mordaunt look like?"

"Very pretty, about seventeen, a brilliant blonde, witty, frolicsome, absurd—in fact, more like a sportive child than a young lady; the most utter butterfly I ever saw."

"No resemblance there," said Kane Hellmuth, thoughtfully—"no resemblance whatever. She was a brunette—grave and earnest."

"That is what Miss Wyverne is," said Blake.

"Well, go on," said Kane Hellmuth, anxious to hear more of Blake's story.

"I was saying," resumed Blake, "that this party excited in me the strongest interest. Miss Wyverne appeared to me the most beautiful being that I ever saw; and I frankly confess that I fell in love with her at once. This will account for the persistency with which I watched the party. I had no difficulty in doing so, for they spent most of the time in the open air, and Miss Wyverne was always with her father.

"Now, you may take for granted my love for Miss Wyverne. I make no secret of that; and I mention it so that you may understand other things.

"I soon saw, to my surprise, that the elderly gentleman took an evident interest in my humble self. At first I thought that he had heard something of my medical skill; but I soon dismissed that thought as a piece of preposterous vanity. Unfortunately, whatever my medical skill may be, the world knows nothing at all about it; so that an invalid at St. Malo would have been the last person to attribute any such quality to me. After a time I began to see that this interest in me grew stronger, and its manifestation more open. As I met him rolling along in his perambulator, or walking feebly up and down near his lodgings, I always caught his eyes fixed upon my face, and they were fixed there with a certain intensity of gaze that was most remarkable. There was, beyond a doubt, something in my face which excited his attention, and he was studying it to find out for himself what it was.

"Well, I was wondering how I could get acquainted with him, and trying to devise some plan of bringing it about so as not to force myself upon him, but I could not hit upon any way that was satisfactory. My passion for Miss Wyverne gave me my chief impulse to this; but at the same time I wish you to understand that I felt an extraordinary interest in the old man, so much so, indeed, that if Miss Wyverne had gone away, I should still have stayed there, so as to try to form an acquaintance with her father.

"Well, at length, this problem was solved for me. Mr. Wyverne himself made the advances—he sought my acquaintance. One day I was standing looking out at sea when he came walking along, accompanied by his daughter, and followed by his footman. He came up to me and raised his hat:

"'Can you tell me,' he asked, 'what that steamer is?'

"He pointed to a large steamer passing along out at sea. I informed him to the best of my ability. He then began a conversation, and turned it to the subject of the climate of St. Malo. He soon found out that I was a doctor. This brought forth a larger confidence on his part, and he began to tell me about his troubles and his motive in coming here. In fact, before an hour we seemed like old friends. He seated himself upon a bench by the road-side, fronting the sea. Miss Wyverne placed herself on one side, I on the other, and we all talked together as though we had known one another for a long time. More than this, he introduced me formally to Miss Wyverne, and made me accompany him to his hotel.

"There is no need for me to go into details. Mr. Wyverne's regard for me was evident, and it was so marked, so strong, and so unvarying, that it afforded perpetual surprise to me. He engaged me regularly as his medical adviser, at a salary that to me was enormous; he delighted to have me with him; he encouraged my attentions to Miss Wyverne; and, as she was always with her father, and as he wanted me to be always with him, the consequence was, that she and I were together far more than is commonly the case with two young people even when they are in tender relations with one another.

"Mr. Wyverne was troubled with disease of the heart. He had been ordered to this place by his London physician, with the injunction to refrain from all excitement. That injunction I enforced upon him with the utmost emphasis. St. Malo afforded many advantages, and we remained there four weeks after I had made his acquaintance. During that time I noticed his unfailing regard; but,

more than this, I was often struck by the peculiar expression which would come to his face when his eyes rested on me—an expression which had in it a meaning that absolutely confounded me. It was a parental look, but more yearning—more maternal, in fact, than paternal; yet why he, a perfect stranger, should regard me, another stranger, with such an expression, was utterly and completely out of my power to imagine.

"My mother lives in England. I correspond with her regularly. Of course, I wrote her all the particulars of my acquaintance with these new friends. I was already sufficiently confounded, but the letter which I received from my mother in answer to mine completed my bewilderment. It was the most extraordinary epistle that ever was written. My first impression was that the poor, dear lady had suddenly gone mad. My ultimate conclusion was, that there was about this Mr. Wyverne an unfathomable mystery, and, what was more, that my mother held the key to it. She remarked that Providence had brought us two together—had brought me and Mr. Wyverne face to face. She said that she was full of amazement and gratitude at the wonder that had come to pass; that at first she had felt like warning me against him, and advising me to leave him; but that she had prayed fervently over it, and her mind had been changed. She concluded by urging me to devote myself to Mr. Wyverne; to follow him wherever he went; to give him my love, and try to win his; to watch over him, and try to prolong his life.

"Such was the unaccountable letter with which my mother made my confusion worse confounded.

"At length I became satisfied that the sea-air was not so good as it might be. It was what is commonly called 'too strong' for one in Mr. Wyverne's peculiar delicacy of health and feebleness of constitution. I recommended Villeneuve, which place was well known to me. Mr. Wyverne at once decided to go. He did not seem to have any will but mine. His reliance upon me had in it something exceedingly touching, and there was that in his look and in his tone in addressing me which was full of a profound pathos. We travelled by easy stages, and arrived there without any accident."

After this Blake proceeded to recount the events which have already been narrated

The letter which had prostrated Mr. Wyverne he had never seen. It had been picked up by Bessie, and handed to Miss Wyverne.

The points upon which Blake laid emphasis may be summed up briefly in the following way:

First.—That Mr. Wyverne exhibited a regard for him which was unmistakable and extraordinary.

Secondly.—That Mr. Wyverne's expression, when looking at him, had in it something most striking, and might be called paternal.

Thirdly.—That his mother's letter pointed at some knowledge on her part which made it desirable for him to continue his connection with Mr. Wyverne, and also led to the suspicion that she herself might have been acquainted with Mr. Wyverne in some way in past years.

Fourthly.—Coming upon all these, and gaining new meaning from these things, while it gave new emphasis to them, was the deathbed declaration of Mr. Wyverne, in which he claimed Basil Blake as his own son. At this same time he said that Miss Wyverne was not his daughter. Moreover, he wished Basil Blake to marry her.

Fifthly.—Wyverne's declaration was accompanied with remorseful allusions to two persons. One of these was Blake's mother. The other was Miss Wyverne's father. In his manner of allusion to these two there were manifest the signs of conscious guilt of some sort at their expense.

Sixthly.—Wyverne had hastily sent for a priest. He had not seemed to be so near death as to be unable to receive holy communion; but the result had been most unexpected. The moment that his eyes had caught sight of the priest he seemed horror-stricken. To Blake that death seemed caused by sheer terror. About the priest he had discovered nothing. He did not know his name. The question yet remained whether his fear was owing to the priest, or to some resemblance which he had fancied in the priest to some other person.

Finally, after making all due allowance for every thing, there arose the question which of two alternatives to choose. One of these was the theory that he was delirious all through his last illness. In this case these events must all go for nothing. The other was, that he was conscious and perfectly reasonable. In this case the events of that dying bed towered up to supreme importance. They interwove themselves with other things. They joined themselves to the incidents which had gone before them, and gave to all these a tremendous significance. Beyond all these preliminary incidents these last events rose up to that appalling climax of death, and gave to Blake a new character, a new name, a new place in the world, and a new duty in life.

How should this be decided?

The two friends talked over this subject from every point of view.

"It cannot be decided now," said Kane Hellmuth. "You must make further inquiries. Before you can pretend to decide a question of such momentous importance to yourself, there are two persons whom it is absolutely necessary for you to see. One of these is that priest, if you can possibly trace him. The other is, of course, your mother."

"I will write to her," said Blake.

"Have you not yet done so?" asked Kane Hellmuth, in surprise.

"No."

"Then, do not write. Go in person. See her. Tell her all. See how she looks."

Blake hesitated.

"You do not understand," said he. "It is not a subject that a son can talk over with his mother. In fact, I feel a reluctance to mention it even in writing. She has made a profound secret of it, and—in short—I do not know what—painful memories—I may awaken—or what anguish I may cause her—by—by bringing such a subject before her."

Kane Hellmuth looked solemnly at Blake for a few moments, and then asked:

"Are you sure that she is your mother?"

"My mother!" exclaimed Blake. "What! she—she not my mother! What! confident of that? She! No other thought is possible. She? Oh, yes; there is no doubt about that. All the memories of my life centre about her, and all the happiness of my life has come from her. From my earliest thoughts, I have the recollection of her sweet face, her yearning love, her tender words, and more tender looks and caresses. Whatever may be the mystery of my life, there is none about her. She never could so play the mother with another woman's child."

"Well," said Kane Hellmuth, "you have

means of judging which are superior to argument. A mother's love cannot easily be counterfeited. The things you mention are the surest proof that she is your mother; and so, if she is, I can understand your hesitation, of course. The priest, also, will be difficult, if not impossible, to find, for the reason that you have not the slightest clew to him. Should you recognize his face if you were to see it again?"

"I should," said Blake, "instantly. It is so remarkable a face that I could not possibly mistake it. I could pick out that priest from among any crowd, and swear to his identity."

"That is well," said Kane Hellmuth, thoughtfully. "There is one other person, by-the-way, who ought to be seen. This Miss Mordaunt. Surely, she knows something. Perhaps she could tell about—Clara."

"There would be no necessity for me to see her," said Blake. "She can know nothing of my parentage. You are the one who ought to see her. If, as is possible, she is the younger sister of your Clara, she can give you some information as to the fate of her father, and possibly may tell you something about that point which we were discussing."

"I have nothing to ask about," said Kane Hellmuth, calmly. "It was a theory of yours. My belief is fixed. You, in order to suggest a commonplace explanation to this apparition, and to avoid the supernatural, in which I believe, suggested that this was herself—in life —and, consequently, that she—did not—in short, that she escaped, as I did. I maintained that such an escape was inconceivable in the face of her guardian's testimony and the actual grave. You then proceeded to show that the guardian's conduct was suspicious, that he might have had reasons for putting her out of the way, and concealing the fact by a pretended death and burial. It was your theory; it was not mine. What do you now say? You yourself have seen this guardian; he was Hennigar Wyverne. You knew him. Answer now. Was Hennigar Wyverne the kind of man who would have been capable of an infernal conspiracy, such as you suggested?"

At this question Blake turned pale.

"When you speak of Hennigar Wyverne," said he, "you speak of one for whom I had already formed a strong regard before that moment when he claimed me as his son. His evident regard for me inspired equal regard in my breast. His daughter, too, made my regard for the father still stronger. He seemed to me to be an honorable gentleman. Since you ask me that question now, I can only say to you, Kane Hellmuth—and I say it solemnly—I do *not* believe that Hennigar Wyverne was capable of such an act as the one that I have suggested. Besides, the motive which I have imputed to him was false. Here is another Miss Mordaunt in his family, treated like a daughter, just as your Clara would have been, no doubt, had she lived. Whether there is any inheritance or not, I do not know; but it could have had nothing to do with the dealings between guardian and ward of which you spoke. I believe that Hennigar Wyverne's letters to you contained the truth. Harsh he may have been, but I do not believe that he was capable of any act of crime. I take it all back; and I can only say that the mystery of your apparition remains at this moment unaccountable."

A long silence followed. Such a sudden change in Blake's sentiments surprised Hellmuth so much that he had nothing to say; and this testimony to the character of Clara's guardian at once destroyed all suspicion that he might have begun to have of any deception on his part. These last words of Blake had also destroyed the very argument which he had framed but a short time before.

"Well," said Kane Hellmuth at last, "dropping my own affairs for the present, I should like to ask you what you intend to do now. Do you intend to make any examination about the—ah—the truth of the—this strange statement of Wyverne's?"

To this Blake did not return any immediate answer, but sat in deep thought for a long time.

"You see," said he, at length, "I am prevented from taking any immediate action by various important circumstances. In the first place, the only persons who can give me any direct information, or rather whom I can ask for such information, are cut off from me. The priest has passed away, and has left no sign. There is no conceivable way of tracing him. I have already done every thing that man could do to find out something about him, but have been utterly unsuccessful. The other person is my mother; but how can a son mention to a mother such a subject as this which Hennigar Wyverne's declaration forces upon me? No. Rather than mention it to her I would allow it to remain an eternal mystery, and live in ignorance always. But, in addition to this, there is another thing that ties my hands," continued Blake, in a more earnest tone. "This affair does not concern me only. It concerns another, and one, too, who, as you may have gathered from what I told you, is very—dear to me—yes—dearer to me—than—than life. It is true, no words of love have ever passed between me and Miss Wyverne—for certain reasons which are easily explained—but yet her woman's instinct must have revealed to her long ago the nature of my feelings toward her. Her father encouraged my attentions, as I told you; but I was held back by a consideration which would have weight with every high-spirited man. It is this: I am poor. She is rich; she is an heiress. I could not bring myself, as I was and am, to do any thing which would make me liable to be stigmatized by the world as a miserable fortune-hunter. No; not one word of love would I ever speak to her till I had in some way lessened the immense distance between us, and had at least raised myself above the reach of sneers. I did not wish to get rich, nor do I hope to do so; my aim was, and is, in some way to gain reputation among men. At present I am utterly obscure; but, if I could only gain some fame for myself, I should then be able to come to her on more equal terms, and ask her to be mine. I know very well how hard it is for a man to push himself above the level of his fellows, but I mean to try. The only trouble is, it will take too much time. But never mind about this.

"I am speaking about what I intend to do in this matter of Mr. Wyverne's strange declaration. Now, that declaration, as you see yourself, was twofold. He claimed me as his son. Very well. But then he also disowned her as his daughter. He took me to his heart, and addressed me in the language of a father; but he also thrust her away, and spoke to her as one who was of no value to him, and of no interest in his eyes. And that, too, on his death-bed! With his dying voice he informed her that she was not his daughter—worse, he declared to her that she was the daughter of his worst enemy—an enemy, too, who does not seem to have injured him, and upon whom he had inflicted

injuries so terrible that they had caused not only the most poignant remorse, but also excited in his mind the sharpest terrors of some strange vengeance that his enemy meant to inflict.

"Now, you see, if I aim to prove the truth of this statement of Mr. Wyverne's, or even examine into it, what is it that I must do? I must enter upon a course of inquiries, the result of which will affect not only myself but her. Suppose, for the sake of argument, that I should at last succeed in finding out and in proving that Mr. Wyverne's words were literally true, and not the ravings of delirium, I should then, of course, discover, first of all, that I am his son, though how in the world that could be I do not pretend just now even to conjecture. But that would not be all. That same discovery would show that she is not his daughter. Who, then, is she? She is some unknown person. Who is her father, if Mr. Wyverne is not? Where did she come from? What dishonor—what shame—yes, what infamy would such a discovery heap upon her innocent head! Good Heavens! could I have the heart; would it even be possible for me to cause such misery, such anguish, to any one in her position, even if she were a total stranger? I hope not; I am sure not. But she is not a stranger. She is the one whom I love better than life, and I say now honestly and calmly that I would rather die than do any thing that would interfere with her happiness. She! why I am so situated now that my only hope is to be able at some time to gain her for myself; and how could I now do such a thing as this? No; my hands are tied. I cannot move a step in this matter. I am only afraid that she may do something to satisfy her own mind; and, if there should happen to be any thing in this; if she should discover that she is really not the daughter of Mr. Wyverne, but of some other man; and that I am the one who is to supplant her and usurp her place—why, good Heavens! what a gulf would that discovery place between her and me! And she is far enough removed from me already, Heaven knows! Besides, there is the grief, the suffering, that such a discovery would cause. She, poor girl, has already suffered enough from the mere suspicion of such a thing as this. How could I do any thing that might change that suspicion into conviction, and thus increase her troubles? Mr. Wy-

verne's unfortunate words have already resulted in changing her whole nature, in making
her brood incessantly over this one mystery
which has been suggested to her. Her former
kindness and friendly feeling toward me have
been changed into what is at the best mere
indifference; and, if I have any hope at
all now, it is that, if nothing more is done,
these cares of hers may eventually pass away.
So, you see, these are the things that tie my
hands just now, and force me to inaction."

Blake had spoken earnestly and frankly,
as though he were giving utterance without
reserve to his inmost thoughts. Hellmuth
listened in silence, and, when he had finished,
made no observation whatever. Perhaps he
thought Blake's conclusions unassailable, or
perhaps, wrapped up in his own thoughts, he
had not heard a word that his friend had
been saying.

———

CHAPTER XIII.

MAKING INQUIRIES.

THE result of the examination of the casket had served to complicate still further the
difficulties by which Inez was surrounded, and
to introduce among them new actors, most
conspicuous among whom was Bessie. Hitherto, in her profound abstraction, Bessie had
been quite lost sight of, and her only aim had
been to hide from her, as much as possible,
the troubles that had come upon herself.
But now the revelation of the true name indicated by the initial "M.," at once seemed
to bring Bessie into the circle of circumstances, and suggested her as a possible act-
or in the events which might be forthcoming.
The name showed that Bessie might be connected with that same family to which Mr.
Wyverne had said she herself belonged; her
connection with Mr. Wyverne appeared to
make it certain; and, if this were so, Bessie
might be some relation to herself. What relation? This was impossible for her to say.

This discovery of the name of Mordaunt
thus put Bessie at once in a different position. It seemed to Inez that all along, under
the appearance of childish innocence and
friendly sympathy, she had possessed the full
knowledge of that secret which she had been
trying so hard to keep from her. She now
recalled the incident at Villeneuve with regard to the letter. Bessie had picked it up.

She had read it. She knew all that was in
it. Doubtless, she may have thought over
the meaning of its contents as earnestly as
she herself had done, and had superior means
of information about its statements to help
her to a conclusion.

To regard Bessie in so new and unusual a
light was unpleasant to Inez. She had always thought of her as a frolicsome child;
it did violence to her feelings to think of her
as one who was as capable as herself of keeping her own counsel and preserving a secret.
It seemed to her now to be of no use to
maintain her own reserve any longer. In
fact, it was impossible to do so, and, more
than this, it was absolutely necessary for her
to ask some questions of Bessie. She wished
to find out who Bessie's relations really were,
and to learn how much she really knew about
this matter. She had understood that Bessie
was an orphan child—the ward of Mr. Wyverne—who would in due time inherit a respectable fortune, but had never known any-
thing more definite, partly because Bessie
was reticent on the subject of her family,
and partly because she herself felt a natural
delicacy preventing her from asking questions
of a private nature.

Thus, therefore, a full explanation with
Bessie was absolutely necessary. But Inez
felt a strange repugnance to it. Bessie
seemed now no longer the same, and the en-
tire confidence she once had in her had been
shaken during the past week. Still Inez was
of a frank nature, and so she quelled her repugnance, and lost no time in seeing her
friend.

Bessie met her more than half-way. As
Inez entered her room to engage in the conversation which she proposed, Bessie's face
brightened, and she ran toward her, flung her
arms around her, and kissed her over and
over again.

"Why, my own darling Inez!" she exclaimed, "is it possible? And so you won't
mope any longer. You have been so sad, you
know. You have quite broken my heart. I
knew, of course, dear, that you could not
help being sad, yet still it was very hard for
me to see you so absent. And you never
favored your poor little Bessie with one single look—no, not one! And now, dear, you
must cheer up. I'll never, never, never let
you mope any more."

Prattling in this way, with the utmost exuberance of affection, Bessie clung to Inez, and drew her toward the sofa, where they sat down, Bessie with her arms fondly twined around her, with her fresh, smiling face close to that of Inez, and her clear blue eyes fixed lovingly upon those of her friend.

"You shall never mope again, Inez dear—no, never, never. You have others who love you. Do you think it is right to be so cruel to a loving heart like mine?"

By such gushing affection as this, by these fond caresses and loving reproaches, Inez felt at first completely overwhelmed, and, for a time, the faint suspicions that had entered her mind faded away. She returned Bessie's caresses, and they talked together, for a little while, in the old strain of perfect confidence and sisterly love. At last, however, the suspense in which she was, and the intense desire she felt to get at the bottom of this secret, brought her back to the purpose for which she had come.

"Bessie, dearest," said she, "you know what I have had to bear of late, and will make allowances for me, I am sure, if I appeared to be cold toward you. If I were to tell you all, you will wonder how I endured it at all. And I will tell you all some day when I feel able to speak calmly about it. But there is something now that I want to ask about, and the person I wish to ask is yourself."

"Me?" said Bessie, opening her eyes wide.

"I am in great trouble, dear," said Inez, "apart from the sorrow I feel about poor papa, and I want you to help me."

"Sorrow — what! more sorrow?" cried Bessie, in mournful accents. "Oh, my own poor, dear darling, unfortunate Inez, what can have happened? Oh, how sorry I am, and oh, how glad I shall be if I can do any thing for you!"

"It was something that poor papa said on his death-bed—the last words he spoke. He said them to me, and they trouble me awfully. I cannot bear to think of them, dear, and so I cannot tell you now, but I will soon. He could not have meant what he said. It must have been his delirium."

"So it was, surely," said Bessie, vehemently, in her slightly Irish way. "Never could he have said any thing at all—at all—that would hurt your feelings if it hadn't been for his delirium. They tell me he was

out of his mind entirely, poor dear! So don't think any thing more about it, but try to be your own self again, Inez jewel."

"I hope it was so, I'm sure," said Inez, sadly, "but I don't know, and I can't help my own feelings. Still, there is something that I want to ask from you. Part of my troubles arise out of something which poor papa said about some person whose name is Mordaunt."

As Inez said this she looked steadily at Bessie. Bessie returned her look calmly.

"Mordaunt!" she repeated, with a slight smile. "Sure that's my name. How very, very funny, Inez darling! Was it me he meant, jewel? I'm sure I don't see why you should worry about that?"

"Would you have any objection to tell me a little about your papa, Bessie dear? I want so much to know. If it is a painful subject, you need not answer, and I beg pardon for asking."

"Objection? Why, my poor, dear Inez, not the least in life. I'd be only too happy, darling, to do that same if I only could. But it's little or nothing I know about that same. Poor dear, darling papa died when I was very, very little, and I have only heard from others what I know about him, and that's little enough, so it is. Unfortunately, all that I know is told in a few words, dear. His name was Bernal Mordaunt, and he died when I was a bit of a child, not more than three years old. He was in some foreign country when he died, and I really do not know even the name of the place. But a child only one year old cannot be supposed to know much, can she, Inez dearest?"

The last part of this Inez had not heard. She had heard the name *Bernal Mordaunt*, and no more. She had heard Bessie quietly claim him as her father. After that, she heard nothing. Her heart throbbed wildly, and her mind was confused with a whirl of fancies that came to her.

"So your father's name was Bernal Mordaunt?" said she, at length, in a steady voice.

"Dear Inez! how very, very sad you look! Why, what possible interest can you take in poor papa?" said Bessie, in a sympathizing tone.

"Do you remember any thing about your mamma, Bessie?" asked Inez again, after a pause.

"My darling mamma died before I was born," said Bessie, in a childish voice. "I never saw her in my life. I have heard that poor papa's grief for poor darling mamma was so violent that he ran away from the country, and died of a broken heart. But I never saw either of them. Sure and it's myself would be the happy girl if I had some recollection of a papa or mamma to look back upon; but I never, never had one, Inez darling. That is the reason why I never spoke about them to you before. It's so very, very sad, dear."

Again Bessie's words made the heart of Inez throb with strange vehemence. Every word seemed to assure her of that which she half dreaded to know. In this unknown Bernal Mordaunt, and in that beautiful lady that bore her own name, Inez, she saw those whom Mr. Wyverne's words made her own parents; in the two portraits of these children, she saw "Clara" and "Inez." She saw no "Bessie." What place was there for a "Bessie" in that little family group? Yet, Bessie's words seemed to indicate this. One thing alone made it seem impossible, and that was the statement that her mother had died at her birth, or, as she expressed it, "before she was born." Could she have been a younger child, whose portrait had never been taken, and never included among the others? But that was impossible. If she herself wore the "Inez" of the portrait, then Bessie could not possibly belong to that family. Bessie was, in fact, several months older than herself, and there was no place for her. On the other hand, Bessie could not be the child of the portrait, for, apart from the difference in the names, which might be passed over, there was an insuperable difficulty in the faces. That child was a brunette. Bessie was a golden-haired blonde.

These thoughts passed through her mind while Bessie was speaking, and, as she ended, Inez asked her, in the same tone as before:

"Were there any others of you?"

"There were, surely," said Bessie, "as I've heard, though I never saw them. Two sisters older than me. I was the baby, and —oh, Inez dear, I'm so fond of babies. Are you not fond of them, Inez dearest?"

Bessie raised her large blue eyes to her friend's face as she said this, and looked at her with a loving smile.

"Sisters?" said Inez, without noticing her question—"sisters, and older than you? Why, I never knew that you had sisters."

"And no wonder," said Bessie. "It was a sad world for all of us; for my two sisters died when I was a child, and it's only the names of them that were left me. You will not wonder now, darling, that I have never chosen to make you my confidante about my family, when there is nothing but so very, very sad a story to tell. It's me that never could bear to speak of that same."

"What were their names?" asked Inez.

"Their names?" said Bessie, with a long sigh. "There were two, one several years older than the other. The eldest one was named Clara, and the youngest one had the same name as you have, Inez. And isn't that awfully funny, Inez dear? But I believe your dear mamma was some sort of a relation to my dear mamma, and that accounts, I suppose, for their both taking the same name for their children. But my sister Inez must have been about three years older than me. Sure it's a mournful subject, and I can't bear to think of it at all at all. Do you know, Inez darling, it's really very hard for you to talk about this? You really almost make me cry. And I hate crying so."

Saying this, Bessie turned her eyes on Inez, who saw that those calm, blue orbs were moist with tears.

"They all died—all," said Bessie, mournfully. "My sisters died while I was a child, and I never saw them. My dear grandpapa took charge of me, and I was brought up in Ireland, you know, till your poor dear papa sent for me, three years ago."

All this Inez heard with the same feelings of perplexity. If Bessie was right, then she saw that her own suspicions were utterly wrong; but, on the contrary, if she was right, then how could Bessie have ever grown up with such an unaccountable belief as this? The Inez of the portrait might not be herself, after all. What foundation had she for her suspicions but a sick man's delirious words? She was younger than Bessie, instead of being older. If Bessie was right, then she was engaged in a foolish task, and heaping up endless trouble for herself to no purpose whatever.

Still, Inez had, after all, so strong a belief that her suspicions were well founded, that she was unable to dismiss them as yet.

There were other things in addition to this about which she wished to ask Bessie.

"Bessie, dear," said she, "you remember that letter that you picked up in the hotel at Villeneuve and handed to me?"

"Yes, darling."

"You read it."

At this Bessie's fair face flushed scarlet, and the bright and sunny smile that usually irradiated it was chased away by a frown, and a sudden flush swept over it. But this passed instantly, and Bessie said:

"Well, really, Inez darling, I hardly knew what I was doing, I was so terrified, and I wondered so much what had happened, and I was so fond of your poor dear papa, that I read it without thinking that it was his letter. I would not have dreamed of reading it though, Inez dearest, but the writing was so familiar that I thought it was no harm. It was my own dear grandpapa's writing, and I thought it was something about me. Sure and anybody would have done that same, and never have given it a thought."

At this new piece of information, Inez started in fresh amazement.

"Your grandpapa!" she exclaimed.

"True for you, Inez dearest, my own darling grandpapa; and wouldn't you have read a letter written by your grandpapa if you had been so excited, and so frightened, and didn't know what you were doing? And, after all, there wasn't much in it at all, at all. Really, I could not make it out—not one single word, dear. Why your poor dear papa should feel shocked at such a letter is quite beyond me—quite. And, really, now that same I don't believe at all, and I don't think the letter had any thing to do with it."

"What is your grandpapa's name, Bessie?" asked Inez, anxiously.

"Kevin Magrath, sure," said Bessie.

"It is a very unusual name," said Inez; "I never heard it before."

"Well, Inez dear," said Bessie, "poor grandpapa is in—in trouble—most of the time—and I don't generally introduce his name into conversation. He's never done the least harm in life—poor, dear grandpapa! —but the world is hard on him."

"Do you know what he meant by those letters B. M.?"

"Surely not. How should I know that?"

"He said that B. M. is alive, and had come back."

"Did he? Really, the words had no meaning to me, Inez dearest, and I have forgotten all about them."

"Don't you think that B. M. means Bernal Mordaunt?"

"Bernal Mordaunt? Why, that's poor papa! Why, Inez dearest, what can you possibly mean? Sure and it's joking you are!"

"Didn't you think of that?"

"Never, till this moment," said Bessie, solemnly. "How should I? I read the letter without understanding one single word. It seemed to me like one of the puzzles one reads in the magazines. But what do you mean by all this about my poor papa, Inez dear? Really, do you know you make me feel quite timid? It's like raising the dead —so it is."

"And this Kevin Magrath is your grandpapa?" said Inez, in whom this information had created unbounded amazement.

"Yes," said Bessie, "he is my own dear grandpapa. He's awfully fond of me, too; but he has his trials. I'm afraid he's not very happy. He's so funny, too! I'm sure I sometimes wonder how he can ever have been my dear mamma's papa; but he is so, entirely."

"Your mamma's name was Magrath, then?"

"Of course, it must have been," said Bessie, simply. "But, Inez dearest, are you almost through? Do you know you really make me feel nervous? I never was cross-questioned so in my life, and, if you don't stop soon, you will positively make me feel quite cross with you. I never saw dear mamma, you know; and I hate to be reminded of my lone and lorn condition."

"Forgive me, Bessie dearest," said Inez, who saw that Bessie's patience was giving way. "I will only ask you one or two questions more, and only about that letter. Do you remember noticing a tone of alarm running through your grandpapa's letter?"

"Never a bit," said Bessie. "Was there any?"

"Yes," said Inez, "very much alarm. The writer seemed frightened at discovering that B. M. was alive."

"And where's the wonder? Sure, I myself would be frightened out of my senses at that same. Now, wouldn't you, Inez dearest—wouldn't you yourself be frightened? Now, wouldn't you—say?"

"Of course; but, then, this letter spoke of some danger that my papa would incur, if this 'B. M.' found him. He advised him to run away—to Russia, or America."

"Did he?" said Bessie, with a bright smile. "Haha! the omadhawn! Sure and it's just like him, for all the world! He's always running away and hiding himself. Sure and I can explain it all to you, Inez jewel. This B. M. is some creditor."

"Creditor!"

"Why not? Don't I know all about it? Isn't poor, dear grandpapa head over heels in debt, and always in hiding? Isn't he afraid to show his nose in England? Sure and he is. And so, you see, Inez dearest, that must be what he meant. Your poor, dear papa must have owed money to this B. M., and, of course, this B. M. is going, or was going, to dun him. Oh, if you had been brought up in Ireland, you'd understand all about that same. 'Deed and you would. So now, my poor Inez, don't worry yourself about nothing. Don't think and talk about things like these. I cannot imagine what in the wide world has come over you. You really shock me. And all about a stupid letter about some stupid money!"

With these words, Bessie wound her arms fondly about Inez; and, when Inez opened her mouth to ask some new question, she playfully put her hand against it, and declared she would not let her speak unless she promised not to say any thing more about this subject.

"You are talking stupid genealogy, Inez dear," said she, "and I positively will not listen to another word. I certainly shall be angry if you continue your cross-questions a moment longer. They make my head ache; and I think you are very, very unkind, and I wouldn't treat you so—so I wouldn't."

Inez found it impossible to resist Bessie, and, though there were many other things which she wished to ask, she was compelled to leave them, for the present at least.

But what she had learned from Bessie did not in the slightest degree quell her curiosity, or satisfy her doubts, or soothe her suspicions. Still there rang in her ears the dying words of Mr. Wyverne—"You are not my daughter!"—and still the images of the three portraits floated before her eyes.

CHAPTER XIV.

MRS. KLEIN.

THE conversation with Bessie left Inez in a great state of doubt and hesitation. As far as she could see, Bessie had been perfectly frank and unembarrassed in all her statements. Those statements were all as plain and simple as they possibly could be. And yet they were completely at variance with the suspicion which she had been cherishing ever since Mr. Wyverne's death.

Bessie's story was plain, simple, and intelligible. It was also very plausible, and, indeed, far more credible than the theory of her own parentage, which she had raised out of Mr. Wyverne's declaration.

It was this:

Bernal Mordaunt had a wife and two children—Clara and Inez. To these he was tenderly attached.

At the birth of the third child Mrs. Mordaunt had died.

This third child was Bessie, and she was three years younger than the "Inez" of the portrait.

But Bernal Mordaunt's grief at the death of his wife was so excessive that he could endure his home no longer. He left the country, and soon after died.

Mrs. Mordaunt's father now took these children under his care. He was this same Kevin Magrath who had written that ill-omened letter. Judging from Bessie's feelings toward him he must have been a kind-hearted man. He took care of these orphan children. Two of them died, and Bessie Mordaunt was left alone, the last of that family.

Now, in some way, her father seemed to be brought into connection with these Mordaunts.

How?

No doubt as guardian, executor, or agent. Perhaps, in his management of Bessie's property, he had done her some injustice.

And now, out of all this, quick as lightning there flashed across her mind what might be the true theory of all this trouble.

Her father might have mistaken her for Bessie!

No sooner had she thought of this than an immense feeling of relief came to her. It seemed so very probable, so perfectly natural.

There had evidently been some sorrow on her father's soul, arising from the consciousness of wrong done. It was this that gave to him that remorse which he felt, and of which he spoke. To whom, then, had this wrong been done of which he spoke?

There was no doubt, both from the letter of Kevin Magrath and from Mr. Wyverne's own words, that this wrong had been done to Bernal Mordaunt. Bessie herself had indicated the nature of that wrong. Her grandfather, she said, was in debt, and perhaps Mr. Wyverne, too. It may have been that these two men had in some way mismanaged the estate of Bernal Mordaunt, and for this cause they dreaded him when he reappeared. Bessie, then, was the one whom her father had wronged. In his illness his delirious fancies brought all his crimes back. She, his own daughter, appeared to him like the injured Bessie, and thus it was that as she came near he had repelled her with those words, " *You are not my daughter!* " It was not herself, then, but Bessie, from whom he had shrunk ; and it was not hers but Bessie's hand that he had placed in the hand of Dr. Blake. Perhaps all along he had misunderstood Dr. Blake's attentions; had thought they were given to Bessie ; had encouraged them for this reason ; and, finally, had at last sought to make some recompense to her by giving her to be the wife of an honorable man.

It was not without a sharp pang that this last thought came to Inez, but no sooner had Dr. Blake occurred to her mind than the thought and the pang passed, and away in an instant went the soundness and stability of Bessie's theory.

For with the thought of Dr. Blake came the recollection that Mr. Wyverne had claimed him as his son. How should she explain this?

Again, in Kevin Magrath's letter, he had laid particular stress, not on *Bessie*, but on *Inez!* How should she explain that?

Again, and above all, how should she explain those mysterious memories of her childhood; how account for her dim recognition of that mother's face in the portrait—that elder sister? To do so was impossible. Had they lived at her father's house when she was a child, and had she thus become acquainted with those haunting faces? It might be so,

yet to her they seemed more, far more than pleasant acquaintances. What was the secret cause of that deep emotion which she felt at the sight of them? Whence arose that profound yearning of her soul over that mother and that elder sister, as over dear ones once loved and lost?

It was evident to Inez that the past must be looked into by means of the help of others besides Bessie. Among the domestics of the household could any one be found whose memory reached back far enough .to make him or her of any use in the present inquiry?

No sooner did this question occur to Inez than she at once thought of an old domestic who occupied a very peculiar position in the house. Mrs. Klein had once been housekeeper, but, having fallen into a species of what may charitably be termed decrepitude, with which, however, *gin* had something to do, the active duties of her position were handed over to another, and Mrs. Klein was pensioned off. Mrs. Klein's present residence was well known to Inez, for she had been in the habit of paying frequent visits to the retired potentate, and she now determined to seek her without delay. Accordingly the carriage was ordered, and, after about an hour's drive, Inez found herself before the humble abode of her old friend.

It was about two o'clock, and Mrs. Klein was at home. Indeed, the first glance showed Inez that it would have been difficult for her to have left her home ; for there was in her gait an unsteadiness, and in her eye a rolling, watery leer, which would infallibly have drawn down upon her the attentions of the police had she ventured forth to any distance from her humble cot. She was about sixty years of age, dressed in black, with a frilled cap on her head, and a bunch of keys dangling from her waist—these last the emblems of her lost sovereignty, but still lovingly retained from the force of habit. She was stout and decidedly "beery" in her aspect and manner, and there was a fuddled unctuousness of voice in the way in which she greeted Inez, and a maudlin tearfulness of eye which showed that her naturally keen sensibilities had been subjected to the impulse of some gentle stimulant.

"Which it's welcome you truly air this day, my own dear child, Miss Hiny," she began, in a whimpering voice. "An' me think-

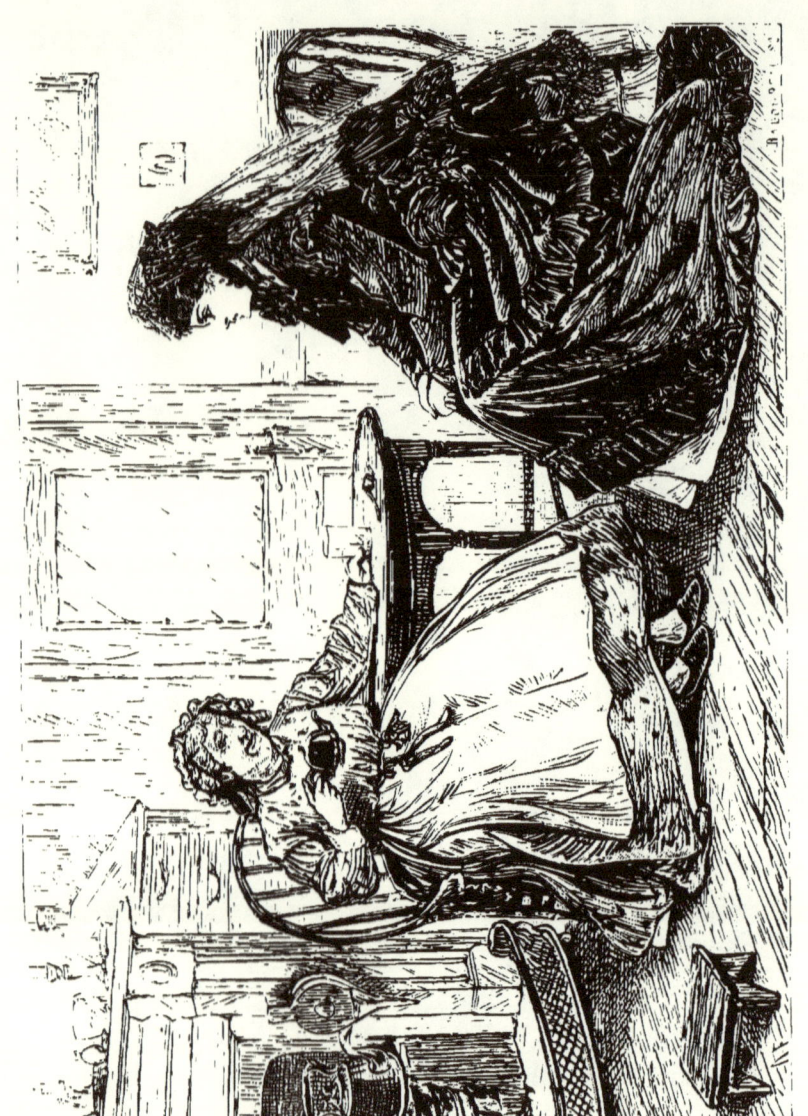

"Nothink so 'olesome an' 'ealthy as a drop of this."—Page 61.

in' that I'd die without the sight of your sweet face, an' left 'ere alone in the cold world that leaves me to pine and languitch, an' no one left to love me now, an' you too may forget, as the good book says! An' so he's dead an' gone, an' the grass waves over he, which he was ever a kind friend to me, an' a brave soger, well used to war's alarms, though he did pension me off, an' me as hactyve an' as nimble as a kitten, an' never 'ad a day's illness in all my life, since I was a child with the measles, an' managed that 'ouse like clock-work nigh on twenty year, which he says there was never any other 'ousekeeper that could 'old a candle, and 'im dead an' gone below!"

And with this rather equivocal conclusion to her somewhat incoherent address Mrs. Klein drew forth an enormous bandanna handkerchief, and mopped away vigorously at her eyes.

Inez took a seat, and waited patiently for Mrs. Klein to overcome her emotions. At length, the old lady drew a long sigh, and, putting out her hand, took an old teapot from the table near her, and poured from this into a tumbler a colorless liquid that looked like water, but whose pungent odor announced the presence of gin.

"Which, after bereavement and melancholick," she said, "there's nothink so 'olesome an' 'ealthy as a drop of this, took, Miss Hiny, only as a medicink, an' to stimmylate the mind an' hease the 'art, which I allus does before I hever goes to my blessed bed at night, an' would 'umbly recommend the same, with my 'umble dooty an' best wishes, for you an' yours, an' 'opin' your dear benefactor left you comfortable, which we shall not see his like again in this vale of tears, an' 'e was as good as a father to you—"

The old lady's booziness and twaddle had begun to discourage Inez, who saw no chance of getting any intelligible information from such a fuddled brain; but suddenly, in the midst of this, the last remark of Mrs. Klein startled her, and she began to think that perhaps, by humoring the drunken creature's fancy, she might get more out of her than she would be able to do if she were sober. For, in the old days, she had never given utterance to any thing that came so near to Inez's suspicions as this. In her later days, she had been occasionally a little excited by gin, but never so much as to be off her guard.

"Yes," chimed in Inez, anxious to see how much Mrs. Klein would tell, "he was as good as a father; he couldn't have done more if he had really been my father."

"Which there never was a truer word, an' 'im with 'is own son lost to 'im, as a body may say, an' the wife of 'is boosom turned agin 'im, an' you not 'is hown, an' in this world men 'ave 'ard 'arts when they 'ave to bring up them as is not their hown—all but 'im, as never spoke of you but with lovin' kindness an' tender mussies, an' ever shall be. 'Mrs. Klein,' says he, ' you 'ave a lovink 'art, an' I hintrust this 'ere lone babe of the woods to you to brink hup as my hown. Call her by my hown name; treat 'er as your young missus; be virtoous, an 'you will be 'appy—to be brunk hup in Wisdom's ways, which is ways of pleasantness, an' hall her paths is paths hof peace.' Which them's 'is hown words, Miss Hiny, as hever was, an' 'im a-confidink in me, as knoo 'ow fully 'e might confide. An', 'Don't you hever tell 'er,' 'e says, ' but what she's my hown, for hit'll be hall the same to 'er in the hend; an' to be brunk up soberly, righteously, an' piously, hall the days hof her life, an' has my hown daughter—Miss Wyverne—hany think to the contrairy 'ereof in hany wise notwithstandink.' "

"How old was I then?" asked Inez, in a tremulous voice.

These wandering words were certainly confirming her worst fears, and bringing back all her worst suspicions.

"Ay, 'ow hold," the old creature went chattering on—"which it's a mere child you was, not hover fower year, an' not as much; an' there was your sister, a fine girl of twelve, that was sent to the nunnery in France—"

"France!" exclaimed Inez, in deep excitement.

"Oh, I know it; I remember it," said Mrs. Klein, positively. "An' me 'carin' all about the proposules, an' she a-cryink like a babby at leavink of you. But I comforted 'er, an' I says: 'Cheer up, little Clara; you shall see Hiny soon, if so be as you be a good girl, an' go hoff quiet.' An' so she bade a long adoo to things below."

"Was Mrs. Mordaunt there?" asked Inez.

Her heart was throbbing painfully, and she could speak with difficulty. She asked this question and named this name so as to

5

test her suspicions to the uttermost, and put them beyond a doubt.

"Oh, ay, ay! an' so you remember the name—poor lady!—which 'er name I remember well, though never seeink 'er, beink dead an' gone before, an' you two being horphans in the cold world below. An' my poor 'art bled for you two in your dissolute state, which your ma beink dead, an' your pa beink fled far away into strange lands, an' me 'earin' afterward that 'e died in heggsile—which Mr. Wyverne 'e stood for'ard, an' says to me: 'That child shall be mine, to be brunk up in the lap of lugsury, an' you be kind an' faithful, an' name your hown reward.' But I ups an' says: 'My reward, sir, axin' your 'umble pardink for bein' so bold, his to be a father to the fatherless an' a mother to the motherless.' An' he says: 'You are right, an' I commend 'er to your faithful boosom.'"

"Why did Mrs. Wyverne leave her husband?" asked Inez once more.

"Which 'e wus allus a kind 'usband an' a faithful father, an' nobody can deny—no, not heven 'er as left him to die hof a broken 'art —an' ever 'ad a kind word for hall the 'ouse-'old; an' took 'er son an' 'is—Basil—'im bein' not hover six year hold, an' in long curls, the be-e-e-eautiful child! An' 'e says to me, 'Mrs. Klein,' an' I says, 'Sir,' an' 'e says, 'They've gone,' an' I says, 'Who?' an' 'e says, with a 'alf whimper, 'My wife,' 'e says, 'an' my son—my boy—my Basil!' An' I says, 'Sir,' says I, ''opin' no hoffence, an' axin' your pardink—they'll come back.' An' 'e says, 'Never; she's too hobstinate, an' 'as bid a heternal haydoo.' Says I, 'Sir, what for? Isn't this 'ere their proper 'ome?' Says 'e, 'We've 'ad a fight, an' she's gone.' Says I, 'About what?' Says 'e, 'About 'er, about little Hiny.' An' 'im so kind an' lovin' that 'e treated 'er like a man, an' never heven advertised her, nor sood for a separation, nor nothink; an' me hexpectin', day hafter day an' year hafter year, that she'd relent an' come 'ome; but relent she did not, an' come 'ome she did never, but 'id 'erself close, an' 'as never been 'eard hof from that day to this blessed momink. Which 'er 'usband bore the cruel blow like a hangel, an' never repined, but showed a Christiang fortitood, an' forguv 'is henemies, an' 'im a good 'usband to 'er, never a-comin' 'ome drunk an' beatin' 'er about the 'ead with a broom-'andle, as is the case with many wives, but kind and true as

'e promised an' vowed in his marriage-bond before the haltar. Which if it's the last word I hever spake, I'd go to that woman, an' look 'er in the heyes, an' I'd say unto 'er: 'My dear, axin' your 'umble pardink, I'd advise you to pack hup your duds an' Go 'ome, for hif you don't hit's a-goink to be the wuss for you an' your boy; which 'ere is Miss Hiny a-twinink 'erself hayround 'is 'art, an' a daughter to 'im, 'avin' lost one father to find a father in 'im, an' bein' deservink of it, too, as a warm-'arted girl, an' as dear to me as a child of my hown.'"

Inez had heard enough. She had no heart to ask any further questions. One thing she had learned which was altogether new, and that was, that this sister Clara had been sent to France—to a "nunnery," as Mrs. Klein said. And there, thought Inez, she must have died. Deeply was she touched by Mrs. Klein's remarks about Clara's love for the little sister from whom she had to part, and her heart was filled with unutterable regrets and unutterable longings after that lost dear one, who loved her once so fondly.

Mrs. Klein now, being no longer directed by any leading questions, went off in a series of remarks of a highly-desultory character. She began by pressing a half-tumbler of gin upon Inez, and wept freely because Inez refused. She then, still weeping, swallowed it herself. After this she began a lamentation over the wickedness of the world and the depravity of the human heart, as exemplified in some recent bad bargains which she had made in her favorite beverage. She urged Inez to take her back, to live with her as companion or chaperon. Finally, she produced an old clay pipe and lighted it.

Inez had scarcely heard a word for some time past. During Mrs. Klein's desultory rambling she had been buried in her own reflections, but out of these she was suddenly and violently drawn by a strangling and choking sensation, caused by the smoke of the particularly villanous tobacco in Mrs. Klein's pipe. She hastily rose, and, without a word, rushed to the door, leaving Mrs. Klein talking to the walls of her house.

About the truth of Mrs. Klein's statements Inez had not the slightest doubt. Had she been perfectly sober, it might have been possible to suspect her of acting up to some plan devised long ago in Mr. Wyverne's life. As it was, such a suspicion was impossible. The circumstances under which this had been said, and the way in which she had said it, all combined to show Inez that it must be true.

In this state of mind she drove home. And now Bessie met her. She rushed down the stairs, and, clasping her in her arms, kissed her, and reproached her lovingly for going out alone.

"Sure and you'll never be your own old self again, Inez darling," she exclaimed. "I had begun to hope that you had got over your reserve, and reticence, and sadness, and solitary ways, and all that sort of thing. I can't stand this at all, at all. Really, Inez darling, you'll break my heart. Why should you hold yourself aloof from me, and why won't you come back to your old familiar ways, dear? Positively, if you treat me so, I shall have to go away, for I shall feel that you no longer lil—lil—love mum—mum—me."

And here Bessie burst into tears.

Inez kissed her, and tried to soothe her, and felt real self-reproach at having inflicted so much pain on this innocent child.

"It was only some foolish business of mine," said she.

"But you have no business to have any foolish business at all," said Bessie, fretfully. "You have no right to wound me so. It was hard enough before, but, after we made friends again, it was very, very cruel in you, Inez dear. It's myself that's been the miserable girl this day, and it's fairly heart-broken that I am with you; and you won't do so again, darling, now will you? You will not be so cold and unkind, now will you, Inez dearest?"

Inez promised not to offend again, whereupon Bessie grew calm, and the two spent the rest of the day together as much on their old terms as was possible, when the heart of one of them was wrung with the remembrance of that which she had heard, and when her mind was perplexed with the problem of her life, and the image of the gentle sister Clara was ever floating before her imagination.

She retired early that night, and at last found herself alone.

Here there was one thought that perplexed her.

This was Bessie Mordaunt—this girl who bore that name, and gave that account of her parentage.

Inez had now not a doubt left that she was, in very truth, Inez Mordaunt, daughter of Bernal Mordaunt.

She had now not the slightest doubt that Bessie's account of herself was utterly false.

Did Bessie know this? Impossible. Bessie would not deceive. Bessie herself must be deceived.

But how?

Evidently Bessie must have been brought up all her life in this belief. She stated it so calmly and so simply, and it agreed so perfectly with her mode of thought and her position in this house, past and present, that she must believe in what she said. Yet it was all false, and Bessie had been carefully brought up to believe it as true.

How could this have happened? Who could have instilled into her so long and so carefully all these lies? What could have been the motive of it? Could it have been Mr. Wyverne? If so, why had he done it? Or could it have been that man who had brought Bessie up—her "dear grandpapa," Kevin Magrath?

That was the question.

THAT she had been all along the victim of some dark plot, Inez now felt confident; but whether Mr. Wyverne was the originator of the plot or not, she could not tell. There were many other things also which perplexed her. What was the position of Bessie? Taking her honesty, good faith, and perfect innocence for granted, what was her place in this involved net-work of circumstances? Was she too a victim? or was she the protégée of the unknown conspirators? Who was her "grandpapa?" What part had he borne in all this? What was his attitude with regard to her? and what had been his attitude toward Mr. Wyverne? Above all, what was the motive of the conspiracy? That it was a conspiracy of no common kind, she felt sure. It had begun long ago, and had been carried on for years. What was the purpose of these two confederates—Wyverne and Magrath? What end did they propose? Was it revenge? or was it avarice? Was there any thing of hers that they might gain?

Of course, these questions could not be answered, and this last one was the greatest puzzle of all, for it was impossible for her to imagine what could have been the cause for which these men had framed so deep a plot, and elaborated it so patiently, and carried it out so carefully.

Bernal Mordaunt was her father. She now believed this without the slightest lingering doubt.

Bernal Mordaunt was a priest. What was the meaning of this? This was a point that she could not comprehend. That he was a Roman Catholic and not an Anglican priest, she knew from the allusion in the letter to his " ecclesiastical business " at Rome. What was the meaning of that? Was this, then, the cause why her parentage had been so carefully concealed? Was this the cause of his flight—his neglect of his children? Was it the affection of Mr. Wyverne, seeking to save her from shame, that had surrounded her with all this mystery? Was this the reason that her sister Clara had been sent to a nunnery, and herself brought up as Mr. Wyverne's daughter? Was this so? and, if so, was it not possible that Mrs. Wyverne may have quarrelled with her husband on the ground that he was receiving a child of shame into his household, and had taken herself and her son from the presence of such pollution? Could this be so?

This? Impossible. It was not of affection and self-sacrifice that Mr Wyverne spoke on his dying-bed. It was of repentance for crime. It was remorse. It was the agonizing desire to make an atonement for wrongs which he had done to her father.

That father had come to him there at that bedside—the injured man had seen the offender, with what result she had heard from Dr. Blake. Of the real horror of that meeting, however, she knew nothing, for Blake had kept that a profound secret from her. She had merely understood from him that Mr. Wyverne had died the moment the priest had entered the room, and that not one word had passed between them.

There were various questions, consequent upon her knowledge of the fact of this meeting, which served to perplex her mind still further.

Had her father recognized Mr. Wyverne?

She thought not, and for various reasons. In the first place, she remembered the fearful change that had taken place in Mr. Wyverne's face, and judged, rightly enough, that such a change would make all recognition impossible, especially on the part of one who had not seen him for fourteen years.

If he had not recognized him, had he at least known his name?

This also she thought impossible. If he had heard so uncommon a name as Wyverne mentioned, particularly the full name Hennigar Wyverne, he would have been struck by it at once. If so, he would not have gone away so hurriedly after that death—making no inquiries after those whose guardian Hennigar Wyverne had been. No; the priest had probably arrived late, as Blake said, from a hurried journey; had been summoned almost from his bed to the dying man; and then, without recognizing him, or learning his name, had continued his hurried journey.

The question now arose whether he had not found out since who this man was. He must have done so. The notice of Hennigar Wyverne's death had been published, and would of course meet her father's eyes. He would then learn who it was that had died so suddenly.

And what then? What, in fact, would be his action? The letter of Kevin Magrath stated that her father was at Rome, and was going to England to see Wyverne. About what? The answer was given in the letter, in part at least: " Inez must be got rid of." It was for her, then, that her father was coming. She was in part, at least, the object of his journey, and of his business in England.

Would the death of Hennigar Wyverne, now no doubt well known to her father, make any difference in his movements? Would he still come to seek after her? What if lies had reached him, such as those amid which Bessie had been brought up? What if he had heard and believed that his daughters, Clara and Inez, were dead long ago? Could she expect that he would ever search after her? Wyverne being dead, what business would he have in England? On the other hand, how should she find him, or effect communication with him in any way?

Of the two plotters to whom she could trace the great conspiracy which had enfolded her and Bessie in its grasp from earliest childhood, one was dead. But the other remained. What would he do? Would he give up, confess all, and set things straight before the world? or would he continue to carry on his work? He was Bessie's "grandpapa." He was, no doubt, using her as a tool for his own purposes. Would he still try to baffle Bernal Mordaunt?

Kevin Magrath, in the letter which he had written to Hennigar Wyverne, had spoken about Bernal Mordaunt with undisguised alarm; but from that letter it was Wyverne who had chief cause for fear. So formidable an enemy was Bernal Mordaunt, that flight or pretended death were the only ways by which the terrors of his presence could be evaded. Was the danger which had been so dreadful to Wyverne less dreadful to Kevin Magrath?

Not one of these questions could she answer. The one which was most important to her was about her father's possible movements. Did he know that she was alive? Would he come to England?

Since that memorable death at Villeneuve a fortnight had passed away. No signs had presented themselves as yet of his appearance. This did not look like haste on his part. The delay seemed unnecessary, even though he did not know of her existence. It looked as though he had heard of Wyverne's death, and had given up his design of going to England.

After breakfast that day, a letter was handed to Inez.

She looked at it in amazement; it bore the postmark of Paris. Who could write her from Paris? There was only one—Dr. Blake. But why should he write? Perhaps it was something with reference to Mr. Wyverne, or perhaps something the thought of which excited her indignation. Could it be possible? No, it could not be; he would not dare, at such a time, to write to her a confession of his feelings.

With this thought she left the table, and retired to her room to read the letter. There was no reason why she should not think so. Dr. Blake lived at Paris, or lodged there for the present; she had no other acquaintance there; and she did not know enough of his handwriting to judge of the writer of the letter by the address.

But the first words of the letter at once put this notion to flight. On opening it, she read the following:

"MY DEAREST CHILD:

"By this time you know all, and therefore will not be surprised at finding that there is one alive who has a right to call you by that tender name. Returning home after a long absence, during which you have been taught to believe me dead, or rather have been kept in ignorance of me altogether, my only business now is to fold my beloved daughter in my arms, and save her from the machinations of those who so long have had her in their power.

"It was my astonishing fate to meet Mr. Hennigar Wyverne at Villeneuve. I was on my way from Rome to England with no other purpose than to see that very man, and receive from him an account of those dear ones whom I had intrusted to him years before. At that inn, just after a short night's rest, I was requested to visit a dying man. I at once went to the room, and, to my utter amazement, found before me the very man I sought. Fearfully changed though he was, I recognized him; for beneath the mere outline of features there is always something more, which, as long as life lasts, betrays the man. And here the recognition was mutual.

"Although he was evidently surprised, yet my presence was, after all, not altogether unaccountable to him; for he had heard of my return, as he told me himself, and the dread of meeting with me had brought him to this. I will not tell you now all the particulars of that interview, when the soul of the dying man, already hovering on the verge of the eternal world, and going to its last account, lingered for a moment to try to atone for the crimes which he had committed, to try to obtain forgiveness from the man whom he had wronged, before passing into the presence of his Maker. I need only say now that he told all, without reservation. All—all was confessed. I have the consolation of knowing that I was not harsh to my false friend, nor deaf to his appeal for mercy, but forgave him all, freely; and, while as man I forgave the injuries that he had done to man, as priest I gave him absolution for the sins which he had committed against God.

"In the midst of the tremendous agitations of that unparalleled hour, it never occurred to the poor dying man to mention that you were in the hotel, and close by us, even though much was said about you. He informed me that he had already told you the truth, though not all. As it did not occur to him to tell me of your presence, it never occurred to me to suspect it. I had thought of you always as a child, and imagined you at boarding-school somewhere. It was not until I came here that I learned where you really were then, and where you are now.

"As it was, I should have remained in Villeneuve long enough, at least, to perform the last, sad funeral-rites over one who, in spite of his treachery, had once been my most intimate friend. But I could not; business of an urgent nature required my immediate presence here in Paris, and I had no remedy but to hurry forward.

"But the emotions called up by that meeting have been too much for me. I am not so young, dear child, as I once was, and I have suffered very much in body and in mind during the years of my absence. Do not be alarmed, my own child Inez, if I now inform you that I am unable to leave my chamber. I have delayed writing to you thus far from the hope that I might go in person, but the prospect of this is too remote for my impatience. Do not imagine by this that my illness is at all dangerous. It is not; it is serious—that is all. But there is one thing which, more than all drugs and remedies, will give me new life, and raise me up from my bed; and that is the sight of my own beloved child—sweet memorial of my sainted wife, whose image is still enshrined in my heart, for whom my love can never die. Come, then, my daughter — come to your father! Come, my sweet Inez, my only treasure in life! I long and yearn to look upon your face. Do not delay. Do not stop to make any preparations. Do not even think of money. You will find every thing with me that you may need. Come! I shall expect you to leave on the very day when you receive this, and I shall count the hours till you reach me. But I fear I am too urgent. I shall give you one day, then, dearest daughter; and after that I shall look for you. My address is No. 123 Rue de la Ferronière, Paris. A carriage will be at the station, and my servants will be ready. I shall send some friend to receive you.

"I can write no more now, as I feel exhausted, and must reserve any more until you come. Au revoir, my dearest child! Make haste; for my strength is failing, and you are my last hope. I embrace you with all my

heart, and wait for you, my own precious child, with indescribable longing.

"Your affectionate father,
"BERNAL MORDAUNT."

The handwriting of this letter was different from that of the address. In the address it was directed in a round, bold, flowing hand; but in the letter itself it was written in a tremulous hand, with frequent breaks, and words written indistinctly. It looked as though it had been written by some one who was feeble and ill, and had scarce strength enough to conclude his task; for toward the close it became very much less legible, as if, having finished it, the writer had been too exhausted to do more, but had to commission another to write the address.

There were certain circumstances in this letter which at another time would have bewildered Inez exceedingly. One was the story of the conversation between Bernal Mordaunt and Hennigar Wyverne, followed by extreme unction. Dr. Blake's account was altogether the opposite. He had said positively that not one word had been spoken by either; but that, as the priest came in, Wyverne died. Here was a discrepancy so immense that each version destroyed the other utterly. The other difficulty lay in the fact that the handwriting of Bernal Mordaunt was not, in the slightest degree, like the writing of that Bernal Mordaunt whose short note to Hennigar Wyverne, accompanying the portrait, lay in the casket. This in itself was a slight thing, and could easily be accounted for on the ground of weakness, change wrought by a new mode of life and increasing years, or the nervous irregularity of a hand unused of late years to hold the pen; but still, in connection with the first-mentioned fact, it was significant.

Both of these things, and others, also, Inez certainly noticed, but failed to lay any stress upon them whatever. She was, indeed, quite incapable now of weighing any thing calmly. That letter had produced upon her so overwhelming an effect, that there was only one idea in her mind—her father ill in Paris—seriously ill—longing to see her—calling to her to come to him—counting the hours—her father looking upon her as his only hope in life—looking to her for strength to draw him up from his bed of languishing—her father, with his unutterable love for her, and yearning over her. How piteous seemed to her those letters, traced with so feeble a hand, growing fainter and feebler as they approached the end of the sheet! How pathetic that allusion to her mother—how resistless that call to her to come—how tender and sweet that loving urgency, which could scarce allow one day for making her preparations to travel!

No idea of refusing entered her mind. Such a call must be obeyed. She must go. Besides, it was the thing that she herself now longed most of all to do. She began, then, at once to pack up a few things. She had money enough in her purse to take her to Paris. She needed no more than enough to take her to his bedside.

One thought of Bessie came to her, and a slight feeling of sadness at thus being compelled to quit her so abruptly. She wondered, also, what excuse she should make. She could not show her the letter. Though her own frank nature would have prompted such a course, her consideration for Bessie restrained her. It would only bewilder her and give her pain. Bernal Mordaunt she believed to be her own father. If she was ever to be undeceived, the explanation would have to come from those who had deceived her—from her "grandpapa," Kevin Magrath. On the other hand, Inez could not stoop to deceit of any kind, and therefore was unable to make up any plausible pretext for her sudden departure. In the end she solved this particular difficulty by telling Bessie that she had to go to Paris immediately on "business."

This intelligence Bessie received in a much better manner than Inez had anticipated. She appeared startled, but said nothing against it. She was mournful, and affectionate, and very pathetic.

"Oh, I know it," she said, sadly. "I saw it was coming to this. I knew, Inez dearest, that you were changed and didn't love me any longer. But there's no use in life to say any thing, for, when love grows cold, there's not the least use of complaining at all, at all. It's a changed nature you're seeming to have just now entirely, Inez jewel, but I hope you'll be your own dear self again before very long. And won't you promise to write me, Inez darling, as often as you can, for I shall be perfectly frantic till I hear from you? It seems awfully bold and brave in you, so it does, to go off travelling this way. I'm sure I should never be able to do it—never."

Inez found that she could not leave till the next day. Her preparations, however, were very simple. She took Saunders with her, and a footman was to accompany her as far as Southampton.

When Inez prepared to start, she found, to her surprise, that Bessie was dressed for a journey also.

"You need not think you're going to get rid of me so easily," said Bessie. "It's myself that'll be the lone girl when you go, and what in the wide world I'll be after doing with myself without you I don't know, so I don't. And so I mean to stay with you till the very last moment, Inez darling, and I'm going all the way to Southampton. I shall bid you good-by on the pier, and I'm sure I think you might be just a little bit affectionate to-day, dear."

Inez was deeply touched by this mark of Bessie's affection, and embraced her, and kissed her fondly. They then drove to the station.

During the drive to Southampton Bessie was loving, tender, pathetic, and occasionally lachrymose. She appeared to cling to Inez with so much tenderness, that Inez felt herself drawn to the fair young girl more than ever, and wondered how one like her would bear the blow of being told that her name and her life were a deceit. She was glad that it did not fall to her lot to tell Bessie.

On the pier at Southampton they parted. Inez went with Saunders, and Bessie, after waiting on the wharf and waving her handkerchief till she could no longer distinguish Inez, returned to London.

CHAPTER XVI.

FATHER MAGRATH.

As Inez, with her maid, Saunders, landed upon the pier at Havre, several persons were passing down on their way to another steamer which was just about to leave for Southampton. Among these was one man, and, if it had been possible for her to recognize that one man upon that spot, the recognition would have changed altogether the progress of circumstances, and have snatched her from the fate upon which she was blindly rushing. But such a recognition was impossible, and Inez passed on her way—away from the one man who could have solved every mystery, and removed every difficulty—away from the man who could have saved her, and on to the station to take the train for Paris. He was dressed as a priest. He was a man of medium stature, with a very remarkable face, the expression of which was so strangely compounded of force and gentleness, of energy and meekness, of resolute will and sadness, that the eye of the most casual observer was irresistibly drawn to take a longer observation. He carried in one hand some wraps, and in the other an old leather valise, worn and battered as though it had accompanied its owner over thousands of miles of journeyings, and bearing upon one end, in white painted letters, the mark B. M.

Following this man was one whose tall figure, stern and strongly-marked features, and shaggy mustache, revealed the person of Kane Hellmuth. This journey had been the result of his recent conversation with Blake. The mystery of his apparition had now come to be a leading idea in his mind, and, as his friend had hinted at the possibility that his wife might not have died, he had resolved upon this journey so as to satisfy his mind once for all. As Mr. Wyverne, her guardian, was dead, that resource was taken away from him, and he could think of no one to whom he could apply for information except that Miss Mordaunt, to whom also Mr. Wyverne had been guardian. It was, therefore, to no less a person than Miss Bessie that Kane Hellmuth was making this journey.

As the steamer was leaving the pier, the priest stood on the deck along with the other passengers, and Kane Hellmuth found in this man a mysterious attraction that riveted his gaze in spite of himself. The last man was he of all men to feel or to yield to, if he did feel, any impulse of idle curiosity; yet, in this case, in spite of his efforts to check himself, he found his eyes, no matter how often he would force them to look elsewhere, irresistibly drawn back again to fix themselves upon that sun-browned face, with the deep, earnest glance, the resolute purpose, the indescribable pathos—that face which, in its expression, and in the traces of the years, showed such a record. It was a record of a life of no common kind—a life of struggle and of suffering —an heroic life, yet at the same time a life which must have been not without some fulfilment of the holiest duties of that office

which his garb indicated—the office of a Christian priest. Kane Hellmuth thus felt his eyes attracted, and with his eyes his heart; but there was no opportunity of making the acquaintance of this singular man. Kane Hellmuth was naturally of a reserved disposition; the priest, on the other hand, was too much absorbed in his own thoughts to be conscious of the interest which he had awakened in the mind of another, and so these two, who might have found much in common if they had become acquainted, passed on their different ways, without exchanging any word with one another. After leaving the harbor the priest retired, and was seen no more; and Kane Hellmuth, who felt no desire to rest, and no capability of obtaining it if he had desired it, paced the deck for hours. Arriving at Southampton, he saw the priest on landing, and then lost sight of him in the bustle and confusion of the train for London.

Kane Hellmuth found out the location of the house of the late Mr. Wyverne from the directory, and went there as soon as possible. It was about four o'clock in the afternoon.

To his immense disappointment, he learned that Miss Mordaunt was not at home, and, upon further and more persistent inquiry, found that she was not in town. Upon still more urgent inquiry as to her movements, John Thomas, with whom he had been speaking, thought that it could be no other than a lover who could be so persistent; and, though Kane Hellmuth's appearance was not that of the one whom John Thomas might imagine as a suitor for one like Miss Bessie, at the same time John Thomas's heart was not without some sentiment of its own, and he thought that such a visitor should not be dismissed too hastily. So he went into the house to make some inquiries before giving any final answer.

After a brief absence he returned, and informed Kane Hellmuth that he could find out all he wanted from Father Magrath, who was in the house, and had sent an invitation for him to come in.

This invitation Kane Hellmuth accepted. He entered the drawing-room, and, in a few moments, a person came in who introduced himself as the Rev. Mr. Magrath.

Father Magrath, as John Thomas called him, was a man of very remarkable appearance. He was dressed in the usual garb of a priest, but his face was not altogether in keeping with his costume. He was apparently about fifty years of age, of medium height, with a frame whose nervous strength and powerful development had not yet felt the advance of years. His hair was curly, and only slightly sprinkled with gray; he had bright keen eyes, straight thin nose, and thin lips, which were curved into a good - humored smile. The pervading expression of his face was one of jovial and hilarious good-nature. He wore spectacles, which, however, did not conceal the keen glitter of his penetrating eyes. His face was unmistakably Celtic in its character; in fact, it was the face of an Irishman, and, if Father Magrath's name had been less Irish, his face would of itself have been sufficient to proclaim his nationality.

A few questions served to make him acquainted with the fact that Kane Hellmuth wished to see Miss Mordaunt for the sake of making inquiries of her about some family matters.

"Well," said Father Magrath, "she's away out of town, and, what's more, she won't be back at all, at any rate not to this house; but I'm her father confissor, and any quistions that ye may have to ask, of a raysonable chyaracter, I'll be quite happy to answer. Ye'll have to excuse me for the prisint, however, as I'm ingaged on some business of the most prissing kind, and perhaps ye can nceme some hour whin I can mate ye."

Kane Hellmuth thanked him, and informed him that his time was limited, and that the earliest possible meeting would be most acceptable.

"Sure, thin," said Father Magrath, "it's meself that's sorry that I can't stee with ye just now, and for that matter any time this dee, an' not before to-morrow ayvenin'. Could ye make it convaynient to come to-morrow, in the ayvenin', about eight o'clock? If so, I'll be happy to have ye. Come and spind the ayvenin'," he continued, in a warm and cordial tone; "I'll be alone, an' I assure ye I'll be dayloighted to have the plisure of your company."

This invitation, so cordially extended, Kane Hellmuth accepted with thanks, and, bidding the friendly priest adieu, he retired to pass the time as best he could till the hour of that meeting should arrive.

Punctual at the hour, on the following day, Kane Hellmuth reached the house, and was at once shown into the brightly-lighted parlor. Father Magrath was not at home, but had left a polite request for his visitor to wait. In about a quarter of an hour he returned, and, after a slight delay, he entered the room, and greeted his visitor with very great warmth and cordiality.

"Sure and it's glad I am to see you this night," said Father Magrath. "It's me that's not fond of loneliness at all at all. We'll make an ayveniu' of it between us, thin. I'm of a convivial timpirament, and I howld that convivialectee is one of the issinces of true injoymint in loife. So we'll get up something. Is it whiskey ye take, thin, or cognac, or do ye prifir woine, or eel? For me own part, I always teek whiskey."

"I shall be happy," said Kane Hellmuth, pleasantly, "to join you in any drink that may be most agreeable to yourself. I think that whiskey, as you say, is as good as any thing."

"Sure and ye nivir spoke a truer word," said Father Magrath.—"Jeemes, my boy," said he, turning to a footman, "the whiskey; bring a daycanter of Scotch and Irish, and the hot wather, with the it ceteras.—And ye smoke, too, of coorse?"

"Yes."

"Jeemes, whin ye're about it, bring the poipes and tobacco," added Father Magrath.

At this Jeemes retired, and soon returned with a tray upon which were all the articles which, in the opinion of Father Magrath, went toward making up the requisites for a pleasant evening.

"Yis," said Father Magrath, continuing pleasantly, in a half-serious, half-jocular way, some remarks which he had been making; "as I said, there is no plisintniss in loife without convivialectee. Of coorse, I main it in a harrumless sinse. It was not in veen that the ancients ileevatid convivialcetce to the skois, and made it one of the occupections of the Olympian dayectics. I'm no ascitic. I belaive in harrumliss and innocint joys, and so I take an occasional drop of somethin' warrum, and an odd whiff of the poipe at inthervals. Now, here ye have whiskey, both Scotch and Irish, and I don't know which of them ye prefer, an' I don't know meself for that matter. And it's a moighty difficult thing to decoide. For, ye see, there are two great laiding schools, if I may use the ixprission, of whiskey, the Scotch and the Irish, or, to ixpriss mesilf more corrictly, the Erse and the Gaelic. Both schools, like both liquors, are an imeencetion of the radiant Celtic jaynius, which, amid all its gifts to man, has conthributed this last and this best one, whiskey. Now, there is a very remarkable distinction between these two outcomes of the Celtic jaynius. One, the Gaelic, is best, whin mixed with hot wather and taken in the shape of toddy ; the other, the Erse, naids not the foreign adarrunment of hot wather, but stands on its own beesis, as a pure, unmixed drink, which in itsilf is a deloight. There's a deep philosophical and symbolical mayning in this which I haven't time to go into just now, but I may suggist, in passing, that these two drinks ixpleen in some misure the varying jaynius of the rispictive races, and the internal qualeetees of the two may be seen in their liquors. The Irish is best taken raw, without admixture ; the Scotch is best, like the nation, mixed—that is to say, as the liquor is best with hot wather, so the Gaelic race in Scotland has achieved the most by intermixing and blinding with the Lowland Saxon populection."

All this Father Magrath rattled off in a quick, jovial way, pouring out glasses for himself and his guest, so as to allow themselves a taste of each of the liquors with which he professed so close an acquaintance. He poured out the Irish whiskey raw in two wine-glasses ; but the Scotch whiskey he poured into tumblers, and manufactured into toddy, in accordance with his own curious theory about the utility of mixing the Gaelic race and the Gaelic whiskey. Kane Hellmuth tasted the Irish liquor, and then sipped the Scotch in its form of toddy.

"Ye'll be smoking," said Father Magrath. "Here are two kinds of tobacco, the Turkish and the Virginian. Which'll ye have ? Here are poipes, unless ye've brought yer own iu yer pocket, which I always do myself."

"I have one," said Kane Hellmuth, producing from his pocket a short meerschaum in a case.

"That's my way," said Father Magrath, with a sigh of appreciation. "Ye do right. Your own poipe, and your own silf, that's the true smoker's motto.

"I''s a mighty quare thing, too," continued Father Magrath, as he filled his pipe, "about this same fashun of smoking, and this same tobacco. Have ye ivir thought where it origeenatid ? Yo know the popular

thayory that it came from America. Don't believe a word of it. Columbus did enough for the wurruld, but it wasn't him or his discovery that gave tobacco to civeeleezcetion.

"Ye see," he continued, "there's this diffeecultee staring ye in the face. Ye've got to account for the uneversalcetee of its use. One quarter of the human race use tobacco. How has it ixtindid so widely in liss thin fower cinturies ? If Columbus is the earliest date for the use of tobacco, how did it pinitrate into India and China in that toime ? Now, my thayory is this : ye know China. Ye know how all the great invintions and discoveries of civeeleezcetion have been traced there; paper, printing, powder, the mariner's compass, and other things. Now, I trace tobacco there. It wasn't America that gave tobacco to the wurruld. It was China. China gave tay. China gave also tobacco. If researches are made into Chinese history, I don't doubt that it will be found that tobacco has been used there for thousands of years ; that Confucius snuffed ; Mencius chewed ; that Fo-hi smoked ; and that the Tartar nomads, and the Persians, and the Indians, received their knowledge of the 'sublime weed,' as Byron calls it, from China. And I don't know but that America may have received it from China also, for if, as some suppose, America was peopled by the Mongol race, there isn't the laste doubt in life but that they carried their poipes with thim.

"Now, whin ye look at tobacco," continued the priest, in an animated way, "ye see three grand classeefeccetions, corrisponding with the three grand divisions which we notice in modern civeeleezeetion. First, there is the Aseeatic; it is manipuleeted, and drugged, and spoiced, and made into a luxureeous arteeficial substance for the use of the upper classes of socicetee. It riprisints Art. Then there is the American, which comes to us in its purity. This riprisints Nature. Finally, we have the stuff made here in the vareeous countries of Europe; giving a rivinue to the governmints, and grinding the face of the poor. This riprisints the Brummagin system of manufactures, which is swallowing up all Art, and all Nature, and thritening to swallow up modern civeeleezcetion itsilf. But, mark me, ther'll be a rayaction among the nations. The peoples will no longer be opprissed. Governmints will no longer tread down humaneetee in the dust. The many

" Your own pipe, and your own silf, that's the true smoker's motto."—Page 70.

will at last force their wants upon the notice of the few. The days of the priveeleged classes are wellnigh indid. If modern civeeleezeetion means any thing it means the rights of man. Those rights man will have. First among them, he will insist on having free tobacco; he will wrist this great luxury of the human race from the grasp of tyrannical governmints, and stand up in all the dignity and grandeur of manhood to smoke, or to chew, or to do any thing ilse to which the great heart of humanity may impil him."

Thus far Kane Hellmuth had listened to the priest without any comment. Just here, however, partly because Father Magrath happened to pause, and partly because he was surprised at this cropping out of revolutionary sentiments from one who belonged to the most conservative class of mankind, he said:

"You talk as though you had embraced the radical gospel. Is radicalism common with the priests of your church?"

Father Magrath looked at him with a keen glance for a few moments.

"Oh," said he at last, "this is only talk. A man's banter never shows his real sintimints. For my part, my life and my thoughts are all taken up with a work in which modern civeeleezeetion, and radicalism, and conservatism, and all the other isms, niver inter. How should they? I'm an anteequarian. I gave up all my time to the most zilous anteequarian rascarches. Most of my life I live at Rome. There I come into immaydeeate contact with the Holy Father, and the whole College of Kyardeenals. If there's any one man they know, that man's Father Magrath. The ixhumeections I've made, and the explorections, and the discoveeries, would take all night to tell. Why, it was only the other day I found at Civita Castellano, in an owld Aytruscan tomb, an antique urrun, and I've got it here now, and that same urrun is worth more thin its weight in solid gold, so it is. There's people that's offerred me more already, and I refused. Me a radical! I'd like to see meself botherin' me head about modern politics. Put me in Florence in the days of Cosmo de Medici, and I'll take my stand with one party or the other but this vulgar nineteenth cintury, with its miserable party squabbles, seems like child's play to me.

"The worst of it is," continued Father Magrath in a pensive tone—"the worst of it

is the lack of a proper spirit at Rome. Why, here I am; and I've been urging for years upon the Roman Government a course of action that might have given them untold wealth. First, I've urged the ixhumeection of the Palatine—the palace of the Cæsars, the *Aurea Domus Neronis*. The trisures that must lie buried there would be enough to give them means for carrying out the boldest designs that Antonelli or anybody else might wish. Secondly, and still more carnestly, I've urged upon them the plan of diverting the Tiber from its bed. It would cost something, it is true; but the cost would be nothing whin compared with the raysult. Why, only think of the trisures that lie buried there—the gold, the silver, the diamonds, the gims, and precious stones; the statues, the carvings, the orniments innumerable. Trisure! Why, in the bed of the Tiber is enough trisure to buy up all Italy! And yet the Papal Government is hard up. And why—?"

Father Magrath paused and looked carnestly for a few moments at Kane Hellmuth.

"Why?" he resumed. "I'll tell you why. It's because they want an Irish pope!"

"An Irish pope!" repeated Kane Hellmuth, as Father Magrath paused.

"Yis," said Father Magrath, solemnly—"an Irish pope! Rome, Italy, Christendom, all need an Irish pope. The Italians cannot govern Rome, or the Church, in the nineteenth cintury. They are a worn-out race. It's not poverty that ails thim. It's indolince, inertia, want of interproise, cowardice, and all that. Give Christendom an Irish pope, and she'd be redeemed. The worruld would wear a diffirint aspict altogither, the day after the iliction of a born Paddy to the chair of Saint Payter should be made known. No country but Ireland, no race but the Irish, could furnish the riquisite qualeefeeceeetions. Ireland has the piety, and the loyalty to the Roman Catholic faith, and at the same time it has the spirit of indipindince, the love of freedom, and above all the ristliss, bounding, invincible, indefatigable inirgy, that makes this age what it is. What is now the layding nation in the wurruld? America. Who have made America what it is? The Irish people. And, therefore, the Irish people, being at once the most pious and the most inirgitic of all the races of man, are the ones from whom, above all, the next Pope of Rome should be ilicted!"

Upon this Father Magrath at length succeeded in lighting his pipe, an attempt in which for some time he had been baffled by his own eloquence, and then, puffing out heavy volumes of smoke, he relapsed for a time into silence.

CHAPTER XVII.

FAMILY MATTERS.

FATHER MAGRATH thus succeeded at last in lighting his pipe, and for a few moments his flow of conversation was checked. He sat holding the pipe with his left hand to his mouth, while his right hand stirred a spoon round the tumbler of toddy. Clouds of smoke rolled up around his head, through which his eyes occasionally peered forth in a furtive way, yet with a quick, keen, penetrating glance at the rugged face and sombre brow of Kane Hellmuth. The latter surveyed the priest calmly, but said nothing. He had come to this interview out of no desire for society, out of no love of conversation, and no taste for that conviviality upon which his companion laid stress. He had come simply because he hoped that he might be able to learn something directly or indirectly about Clara, his late wife; and it seemed to him that one who filled the responsible post of father-confessor to this family would be the very man who, of all others, would be the most likely to give him that information which he needed. He listened, therefore, in silence and with patience to the priest's remarks, thinking that his wandering fancy would soon exhaust itself, and his mind come to business matters.

"I rigrit extramely," said Father Magrath, at length, "that Miss Mordaunt isn't at home. But she couldn't stay here any longer. The raycint sad occurrince, the dith of her vinirible frind, preed daiply upon her mind, and she has been compilled to quit the city. For me own part, I must say that, although I was not altogither surprised at poor Wyverne's dith, I filt it extramely."

"Yes," said Kane Hellmuth, who, now that Father Magrath had got to a topic like this, was anxious to keep him to it and to draw him out, "yes, I suppose so, but it was

very sudden, and I did not know that any one could be expecting it."

Father Magrath sighed and shook his head.

"I was acquainted with the doctor who attended him."

"The doctor that attindid him?" repeated Father Magrath. "That'll be Dr. Burke—no, Black—no, that's not it—it's something like it."

"Dr. Blake."

"Blake—yis, that's the name, so it is. A young man—yis. Miss Mordaunt infarrumed me all about it, and she mintioned him with much rayspict."

"There was some trouble on Mr. Wyverne's mind toward the last," suggested Kane Hellmuth. "The doctor said that Miss Wyverne seemed to feel uneasy. I hope that she has overcome that feeling."

"Miss Wyverne—what?" said Father Magrath. "What's that? Why, ye don't mane that wild fancy of his? Sure and did yer frind the doctor let her go off with such a fool's fancy in her poor little head? D'ye mane his notion about not knowing her? Sure and it's wild he was. Didn't I hear all about it. He didn't ricognize his own choild. It was delirium. He was out of his sinsis. Yer frind the doctor must be very young to take the language of faver and delirium for sober sinse. I'm afraid he hadn't his wits about him; but, most of all, I blame him for not explaining to her, poor girl. Faith, thin, there's no fear that she'll be troubled about that. She's got a black future before her, I'm afraid."

"I sincerely hope that no new affliction has happened to Miss Wyverne."

"Well, it's ginerally considered an affliction," said Father Magrath, "to be lift distichoot."

"Destitute? Why, wasn't her father a very rich man?"

Father Magrath shook his head with solemn and mournful emphasis.

"No," said he, "Miss Wyverne has nothing. Her father had nothing to layve her. He was head over heels in dibt. Under the show of great apparent wilth, he concealed utter poverty."

"You amaze me," said Kane Hellmuth, in a sympathizing tone.

"It was an old dibt," continued Father Magrath, "contracted years ago—he niver was able to do any thing with it. He had to kape up a certain style, and this, of coorse, necissitated a great ixpinditure; consequently he wint from bad to worse. One man was his chief creditor, and he was lenient for a long time, until this last year or so, whin he changed his chune, and demanded a sittlemint or some sort of security. All this preyed greatly upon my poor frind's mind, and, in conniction with the life-long anxieties of his business, resulted in some affiction of the heart, some inflammeetion of the pericarjum. And here now ye see the ind. Here he is—a did man—and here is his daughter literally pinniliss. What's wust, she doesn't know any thing about it yit, and I'm bothered out of me life about it, for it is my milancholy juty to infarrum her of these facts, but how I'm to do it I don't for the life of me know."

Father Magrath was silent for a few moments, and pensively sipped his toddy.

"By-the-way," said he, at length, "this frind of yours, the doctor, do ye know where he is?"

"Oh, yes; he's in Paris."

"In Paris? Well, that's very convaynient. I find that it is nicissary for me to obtain some sort of a formal steetment from his medical man, if possible, rilitiv to the disease of poor Wyverne, and to have it jewly attested before some magistrate. If yer frind is so handy as that, maybe I might write and he'd forward the nicissary documents. Would ye have the kindniss to give me his address? and, perhaps, ye'd better write it out in this mimorandum-book."

With this Father Magrath drew a memorandum-book and a pencil from his pocket. Opening the former, he handed it to Kane Hellmuth. The latter took it, and, on the page indicated by the priest, he wrote down the address of Dr. Blake in full. The priest thanked him, and restored the memorandum-book to his pocket.

"Yis," he continued, in a soliloquizing tone, "it was very sad the whole affair, poor Wyverne's life and his dith. His money-troubles killed him at last. He was always hard up—his wilth all show, and a grasping criditor, and him as poor as a rat, with nothing to leave his daughter, poor girl."

"What'll become of Miss Wyverne?" asked Kane Hellmuth, with some interest.

Father Magrath smiled.

"Oh, for that matter, there's no danger,

after all. It's only the sinse of indipindince that she'll lose. She has frinds that love her far too dearly to see her suffer, and they'll know how to keep her from knowing any thing of want."

"Was Mr. Wyverne any relation to Miss Mordaunt?" asked Kane Hellmuth, who now felt anxious to bring the conversation nearer to the subject of his thought.

"A distant relation. Mr. Wyverne was her guardian."

"She has something, I suppose, to live upon?"

"Oh, yes; she is sufficiently well provided for to make her feel jew contintmint. Her wants are not ixtravagant. She has been brought up with very simple tastes, and, for that matter, if the worst comes to the worst, she could be a governess. It's very different with her from what it is with Miss Wyverne, that's looked on hersilf all her life as an heiress."

"Has Miss Mordaunt any brothers or sisters?"

"No," said the priest; "she's alone in the wurruld. There were others, but they're dead and gone. She's had a sad lot in life—orphaned in her infancy—alone without any rilitives to spake of—but she's got a good, and a gintle, and an angilic disposition of her own."

"Had she no sisters?" asked Kane Hellmuth, in a voice which he tried to make as steady as possible, but in which, in spite of his efforts, there was a perceptible tremor. The priest took a hasty glance at him, and saw that his head was bowed, leaning upon his hand.

"She had," said the priest, after a short hesitation—"she had a sister."

"A sister? I thought so," said Kane Hellmuth. "Was she older or younger?"

"Older—tin years older."

"Do you know her name?"

"Clara."

With every new word the agitation of Kane Hellmuth had increased, so that it would have been perceptible to duller eyes than those keen and scrutinizing ones of Father Magrath, which were fastened so vigilantly and so searchingly upon him.

"Bessie," said the priest, in a mournful tone, "comes from an ill-fated family. I hope she may be an ixception to the mournful distinies that seem to purshoo her rilitives. There was the mother, died in the prime of her life; there was the father, wint mad with sorrow, and took himsilf off to foreign parts, where he wint and died. Thin, there was this elder sister. Whin Mr. Mordaunt died, Mr. Wyverne stipped forward and took the two poor orphans under his own protiction. He didn't take thim into his own house, because it wasn't convaynent, owing to family diffeeculties of his own with his wife; but he put the two orphans in good hands, as I can tistify. He was as good as a father to thim. He took care of their little means, and, for that matter, ye might say he gave it to thim."

"What became of this elder sister?" asked Kane Hellmuth, in a scarcely audible voice.

"It was a very sade fate, the saddest I iver knew," said the priest. "Mr. Wyverne had determined to give her the best education possible, and sint her to a boarding-school in Paris."

"Well?"

"Well, it's almost too sad to talk about. Remimber, she was very young — a mere choild—not over sixteen, and that, too, in a Frinch school, where gyerruls are so secludid. Well, it happened that some prowling advinturer—some unprincipled and ficudish deludherin' riptoile—managed to make her acquaintince. Ye know the ind of that. There is only one ind. That ind was hers. Clara Mordaunt was ruined by the macheeneetions of a scoundril that I hope and trust is ayvin now gittin his jew in this life or the other."

At this, Kane Hellmuth's face turned to a ghastly pallor. It was hard indeed for him to listen to this, and yet say nothing.

"I have heard something about it," said he. "A friend of mine once told me, some years ago, but he said they were married."

"Married!" said the priest, with a sneer. "There were no pains taken to lit the marriage be known, at any rate, and the scandal about her was as bad as if she had not been. No, depind upon it, there was no marriage. She was run away with. It was the old story, and it came to the same ind."

"The end? what was the end?" gasped Hellmuth.

"The villain deserted her, and—"

"He did not!" cried Hellmuth, in a terrible voice, starting up and looking at the priest.

"I only say what I've heard, and what the frinds of the poor gyerrul have heard and have believed," said the priest, mildly. "Perhaps ye know more about it than I do. If ye were livin' in Paris that toime, ye might have found out, and in that case ye can tell me."

Kane Hellmuth made a mighty effort, and regained his self-control.

"Excuse me," said he; "but years ago I saw the man that you speak of. He was my friend. He said that he was married."

The priest shrugged his shoulders incredulously.

"Oh, of course, he said so," he remarked; "that's what they always say. At any rate, there is the fact that she was virtually betrayed, deserted, and died the worst of deaths, brought down to that by a brokin heart. What matter his impty protistations about farrums of matremoncy, I ask ye, in the face of sich a catasthrophe as that?"

To this Kane Hellmuth made no answer. He came to get information, not to argue or to apologize. He knew better than any other what was the actual extent of the guilt of that man of whom the priest spoke so severely; but he had no heart to offer an apology. Was not the deed itself full of horror? had it not crushed his life down into the dust of never-ending self-reproach?

"Did she die?" he asked, in a faint voice, returning to the subject.

"She did, and by the worst of deaths. She died—and—by her own hand."

The priest paused. Kane Hellmuth listened breathlessly. At last the revelation was coming.

"It was found out by their landlord, who told her frinds afterward all about it. According to his story, the two had high words togither that morning. Toward ayvenin' he suspictid something, and knocked at the dure. There was no answer, which made him break open the dure. There he saw a sight that filled him with horror. The poor gyerrul lay did, stone did, on the flure, and the scoundril that had killed her was in some drunken fit on a sofa, or in bed. He was sint off to his frinds — she was buried. He disappeared, and I hope he's did. I wouldn't like to be sittin' near that man. Priest though I am, I fear I should feel a murderous inclination stealing over me. I wouldn't have any confidince in mesilf, at all at all—not me. Ye say ye're his frind. Can ye tell me what became of him ? "

" He's dead," said Kane Hellmuth, in a faint, choking voice.

" Dead ? Thin I hope he killed himsilf. That was the best thing left for him to do after killing that poor gyerrul."

At this Kane Hellmuth bowed down his head, and buried his face in his hands. Was there any thing more now for him to learn? Was not this enough, this confident declaration of Father Magrath ? Did he wish any more ? Could he venture to go into details about such a subject, and ask the particulars of that most terrible of tragedies from a man like this, who uttered words that pierced like daggers ? That were too hard a task. The information which he had already gained seemed sufficient.

" Her frinds," continued the priest, still pursuing the train of thought which had been started, "buried her, and strove to save her name from stain by putting the name of the man on the stone, just as if he had been her husband. And so, if ye iver go to the cimetery of Père-la-Chaise, ye'll see on that stone, not the name of *Clara Mordaunt* but *Clara Ruthven*. Ruthven, ye know, is the name of the villain that killed her."

At this a deep groan burst from Kane Hellmuth.

" Sure, ye don't seem well," said the priest, in a tone which was meant to express sympathy. " Won't ye take some more whiskey ? Try it—neat. Its moighty ifflictive, whin taken that way, for dispilling mintal deprission, and shuperinjewcing a contintmint and placidity of moind."

Kane Hellmuth shook his head.

" Well," said the priest, " I'll power out a thimbleful for mesilf, for the subject is a distrissing one intirely. And so ye say," he continued, " that this man is a frind of yours, or was ? Sure, and I'd like to know, thin, is he alive now ? "

Kane Hellmuth drew a deep breath.

" He's dead," said he again, in a hollow voice.

" Dead ! Oh, yis. So ye said before. Whin did he die ? "

" Ten years ago," said Kane Hellmuth.

" Tin years ago ! Why, that was the same toime ! "

" He died when she died," said Kane Hellmuth, in the same tone.

" Sure, and I nivir heard a word of that afore. And what was it that he died of? Min, like that, don't often die off so aisy. They live long, whin their betters die ; and that's the way of the wurruld. What was it that he died of, thin ? "

" He killed himself," said Kane Hellmuth, in harsh, discordant tones, that seemed wrung out of him.

" Killed himself!" repeated the priest. " Well, it's well he did ; for, if that man were alive now at this moment, it would be enough to make poor Clara rise from her grave."

These last words were too much. Thus far this priest had shown an astonishing capacity for saying things that cut his companion to the very soul, and saying them, too, in a casual, off-hand, unconscious way, as if they were elicited by the subject of their conversation. It had been hard for Kane Hellmuth to endure it thus far, but he could endure it no longer. These last words summed up briefly the whole horror of his present situation, to avert which, or to escape from which, he had made this journey.

He started to his feet. He did not look at the priest.

" I'm much obliged to you," said he, " for the information which you have given."

At this the priest stared at him in astonishment, which, if not real, was certainly well feigned.

" What's this ? " he said, " what's this ? Why, man ! What d'ye mane ? Ye can't be going ! And the ayvenin' not fairly begun."

" I must go now," said Kane Hellmuth, abruptly, in a hoarse voice. " My—my time is limited." He stood swaying backward and forward, his face ghastly, his eyes glazed, and staring wildly at vacancy. He did not see the keen glance of the priest as he earnestly regarded him.

Kane Hellmuth staggered toward the door. The priest followed.

" Sure," said he, " it's sick ye are. And ye won't take another glass ? Perhaps, ye'd like cognac. In the name of wonder, what's come over ye, man ? Take some cognac, or ye'll niver get home. Sure, and I'll niver let ye go this way. Wait, and get some cognac. Faith, and ye must wait, thin."

Saying this, the priest laid his hand on Kane Hellmuth's arm, and drew him back. Kane Hellmuth stood with a dazed look in his eyes, and an expression of anguish on his face. The priest hurried to the sideboard, and, pouring out a tumbler nearly full of cognac, offered it to his companion, who took it eagerly and gulped it down. The fiery draught seemed to bring him back to himself, out of that temporary state of semi-unconsciousness into which he had fallen. His eyes fell upon the priest, and the wild light faded out of them.

"Pardon me, sir," said he, in a perfectly cool and courteous manner, which offered a striking contrast to the tone of his voice but a minute before. "I am subject to spasms of the heart, and I'm afraid I've caused you some alarm. But they do not last long, and your kind and prompt assistance has helped me."

"Won't ye sit down again, thin?" said the priest, earnestly, "and finish the ayvenin'?"

"You're very kind," said Kane Hellmuth, "but, after this attack, I might have another, and, under the circumstances, I think I had better go."

"Won't ye stay and rest, thin, till ye feel stronger?" persisted the priest.

"Thank you," said Kane Hellmuth, "but I require the open air just now. A walk of a mile or so is the best thing for me. I shall, therefore, bid you good-by, with many thanks for your courtesy."

Saying this, he held out his hand. The priest took it and shook it heartily.

"I won't say good-by," said the priest. "We'll meet again, I hope. So I'll say *au revoir*."

"*Au revoir*," said Kane Hellmuth, courteously, falling in with the priest's mood.

They thus shook hands, and Kane Hellmuth departed.

The priest accompanied him to the door. He then returned to the room. He poured out a fresh glass of toddy, lighted a fresh pipe, and then, flinging himself into an arm-chair, sat meditating, smoking, and sipping toddy, far into the night.

CHAPTER XVIII.

MORDAUNT MANOR.

SEVERAL miles away from Keswick, Cumberland, lay some extensive estates, surrounding a first-class country-house, known as Mordaunt Manor. About a fortnight after the departure of Inez for the Continent, a solitary horseman stopped at the gates of Mordaunt Manor, and was admitted by the porter.

A broad avenue lay before him, winding onward amid groves and meadows, lined on each side by majestic trees, among which clouds of rooks were fluttering and screaming. Riding along this avenue for about a mile, he at length came in sight of the manor-house. It was a stately edifice, in a style which spoke of the days of the Restoration and Queen Anne—one of those massive and heavy houses which might have been built by a disciple of Vanbrugh, or Vanbrugh himself—a false classicism employed for domestic purposes, and therefore thoroughly out of place, yet, on the whole, undeniably grand. There were gardens around, which still had that artificial French character that was loved by those who reared this edifice. There was any quantity of box-wood vases, and plants cut to resemble animals, and a complete population of nymphs and Olympian gods.

The horseman dismounted, at length, and, throwing the bridle to one of the servants, ascended the steps and entered the house. He gave his name as Sir Gwyn Ruthven.

Sir Gwyn Ruthven seemed to be an average young man of the period. He was under twenty-five years of age, of medium height, with regular features, brown hair cut short and parted in the middle, side-whiskers not extravagantly long, bright, animated eyes, and genial smile. An eye-glass dangled from his button-hole, and a general air of easy self-possession pervaded him.

Two ladies were in the drawing-room as he entered. One of these was an elderly personage, with a face full of placidity, self-content, and torpid good-nature. The other was a young lady, whose vivid blue eyes, golden hair all flowing in innumerable crimps and frizzles, *retroussé* nose, perpetual smile, and animated expression, could belong to no other person in the world than Bessie Mordaunt.

Bessie had already risen, and greeted the new-comer with the cordial air of an old acquaintance. She then introduced her companion, who seemed to act in the general capacity of *duenna*, guardian, chaperon, guide, philosopher, and friend.

"Let me make you acquainted with my dearest auntie—Mrs. Hicks Lugrin."

"At this Sir Gwyn looked deeply distressed, and tried to change the conversation."—Page 97.

"I could scarcely believe what I heard," said Sir Gwyn. "I had no idea that the Miss Mordaunt of Mordaunt Manor was you; but, from what they told me, I saw it must be. Even then I could hardly believe that I should be so fortunate as to have you for so near a neighbor; and so, you see, I've dropped ceremony, and come at once, without giving you time to rest after the fatigues of your journey. But, 'pon my life, Miss Mordaunt, I couldn't help it; and it's awfully good in you, you know, to see me."

To this Bessie listened with her archest look and merriest smile. It was evident that they were very good friends, and that the pleasure which Sir Gwyn so plainly expressed was not disagreeable to her.

"Sure," said she, "a month ago this day I hadn't the least idea I'd be here now; and I don't know what to make of it at all, at all. But it was so very, very sad about poor, dear Mr. Wyverne! It almost makes me cry. But, then, you know, it's such a comfort to be with my dearest auntie again!"

Sir Gwyn looked at her admiringly.

"You vanished out of London so suddenly, you know," said he, "that I began to think I should never see you again. And Mr. Wyverne—ah!—yes—very sad—to be sure—as you say. I suppose, however, he was no relative—"

Bessie sighed.

"No, not a relative," said she; "but then, you know, he was always so awfully kind to me, and he was my dear old guardy, and, really, I loved him almost like—like—an—an uncle, you know; and it's myself that was fairly heart-broken—when—when I lost him."

Another sigh followed. It was a mournful theme, and Sir Gwyn's face was full of sympathy for this lovely mourner.

"How is Miss Wyverne?" he asked, gently.

Bessie sighed, and shook her pretty little head.

"She feels it very, very deeply," said she, "of course—she is such a very affectionate nature—and it was all so awfully sudden, you know! I was so anxious for her to come here with me—poor darling!—but I couldn't get her to do so. And it's fairly dead with grief she is this day. I told her how I sympathized with her, but it was no use. Oh, yes, Sir Gwyn! it's myself that knows what it is to lose a papa, and a dear mamma, too, by the

6

same token; for I've been through it all, and it's awfully sad. It almost makes me cry."

At this Sir Gwyn looked deeply distressed, and tried to change the conversation.

"I suppose," said he, "Miss Mordaunt, you have not been here for a long time?"

"No," said Bessie, "not since I was a child. It's perfectly strange to me. I don't remember one single thing about it. But I was so very, very young, you know—a child in arms, positively! So, of course, I remember nothing. I was taken away to France, you know."

"To France?" repeated Sir Gwyn, in some surprise.

He knew nothing about the history of Bessie's life, and was quite eager to get her to tell something about a subject which was evidently so deeply interesting to him.

"Yes," said Bessie; "and so, as I was taken away so early, I really know nothing whatever about Mordaunt Manor, though it is my own sweet home. My dearest auntie knows all about it, and many's the time she's took up whole days telling me about my ancestors."

At this, Sir Gwyn regarded Mrs. Hicks Lugrin with a bland and benevolent smile, as though her close connection with Bessie was of itself enough to give her interest in his eyes.

"Perhaps you don't know, then," said he, with a smile, "that I am your nearest neighbor. I should have told you that in London, if I had only known it."

"Oh, auntie told me," said Bessie.

"I hope," said Sir Gwyn, "that Mordaunt Manor won't be any the less pleasant to you on that account."

"Well," said Bessie, with a droll smile, "there's no knowing. You may be after finding me a disagreeable neighbor, and, before we know it, we may be engaged in litigation with each other. And I never knew till yesterday, and I think it's the awfullest, funniest thing!"

"It's a remarkable coincidence," said Mrs. Hicks Lugrin, suddenly, after a period of deep thought, "and one, my dear Bessie, which, I may say, is as pleasant as it is remarkable."

There was some degree of abruptness in this speech, and in the tone of Mrs. Hicks Lugrin there was something that was a little stiff and "school-ma'amish," but Sir Gwyn was too amiable to criticise the tone of a kindly remark, and was too well pleased to think of such a thing. He looked more benignantly than ever at Mrs. Hicks Lugrin, and a thought came to him that she was a very admirable sort of woman.

"Oh, thanks," he laughed, "but really when you come to talk of pleasure about this discovery, I am dumb. Pleasure isn't the word. I assure you Ruthven Towers will know a great deal more of me now than it has thus far. I've been deserting it too much. It's a pity, too; for it is one of the finest places in the country. Perhaps some day I may hope to have the honor of showing it to you and your—your amiable aunt. I'm awfully sorry that I have no one there to do the honors, but you know I'm alone in the world, like yourself, Miss Mordaunt."

Saying this, Sir Gwyn looked at her with very much tenderness of expression and a world of eloquent suggestiveness in his eye.

"How very, very funny—that is, sad!" said Bessie, hastily correcting herself.

"That," remarked Mrs. Hicks Lugrin, with her usual abruptness, "is a circumstance which can easily be remedied."

This remark conveyed a meaning to Sir Gwyn which, though not in very good taste, was nevertheless so very agreeable to him that his face flushed with delight, and he thought more highly of Mrs. Lugrin than ever. But Bessie did not seem to apprehend its implied meaning in the slightest degree.

"Ruthven Towers," she said; "what a perfectly lovely name—so romantic, you know —and I do hope, Sir Gwyn, that it is a dear old romantic ruin. I'm so awfully fond of ruins!"

"No," said Sir Gwyn. "I'm very sorry, but, unfortunately, it's in excellent preservation."

"How very, very sad!" said Bessie. "I do so dote on old ruins!"

At this Sir Gwyn looked pained. For the moment he actually regretted that his grand old home was not a heap of ruins, so that he might have the happiness of gratifying the romantic enthusiasm of this lovely girl.

"Ruins," interrupted Mrs. Hicks Lugrin, "may be very congenial to the artistic taste, but, for a young man that has life before him, there is nothing so wholesome as a whole house over his head."

This remark Sir Gwyn entirely approved of, and acknowledged it by another of his benignant smiles.

The conversation now wandered off to other things. Sir Gwyn and Bessie had much to say about the last London season. He had met her then, and had seen her several times, during which interviews he had gained a friendly footing, and had begun to manifest for her an interest very much deeper than usual, which Bessie could not have been altogether ignorant of. Upon the present occasion he was evidently most eager to avail himself of all the advantages which grew out of this former acquaintance; combined with the additional advantages of his position in the county, and his close neighborhood to her, it gave him occasion to offer her many little services. He knew all about Mordaunt, and could tell her all about it. He could also show her Ruthven Towers. These were the things that first occurred to him as being at once most desirable, most pleasant, and most natural, under the circumstances.

Bessie's chaperon seemed to be pleased with Sir Gwyn's polite attentions, but Bessie herself was very non-committal. She spoke of the necessity of seclusion, and alluded to the death of her guardian as something which she ought to observe in some way commensurate with her own grief. Sir Gwyn, upon this, was too delicate to press the matter, and postponed it until another time.

"English country-life," said Bessie, in the course of these remarks, "is a strange thing to me entirely. I've never seen any thing of it, at all, at all; and really it will be quite a new world to me. She spoke so young when I was taken to France, you know, Sir Gwyn, and all that I know of English country-life is what I have heard from dear auntie—isn't it, auntie, dearest?"

"Your observations are entirely correct," said Mrs. Hicks Lugrin.

"Then let me hope," said Sir Gwyn, politely, "that you will find it as pleasant as London life."

"Oh, I'm sure I found London life perfectly charming," said Bessie, with enthusiasm. "And you know I had just come from France, and you may imagine what a change it was."

"You must have lived there all your life."

"Yes," said Bessie. "It was at St.-Malo. Have you ever been there, Sir Gwyn?"

"No, never."

"Oh, it's such a perfectly charming place," said Bessie, "and it's more like my home than any other place. It's so lovely. And I was taken there when I was—oh, only the littlest mite of a little thing, and lived there till only a year ago, Sir Gwyn, and sure it was myself that had the sore heart when poor, dear, darling guardy came to take me away, so it was."

"I'm sure it must have been," said Sir Gwyn, in tones full of tenderest sympathy.

"I'm sure it was awfully sad to lose my papa and mamma," said Bessie, mournfully, "but to lose my home seemed worse, so it did; and that's why I feel so awfully sorry about my poor, darling Iny. Not but that she has a home—but then it doesn't seem like it at all, at all."

"I suppose not," said Sir Gwyn.

"And it's worse for poor, dear, darling Iny than it is for me," continued Bessie, "for you know she has no one, and I have my other dear guardy, my poor mamma's dear papa, you know, Sir Gwyn. And he's the very nicest person! You can't imagine!"

Sir Gwyn looked as if he were trying to imagine, but was unable.

"You know her, my own dear, darling Iny—do you not, Sir Gwyn?"

"Iny? You mean Miss Wyverne?"

"Yes—Inez her name is—the same name as mine, you know," continued Bessie, gently and sadly.

"The same as yours!" exclaimed Sir Gwyn. "Why, I thought that yours was Elizabeth? I remember Miss Wyverne, of course, and she always called you Bessie."

As Sir Gwyn uttered this name there was an indescribable tenderness in the tone of his voice which did not by any means escape the notice of Miss Bessie, but she gave no sign to that effect. She merely went on, in a calm way:

"Oh, yes; she always insisted on calling me Bessie. She said it was awkward for both of us to be Iny. My name, you know, is Inez Elizabeth—Inez Elizabeth Mordaunt."

"I think Inez is a perfectly beautiful name," said Sir Gwyn, enthusiastically.

"So do I, surely," said Bessie; "it is so entirely. In France they all called me Inez, but dear, darling Iny set the fashion of calling me Bessie; and, after all, it would have been awkward to have two in the house

named Inez, and so it was nothing else but Bessie, Miss Bessie, and so I grew to love that name, because I loved so the dear, darling friends who called me by it. Still, I think Inez is awfully lovely, and it's uncommon and romantic. Dear, darling Iny and I are second cousins, and Inez is a family name, you know, so we both had it."

All this was news to Sir Gwyn, of course, who, as he said, had heard her called "Bessie," and had always thought of her under that name. Still, "Inez" was undeniably a beautiful name, and Miss Mordaunt was no less lovely under this sweet foreign name than she had been under the plainer one of "Bessie." He lamented that he was not at liberty to make use of either one of these names and call her by it. The time for that, however, had hardly come as yet, and he could only indulge in the hope that it might come before very long.

This preference which Bessie expressed for the name "Inez," was also sanctioned and solemnly confirmed by Mrs. Hicks Lugrin, who said, in her characteristic manner:

"My dear, your preference is every way justifiable, and you should insist now on all your friends calling you by the name for which you yourself have so decided a preference."

When Sir Gwyn at length took his departure, it was in a state of mind that may be described as made up of exultation, expectation, anticipation, elevation, and all other "ations" which go to set forth the state of mind which humanity experiences under the stimulus of Love's young dream. Already, in that London season above referred to, he had been smitten with Bessie's charms; and, though her absence had weakened this effect to some extent, yet now the sight of her face more than revived these old feelings. The circumstances under which he now saw her tended to deepen this effect. She was in a quasi state of mourning. She announced that she intended to keep herself secluded, for a time at least, and avoid the gayeties of society. Her "mourning" was thus deep enough to keep her restricted within the very sphere where she would be most accessible to him. Her face now seemed to him more piquant than ever; the perpetual smile which Nature had stamped upon her lips did not readily adapt itself to a sombre expression of grief; and thus Bessie's attempts to look bereaved and afflicted were only successful in so far as they served to call up to her face a new expression, and one, too, of a very attractive kind. The circumstances that had thus brought her here and given him such access to her, could not be regarded by him with any other feelings than those of the deepest satisfaction; and he determined to avail himself to the very utmost of the rare privileges which chance had accorded to him.

And so Sir Gwyn, on the very next day, found a pretext for riding over to Mordaunt Manor. He found Bessie as cordial as ever.

She received him with a smile, that bewitched him, and with a simple, frank friendliness that was most touching. She told him it was "awfully kind" in him to come to see her again when she was so lonely. She remarked that Mordaunt Manor was "awfully stupid," with other things of the same kind. Mrs. Hicks Lugrin also chimed in with similar sentiments. On this visit Sir Gwyn ventured to hint at a drive through the country. Mrs. Hicks Lugrin thought that it would benefit Bessie's health, and that a companion like Sir Gwyn, who knew all the history of the county, would be a benefit to the minds of both of them.

The drive was very successful, and was repeated. In a few days Bessie went out riding with Sir Gwyn, first confining herself to the park, and afterward going into the outer world. Then it began to be interrupted, for the great world was in motion, and everybody who pretended to be anybody was hurrying to Mordaunt Manor to welcome its lovely young mistress to her ancestral home and to her native county.

CHAPTER XIX.

THE LOST ONE FOUND.

FROM what has been related it will be seen that Miss Bessie had experienced a great change in her life, having thus suddenly advanced from the position of certainly not much more than ward to the conspicuous elevation which was given by becoming mistress of Mordaunt Manor. Nor in coming to what she called her ancestral home did she find any lack of any thing which she might have conceived of as necessary to the grandeur of her position. There was the Hall itself, and the broad estate, and every thing corresponded, without and within. Troops of servants stood ready to do the slightest bidding of their young mistress; men-servants and maid-servants, footmen, grooms, coachmen, pages, appeared before her wherever she wandered. Prominent among these were several dignified functionaries—the butler first; then the French chef de cuisine and the housekeeper, Mrs. Spiller. Over all these Miss Bessie reigned as queen; while, as her prime-minister, Mrs. Hicks Lugrin stood at her side to give her counsel, or to carry into execution her wishes. Thus Mordaunt Manor, on once more being open to the great world, appeared fully equipped. During the years in which it had been closed every thing had been managed with the utmost care; and now it seemed about to enter upon a new career, under auspices at least as brilliant as any which it had ever known.

As the eye of the great world thus came to turn itself upon the young mistress of Mordaunt Hall, and to subject her to its scrutinizing gaze and its cold criticism, Bessie bore the ordeal in a manner which could not be surpassed if she had been trained all her life for this very thing. Perfectly calm and self-possessed, she yet showed nothing which was in any way inconsistent with the most sensitive delicacy and maiden modesty; she appeared like the type of innocence and self-poise combined; and around all this was thrown the charm of her rare and radiant beauty. Society, which thus came to criticise, remained to admire; so beautiful, and at the same time so wealthy an heiress had but seldom been seen; and she was evidently one who was adapted to shine in the lofty sphere to which she had been born. Society thus took note of all her charms. Society decided that Miss Bessie had a remarkably tender and affectionate nature. Society noticed the slight touch of Irish brogue in her accent, and thought that it added a zest to her already bewitching manner. Society also noticed the attentions of Sir Gwyn Ruthven, and smiled approvingly. It was without doubt a most excellent and suitable thing; and, if Sir Gwyn Ruthven could win her, the match would be unexceptionable. The two largest estates in the county already adjoined one another; and this would unite them into one magnificent property. Society, in fact, admired this prospect so very greatly that it unanimously declared Sir Gwyn's attentions to be "really quite providential."

The blandishments of the great world and the devoted attentions of Sir Gwyn Ruthven did not make up the whole of Bessie's life, however. One part of it was taken up in a correspondence which, though not large, was yet of immense importance. It was not large, for it consisted of but one letter every other day or so, yet that one letter was so important that most of her time when alone was taken up with the study of it, and with writing her answer. The letter which she sent in reply was always dropped into the mail-bag with her own hand, and it always bore the same address—*Kevin Magrath.*

Several weeks of Bessie's new life passed away, and at length, one day, she received a letter from this one correspondent which conveyed intelligence of such unusual importance to her that she remained most of her time in her room with the letter before her, pondering over its startling intelligence. To Sir Gwyn, who called on her as usual, she did not deny herself, but appeared as animated, as careless, and as joyous as usual; but, after his departure, she once more sought her own apartment, and there sat motionless for hours, with the letter in her hands, plunged into the deepest thought, and with such an expression of anxiety on her brow, and such a deep abstraction in her gaze, that if Sir Gwyn Ruthven could have seen her he would scarce have been able to recognize the face of the smiling, joyous, exuberant, and careless girl, whose image had been stamped so deeply upon his memory, and upon his heart.

After receiving that letter, Bessie sat up late into the night, and it was well advanced toward morning when she wrote a reply. She then retired, slept a few hours, and, after rising and taking a slight breakfast, she went herself, as usual, to mail her letter.

About a week after this, a gentleman drove up to the gates of Mordaunt Park. Dismounting from his carriage, which was evidently a hired one, he paid the driver, who at once returned in the direction of Keswick. Upon this the gentleman went to the porter's lodge and stood talking for a few minutes with the porter.

This new-comer was a man of medium stature, with dark complexion, which had a sun-browned, weather-beaten appearance, like

the face of a sailor; but the refinement of the features, and a certain indescribable something in the expression, showed that he was something very different. His dress showed him to be a clergyman. He had heavy eyebrows, from beneath which glowed piercing black eyes. His jaw was square and massive, and yet, in spite of these signs of strength, vigor, and resolute will, the prevalent expression of his face was one of gentleness; and there were sufficient indications there of a nature which was full of warm human sympathies. His hair was sprinkled with gray, and he seemed somewhere between fifty and sixty years of age. He walked with a slow pace, and in his gait and in his manner there were certain unmistakable signs of feebleness.

This man stood talking with the porter for some time, and at length, having satisfied himself, he turned away and walked up the avenue toward the Hall. He walked slowly, and with feeble steps, as has been said, and used a cane, which he carried to assist his walk. He frequently paused, and looked around; but, whether this was through curiosity or through weariness, did not appear. At length he came within sight of the Hall. Here there was, by the side of the avenue and under the trees, a rustic seat, and upon this the clergyman wearily placed himself.

He had not been there long, when the sounds of galloping horses arose in the distance, coming apparently from somewhere down the avenue. The old man was sitting on the rustic seat, with his eyes fixed upon Mordaunt Manor-house, and did not appear to hear those sounds. Soon, however, they drew nearer; and at length a gentleman and lady came galloping by, on their way to the house. The gentleman was Sir Gwyn Ruthven. The lady was Bessie. They had been riding. Sir Gwyn did not notice the old man, being too much absorbed in his fascinating companion to be at all conscious of any other thing; nor did he see the start which the old man gave, and the eager gaze which he directed toward them. Bessie caught one glimpse of him and of his rapid gaze, but appeared not to see him, for she instantly turned her eyes away, and went speeding past. Thus, to the old man, as he fixed his eyes on her, there appeared this flitting vision of loveliness; the round, rosy, dimpled face, the sunny blue eyes, the beautiful perpetual smile, and the gleaming golden hair of the young heiress, forming an image of beauty that might have excited the admiration of the most world-worn or the most cold-hearted. She rode with admirable grace, her elegant figure seemed formed for horsemanship, and, thus speeding by, she was borne swiftly away toward the house.

The old man still sat, and, after she had dismounted, and had disappeared within, he still kept his eyes fixed upon the door-way through which she had vanished from his gaze. An hour passed, but he did not move. At length, Sir Gwyn reappeared and rode past toward the gate. Upon this, the old man rose and went toward the house.

Upon Bessie's return, she had allowed Sir Gwyn to bask for a time in the sunshine of her presence, together with the shadow of the presence of Mrs. Hicks Lugrin, and had been as gay and as charming as ever. Upon his departure, however, she had flown at once to her room. Here all her abstraction returned; she seated herself by the window, and breathlessly watched the movements of the old man. She had seen him! What would he do?

She saw Sir Gwyn ride past.

She saw the old man then rise and walk toward the house. Then she retreated to the middle of the room and waited.

A servant brought up a card:

"*M. l'Abbé Bernal.*"

Bessie took it in silence, and looked at it carefully.

"Tell him that I shall be down presently," said she, very quietly, "and tell Mrs. Hicks Lugrin that I should be obliged to her if she would come here."

The servant retired.

In a few minutes Mrs. Hicks Lugrin entered.

Bessie handed her the card.

Mrs. Hicks Lugrin read it, and said not a word.

"I have been thinking," said Bessie, "that, on the whole, it would be as well, auntie, if you were not to be present at our interview."

"Oh, most undoubtedly," said Mrs. Hicks Lugrin. "I only thought that perhaps you might require my presence for purposes of corroboration or identification."

"Never a bit," said Bessie; "trust me

for that, auntie. Am I an owl? Sure, it's me that's well able to take care of myself without any help at all at all—and there ye have it. But it's really getting awfully exciting," she added, in a different tone, "and do you know, auntie dear, I really begin to feel a little nervous?"

Mrs. Hicks Lugrin said nothing, and Bessie soon after went down to the drawing-room.

The old man was seated in the middle of the room, with his face turned toward the door. As she entered, she saw his face, figure, and expression, most distinctly. A window which was on his left threw light upon him, and gave the most distinct view possible. She herself also, as she came in, was revealed to him as fully and completely. She came in as light as a dream, with her ethereal beauty, her large, tender, deep-blue eyes, her golden hair, her dimpled cheeks, her sweet smile of innocence; there was on her face a simple expression of courteous inquiry, blended with gracious welcome; and, with this on her face, she looked at him steadily, with the fixed glance of an innocent child, and came toward him.

He rose and bowed; then she sat down, and he resumed his seat, drawing himself nearer to her as he did so. He then looked at her earnestly for some time. He appeared agitated. His hands trembled; there was a certain solemn sadness and melancholy on his face.

"And you are Inez?" he at length said, in a tremulous voice.

At this, there came up in Bessie's face the deep, wondering look which often arose in her eyes. She said, softly:

"Inez Mordaunt."

"Inez Mordaunt?" repeated the old man, "I saw you when you were a child. I—I knew your—your parents. You have changed so much that I should not have recognized you, and you do not look like either of your parents."

"How very funny!" said Bessie; "and did you really see me? and so long ago? Indeed, then, and it's true what you say, that I've changed; for, when I was a child, my hair and eyes were darker. I've got some of my hair now—cut off by poor dear darling mamma—and really do you know it's quite brown? and isn't it funny, when I'm *such* a blonde now?"

" The old man still sat with his eyes fixed upon the door-way."—Page 88.

A melancholy smile came upon the old man's face, and a look of tenderness appeared in his eyes as he listened to Bessie's prattle.

"And you are Inez?" he said once more, slowly, in a tremulous voice, which was full of indescribable pathos.

Bessie said nothing, but smiled sweetly.

Thus far this interview had certainly been an unusual one. The old man's address had been abrupt and odd in the extreme. Evidently he had no desire to be otherwise than courteous; and yet his manner showed a strange lack of the commonest observances of civility. Bessie, on her part, showed herself quite at her ease; altogether frank, unconventional, and communicative. She evinced no surprise whatever at the old man's singular mode of address, but accepted it as a matter of course, and certainly such a reception by her was quite as extraordinary as the behavior of the visitor.

"You don't know me," said the stranger; "you do not recognize the name which I sent up. I wonder if it is possible for you to guess the errand upon which I have come? I wonder how you will bear the news which I have to tell?"

He spoke in a tone of profound sadness, yet infinite sweetness and tenderness, fixing upon Bessie the same gentle and loving look which he had already turned toward her. Bessie looked back at him inquiringly, and now a change came gradually over her own face.

"I don't know, I am sure," she said, in a faltering voice. "You seem to have something dreadful on your mind; and I don't remember ever seeing you in all my life. Oh, what is it? Tell me, and do not—oh, do not!—keep me in suspense. It's something awful; I know it is. It is some sad news!"

As Bessie said this, a sudden expression of terror passed across her face, and she clasped her hands and started back.

"Do you remember your parents?" asked the old man, in the same tone, and regarding her with the same look.

"My parents?" said Bessie. "Oh, no—only a little. My dear, darling mamma died when I was only three years old; and my poor dear papa left me then, and went away somewhere, and died. And I have often wept—oh, how bitterly!—as I thought of those darling ones—lost entirely—that I was

never going to see again at all, at all! And, do you know, really, it's quite awful?"

Bessie sighed, and rubbed her little handkerchief over her bright-blue eyes.

The old man's eyes now seemed to devour her, as they rested upon her in the intensity of their gaze. There was also in them a certain expression of longing, yearning love—something deeper than any thing which had yet appeared, and yet something which was the natural development of that gentleness and tenderness with which he had gazed at her from the first.

It cost him an effort to speak.

"Your parents," he said, in a low voice, "did not both die. Your father did not—"

"No," said Bessie; "poor dear papa, as I was saying, was so upset by the death of poor dear, darling mamma that he left the country, and died abroad, so he did. And, oh! it is so very, very sad!"

The old man's eyes glistened. Was it a tear that trembled there?

"Your father," said he, in tremulous tones, "did not die. He—is—alive."

"Oh, really, now," said Bessie, "you're altogether wrong, you know. Pardon me—but I ought to know, when I've been mourning over him all my life. Sorrow a day has passed that I haven't felt what it is to be an orphan! It's fairly heart-broke with grief I am when I think of it. And then, you know, it was so very, very hard for poor darling papa to go and die so far, so very far away!"

"It was all wrong; it was all a mistake," said the old man, drawing his chair nearer, and looking at her with more longing eyes, and speaking in more tremulous tones. "It was a false report. He was on his way East. He was very ill at Alexandria. It was the plague. But he recovered. He had given up the world, and so he never wrote. But he did not die—"

"Sure, then," interrupted Bessie, "he might have dropped a line to me. Oh, if I could but have heard from him only one word! And me all alone in the wide world —none to love me—none for me to love—an orphan! It was heart-breaking entirely, so it was; and really, now that I think of it, I wonder how I was able to bear up."

Again Bessie rubbed her eyes.

The old man said nothing for some time. He was struggling with profound emotion, and for a few minutes was quite unable to speak.

"Inez!" said he at last, in a voice deep, low, tremulous with unutterable tenderness.

At this Bessie looked up with the same frightened face which she had shown a short time before.

"Inez," said the old man, "it was hard for you to be left so many years alone, as you thought, in the world; but the reasons will all be explained some day. Your father, Inez—your father now mourns over this, and sees that he indulged a selfish grief, and was too forgetful of you in one sense, though he never ceased, even in his deepest grief, to love you passionately—you and that other dear one, your sister. But now, Inez—now it is over. Your father has come back to you. Look, Inez—look at me! I am changed, I know. Look! Do you not see something in my face that you remember?"

At this Bessie rose from her chair, clasped her hands, stared at him, and started back a few paces.

Tears fell from the old man's eyes.

"Inez!" he said, and then was silent.

"O sir! what do you mean by this?" cried Bessie. "Is this real? Do you mean it? In Heaven's name, is this true? You are mocking me. How can I know it? How can I believe it? And so sudden!"

"Inez!" said the old man again; "it is all true. I tell you that I am your father!"

Bessie now stared at him, and her face underwent several very remarkable changes. It was a face so mobile and so expressive that it was wonderful how strongly the feelings that she might wish to show were shown forth there. First, then, came surprise, then fear, then timid hope, then joy. The old man watched all these changes breathlessly, and with tremulous agitation. At last, Bessie seemed to comprehend the truth; and, as this last joyous change came over her eloquent face, she sprung forward, and flung herself into the old man's arms.

And Bernal Mordaunt pressed her to his heart, and kissed her tenderly, and murmured words of love over her fair young head:

"Inez! my own Inez! my daughter! my darling! I have found you at last, and we must never part again!"

————

CHAPTER XX.

AT HOME.

THUS it was, then, that Bernal Mordaunt, after so long an absence, came back to his own home.

The joy of this meeting filled all his heart, and he surrendered himself to it completely. The sadness which years had stamped upon his face was succeeded by the sunshine of happiness; and he could not remove his loving gaze from Bessie's face. She, on her part, conducted herself admirably; and there was no lack of tender caresses, and of all the manifold signs of filial affection with which a loving daughter should receive a father so suddenly and unexpectedly restored. Bessie's whole nature seemed singularly gentle, and tender, and feminine, and soft, and caressing; and so her father, after years of exile and sorrow, found himself at last once more in the possession of those sweet, domestic joys which he had thought were lost forever.

Mrs. Hicks Lugrin was very properly overwhelmed with surprise when she learned what had happened; but Bernal Mordaunt, who had been informed of her office in the household, greeted her with warm yet gentle courtesy, as his daughter's friend and benefactor.

There was a whole world of things to be talked over between these two—Bessie and Mordaunt—and each had something to tell to satisfy the curious inquiries of the other.

"Do you not remember me at all, dearest daughter—not at all?" was a frequent inquiry made by Mordaunt.

"Well, only just a little bit—a little tiny, tiny bit, papa dearest," said Bessie. "You know I was only three years old when you left; and I only remember a dark-haired, handsome man; but now you're not dark-haired at all, at all—that is, at any rate it's as gray as it is dark, now isn't it, papa dearest? And, besides, you would never have known me, for I'm so awfully changed, if you had seen me anywhere else, you know—now would you, papa dearest?"

And Bernal Mordaunt, looking at her lovingly, could only say:

"Well, dear child, I must confess that the Inez I expected to see was different from you."

Bessie gave a gentle sigh. Then she

smiled. Then she stooped forward and kissed his forehead.

"But you love your poor little Inez all the same, if she has grown to be an ugly little blonde—now don't you, papa dearest?"

Mordaunt stroked her head fondly.

"Ah, my child!" said he, "I take you as you are, and thank Heaven for finding you so loving and so dear. Sorrow and hardship, dearest Inez, have made your father a very different man from the one you remember, and the father who comes back to you has not long to live."

"O papa!" murmured Bessie—"O papa! dearest, dearest papa, don't—don't—don't talk so! You really almost make me cry."

Mordaunt looked at her lovingly. Such affection as this, so tender, so devoted, was sweet indeed to him.

Mordaunt's account of his past life was not a very long one. It was the death of his wife that had been the cause of his departure from home, as Bessie already knew. Before that he had lived a life of unalloyed happiness and prosperity; living in splendor at Mordaunt Manor, and holding a leading position in the county. From all this the death of his wife had suddenly dashed him down. He had been passionately attached to her. Her death had been very sudden. In an instant all interest in life was lost, and all the sweetness and light of existence died out utterly, and were buried in her grave.

A resolution was then taken by him, which, under such circumstances, was not by any means so unusual as may be supposed. It was to devote himself to a religious life for the rest of his days. He was a Roman Catholic, and his Church afforded ample opportunities for the gratification of such a wish as this. His devotion to religion was profound and earnest. To him, in his dark and bitter grief, religion alone gave him any consolation; and amid such consolations he sought to bury himself. He flung himself into the arms of the Church. He became a priest. Finally, in order to carry out to the farthest his new desires, he sought to become a missionary to heathen countries. This desire was gratified without any very great difficulty.

At the outset he had taken steps to secure a fitting home for his children; and for this purpose had applied to Mr. Hennigar Wyverne, who was an intimate friend, and was,

also, a connection. This gentleman had consented to do what Mordaunt requested, and was appointed guardian of the Mordaunt children, and trustee of the estate till they should come of age. It was, therefore, with a feeling of perfect peace on his children's account that he had gone to his distant field of labor. While on his way to the East he had been attacked by the plague at Alexandria, and had the narrowest possible escape from death. Recovering, he had resumed his journey, and had spent many years in India. Finally, his health had broken down, and he was compelled to return to Europe.

Now, no sooner had his back been turned upon the scene of his labors and his face set toward Europe, than there arose within him a great longing to see his children, or at least to learn what had become of them. He had given himself up so entirely to the work which he had imposed upon himself, that he had held no communication of any kind with Mr. Wyverne; and so, on returning home, he was in perfect ignorance about their fate. He remained for a few days in Rome, and then travelled to London. He had to visit Milan and Geneva on his way. This took him through a part of Switzerland, and brought him to Villeneuve. There he was, without knowing it, brought face to face with Wyverne himself. Not until he reached Paris had he learned this, and then it was only from the papers and from certain inquiries which he made that he was able to find out the truth. This discovery was a most distressing one. He longed to see Wyverne, but now it was too late. He hurried back to Villeneuve, but the party had left, and the remains of the dead had been sent forward to London. He returned to Paris, and was detained there by ecclesiastical affairs for some time, after which he hurried to London.

On inquiring at Wyverne's house, he found that Miss Wyverne had gone away, and that the house was about to be closed. No one but servants were there, and none of these could give him any information. After laborious inquiries, he was able to find out Wyverne's solicitors, and called on them for information as to his daughters. But the information which they gave was only of the most general character. Their relations toward the late Mr. Wyverne, they told him, were not at all confidential, but only of an ordinary business character; and, consequently, they

knew nothing about his private affairs. Some
years ago they had heard that the elder Miss
Mordaunt had died abroad. The other one
they believed was still alive, though they
knew nothing at all about her.

The mournful intelligence of the death of
one of his children was thus the first definite
information which he had received; and beyond
this it seemed difficult, if not impossible, to
learn any thing. But his desire was now
stimulated, if possible, still more to learn the
whereabouts of his surviving child. He went
back once more to Mr. Wyverne's house to
question the servants. Most of them were
new ones, none had been there more than
three years, and of the affairs of the family
they knew nothing, except what they had
heard as the gossip of their predecessors.
This was to the effect that Mrs. Wyverne had
separated from her husband and was dead;
that Miss Wyverne had lived at a boarding-
school until the last year or so, and had gone
to live with some relatives, they knew not
where. He recalled the name of the old
house-keeper who had once been there. It
was Klein. He asked after her. He was
informed that she had been dismissed for
drunkenness. This was all.

He now sought after this Mrs. Klein.
With the help of the police, he at last found
her residence; but from the woman herself
he could learn absolutely nothing. This
arose partly from the drunken confusion of
her brain, but partly also from some unaccountable suspicion which she seemed to entertain that he was meditating some injury to
Miss Wyverne. She remained obstinate in
her stupid unbelief in him, and from her
disjointed and incoherent answers he could
gather nothing.

After this there remained nothing for him
but to go to Mordaunt Manor. At Keswick
he had learned that Miss Mordaunt had returned home, and was living there now. This
filled him with hope, and he had come onward without delay. The concealment of his
name arose merely from the desire to spare
her the shock that might arise from too sudden a revelation, and also from a desire to see
how far she might remember him.

Such was the substance of Mordaunt's
story, and, of course, where he was in ignorance, Bessie was able to give him all the information that he desired.

She informed him, therefore, that Mr. Wyverne had been the kindest, the most affectionate, and the most thoughtful of guardians;
that he had sent her away after his wife's departure to live with a relative of his, Mrs.
Hicks Lugrin; and that she had lived with
her ever since, with one interruption. A year
ago, Mr. Wyverne had invited her to come
and stay with his daughter for a time; and
she had been travelling with them when he
died. She informed Mordaunt, to his intense
amazement, that she had been at Villeneuve
at the time of Mr. Wyverne's death; and,
therefore, that they must have been in close
proximity without suspecting it. Mr. Wyverne, she said, had suffered for years, and
had been sent to the Continent by his physicians as a last resort. About Mrs. Wyverne
she knew nothing whatever, nor had Miss
Wyverne even mentioned her name.

About Clara Mordaunt Bessie had but little to say. Clara had been very much older
than she was, nearly ten years, and had been
sent to a boarding-school. She had died
there, and her death had taken place about
ten years ago.

Bessie's information, meagre as it was,
gave Mordaunt all that he could learn now,
since Mr. Wyverne, who alone could tell all,
was dead. Her story was interlarded with
characteristic remarks about Mr. Wyverne's
kindness; about her "dear auntie's" affectionate care; about Miss Wyverne's gentle
friendship, and her deep grief over her father's death; and about her own joy at such
an unexpected termination to her own troubles.

"And as for poor, dear, darling Iny, you
know, she has the same name that I have,
papa dearest, and isn't that funny? and she
used to call me Bessie, to prevent confusion,
while I was living at poor, dear Mr. Wyverne's—she was the dearest and best of
girls—and oh, so affectionate. It almost
killed her, papa dear, for her to lose her
dear papa. And wasn't it awfully sad, now?
And she with never a care in the wide world
before! Oh, but it was myself that had the
sore heart for her! It was too hard for her
to bear that same. She wasn't the one that
would stand grief at all at all! And no more
was I, by the same token; but, papa dear, really you know it seemed worse for her, because
I was so very, very young. But she became
quite changed. Her grief was too much for
her, and you wouldn't have known her. For

my part, I should have stayed with her till death, but I saw that she did not wish to have me; in fact, she herself went away to some of her friends, and wouldn't let me go with her, though I wished to so. But, then, I need not be sorry for that, for, by coming here, I've found you all the sooner—haven't I, papa dearest?"

While talking about Villeneuve, Mordaunt informed her of a cross which he had lost, and which he afterward thought had been lost there. On his return he had made inquiries about it, but without effect. No one had seen it. It was a precious relic—one which he had got made in memory of his dear wife, and had worn ever since.

Of this cross Bessie knew nothing whatever.

Mordaunt also mentioned some lockets which he had left with Wyverne.

"They were three—one of my wife; one of Clara; and one of yourself, Inez. I at first took them with me, but I found that they only served as reminders of my incurable grief, and caused a distraction to my thoughts and affections, which, henceforth, I hoped would be centred exclusively on religion. For this cause I made a final sacrifice of my feelings, and concluded to leave them behind me. I sent them to poor Wyverne, but never heard from him about them. Did you ever see them? Did he ever mention them?"

Bessie shook her head.

"Oh, no, papa dear; no, never. For you know, of course, if I had seen them ever, I should remember; and how awfully nice it would be to see myself how I looked as a child—and only three—and much darker than I am now. Only fancy! Oh, but it's a strange thing entirely! But, of course, poor, dear Mr. Wyverne could never have received them, you know, papa dear—now, could he?"

To Mordaunt, this suggestion seemed a probable one, and he thought that Wyverne must have failed to receive those precious lockets, for, if he had, he would certainly have shown them to his dear daughter.

So remarkable an event as the return of Bernal Mordaunt after so long an absence, and after a general belief in his death, could not be long unknown. Society hastened to offer its congratulations, and to welcome the wanderer back to its fold. But the wanderer did not show any very strong desire to be wel-

comed. Society soon became aware of the fact that Bernal Mordaunt was desirous of quiet and seclusion. The sorrows and hardships of years had produced their natural effect upon his constitution, and he felt himself to be, as he told Bessie, a broken man. Aside from this, the profession which he had adopted, and the life that he had lived, had drawn him away altogether from the great world; nor could he any longer bring himself to feel any sympathy with that world, or its tastes, or its ways. What had he, the world-worn man, the missionary priest—what had he in common with a gay, thoughtless, and frivolous crowd; with a society as light and shallow as that which he saw around him? But there were yet a number of his old friends living who heard of his return with joy, and hastened to greet him. These, of course, were different from the common run, and Mordaunt received them with unfeigned pleasure and cordiality. Yet even these visitors could not help seeing that the old Bernal Mordaunt lived no longer. This man was like another person; his sympathies, and tastes, and feelings, had all changed. A few words of conversation about the old days served to exhaust the subject of the past; and then there remained no subject of common interest in the present. So, though Bernal Mordaunt tried to be cordial, and his old friends tried to be enthusiastic, yet the conditions of each had so changed that a feeling of dissatisfaction was the only result.

Bernal Mordaunt thus showed no desire to regain that position in the great world which had once been his; and might now be his if he had chosen to claim it. He had come home as a broken-down man, and he wished to remain home as quietly as possible. The calm of domestic joys, the dear delight of a daughter's fond affection, these were the only things which he now valued. A return to Mordaunt Manor brought back old associations, and revived all those memories which the years had only partially dimmed. Bessie became more beloved, more dear, and more precious to him every day. The old man had only this one object in all the world to love, and upon her he lavished all his affections. For her part, it must be confessed that no daughter could have been more affectionate, more attentive, more watchful of every mood of his, more solicitous of his comfort. She gave herself up to him completely.

There was an incessant vigilance in Bessie's watchful care of Mordaunt which surprised and delighted him, exciting his tenderest gratitude, and leading to most touching expressions of affection on his part. Even Sir Gwyn was now put in a secondary place. Bernal Mordaunt was supreme in Mordaunt Manor. Bessie was his daughter and his slave. Sir Gwyn saw the new idol of Bessie's heart, and had nothing to say or do but join in the common reverence. And this he did honestly and cordially.

The fact is, there never was a better fellow than this same Sir Gwyn Ruthven. He was desperately in love with Bessie by this time, and, though no formal declaration had as yet escaped his lips, still there was an evident understanding between them, and he felt that Bessie was aware of his feelings and desires. Now it happened that Bernal Mordaunt had come home at the very juncture when he wished to have Bessie most to himself, and the most critical time for his own prospects. Still the young fellow scarcely complained, even to himself. The restoration of a father, long mourned as dead, seemed to him to be an event which could be thought of with no other feelings than those of solemn joy; and Bernal Mordaunt had that in his face which excited in the mind of the young man the deepest reverence and even affection. Among those who greeted Bernal Mordaunt none was so cordial, so sincere, and so respectful, as Sir Gwyn.

Bernal Mordaunt scarcely noticed any others in that society which sent its representatives to welcome him; but Sir Gwyn Ruthven could not escape his notice, and, out of Mordaunt's own tender and vigilant parental feeling, he soon detected the love which Sir Gwyn had for Bessie. This discovery made him anxious to know more about the young baronet, and thus he sought him out; and the result was to create in his mind feelings of strong esteem for Sir Gwyn, and of thankfulness that his daughter should have won the regard of so worthy a man. This discovery also produced a change in his own attitude. He began to fear that he had been too selfish, and had been monopolizing too much of his daughter's time and care. He, therefore, tried to remain more by himself, so that he might not interfere in the slightest degree with his beloved daughter's happiness. Yet, strange to say, Bessie would not allow

this. She began to reproach him for growing tired of her already, and so Bernal Mordaunt had to give up his little plan of self-sacrifice, and indulge his paternal fondness for his daughter without any further fear of being de trop. But Sir Gwyn had no reason to complain, for he was always made cordially welcome by Mordaunt; and this species of domestic footing upon which he found himself could not be otherwise than pleasing.

CHAPTER XXI.

BAFFLED FANCIES.

AFTER that interview with Father Magrath, Kane Hellmuth returned to Paris with a graver sense of mystery, and a profounder feeling of gloom. The remarks of the priest had stung him to the very soul; and yet he did not see how they could have been intentional. He did not think it possible that this priest—a man whom he had never seen before, and one who certainly could never have seen him—could have penetrated that deep disguise which years and grief had thrown over him—a disguise far more effectual for concealment than any mere change of attire or arrangement of hair and beard. It seemed evident to him then that the priest's words, sharp and incisive though they were, must have been uttered quite spontaneously, and arose from his indignant sympathy with the injured Clara Mordaunt, without any suspicion that he was speaking to her murderer.

The faint hope, therefore, that had been raised within his mind by Blake's suggestions, had been dissipated by this interview with the priest, and his journey had proved worse than useless. All that he had heard had only served to confirm his worst fears, and to tear open afresh the old wound of his sorrow and remorse. But, in addition to this, there remained the mystery of the apparition, which was now even more inexplicable than ever. Had he been able to think for one moment that his brain, or his optic nerve, or even his digestive organs, might be in a diseased condition, or in a condition even approximating to it, he might then have had an easy explanation. But nothing of this was the case. His bodily frame in every part and every function had never been more sound and vigorous. The apparition, he believed, must have an objective existence, whatever it was. Its mysterious movements, the tremendous effect which it produced upon him in mind and body, the extraordinary expression of its face, and the never-to-be-forgotten look of its eyes as they rested upon him, all conspired to increase his conviction that there was something of the supernatural about it. He now could have no other expectation but that it would repeat its visits. With this expectation, he tried to nerve himself to a resolution to force himself out of that passive state in which he had sunk on former occasions, and to take some action—to accost it—or at least to follow it. In this way, if it were possible, he might be better able to fathom the mystery. But to nerve one's self up to a resolution in the absence of the terror was a far different thing from effecting it in its face and presence; no one knew this fact better than Kane Hellmuth, and he was too conscious of his weakness to make resolutions which could not be carried out. He could only resolve, in a general way, to struggle more strenuously against his weakness, and hope that another meeting would find him less unprepared.

It was in this frame of mind that Kane Hellmuth returned to his lodgings. Blake had not expected him back so soon, and therefore was surprised when his friend called at his own rooms. He had not entertained a visitor in those rooms since that memorable evening when Dr. O'Rourke told him the appalling story of the monk Aloysius. When Kane Hellmuth's knock came, he was thinking over that very circumstance, and wondering what had become of O'Rourke, from whom he had not heard a word since his departure. Various circumstances had intensified his interest in O'Rourke's project, which had at first seemed so wild, but which had been presented to him as so feasible. At the present time, he jumped up hastily and sprung to the door, expecting O'Rourke, and it was with a momentary feeling of disappointment that he saw Kane Hellmuth. But this visitor was also welcome, for he had been to London; he had perhaps seen Inez, and he could tell him how she was bearing the bereavement with which she had been afflicted.

So, no sooner had he recognized his friend, than he poured forth a current of questions. Had he actually been to London? Why had he come back so soon? Had he found out any thing? Had he seen Miss Wyverne? Had he heard any thing about her? Had he asked any thing about her? To all these questions Hellmuth listened in gloomy silence. At length, he seated himself, and then leisurely told the general outlines of his story. To this Blake listened with an impatience which he tried in vain to repress; and at length, as Hellmuth ended without having made any mention of the only subject about which he cared to hear, he once more reiterated his questions. To these, of course, Hellmuth could give no satisfactory answers. He had not seen her, and she had only been spoken of in a casual way by Father Magrath. He had mentioned her name merely in connection with her recent bereavement. He told what the priest had said about the condition of Mr. Wyverne's affairs, and Blake was astonished and shocked to learn that the lady whom he had regarded as a great heiress was really no better than a penniless dependant. Of course, no idea ever entered his mind about the credibility of the priest's statements. The testimony of one who occupied so important and so confidential a position in the family as this man evidently did, was of itself final, and left no room for doubt in the mind of either.

Another deep impression was produced upon Blake by Father Magrath's treatment of Mr. Wyverne's dying declaration. He had half believed in their actual truth, and had led Inez to feel the same, though that truth seemed to him most bewildering and most incredible. Now, however, all such ideas would have to be dismissed. Father Magrath must know perfectly well the truth about the past life of his friend, and his summary rejection of Mr. Wyverne's declaration as utter nonsense, together with his very clear and natural explanation of the facts of the case, left no room for further discussion on that subject. After all, from almost any point of view, it was far easier to consider his words, as Father Magrath expressed it, the ravings of delirium, than as the sober utterance of reason. If any perplexity now remained on Blake's mind with regard to this subject, it arose wholly out of his mother's mysterious language with reference to that man with whom he had become acquainted in so singular a manner, and Mr. Wyverne's own very remarkable regard for himself. Still, perplexing as these things might be, he was now forced to conclude that they must be accounted for in any other way rather than that in which he had lately been interpreting them.

Both of these men, then, had been indulging in fancies, which now seemed to them not only untenable but nonsensical.

These may be enumerated:

First. Kane Hellmuth had indulged in a vague hope that the wife who had died ten years ago might not have died at that time, as he supposed.

Secondly. That the mysterious apparition which so strongly resembled her might be accounted for on the ground that it was really herself.

Thirdly. Blake had fancied that Mr. Wyverne, when in the evident delirium of mortal illness, had been speaking the language of calm and sober reason.

Fourthly. He had, therefore, been led to believe in these delirious words, and to suppose that Inez Wyverne was not the daughter of Hennigar Wyverne.

Fifthly. For the same reason he had brought himself almost to the belief that he—Basil Blake, M. D.—was the son of this Hennigar Wyverne.

Now, all these fancies, and all other fancies connected with these more or less directly, were at once scattered to the winds; and Basil Blake could only congratulate himself that his unselfish consideration for Inez had prevented him from entering upon so absurd a search as this would have been. It was gratifying in other ways, too. He saw now that one trouble, which had so distressed Inez, would be dissipated; and he saw also that the false position, in which his own tenderly beloved and honored mother had been placed by Hennigar Wyverne's declaration, had no existence whatever.

All this time, as will be seen, both Kane Hellmuth and Blake remained in ignorance of one important fact. Neither of them had the slightest idea that Inez had left her home. If Father Magrath had known this, he had at least chosen to say nothing whatever about it. According to his statement, Bernal Mordaunt was the father of Bessie; and, therefore, the belief which had caused the flight of Inez had apparently no place in his mind. The story which he had told Kane Hellmuth accorded in all points with the account which Bessie had given of herself to Inez, though not altogether with the story which she had told Sir Gwyn, or the reminiscences of the past which she had narrated to Bernal Mordaunt himself. Inez, however, had indulged her own beliefs, and had acted upon her own impulses; and now, as has been seen, at the very time when Blake and Kane Hellmuth were holding this conversation, she was far away from her own home. While, therefore, Blake was eagerly questioning Kane Hellmuth about her, he had no idea that she had left her home, and that, too, with Paris for her destination—that she might, even now, be not very far from him. But such a thing could not possibly be suspected under any circumstances, and the dismissal of his fancies made it inconceivable to him that she should be anywhere else than at home.

Among all the facts which Blake gathered from Kane Hellmuth's account of his visit, the one that produced, perhaps, after all, the most profound effect upon him, was the startling and unexpected announcement of her poverty.

At first this shocked him, but afterward other feelings arose within him. She was no longer a great heiress! Her father's wealth, it seemed, was all fictitious. The great heiress was an utterly destitute and penniless dependant. She would have, henceforth, to trust for her very daily bread to the bounty or the pity of her friends.

A tumult of emotion arose within Blake's heart; and, after the first natural feeling of pity or regret, there came a sense of gratification and triumph. Such feelings were quite natural. For, hitherto, the great wealth of Miss Wyverne had seemed almost appalling to one in his situation, with his feelings toward her, and hopes. Her wealth elevated her far above him, so far, indeed, that he almost despaired of ever reaching so high. He could only hope to attain to an equality with her by some sudden stroke of Fortune. He shrunk from the position of even an apparent fortune-hunter; and his high sense of honor and manly pride recoiled from the apprehension of the world's comments upon him, even if it should be possible for him to win so great an heiress. It was this great difference in their positions that had held him back even when Mr. Wyverne had so strongly favored his advances, and had over and over again prevented him from saying to her that which he longed to say, and which she herself sometimes seemed not unwilling to hear. Now, however, the difference was destroyed. He found himself on a level with her, not by his own elevation, but through her depression. Had he been merely a friend, he would have felt sorrow, but, being an ardent lover, he rejoiced. It gave him hope. As soon as the first sharpness of her recent bereavement should be mitigated, he might go to her and tell her all. It only remained for him to make himself able to give her a home in order to ask her to be his.

This now became his one idea—to win Inez.

But, in order to win her, it would be necessary for him greatly to improve his present position. Just now, he was doing no more than enabled him to support himself and assist his mother. Under present circumstances, he could not gain her. The one thing that he wanted was a rise in life. He wanted it immediately. He was burning with impatience, if not to win Inez at once, at least to see his way toward gaining such a prize.

Kane Hellmuth left, and Basil Blake was alone. Now, there came back the thought which he had entertained when Kane Hellmuth's knock had startled him. He recalled the memorable interview with Dr. O'Rourke—the story of Aloysius. One thought arose, and stood forth prominently in his mind, rising up to grander proportions, till all his excited soul was filled with one vision—a vision of splendor unutterable—of wealth illimitable—the vision which O'Rourke's vehement words had once before imparted to his imagination, and which now once more arose and would not be driven away—the treasure of the Cæsars.

At another time, and under other circumstances, Blake might have reasoned away his gathering faith in O'Rourke's theory; but now his love for Inez, his impatience to win her, his own poverty, her dependence, his intense desire for some immediate action, all forced his thoughts to dwell upon this, and caused him to give to it that faith which his will rather than his reason dictated. Some treasure might be there, at any rate. Whether it had been buried there in ancient or in mediæval times mattered not. As long as any treasure might be there, whether of the Cæsars or the popes, the Hohenstaufens or the Roman barons, it was worth a search.

Failure could do no harm; it could involve no loss; while success would give him all that his wildest fancies could portray. In spite of himself, therefore, his thoughts constantly reverted more and more every day to this dazzling, this transcendent, this unparalleled project; and, while he struggled to repress too great eagerness of hope, the remembrance came to his mind of all those vehement arguments with which O'Rourke had once before reasoned down his incredulity, and enforced at least a temporary acquiescence in the credibility of his theory. He recalled also the minuteness of details which had characterized the story of Aloysius, and the stress which O'Rourke had laid upon this; he recalled what he knew of the character of O'Rourke himself, a man who, as far as he could judge, seemed too hard and practical, too much possessed of common-sense, to become a prey to visionary projects; and, to Blake's mind, O'Rourke's own character appeared one of the strongest arguments in favor of the bulk of his theory.

During Blake's stay at St. Malo, the events of his life had been so interesting that O'Rourke's plan had become, if not forgotten, at least obscured by other things. In the presence of Inez, even the treasure of the Cæsars became a matter of small importance. The days passed, and, as every day Inez Wyverne occupied a larger space in his thoughts, so O'Rourke and his projects became less and less prominent. At length the tragedy of Villeneuve occurred, and Inez suddenly became alienated. Between him and her a gulf seemed to have opened, arising from that mysterious declaration of the delirious father, which seemed to place them both in so false a position toward one another. This last occurrence had furnished Blake's mind with new thoughts, and the alienation of Inez had given him new anxieties. Thus they had separated; and, while the coldness of Inez had prevented her from exhibiting the warmth of common friendship, his own delicacy and his respect for her grief had prevented him from showing in any way the deeper feelings of his own heart.

But now, under these new circumstances, every feeling that could influence him combined to direct his thoughts once more to the forgotten plan of O'Rourke. Day succeeded to day, and the more he thought of it the more did his thoughts cling to it. Week succeeded to week, and these thoughts came to be upper-most in his mind. It came at last to this: that it was simply impossible for him to take any interest in any other thing so long as this should be undecided. So brilliant a plan for securing at one stroke the fortunes of his life was not to be easily set aside or lightly dis-regarded; more than this, it forced itself more and more upon his attention, and finally engrossed all his thoughts.

So aggressive were these thoughts, and so absorbing, that all other things at length lost their interest; and, so long as this was held in suspense, he was unfit for any thing else. Kane Hellmuth could not help seeing that Blake was preoccupied, and profoundly inter-ested in some purpose; but what it was he forbore to inquire. Blake never alluded to the subject, even in the remotest way. He remembered O'Rourke's warning, and was re-solved that no carelessness or rash confidence of his should endanger the success of this great enterprise.

Meanwhile, the days passed on, and the weeks also, and O'Rourke gave no sign. As the time passed, Blake waited, expecting every day to hear from him or see him. Between his interview with O'Rourke and his return to Paris, eight weeks had elapsed; several weeks more had passed away since, and still there was no sign. The three months would soon be up.

What then?

The longer his suspense lasted the greater his impatience grew, and at length that im-patience became intolerable. It caused in-numerable speculations as to the result of O'Rourke's attempts thus far. Sometimes he feared that O'Rourke had changed his mind about taking an assistant, and had resolved to do all the work himself. At other times he feared that some disaster might have oc-curred, and that the bold explorer into those subterranean realms had paid for his temerity with his life. Again his fears took a new shape, and led him to suppose that the ex-periment had been tried, the search had been made, and had resulted in such a total failure that O'Rourke had retired in shame and disappointment too deep to al-low him even to give notice of his failure to his proposed confederate. This fact of Blake's anxiety, and of his numerous specu-lations about the causes of O'Rourke's silence, shows better than any thing else how com-pletely this treasure-hunting scheme had taken possession of his soul.

CHAPTER XXII.

THE RETURN OF ANOTHER MESSENGER.

At length one day a telegraphic dispatch was brought to Blake. He opened it, with a vague thought that it might be some ill news from his mother, from whom he had heard nothing for some time. It was not from England. It was from Rome. It was from O'Rourke. Blake's heart beat high with hope as he read it, though in those few words there was but little of a definite char-acter. The dispatch was as follows:

"*Have made good beginning. Be Paris two days. Be ready.*"

The three months were almost up when this came. Blake's fever of excitement had reached its height. His suspense was be-coming intolerable. In the midst of such feelings this message came, and served to stimulate his hope to the utmost. In that meagre dispatch there was no mention made of the particulars of the Roman expedition, but O'Rourke spoke of a "good beginning," and told him to be ready. He could not wish for any thing better. It was all that O'Rourke had proposed to do by himself. Any thing more he had already decided to defer, even to attempt, until he should have a companion and an assistant. Best of all, O'Rourke would be here in two days, and he would know all.

The two days passed slowly. Blake saw Kane Hellmuth once. The two friends had but little to say. Hellmuth was preoccupied. Something unusual had occurred, but Blake had too much on his own mind to notice it. Had not Blake himself been so taken up with that dazzling plan which now filled all his thoughts, and lured him on constantly with a resistless fascination, he could not have failed to notice the troubled aspect of his friend's face. Some new thing had evidently hap-pened, but what it was Blake did not ask, nor did Kane Hellmuth tell.

That same evening Blake was alone in his room. He expected O'Rourke on the arrival of the Marseilles train; and, if he did come by that, he could not hope to see him much before midnight. Time passed. At last mid-night came. About half an hour afterward

Blake heard steps ascending the stairway. In uncontrollable excitement he sprang to the door and looked out. He met O'Rourke face to face.

"Well, me boy," said the latter, wringing Blake's hand heartily, "here I am again. I haven't disappointed ye, have I? Oh, by the powers! but isn't it the hard time I've had! Sure it's meself that's been going to give up intirely, over and over agin. Still for all, mind ye, it wasn't the trisure, or the catacombs, at all, at all. The difficulties arose merely in the attimpt to get a futhold, and juring the failure that was consequint from the obchooseniss of the people. But I'll tell ye all. Have ye iver a drop of whiskey, thin?"

Blake hurried to his closet and brought forth a bottle, which he placed by the side of a decanter of wine, that already stood upon the table, and then produced a glass.

"I have cognac," said he, "but I'm sorry to say I have no whiskey."

O'Rourke gave a sigh.

"Well, well," said he, "it's no bad substichoot," and, with these words, he poured out some cognac. Then he flung himself into an easy-chair, and, holding the glass in his hand, sat leaning back for a few minutes sipping the cognac. At length he put down the glass, and then drew a long breath of satisfaction.

"Well, Blake, me boy," said he, "I'll tell ye all about it from beginning to ind; all the whirrul and chumult of ivints that have happened juring my absince, and ye'll discerrun for yerself the difficulties I've had to contind with.

"In the first place, ye'll be surprised to hear that all this time thus far has been conshumed, not in any subterranean labor, but simply in the attimpt to get a house. Ye see, it isn't ivery house that'd do. There were only a certain number in the immajiate vicinity of the monastery of San Antonio. It would have been quite useless to git a house any distance away. Now, ye know, the monastery is on the Via dei Conti, and the passage of Aloysius takes its beginning from the west wall—in the very middle of that wall, according to the description of me own cousin Malachi, monk that was, and is now in glory. This passage, as I have all along infarrumed you, runs in a direction which must lead to the Roman Forum—now the Campo

Vacchino—and the Palatine Hill. Of coorse, any house I'd be after rinting must be situated in sufficient proximity to the monastery to allow of the possebelty of enginecring a way to the passage of Aloysius; or, if I could get a house on the ground, in the rear of the monastery, it would do as well, for thin the passage could be tackled more directly. Well, this, of coorse, was the thing I tried to do, but it was the very thing I couldn't do. I could git upper rooms plinty enough, but the lower flure was the thing I couldn't git. Thin, there was sich indiffierince, sich a lack of interprise, sich churrulishniss and shupineness, that over and over I filt inclined to throw up the kyards and returrun home in dispair.

"Howandiver, sich a prize as the one I had before me was not one that was to be given up, merely because there happined to be a few obstacles at the outsit, ispicially when these obstacles arose from nothing more than the obchuseness and shupineness of min, and other things which could easily be continded with. So I kipt on; and, though week after week passed away without any thing being done, yet I persevered, and finally mit with an opporchunity, which I at once seized a holt of. This opporchunity was a large house, which was one of the foulest, and vilest, and most dilapidated in the city. For this cause I had niver so much as given it a thought; for, ye see, my idea was to hire the lower story of some house, which might pass for a shuitable risidence for a man in moderate circumstances, who was indivoring to live economically. Now, the momint that I saw this old rack of a house, the thought came to me that this would be the place. I need not take it as a lodger, but I might rint the intire structure. It was a large, quadrangular idifice, and was crammed and crowded with the lowest class of the population. I wint to the ouner, and riprisinted that I wanted to instichoot a manufactory there of a new kind of maccaroni, and offerred to rint the whole building. There was no difficulty about that. I offerred him a good price, and he accepted it; but the real difficulty was with the tinints, who were unwilling to go. Howandiver, they were all poor, and tinints by the week, and a few baiocchi apiece sufficed to make thim, one and all, leave very contintedly. So at last the big house came impty into my hands, but the delay in gitting the tinints all moved out was so great, that it was not till a week ago

7

that I was able to inter in and take forramel possission.

"Well, sir, there niver was a luckier chance in the wide wurruld than the one that put me in possission of that particular house. It was four stories high. It was at least five cinturies old, and maybe tin. The walls were solid and massive; the windows small and iron-grated; on the lower stories the windows worn't open to the street at all, but looked out on the court-yard. Only the upper stories had windows on the street, and these were barred and grated, as I said. It was quadrangular in shape; and the dure was of massive oak, studded with iron spikes. I had a bit of a hinge put on one the first day, and that's about the ixtint of the repairs which I've put on it thus far. Ye see, whin I open my maccaroni manufacture, the repairs can be inlarged. 'Deed, thin, but repairs are needed; the roof is open in half a dozen places, and the plaster everywhere is tumbling from the walls. But the massiveness of the house is wonderful. It was undoubtedly built in the old days of faction and street-fighting; perhaps in the days of Boniface VIII., or maybe in those of old Hildebrand, or maybe as far back as the times of Theodora and Marozia. Ye may depind upon it, I was the happy man that day as I saw this.

"Thin, apart from this, the situation was the very one that was best shuited to my purposes. In the seclusion of this obscure street, one's operations need not be inquired into, nor need they be so carefully gyarded as they would have to be ilsewhere. Thin, it lies in the rear of the Monastery of San Antonio. Take a point in the middle of the west wall of the monastery as one point, and thin take the Arch of Titus as another, and between these two points draw a straight line. Well, the north wall of this old house won't be more'n a few feet distant from that line. What d'ye think of that, now? Wasn't that luck? Wasn't that worth waiting for?

"Well, of course, my only idea was to examine without delay the lower portions of the house. So, first of all, I had the bit of a hinge put on, and thin had the bolts fixed so that I could shut the dures and bar thim. Whin I did that, I could defy the wurruld. Before I did so, I had a bit of a pick brought in, and that was all, barrin' lights, and a bit of food and drink. Ye may depind upon it,

when I shut mesilf inside, thin I felt safe. It was a fortress. No one could spy me, no one could assail me. The walls, of schupindous thickness, enclosed me; and, if the old roof was a bit dilapidated, sorra a bit of difference did that make.

"Well, now, you must know this, and it's a great thing in our favor. The Monastery of San Antonio is on ground that is a little higher than that on which the old house stands; about six or eight feet, no more. That was another thing I deticted at a glance, and, of course, congratulated mesilf about it. For why? Why, ye see, the cellars of the house would then be thereabouts on somewhere the same gineral livil with the livil of the lowermost vaults of San Antonio. Of course, my first visit was made to the cellars. They were very spacious, and ran all underneath the house. I merely wished to see their ixtint, and also to test the rock, to try how hard it was, whether it would yield easily to the pick, or whether I would have to make use of gunpowder. If it was the same rock as that in which the Catacombs are ixcavated, of course I knew I should have no difficulty; but, unfortunately, I couldn't be sure of that; for there's another stratum of rock that lies under Rome, of a very different character. This is travertine, a stone of wonderful nature, as porous as a sponge, looking like the petrifactions of innumerable little twigs, yet as hard as flint; and, with stone like that, I knew I couldn't do any thing. I also wished to pound upon the walls of the cellar to find out if there might be ixcavations or hollows beyond, on the south side; for, if there was any such, it would show me that the Catacombs were near.

"Well, ye may be sure I wint to the south wall first and forrumost. I wasn't going to waste any time on other places. Well, the south wall was all built up of stones of different sizes. This surprised me a little at first, for I had a vague idea that I'd find solid rock, but such an idea was shuperlatively absurrud, for what could they do without a regular, firrumly-built foundation? Well, I pounded along this wall all the whole length without obtaining any satisfactory results, for there was the same sound all along, and, if there was any hollow behind, it didn't show itself that way. My chief hope was that I might break away the wall and git to the soft Catacomb rock; my dread was that I should

" ' I rushed forward, and held my light far in.' "—Page 93.

find the hard travertine, or the soft sand. Under Rome there are these three strata: the hard travertine, such as is used for building purposes; the soft sand, out of which the Roman cemint is made; and the soft sandstone, where the excavations were made for the Catacombs. It is only where this last occurs that the Catacombs exist, and so all my hopes depindid upon the kind of ground that I might incounter behind the wall.

"I wint to work vigorously. The stones begán to give way after a few blows of the pick. I got out the small ones first, and thin wint to work at a good-sized bit of a rock, and, afther about two hours' hard work, I fetched it out on the flure.

"Well, there was plasther behind that again, and other stones, so I had to enlarge the breach to an ixtint comminsurate with what now appeared the evidint thickness of the wall. It was the foundation-wall, ye'll understand, of an idifice, built in the middle ages, whin ivory house had to be a man's castle, and this was as strong as a castle. I worked all night long, and still the more rocks I pulled out the more there were behind. By morrunin' I had a hole six feet wide and six feet deep, and still there were no signs of any ind. Well, I had to leave off and seek some repose. I slipt, risted, and refrished mesilf all that day, and on the following night returned to my work. I had worked out another big stone that lay at the ind of my ixcavation. It rolled down the slanting line of the rubbish that lay in the hole, and it was a wonder it didn't take me with it. As it left its place, I discerruned something dark. I rushed forward, and held my light far in. It was an opening. I thrust my arrum forward. I could feel that I had reached the outside of the foundation-wall, and that beyond this there was imptiniss.

"Tare and ages, Blake! but I was the wonderful man at that momint. I fell to trimbling all over. Me hand shuk to that ixtint that I had to leave down the light on the flure, and stand still, panting and suffocating, with me eyes fixed on that same. Me head seemed as impty as that imptiness beyond, and inside of me skull me brain wint round in a wild whurrul, and I was for a few momints rejuced to a state of prostration so ixtreme that I couldn't rezhume me work for iver so long. Howandiver, I picked up me scattered sinses at last, and me lamp too, and

thin, returruning to the hole I'd made, I tried to enlarge it. It was rather dangerous work just thin—and, indeed, it had been so for some time past—but I was too ixcited to think much about it, and so I succeeded, after a half-hour's desperate work, in making a hole large enough for me to put me head and shoulders through. By that time I had got over me ixcitemint altogether, and I wasn't going to let mesilf be thrown off me gyard agin. So I tuk me bit of a light and stuck it through, and thin pushed me head and shoulders in after it. Well, my first feeling was one of deep disappointmint, but this was instantly succeeded by one of wonder. The imptiness that lay there was only of a small ixtint. It was a hollow cavity, that was all; horizontal; about six feet long, and three feet wide, and two feet high. Beyond this, on the other side, was the rock, which here was white and smooth. I say I first felt disappointmint, but, after about seventeen seconds, as I said, I was filled with wonder. There could be no doubt that it was a grave, and, as I believed firrumly, a Catacomb grave. But how had it come here? I accounted for it at once in the easiest way possible. The builders of this house, in digging for a cellar, had come to this grave, and perhaps even to one of the passage-ways with many other graves. They, no doubt, considered them as the graves of the old pagans, and scattered their ashes to the winds; or, if any one of them could read—or, if they sint for a priest to decipher the tablets, they, no doubt, saw that they were Christian dead, and had thim all riverintially removed to another place, after which they continued their work of building. That was the way I accounted for it in my own mind during the few minutes that I lay there with me head and shoulders poked through, looking at this impty sipulchre.

"Well, as I lay there, staring all around, me attintion was suddenly arrested by the great difference that there was between the stone that faced me, forming the back of the sepulchre, and the rock in which the tomb was cut; for the rock was brown sandstone, quite rough, too, with the marks of the chisel plainly discernible; while the stone at the rear was white and smooth, with no chisel-marks in particular. A closer look showed me that it was marble, and that it was joined on from another side which lay outside of this where I was. In a momint I comprehindid the facts of the case. The ixcavations had been cut in the rear of the grave; that slab showed the front of it. If so, there must be a passage-way on the other side. The momint that this thought came to me, I scrambled back, seized the pick, returruned once more to the hole, and thin dealt a dozen punches with all me force at the marble. I was right. The marble yielded; a few more blows forced it farther away; and, finally, with a dull thud and a low crash, fell in. In another minit I was in after it, with me lamp in me hand, looking around me with wild eyes. And oh, but wasn't that the momint of all momints! Holy saints and angels! but wasn't I the frantic and delirious man! It was a passage-way; with all the marks, and signs, and appurtenances, which characterize the passages of the Catacombs; with the slabs, and the inscriptions, and the tiers of tombs, and the black darkness in the distance, into which the faint lamp-light only struggled a few feet or so, and thin died out. And, oh, but I was fairly overwhellumed once more, so that I just sat down there and biut me head down, and cried like a child!"

O'Rourke hastily poured out another glass of cognac, which he gulped down, and then went on:

"Well, there I was, in the Catacombs, in the very part of the Catacombs I wished to be, that is, the Palatine Catacombs, and in the rear, that is toward the west of the Monastery of San Antonio. Still, the question remained—what the passage was. No doubt, as I had all along considered, there were numerous passage-ways here, just like the one which I wished to find. I could not be satisfied till I had learned something more about this. So I tuk me lamp, and I started to walk along on me left, for I knew that the Monastery of San Antonio lay in that quarter. Well, as I wint along, I saw nothing but the slabs that covered the tombs and bore the usual inscriptions. They were familiar enough to me, for I'd seen the likes of thim over and over in the Lapidarian Gallery, or the Vatican Museum. So I strolled along without paying any special attintion to any of thim. I was surprised to find that there were no transverse passages, and thought this was a good sign. At length, I began to wonder at the distance I had gone, and to fear that, after all, this was the wrong passage-way, wbin suddenly I found mesilf brought up full

in front of a wall. The ind was walled up. I could go no farther. There was no doubt about it. This was the Monastery of San Antonio; this was, injubitably, the intrance into the vault—walled up—and this was most certainly the *Passage of Aloysius.*

CHAPTER XXIII.

BLAKE TAKES LEAVE OF HIS FRIENDS.

DURING this account of himself, O'Rourke had watched Blake very intently, to see the effect produced upon him. If he had wished to create an excitement in Blake's mind, he certainly had every reason to feel gratified. Already, even before he had come, Blake's tumult of hopes and fears had been excessive; and now, during this singular narrative, his emotion reached its climax; so great was it, in fact, that it seemed to deprive him of the power of speech; and he had sat there spellbound and mute. Not one word did he say all this time; but, by his rigid attitude, his clasped hands, his heightened color, his glistening eyes, he plainly showed how intense was the excitement within him. Yet the story of O'Rourke had been so narrated that he had all along been kept in suspense, and therefore his attention had been quickened, and his excitement increased, all through, until finally it reached its climax at the end, when O'Rourke came to the convincing proof, and the plain declaration, that he had discovered and traversed the passage of Aloysius.

"By Heaven!" he burst forth; "I swear, O'Rourke, all this seems almost incredible."

O'Rourke smiled.

"I've got something," said he, "that'll settle the doubts of any man. Look here."

And he slowly produced from his pocket a rosary. It was old, and stained, and discolored. It seemed as though it had been exposed to damp for a long time.

"What's that?" asked Blake.

"Well, that's more than I can say, for certain; but I'll tell you how I got it. I've told ye how I got to the ind of the passage—by the Monastery of San Antonio. Well, I stayed there a few moments, and thin returruned to the place of interrance. Arriving there, I did not feel inclined to leave just yit, so I tuk to wanderin' along, thinking that I might go at least as far as some transverse passage, especially as this had been mintioned in the manuscript. So I walked on, and, at length, after I had gone about as far from the interrance as it was from that spot to the monastery, I found another passage crossing, and, looking forward, I could see where the passage of Aloysius still ran on, losing itself in the darkness. Well, I wasn't prepared for an ixploration, so I felt satisfied, and returruned in a leisurely way. This fust transverse passage corroborated, as you see, the manuscript story, together with the story of me cousin Malachi, in ivery particular. And now, as I walked back, I noticed the slabs with the inscriptions. I stopped to look at a few. I noticed the mixture of letters which Aloysius mintioned; that is to say, Greek characters were mingled with Latin, and Greek names and words were spelled with Latin letters. It was this that confused Aloysius, no doubt, who couldn't have known a word of Greek, nor even the Greek alphabet. Most of these slabs were dingy and grimy, and the letters were not very deep cut or well formed. At length I noticed one that was less dingy. It was the second from the floor, in a tier of four, and the letters were deep cut and well made. I stopped, and held up my lamp to read it. Well, there I saw the usual monogram, which I described to you before, ye remember, and under it I read these words:

"'*In Christo. Pax. Antonino Imperatore, Marius miles sanguinem effudit pro Christo. Dormit in Pace.*'"

"By Jove!" cried Blake. "You didn't though, did you? Why, that's the very inscription that Aloysius mentioned!"

"The very inscription," said O'Rourke, solemnly. "You may imagine how I felt. I can't describe. Anyhow, there I stood, leaning forward, and reading this, whin suddenly I trod on something that gave a dull rattle like gravel. I stooped down, and saw a lot of these beads. Some were lying in a line, others had been thrust aside by my feet. The string that had fastened them together was gone. It had, no doubt, mouldered away. Now, whose could that have been? Not the rosary of an ancient Christian, for they didn't have thim. Not the rosary of me cousin Malachi, for the string couldn't have rotted away in so short a time; it must, thin, have been

the rosary of the monk Aloysius, or of the poor Onofrio; one of those two, no doubt; and, perhaps, whin they stopped to read this epitaph, it fell from the one it belonged to without its fall being noticed. I picked up all the beads, and I put a bit of a string through thim, for convenience' sake."

Blake took the rosary, and looked at it with indescribable interest.

"Yes," said he, "it must be, as you say, the rosary of Aloysius."

"Of course, it must," said O'Rourke.

"It's perfectly amazing," said Blake.

"Excuse me," said O'Rourke, "it's all perfectly natural. The only wonderful thing about it all is, that I should have been lucky enough to break into the grave. If I had come to the solid stone, I might have had a month's hard work, at least. But, whin once I got inside, it was quite natural, whin you think of it, that I should find this very passage of Aloysius."

"I suppose it is," said Blake, still looking at the beads.

O'Rourke now poured out another glass of cognac.

"Well," said he, as he sipped it, "what are ye going to do? Are ye ready?"

"Of course," said Blake, "not only ready, but eager. I'm ready to start off now, this very instant."

"That's right," said O'Rourke; "and ye haven't told any one?"

"Not a soul—of course not."

"Well, I didn't know; a man sometimes has connections that it's difficult to keep a secret from. Ye're a young man, ye know; handsome, and mighty taking with the ladies; and, if ye had one in tow, she might see in yer face that ye were after something, and worrum it out of ye."

"Oh, no; there's nothing of that kind going on," said Blake, with a mournful thought of Inez.

"Well, I'm glad to hear it, for it would spoil all," said O'Rourke. "At any rate, here I am, and here you are, and every thing's ready. We needn't leave this moment, but we'd better start as soon as we can. Will ye be able to go by the morruning's train?"

"Yes."

"Any letters ye have to write ye can write to-night, and mail as we go to the station, only ye won't say any thing about what it is ye're after?"

"Of course not. I shall simply write one or two letters, and mention that I am going out of town on business for a month or so."

"That's right," said O'Rourke, with evident gratification. "Thin, if nothing does come of it, ye won't git laughed at. We'll keep our own secret, and, if we fail, there'll be no harrum done at all, at all. I'm glad ye kept the secret so well. It shows that my judgmint about ye was right, and I'm glad of it. A companion and assistant I must have, and I'd rather have you than anybody I know of. Ye'll be not only a fellow-laborer and business partner, but also a friend in case of need. I couldn't get on alone at all, at all. I'm not timid, and I'm not what you'd call shuperstitious, but working alone down there in a place like that is a test of a man's nerruves that I don't care to impose on me-silf. Besides, apart from that, there's worruk required down there that one man wouldn't be enough for. We've got to take ropes, and ladders, and lights, and, in the evint of success, we've got to carry some store of articles that'll be likely to have some weight in thim for a long distance. There ought to be enough down there to satisfy two min, or, for that matter, two thousand, so I don't objict to go halves with ye for the plisure of yer company."

"Well, old fellow, come now, it don't seem hardly fair to you to come in for so much, when you have had all the trouble thus far, and the secret is yours, too."

"Pooh! we needn't talk now about the division," said O'Rourke; "that's counting the chickens before they're hatched in the worrust way. It may be a total failure, so it may. Ye'd best be after trying to prepare yersilf for any disappointmint."

"Oh, well, of course I shall do that, you know."

"And ye'll have time to write to yer friends."

"Yes."

"How many letters did ye say ye'd have to write?"

"Two."

"Two? Hm! and ye'll have to be ready to start at five, and it's now half-past one," said O'Rourke. "I must be after going."

"Half-past one!" said Blake, in surprise. "Why, so it is; I had no idea it was so late."

"Well, I'll be going," said O'Rourke; "so ye'll write yer letters at once to yer two friends? I hope they're not both ladies?"

"Oh, no, only one of them is a lady."

"And ye'll be very guarded, so as not to let on what ye're after doing?" said O'Rourke, cautiously.

"Oh, you may trust me for that."

"Well, I'll be going, and let me advise ye to try to get some sleep. Ye're too excited, man. Write yer letters, go to bed, and sleep the sleep of the just. Thin ye'll be better prepared for future werruk and future excitemint. Ye're altogether too flushed, and excited, and feverish-looking just now."

"Well, I dare say I am just a little more excited than usual," said Blake; "but it will pass away soon enough."

"Well, I'll be going," said O'Rourke again. "I'll come here for ye in the morruning. Good-night."

He wrung Blake's hand with his usual heartiness, and then left.

After his departure, Blake sat for sometime without moving. The intense excitement into which he had been thrown by O'Rourke's story still affected him. His heart beat fast and furious, and a thousand dazzling visions of endless treasures swept before his mind. All the accumulated fancies of the last few days now arose up together in one vast assemblage, till his brain fairly reeled beneath their overmastering power. He was confounded by the magnitude of his own hopes; he was bewildered by the immensity of the treasure which O'Rourke had suggested.

He sat motionless for about an hour, when suddenly he started to his feet.

"This will never do," he murmured; "I must write those letters."

He then went to the table and poured out some cognac, which he drank off hurriedly. Then he procured writing-materials, and sat down to write. But it was a very difficult task. His mind was so full of other things that his dazzling thoughts intruded themselves into his letter, making nonsense of it. Three or four were torn up and thrown aside. At last he managed to write out a rough draft, full of corrections, and, after reading this over, it seemed as well as any thing else that he could write under the circumstances. This, then, he copied out, and what he wrote was the following:

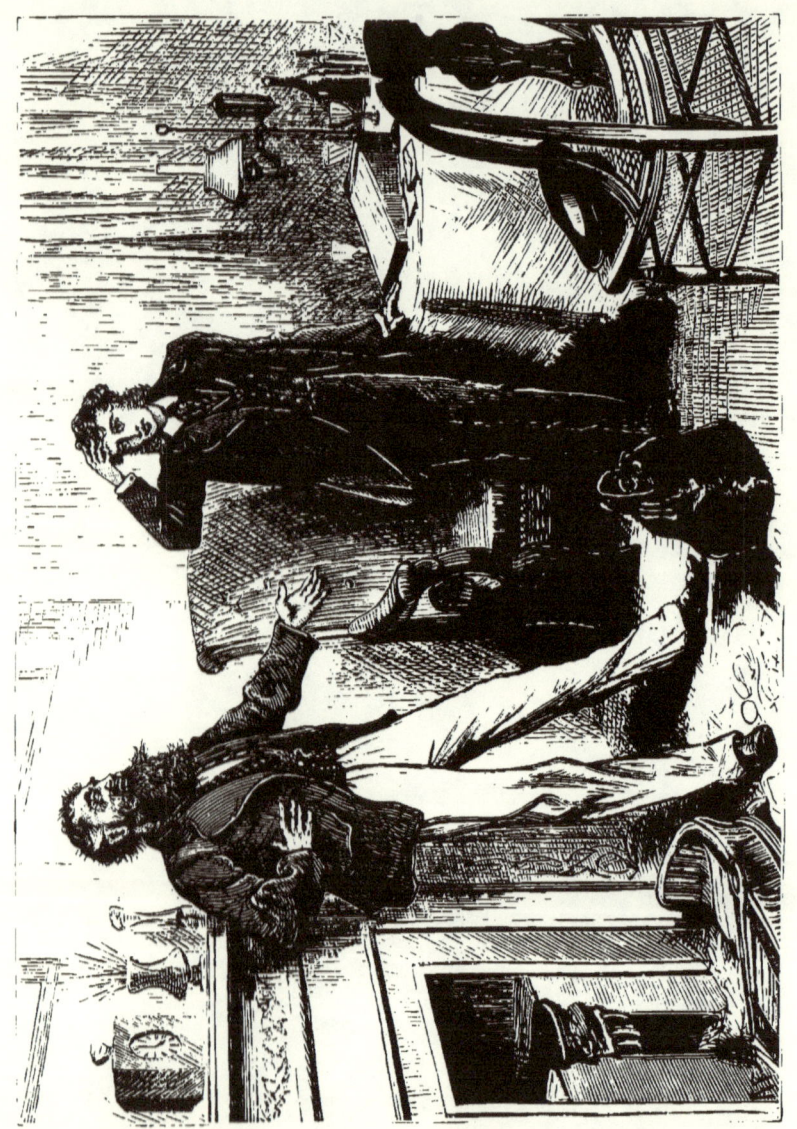

" He sprang up, and saw O'Rourke, who burst into a shout of laughter."—Page 99.

"MY DEAR HELLMUTH: I intend to start off in the first train to-morrow on business. I have heard of a chance of doing something in the South, and think it advisable to try. I may be gone some time, and I may return in less time. A party is going to accompany me, with whom I propose to associate myself. Nothing may come of this, but I think it is best, under the circumstances, for me to try what can be done. On the whole, I think it is advisable to try. It is somewhere in the South, and my friend who goes with me will do what he can. I may return soon, but I don't know, and if I can do any thing I may not come back for some time.

"Yours very truly,
"BASIL BLAKE."

On reading this over, it struck Blake as a most absurd production, but he had already made some half-dozen previous attempts which were even worse, and so, in despair, he concluded to let it go as it was, and not attempt another. It was better to write something than to vanish suddenly without a word, and, at any rate, in spite of the absurdity of the note, it did convey a friendly notice to Hellmuth of his departure. So Blake folded this, and addressed it to Kane Hellmuth.

The next letter was even a greater task, for the effort to write the first one had in some measure increased his confusion of mind, and caused him to express himself even more awkwardly. After over an hour of hard work he accomplished the following:

"MY DEAR MOTHER: I have not heard from you for some time. It is more than a month since I have heard from you. You informed me that you were going to go to London, and I have not heard from you since. I would go home and see how you are, for I feel some anxiety about you, but just now an event has occurred which seems to promise something in the way of professional advancement. If it turns out well, I may stay there some time. If it does not turn out well, I may not stay there some time. The party who is going there with me is a friend of mine, and a professional friend of mine. He thinks the chances there are good, and, if so, we shall both of us probably remain there some time probably. However, I do not know exactly how long we shall stay there; some time, however, in case of success; but,

if not, of course not. You need not write unless you write to me; however, we may not be gone very long probably.

"A party has mentioned a good prospect of success in the South—a professional friend of mine, and we shall probably work together. I shall not probably write to you again until the next time I write. I think, therefore, that I had better leave in the first train to-morrow morning; but, if we are not successful, of course I shall probably be back soon. Unless we succeed, I shall, however, not make a very long stay. However, that depends upon circumstances to some extent.

"You will probably be surprised, dear mother, to learn that it is my intention to leave this city by the first train to-morrow morning for the South. The reason of this somewhat sudden departure is this: there is a professional friend of mine who has been talking to me about that country, and he would like me to go with him. If we are successful, we may not, however, return long. I have decided to go in the first train to-morrow morning to the South with a party who is a professional friend of mine, and we both hope to find a place there where we shall be able to do better for ourselves. In case I am successful, I hope, of course, that you will write me as often as you possibly can, for I am beginning to feel quite anxious about you. Hoping soon to hear from you —I shall, therefore, go and see for myself. Write me often, dear mother, and believe me your affectionate son,
"BASIL."

Blake did not read this letter over, but managed to fold it and put it in the envelop. He had not enough of consciousness left to address it; but, having gone that far, his head fell forward on the table, and he slept profoundly.

He had not been sleeping long before he was roused by a rough shaking. He sprang up and saw O'Rourke, who burst into a shout of laughter.

"So this is the way you sleep, is it?" he cried. "Your head on the table and your door open to the public. So you've got your letters written, though one of them isn't addressed. It might go strayhter if you were to address it."

Blake stared and stammered, and it was some time before he could collect his scattered faculties.

" Why—why—you just left—"
"Tare and ages, man! why, it's five
o'clock," cried O'Rourke.
" Five o'clock!" gasped Blake.
" Yes. Are you ready? Are your trunks
packed? Ye needn't take mor'n a valise with
ye. But ye'll be after gathering up yer duds,
and not leaving thim scattered about."

Upon this Blake hurriedly went about
gathering some things which he threw into a
valise. Those which he did not want to take
with him he flung into a trunk, and then
locked it. Then, at O' Rourke's suggestion,
he addressed the letter to his mother, and
stuffed the two in his pockets. Then, hurriedly attending to his toilet, he announced
that he was ready.

They then went down. A cab was ready.
Blake told the *concierge* to take care of his
trunk.

On their way to the station he dropped
his letters in the post-office box.

CHAPTER XXIV.

DESCENSUS AVERNI!

It was Blake's first visit to Rome. Under
any other circumstances, he would have yielded to that manifold charm which the Eternal
City exercises over every mind that possesses
a particle of enthusiasm, and would have
found himself at once examining the treasures which here, more than in any other part
of the world, are stored up, and serve to il-
lustrate and to emphasize the teachings of
antiquity, of religion, and of art. But the
circumstances were unusual, and Blake's
mind was all preoccupied with thoughts of a
treasure of a different kind. Already the
wonderful story of Aloysius had borne fruit
within his mind, as we have seen; and, since
his departure from Paris, O'Rourke had left
nothing unsaid which could stimulate his
imagination, or excite his most sanguine
hope. His efforts in this direction were not
made by means of any attempts at direct
description, but rather through what might
be regarded as dry details or formal statistics.
He talked learnedly about the revenue of the
Roman Empire; of the arbitrary modes by
which the emperors extorted money; of the
wealth of Rome, created out of the plunder
of the world; of the immunity from plunder

which Rome itself had enjoyed; and of the
condition of the city at the time of Alaric's
approach. He made estimates of the wealth
of the imperial palace, and other estimates
of the probable value of the plunder which
was carried away by the army of Alaric. All
his figures were in millions. He assumed a
confident air in speaking about the treasure
which was concealed in the Catacombs, and
sometimes allowed himself to speculate on
the value of that treasure.

By this means he kept Blake's mind strung
up to the proper degree of enthusiasm and
excitement; so that at length, on reaching
Rome, he had no other thought or desire than
to enter upon the search without delay. Indeed, so eager was he, and so much did his
excitement surpass that of his friend, that he
would have hurried to the spot at once, had
not O'Rourke objected.

" Sure and this'll niver do entirely," said
the latter. " Don't ye remimber the proverb,
'The more haste, the less speed?' D'ye
think we're in a fit state to begin a laborious
task like ours, whin we're overwhelmed by
fatigue and starvation? For my part, I want
a good dinner, a good night's rist, and a good
breakfast. We have also to make jue preparations. I've got a list of things that we require, that we can't get till to-morrow. So
ye'll have to make up yer mind to wait. It's
lucky that ye've got me to think for ye, so it
is."

Blake's impatience rebelled against any
delay, however necessary; but he had to yield
to the sober sense, the prudent counsels, and
the wise forethought of his companion. In
fact, there was no help for it, as O'Rourke had
the matter all in his own hands, and no movement could be made without him. By this
delay Blake's impatience and excitement were,
if possible, only increased. He had scarcely
slept since O'Rourke's last meeting with him;
and this night of waiting, from the very fact
that it separated him from the wonders that
awaited him on the morrow, afforded too
much stimulus to his fancy to allow of any
thing like real sleep. His brain was in a
whirl, and the fitful snatches of sleep that he
caught in the intervals of his wild speculations were filled with dreams that were, if
possible, wilder still.

On the following morning, Blake arose at
a very early hour, and waited with much impatience the movements of O'Rourke. The

latter, however, seemed in no hurry whatever. Several times Blake knocked at his door, but received only a half-sleepy assurance that he was not awake yet. It was as late as ten o'clock when O'Rourke made his appearance. "*Salve!*" said he; "in Room I salute ye as a Roman. In other terrums, the top of the morruning to ye."

"Good-morning," said Blake. "Shall we go now?"

O'Rourke looked at him for a few moments with a reproachful gaze.

"How impatient ye are," said he, "to go down to the tomb!"

"Don't you think we're losing time?" said Blake, a little disturbed, in spite of himself, at an indescribable quality in O'Rourke's tone.

"Losing time, is it? Gaining time, I call it. Let's not go down there till we've seen the sun set in glory from one of the sivin hills of Room. For my part, I'm not going down till night—and there ye have it."

This resolution Blake found it impossible to change; so he was compelled to smother his impatience as best he might, and wait for O'Rourke to lead the way.

All that day O'Rourke obstinately refused to say one word about the Catacombs, or the treasure of the Cæsars, or the history of the middle ages. He frowned whenever Blake introduced those subjects. He sought pertinaciously and resolutely to keep his own mind and that of Blake fixed upon other subjects, as far removed from these as possible.

"Ye'll have enough of it when ye get down there. Sure, it's bracing yer mind that I am, in preparation for the orjeal that's before ye."

O'Rourke took him first to the Pincian Hill, and insisted on showing him the view from that place. After this he dragged him to the Villa Borghese, and thence to the Coliseum. Here he pointed out the peculiarities of the structure, regarding it both from an archæological and an artistic point of view. From this place he set out for St. Peter's.

"I wish ye to notice," said he, "the sharp contrast existing between each of these schupindous monimints. The one is the imblim of pagan, the other of Christian Room. They are each symbols of the instichutions out of which they sprung. The one is the fit exponent of that material Room that wielded its shuprimacy through the mejium of brute force; the other the exponint of that spiritual Room that exercised its shuprimacy through the higher mejium of the abstract, the immaterial, the shupernatural. And, as this mighty fane is grander and nobler thin the pagan amphitheatre, so also is the Room of the popes a grander and nobler thing thin the Room of the impirors."

To most of these discourses Blake was not in a mood for listening; but the manner of O'Rourke surprised him and impressed him. He felt puzzled, yet he tried to think that it was some eccentric plan of his friend's to draw his mind out of its too-excited state, and reduce it to a common-sense calm and self-contained repose. This O'Rourke announced as his purpose, and, as no other explanation was forthcoming, Blake was forced to accept it.

At length the day began to decline, and O'Rourke announced his intention of going to their place of destination.

The darkness came on rapidly, as is the case in this southern clime, and Blake noticed but little of the scenes through which he passed. Even had it been light, his ignorance of Rome would have prevented him from observing any thing with intelligent interest. Once O'Rourke pointed to a large building and said, "We're coming near, that's the Monastery of San Antonio." Blake saw a gloomy and shadowy pile in a narrow street, but could not make much out of it. They had not much farther to walk after this, but soon reached a dilapidated house of ancient architecture and large size, corresponding in appearance with the description which O'Rourke had given of the house that he had rented. The doorway was low, and consisted of an archway of massive stones. The doors were massive, and studded with large iron bolts. The street in which it stood was narrow and dark, and the exterior of the sombre edifice threw an additional gloom over the scene around.

O'Rourke opened the door in silence, and motioned to Blake to go in. Blake did so. Thereupon O'Rourke followed, and carefully bolted the massive door. Blake threw a glance about him. He saw that there was a court-yard, around which appeared the sides of the gloomy edifice, from which a deep shadow was thrown down. O'Rourke did not allow him to look long upon this uninviting scene, but went to a door which he unlocked.

Blake followed him. They entered a narrow hall, and O'Rourke carefully closed the door behind him and locked it.

He then lighted a lantern, and, without a word, walked along the hall till he came to a narrow stone stairway. Blake followed him. Down this narrow stone stairway the two went, and at length reached a chamber underneath. This chamber was vaulted, and the walls were composed of large stones, white-washed. O'Rourke did not wait here a moment, but walked on, followed by Blake. A narrow arched passage led from this vaulted chamber, and, passing through this, they came to a large cellar, from which the chamber had evidently been walled off. The cellar was about eight feet in height, and was formed of solid piers, which were vaulted over, so as to support the massive structure above. These piers and the vaulted roof were all grimy with dust and smoke, and covered with mould. The floor was formed of large slabs of stone.

O'Rourke still walked on, and, after passing several piers, at length stopped.

As he stopped, he turned and looked for a moment at Blake. Then, without a word, he pointed toward his left, holding up his lantern at the same time so that its light might shine upon the place. Blake looked, and saw a pile of rubbish. The next moment he sprang toward it, and O'Rourke, moving nearer, held his lantern so as to light up the place.

Blake stooped down and looked forward with a new outburst of those excited feelings which had been repressed all day. The pile of rubbish lay against the wall in which there was a large excavation, terminating in a black hole of oblong shape. It was the hole that O'Rourke had told him of. This was the place, and this was the entrance to those dazzling fortunes that awaited him.

Carried away by a sudden impulse, he hurried forward, and would have gone through that black opening; but O'Rourke laid his hand upon his shoulder, and drew him back in silence.

O'Rourke now went to the middle of the cellar to a place about twenty feet from the opening, and put down his lantern on the stone floor. Blake came up to the place and saw a number of articles lying there. Prominent among these was a light wooden ladder about ten feet long. There was also a box

of solid construction on four small wheels; a stout wicker basket with two handles; a coil of rope; a roll of canvas; a small furnace; a crucible; three lanterns; a vessel of oil; two pickaxes; two crow-bars; an axe; several balls of twine; together with some smaller articles of a miscellaneous character. O'Rourke had already informed Blake that he had made a hurried collection of all the articles of immediate necessity before he had left Rome for Paris, and the present spectacle showed the latter how diligent he had been. These served as eloquent reminders of O'Rourke's story, and as forcible suggestions of the work that lay before them.

Blake's first act was to take one of the lanterns. He drew some matches from his pocket, and proceeded to light it. Being a smoker, he always carried matches. These were destined to be useful afterward. Having succeeded in lighting his lantern, he looked at O'Rourke, and waited for the next movement. He caught O'Rourke's eyes fixed on him with an intent air of watchfulness. For a moment Blake felt a slight uneasiness, but at once shook it off. O'Rourke's look had struck him as being slightly unpleasant, but the thought immediately came to him that his friend was merely watching to see whether he was cool or excited. So the only effect of this apparently-sinister glance was to cool off a little of Blake's excitement.

O'Rourke now took the ladder and walked toward the excavation in the wall. Blake followed him, carrying his lantern, and nothing else. O'Rourke crawled through the oblong opening, and then drew his ladder after him. Blake followed in silence. He put his feet through first. About four feet below the opening, his feet touched a foothold, and then he drew himself altogether inside, and, holding up his lantern, stared eagerly around him.

It was not much that met his view. He found himself inside a passage-way excavated in the solid rock. The rock was a species of sandstone. Its hue was dark, and its surface still bore rough marks made by the tools of the ancient excavators. The height was about seven feet, or a little over. The wall was covered with slabs which bore rudely-cut inscriptions. These slabs were of a lighter color than the wall, and of a smoother finish. They were placed against the wall, one over the other. Immediately opposite him were three, and above and below the opening through which he had come were two others. Before and behind him was thick and impenetrable darkness.

Before him O'Rourke was standing. His back was turned toward him. The ladder which he had brought was standing on the ground, and the upper part resting against his shoulder. He seemed not to be looking at any thing in particular, for his head was bent forward as though he was in deep thought— as though he was meditating the best plan of advancing. Blake waited for a few moments, and then, feeling eager to go on, he touched O'Rourke's shoulder.

Thus far O'Rourke's behavior had been most extraordinary. From the moment that he had locked the outer doors he had not spoken a word. Blake had been impressed in spite of himself by the silence of his companion, and had said nothing. Now, however, as Blake touched O'Rourke's shoulder, the latter started and half turned.

"Well, Blake, me boy," said he, in a cheerful tone, "here we are at last amid the mouldering rimnints of the apostolic marchures that deposited their bones and raised thim ipitaphs ; sure, but it's meself that would be the proud man to linger here and dally with me archœological riminiscincis. It's a fine field, so it is, for classical inthusiasm. The actual fact bangs all the ilivatid splindors of Virgilian diction. Sure, but it's careful we've got to be here ; it's easy enough, so it is, to go, but we've got to take precautionary misures about securing a returrun. Sure ye know yerself how it is :

. . . . 'Facilis descinsus Averni ;
Noctes atque dies patot atri janua Ditis ;
Sed revocare gradum, shuperasque evadere ad auras
Hoc opus, hic labor est. Panci, quos acqnns amavit Jupiter, aut ardens evexit ad acthern virtus,
Dis geniti, potuere."

"By-the-way, now that I come to think of it," he continued, "it would be an iligant question intirely whither Virgil didn't get some of his conceptions of the under worruld from these Catacombs ; but thin, howlding, as I do, the theory of their Christian origin, that position would be altogether ontinible."

"Oh, yes ; I dare say," said Blake, indifferently ; "but don't you think we had better be moving ? "

At this O'Rourke turned and looked at him with a fixed gaze and a slight smile.

"Blake, me boy," said he, "I have detected in you all this day and evening a deplorable tindincy to unjue excitemint. Now, if one thing is prayimintly necissitatid in an ixploration of this discription, it's perfect coolniss and *sang-froid.* Ye are too feverish ; ye must git cooler. Ye'll lose yer head like poor Onofrio, and vanish from me gaze in some of these schupindis labyrinthine wildernissis. Try, thin, if ye can, to banish from yer mind the dazzling visions that are luring ye out of yer sinses. The conversation that I mean to maintain here isn't going to be about any thing ixciting or sinsational, but rather upon those august subjicts that give tone and inergy to the mind. Let us wander onward, thin, not as vulgar money-diggers or trisurehunters, but as learned archœologists."

With these words O'Rourke shouldered his ladder, and walked on at a moderate pace. Blake followed. The passage as they went on continued to preserve the same dimensions. On either side appeared the tablets that covered the tombs, bearing their inscriptions. Its course was not exactly straight, yet the curve was a gentle one. No side-passages or crossings appeared for some time.

At length a crossing appeared, and here O'Rourke paused. This crossing consisted of a passage of about the same size and general appearance as the one which they were traversing ; and the eye, in glancing into it from either side, soon lost itself in the impenetrable gloom. Here O'Rourke put down his ladder and the lantern, and then taking a ball of twine from his pocket, he fastened one end to an iron bolt which he had brought for that purpose. This he placed on the floor. It was to be their clew. Thus far all was plain ; but beyond this he dared not trust himself without this safeguard. He now took up his ladder and his lantern. Blake insisted on carrying the former, and, after some friendly altercation, succeeded in doing so. O'Rourke now held the lantern in one hand, and, putting the ball in his pocket, he prepared to unroll it as he walked, so as to leave the clew behind him.

"Sure, Blake, me boy," said he, "but this is the descint into the inferrunal worruld that we've read about at school. Here we are, : we're Æneas and Achates, or, better yet, we're Alcides and Theseus—we won't dispute which is which.—Have ye ever read the 'Hercules Furens?' I warrant ye haven't.

Well, it's a fine worruk ; and I've been maundering and soliloquizing over some of its lines that are mighty appropriate to our prisint adventurous jourreny :

'Non prata viridi laeta facie germinant,
Nec adulta leni fluctuat zephyro seges ;
Non ulla ramos silva pomiferos habet ;
Sterilis profundi vastitas squalet soli,
Et foeda tellus torpet aeterno situ,
Rerumque moestus finis et mundi ultima,
Immotus aer haeret, et pigro sedet
Nox atra mundo ; cuncta moerore horrida,
Ipsaque morte pejor est mortis locus.'

"Now, that's what I call mighty fine poetry," said O'Rourke, " and I'll jist invite ye to projuice any other passage in ancient or modern poetry that'll beat it. Yes, Blake, me boy, that's it—' ipsaque morte pejor est mortis locus ! '——"

He stopped abruptly, and then, unwinding the string, went forward.

Blake followed.

Yes, O'Rourke was trying to quiet his nerves by quoting Latin. Now if that Latin had been pronounced Oxford-fashion, it would not have been very intelligible to Blake, but, being spoken with the Continental pronunciation, and with a dash of Irish brogue running through it, he did not comprehend one single word.

CHAPTER XXV.

THE CITY OF THE DEAD.

. O'ROURKE thus went first, unwinding the string, while Blake followed, carrying the ladder. The strange silence that O'Rourke had maintained while in the house had been succeeded by a talkativeness which was equally strange.

" For me own part," said he, as he walked along, "we may as well begyile the solichude of the jourreny by cheerful though not exciting conversation ; and, by the same token, I may remark that I have always taken a deep interist in the Catucombs. Here we have an unequalled opporchunity of seeing thim in their frish virgin condition. These interesting subjects are very useful to keep us in a cool state of moind, and to act as a privintive against unjue excitemint.

" It's ividint," he continued, " that these are all Christian tombs, for on most of thim ye may see the monogram that I mintioned to you. Here, for instince, is one."

He stopped in front of one of the tombs, and held up his lamp. Blake stopped, also, and looked at it, though with much less interest than that which was felt, or at least affected, by his companion. There were four slabs here, one above another, enclosing four grayes. The inscriptions were rudely cut in all these. Some of the names, which were Greek, were spelled with Greek letters.

"Many of these tombs are ividently occupied," said O'Rourke, "by min of the lower classes, but it doesn't follow that the Christians of the age which buried these bodies had no shuparior min. Of course, the majority among thim, as in all other communities, was ignorant, and the majority asserts itself even in this sublime naycropolis. Still, that's a fine ipitaph," said he, pointing to the one before him. "It's laconic, and yet full of profound meaning. Spartan brivity with Christian pathos."

The epitaph to which he pointed consisted but of a few words. They were these :

" *Faustina, cruciata, dormit, resurget.*"

Another bore the inscription :

" *Dormitorium Cæcili.*"

Another :

"*Aselus dormit in pace. Vidalia fecit.*"

O'Rourke walked on farther, stopping at times in front of those tablets which bore longer inscriptions than usual, and translating them for the benefit of his companion, of whose classical acquirements and intelligent appreciation of the scene around him he seemed to have doubts, which were probably well founded.

"Here," said he, "is one that reminds me of that one of Marius behind us, that I forgot to show you :

" ' *Lavinia, of wonderful amiability, who lived eighteen years and sixteen days. Lavinia sleeps in peace. Her father and mother set up this.*'

"Here, Blake, is a long one :

" ' *Adsertor, our son, is not dead, but lives in heaven. An innocent boy, you have already begun to live among the innocent ones. How gladly will your mother, the Church of God, receive you returning from this world ! Let us restrain our tears and cease from lamentations.*'

"Here," said O'Rourke, as he stopped in

frout of another, "is ono of the most interesting. It is a *besomum*. D'ye happen to
know what a *besomum* is ? Well, it's a place
where two aro buried—or sleep together, as
the holy Christians called it."

A few steps farther on, the attention of
O'Rourke was arrested by an inscription
which was far longer than any which had yet
met his eyes.

"See here," said he, "this one tolls a long
story." And then he read it:

*"'Phocius sleeps here. A faithful bishop.
He ended his life under the Emperor Decius.
On his knees, and among the faithful, he was
arrested and led away to execution. His friends
placed him here, with tears and in fear. Oh,
sad times ! in which even among sacred rites
and prayers, not even in caverns and among
tombs can we be safe. What can be more
wretched than such a life, and what than such
a death, where they cannot be buried by their
friends and relations ? He has scarcely lived
who has lived in Christian times.'"*

O'Rourke stood for a few moments musing.

"It's been a theme of frequint meditation with me," said he, "the wonderful differince between these Christians and their
pagan contimporaries with rifirince to their
regyard of death. Go read the inscriptions
on the pagan tombs. What are they all ?
Terror unspeakable, mourning, lamentation,
and woe. Not a ray of hope. 'I lift up my
hands,' says one, 'against the gods, who have
snatched away me innocent.' But what do
we see here ? Not a sad longing after the
vanished plisures of life, but a confident
expectation of a better life to come."

O'Rourke here gave a deep sigh, and again
resumed his walk. This time he paid no further attention to the epitaphs. It seemed to
Blake as though he had been carried away
beyond himself, and beyond all immediate
recollection of his errand here, by the solemn
memorials of the sainted dead. For such
feelings as these Blake felt nothing but profound respect. It heightened his estimate of
O'Rourke's character; and, though the conversation was one in which he had not felt
able to take part, yet it had produced a
marked effect upon him. The translations
of these epitaphs drove away the wild fever
of excitement which had so long clung to
him. In the presence of these solemn memo-

rials of Christian suffering and constancy and
faith, his longings after treasure and riches appeared paltry and trivial, and there was communicated to his mind a feeling of shame at
coming on such an errand to such a place.
With the cessation of his hot excitement
there came, also, a feeling of something akin
to indifference about the result of his search,
and he began to contemplate a possible failure with equanimity.

Already as they advanced they had come
to places where other passage-ways crossed
their path, and disclosed depths of viewless
gloom on either side. There was something
appalling in the suggestions which these afforded of endless labyrinths, in which to venture for even a few paces would be a death
of horror. They served to remind Blake of
the terrible fate of Onofrio, and gave to that
slender thread which O'Rourke was unwinding an inconceivable importance. Upon that
slender thread now hung their two lives—that
was the tie that bound them to the world of
the living, and by the help of which they
could alone hope to retrace their steps to the
upper air.

For already the passage-way had wound
about in various directions, and they had
come to other passages which led into this at
such an angle that it would be only too easy
to choose the wrong path on returning. None
of these passages were crooked, but the difficulty lay in the way in which they opened
into one another, and in the confusion which
their general similarity would create in any
mind.

"I think I'm going right," said O'Rourke;
"but that last passage-way may have been
the proper course for us. Howandiver, we're
on the way to the Painted Chamber. That's
the nixt objictive point to aim at. Once
there, the opening in the flure'll be a
gyide."

They walked on for some distance farther,
and then O'Rourke stopped and half turned.
Blake came up and found that the passage-
way here had been enlarged. There was a
species of chamber—the roof was vaulted—
the sides were covered with a thin coating of
stucco, upon which were some faded pictures,
roughly drawn and rudely colored. At once
he recognized the place as the one which had
been mentioned in the story of Aloysius.

"The Painted Chamber !" exclaimed
Blake

O'Rourke smiled.

"True for you," said he. "And so we're right thus far. It's mighty incouraging, so it is—and I must say, ye see yersilf, how much better it is for two to come than one. I confess, Blake, me boy, there's a solimnity about this place that overawes me; and, if I'd been alone, I'd have—well, I'd not have come so far this time. I'd have returreened, so I would. And sure and this is a great place intirely, so it is. Sure, and the paintings are on the walls yit, as any one may discerrun, just as me cousin Malachi said they were—and what is this?" he continued, going up to the wall and holding up his lantern. "Sure, and it's the Noachian diluge, though rudely enough drawn—and here," he continued, going to another place, "is a galley with a sail. I've seen that afore in the Lapidarian gallery, and they interpret it to riprisint the immortality of the soul. Here's a palm-branch—here's another ship, and a fish—and a man—maybe it's Jonah they meant. I tell you what it is, Blake, me boy, there's a power of symbolical meaning in all this, and I'd be proud to explain it all to ye some time; but just now, perhaps, we'd better reshume our wanderings."

Upon all these, which O'Rourke thus pointed out, Blake looked with an interest which had been increased by the scenes through which he had been passing, and by the solemn thoughts which they had created within his mind. Not unwillingly would he have delayed a little to listen to his companion, who seemed to have such a wonderful comprehension of the meaning of these drawings, so rude and so meaningless to his inexperienced eyes; but O'Rourke's proposal to go on drew away his attention, and he at once acquiesced without a word.

"We've got to go straight on," said O'Rourke, "and we ought to come to the hole before long."

The chamber was circular, and about twelve feet in diameter. It seemed to be a simple enlargement of the intersection of two passages. Once enlarged, it had been decorated in the manner already noticed.

O'Rourke turned away, but still hesitated, in that manner which had marked his progress here all along. There was evidently something on his mind. Blake noticed it, but thought that it was simply his meditations upon the early Christians.

"It's a small place, too, for such a purpose," said O'Rourke, speaking as if at the conclusion of a train of solemn thought. "It couldn't have held many. It must have been crowdid, so it must."

"What do you mean?" asked Blake. "What purpose?"

"Well, you see, Blake, me boy," said O'Rourke, "this place was once used as a Christian chapel."

"A chapel!"

"Yis. Juring times of persecution, the Christians had often to fly to these receptacles, and hide here. In these chapels they had to conduct their sacred cirimonies. Here, too, they had their burial-services. Oh, sure, if these walls could but speak, what a tale they could tell! Mind ye, I don't hold with some that there iver was a time whin the Christian population came down here *en masse;* I hold that it was only the shuparior clergy—the bishops, and sich like—or the iminint min that hid themselves here. But they held their services here, no doubt; and on Sundays there would be a large crowd wandering about here, as they were being conducted to these chapels, or as they came to bury the remains of some frind. But what puzzles me is, that I don't see any remains of an altar, or any thing of that kind. If it had been used as a chapel, there'd have been an altar, and, if so, there'd have been some remains, unless they afterward removed thim to some church overhead. And that may have been—but the fact is, the quistion is a complicated one, and cannot be fairly and fully discussed on an occasion like this."

With this, O'Rourke turned abruptly away, and, unrolling the string, he walked out of the chapel through that passage-way which was a continuation of the path along which they had hitherto been advancing.

He walked on, unrolling the string as before, holding the light very carefully so as to see his way, and not saying a word. Blake followed in silence. In this way they went on for about fifty paces.

Then O'Rourke stopped, and looked earnestly downward at the pathway before him. Then he advanced two steps farther. Then he turned and held out his hand with a warning gesture.

"It's the hole! we've come to it!" said he, in a low whisper.

"Where? where?" asked Blake, hurrying up.

"There!" said O'Rourke.

As he said this, he pointed to a blackness in the path before him. Blake looked, and saw an opening in the path, yawning immediately beneath them. An involuntary shudder passed through him, as he thought of the danger which this presented to the incautious explorer. But the danger here was not real, after all; for no explorers came to this place, except themselves, and they had been sufficiently cautious to avoid it.

"Me cousin Malachi was right," said O'Rourke. "He came as far as this. It now remains to see whether the monk Aloysius was right or not. If so—thin—soon—we—shall—know—all."

O'Rourke spoke slowly. Blake made no answer. He had reached this spot about which he had thought with intense excitement of late—this spot which seemed the last stage in the journey to endless wealth; but now his imagination, which but lately had so kindled itself at this thought, lay dull and dormant within him. Already there was a load on his mind, a dull presentiment of evil. He was conscious of this change. He wondered at it. He attributed it to various things—to the reaction consequent upon over-excitement long continued; to the sermonizing of O'Rourke, who had discoursed upon semi-sacred things ever since they had entered here; to the presence of the dead, whose holy lives, and glorious deaths, and immortal hopes beyond the grave, seemed to throw such contempt upon so mean a quest as this, for the sake of which he had violated their last resting-place. But, whichever of these was the cause, there he stood, not indifferent, but strangely melancholy, and disturbed in soul with vague alarms and dark forebodings.

O'Rourke stood looking down in silence into the yawning abyss beneath. Then, drawing a long breath, he put his lamp down on one side of the pathway, and, turning to Blake, he took the ladder from him. This ladder he then proceeded to let down. He did this slowly and cautiously. In a few minutes it touched the bottom, and the top of it projected about one inch. The ladder, being ten feet long, showed thus the depth of the passage beneath from the place in which they were standing.

"My calculation," said O'Rourke, "was based upon the statemints of the monk Aloysius. This proves that the statemints were true. Every thing in that manuscript has thus far turrened out true, and I only hope the rest of our undertaking will be equally successful. So now, here goes!"

Saying this, O'Rourke began to descend. Blake watched him till he reached the bottom. He saw that the passage below was, in all respects, the counterpart of the one above. But he did not delay to look. The moment that O'Rourke had reached the bottom, he began to descend, and in a few moments stood by his side.

O'Rourke now went on very cautiously, unwinding the string.

"Shall I take the ladder?" said Blake.

"No," said O'Rourke; "if Aloysius is right, there'll be no need for the ladder; and, if he's wrong, thin our game's up—that's all. Besides, I don't believe there'd be any ixcavation beneath this. We must now be on a level with the Tiber."

Blake, upon this, followed his companion, leaving the ladder where it had been placed.

They walked about thirty paces.

Suddenly, O'Rourke stopped, and turned round with a blank expression, feeling his coat-pockets, one after the other.

"What's the matter?" asked Blake.

"Tare an' ages!" exclaimed O'Rourke, "if I haven't dropped me other ball of twine, and this one is nearly used up! I wouldn't trust meself a step farther."

"Why! did you leave it behind in the cellar?"

"Sure and I took it with me, so I did, and —by the powers! I have it—I moind pulling out me handkerchief in the chapel, and I moind hearing a thud on the flure. I must have dropped it. I'll go straight back for it, and you wait here—unless you're afraid of the ghosts—you wait here, and I'll be back in a giffy, so I will."

Saying this, O'Rourke brushed past Blake, on his way back to the chapel to get the ball of twine.

"Ye may be going on," said he to Blake, "till ye come to any new passage-way—it seems like a straight course—or ye may wait for me."

"Oh, I'll wait for you!" said Blake. "We'll find it, or miss it in company."

He spoke in a melancholy voice. He had

begun to feel half vexed with himself for his own indifference; yet he was indifferent. Nor was it unaccountable. Often does it happen, in the lives of men, that an object, pursued with absorbing eagerness from 'a distance, grows tame at a closer approach. Thus the lover's ardor is sometimes dispelled on the approach of the marriage-day; and thus Mont Blanc, which had inspired such a glow of enthusiasm when seen from the Vale of Chamouni, becomes a freezing mass of ice, killing all enthusiasm, when the climber approaches its summit.

So, in profound dejection, Blake stood still, waiting for O'Rourke. He had lost his enthusiasm; his excitement was gone. Avarice, ambition—even these feelings ceased to inspire him.

At length, it struck him that O'Rourke had been gone for a long time. A slight fear arose. It was instantly quelled.

He determined to go back in search of him.

He walked back for some time.

Suddenly, he stood still.

He was confounded.

He had walked back a distance greater than that which he had followed O'Rourke after descending the ladder, yet he had not come to the ladder. Only twenty-five paces or so! He had walked fifty.

Where was the ladder?

He looked along the arch of the vaulted passage overhead, holding up his lamp.

He walked back for twenty-five paces.

Overhead was an opening in the vault, black, impenetrable, terrible! Was that the place through which he had descended?

It was!

Where was the ladder?

The ladder was gone!

CHAPTER XXVI.

BETRAYED.

For a long time Blake stood staring at that black opening overhead. Not a vestige of any thing was there. The string had gone. O'Rourke had taken away from him not merely the means of return, but the clew which showed the way. And this was all of which he was conscious. Even of this he was only conscious in a vague way, for his brain was

in a whirl, and his whole frame tingled at the horror of his thoughts, and, in the immensity of this sudden calamity, he stood bewildered, incapable of speech or motion—incapable even of thought. Not a sound came to his ears. It was silence all around—the silence of death. Yet his attitude was one of expectancy. As yet he could not believe all, or realize the full extent of his appalling condition. His expectation rested on O'Rourke, and his ears tried to catch the sound of returning footsteps. But his ears listened in vain, and the time passed, and horror deepened in his soul, till, from this faint hope he descended slowly into the abyss of despair.

One thought now overspread all his mind, and this was that O'Rourke had betrayed him, and had lured him here for this very purpose. Why he had done this he did not at that time try to conjecture. He was not yet sufficiently master of his own thoughts to speculate upon this. He had only the one supreme and overwhelming idea of treachery—treachery dark, deep, demoniacal, far-reaching—which had laid this trap for him, and had brought him to it. To this feeling he yielded. His head sank down from that upward stretch into which, for a time, it had been frozen; the rigidity of his limbs, wrought by one moment of unutterable horror, relaxed; a shudder passed through him; he trembled like a palsied man, and his nerveless hands could scarcely hold the lantern. But this light now shone before him as his very last hope—if there was, indeed, any such thing as hope remaining—and to save this he clutched it with a convulsive grasp. This effort roused him from his stupor; and, though his bodily strength was still beyond his recall, yet the faculties of his mind were restored and rallied at the impulse of the instinct of self-preservation. Too weak to stand erect any longer, he seated himself, still clutching his lantern, with his back supported against the wall, and then, in his despair, began to think what might be the meaning of this.

Had O'Rourke really left him? Of this he had no doubt. But why had he done this? To this he could give no answer whatever.

Suddenly he sprang to his feet, and began to call in his loudest voice. His terrors, after all, might be unfounded, and O'Rourke might, perhaps, return. At least he might answer and tell him the meaning of this. With this hope he called, and, for some time, his cries sounded forth as he uttered every form of appeal, of entreaty, of reproach, of despair. His voice rang mournfully down the long passages ; but to him, as he listened, there came no reply except the dull, distant echoes returned from the gloomy recesses of the Catacombs. Whether O'Rourke heard him or not he could not tell. Perhaps he had hurried away at once, so as to be out of the hearing of his cries ; perhaps he was waiting close by, and listening coolly to the despairing entreaties of his victim ; but, whatever he had done or was doing, he gave no sign. Above, all was dark. Blake covered up his own light as he looked up, to see if there was any gleam from O'Rourke's lantern visible in that upper passage-way, but his most searching scrutiny failed to distinguish the slightest possible glimmer of light in that intense gloom. It was the blackness of darkness.

Once more Blake sank down into the despair of his own thoughts. With this despair there was mingled unspeakable wonder at O'Rourke's treachery. The motive that had impelled him to this was utterly beyond his conception. He had known him for a year. He had made his acquaintance in the most casual manner. They had gradually drifted into one another's way. What had he ever done, or what could O'Rourke have imagined him to have done, that he should plan for him so terrible a fate as this ? Or what possible purpose of any possible kind could O'Rourke have before himself that could be promoted by such a crime ?

It was no panic-flight of O'Rourke's. It was deliberate. He had taken the ladder so noiselessly that no sound had indicated what he was doing. He had even removed the clew.

It was, therefore deliberate ; and this treachery joined itself to all that had gone before—formed the climax to it all. It was now evident that the whole story of the treasure had been planned for the purpose of luring him to this place and to this fate. The story of Aloysius had been, no doubt, a fiction of O'Rourke's, from beginning to end. His cousin Malachi had never existed. The Monastery of San Antonio probably was a fiction. The old manuscript was another. O'Rourke had never produced it. He had told an exciting story, and worked upon his credulity, his necessities, his ambition, and

his avarice. As to the treasure, it was the wildest of dreams. If there had been any, he would not have been betrayed to this fate.

Such was the sudden awakening of Basil Blake from his dreams of boundless wealth.

But there remained the dark and inexplicable problem of the motives of O'Rourke. Could it be that he was mad ?

This would account for it all. O'Rourke was certainly eccentric. His eccentricity might be madness. He might have been one of those homicidal madmen who plan craftily the deaths of others ; and his very acquaintance with him might have been sufficient to suggest to O'Rourke a plan for his destruction. He recalled his strange demeanor since their arrival at Rome ; his singular silence in the cellar ; his unwonted talkativeness on the way through the passages ; his odd gestures, mysterious looks, and significant words. Were not all these the signs of a disordered brain ?

On the other hand, if he were not mad, what possible motive could he have for his treachery ? Blake could think of nothing whatever in his life that could account for any hostile plot against him. All his life had been commonplace, and his position was sufficiently obscure to guard him against the machinations of enemies. One thing only in all that life of his stood forth as beyond the obscure and the commonplace. That was the mysterious friendship of Mr. Wyverne, his mother's singular words, and, above all, the strange and incredible declarations of the dying man. But that had already been declared false by another authority. Even if it should be true, could there be any thing in that which could connect itself in any way with O'Rourke's plot, and be a reasonable cause for such a terrible betrayal as this ? How should O'Rourke know Wyverne ? How could he be benefited ? Or were there others who wished to get him out of the way—by such a mode of destruction as would render it impossible that he could ever again be heard of ? Alas ! if there were any who had sent O'Rourke to do this, they had certainly chosen their agent well. Blake now remembered how completely he had concealed his movements ; and he recalled those letters which he had written to Kane Hellmuth and his mother, in which not the slightest indication was given of the place to which he was bound, or the purpose for which he was going. He was now alone—no friend could help—no one could ever track him here; and here he must die, and exhibit the fullest reality of that dread fate which O'Rourke had ascribed to her imaginary Onofrio.

But now another change came over Blake —a reaction from this despair—a recoil from that paralysis of all his energies which had come upon him. He started to his feet. There was yet time. Could he not retrace his steps? How much time had already passed he did not know, but, if he could find his way back along the passages to that opening in the wall, he might yet save himself.

This thought at once restored all his strength of body and vigor of mind to the utmost. He started to his feet, and once more looked upward, scanning eagerly that opening above him. The distance was not great. Was it impossible for him to climb up there and regain that passage-way? True, there was nothing but the smooth wall, which presented no foothold just here, except the slabs that covered over the graves. He could not jump up, he was not sufficiently agile for that. How, then, could he contrive to scale that bare wall of ten feet between himself and the floor above?

The wall itself afforded a ready answer to this. On that wall there were three slabs, covering three tombs, one above the other, in the mode which has already been mentioned so frequently. If those slabs could but be removed, or if only one of them could be displaced, then Blake would have a foothold by which he could reach the upper passage-way. These slabs he now examined most carefully. He struck them with his hands; he tried to find some crevice by which he could get a sufficient hold of them to pull them from their places. But these efforts were vain; for, though ages had passed away since they were placed here, still the cement was firm, and none of the slabs would yield.

But Blake would not yet give up. Every thing now seemed to depend upon the promptness with which he worked. He drew his knife, and, opening the large blade, began to cut at the stone over the slab. His intention was to try to cut away the stone to such an extent that he could pass his fingers through and grasp the slab. He began with the middle slab. The rock was soft sandstone; and as he cut and dug with his knife he had the satisfaction of seeing that he was gradually working it away, so that he had the

prospect in time of making a hole large enough for his purposes. But his work was slow, and he discovered very soon that his knife was wearing away rapidly under it. At length, when his hand ached with the effort, and was bleeding from blisters, when so much of his knife was worn away that the prospect of continuing much longer at this task was faint indeed, he discovered that the thickness of this particular slab was too great to give any prospect of removing it in this way.

Yet the moment that he made this discovery, he made also another, which counterbalanced the first, and changed despair once more into hope.

The hole that he had made, though not large enough to enable him to remove the slab, was still large enough to assist him to scale the wall. All that he needed was a few others like it. Two more would suffice. If he could cut one over each slab, even smaller than this, he could then climb up.

Instantly he set to work once more, this time at the lower slab, and here at length he succeeded in cutting a small slit large enough for him to insert the toe of his boot. It was not so large as the first hole that he had cut, but suited his purpose quite as well.

He then turned his attention to the uppermost slab. The others were flush with the wall. This one, however, projected in one corner about half an inch. No cutting was therefore required, for he could grasp this with his fingers so as to draw himself up to some extent.

He now prepared to ascend. But first it was necessary to secure the safety of his lantern. In order to effect this, he tore up his pocket-handkerchief and his cravat into thin strips, and tied them all together until at length he had a line fifteen feet long at least. One end of this he fastened to the lantern, the other he tied to his knife. Then he flung his knife up through the opening. It fell on the floor there, and thus held the line that was fastened to the lantern below.

Blake now braced himself for this great effort to climb the wall. Grasping the upper slab, he put his right foot in the lower hole, and drew himself up thus till he was able to thrust his left foot into the larger hole that he had scraped away over the middle slab. Here there was a firmer foothold, and here, with one vigorous effort, he raised himself up higher, clinging to the upper slab with his right hand, and grasping with his left at the upper floor. He reached it, and, assisted by his firm foothold, raised himself up higher. Then, with a final spring, he threw himself up, and, catching his toe on the upper slab, he succeeded in working himself through the opening and on to the floor of the upper passage-way. Then he drew up the lamp, and put the line in his pocket, so as to use it in case of any further need.

Once more, then, Blake found himself in this upper passage, and now he proceeded to hurry back the way he had come. In a short time he reached the Painted Chamber. Here, even if he had felt any lingering doubts as to O'Rourke's treachery, the first sight would have served to dispel them, and confirm his worst suspicions; for the chamber was empty, and O'Rourke had taken his ladder and his string.

But there was no time to lose. Haste was needed, and yet, at the same time, the utmost caution was equally needed; for how could he find his way back? True, the pathway had not been very crooked, and therefore, if he were to keep in the straightest possible course, he would be most certain to find the true way; yet still there were places where, among several passages branching off in the same way, it would be difficult to tell the true one. But, until that place was reached, he might hurry on with less circumspection.

Accordingly, he advanced as fast as a vigilant outlook would allow him, and for some time had no difficulty. At length, to his intense joy, he discovered something on the floor. On stooping to examine it, he found that it was the clew. O'Rourke had apparently gone back, winding it up as he went; but at length, becoming perhaps weary of this, and feeling certain of the destruction of his victim, he had contemptuously thrown it down.

Blake now hurried on faster than ever, with nothing to prevent the most rapid progress, since he was guided by the string that ran along the path. Before long, he came to the ladder, which lay obliquely across the path, as if carelessly flung down by one who was weary of carrying it, and had no further need of it. This ladder was of no use, however, to Blake, though a short time before all his life seemed to depend upon it; so he hur-

ried on, seeing in it only a sign that he might yet reach the house before O'Rourke had left.

On he went, faster and faster. At length, the clew ended. Blake recognized this place. It was at that first crossing to which they had come, and beyond this he knew that there were no other crossings till he reached the aperture by which he had entered. To arrive at this point, at last, was almost like an escape; but still his escape was not yet effected, and so he hurried onward. The aperture for which he was now looking was on his left, and, as he went, he watched that side narrowly.

At last he saw it.

All the other slabs were in their places, but this one was off. It lay on the ground below. The aperture was all dark. Blake sprung toward it, and thrust in his lamp and his head.

The next moment he stood there, rooted to the spot, staring with wild eyes at the sight before him, while a new despair deprived him of strength and almost of consciousness.

For there, full before him, in the place where that opening had been through which he had crawled after O'Rourke, was now a wall of stone, presenting a barrier which stopped all escape. There were two large stones. They had been pushed up here from within—by the malignant and relentless purpose of his enemy—not fastened with cement, but lying there solid, irremovable, and beyond the reach of any efforts of his.

At this sight he reached the last extremity of his prostration and of his despair. The lamp fell from his hands into the stony sepulchre, and he burst into a torrent of tears.

And now, at this moment, while his lamp lay extinguished, and all around there was a darkness utter and impenetrable—a darkness, also, fully commensurate with the darkness of his despair—there came to his ears a dull sound from beyond that wall, as if some one was moving there.

At once Blake roused himself, and listened.

The sounds continued. Some one was moving. There was the rattling, shuffling sound as of some one piling up stones. It was as though O'Rourke had not been satisfied with any common barrier to Blake's escape, but had resolved to replace the whole wall in all its thickness, and leave it as he had found it. There, then, was his enemy, within a few feet, yet inaccessible and invisible—not remorseful for what he had done, but actively malignant still, and still toiling to accomplish, in its fullest perfection, the terrible task which he had undertaken.

Blake listened in dumb horror, unable to speak a word, even if words had been of any avail. But no words were forthcoming, and he leaned there in that thick darkness, clinging to the sepulchre with a convulsive grasp, and all his soul centred in his sense of hearing. That sense seemed now to have taken an almost superhuman power and acuteness, as though all his other senses had lent their aid to this. The rattle, the sliding, the dull thud, the harsh grating of the stones as they were handled by the terrible workman on the other side, still went on; and still the sounds penetrated the wall, and came to the silent place of the dead beyond.

Blake listened, unconscious of time, and only conscious of the slow approach of his appalling doom.

At last all ceased.

Then there came the sound of a human voice—low, muffled, sepulchral, but, to Blake's acute hearing, sounding with terrific distinctness. There were but four words that thus came to his ears through the thick wall where the stones stood, piled up without plaster, and allowing the awful words to pass through ·

"*Blake Wyverne, farewell forever!*"

Then all was still.

CHAPTER XXVII.

FILIAL AFFECTION.

THE time passed pleasantly indeed with Bernal Mordaunt. The worn-out man felt this rest to be sweet after his weary life; and it was sweeter still, after so many years of loneliness and exile and wandering, to find around him once more the tender embrace of kindred and of affection. In his far-distant home, as missionary, the Abbé Mordaunt had not been without those lofty consolations which the active performance of a high duty, and zealous labor for the good of man, and fervent faith, can give to the soul, even when all earthly joys have been torn from its grasp; but such labors and such zeal were only possible in the days of his vigorous manhood.

Now, when vigor had gone, and such apostolic labors were no longer possible, his heart yearned for some close human tie, and some tender human affection. For this cause he had thought of his daughters, and had come home to find them. One was gone, but one was left; and that heart of his, which had so long been destitute of the treasures of human love, now expanded, and filled itself with that tender affection which was lavished by her whom he called "his own," "his only one," "his darling daughter," "his most precious Inez."

In spite of all his deep yearning for this filial love, Bernal Mordaunt was not exacting; and it has been seen how carefully he tried to avoid standing between Bessie and one whom he supposed to be the object of tenderer and stronger affections than any which she could bestow upon himself. It has been seen also how Bessie frustrated his self-denying plans, and met this sacrifice of love, by another sacrifice of love on her part, and refused to accord to Sir Gwyn any privileges which might draw her away from Bernal Mordaunt. This Bernal Mordaunt felt more than any thing that had occurred since his return home. He believed that it must be a sacrifice on her part; yet in his secret soul he exulted over such a sacrifice, since it had been made for his sake. He deprecated it as greatly as he could to her, but Bessie met such deprecatory language in a way of her own which was thoroughly characteristic, by the profession of still greater love, and by the declaration that she would give herself up altogether to him, and for his sake cut herself off from all society. This, however, Bernal Mordaunt did not wish her to do. In his love for her, he regarded not only her present but her future, and he was not selfish enough to permit his own happiness to stand in the way of what he considered her permanent good. The regard which he had from the first conceived for Sir Gwyn Ruthven had steadily increased with the progress of their acquaintance; and it seemed to him that Sir Gwyn was in every respect a man to whom he might gladly intrust the daughter whom he loved so fondly, and for whose future welfare he was so solicitous.

Meanwhile, Sir Gwyn, though full of a sincere and devoted regard for Bernal Mordaunt, had not by any means lost sight of the great aim of his present life. Bessie, in her new *rôle* of affectionate daughter, appeared to him to be more charming than ever. It needed but this to complete her charms in his eyes, and to transform her into an angel. What was best, the cordiality and evident regard which Bernal Mordaunt always exhibited toward himself had placed him upon a footing of familiar and intimate friendship, and thus enabled him to see to the best advantage the tender, the incessant, the self-denying care of Bessie for the old man. Still, in spite of this surrender of herself, Bessie was not separated from him; in fact, she appeared to be drawn nearer to him, and never had Sir Gwyn more profoundly enjoyed himself. Bernal Mordaunt himself was willing to favor the lovers in every possible way; and often, when Bessie would not leave him, he pretended to be asleep, so as to leave an open field to Sir Gwyn. At other times he would occupy himself with reading, and watch those two who were both so dear to him, with a quiet smile, which showed with what tender human sympathy he noticed the progress of affairs.

Bessie showed herself in all respects a daughter beyond all praise. She walked with the old man, making him lean on her slender arm; she read to him all the daily papers; she assisted in finding out what books he preferred; and used to sit at his feet on a low stool reading to him for hours, while he rested his hand on her golden hair, and watched her with a look of unspeakable love. She was quick to discover that he liked her conversation, and was amused with her little Hibernicisms, and occasional outcropping of the brogue which distinguished it; and so she took pains every day to have some amusing story to tell him, and to tell it too in her oddest manner, with her oddest idioms, well satisfied if she could succeed in raising a laugh at the point of this story, which she took good care to introduce always in the most effective way. When local events failed, she would fall back upon her early reminiscences, and these were invariably of so grotesque a kind that Bernal Mordaunt relished them more than any thing else.

Bernal Mordaunt thus was happy—more truly and calmly happy than he had been for years. It was not, indeed, so elevated a sentiment as some which he had known during his active missionary life; not that high spiritual rapture which had sometimes visited his soul; yet it was true happiness, tender and human and domestic, a feeling well deserved, and well befitting the man whom years and hard labor and sorrow had enfeebled. For, in spite of the calm and quiet life into which he had passed; in spite of the pure and invigorating air; in spite of his own peace of mind and happiness; in spite even of the incessant and vigilant and most tender care of the devoted Bessie, Bernal Mordaunt's health did not improve, but, on the contrary, strange as it may appear, from the moment that he came to Mordaunt Manor, his health and strength gradually yet steadily failed. There was no visible cause for this. Every thing around him seemed adapted to build up a weakened constitution, and give tone and vigor to an enfeebled frame, yet still there was the mysterious fact, and Bernal Mordaunt himself knew it and felt it, accepting it, however, with solemn and placid resignation as the inevitable will of Heaven.

One morning, as he and Bessie were together, Sir Gwyn found them, and after a short time Bessie meekly withdrew. Bernal Mordaunt was struck by this occurrence, which was quite singular, for Bessie had always chosen to remain on former occasions; but at length it was explained, for Sir Gwyn, with all the embarrassment which is usual in such cases, proceeded to inform him that he had come to ask his daughter's hand.

The reception of this request was all that Sir Gwyn could have desired. Bernal Mordaunt pressed the young man's hand, and looked at him earnestly, with moistened eyes.

" My dear Gwyn," said he, addressing him in the familiar style which the young man had himself requested that he would use—" my dear Gwyn, the object of my dearest regard on earth is my sweet daughter Inez, and her future happiness. You know how dear she is to me, and how I live in her presence. You know, too, what a heart of love she has—how tender she is, how true, how devoted, how forgetful of self. I never cease to thank Heaven for the mercy bestowed upon one so undeserving as I am, in the gift of an angel upon earth, to be my daughter, to love me, to tend me, to devote herself to me, as she does. But still I am not forgetful of the future, my boy; and I know that the best thing for her to win is the heart of a brave, loyal gentleman, who may be her protector through life. I have seen all this in you, Gwyn, my dear boy, and I am happy in the thought that you love her; and, if you can win her love, you have, not only my consent, but my grateful and earnest good wishes. You have my consent, Gwyn, and more—you have my most affectionate sympathies; for it will give me sincere happiness to receive you as my son."

Gwyn was quite overcome at such a reception of his request, and murmured some words of acknowledgment. There was evidently something on his mind, however; and this, after some further conversation, all came out.

"I had to ask this first," said he; "but I've got something else that I'm anxious to tell you, before this goes any further. It's something that you ought to know, and I ought to tell. It's about my own affairs."

Bernal Mordaunt at this looked at him with a pleasant smile of encouragement.

"The fact is," said Gwyn, "there's some difficulty in my present position, some uncertainty as to my right, not only to my title, but also to my estate. I will explain. I am the youngest of three brothers. My eldest brother died a few years ago, leaving no heirs. Now, between me and him there was a second brother; and it is this one that makes my present position uncertain. About ten years ago, he vanished. He lived in Paris when he was last heard from. He had been very dissipated. As the second son, he had no prospects; and the wild life which he had lived had already exhausted what my father had allowed him. There was some talk of a hasty marriage that he had made with some grisette or some unworthy creature. Be that as it may, he vanished, and has never been heard of since.

"Well, you know, my elder brother died, as I have said; and, as my second brother was not to be found, I came in for the inheritance. As to my second brother, I have heard various rumors. Some say that he committed suicide; others, that he died in extreme poverty in Genoa; others, that he went to India, and died there. But, among all these rumors, no proof has ever been brought forward that he is dead. He may be living yet, and the only actual proof that I can adduce in favor of his death is the improbability of any man in needy circumstances allowing a great inheritance to pass into other hands, when he has only to come forward to claim it. At the same time, I know this, that he was always different from other men; and, if he had

chanced to be engaged in some mode of life that suited his tastes for the time, he would let the inheritance pass, and not come forward till it suited him to do so. As to my elder brother's death, he must have heard of that, for it was mentioned in all the papers at the time, and, what is more, notices of it were inserted in the leading journals on the Continent and in America. So, you see, as it is possible that he may be alive, it is also possible that I may not be the rightful owner of the Ruthven estates; and, if he should ever appear, I should have to give them all up to him. The probability of his appearance is certainly somewhat remote, but still I thought it my duty to explain this matter."

To all this Bernal Mordaunt listened with a pleasant smile.

"My dear boy," said he, as Gwyn finished, "I am grateful to you for your frankness and for your confidence. At the same time, all this makes not the slightest difference in my feelings. When I accepted the proposal which you made, it was not the baronet that I regarded, or the heir of the Ruthven estates, but the young man Gwyn Ruthven, whom I consider as a noble-hearted and loyal gentleman, and whom I esteem, not for what he *has*, but for what he *is*. I assure you that it makes no difference to me whether you are rich or poor. The life that I have lived, and the principles that have animated me, have all caused me to regard riches as of less importance than the world supposes. Inez has Mordaunt Manor; and, if you should be stripped of every thing, this would remain, and this would be enough. So do not let any considerations of this sort interfere with your hopes and plans. If you love her, go and try to win her. If she accepts you, I give you my blessing. But, as for this missing brother of whom you speak, of course you have duties there, which I am sure you have already tried to fulfil."

"You are right," said Gwyn, earnestly; "I have tried to find him. I have sent out notices, and have even communicated with the police in Paris, in Vienna, in New York, and in several other places. If he is alive, the place is his, and I am ready to give it up."

"My boy," said Bernal Mordaunt, in tones more tender than any which he had ever, thus far, used to Gwyn, "once upon a time, many years ago, your father and I made an agreement. We were very old friends. We were boys together. We were together at Eton, at Magdalen College, Oxford, and in the same regiment in the army for a few years. We married at about the same time. I lived here, he in London; but, though our families were separated, he and I saw very much of one another, and kept up our friendship. I remember your brothers. On my last visit to London, where his duties kept him for the greater part of the year, they were at home—Bruce and Kane, fine, manly boys, though Bruce was not much to my taste. It was Kane that I admired. You, Gwyn, must have been a baby. I didn't see you. Your father and I were speaking of our children. He had only sons; I had only daughters. We thought that it would be a good thing if one of his sons should marry one of my daughters, and thus join those two noble estates. We talked it over with enthusiasm, and we both agreed that it would be too desirable a thing to neglect; and we parted with the wish that it might eventually result in this. Alas! man proposes, but God disposes: our lives were strangely altered from what we anticipated, and I never saw him again. But in you, my dear boy, I see him; and, when I first saw you with my sweet Inez, I could not help wishing that the old hope of years ago might be fulfilled in you and her. Still, you must remember that it is not the union of the estates that I now regard; these things I consider as of small importance, in comparison with the welfare of my sweet Inez. As to your brother, if there is any mode of search that you can yet think of, you had better try it.—And that was the end of poor Kane? And such a noble boy! Poor lad! poor, poor lad!"

"You may rely upon it," said Gwyn, "if there is any conceivable way by which I may hear of him, I will make use of it."

"I know that, of course, my boy," said Bernal Mordaunt, kindly.

After this there was a new tenderness on Bernal Mordaunt's part toward Bessie, which also extended itself to Gwyn. The two young people had evidently come to an understanding; and Bernal Mordaunt, in all his words and looks, showed plainly that he was well pleased for this to be so.

"Gwyn, my dear boy," said he, one day, taking advantage of an occasion on which they happened to be alone, "I wish to speak to you about that subject which we were discussing the other day. You know how dear to my heart is the welfare of my beloved Inez. Every day I think of it more and more, and all the more as I feel that my own end is approaching."

"O sir!" began Gwyn; but Bernal Mordaunt checked him.

"No, no," said he, "I know well what you wish to say, but it is not necessary. Believe me, my own feelings in this matter are a sure guide. See how it is with me. See how much weaker I now am than I was when you first knew me. I came home somewhat broken in health, it is true, yet still not so much invalided but that I might indulge in a reasonable hope of recovery. I had worked hard and suffered much, yet not more so than many of my brethren in the same holy cause. Under ordinary circumstances I might hope for a complete restoration to health from a return to Europe. Indeed, the voyage home proved wonderfully beneficial, so much so that, when I reached Rome, I was congratulated by every one on my vigor and energy. I went to Paris and to London, and my health continued to improve in spite of bad news which I heard, and distressing doubts, and great fatigue. When I came here I felt strong.

"Yet all these hopes which I had formed of renewed health and prolonged life, it has pleased Heaven to make of no avail. It may be that the purpose which lay before me called forth certain latent energies, the exercise of which was beneficial; and that, when all was gained, and there was nothing more to work for, the cessation of the play of these energies threw me back upon myself, and left me to sink helplessly into this weakness where I now find myself. I put it in this way, for I know no other way in which I may account for it yet still, whatever be the cause, it is a fact that, since my return to Mordaunt Manor, I have grown steadily worse and worse every day. At this moment I feel a profound weakness and a failure of vital power, which I am sure must soon have a fatal result. There is no help for it. You know, for you have seen, how tenderly, how assiduously, how devotedly, my sweet Inez has nursed me and cared for me. My very food comes from her hands. Her deep love for me will allow no other hands than her own to prepare certain little dainties which she knows I like. She watches me night and day. She hovers around me incessantly. And yet, what can she do? If tenderest love could restore me, hers would do it; but, as it is, Gwyn"—and Bernal Mordaunt's face assumed a look which afterward haunted Gwyn for many a day—"as it is, it really seems as if all her fond care and all her assiduous atten- tion only served to draw me down more surely to death.

"And now, Gwyn, my dear boy," he con- tinued, after a pause, "what I wish to say is this: My days I feel are numbered. I must soon leave her; but, before I go, it is the one desire of my heart to see her future se- cured; to see her, in short, under your pro- tection before she loses mine. I mention this, my dear boy, because I have it so much at heart, and because it really seems to me that, if this were accomplished, I should die content. Will you not try to do what you can to persuade her to grant this desire of the father whom she loves so tenderly?"

"Oh, come," said Gwyn, "I really think you take too desponding a view of things, and, as to what you mention, I'm sure I'd give my eyes if I could only induce her to consent. Perhaps, if you mentioned it to her, she might be more willing to listen to me."

"I think I had better do so," said Bernal Mordaunt, thoughtfully.

———

CHAPTER XXVIII.

SELF-SACRIFICE.

THE matter upon which Bernal Mordaunt had spoken to Sir Gwyn was one which had been prominent in his thoughts before, and remained afterward a subject of still more absorbing importance. His deep love for his daughter forced him to dwell upon this idea; and the more he felt his own increasing weakness, the more anxious he was to secure his daughter's future before he should leave her forever. All that he had said to Sir Gwyn he felt to be true. It was true that his health had improved after leaving the East, and that he had constantly gained strength up to that moment when he had reached Mordaunt Manor. It was true that, since that time, a change had taken place for the worst, and that ever since he had steadily and uninterruptedly grown weaker; and, con-

sequently, if he looked forward to the worst, and confidently expected that death alone could end this, he was justified in his opin- ion. What might be the cause of this change for the worse Bernal Mordaunt himself did not know. It might be supposed that the pleasant surroundings of home, the perfect rest and calm, and, above all, the unwearied attentions of Bessie, would have had nothing but a beneficial effect upon him; yet Bernal Mordaunt had plainly stated his belief that they had produced upon him an effect which was the very opposite.

But his daughter's future was now the chief thing upon his mind, and soon he felt too impatient to postpone any further the arrangement which he longed to have made.

"My dearest Inez," said he, one evening, after Sir Gwyn had left them, "there is some- thing that I wish to speak to you about."

"What is it, papa dear?" said Bessie.

They were alone together—he in an arm- chair, she on a stool at his feet—and, as he spoke, she put her little hand in his. He pressed it between his own, and went on:

"It concerns you, my dearest Inez, and is, therefore, the fondest wish of my heart. You see how I am now and how I have been, dear, since my return home. I grow weaker and weaker every day, and I cannot help looking forward to the time when I shall have to leave you."

"Leave me, papa dearest? Why, what do you mean? What are you going to leave me for? Are you tired of me? Are you going back to those horrid Chinamen and Turks? You shall never go near them, or, if you do, I will go with you, so I will."

Bernal Mordaunt shook his head mourn- fully.

"I meant a different journey, Inez dar- ling," said he, "and one on which no earthly friend, however true and loving, could ever accompany me. It is a journey which I and you and all must go alone, and that journey is nearer, I think, now than ever it was be- fore; and this is the journey that I speak of; and I do not wish to go on it until I accom- plish something that is very important."

At this, Bessie withdrew her hand, and clasped this and the other together. Then, shrinking back, she fixed her large blue eyes on Bernal Mordaunt with a look of fear.

"O, papa!" she cried. "O, papa! dear, dearest papa! how horrid it is for you to

"'And sure but it's meself that's the heart-broken girl this day!'"—Page 117.

talk so! O, papa! why do you talk so? O, papa! what makes you so cruel? You cannot mean what you say. It's false, so it is. You're not worse, at all, at all. Oh, how terrible it is for you to speak such words, and sure but it's meself that's the heart-broken girl this day!"

"My dearest child," said Bernal Mordaunt, leaning forward and placing his hand tenderly on her golden, rippling hair, "my own Inez, these things must be said. If there is a sorrow to come, it is better to be prepared."

"But I don't want any sorrow to come," said Bessie, "and I can't bear it. If any sorrow comes, I'm sure I shall die."

Bernal Mordaunt sighed. The thought of her loving and tender nature was too much for him. She was so profound and absorbed in her affection. How could this slender young girl, whose whole nature seemed made up of tenderness, who lived only to love or be loved, bear the rude shock of affliction, of bereavement?

"My sweet child," said he, in a tremulous voice, "Heaven knows how gladly I would do any thing to save you from sorrow—how gladly I would put myself between you and every possible evil. But such things cannot be, and there are none so pure and so innocent but that they must bear their share of the ills of our common humanity. If I am to leave you, and if my loss gives you such sorrow, I might almost regret, for your sake, Inez dearest, that I ever came home, and called forth so much love from you, only to wring your tender heart; yet, for my own sake, I cannot but rejoice that I have found you and known you, and felt your tender love before I go."

At this Bessie bowed herself down and hid her face in her hands. Her form trembled violently, and gave signs of deep emotion.

Bernal Mordaunt was himself overcome by the sight of this, and therefore changed the conversation to something else.

A few days afterward, however, he returned to the point, and this time he did not dwell so much upon that mournful theme which proved so painful to Bessie.

"You see, my dearest Inez," said he, after some preliminary explanations, "how my heart is set upon this. I really suffer from the thought that your only protector and guardian is a feeble old man. Now, if any thing should happen to me, what would become of you?"

"But nothing shall happen to you, papa dearest; and if any thing should, why—why —I—I—don't—don't want any thing to become of me at all. I want to lie down and die, so I do, and there you have it."

"I know well your devoted love, my own darling daughter," said Bernal Mordaunt, fondly, yet sadly, "but I am now speaking about my own feelings. I may be utterly in the wrong about myself and my health, as you say I am; yet still I feel this way. Now, my own child, you always think of my wishes and make them your law. Do you think that you would grant a request of mine which lies very near my heart?"

Bessie looked up with childish innocence.

"What is it, papa dear?" she asked.

"It is this, my child: I wish to see you with some protector—less frail and feeble than I am. I might nominate a guardian, but I know of none. Poor Wyverne is gone. None of my acquaintances here are congenial except one; and it is this one under whose guardianship I should like to see you before I —before I grow any worse."

"Who is he papa, dear?" asked Bessie, in the most unsuspicious manner.

"Our dear friend Gwyn."

"Gwyn!" exclaimed Bessie, "my guardian!" She looked at him in astonishment.

"Yes my dearest Inez. He shall be your guardian, the kind of guardian which his love for you and your feelings toward him would make most fitting. In short, the highest desire of my life is to see you his wife before I grow any worse."

At this Bessie buried her face in her hands, bowed down, and said not a word.

"You are betrothed, why should you wait? Why not grant an old man's wish when it lies so near his heart? This is my strongest desire, Inez darling. You will not refuse it when I ask it so earnestly. And it is all for your own sake. Can you decide now?"

"Oh, papa! dear, dear papa! I do so wish that you would get this absurd idea out of your head."

"It's my wish, dearest Inez," said Mordaunt, earnestly.

"Oh, papa dear, how you do put things! You know how eager I always am to do even the slightest little thing that you want me to, but this is like asking me to desert you, and how can I possibly do that? No, papa—my own papa—I know that poor dear Gwyn is awfully fond of me, and I like him too, and I have told him so; but if it comes to leaving you, papa dearest, why I won't, and I'd give him up before you, so I would, and there you have it."

Saying this, Bessie seized Mordaunt's hands, and, hiding her face in them, she covered them with kisses. Tears stood in Mordaunt's eyes; the devotion of this daughter was wonderful. His father's heart yearned over her with inexpressible tenderness; and yet out of that very tenderness he still was firm in his resolve to exert all his power to bring the marriage about. It was for her sake. Should he die, the marriage would be postponed for a long time, and during such a postponement it might be prevented altogether by some casualty.

All this he pointed out to Bessie, and, together with this, he brought forward other persuasives, but urged most of all his own wish, which, whether reasonable or unreasonable, was so set upon this that a disappointment would grieve him sorely. One by one Bessie's objections and scruples, and they were many, were argued away or set aside, and at last she had no other resource than to assent. Yet, even then, she made a most express stipulation that her marriage with Sir Gwyn should make no difference in their mode of life—that they should still live at Mordaunt Manor, and that she should be his nurse and his attendant as before. To these things Mordaunt consented, and Sir Gwyn was only too glad to win Bessie under any circumstances.

Having thus gained Bessie's consent, Mordaunt was urgent in pressing her to arrange it at an early date. His own health now declined even more rapidly, and this made him all the more impatient. Sir Gwyn, also, who saw Mordaunt's impatience, united his own ardent entreaties, and Bessie was unable to refuse.

The marriage thus took place about a month after Mordaunt had gained Bessie's acquiescence. Prominent among those who witnessed the ceremony was Mordaunt, who sat in a chair in the centre aisle, propped up with pillows. His strength had failed so much that he had come to this. But the ef-

fort was too much, and he was so exhausted that on his way home he fainted.

Sir Gwyn and Lady Ruthven went on a short tour through the Highlands, but were not gone more than a fortnight. Bessie's anxiety would not allow her to remain away longer. She had to fly back to her "dear, dear papa." Mordaunt seemed somewhat better, in spite of the over-exertion at the wedding. There was more strength in his frame, more color in his cheeks. When the bridal pair left, he was unable to stand alone. Now he could walk about the house, and up and down the piazza.

Sir Gwyn was overjoyed, and Bessie expressed herself in terms of the highest delight.

Encouraging as this improvement in Mordaunt was, however, it proved but temporary; and Bessie had scarce resumed her former fond attendance upon her "dearest, darling papa," when the strength that had begun to return, once more began to leave him. This created the deepest dejection in him. He had begun to hope. All hope seemed now to be gone.

Lady Ruthven received the congratulatory visits of the country people, who found her in her new dignity more charming than ever. But the universal popularity which she had gained in no way changed the simplicity of her character and manner. There was no affectation, nor was there any attempt to lay aside the little peculiarities which had always formed at once her distinction and no little of her charm.

Nor did the new social duties which now devolved upon her draw Lady Ruthven away from those duties to which Bessie had been so devoted. Mordaunt saw, with new tenderness, that her promise to him had not been a vain one; and that the husband had not eclipsed the father. To Mordaunt she allotted more time than either to her husband or to the world. The attendant physicians thought that her unremitting care had prolonged the old man's life beyond what would have been its term under other circumstances; and society, which already admired her for her beauty and amiability, now adored her for her tender devotion and her filial piety. Gwyn, also, in winning the daughter, had not forgotten the father; but, as the lover had been, so was the husband, and he found the society of his wife none the less pleasant in Mordaunt's chamber than else-where.

But, Mordaunt's days were numbered. This was evident. Ho knew it himself. Gwyn knew it. Bessie tried to reject the belief, but it could be seen that she dreaded the worst. There was about her, at times, a hurried nervousness, a dreamy abstraction, a fearful, furtive glance, unlike any thing that had ever before been seen in her by her friends. Gwyn noticed this, and urged her in his loving way to take more rest, but Bessie turned it off with a smile and a sigh.

Mordaunt's days were numbered. Since the return of the newly-married pair, his strength began to fail him, and he descended by ever-accelerated degrees down toward the last verge of life. But, with each succeeding stage of weakness, Bessie's care grew more and more unremitting. At length she had to deny herself to all visitors, and confine herself to Mordaunt's chamber.

As the old man descended deeper and deeper into the dark waters of death, his heart still turned with yearning affection and inexpressible gratitude to this bright young being whose love had so glorified the last days of his life. He had come home, as he now saw, to die; but how sweet it was to descend to death in such society; to feel her soft touch, to hear her voice of love, her low-breathed tones of tender affection, all the way! To the worn-out man death that came in this way could scarce be deemed unwelcome. Could any death be better or brighter?

It was Bessie who thus cheered his last hours. She read to him when he wished it. She sung to him the hymns or the chants which she loved—hymns and chants which she had already learned for his sake. He loved to listen to her voice as she thus sung, clasping her hand the while as though he gathered strength from her. She also, as always before, poured out all his draughts, and administered to him all his medicines. This was a privilege which she had claimed from the first, and the old man expected it; and, during her absence on the bridal tour, he missed this tender attention, even though his health had been better without it.

So the days passed, and Bessie showed her tender and solicitous love.

Thus the last hour drew near.

For a whole day he had been at the verge of dissolution. Bessie had refused to leave his bedside. She sat there, holding his hand, and wiping the cold dews of death from his brow. In that same room was Gwyn, watching the dying face of Mordaunt; watching also the pale face of his devoted wife, who in her deep love for a father thought nothing of herself. He was afraid of the reaction from all this; yet he did not know what to do. Bessie refused to leave the room till all was over; and he knew not what arguments to bring forward at such a time. The family physician was also there, counting the moments that might elapse till all should be over, and looking with unfeigned emotion upon the scene before him, where the daughter clung so to the dying father, as though she would drag him back from death unto life.

Suddenly the dying man opened his eyes, and fixed them on Bessie. His lips moved. She bent down low to listen.

"Inez," said he.

"Yes, papa dearest," said Bessie.

Mordaunt stared at her.

"You are not Inez!" said he, in a voice which was audible to all in the room.

Bessie shook her head mournfully, and looked at her husband.

"His mind is wandering still, poor papa! He is thinking of poor, dear, darling mamma, so he is. Her name was Inez, too, the same as mine."

Mordaunt's eyes closed.

After about an hour he opened them once more, and again they rested on Bessie. Those who looked at his face now saw that the last great change had come over it. Death-struck was that face now, yet the eyes were full of intelligence, and beamed with inexpressible tenderness as they rested on Bessie.

"Inez — dearest — best — daughter!" he said.

Bessie bent down low over him.

"Kiss—me—Inez!"

Bessie pressed her lips to his cold forehead.

Such were the last words of Bernal Mordaunt. He was buried in a manner worthy of the great house of which he was the last representative.

Lady Ruthven was greatly prostrated by this last blow, yet she rallied from it with unexpected rapidity. But the melancholy event that had just occurred made Mordaunt Manor distasteful to her now; and so she yielded to her husband's earnest solicitations, and went with him to take up her permanent abode at Ruthven Towers.

THE letter which Blake had written was delivered to Kane Hellmuth on the following day. It excited much surprise on the part of the latter, and for a twofold reason: first, because his friend's departure was so sudden; and, secondly, because the letter itself was so incoherent and unsatisfactory. The construction of the sentences was most confused and awkward; and it was impossible to find out where he had gone, and what he had gone for. Kane Hellmuth could not suspect so frank a nature as that of Blake of any thing like deceit; and, if the letter was ambiguous or unintelligible, he chose rather to attribute it to haste, or sleepiness, on the part of the writer. He had seen him on the previous day, and Blake had made no mention of any thing of the kind; nor did he seem to have any idea of going on a journey. He was certainly a little abstracted in his manner, for Kane Hellmuth's own cares had not altogether prevented him from noticing that; but this may have arisen from his anxiety about his mother, from whom, as he himself had said, he had not heard for some time. He could only understand this mysterious letter by supposing that some friend of Blake's had written to him, or come to him, and given him information of some sudden opening which he had to accept at once. Thinking, therefore, that Blake would either be back, or write more fully before long, he put the letter away, and waited in the expectation of hearing more.

Days passed, however, and weeks also, and even months, without any further communication. This surprised Kane Hellmuth, for he had expected different things; and, taken in connection with the incoherent letter, it gave him some anxiety. He also felt this another way, for he had conceived a strong regard for his friend, and liked to run in to see him, or have him drop in to his own apartments. The matter, therefore, took up a good share of his thoughts, and he could not help the suspicion that there was some

evil involved in this sudden and mysterious flight. What it could be he did not know, for he was not aware of any circumstances which might inspire any one with evil designs against him; and so, in default of other things, his mind dwelt upon that strange intercourse which Blake had held with Mr. Wyverne, which was terminated by the wonderful declaration of the latter, and his death. Although he had heard Father Magrath's explanation of that affair, and fully believed it, yet still, in spite of this, he could not help connecting it in some way with Blake's present disappearance, and the thought occurred to him often and often that if, after all, it were true, Blake might have enemies; though who they could be, and what motive for enmity they could possibly have, was utterly beyond his comprehension.

Thus the time passed, and as the months went by without any news from his friend, he began to fear the worst, though such was his ignorance of Blake's movements that he did not know what to do to search him out. The *concierge* of the house where Blake had stopped could tell him nothing except that on a certain morning he had gone in company with another person, and had left directions that his trunk should be taken care of. He did not know who the other person was, and the description which he gave of him afforded no intelligence to Kane Hellmuth. To the police it was, of course, useless to apply, for the meagre information which he could supply them with would not be enough to yield them any clew by which they might be guided to a search. His helplessness in this matter was therefore complete, and that very helplessness made the whole affair more painful to him.

Before this he had been the prey of one great and engrossing trouble, which arose from that mysterious and inexplicable apparition whose visitations he had described to Blake. Now this new trouble had taken up his thoughts more and more, until at length his own affair had come to occupy but a small portion of his attention. It was not forgotten by any means; it was only pushed over into a subordinate place, and ceased to be a supreme care. The possible evil impending over Blake seemed to him more formidable than any thing that could arise from his own experiences; and so it was that, in the mystery which had gathered around Blake, his own peculiar mystery had grown to be a matter of minor importance.

Such was the state of Kane Hellmuth's mind, when one day he was wandering through the streets on the way to his rooms. He was approaching the street up which he intended to turn, and was about six feet from the corner, when suddenly at the opposite corner he caught sight of a figure which at once drove from his mind all thoughts of Blake, and restored in its fullest intensity all those mysterious feelings which he had described in narrating his story of the apparition. It was a female figure. The face was thin, and pallid, and careworn; the eyes were large and dark, and rested for a moment upon him. The very first glance showed him that this was the face of his "apparition" in very truth, and beyond a doubt; and so profound was the shock that, for a moment, as he stared back, he felt rooted to the spot.

But about this apparition there were certain peculiarities of an important kind. The face was precisely the same—the same pallor—the same deep, dark eyes—the same fixed, unfathomable gaze; yet in other things a change was observable. The expression was no longer one of reproach; it was rather one of sudden terror—a terror like his own; the glance was not long and sustained—it was rather furtive and hasty. Moreover, though this apparition was dressed in black, it was not the costume of a nun; it was simple and sober, yet it was the fashion of the day; and this change from the weird and unfamiliar, to the commonplace and familiar, of itself went far to steady Kane Hellmuth's nerves, and prevent him from sinking into that lamentable weakness which had characterized his former meetings with this mysterious being.

He stopped there for a moment, rooted to the spot, with his brain in a whirl, and all his former feelings overwhelming him; but the emotion was more short-lived than before, since these changes in the form and fashion and expression of the figure were noticed at once, and went far to reassure him. The figure threw one hasty, furtive look at him, and then, sharply turning the opposite corner, walked quickly up the street.

In an instant Kane Hellmuth started in pursuit. It was an irresistible fascination that drew him on. He was resolved now to do what he could to fathom this mystery that so long had troubled him. Every step that he took seemed

to bring back his presence of mind, and drive away those feelings of superstitious terror that had at first been thrown over his soul. Every step that he took seemed to show him that he was the stronger, and that the other was the weaker. Every thing was now on his side. Surrounding circumstances favored him. It was broad day. It was a public street, on which people were passing to and fro, and the ordinary every-day traffic was going on. There was no chance here for any of that jugglery which might deceive the senses; or any of those associations of night, and gloom, and solemnity, which on the last memorable meeting had baffled his search. Moreover, the face of the Figure was turned away. It was Its back that he saw. The Figure moved rapidly on, yet not so rapidly but that he could keep up with It, or even overtake It. It seemed to him that he was the pursuer, and the Figure the pursued, and that now, if he followed vigorously, all might be at last revealed.

Kane Hellmuth thus followed from one corner to the next. Then the Figure crossed the street to the opposite corner. He followed. Then the Figure turned, and fixed its eyes again on Kane Hellmuth. It was the same glance as before, intensified. It was a sudden glance, and one, too, which showed signs of unmistakable fear. Yet the face was the same—it was the face of his apparition—the face that had haunted him for years—the face that was associated with the brightest and the darkest hours of all his life. The look of fear was something new, yet it seemed to heighten his own resolution and strengthen his own heart; for now it seemed as though the tables had been turned, and all the fear which once had been felt by him had passed over to the other.

The Figure now walked on faster. Evidently It was trying to fly from him. He himself increased his pace. Easy enough was it for him to keep up even with this utmost exertion of the other. In a race like this he was the superior. He saw it; he felt it. There was nothing of the supernatural here. Could it indeed be? Was she, then, alive? But, if so, why did she fly? What did she mean? It was a living woman that was before his eyes, fearing him, flying from him, overcome with human terror.

The woman hurried on. Kane Hellmuth hurried after. Suddenly she hailed a passing cab. The cab drew up at the sidewalk. The cabman got down to open the door. Already the woman's hand was on the door, and her foot was on the curb, when Kane Hellmuth reached the spot. He did not stand on ceremony. Too deep was his anxiety to learn the truth of this matter for him to observe any of the petty courtesies of life. He was not rude or rough; he was simply earnest, and in his desperate earnestness, and in his deep longing to know all, he laid his hand suddenly and sharply upon the woman's arm.

She turned hastily and stared at him, showing a face that was filled with an anguish of terror. Her lips moved, but no sound escaped them. Then, while Kane Hellmuth's hand still clutched her arm, a low moan escaped her, she reeled, and would have fallen if he had not caught her in his arms.

The cabman stood by observing this scene calmly. It was no business of his. He did not understand it, of course, but then it was often his fortune to be a witness of unintelligible scenes like this.

Meanwhile, the woman hung senseless on Kane Hellmuth's arms. For a moment he was puzzled what to do. Where was her residence? He did not know. Where should he take her? No apparition was this—this being of flesh and blood of whose weight he was sensible; but rather a living human being. But oh! who—and why had she sought him out?

He did not hesitate long. He lifted her into the cab, and then, getting in himself, he gave the cabman his own address. The cabman drove there at once, and, as it was not far away, they soon reached the place. Kane Hellmuth then took the woman in his arms, and carried her up to his own apartments. Then he sent up the women of the house, and waited the result.

The usual restoratives were applied, and the woman came out of her senselessness. She looked wildly around, and for some time was unable to comprehend her situation. Then a sudden look of terror came over her face, and she began to implore the women to let her go.

The women did not know what to say. Kane Hellmuth had hurriedly informed them that he had found her fainting in the street, and this they told her.

"Then I am not a prisoner here?" said the woman, eagerly.

"A prisoner!" exclaimed one of the attendants; "mon Dieu! no, madame. How is that possible? You may go when and where you please; only you must rest a few moments. It was a very kind gentleman who brought you here, and sent us up."

The woman gave a low sigh of relief, and sunk back again. She had been placed on the sofa in Kane Hellmuth's room. She was young, and seemed to have suffered much. She was evidently a lady.

Suddenly she roused herself.

"Who brought me here?" she asked, abruptly.

"Monsieur Hellmuth," said the attendant, pronouncing the name as well as she could.

"Hailmeet," repeated the lady, thoughtfully.

"Would you like to see him—perhaps he can explain — that there is nothing to fear."

"I am not a prisoner, then?" said the lady, earnestly.

"Oh, no—a prisoner? Mon Dieu! impossible!"

"And you are not employed to detain me?"

"Mon Dieu! but mademoiselle is raving—that is a thing altogether impossible. But you must see the good Monsieur Hellmuth."

With these words the woman who had spoken left the room, and informed Kane Hellmuth that the young lady had come to her senses; telling him also, what she had said. Her words excited surprise in Hellmuth's mind, but he was eager to know all, and so he at once entered the room. The woman followed him, and waited there, together with the other attendant.

Kane Hellmuth looked earnestly at the pale face before him, and the lady raised her large, dark, melancholy eyes to his face, and regarded him with equal earnestness, though in her look there was an anxious scrutiny and timid inquiry. But the face that she saw seemed to have no terror for her now, and the first look of fear gave place to one of mournful entreaty.

"Oh, sir," said she, in English, "you are an Englishman; you cannot be capable of injuring one who never harmed you! I have suffered enough, and why I do not know."

"He laid his hand suddenly and sharply upon the woman's arm."—Page 122

At this, Kane Hellmuth felt bewildered. This was, indeed, a strange address from her. He said nothing for a few moments, but regarded her with a solemn face, and a look in which there was nothing save tenderness and longing.

"You do not seem to know me," said he, at length, in a mournful tone.

"I do not," said the lady. "I never saw you before to-day."

"Are you not Clara Ruthven?" asked Kane Hellmuth, in a tremulous voice.

The lady shook her head.

"Is it all a mistake, then?" cried Kane Hellmuth, in a voice that was a wail of despair. "Are you not my Clara? Are you not Clara Mordaunt, who—"

He was interrupted by the lady. At the mention of the name of Clara Mordaunt she started from the sofa to her feet, and stared at him in amazement.

"Clara Mordaunt!" she exclaimed. "Clara Mordaunt! Who are you? What do you know about Clara Mordaunt? Clara Mordaunt!" she repeated, and again the frightened look came to her face. "Oh, sir, if you are in league with those who have so cruelly wronged me, have pity on me! Do not, oh, do not detain me! Let me go. My life is wretched enough, and my only hope is to have my freedom till I die."

"Answer me this," said Kane Hellmuth, in a hoarse voice, which was tremulous still with deepest emotion. "I am no enemy; I have no evil designs; if you are a stranger, after all, you have nothing to fear from me; if you are in trouble, I swear I will do what I can to help you, but only answer me. If you are not Clara Ruthven, she who was born Clara Mordaunt, in Heaven's name who are you, and why have you appeared before me in so many places?"

"I have never appeared before you," said the lady. "I never saw you before. You ask after Clara Mordaunt. I am not Clara Mordaunt. Clara Mordaunt is dead. She died ten years ago. Why do you ask me if I am Clara Mordaunt?"

"Dead!" repeated Kane Hellmuth, in a hollow voice. "Well, that is what every one says, but I swear I never saw in any human face such a resemblance to any other human face as there is in yours to the face of Clara Mordaunt! But what do you mean by saying that you never appeared to me before?

Were you not at Père-la-Chaise Cemetery?"

"Never," said the lady. "I never saw you before."

"What! were not you the one that I saw at Notre-Dame, in the rail-cars, in the Boulevard where—"

"You are utterly mistaken," said the lady; "I never saw you before."

"Have you not been here all these years, appearing and disappearing like a phantom, reminding me of one who you say is dead?"

"Years!" said the lady. "I don't understand you. I have been in Paris only three months, though they seem like many, many years. But oh, sir! you look like one who would not willingly do a wrong. Your face cannot belie you. Will you tell me what you mean by asking after Clara Mordaunt?—what you mean by calling her Clara Ruthven, and tell me what she is to you?"

"To me? O Heavens!" said Kane Hellmuth, "she was so much to me that now it is better not to talk about it. But did you know her? Will you tell me how it is that you have such an extraordinary likeness to her? If you are not Clara Mordaunt, who are you?"

"My fright must have been a mistake," said the lady, looking at Kane Hellmuth with greater interest, "and I can only hope that it has been so. I will tell you who I am, for oh, sir, I think I may trust you. This Clara Mordaunt that you speak of was my own sister, and my name is Inez Mordaunt."

"Her sister! Inez Mordaunt!" cried Kane Hellmuth, in amazement. "Why, she said that her sister Inez was dead!"

The lady stared at him.

"Dead? Did she say that? Then she must have been deceived, like me, all her life. For I, too, lived a life that was all surrounded by deceit, and it was only an accident that revealed to me the truth. I was brought up to believe that my name was Wyverne, and—"

But here Kane Hellmuth interrupted her.

"Wyverne!" he cried. "Wyverne! Inez Wyverne! Are you Inez Wyverne? Oh, Heavens! what is the meaning of all this?"

He stopped, overwhelmed by a rush of emotion consequent upon the mention of that name. He recalled the story of Blake, and Blake's love for this girl, who had thus so strangely come across his way. He recalled his conversation with Father Magrath. He had heard from him that Inez Wyverne had been left penniless, but how had she come here? Why did she take the name of Mordaunt? How was it that she called herself the sister of Clara Mordaunt, his wife? Who was the other Miss Mordaunt whom he had gone to London to see? Was she, too, a sister of his lost Clara? That this Inez was her sister might be proved by her extraordinary resemblance, which had led him to identify her with the apparition; and yet it was impossible that she could be identical with that other mysterious one, for she had disclaimed it. What was the meaning of this?

Such were the thoughts of Kane Hellmuth as he stood there staring at this lady whom he had brought here, and who, whether Inez Wyverne or Inez Mordaunt, was equally inexplicable in that bewilderment of his thoughts.

CHAPTER XXX.

THE STORY OF INEZ.

THE presence of the attendants acted as a check upon Kane Hellmuth, and he was quick to perceive that this was neither the time nor the place for that full explanation which he wished to have. There was much to be said on both sides, and he longed to hear her story, both for his own sake, and also for the sake of his friend to whom this Inez was so dear. Such a thing would, however, have to be postponed until another occasion.

Instead, therefore, of pouring forth that volley of questions which his first impulse prompted him to do, he checked himself, and began to apologize for bringing her to his room, on the ground that it was an utter mistake, which would have to be explained elsewhere. He informed her that the cab was still waiting, and would take her to her lodgings whenever she wished it. Inez at once accepted the offer with evident gratitude; the fear that Kane Hellmuth had but recently inspired was all gone, and she seemed to regard him as one who might be a friend. With her fear much of her weakness had passed, and she was able to walk to the cab without assistance.

Kane Hellmuth accompanied her, and Inez seemed to acquiesce in his offer of companionship with evident satisfaction. As the cab drove off, nothing was said for a few minutes, when at length Kane Hellmuth burst forth abruptly with—

"All this is the most astonishing thing to me that can be imagined. When you mentioned the name of Wyverne just now, I at once recognized you as one of whom I had heard very much from an intimate friend of mine, who also, I think, is a friend of yours— Dr. Basil Blake."

"Dr. Basil Blake!" exclaimed Inez, eagerly. "Do you know him?"

She spoke eagerly and with agitation, and her whole manner showed that Blake was not without interest in her eyes.

"Basil Blake," said he, "is my intimate friend. On his return from Villeneuve, he informed me of what occurred there."

Inez looked at him earnestly.

"Are you his friend? Then, perhaps, he mentioned your name to me. He used to talk about his friend Kane Hellmuth."

"I am Kane Hellmuth."

At this, Inez looked at him more earnestly than ever, and her face was overspread with a sudden expression of inexpressible relief.

"Oh, how glad I am!" she said, simply and innocently. "Oh, I cannot tell you, Mr. Hellmuth, how very, very glad I am. Oh, how fortunate for me this meeting is! You cannot imagine what I have suffered. This very day I have been in the darkest despair. Oh, how glad, how glad I am!—And is Dr. Blake here too?"

"Well, no—not just now," said Kane Hellmuth, with some hesitation. "He left here a while ago for the south, on business."

"Oh, how glad I am!" said Inez again, speaking half to herself, and in a tone of such innocent and unfeigned joy that Kane Hellmuth felt touched to the heart; and it seemed to suggest to him long and severe suffering on her part, out of which she now saw some means of escape by his assistance.

This assistance he hastened to promise her, and not long after they reached their destination. The lodgings of Inez were not very far from the place where he had first seen her, and were of a kind that seemed suitable to genteel poverty. The room into which he followed her seemed like a general parlor, and formed one of a suite on the second floor, hired, as she informed him, by the lady with whom she was lodging.

Situated as these two were with regard to one another, there was very much to be asked and to be answered on both sides; nor was it until several interviews that each became acquainted with the position of the other. The position of Inez was one of so painful a character, that she was eager to tell it all to Kane Hellmuth, so as to get his assistance; and he on his part was equally anxious to tell her his story, partly to explain his late conduct, and partly from the hope that she might give him some information about the mysterious apparition which had so troubled him. As far as that was concerned, however, Inez was not able to throw any light on it whatever, and indeed she knew less of that "Clara Mordaunt," whom she considered her sister, than Kane Hellmuth himself. There was no way in which Inez could account for the apparition. If it was ever explained, the explanation would have to be made in some way quite irrespective of her; and her story showed that she could not have been in Paris at all while those mysterious visitations were occurring.

Her own story, however, was one of such an extraordinary character, that it at once aroused his warmest sympathies, and occupied most of his thoughts. It was not all told at once, but in the course of various interviews; and, without reporting any conversation *verbatim*, it may be best to narrate that story now:

When Inez landed in France, she took the first train for Paris, and for some time had no other thought than to hurry on without delay, so as to see her father as soon as possible. At length she began to feel troubled about the meeting that was before her, and wondered how, in the confusion of a railway-station, she could recognize her father's messengers, or be recognized by them. Her anxiety to reach her father increased her anxiety in this respect, and at length she had to tell her troubles to her maid Saunders. She herself could not speak French very well, but Saunders could speak it as well as English, and no sooner had she learned the anxiety of her mistress, than she hastened to soothe her. She promised to speak to the guard, and did so to such good purpose that this functionary came in person to Inez, and with many gesticulations assured her that he himself

9

would look out for her friends, and see that they should find her. Reassured by this, Inez got the better of her anxiety in this respect, and at length reached Paris.

As the train stopped, Inez felt a strange sense of desolation in her heart. She was weak, too, and weary, for she had travelled all night, and it was a raw, gray, dismal morning. She looked out into the station-house, and saw the twinkling lights, and the crowd moving to and fro. The consciousness that she was in a foreign country, without a home, came to her with oppressive power; nor could even the thought of her father, with which she tried to console herself, enable her to overmaster this sense of loneliness. There was also a time of waiting which seemed unusually long. She had anticipated an earnest welcome, but she was allowed to wait without any, and thus at the very outset her heart sank, and she felt herself a prey to strange, dark fears and forebodings.

At length, Saunders directed her attention to an advancing figure. This one was preceded by the guard, and looked as though he might be the messenger sent to receive her. As he drew near, Inez could see his face quite plainly; for it was turned toward the cars, over which his eyes wandered as though in search of some one. The approach of this messenger might at another time have quelled her rising fears; but the aspect of this man had in it something which Inez did not find at all reassuring; and the face on which she expected to see an air of respectful, if not eager, welcome, had in it now nothing which was not repellent. It was a commonplace face—a coarse and vulgar face—not the face of a man who might be a friend of Bernal Mordaunt. It did not seem bad or vicious; it was simply coarse and commonplace. Nor was the man a servant or a footman, for he was dressed as a priest, and looked like one who might claim the right to associate with Bernal Mordaunt on equal terms. But, though his garb was clerical, there was nothing of the priest either in his face, or attitude, or manner; and the cloth had in this instance failed most completely to contribute its usual professional air to the wearer. Such, then, was the man who came here to receive Inez.

Saunders had already risen, and went outside to speak to the priest. Inez followed shortly after. The priest introduced himself as Père Gounod, and spoke a few words of conventional welcome. Inez was not sufficiently familiar with French to judge whether he was a man of education or not; but there was a certain clumsiness in his manner, and coarseness of intonation, which made her think that he could not be; yet how could she judge? Still, this was a thing of no moment, and her thoughts soon reverted to the one uppermost idea of her mind—her father; and all the deep anxiety which she felt was manifest in her voice as she asked after him.

The priest looked at her with a quick, furtive glance, and then looked away.

"He is very low," said he, slowly.

There was something in his face which frightened Inez. She would have asked more, but could not. She was afraid of hearing the worst. The priest said no more, but turned, and, with a silent gesture, led the way to the carriage. Inez followed. Saunders also followed. On reaching the carriage, Inez saw that it was a close cab. The priest held the door open. She got in, and was followed by Saunders. The priest then went to see about the luggage, and, after a short absence, returned. He then got on the box with the driver.

After about half an hour's drive, the cab stopped. On getting out, Inez found herself in front of a large and gloomy edifice. She followed the priest, who led the way in through a small door, and up a flight of steps, and along a gallery which looked out into a courtyard. He then opened a door which led into a room. It was meagrely furnished, the floor was tiled, and there was a depressing gloom about it which deepened the melancholy despondency that Inez had all along experienced.

The priest motioned toward a sofa, and asked Inez to sit down.

"But I wish to see papa," said she, anxiously.

"I will go and see," said the priest. "You must wait."

Saying this, he left the room. This strange proceeding seemed unaccountable to Inez, and only increased her fears. He was not long gone; but the time of his absence seemed long indeed to her. She did not sit down, but stood, where he had left her, motionless and terrified, and there he found her on his return.

"Will you not sit down?" he asked.

"But I want to see papa," said Inez.

"One moment," said the priest. "Sit down—I have something to say."

At this strange delay Inez grew more agitated than ever. The priest seated himself. She could not move. She stood thus, pale and trembling, and looked at him fixedly.

"I have something to say," repeated the priest, "and I am very sorry to have to say it."

He paused, and leaned his elbow on his knee, bending forward as he did so, with his eyes on the floor. Thus Inez no longer saw his face, but only the top of his head. Now, in moments of the deepest anxiety, and even anguish, it is strange how often the attention is attracted by even trivial circumstances. It was so with Inez at this time. Full of anguish, with her soul racked by suspense, a prey to the gloomiest forebodings, waiting with something like despair the communication of the priest, her eyes, as they rested upon him, noticed this one thing in the midst of all her agitation and her despair, and that was that this priest had no tonsure. His hair was a thick, bushy mass all over his head; and the characteristic mark of his sacred office was altogether wanting. She noticed this, and it was with an additional shock that she did so. Yet it was not till afterward that she learned to place any stress on this one fact, and see it in its full significance. At that time the shock passed away, and yielded to her uncontrollable anxiety about her father.

"Why don't you say what you have to say?" cried Inez at length. "I want to see papa."

The priest raised his head.

"I wish," said he, in a low voice, and speaking very slowly, "to break it as gently as possible."

Every one of these words was terrible to Inez. To such a saying as this, following after such strange actions, there could be but one meaning, and that one meaning must be the worst. Yet, so great was her terror at hearing this, that she dared not ask another question. She stood as before, with her eyes fixed on him, while he kept his eyes averted.

"I did not tell you before," said the priest. "I wished to prepare you. I wished to do it gradually. I must prepare you for the worst—the very worst."

He paused.

Inez stared at him.

"He—is—dead!" she faltered, in a scarce audible voice.

The priest looked at her with a significant glance, and in silence.

"When?" asked Inez, speaking with a great effort, but in a faint voice.

"Three days ago," said the priest.

Inez gave a low moan, and staggered toward the sofa. Saunders sprang up and assisted her. She sank down upon it, and, burying her face in her hands, remained silent and motionless, yet an occasional shudder showed the suffering of her mind. Nor was this suffering without a cause. True, it was not like losing a father whose love she had always known; but still, ever since the discovery of the portraits, she had thought much of Bernal Mordaunt, and had conceived for him all a daughter's feelings. She had recalled many of the reminiscences of early childhood. Above all, his last letter to her had thrown around these feelings additional strength and tenderness. During her journey these feelings had increased, and all her life and all her hope seemed to refer to the meeting with him which she was seeking. Now, in an instant, all this tender love was blighted, and all this eager hope made forever vain. The blow was a severe one, and Inez wellnigh sank under it.

The priest looked at her with close observation, but with no particular sympathy. Thus far he had been somewhat embarrassed while subject to the searching gaze of Inez. Now, when that gaze was removed, and her head buried in her hands, he was able to speak with freedom.

"He died three days ago," said the priest, speaking somewhat less slowly than before, and in what may be described as a wary and vigilant manner; watching Inez all the while most attentively—"three days ago. He wrote a long letter—a very long letter—too long a letter, indeed—to you, asking you to come here. Well, after that he fainted. It was an hour before he revived. Then we knew—and he knew, too—that he was—dying! But there was nothing to be done, for he was beyond hope. . . . Well," continued the priest, after a pause, in which his eyes never removed themselves from Inez, who still remained with her head bowed down and buried in her hands—"well, then the poor man called for writing-materials again. We sup-

plied him with them. We raised him upon his bed, so that he might be in a position to write. He took the pen, and at first could hardly hold it. But at length he made a great effort, and wrote about a page. That was all that he was able to do, and, in my opinion, it was just one page too much; but we had to indulge him, for he was so eager about it—and what can you do with a dying man? Well, that was too much. He fell back exhausted, and never spoke one word more. In two hours all was over, and he had barely life and sense enough to receive the viaticum. That was three days ago. You received his letter, and waited till you could leave, and have spent this third day in travelling here. This brings you here at the close of the third day. It is a pity that you had not come before, for he loved you dearly. But still his last thoughts were of you, and his last words, too, for the letter that he wrote was for you."

At this Inez started up.

"For me!" she exclaimed. "Is there—did he leave any message for me?"

"The letter that I have been telling you about was for you."

"Have you got it?" cried Inez, eagerly.

"It is here—for you—if you wish to see it," said the priest.

"Oh, let me have it—let me see it!" said Inez, in a tone of mournful entreaty.

"You shall see it, of course," said the priest. "It is for you, and it is waiting for you. It is a pity that you have not come in time for something better than a letter. The poor Abbé Mordaunt would have been greatly cheered. We urged him to send for you before, but he was full of hope that he would recover and be able to go to you. He was unwilling to put you to the trouble of a journey. He never knew how ill he was till the last, and then it was too late. He came home from his mission with broken health. He allowed himself no rest. An affair at Villeneuve agitated him greatly, and preyed on his mind. It was something that occurred there, and other things that he heard of after his arrival here. He sank quite rapidly, poor man! And all the time he persisted in the hope that he would recover. At last the doctor told him the truth, and then he wrote for you. But it was too late. The effort of writing hastened the end, and so, as I said, he did not live out that day. Still he left his last instructions for you, and I have kept that letter to be given into your own hands. And here it is. I took it from his own hands, and put it in this envelop, and wrote your name on it."

Saying this, the priest drew forth a letter from his pocket and handed it to Inez. She took it with a quick, nervous, eager grasp. The envelop bore the address in a strange hand, simply—

"*Inez Mordaunt.*"

This the priest had explained. But this she did not notice. All her thoughts were turned to the letter itself—the last words of her father, now lost forever—her father, found so strangely, lost so suddenly. With a trembling hand she tore open the envelop, and the last words of that father lay before her eyes.

CHAPTER XXXI.

IN PRISON.

INEZ tore open the letter and read the following:

"MY DEAREST DAUGHTER: I have just written to you to come to me. It is too late. I am dying. I should have gone on to you. I have scarcely strength enough left to write this. There are many things which I wish to explain. But this explanation cannot now be given by me. My beloved child, I leave you, and forever, but I do not leave you friendless. I have one good and tried friend—the friend of a life; and, though I must leave you, I am able to console myself with the thought that you will be cared for. My dear friend, true and tried, Kevin Magrath, I appoint as your guardian. He will be to you, my daughter, another guardian. He will love the child of his friend as his own child. Trust in him. Love him as your father. He will do for you all that I could have done. He will tell you all about me, and about that past which has been so dark to you. You will have a great grief, but do not give way to it, my child. Trust in Heaven and in my friend Kevin Magrath—father to fatherless—go long journey—never again which—I have —formerly—in vain—mother—just the—last words—not at all—mission—broken—faint—wishes — love—Kevin—Kevin Magrath—forever—father—"

There was no signature. The letter ended with several lines of undecipherable writing, in which a few words were here and there discernible — words without connection and without meaning.

Inez read it all over many times, and was troubled in soul. It was not what she had expected. It was a letter that excited dark fears and anxieties. The circumstantial account which the priest had given her did not at all reassure her. For some time past she had been living in an atmosphere of mystery, and had learned to indulge in a suspicious habit of mind; and so it was that this letter added vague and alarming suspicions to the anxieties which it caused.

All those fears, anxieties, and suspicions, derived their origin from one name mentioned there. It was a name that was mentioned with emphasis—the name of a man that she had learned to regard as an enemy—and yet this man was indicated to her by this letter as her father's true and tried friend, and urged upon her trust and affection. He was to be her guardian. How was it possible for her to read such a letter as this without the darkest suspicions?

For the present, however, these gave way to a yearning desire to see, if possible, all that was left of the man whom she had regarded as her father—her father discovered so strangely, yet lost so suddenly. Was it too late for that? She turned once more to the priest:

"May I not see him?" she asked, in a tremulous voice.

"See him?" repeated the priest.

"Yes," said Inez, "my papa. If I could only see him—one last look—"

"See him!" repeated the priest, in a strange tone—"see him!"

He hesitated and looked away.

"If I only could," said Inez, "if it is not too late."

"Too late?" said the priest, shaking his head. "Alas! it's too late—too late. You've said it. That's what it is. Too late—yes, too late—too late."

"What do you mean?" asked Inez, despairingly. "Can I not have at least the sad satisfaction of seeing him as he is now?"

The priest looked at her with his usual furtive glance.

"But he's gone!" said he.

" ' Buried ! ' "—Page 129.

"Gone!" repeated Inez, in a bewildered voice.

"Yes, gone," said the priest.

"But how?" said Inez. "What do you mean?"

"Buried!" said the priest, in a solemn voice.

"Buried!"

Inez repeated the word, but was so overwhelmed by the thought that she did not seem to know what it meant. "Buried!" she said again, in a low voice, as if to herself, and, as she said this, she shrank back with a frightened look.

Buried!

"It was three days ago that he died," said the priest. "He was buried this morning. You can never see him again."

At this overwhelming intelligence Inez stared at the priest with an expression in her face that seemed like horror. Then she looked wildly around. Then she once more bowed her head, and this time she burst into a torrent of tears. She had reached the lowest point in that abyss of sorrow which she had been descending, and there she found that the last faint consolation was denied her. The faithful Saunders rushed to her aid. The priest sat motionless watching her. But to Inez the faithful Saunders and the priest were both alike objects of indifference, for all her thoughts were now turned toward the sharpness of this sudden bereavement and the desolation of her present state.

For a long time Inez remained in that condition, overwhelmed by grief and racked by convulsive sobs that shook her frame. The priest watched her still with that vigilant gaze which he directed toward her whenever her eyes were not turned toward him. Sometimes he looked toward the faithful Saunders, and the eyes of the faithful Saunders met his; and, as the eyes of the good priest and of the faithful Saunders met, there seemed to be some kind of intelligence between them. But, if there was any such intelligence, it satisfied itself just then with a silent glance, and deferred any expression in words until a more convenient opportunity.

The blow which had thus fallen upon Inez was one from which she could not readily recover. Rousing herself at length from her first prostration, her only desire was for seclusion, where she might give herself up more entirely to her gloomy thoughts. The faith-

ful Saunders accompanied her to the place, which was pointed out to them by an old woman whom the priest sent, and who appeared to be a combination of char-woman, chamber-maid, and lady's-maid. The room to which Inez was thus shown had a greater air of comfort than the other, yet still it was furnished in a scanty manner, and the tiled floor, with one or two small rugs here and there, had a cheerless air. Here Inez found her luggage, and the faithful Saunders proceeded to open her trunks and arrange her things. But Inez paid no attention to her. She flung herself upon a couch, and the faithful Saunders, finding that she was not needed, finished her task, and silently withdrew.

Inez ate nothing that day, and slept none on the following night. In truth, her position was one which might have seemed gloomy indeed, even to a more sanguine temper. There was about it a dreadful sense of desolation, from which she could not escape. It seemed to her that she had lost her father, her home, her country, and every friend that she ever had. In her father's last letter she had read that which seemed to her to put a climax upon all her woes. Before that she had been simply friendless and in exile, but now she found herself handed over to the guardianship of one of whom she had learned to think with abhorrence. She could not forget the letter which had struck down Hennigar Wyverne at Villeneuve, and that this letter had been written by Kevin Magrath.

For several days she gave herself up completely to deep despondency; and, so strongly did it prey upon her spirits, that at length she became quite ill. In this condition she remained for several weeks, and the profound dejection into which she had fallen made her completely indifferent about her recovery. During this time the faithful Saunders nursed her. At length her youth and vigorous constitution triumphed over her illness, and the lapse of time familiarized her mind so much to her new position that, in the ordinary course of things, it began to appear less intolerable. Soon she grew stronger, and the buoyancy of her spirits led her to indulge rather in hopes for the best. At length she was able to go out of her room, and walk up and down the apartments and out into the gallery.

The house was old and gloomy. There was a small court-yard enclosed by its walls.

On the side where she lived was an open gallery, from which her *suite* of rooms opened. No one else seemed to be living in the house except the priest and the old woman, with herself and the faithful Saunders. This last personage was as devoted as ever. Of the priest she saw but little, and of the old woman still less. She was thus left very much to herself, nor did the solitude seem unpleasant. On the contrary, it was rather congenial to that pensive melancholy which had set in after the first outburst of grief and despair.

At length, one day, while thinking over her lonely condition, she reflected that there was one friend of hers in Paris who might be glad to know that she was here. This was Dr. Blake, whose place in her regards had not grown less prominent, in spite of the mournful events of the time that had elapsed since she left Villeneuve. It came to her like a very pleasant thought, and the idea occurred that, if she should go out, it might not be impossible to see him somewhere, or be seen by him. Her loneliness made this one friend seem now more valuable than he had seemed before; and she had no sooner thought of this than she at once sought to put it into execution. Accordingly, she dressed herself for a walk, and was about to go out alone, when Saunders respectfully interfered, and implored her not to do so. To the wondering inquiry of Inez, "Why not?" the faithful Saunders pleaded her weakness, and the dangers of the Paris streets. Finally, Inez consented to take a drive instead of a walk.

The carriage which took her out was not the most cheerful kind of a one. .It was the same close cab which had brought her from the railway-station. The faithful Saunders went with her, though Inez at first seemed rather inclined to go alone. But this seemed so to wound the affectionate heart of the faithful one that Inez good-naturedly consented to let her go.

The drive did not result in any thing. On the whole, Inez felt very much disappointed in Paris. She had heard so much about its splendor that she had expected to find something very different. She mentioned several places whose names were familiar, to which she wished to be driven, but, on seeing them, she found that they did not come up to her expectations. She was driven through a number of narrow streets, finally along a wide but bare-looking place, then into the narrow streets again; then out into the wide place, until she was thoroughly wearied, and did not care to continue her drive any longer.

After this she went out on almost every fine day, and with the same result. Saunders always went with her; she always saw the same commonplace streets; she never saw any one who looked like Dr. Blake.

And this was Paris!

She could not help feeling amazed at the reputation of so mean a city!

Once or twice she thought of shopping. But from this she was prevented by a circumstance which was at once paltry and humiliating—she had no money. The letter of Bernal Mordaunt had told her not to bring more than was needed for her trip, and the small amount which she happened to have in her purse had been exhausted. Even had she needed more, she would not have known at that time whom to ask for it. She could not ask Bessie. Mr. Wyverne, who had always before supplied her liberally, was dead; and she did not know any one else to whom she could apply. For this cause she had left her home thus ill-supplied with money, and now she felt, for the first time in her life, the helplessness of poverty.

It was this poverty, together with her loneliness and friendlessness, that brought the questions before her, over and over, What was she to do? What would become of her? How long would this life go on? She herself could do nothing, and did not know how she ever could do any thing. The world of the past was lost forever to her.

These drives at length became tedious to Inez. She did not like to be always accompanied by Saunders, and the sense of restraint which she felt in the close cab was irksome. She felt strong enough to go alone by herself, and one day resolved to do so. She simply informed the faithful Saunders that she was going out for a short walk, and wished to be alone. Saunders saw by her manner that she was resolved, and said nothing, but meekly acquiesced. Inez was soon ready, and went out into the gallery on her way down.

At the end of the gallery was a door which opened into a stairway. To the surprise of Inez, this door was locked. She had often before noticed that it was closed, but, having not had any reason for trying it, she had never known that it was locked; and, on the occasion of her drives, it had always been open. Now, however, she was vexed to perceive that her plan for going out alone was attended with difficulties. She stood for some time knocking, but to no purpose; and at length concluded that it must be accidental, or rather that it rose from an excess of precaution on the part of the stupid old woman. In spite of this simple mode of accounting for such an unpleasant fact, Inez felt not only disappointed but also troubled; and a vague suspicion arose that her surroundings were not so satisfactory as they might be. There seemed to be too much surveillance. Some one was always with her. The faithful Saunders was a trifle too faithful. Of that personage she knew but little. She had been her maid for not over three months, and Inez had never thought of her personal peculiarities. She had been satisfied with the faithful performance of the duties which pertained to the responsible office of Saunders, and had never had occasion to think about her more deeply. And, though she tried to drive away the thought as ungenerous, she could not help fearing that the faithful Saunders might be watching over her from other motives than those of affectionate and loyal solicitude.

Inez waited all day for that door to open, but it did not. She sat with her things on. Saunders prepared lunch at the usual hour, but Inez was too indignant to touch it. At length, at about six in the evening, the old woman came up with dinner. The first impulse of Inez was to give her a sound rating, but this was repressed, and she contented herself with telling her about her disappointment, and directing her to have the door left open on the following day. At this, the old woman stared, but said nothing.

On the following day, however, the very same thing occurred, and Inez, who had again dressed herself for a walk, was unable to go. This time she could not restrain herself.

"There's something about this that I do not understand," said she to Saunders as she returned to her room. "Do you know what it means, Saunders?"

"Oh, no indeed, miss!" said Saunders; "me?—the idea!"

"Perhaps you can get the door open, or make them hear you, Saunders; you seem to have some understanding with these people."

At this Saunders rolled up her eyes.

"Me, miss! Me an understanding, that

never set eyes on them before in all my born days, and only follered you here to this town because you was wantin' me, and homesick now as I be in this gloomy den! Why, whatever you can mean, miss, beggin' your pardon, is more'n I can tell, and I only hope you don't see any thing in me that's underhand—for, if so, I maybe better go away."

At this Inez was startled. To lose Saunders would be too much. She had spoken too hastily. Her suspicions were wrong. She hastened, therefore, to smooth over the ruffled feelings of the faithful one, and Saunders subsided into her usual calm.

That evening at dinner the priest came in. This man had always been distasteful to Inez, but now was all the more so, since she could not understand what he was or what his intentions were. She had not forgotten that he had no tonsure; she did not believe that he could be a priest at all, and the suspicion that he was disguised was a most unpleasant one. On this occasion Inez at once informed him about the door, and told him that it must not occur again. Her tone was somewhat haughty, and she unconsciously adopted an air of command in addressing him.

The priest looked down, avoiding her eyes as usual.

"You are mistaken," said he; "you have gone out whenever you wished. The door is kept locked—on account of thieves—as there are so few servants—and the woman is so old and stupid."

"Very well," said Inez; "I wish to go out to-morrow, and I should like you to tell the old woman, so that she need not make any more of those stupid mistakes."

CHAPTER XXXII.

LIGHT ON THE SITUATION.

SAUNDERS had always been what is called a "faithful creature," and Inez had thus far found her quite invaluable. It was on the morning after her last interview with Gounod, however, that Inez made the discovery that there were limits to the fidelity of her maid. On that morning the faithful Saunders did not make her appearance; and Inez, after waiting an unusually long time, concluded that she must be ill. With this idea she went to see after her, but, on going to her room, found that no one was there. At this she felt annoyed; it looked like neglect, and she went immediately to the parlor in search of her maid, with the intention of administering a pretty sharp rebuke. Here, however, there were no signs of her; and a little further search showed her that she must have gone away. A sudden suspicion then darted across her mind. She hurried back to the maid's room. On entering, the suspicion was confirmed. The trunk was not there. Saunders must have left her, for she had taken her trunk.

This discovery was so painful that at first she felt quite stupefied. She could not imagine how Saunders could have done it, or how Gounod could have allowed it; but, for the present, her mind was less occupied with speculations about the mode of her departure than with painful efforts to imagine the cause of it. Saunders had always been so profuse in her protestations of fidelity, and so unremitting in her services, that this sudden departure seemed to give the lie to it all. It seemed like treachery, and the ease with which she had gone made it appear as though Gounod had connived at it.

In the midst of these thoughts the old woman arrived, and began her ordinary routine of duties, which consisted in laying the breakfast table and making the beds. Inez did not think it worth while to say any thing to her, but waited patiently until she had finished her task, when she asked her to tell Gounod that she would like to see him. In about half an hour, Gounod came.

To her story about the sudden departure of the maid, Gounod listened respectfully, and at once explained. He informed Inez that Saunders told him, the evening before, that she had received sudden intelligence of the dangerous illness of her mother, and would have to go and see her at once; and that he had got a cab, and taken her to the railway-station. The maid, he added, had told him that she did not like to tell her mistress about it; that she felt very badly at leaving her under such circumstances, and requested Gounod to make all necessary explanations. Finally, Gounod offered to procure her another maid, either a French or an English one, whichever she preferred.

Inez thanked him, but replied that for the present she did not feel inclined to have a

maid; and, after a few more words, Gounod withdrew.

Gounod's explanation had not altogether satisfied Inez. It was certainly a very natural and a very probable cause for the departure of Saunders; but still Inez could not help thinking that there was something else at the bottom of this. Either Saunders might have grown weary of her lonely life, or else, as she had thought before, she might be in some mysterious league with Gounod. The peculiar conduct of that personage had already seemed suspicious, and now it seemed still more so.

After all, however, in spite of a certain degree of inconvenience which resulted from it, Inez was not altogether sorry to be without a maid. She felt somewhat vexed at the manner in which Saunders had left her, and there were circumstances connected with her departure which excited vague suspicions in her mind; yet, on the whole, she was not particularly distressed about it. The fact is, the constant attendance of Saunders during the drives had grown to be excessively irksome. Her plea had been fidelity; but Inez had begun to suspect that it might be, at best, officiousness, and even something worse. At any rate, it had grown to be so unpleasant that Inez had about resolved not to go out again until she could go alone. The departure of Saunders seemed to leave her free to do this.

Accordingly, to prevent a recurrence of that mistake which had prevented her from going out the last time that she had tried, she sent for Gounod in the following morning. He came in a short time.

"I wish to go out to-day, at noon," said Inez; "and I want you to leave the key of that door with me, or, at least, to leave it open, so that I may not be prevented again by the stupidity of that old woman."

"Certainly," said Gounod. "At what time shall I have the cab ready?"

"I do not want the cab," said Inez. "I wish to go alone."

"Alone!" exclaimed Gounod, in surprise. "You must, of course, have some attendant."

"No," said Inez; "that is the very thing that I do not wish to have. I wish to go alone."

"Alone! But, Heavens! that is impossible. Why, you would be utterly lost. Paris is a labyrinth. You never were here before. You could never find your way back."

"Nonsense!" said Inez. "I shall take the address of the house, and, if I lose my way, I can come back in a cab."

"But, mademoiselle, you do not know the danger here in Paris to a young girl, a stranger, unattended. You do not know, or you would not ask this. It is impossible. Some one must accompany you. Here no young girl ever ventures out into the streets without her *chaperon*."

At these objections Inez felt irritated and suspicious. There might be greater restraint over girls in France than in England; but to her the idea of danger in the streets of Paris, in broad day, seemed preposterous. Yet she did not know exactly what to say in answer to Gounod's strong assertions. She felt eager to go, and throw off this restraint.

"I must go; I insist upon it," she said. "This imprisonment is too painful. I am always watched. I cannot breathe freely."

"Mademoiselle," said Gounod, "this is not England. Do not talk of a prison. It is a home, a French home; you are simply living like a French girl. Be patient, I pray you. The Abbé Magrath will soon be here. It is painful to me to be obliged to refuse the slightest request of yours, but this one is clearly unreasonable—and what can I do?"

"I cannot understand this at all," said Inez. "This danger is purely imaginary. I shall die if I am shut up this way."

"Mademoiselle, you need not be shut up. You may go out with your attendants."

"My jailers!" exclaimed Inez, indignantly.

"Pardon, mademoiselle, I must ask you not to use such language; it wounds me, and I cannot believe that you have that intention."

"I have no intention of giving pain to any one," said Inez, "but I must insist on being allowed some slight degree of liberty."

"Mademoiselle, I dare not," said Gounod. "What answer could I make to the good Abbé Magrath if any evil should happen to you?"

"The Abbé Magrath is nothing to me," said Inez, fretfully.

"Pardon, mademoiselle. Is he not your guardian? Even now he is engaged in your affairs; he is endeavoring to procure for you a happy home, and I dare not let you expose yourself to danger."

This was Gounod's position, and in this he was immovable. Inez remonstrated, but her remonstrances were in vain. He offered again to find attendants for her, but the offer was of course rejected; and, when he at length took his departure, Inez found herself the lonely occupant of this suite of rooms, which seemed to her already nothing else than a prison-house.

In her deep indignation at Gounod's strictness, and in the impatience with which she chafed at these prison-walls, she imagined a deeper purpose beneath all this than those commonplace precautions which Gounod professed; and, in the effort to find out what this purpose might be, she found herself looking beyond Gounod to that other one who seemed to her to be the real master here—the one whom Gounod quoted, and whom he called the good Abbé Magrath.

This Abbé Magrath was no other than Kevin Magrath. His name was always associated in her thoughts with those mournful events at Villeneuve, of which his letter to Hennigar Wyverne had been the cause. That letter had ever since been in her possession. Its language was familiar to her memory. She knew every word. It seemed singularly ill-omened, and gave the writer the character of a dark intriguer, to her mind—and a partner with Hennigar Wyverne in his crime, whatever that might have been. This was the opinion which she had formed of Kevin Magrath from that letter of his, and she had never ceased to wonder how it had happened that her dying father had intrusted her to the care of such a man. Either her father had been terribly mistaken in his friend, or she herself must have formed an utterly false opinion with regard to him.

Thoughts like these led her to examine these letters once more, so as to reassure herself about the nature of their contents, and to see if there would now appear in the letter of Kevin Magrath to Hennigar Wyverne all that dark and baleful meaning which she had seen in it at Villeneuve. In her eagerness to ascertain this, Inez brought forth this letter and the letters of Bernal Mordaunt from her pocket-book, where she kept them as her most precious possessions, and little else did that pocket-book contain. These she laid on the table before her, and then spread them all open.

And now, scarcely had she done this, when

an extraordinary thing attracted her attention, and a suspicion darted into her mind,
so wild, so terrible, that she started back in
horror, and for a moment averted her eyes.
Yet the thing was there visible enough, and
the suspicion was natural enough, for, as her
eyes hurried again to the papers, she saw it
plainly. It was this:

The writing of these letters was sufficiently
alike for them all to have been written by the
same man.

One of them was from Kevin Magrath to
Hennigar Wyverne. The others purported to
be from her father, Bernal Mordaunt, to herself, Inez Mordaunt, his child. Yet all these
might have been written by the same man.

What was the meaning of this?

Was it possible that Bernal Mordaunt had
been too weak to write, and had employed
Kevin Magrath as his amanuensis? It did
not seem possible to Inez, for the writing of
these letters evidently purported to be that
of Bernal Mordaunt himself, and no other;
and the characters which grew more and
more illegible toward the close were evidently
designed to indicate the weakness of a dying
man.

What was the meaning of this?

With a trembling hand, and a heart that
was now throbbing wildly with terrible excitement, she placed all the letters side by
side, confronted by the frightful fact that the
handwriting in all three was essentially the
same. So appalling was this discovery that
Inez sat motionless for some time, incapable
of movement, incapable almost of thought,
paralyzed by the tumult of feeling which now
agitated her heart. At length she rose to her
feet, and, with an unsteady step, and a face
more ghastly than it had been ever since the
first awful moment of her arrival here, she
tottered toward the window, and, sinking
down upon a seat there, she looked vacantly
and dreamily out. Only one thought was in
her mind, a question which she knew not how
to answer. What was the meaning of all
this?

Thus far Inez had allowed herself to be
borne onward by circumstances, and had accepted in good faith what others had told her,
whether by letter or by word of mouth. But
this last discovery had destroyed her blind
faith. It had roused the worst suspicions.
It had thrown her back upon her own reason,
even as the tragedy at Villeneuve had thrown

her; and thus, as the first shock passed, and
she gained more control over herself, she began to collect her thoughts, and to review her
whole position.

One of two things at length seemed evident to her:

First, the writing of Kevin Magrath and
that of Bernal Mordaunt may possibly have
been very much alike.

Secondly, Kevin Magrath may have forged
these letters.

These were the two alternatives before
her, unless indeed she could suppose that
Bernal Mordaunt had himself written that first
letter to Hennigar Wyverne in Kevin Magrath's name—a thing which, from the nature of the case, was of course impossible.

First, then, was it at all likely that Bernal
Mordaunt's handwriting was like Kevin Magrath's? It was certainly possible. How
could she know? Could she find out what
Bernal Mordaunt's handwriting was really
like? Scarce had she asked herself this question when the answer came. She could. In
an instant she recollected that little note accompanying the portraits addressed to Hennigar Wyverne years before. She had it yet.
The casket was in her trunk. She hurried to
the trunk and opened it. With a trembling
hand she took out the note, and laid it on the
table beside the other papers.

In that moment the answer was given.

The letter of Bernal Mordaunt to Hennigar Wyverne was in writing which had nothing in common with that of the letters pur-
porting to have been written by him to herself. Years of course might make a difference, but the difference here was not that
which is produced by time. The difference
lay in the essential style of writing. Bernal
Mordaunt's was round, Kevin Magrath's sharp
and angular. The one who had written these
letters in Bernal Mordaunt's name seemed to
Inez to have taken it for granted that she
knew nothing of Bernal Mordaunt's handwriting, and had therefore taken no pains to imitate it or to disguise his own. And this one
was proved to be Kevin Magrath's by his own
letter.

How he had managed to send these letters
at such a time Inez could not imagine. He
must have had some secret knowledge of her
movements, and of the state of her mind. He
must have known that she would be prepared
to receive Bernal Mordaunt's claim to be her

father. From whom could he have obtained this knowledge of her thoughts and feelings? Could Saunders have been his spy and agent? She recalled the noise which had startled her on the night when she searched the cabinet, and wondered now whether she had been watched then, and if the watcher could have been Saunders. It seemed probable. No one was so likely as her own maid to give to Kevin Magrath such information.

It seemed to Inez now that these letters in Bernal Mordaunt's hand were forged. And what followed? A whole world of results—results so important that her brain reeled under the complication of thoughts that arose. If these letters were forged, then Bernal Mordaunt could not have sent for her. He might never have been in Paris. He might even now be searching for her in England. More; she might not be his daughter after all. How could she now believe any thing? How could she tell who she was? Thus there arose in her mind a doubt as to herself and her personal identity, out of which grew fresh perplexity. But this soon passed. Deep down in her heart there was an instinct, undefinable yet strong, which forced her to believe that she was Inez Mordaunt, the daughter of Bernal Mordaunt. Deep down in her heart there was a yearning love which had quickened into active life at the first sight of those portraits; strange feelings and memories had been awakened by the sight of those faces; and her heart claimed them as mother and sister.

The motive that might have animated Kevin Magrath toward weaving around her this dark plot was an impenetrable mystery to her; but that he had woven a plot was now but too painfully evident. His aim seemed evidently to have been to entrap her into his own power through her own consent and co-operation; and, to accomplish this, he had been working most subtly and most assiduously. She recalled the language of his letter to Hennigar Wyverne, with reference to herself, that she (Inez) must be removed from Bernal Mordaunt's way. She now saw that the death of Wyverne had not changed Kevin Magrath's views, but had only caused him to take the matter into his own hands. She saw, too, that a plot of this kind, which had been so successful, and had only been discovered by an accident, could not have been carried out at all without the coöperation of

some of the inmates of the house—that one being, as she had already suspected, her maid Saunders.

In the midst of all this she saw that the death of her father in this house must be as false as the dying appeal to her. She considered the whole thing a deception. Affairs had been so managed that she had not caught one glimpse of her father either alive or dead. He had never been here! He was probably alive and searching for her, and she had fallen into the trap set for her. And now, since she was here in this trap, many little circumstances explained themselves — the stealthy journey from the railway-station, the strange behavior of the man Gounod, whom she had detected as not being really a priest, but only some common man in a priest's dress; the cautious drives out in a close cab; the locked doors; the constant watch—in all this also the faithful Saunders was implicated, for she, under the mask of devotion, had contrived to be with her always. And now here she was, in this deserted building, alone, a prisoner, under lock and key, with the man Gounod and the old woman as her jailers.

What could she do? Could she hope ever to escape?

Dark, indeed, the prospect seemed; nor could she, with all her most anxious thoughts, discern any way by which escape might be effected. This she would have to leave to circumstances in the future. Perhaps she might be removed from this to some other place where an opportunity might arise. She could not hope for more than this, and she could only make up her mind to be as cautious as possible, so as to avoid suspicion, and throw her enemies off their guard.

Night came, but it was a sleepless one to Inez. These new circumstances kept her in a state of constant excitement. Yet, though the discovery which she had made was in one sense so terrible, it was not without its alleviations. Out of this discovery followed an assurance to her, or at least a hope, that her father might yet be alive, that he might be even now seeking for her, and might at last find her. Bessie would see him; she would tell him all that she knew about this journey to Paris. Her father would come here; he would employ the aid of the police; he would at last rescue her. Thus she tried to hope, and this hope was the brightest thing that had occurred to her since her arrival here.

CHAPTER XXXIII.

A FLIGHT FOR LIFE.

INEZ had now but one thought, and that was escape. Her situation was one which, in spite of its difficulties, did not prevent hope altogether. She was a prisoner, it is true, but the departure of Saunders deprived her of what she now felt to be the most dangerous of all the spies around her. Gounod and the old woman remained, but neither of these seemed capable of keeping up any very effective or very vigilant system of spying. Kevin Magrath was not here, and he had probably been so confident in the security of this prison that he had sent Saunders away, or taken her away elsewhere.

All the thoughts of Inez for the next few days were directed toward her surroundings, in the endeavor to discover some way by which she might carry into execution her plan of escape. This endeavor, however, was not very successful. The house was uninhabited except by herself and her jailers. Her apartments were on one side; the windows of her rooms opened upon the gallery, and not upon any street. This gallery was also shut off from the rest of the house; and the door by which escape could be made from it was kept locked always. Twice a day the old woman unlocked it and made her appearance: once with breakfast, and also to make the beds and clear up the rooms; and a second time with dinner. Sometimes Gounod would look in during the day. His calls were, however, irregular, and Inez never took any notice of him.

Now, the policy of Inez was very simple, and at once the best and the easiest for her under the circumstances. She appeared quite content. She was wrapped up in herself. She never spoke one word, good or bad, to the old woman or Gounod. She ate her meals, slept at night, and, during the day, sat patiently in her room. Neither Gounod nor the old woman ever saw any sign of impatience in her. To neither of them did she ever hint that she was discontented or unhappy. She never asked to go out, or to drive out. As far as they could judge by outward appearances, she was content. They had every reason to believe that she had acquiesced in the plan of Kevin Magrath, and was now placidly waiting for his return so as

to accompany him to Rome. Gradually this conviction became strengthened in the minds of her jailers. The old woman, who at first used to look at her anxiously every time she came in, grew at length to accept her calm and peaceful face as a matter of course. Gounod became less vigilant, and his visits became more and more infrequent. Many little things, indeed, showed a relaxation of the strictness of their watch.

Meanwhile, though Inez thus succeeded in maintaining an outward calm so perfectly as to impose upon her watchful jailers, she herself was by no means free from agitation and tumultuous feelings. It was one long state of suspense, and all the harassing conditions of suspense were experienced by her to the uttermost. Yet, Inez came to this task not without preparation. She had already endured much; already had she learned to subdue her emotions, and exercise self-control. This new task was, therefore, the easier to her from the preparation which she had undergone. Under cover, then, of profound calm and placid content, she carried an incessant watchfulness, an eager, sleepless outlook, a vigilant attention to all that went on around her. Not a change took place in the action or demeanor of her jailers which she failed to notice; and these changes seemed to promise something.

Already she had placed all her hope in the door at the end of the gallery. Through that only could she hope to escape. Her gallery was too high above the court-yard for her to let herself down. There were no other ways by which she could leave this story on which she was, either to go up or down. Since, then, this door was the only pathway to liberty, it became the centre of all her thoughts and watchfulness.

It was with reference to this, then, that certain things were noticed by her.

The old woman came, as has been said, regularly twice a day. At first she was most painfully careful and guarded in all her actions. Upon passing through the gallery-door, she always spent about a quarter of an hour in locking it, putting the key in her pocket, and in trying the lock over and over, to see whether it was really locked or not. Then she would come to the parlor, and look in with painful and eager inquiry.

But the cool and patient indifference of Inez affected the old woman in spite of herself. Gradually, she spent less and less time at the door. This Inez noticed as she sat in the parlor. This parlor was near the door, and through the window, which opened out into the gallery, she could see it very plainly. The old woman would bring in breakfast, and then, while Inez was eating, she would go to her bedroom, at the other end of the gallery, to attend to her duties there.

Now, the decreasing vigilance of the old woman became a matter of immense importance to Inez, especially with regard to the gallery-door. Upon this all her attention became exclusively centred. Every day made some trifling change which was in her favor. The old woman at length turned the key in the lock quite carelessly, and once even left it in the lock and walked into the parlor, leaving it there. Something, however, put her in mind of it, and she returned and took it out. A few days passed, and the same thing occurred again. This was the thing for which Inez had been waiting. This was the thing for which she had been preparing. The old woman spread the breakfast, and never remembered about the key, and then, as usual, turned toward the bedroom. As she left the parlor, Inez started up, and, at the very moment when she disappeared through her bedroom-door, she stole with a swift yet stealthy step to the gallery-door. In an instant she unlocked it, snatched out the key, transferred it to the other side, and locked it there.

Thus the old woman herself was imprisoned.

But for Inez there was no time to lose. The old woman might discover what had happened at any moment; and, if Gounod was in the house, he would hear her cries. Inez, therefore, hurried along down a flight of steps that was before her swiftly, yet cautiously, and thus she reached the story below. Now there was a narrow corridor that ran for some distance, and at the end of this a flight of steps. Down this she also went in the same way. Reaching the bottom, she found herself on the ground-floor, inside a hall that ran across the building. At the bottom of this stairway there was a door that opened into the court-yard, and this lower hall ran back from this door to the front of the house, where there was another door.

Inez stopped at the foot of the stairs close by this back-door, and peeped cautiously forth

at the front-door. In an instant she drew back. It was the *conciergerie*. There was a man there. It was Gounod. The front-door was open, but Gounod sat there, smoking, reading a morning paper, barring her way to liberty.

For a moment she stood still, overcome by despair, but in another moment it passed. Then, with the same swift resolution and presence of mind which had marked all her acts thus far, she stepped noiselessly out through the door into the court-yard. The stairway concealed her from Gounod, and she made no noise to betray her movement.

This back-door was double; there was an inner and an outer one. The outer one was of massive construction; the inner one was lighter, and had windows in the sides.

One look around the court-yard showed that there was no avenue of escape there. The main portal was closed and locked. There was only one hope, and that was through the *conciergerie*. Perhaps Gounod would move. Perhaps he would go up-stairs, or out into the street, or into the court-yard; perhaps he might fall asleep; perhaps, if all else failed, she might make a mad rush for liberty.

One of these things might happen. It was necessary for her to hold herself in readiness. The space between the two doors seemed adapted for a hiding-place. Through the glass of the inner door she could watch the movements of Gounod; while the massive outer door, as it swung back, would shut her in and save her from detection. The moment that this thought suggested itself she acted upon it. Quietly pulling back the door, she slipped into the place, and then drew the door so as to shut herself in. The glass was dusty, but, by breathing upon it and rubbing it gently, she was able to watch the *conciergerie*, and see Gounod with sufficient distinction.

There she waited—watchful, motionless, scarce daring to breathe, looking with all her eyes, and listening with all her ears. She was straining her eyes to see if Gounod would move, or if any favorable change would take place in his position. But Gounod made no change for the better. He smoked on, and shifted and changed his position, and leaned at times back in his chair, and yawned, and read his paper, and smoked again, and so on, till Inez thought that hours must have passed, and wondered what sort of a paper this could be which could thus take so long a time to read.

She had been listening all this time—listening to hear whether the old woman had discovered her flight. This discovery might take place at any moment. A long time had passed, and it seemed far longer than it really was; and, as it passed, the attention of Inez only grew the more eager.

Suddenly it came.

She heard it.

The cry!

Her flight was discovered. The old woman had found it out.

There was a wild, shrill, piercing yell from the upper part of the house—a yell so clear and penetrating that Inez actually felt it thrill through all her frame, and Gounod sprang to his feet, while the paper fell from his hands and the pipe from his mouth. He stood listening.

There came another yell—a yell of wild lament, intermingled with words, which, however, were quite unintelligible. Gounod threw a quick look around him, and then darted from the *conciergerie*, and ran hastily toward the back-door. He advanced straight toward the hiding-place where Inez was standing, and then, reaching the foot of the stairs, stood listening once more. At that moment he was not more than twelve inches from Inez.

Horror paralyzed her. She could not even breathe. It was terrible, beyond expression, to be so near to escape, and yet to have so near her the relentless jailer. But her suspense did not last long. Gounod waited, and then another yell, more impatient, more prolonged, and more eager, came down to his ears. Upon this he started, and, springing forward, rushed up the stairs, taking three steps at a time.

Now was the moment! Before Gounod had gained the top of that stairway, Inez had slipped out from her hiding-place; and, as he was running along the upper gallery, she was hurrying toward the *conciergerie*. Here a sudden impulse seized her to take some kind of a disguise, so as to prevent observation. In her present dress she would look strange in the streets, without jacket or bonnet. One quick look around the *conciergerie* was enough. There was an old water-proof cloak there and a hat, evidently the property of the old woman. Inez felt some reluctance about using

these things, especially the hat, but there was no help for it. She could not stop to reason. She seized the cloak, flung it over her, thrust the hat on her head, and then sprang out through the open door into the street.

Away and away! She was afraid to run, but she walked as rapidly as possible. At length this street ran into another which was more crowded. Here she mingled with the throng of people and soon lost herself. But it was not easy for her to feel safe. So terrible was her sense of pursuit and her dread of capture that she walked on and on, turning into one street after another, rounding corners, walking up lanes, and losing herself inextricably. The streets, as she went, grew more and more populous, the houses grew handsomer, the public buildings more stately. At length she came to a river, over which there were thrown numerous magnificent bridges, and beyond there arose the lordly outline of splendid palaces and noble monuments. In these she beheld, at length revealed, all the glories of Paris; and, in spite of the terrors of pursuit and the agitation of her flight, she could not help accepting this as a fresh proof of the vigilance of her jailers and the treachery of Saunders, who had never driven her near this part of Paris, but had diligently kept her in streets where she could see nothing of the splendor of the great city.

But there was no time now either to recall past treachery or to admire the splendors of the surrounding scene. Escape was her only thought—security in some place of refuge, where she might collect her thoughts and consider her future. On, then, she went, and still on. She crossed a bridge that was nearest, and then once more plunged into a crowd of streets.

At length, her attention was arrested by a notice on the window of a house. It looked like a place suited to one of moderate means. It was a notice to lodgers. She entered here, and made inquiries. She was pleased with the look of the place, and also with the appearance, the tone, and the manner of the landlady. Here, then, she took lodgings.

Her first thoughts now were about regaining her friends. She had no money, and therefore could not travel. She could think of only one thing to do, and that was to write to Bessie. Bessie would feel for her, and either send her money or fly to her relief.

Bessie also might know about her father by this time, and would send him. So afraid, however, was Inez of letting her secret be known that she did not give Bessie the address of her lodgings, but simply told her to address the letter *poste restante* at Paris. In her letter she informed Bessie that she had come to Paris owing to false information which she had received, that she had been in great distress; and, after a brief outline of her sufferings, implored her to send her at once as much money as would be sufficient to take her to England.

Having written this, she waited impatiently for an answer. Afraid to go to the post-office herself, for fear of being discovered and recaptured by some agent of Magrath's, Inez appealed to the landlady, who sent her daughter there. There was no answer.

Several days passed.

Every day some one went there, either the landlady or the landlady's daughter, or some other member of the family. All were full of sympathy for the beautiful English girl who was so lonely and so sad. But the days passed, and still no answer came.

Then Inez wrote again. Her letter was more urgent and more full of entreaty than before. She drew a picture of her past sufferings and present desolation that would have moved the most callous heart, and implored Bessie not to delay in sending her assistance.

After this she again waited in a fever of impatience. Day after day passed, and week after week. No answer came. At length, so great was the anxiety of Inez that it surmounted even the haunting dread of pursuit and recapture; and, fearing that the landlady might have made a mistake of some sort, she ventured forth to the post-office herself. But she met with no better success.

There was no letter at all for any such person as Inez Mordaunt. There was no letter for any such person as Inez Wyverne—nor for Miss Mordaunt, nor for Miss Wyverne. Inez named herself in every possible way; but the end of it all was, that no answer at all had been sent to either of her letters.

Upon this she lost all hope, and the only conclusion that she could come to was, that Bessie herself had perhaps been foully dealt with by Kevin Magrath. This fear seemed so justifiable that it preyed more and more upon her mind, and finally became a convic-

tion. The picture which her imagination formed of the childish and light-hearted Bessie, drawn helplessly into the power of the unscrupulous Magrath, was too terrible to be endured. The sufferings through which she had passed since her flight reached a climax. This last disappointment broke down all her fortitude. Strength and hope alike gave way, and a severe attack of illness followed, in which she once more went down to the extreme verge of life. But the kind care of the landlady watched over her, and those good people showed warm and loving hearts. Their care saved her, and Inez was once more brought back to life.

As she found herself convalescent, she became every day more and more aware of the necessity that there was to get money in some way. Her debt to the landlady was heavy already; and, more than this, she was eager to return to England.

How could she do this?

There was only one way possible.

That gold cross which she had found at Villeneuve she had ever since worn around her neck, and had it still. There was no other way to save herself than by the sacrifice of this. It was a bitter thing, but it had to be done. It was necessary to pawn it, and thus get that money which alone could save her now.

She had, therefore, nerved herself up to this. She had set forth in search of a pawnbroker or something equivalent, and was on this errand at the time she met Kane Hellmuth. Full of terror, fearing pursuit and recapture, every one seemed a possible enemy; and the earnest stare of Kane Hellmuth was sufficient to rouse all her fears. He seemed some agent of her enemy, and, when she knew that she was being pursued by him, she lost all hope. As a last resource, she sought to take a cab, but at that instant her strength gave way.

CHAPTER XXXIV.

A FRESH INVESTIGATION.

THE story of Inez had been communicated to Kane Hellmuth in the course of several interviews. The confidence which thus began between them, soon became of the most familiar kind. From the first, the sore necessities

of Inez made her cling to this strange Englishman upon whom she had been thrown,
and who had been so ready in the offer of his
assistance; but, after she learned who he was,
her trust in him became boundless. The confidence which she put in him was met with
the fullest return on his part; and Inez, who
had trusted in him, when she discovered that
he was the friend of Dr. Blake, at length
learned, to her amazement, that he was the
husband of her elder sister Clara. This discovery she hailed with the utmost joy. This
one fact gave her a friend and protector.
More, it gave her a relative. Kane Hellmuth
was thus her brother, since he was her sister's
husband. Could any thing be more consoling
than this? To this man, then, the friend of
her lover, and the husband of her sister, she
gave all her trust and confidence.

As brother of Inez, Kane Hellmuth took
her at once under his protection. He redeemed her from her difficulties, and let her
have sufficient money to extricate herself
from her embarrassments without the sacrifice of the precious relic of her father. As
her brother, he visited her at the house, and
was received with smiles of welcome by the
kind-hearted landlady and her daughter, who
were filled with joy at this sudden improvement in the fortunes of the sweet young English lady that had become so dear to them.

In the course of their conversations Kane
Hellmuth had mentioned to her what he
knew of Dr. Blake, but did not show her his
letter. It was so incoherent that he was
afraid that it might increase her anxieties if,
as he strongly suspected, she cared much for
him. His own anxieties about Blake he kept
to himself; and, indeed, these were now completely eclipsed by his anxieties about Inez.

The story of Inez had excited within him
an extraordinary tumult of contending emotion. The new position in which it placed
Kevin Magrath, was the most astonishing
thing to him. He had a very vivid remembrance of that man, of his rollicking Irish extravagance, and his bitter denunciation of
the "destroyer of Clara Mordaunt." He had
been accustomed to think of him as a sort
of accusing witness against himself; but now
this accusing witness was transformed into a
remorseless villain, who had been the framer
of an infamous plot against a defenceless
girl. A new motive for action was roused
within him: to meet this man again, to ex-

tort from him some satisfaction for his mis-
deeds, or bring him to punishment.

Apart from the villany of Magrath, there
stood forward, prominently, the contradiction
between what he said to himself and what he
communicated to Inez. To himself he had
said that Inez was Inez Wyverne; that her
father, Hennigar Wyverne, had left her penniless, and that she would be dependent. To
Inez he had plainly declared, by his letters,
that she was the daughter of Bernal Mordaunt.

To himself he had said that Hennigar
Wyverne owed Bernal Mordaunt money; to
Inez he had told a story of the most absurd
and extravagant kind.

In short, all that Magrath had said to him
was utterly opposed in every respect to what
he had said to Inez.

As he had thus lied about Inez, might he
not also have lied about Clara?

This thought started up in Kane Hellmuth's mind, and at once roused his eager
desire to make new inquiries about the death
of his lost wife. The theory that Dr. Blake
had suggested had once before deeply impressed him; the statements of Magrath
seemed to have destroyed that theory; but
now, since Magrath had been proved to be a
villain and a liar, his old feelings rose up,
and, for his own sake, as well as for the sake
of Inez, he resolved to enter upon a fresh
search into the whole of this dark mystery.

It was a mystery before which he was
completely baffled. It seemed to be a fact,
after all, that Hennigar Wyverne's dying
declaration was true. Inez was clearly the
daughter of Bernal Mordaunt. Would it be
equally true that Dr. Blake was the son of
Hennigar Wyverne? He remembered how
strongly Blake himself had at one time been
inclined to this belief, and for whose sake he
had refrained from entering upon a search.
It was the statement of Magrath which had
driven this belief out of Blake's mind, but
now this statement had turned out to be a
lie. More than this, Magrath himself had
been shown to have a deep interest in this
lie; he had come forward as an active persecutor, and, in intention, a destroyer of Inez.
Would he have the same motive to act against
Blake? Could Blake's extraordinary disappearance, and still more extraordinary silence,
be due to the same subtle agency? Could
the man who had beguiled Inez to Paris and

entrapped her, have beguiled Blake also to some place where he might work his will upon him? Blake, in his letter, spoke of going "south" with a friend. Could this friend be Magrath? Could that "south" be Rome?

Such were the thoughts that filled Kane Hellmuth's mind. The whole situation became a dark and inscrutable problem. It was impossible to solve it while resting inactive at Paris. It was necessary for him to act, and to act immediately, both for the sake of Inez and also for the sake of Blake.

Another also appeared to Inez to be involved in this mystery, and that was Bessie. About Bessie, Kane Hellmuth was greatly troubled. Inez had informed him of Bessie's own account of herself, and her belief that she was the daughter of Bernal Mordaunt. The name Mordaunt had struck him very forcibly once before, and now it afforded equal matter for conjecture. He was puzzled, but he could not help thinking that, as Inez knew her best, her conjectures about her were more just than his. The fact that she, too, was involved in this wide-spreading difficulty, only afforded a fresh reason for instant action on his part.

This decision he announced to Inez, who at once begged that he would take her to England.

To this, however, Kane Hellmuth objected.

"My dear Inez," said he, addressing her in that familiar manner which was justified by his near relationship, "you are really safer here than anywhere else. There are many reasons why you had better not go. Your enemies will think that you are in England even now, and will search after you there. In travelling there with me you would be certain to be discovered, and I also would be known as your friend and companion. They would know that I had found out all—our relationship, also—and would be in a position to baffle me in my search. You, too, would be watched; and, as I should have to leave you, I could never feel comfortable about you."

"But isn't this place far more dangerous?"

"No," said Kane Hellmuth; "on the contrary, it's the safest place in the world. They will never look for you in Paris. Then, again, even if they were to find you, they could do nothing. Paris is the best-governed city in the world. The police here are omniscient; no one could be illegally carried off. You are absolutely safe. The moment you left that house, you were safe. If the old woman and Gounod had both chased and captured you, they would not have dared to take you back, unless you yourself wished. Any remonstrance of yours would have drawn the attention of the police. Gounod and the old woman would have been arrested and examined; and that, I imagine, is about the last thing that they would wish to happen to them. Men of Gounod's order are particularly anxious not to get into the hands of the police. The fact is, there is no place in the world where you are so absolutely safe as you are here. In London you would be in danger. In any small town anywhere you might be in danger. Here, however, no danger can befall you. I assure you solemnly, my dear Inez, it is absolutely impossible for you to get into the hands of that miscreant again, unless you yourself voluntarily go there."

At this Inez smiled. Kane Hellmuth's tone completely reassured her. The idea of putting herself voluntarily into the hands of Kevin Magrath was, however, excessively amusing to her.

"You may laugh," said Kane Hellmuth, "but that is a real danger. Be on your guard. Don't let him entrap you again."

"I shouldn't go with him," said Inez, "not even if he should declare that my papa was dying, as he did before."

"Oh, well, he wouldn't use that trap again; he would have something else the next time."

"There is nothing else," said Inez; "there is no other living being through whom he could work upon me."

Kane Hellmuth looked at her earnestly.

"I am very much mistaken, my poor Inez," said he, "if there is not. There is, I think, one other human being. Be on your guard, dear; don't allow yourself to be deceived. You know whom I mean. Now, if it should happen that you should hear of him in any way that is not perfectly free from suspicion, be on your guard."

Inez looked down on the floor with a heightened color, and in some surprise. She did not know about Kane Hellmuth's fears for Blake, or his suspicions about Magrath's possible intentions toward him also.

10

"I'm sure I don't see how that could be," said she.

"Well, no matter," said Kane Hellmuth. "Only promise me that you will not go anywhere without ample protection and security."

"Oh, of course," said Inez; "I'm sure I've learned too hard a lesson to forget it easily."

"I hope you may not," said Kane Hellmuth.

In view of this proposed journey, Inez would have been glad, indeed, if she could have given him any information which might assist him in the search. But this she was unable to do. She knew of no one who was acquainted with the past of herself, except, perhaps, old Mrs. Klein. That person had certainly given her some valuable information, but she did it incidentally, and in a haphazard fashion. An old creature, so sodden with drink as she was, could not be expected to give any coherent answers to a regular series of questions. Of this she informed Kane Hellmuth, who took down her name and address, and thought that it might be worth while to pay the old woman a visit.

When he bade her good-by that evening, it was with a certain solemn foreboding of indefinable evil that was possible—some evil that might happen to her or to himself, before they might meet again.

"Good-by, Inez, dear sister! Remember what you promised."

"Good-by, Kane!" said Inez, in a voice full of emotion.

She felt as though she was losing her only friend. A tear stood in her eye. Kane Hellmuth held her hand in his, and looked at her with a softened expression on his stern face.

Then he stooped, and kissed her.

Then he turned, and left the house.

On the following morning he left for London, and arrived there in due time. He had not been there for years, and had no acquaintances in particular. The solicitors of his father were the ones from whom he hoped to find out something, though what that something might be he hardly knew. He did not know what course of action might be required on his own part. He did not know whether it would be best to carry on the work which he had before him in secret, or to break through that law of silence which he had im-

posed on himself since his wife's death. He held himself in readiness to adopt whatever course might be best for the fulfilment of the work in which he was engaged.

His first act was to go to the house in which Mr. Wyverne had lived. Upon reaching it, he found it closed. It was evident, therefore, that Bessie Mordaunt must be sought for elsewhere.

He then thought of Mrs. Klein, and at once drove off to visit her. The address which Inez had given him enabled him to find her without difficulty, as she was still living in the same place.

Although Inez had given him a very good idea of her interview with Mrs. Klein, still the sight of the old woman was somewhat disheartening to one who came, like Kane Hellmuth, in the character of an investigator after truth, and an eager questioner. It was not the bottle at her elbow, nor her bleary eyes, nor her confused manner, that troubled him. For this he was prepared. It was rather the attitude which Mrs. Klein chose to take up toward him. She threw at him one look of sharp, cunning suspicion, as he announced to her that he had come to ask her a few questions, and then obstinately refused to answer a single word.

The fact is, Kane Hellmuth was a bad diplomatist, and soon perceived that he had made a mistake. This he hastened to rectify in a way which seemed to him best adapted to mollify one of Mrs. Klein's appearance, which was the somewhat coarse but at the same time very efficacious offer of a sovereign.

The effect was magical.

Her fat, flabby fingers closed lovingly around it; and she surveyed Kane Hellmuth with a mild, maternal look, which beamed benevolently upon him from her watery eyes.

"Deary me!" she said; "and you such a 'andsome young gentleman, as is comin' to visit a poor old creetur as is deserted by all kith and kin, which it's truly lavish and bountiful you are as ever was, and him as gives to the poor lends to the Lord, and may it be restored to you a 'undredfold, with my 'umble dooty, and prayer that your days may be long in the land, for evermore, and me a 'oman as has seen better days, which I'm now brought down to this; and many thanks, my kind, kind gentleman, for all your kindness shown."

"See here, now, Mrs. Klein," said Kane Hellmuth, sharply—"gather up your wits, if you can. I want you to answer one or two questions. You know all about Hennigar Wyverne's family."

Mrs. Klein gave a sigh:

"Which 'im as is dead and gone, and was the kindest and mildest-mannered gentleman as ever I set heyes on, and allus treated me that generous that I could have blacked his boots for very love, and his—"

"All right. Now, see here. There was Inez Mordaunt, that lived in his house—"

"Miss Hiny—my own sweet child alive—and me that loved her like—"

"Oh, of course. You see I know all about her. But I want to ask you about another. Who is this other girl that lived at Mr. Wyverne's, and called herself Bessie Mordaunt?"

"Which there never was no girl called Bessie, and she didn't live there. She was sent off to France, and her a young thing as had just lost her mother. For my part, I allus says to Mr. Wyverne—says I, 'Sir,' says I, 'Miss Clara's too young to—'"

"Clara!" exclaimed Hellmuth, with a strange intonation. "What became of her? Tell me—tell me—tell me!"

Mrs. Klein gave a doleful sigh, and shook her head solemnly.

"Which she's dead and gone, and is a blessed angel these many years, kind sir; and beggin' yer humble pardon, but it's better for her as is far away from a world of sin and woe, and all the chances and chanjues of this mortial spere. And I allus said as—"

"Yes, yes," said Hellmuth, with some impatience, hastily changing the conversation. "But this one I mean called herself Bessie."

Mrs. Klein shook her head.

"She was named Clara—I don't know any Bessie—and I take my Bible oath—and never fear—"

"She may have come to the house after you left."

"And very likely, and me 'as allus, kind sir, kep' that house that orderly as was beautiful to be'old; but what goin's on there was there after I left, Lord only knows, an' Mr. Wyverne that mild that anybody could impose on 'im same as if he was a new-born babe—"

"Do you know a man named Kevin Ma-

grath?" said Kane Hellmuth, rigidly holding her to the points about which he wished to question her, and checking her headlong garrulity.

Mrs. Klein looked at him with a bleary gaze, and again wagged her fat old head.

"Won't you take somethin' warm, kind sir?" she asked.

"No," said Kane Hellmuth. "But about Kevin Magrath—can you tell me any thing?"

Mrs. Klein poured out a glass of liquor, and slowly swallowed it. Then she smacked her lips. Then she drew a long breath.

"'Im," said she, "as was the serpent that stole into that Heden, and me allus tellin' Mr. Wyverne. Says I, 'Sir, beware; 'e'll put your neck inside the gallus'-noose.' And where he came and where he went I do not know, nor can tell, savin' an' except as he wos a willain—a out-an'-outer—and me as knows no more about him than that."

Mrs. Klein evidently could say nothing about Magrath more definite than this. Kane Hellmuth questioned her again and again, but the answer was always of the same kind. His visit here seemed, therefore, a failure, and he felt inclined to retire and leave Mrs. Klein alone with the beloved society of her bottle. But he had one question yet to ask, and upon her answer to this very much depended.

"See here," said he. "Can you tell me any thing more about Bernal Mordaunt? Where did he come from? Who was he?"

Mrs. Klein seemed to rouse herself at this last question. She looked at him with less stupidity in her sodden, boozy face.

"Which as hevery one knows," said she, "and I wonders much as 'ow hever a fine gentleman like you turns up and 'as never 'eard of Bernal Mordaunt. They kept it close from Clara, and made out as 'ow it was 'er huncle's 'ome, or second cousin, and hit 'er father's hown place, and one of the grandest and gorgeousest in the kingdom; for, as I allus says, 'tisn't hevery girl as has a in'oritance like Mordaunt Manor."

"Mordaunt Manor!" cried Kane Hellmuth.

He shrunk away from the old woman, and sat looking at her with a pale face and glowing eyes.

"Mordaunt Manor, as hever was," said Mrs. Klein, "which I knowed it all along, and pore Mr. Wyverne, as is dead and gone, knowed as I knowed it, though them children were that lied to that they didn't know their own father's 'ouse."

"Mordaunt Manor!" exclaimed Kane Hellmuth again, upon whom this information had produced a most extraordinary effect. "In what county?"

"Mordaunt Manor as is in Cumberland County—which there never was but one Mordaunt Manor, as anybody hever 'card hon."

Kane Hellmuth started to his feet. He had heard enough. His mind was made up to some sudden course, revealed by this new information. He left abruptly, and hurried back to his hotel.

That evening he was hurrying on by express out of London toward the north.

CHAPTER XXXV.

THE TWO BROTHERS.

THE sudden resolution which Kane Hellmuth had taken was not without a sufficient cause. The connection which Mrs. Klein's information had established between the children of Bernal Mordaunt and Mordaunt Manor gave rise to numerous suspicions in his mind. If they were the heiresses of Mordaunt Manor, then there was supplied that which his mind had long sought after—namely, a motive for the plot against Inez, and for that plot in which it now appeared that Clara had been involved. Yet, if this were so, why had not Clara known it? If Mordaunt Manor was her home, why had she never said so? The only answer to this lay in Mrs. Klein's incoherent remarks about "lies" which were told her, so that she didn't know her own father's house. She may have left it at so early an age that she had no certainty about its being her home, and afterward may have been made to believe that it belonged to some one else.

In any case, however, it now seemed to Kane Hellmuth that Mordaunt Manor itself was the best place for him to go to. If it belonged to Bernal Mordaunt, he himself would be more likely to be there than anywhere else; and, if he was not there, he might find out where he really was. If Kevin Magrath's plot really had reference to this, he might possibly find out there something about him. Or, if neither of these could be found, there was a remote probability that he

might hear something about Bessie. For all these reasons, then, and for others which will afterward appear, Mordaunt Manor seemed to him to be by far the best place that could be found for a centre of operations.

On reaching Keswick he stopped at the inn, where he obtained answers to all the questions that he chose to ask; and these answers filled him with amazement. In these answers there was communicated to him a number of facts which were incomprehensible, bewildering, overwhelming!

The first thing that he learned was that Bernal Mordaunt had returned home after an absence of years, and, after a brief decline, had died there.

Moreover, he had been welcomed home by his daughter.

This daughter had herself come home but a short time before, after an absence of years.

This daughter had cheered the declining days of the feeble old man, had given herself up to him with a devotion and a tender love that was almost superhuman. In that love the old man had solaced himself, and he had died in her loving arms.

Moreover, the name of this daughter was *Inez Mordaunt!*

This Inez Mordaunt had filled men of every degree with admiration for her beauty, her fascinating grace, her accessibility, her generosity, and, above all, for her tender love and unparalleled devotion to her aged father.

This Inez Mordaunt also had married a man who was worthier of her than any other; he was also a resident of the county, and thus she would not be lost to the society which admired her so greatly and so justly. Her father had hastened on the marriage before his death, so that he should not leave her alone in the world. Even after her marriage this noble daughter showed the same deathless devotion to that father for whom she had done so much.

The happy man who had won so noble a woman for his wife was Sir Gwyn Ruthven, of Ruthven Towers.

All this is familiar to the reader, but all was not familiar to Kane Hellmuth. One by one these facts came to him like so many successive blows—blows of tremendous power—blows resistless, bewildering, overwhelming, falling upon his soul in ever-accumulating force, until the last one descended and left him in a state of utter confusion and helpless uncertainty.

With the first fact he was able to grapple. It was intelligible that Bernal Mordaunt had, after all, come home, here, to Mordaunt Manor. It was intelligible that he had reached his home weak and worn out; and that he had died. It was intelligible and probable that Bernal Mordaunt was now dead, and buried, and that his remains were actually in the family vaults of Mordaunt Manor.

So far, so good; but now, when Kane Hellmuth advanced thus far on this solid ground, and looked out beyond, he found every thing misty, gloomy, uncertain, chaotic, and unintelligible.

What was the meaning of this daughter? She had reached home not long before her father. He had recognized her. He had found happiness in her. Her love and devotion for him was spoken of as something nearly superhuman. Had Bernal Mordaunt, then, another daughter?

The name of this daughter was Inez Mordaunt.

Inez Mordaunt! But he had left Inez Mordaunt in Paris, where she had been decoyed by letters forged in the name of her father, Bernal Mordaunt. What Inez Mordaunt was this?

Could his Inez—his sister Inez—be mistaken? Impossible. His Inez was the sister of his Clara. The likeness between them was so extraordinary that he had stopped her in the street, and carried her senseless to his lodgings. Since then he had heard her whole story. He had the testimony of Mrs. Klein to the identity of his Inez with her who was once called Inez Wyverne. His Inez was the sister of his lost Clara beyond a doubt.

Were they, or were they not, the children of Bernal Mordaunt? He knew that they must be. His Clara was, he knew; and that Inez was, he also knew.

Could there be two Bernal Mordaunts? One, the father of his Inez; the other, the father of this strange Inez here? Impossible. Mrs. Klein's testimony pointed to Mordaunt Manor as the home of Clara and of Inez. But, if so, why had not his Clara known this in her life? Or was a creature like Mrs. Klein to be trusted in any thing whatever? Might he not have come here on a fool's errand?

No.

The answer to this lay in Kevin Magrath's plots, and in the fact that Mordaunt Manor alone formed a sufficient cause and motive for them. Without Mordaunt Manor he was an insane schemer; with Mordaunt Manor he was a villain aiming at a magnificent prize.

But, if this was so, what part had he in the magnificent prize? Was it not already held by this other Inez, this wonder among women, this pious daughter, this paragon? And what was there in common between her and one like Kevin Magrath? Yet Bernal Mordaunt had come home, from his years of exile and sorrow, to Mordaunt Manor, and there was his daughter Inez to welcome him, his daughter whom he loved, and in whose arms he died.

But beyond all these bewildering and contradictory facts lay another which produced upon Kane Hellmuth's mind an effect so strong that it may be called the climax of them all.

This Inez Mordaunt had married Gwyn Ruthven. They were living now at Ruthven Towers.

Over this, Kane Hellmuth brooded long and solemnly. In this last fact he saw that which would open to him a way by which all the others would be made plain. Yet the way was not one which he would have chosen. He would rather have tried any other way. It came in opposition to his self-inflicted punishment. It would terminate the silence of years. It would put an end to that seclusion in which he had thrust himself, and draw upon him the glare of day. Thus far he had been, as he called himself, a dead man —this would force him to rise from the dead.

This was not what he wished. But it was too late to go back. He had set forth in this path. The way now lay straight before him to Ruthven Towers, to Gwyn Ruthven and his wife, who had called herself Inez Mordaunt. Could he now turn back? Dare he do it?

He dare not. For the sake of Inez, whose wrongs were still in his mind, for the sake of his lost wife, who also had suffered wrongs that seemed to have come from the same source from which had flowed the wrongs of Inez; for his own sake, too; for every reason that can animate a man to action he felt himself impelled to go onward, and to penetrate this mystery.

Now, Kane Hellmuth was a man who, when he had once resolved on any course, had no other idea in his mind than a simple, straightforward, and tenacious pursuit of it till his purpose might be accomplished.

Had this other Inez Mordaunt still been unmarried, he would have avoided Gwyn Ruthven. He would have gone to her. He would have seen her, and questioned her, and thus have satisfied himself, if satisfaction had been possible. But she was now the wife of Gwyn Ruthven. Her identity was merged in his. He could not go and interrogate the wife apart from the husband. The only way to the wife lay through the husband. To the husband, therefore, he must go; and so Kane Hellmuth, on this day, set forth for Ruthven Towers and Gwyn Ruthven.

He rode on horseback.

He was scarce conscious of the scenery around him as he rode along, though that scenery was wondrously beautiful. He was considering what might be the best course of action.

By the time that he reached the gate of Ruthven Towers he had decided. After this, he was less preoccupied. He passed through the gates. He looked all around with strange feelings. He rode up the long avenue. He dismounted. He entered Ruthven Towers.

On inquiry, he learned that Sir Gwyn Ruthven was at home. He gave his name, and was shown to a large room on the right. He entered and waited.

He did not have to wait long. Sir Gwyn was prompt, and soon came down to see his visitor.

Kane Hellmuth was standing in the middle of the room. Sir Gwyn, on entering, bowed courteously. Kane bowed also. Then Sir Gwyn seemed to be struck by something in the appearance of his visitor. He looked hard at him for a moment, then he looked away, then he looked again, this time with an air of perplexity. Kane, on his part, looked at Sir Gwyn, and his stern face softened. Indeed, Sir Gwyn was one upon whom no one could look without a sense of pleasure. It was not because he was what is called handsome, not on account of any mere regularity of feature, but rather on account of a certain fresh, honest, frank expression that reigned there; because of the clear, open gaze, the broad, white brow, the air of high breeding mingled also with a boyish heartiness and simplicity. Sir Gwyn, in short, had that air which is so attractive in a high-bred boy of the best type—the air of naturalness, of frankness, of guilelessness, and generosity. For this reason, the hard look died out of Kane Hellmuth's eyes, and a gentler and softer light shone in them as they rested on Sir Gwyn.

"I hope you will excuse me for troubling you, Sir Gwyn," said Kane Hellmuth, at length, "but I have come a great distance for the purpose of making some inquiries at Mordaunt Manor. I had no idea that Mr. Mordaunt was dead until my arrival here; and, as my business is of the utmost importance, I have thought it probable that I might obtain the information that I wish from yourself, or from Lady Ruthven."

At the sound of Kane Hellmuth's voice, Sir Gwyn gave a start and frowned, and listened with a puzzled expression. He was evidently much perplexed about something, and he himself could scarcely tell what that something was.

"I'm sure," said he, "that both Lady Ruthven and myself will be happy to give you any information that we can."

"It all refers," continued Kane Hellmuth, "to the life of Mr. Mordaunt after his return home. I am well aware of his long absence. Since his return, however, it is very probable that he has spoken of these things about which I wish to ask."

"Very probably," said Sir Gwyn, slowly, with perplexity still in his face. "He was very communicative to me."

"What I should like to ask first," said Kane Hellmuth, "refers to an affair at Villeneuve. Did Mr. Mordaunt ever mention to you any thing about the death of Mr. Wyverne at that place?"

"Oh, yes, he told me all about it."

"Thanks," said Kane Hellmuth. "What I wished to know was whether it was the same Mr. Mordaunt. I did not know but that it might have been another person. He did not give his name, and it was only my conjecture that it was he."

"It was Mr. Mordaunt himself," said Sir Gwyn. "He told me all about that occurrence, and also all about his past connection with Mr. Wyverne."

This reply settled one thing; namely, the identity of this Bernal Mordaunt with the father of his Inez.

"Thanks," said Kane Hellmuth; "and now I wish to ask one or two other things. They refer to his family. They concern myself very nearly, or I should not ask them. They are only of a general character. Would you have any objections to tell me how many children Mr. Mordaunt had?"

"Certainly not," said Sir Gwyn. "He had two daughters, that is all. The name of the oldest was Clara."

"Clara!" said Kane Hellmuth, in a strange voice.

"The other one," continued Sir Gwyn, "was named Inez."

"Is—Clara—alive yet?" asked Kane Hellmuth, in a tremulous voice.

"No," said Sir Gwyn, "she died ten years ago."

"Ah! and the younger one, I presume, is still alive?"

"Yes, the younger one is Lady Ruthven, my wife."

"Ah!" said Kane Hellmuth.

He had heard this before. It was now confirmed. The problem remained a problem still, but he had advanced somewhat nearer to a solution, for the very reason that he had approached so much nearer to the one who had called herself Inez Mordaunt. This was her husband. He had no doubt whatever of the truth of the intelligence which he was giving to his visitor.

"One thing more, Sir Gwyn," said Kane Hellmuth, "I really must apologize for the trouble that I am giving you, and I hope you will not suppose that I am asking out of nothing better than idle curiosity. What I now wish to ask refers to your own family— your own brothers."

Kane Hellmuth paused. Again Sir Gwyn looked at him with that perplexity on his face which had already appeared there. The two thus looked at one another earnestly. Kane Hellmuth felt a pang of sadness as he looked at that noble and generous face, and thought that he might be the means of inflicting pain upon one who did not merit it; but his task had to be done, and went on:

"There were three of you, I think," said he; "Bruce, Kane, and yourself."

Sir Gwyn bowed in silence. The perplexity of his face was now greater than ever.

"Bruce died at home, I believe," continued Kane Hellmuth, "and Kane died in Paris."

"No," said Sir Gwyn.

"I have understood so."

"Mr.—ah—Hellmuth," said Sir Gwyn, earnestly. "Tell me truly, were you ever acquainted with my brother Kane?"

Kane Hellmuth hesitated.

"Yes," said he, slowly, "I was, about ten years ago, in Paris."

"Do you believe that he is dead?" asked Sir Gwyn, sharply and eagerly. "I don't. I never did," he continued. "I tell you I have tried everywhere to find him. Look here, there's something confoundedly queer about you, do you know? odd, isn't it? but it seems to me that we've met before, but hang me if I can remember where. I tell you I've done every thing to find my brother Kane. I've advertised. I've sent out agents. I don't believe he's dead, and I hope to meet him yet. By Jove! And, see here, if you should ever get on his track, tell him this from me: That I am waiting for him, that I am holding this place for him, that I'd give it all up—estate, title, all, for the sake of seeing him once more. Yes, by Heaven! I would; and if I only knew where he was now I'd go to find him if I had to risk my life. I say this to you because, do you know, somehow you've got a confoundedly queer look about you, and, by Jove! you remind me of him somehow. You don't happen to be a relative of the family in any way, I suppose."

The tone in which Sir Gwyn spoke was the tone of a big, honest, warm-hearted boy. Every word went to the very heart of Kane Hellmuth. He was not prepared for this. In the course of his life he had lost much of his faith in man, and had accustomed himself to think of his brother as one who would be glad to hear of his death. He had been trying to make himself known in a gradual way, so as to ease the blow which he supposed would fall on his brother. Lo! now, to his amazement and confusion, here his brother stood there offering to give up all—estates, title, yes, even life itself, if he could find him.

His head sank upon his breast. He struggled to keep down the emotion that had arisen in his soul. It was hard to restrain himself. Sir Gwyn looked at him in wonder. At length Kane Hellmuth raised his head. He fixed his eyes on Gwyn with a strange meaning. Then he spoke.

"Gwyn!" said he.

That was all.

Sir Gwyn started. Then all the truth in a moment burst upon him.

"Oh, by Heavens!" he cried. "O Heavens! Kane! Kane! Kane! By Heavens! Kane himself! You glorious old boy! Didn't I know you? didn't I feel that it was you?"

He grasped both of Kane's hands in his, and clung to them with a fervid, enthusiastic greeting, wringing them, and shaking them over and over.

"Kane, you dear, glorious old boy, where have you been wandering? and why have you stayed away so long? Haven't you seen my frantic advertisements, imploring you to come and get your own? Haven't I felt like a thief for years, holding all this when you might be wanting it? Ah, dear old boy! I know what you once had to suffer. And you might have let me had a word from you. You once used to think something of me when I was a youngster. Don't you remember how I used to look up to you as the pride, and glory, and boast, of the whole race of Ruthvens? You must remember enough about the youngster Gwyn to know that, whatever his faults were, he'd be as true as steel to you. Bruce treated you like a devil, too, and I cursed him for it to his face; and didn't you get my letter, Kane? I was only a boy at school, and I sent all I had to you—my two sovereigns—all I had, Kane. It wasn't much, but I'd have laid down my life for you."

So Sir Gwyn went on. He appeared to be half crying, half laughing. He still clung to his brother. It was the enthusiastic, the wild delight of a warm-hearted boy. As for Kane, he stood overwhelmed. He trembled from head to foot. He tore one hand away, and dashed it across his eyes.

CHAPTER XXXVI.

RUTHVEN.

THUS, then, it was that Kane Ruthven came back to the home of his fathers—to Ruthven Towers. He was a dead man no longer. He was no more Hellmuth, but Ruthven.

He had not anticipated such a reception. He was not prepared for such truth and fidelity—such an example of a brother's love. He was unmanned. He stood and wept.

Yet life seemed sweeter now to him through those tears.

"Dear boy," said he at last, as soon as he had recovered himself somewhat, "don't talk to me about the estate, or the title. They are yours. Do you think I came back for them? They are yours, and they shall be yours. I gave them up years ago. I saw your notices, but I was not going to come back here. Things had happened which made wealth and rank of no importance. I have as much money as I want. I don't care about a title. You shall remain as you are now, and so will I."

"I'll be hanged if I will!" cried Gwyn. "I tell you, this estate and title have been bothering me out of my life."

"Well, then, I'll make out a paper transferring every thing to you."

"You shall do nothing of the sort."

"I will. You don't know how I am situated."

"I swear you shan't. You are the head of the Ruthvens, and I glory in you, and I long to see you in your place, old boy."

"No, Gwyn—my own place is a very different one. I have lived my life. I didn't come back to interfere with yours."

"It's no interference. Come now, Kane, don't be absurd. It's all yours, you know,"

"Very well, and I hereby make it all over to you."

"I won't take it."

"You must. I'll make out the necessary papers, and then go back to my lair that I've just come out of."

"What's that? What!" cried Gwyn. "Go back! Why, you won't go back? You have come home now for good, Kane—haven't you? Go back? No, never! You are here now, and here you must stay."

"Oh, you may be sure, dear boy, we'll see one another often after this; but, for my part, I have a work to accomplish which will require all my care for some time to come, and, at present, I'm still Kane Hellmuth,"

"Hellmuth! what preposterous nonsense! You're Sir Kane Ruthven of Ruthven Tower and you shall remain so."

"No, Gwyn, my purpose is fixed and unalterable. I care nothing for such things. You can enjoy them. I have as much money as I wish. I need nothing more. You have your position, and there is your wife."

"My wife!" exclaimed Gwyn. "Ah,

" Over the fair face there shot, for an instant, an expression of pain,"—Page 149.

Kane, you little know her. Oh, how she will rejoice over this! Oh, she knows all about it! I've told her all. Oh, how glad Bessie will be! Oh, how Bessie will rejoice!"

"Bessie!"

This exclamation burst forth from Kane involuntarily. His voice was harsh and grating. He stood with staring eyes and averted face. The utterance of that one name—"Bessie"—had been sufficient to overturn all his thoughts, and thrust him back into his old bewilderment and gloom. Like lightning, a thousand thoughts swept through his mind, quickened into instant life by that one name. This revealed all.

"The false Inez who had married his brother was Bessie. Bessie who? Bessie Mordaunt—the friend—of the true Inez; the Bessie to whom she had written, but who had refused to answer those letters of despair—Bessie!"

Gwyn noticed the change.

"What's the matter, Kane?" he asked, anxiously.

Kane drew a long breath.

"Oh, nothing!" said he. "By the way—what do you mean by 'Bessie.' I thought your wife's name was Inez."

"So it is, but it is Bessie also. Her full name is Inez Elizabeth Mordaunt. She was living with the Wyvernes, however, at London, you know, where I first became acquainted with her, and they all called her Bessie to prevent confusion, for there was another Inez—Inez Wyverne—a distant relative of hers. So, I knew her as Bessie, and I've called her Bessie ever since. Inez is a pretty name, but it seems unfamiliar to me."

All this was terrible to Kane. It confirmed what had been told him. Inez Wyverne was Inez Mordaunt. Bessie had taken her place. Had Bessie betrayed her? Inez loved her still, and trusted in her. Was it possible that Bessie was a traitor, or had she only been mistaken? But, then, Bernal Mordaunt must himself have received Bessie as his daughter!

Kane Ruthven feared the worst. And there came to his heart a sharp and sudden pang. If Bessie should prove to be the traitor, the impostor, which he now imagined her to be, then what wrong would have been done to this noble, this generous heart! Here was this true and loyal soul, this matchless brother, with his faithful love, his unsullied nature, his young, pure life, linked

to one whose character must be terrible. Could he go on further when his path would only serve to darken this brother's life? He shuddered, he half recoiled. How could he dare? His brother had taken a serpent to his bosom. Could he open his brother's eyes, and show him all?

Just at that moment, in the midst of such gloomy and such terrible thoughts as these, there came a sound which penetrated like sudden sunshine through all the clouds of suspicion and terror that were lowering over the soul of Kane Ruthven, a sudden sound, sweet, silvery, musical—a sound of laughter that was childish in its intonations—a peal of laughter that was full of innocence, and gayety, and mirth.

Then followed a voice—

"Aha, you runaway! So, here you are! and it's meself that's been the heart-broken wife. Really, I began to think that you'd deserted me, so I did. Come, sir, give an account of yourself. How dare you leave me for a whole half-hour!"

The new-comer suddenly stopped. She saw a stranger there.

At the first sound of her silvery, musical laugh, Kane Ruthven started, and looked up.

He saw before him a vision of exquisite loveliness. It was a young lady—who looked like a very young girl, a blonde, with large eyes of a wonderful blue, with a face of indescribable piquancy, with golden hair, flowing in rich masses over her shoulders, with a dress of some material as light as gossamer. This was the one whose laugh had penetrated to his ears, who now came lightly forward with these words addressed to Gwyn.

Gwyn, too, had started at her entrance. At the sight of her the cloud that had come over his face, thrown there by the strange gloom of Kane, was instantly banished, and a joyous light succeeded. He took the lady's hand, and led her forward.

"Kane," said he, "here she is—my own Bessie. O Bessie! who do you think this is? You'd never guess. It's my dear, long-lost old boy—my brother Kane."

The hand that Gwyn held suddenly closed convulsively around his; over the fair face there shot, for an instant, an expression of pain. Bessie shrank back involuntarily, and half raised her other hand, as if to her heart. Yet this was only for an instant. It passed as suddenly as it had come. Kane did not notice it, nor did Gwyn.

"Kane!" exclaimed Bessie, in a sweet and gentle voice; "sure then it's me own brother he is too, and oh, how glad I am!"

She held out her hand with a sweet smile. Kane took it, and the smile on her face drove away the last vestige of his gloomy fears. All evil suspicions passed away. He saw only that perfect loveliness and that bewitching smile; he saw only her charming grace and captivating beauty; he saw only the wife of Gwyn, and the friend of Inez.

He pressed her hand fervently, and in silence.

"Really," said Bessie, "do you know, Gwynnie, dearest, you gave me an awful shock, and I haven't got over it yet. I was so awfully glad, you know, but it was at the same time so awfully sudden, you know; and oh, how we've talked about this. I'm sure I can hardly believe it is so, and I'm sure it's awfully funny to find a brother so suddenly, when you never expected such a thing at all at all. And oh, but it's the blessed thing to think that our brother Kane should turn up after all, so it is."

She looked at Kane as she said this with a sweet smile on her face. Kane noticed this, and was charmed. He noticed, also, the slight "brogue" that was in her tone, which, intermingled as it was with the idiom peculiar to young ladies, seemed to him to be very charming. He believed in her at once. The sight of that face was enough. With such a being suspicion had simply nothing to do. She herself was beyond all suspicion. In her face, her manner, her tone, he could see infinite possibilities for love, for loyalty, for sociability, for friendship, for fun, for drollery, for kindliness, and for gracious self-surrender; such a one seemed a fit companion for Inez or for Gwyn; but to associate her, even in thought, with such foul natures as Kevin Magrath, seemed an unholy thing.

And so it was that Kane Ruthven first met Bessie.

The expression of Kane's face was usually an austere one. His dense growth of crisp hair, his bushy eyebrows, his heavy and somewhat neglected beard, his piercing eyes, his corrugated brow, and, added to all these, the hard outline of his features, all combined to give him a certain saturnine grimness, which would have been repellent had it not been for the lurking tenderness that shone in his glance—a tenderness which was perceptible enough to any one who took more than a superficial observation. On the present occasion, the look with which he regarded Bessie had all of this tenderness, and nothing of this grimness and austerity; it was a look such as an anchorite might give to some child visitor straying near his cell, whose approach might have broken in upon his solemn meditations. To Kane Ruthven there seemed about Bessie a sweetness, and light, and sunshine, which forced him for a time to come forth out of his usual gloom.

"Sure, and it's quite like the parable of the prodigal son entirely," said Bessie; "only of course, you know, I don't mean to say that you were a prodigal son, brother Kane; and then, too, in the parable, it was the younger son that was the prodigal, but you're the older, so you are; now isn't he, Gwynnie, dearest? But, 'deed, and it's no matter which, for it's only the joy over the return that I was thinking of, so it was, and sure we'll kill the fatted calf and be merry, as they did in the parable. I feel," she added, with an absurd look of perplexity, "that my comparison is hopelessly mixed up, but then my intentions are honorable, you know."

As Bessie said this, she stole her hand toward that of Gwyn, and inserted it confidingly in his, quite in the manner of a fond young bride, who is confident of the attachment of her husband, and upon whose marriage still exists something of the bloom of the honeymoon. Gwyn, on his part, did not fail to reciprocate this tender advance, and his hand clasped hers lovingly, and the two stood thus opposite Kane, indulging in this pardonable little bit of sentimentality, or spooneyism, or whatever else the reader may choose to call it, quite regardless of his presence. Upon Kane, however, this little action, which was not unobserved by him, did not produce any unpleasant effect, but rather the opposite. It seemed to him to be a beautiful picture—the young husband, with his frank, open, gentle, and noble face; the fair young bride, with her fragile beauty, and the golden glory of her flowing hair—these two thus standing side by side, with hands clasped in holy love and tenderness.

Kane felt softened more and more, and this scene roused within his mind memories drawn from his own past; memories of a time when he, too, like Gwyn, had one who was as dear to him as this fair young creature was to his brother; memories of a time when the touch of a gentle hand stealing toward his would quicken his heart's pulsation, and send through him a thrill of rapture. Those memories had never been lost, they had lived through all the weary years, they formed a torment to him in his desolation ; but never had they been roused to such life, and with such vividness, as at this moment, when Bessie made this half-unconscious movement of confiding tenderness. The happiness of Gwyn only served to remind him more poignantly than usual of all that he had lost, and a drear sense of solitude came across his soul—

"Oh, for the touch of a gentle hand,
And the sound of a voice that is still."

The sight of his brother's happiness also had another effect. It elicited not envy, for envy was a stranger to his heart, but rather a generous sympathy, and a more tender regard both for this brother and this new-found sister. Inez was one sister, and here stood another as fair as she, and, to all outward seeming, as gentle, as pure, and as good. The sight of these two only served to strengthen his firm resolve already made, to leave his brother here in possession of that estate and title for which he, in his present mode of life, had no need, and of which his nature would not permit him to deprive him.

The loving and tender reception of Kane by these two was met on his part by a grateful reciprocity of feeling; the hearts of all of them were opened to one another; and an interchange of confidences took place, which was unreserved on the part of Gwyn, and only limited on the part of Kane by the nature of those griefs which he suffered, and which could not be lightly spoken of. He laid great stress on his wanderings, and particularly on his adventures in South Africa in search of diamonds. His allusions to this were made with the intention of letting Gwyn see that he had ample means of his own, and of communicating to him, in a delicate way, the fact that he had no intention whatever of taking any steps to deprive him of the estate.

But the chief topic of conversation referred to times far beyond this, and to things which they had in common. Gwyn had much to say about his early boyhood and his remembrances of Kane. He brought forward a thousand things which had faded out of his

brother's recollection, but were recognized as Gwyn mentioned them. About these Gwyn talked with a zest, and a simple, honest delight, which was very touching. His whole tone showed that, in the days of his early life, he had looked up to this brother Kane with all the enthusiastic admiration of a generous boy. It was also quite evident that this enthusiastic admiration had lasted beyond his boyhood and into his maturer years. He seemed to have considered his brother Kane the *beau idéal* of perfect manhood, and one who was the best model for his own imitation. At the same time he regarded his own efforts to imitate him as useless, and the honest humility of his allusions to his own inferiority was almost pathetic, especially when his noble face and his chivalric sentiments were so manifest, and seemed to speak so plainly of a character and a nature which could not suffer from a comparison with even that idealized Kane which he had in his mind.

The minuteness and the accuracy of Gwyn's recollections surprised Kane, who had forgotten many of the occurrences mentioned. They referred chiefly to Kane's last year at home, when Gwyn was a little fellow and Kane a young man. The incidents were very trifling in themselves, but at the time they had appeared wonderful to the boy ; and now, even when he had become a man, they seemed the most important events of his life. It was not long afterward that Kane's misfortunes had occurred, and Gwyn showed, without going into particulars, but merely by a few eloquent statements of facts, that, at the time when Kane was so desolate, there was one loving heart that was sore wrung for him, and one loyal soul that would have faced even death itself if it could have done him good.

Bessie bore herself admirably during the conversation. She did not thrust herself forward too much ; nor did she, on the other hand, subside into silence. A few, well-chosen remarks, now and then thrown in, served to show that she was full of the deepest interest in all that was said, and occasional timely questions served to draw forth a fuller explanation of the subject to which the question referred. Moreover, all the time there was in her expressive face such eager curiosity, such profound interest, such total surrender of self to the one who might be speaking, that her very silence was more eloquent than any words could have been.

Bessie was also gentle and affectionate. Kane was her brother now. With a frankness that was charming she at once began to put herself on the footing of a sister toward him; and proceeded, not abruptly, but delicately and by degrees, to insinuate herself further into confidential terms of intercourse. At first it was Brother Kane, occasionally dropped as if by accident; then the familiar name was repeated more frequently. Then she called him simply Kane. Once, when her sympathies seemed unusually strong, she exclaimed, "O dear brother Kane! it's heart-broke you must have been about that same!" Finally, when they bade one another good-night, she held forth her cheek in the most childish and innocent and sisterly manner in the world, and, as he kissed her, she said:

"Good-night, dear Kane; good-night, and pleasant dreams."

CHAPTER XXXVII.

HUSBAND AND WIFE.

KANE RUTHVEN had come here to Ruthven Towers on an errand. That errand was two-fold: It referred, first, to his lost wife Clara; and, secondly, to his injured sister Inez. He had come here with these things foremost in his mind, and all his thoughts turned toward a dark mystery. But his arrival here had produced a change. The unexpected reception by Gwyn, the meeting with Bessie, the discovery of this loyal, true, and noble-hearted brother, with his fair, and gentle, and tender wife, all tended to expel the darker feelings from his soul. The first sound of Bessie's laugh had been to him what the harp-notes of David had once been to Saul; and, though the dark clouds might again roll over him, yet he none the less enjoyed this brief sunshine. For that day, at any rate, he did not choose to introduce the subject of Inez, and he gave himself up to the spirit of the occasion. Once more he came back to the old world which he had left; and, on becoming a Ruthven again, he allowed his mind to dwell upon the distant past. That night he took up his abode in the home of his fathers, and slept at Ruthven Towers.

The honest and unaffected joy of Gwyn over his brother's return could not be repressed, but was manifest after they had parted for the night, and while he and Bessie sat talking over the wonderful events of the day.

"Isn't it the most wonderful and the jolliest thing you ever heard of, Bessie, dear?" he said; "but, oh, you haven't the faintest idea of what he used to be! He was the most magnificent swell — the bravest, boldest, handsomest, most glorious man I ever saw. He neglects himself, and is reckless about his life; but you can easily judge yet, from his present appearance, what he may once have been. As it was, he was a great, bright vision in my life, that I've never forgotten. His ruin was a great, dark thunder-cloud, and I swear I've never got over that! I almost broke my heart about it, and I used to imagine a thousand things that I would do for him when I got older. And then I've never given him up, you know that; I told your poor father that. I always hoped he would turn up, and here he is at last. But he's an odd sort of a fellow. He always was the soul of honor and generosity; and in this he is the same still, only perhaps even more so. I've already told him how I searched for him, and how bad I had felt all along at keeping the title and estates while they were his. Whereupon, what do you think he said? Why, he declared that he wouldn't have any thing to do with them; but, of course, he'll have to. I'll make him. He's suffered enough, poor old boy! from his family. All I want is to see him have his own. He'll have to take Ruthven Towers, and be Sir Kane. Plain Gwyn Ruthven's enough for me, especially so long as I have my little Bessie with me."

During these last words a cloud had come over Bessie's brow, which, however, Gwyn did not perceive. As he ended, he turned fondly toward her, and kissed her lovingly.

Bessie smiled.

"So he's going to be Sir Kane Ruthven, and you're only Mr. Ruthven, after this," said Bessie, slowly; "and he's going to take up his abode here on his own estates, and Ruthven Towers is all his own entirely, and we're intruders, so we are. Well—well, but it's a queer world we live in, so it is."

As Bessie said this, the forced smile passed off, and the cloud came back to her face. But Gwyn was taken up with his own pleasant thoughts, and did not notice her.

"Yes," he exclaimed, "'the king shall come to his own again.' Hurrah! Kane swears he won't take it, but I swear he shall. And now we'll see who'll win."

"Oh, sure, he'll take it fast enough," said Bessie, gloomily. "No man ever lived that would refuse it—and if it's his—it's his, so it is."

"Yes; but you know he really wouldn't take it if I didn't make him," said Gwyn; "and I'm going to make him."

Bessie was silent for some time. This was so unusual a thing with her that Gwyn at length noticed it, and looked at her smilingly and pleasantly. Her head was half turned, so that he could not see her face, and therefore did not observe the slight frown of her usually serene brow, or the compressed lips, that generally were fixed in so sweet a smile. But serenity and smiles were gone now.

"Isn't it awfully jolly?" cried Gwyn, enthusiastically.

"Awfully," said Bessie, while her little hands clutched each other convulsively, and a deeper frown came over her brow.

"It's almost too good, to get old Kane back," said Gwyn, in the same voice. "I swear I can hardly believe it yet!"

Bessie made no reply for some time. A severe struggle was going on within her. At length she regained her self-control altogether, and turned her face around. Once more her brow was serene, and the old familiar stamp of her sweet smile was on her curved lips.

"Oh, yes, Gwynnie, darling," said Bessie; "it's the awfullest jolliest thing I ever heard of, so it is; and that dear, darling, old Kane, so splendid a man! really, he's just like Olympian Jove, entirely, so he is; and so he's Sir Kane, is he? and you're only Mr. Ruthven, and I'm not Lady Ruthven at all, but only plain Mrs. Ruthven. How very, very funny, is it not, Gwynnie, darling?" •

Gwyn laughed aloud; not so much at the funny idea that Bessie had pointed out to him, but rather out of the joy of his heart over his brother's return.

"Oh, it is very, very funny, it is, entirely," said Bessie; "and so we'll have to quit Ruthven Towers, and Sir Kane will remain in possession."

"Oh, yes," cried Gwyn, "he'll have to do it; of course, the dear old boy. He'll make no end of a row about it, you know; but he'll have to do it. Ha, ha! isn't it jolly? But we'll be close by one another always, that's one comfort."

"How is that, Gwynnie, darling?" asked Bessie, in her softest tone. "How can we always be close by one another if we have to leave Ruthven Towers? Sorrow a one of me knows at all, at all."

"Why, of course, you know, you little goose, we'll go and live at Mordaunt Manor."

"O Gwynnie!" exclaimed Bessie, fixing her eyes mournfully upon her husband, and speaking in tones of the utmost reproach— "O Gwynnie! Mordaunt Manor."

"By Jove!" exclaimed Gwyn, "my own little pet, I really forgot your—your dislike, and all that."

"And pup—pup—poor—did—did—did—dear pup—pup—pup—pa! scarce cold in his grave. How can I go back?" sobbed Bessie; "and you know how sad it was, and how hard it is to avoid giving way. O Gwynnie! how could I ever expect such a thing from you!"

At this Gwyn looked unutterably shocked and distressed. He folded her in his arms —he swore and vowed that he did not mean what she supposed; that there was no necessity to leave Ruthven Towers yet, for a long time, and, even when they did, they need not go to Mordaunt Manor. They could live in London, Paris, anywhere, in a hundred other places. Bessie gradually allowed herself to become mollified, and at length seemed quite herself again.

"But won't it be awfully funny, Gwynnie dear?" she said. "I'll have to support you, won't I? Sure it's turn and turn about it'll be, so it will."

Gwyn laughed at this in his usual uproarious fashion.

"Sure," said Bessie, thoughtfully, "all this reminds me of a thing that I've sometimes thought of. It used to seem impossible, but now sure there's no knowing, and I don't know but that it'll be the next thing that'll happen, so it will; and, if so, then good-by, say I, not only to Ruthven Towers, but also to Mordaunt Manor."

At this Gwyn started and stared at Bessie in amazement.

"What do you mean?" he asked.

"Sure I mean what I say."

"How can we bid good-by to Mordaunt Manor ?"

"Why, the same way that we're going to bid good-by to Ruthven Towers."

"Oh, nonsense ! Why, my elder brother has come home. You haveu't any elder brother, you know, you little goose."

"No, but what prevents me from having an elder sister ? " said Bessie, looking earnestly at her husband.

"An elder sister !" cried Gwyn, in new amazement.

"Just that; it's that entirely what I mean, so it is," said Bessie, "and sorrow the thing else it is, at all at all; and there you have it. Oh, really, Gwynnie darling, you needn't begin to smile. You've done enough laughing for to-day; and this'll help you to feel a little more serious, so it will. I suppose poor, dear papa could never have mentioned it to you," continued Bessie, with a sigh, " but, no wonder, when he was so very, very ill."

"'Pon my life!" exclaimed Gwyn, "I haven't the faintest idea what you're driving at. You have to explain yourself more, Bessie dearest, only you mustn't make your poor little head ache about nothing."

"Oh, never mind my poor little head," said Bessie; "there's enough in this to make more heads ache than mine. Only I do wish poor, dear papa had explained it all to you. I hate so to make explanations. But there's no help for it. Well, you know, Gwynnie dearest, poor, dear papa had two daughters—one Clara and the other Inez."

"But Clara's dead," cried Gwyn.

Bessie shook her head.

"Nobody ever knew about her death, at any rate; she's dead in just the same way that your brother Kane was dead."

"What!" cried Gwyn—"what makes everybody say so, then? And your father, he gave her up as dead. I've heard him speak about the dear child that he had lost."

"Sure enough," said Bessie, "he did that same. This sister Clara disappeared when I was a bit of a child, and, of course, you know, Gwynnie, it certainly is possible, and perhaps even likely, that she is dead; but, at the same time, there is no certainty of that, at all at all, not the least in life. You see, she was sent off to a school in France, and while there she made a runaway match with some adventurer; and that's how it was. Well, there was a will, and there was

a guardian, and the will arranged that, if ever either of the daughters married without the consent of the guardian, she could be disowned, or something. Well, poor papa was supposed to be dead, and poor, dear guardy didn't like the match, and so, I suppose, he treated them rather cruelly, for she disappeared, and was given out as dead, and that's all I know about it, you know. So, you know, I've often thought that poor, dear, darling Clara might yet be alive—and oh, how awfully glad I should be to see her !—and she may come and claim Mordaunt Hall, you know ; and then, you see, Gwynnie darling, we'll be left to our own resources entirely."

"Oh, really now, Bessie, see here, now," said Gwyn, "this is all very different, you know—a different thing entirely. Oh, she's not alive—no—no—depend upon it, she's not alive—no, nothing of the kind—why, it's all nonsense, you know."

"But wouldn't it be awfully funny if she were to turn up, after all, alive and well, and come to take possession of Mordaunt Manor ?"

"Preposterous !" exclaimed Gwyn. "Why, Bessie love, you haven't got a ghost of a foundation for all this."

"No, darling, nor had you any foundation more than this for your belief in the life of dear Kane, yet you always believed he would come—didn't you, darling ? "

Gwyn was silent.

"And so, do you know, Gwynnie, I really have always had a firm belief that some day my poor, dear, darling sister would turn up—and wouldn't that be funny ? "

"Oh, but, you know, Bessie, you see this is a different sort of thing altogether. Oh, quite !"

"But isn't it awfully funny, now ? "

"Oh, yes."

"And now, Gwynnie, I've got another thing to tell you, and it's very, very funny, too—sure and it's getting to be the funniest thing I ever knew—all this is—it is entirely."

"What do you mean now ?" asked Gwyn, curiously, wondering what new revelation Bessie might make.

"Sure and it's this," said Bessie. "Your brother Kane was married, you know."

"Oh, yes ; I know that, of course."

"Did you ever hear the name of the lady ? "

"Never."

"Well, then, I'll tell you who she was, and you must be prepared for a surprise, so you must. The lady that your brother Kane Ruthven married was my own elder sister, Clara Mordaunt!"

At this Gwyn actually bounded from his chair.

"I don't believe it!" he cried.

"It's the truth I'm telling," said Bessie, placidly. "My dear guardy was hers also; it was Mr. Wyverne that you've heard me talk about, and he told me all about it. And oh, but the dear man had the sore heart afterward; really it was very, very sad, Gwynnie dear, to see how he tried to find poor, dear Clara, so as to make amends. He made that last journey to France for the purpose of making a final search."

Some more conversation followed about this. Gwyn had many inquiries to make about Mr. Wyverne and Clara before he could feel satisfied. But Bessie's answers were so clear that there was no room for doubt left in his mind.

"And so, Gwynnie dearest," said Bessie, laying her hand lovingly upon that of her husband, and bending her golden head near to his till her forehead rested on his shoulder, "you see, Clara was really dear Kane's wife, and I dare say she is still alive, and wouldn't it be funny if it should turn out that dear Kane had come here on her business as well as his own?"

Gwyn had begun to caress the lovely head that was leaning on his shoulder, but at this he stopped, and a sudden look of pain flashed across his face. But it passed away instantly.

"Pooh!" said he. "Kane hasn't any secrets from me. If his wife was living, he'd have told me."

"Oh, of course, but you see, dear, he's hardly had time yet. I dare say he'll tell you to-morrow, or next week. He'll break it very, very gradually, of course. Besides, he wouldn't like to mention it before me."

At this, the gloom came over Gwyn's face once more.

"By Jove! Bessie," said he, "you don't know what you're saying."

"I'm sure I don't know why this should not be so," said Bessie.

"Oh, nonsense! it makes him seem like—like—like an underhanded sort of a fellow."

"Well, I'm sure I didn't mean to hint at any thing of that sort about dear Kane. It's your own fancy, Gwynnie dear."

Gwyn frowned, and sat in thought.

"Well, at any rate," said Bessie, "you can't deny that we're both likely to be paupers."

Gwyn drew a long breath, and was silent.

"By paupers I mean, of course, dependants on others, and that I hate, even when it's my own sister. If I were not married, it would be different, but a married woman ought to depend on her husband."

"Oh, nonsense, you little goose!" said Gwyn, hurriedly; "this is all nonsense; but, even if it were so, I can take care of you, you poor, little, precious darling."

"I'm sure I don't see how."

"Why, I'll—I'll—I'll go into the army, of course."

"I never could bear that, dear," said Bessie, with a shudder. "It's too—too dangerous. Besides, darling, do you think the pay of an officer is enough to support a wife? They say not."

"Oh, well," said Gwyn, in an attempt at his old cheerfulness, "I'm young. There's lots of young fellows that fight their way through life."

"Sure, and there are," said Bessie, pleasantly; "but you know, Gwynnie dear, you haven't been brought up to fight your own way—no more have I."

"'Pon my soul, Bessie," said Gwyn, with a short laugh, "you're developing an amount of prudence that I never gave you credit for."

"Sure, and it's the bitter, black prospect before us that's enough to make a fool wise. I'll have to give up being a butterfly, Gwynnie darling, so I will, and turn into a busy bee. It's not prudence, so it isn't. It's fear, for I'm frightened out of my wits. And oh! don't—don't be so hasty, Gwynnie, don't give up all, don't, don't, darling, darling Gwynnie!"

With these words Bessie burst into tears, flung her arms about her husband, and sobbed upon his breast.

"Oh, come, now," said Gwyn, but he could say no more. He was troubled. Bessie held him thus, and entreated him as before.

"I must," said Gwyn, "my own darling. It's dishonor not to—"

"Oh, sure, and what's dishonor compared

to black, biting poverty ? Sorrow the bit do I care for dishonor, and there you have it."

At this, Gwyn shrank back a little. The hand which was fondling her and soothing her again, as before, ceased as if paralyzed. He looked at the golden head and the slender form.

"Well, Bessie," said he, at length, " a lady once told me, in confidence, that women never have any sense of true honor. I was horrified, at the time, at such a sentiment, from a lady too; but, after what you've just said, I'll be hanged if I don't begin to think there must be some truth in it."

"I don't care," said Bessie. "What's sentiment? What's honor? It's only *you* I care for in all the world, only *you*—only *you* —and this will bring darkness and sorrow down on you, Gwynnie. O Gwynnie! O Gwynnie! darling, darling Gwynnie! what will become of you ? "

At such fond words as these, Gwyn's heart overflowed with tenderness. The poor, little, weak, loving creature, thus clinging to him, with her timid, tender, loving heart, how could she be responsible for any sentiments that did not happen to come up to a man's code of honor ? It was enough for him that she loved him so. He kissed her therefore tenderly, and soothed her fears.

"This man," said Bessie — "this man comes like a serpent, to ruin us."

"Oh, nonsense! nonsense! Bessie, darling, you mustn't talk so."

Bessie clung more closely to him.

"I wish he had never, never come ! " she said, passionately.

"O Bessie ! "

"I wish he had died when they thought he had."

"Darling, don't talk so, you don't know how you wring my heart."

"I don't care. I wish he was dead ! " cried Bessie, fiercely and bitterly.

"Bessie," said Gwyn, "you *must* stop."

He spoke sternly. Bessie gave a sob, and clung more closely to him. Her arms were around him. He loved her better than life. He thought her not responsible for these passionate words, and, in the circling clasp of those loving arms, how could he feel anger ?

———

CHAPTER XXXVIII.

REVIVING OLD ASSOCIATIONS.

HOWEVER excited Bessie's feelings may have been, they left no trace behind, for on the following day she greeted "dear brother Kane" with the same cordiality, the same innocent affection, and the same sisterly familiarity which had distinguished their adieux of the evening before. As for Gwyn, there was no change in him, except that he was, if possible, even more cordial than ever. Kane on his part was in no haste to put an end to the happiness which he felt at thus finding himself again the centre of affectionate attentions; he felt as though his business had something in it which would in some way interfere with the sunshine of the present, and therefore was in no immediate haste to introduce it.

That day they passed in visiting the places within and without in which Kane took an interest.

When he was a boy, the Ruthvens had lived in London principally, and had come to this place but seldom. On one of these occasions, Kane had remained several weeks; and all his memories of Ruthven Towers were crowded into this space of time. He was then a boy of fourteen, active, eager, daring, and during this visit had made himself thoroughly familiar with all the past history of Ruthven Towers, with every legend connected with this place or with the surrounding country. He had never been here since, but so vivid was the impression which this visit had made upon his mind, and so retentive was his memory, that every thing almost that he saw served to recall some incident in that bright time of boyish vigor and enjoyment.

To all the reminiscences of that bright past, Gwyn listened with his usual relish and absorbed interest, questioning his brother incessantly, and hanging upon his words with that fond admiration which ever since Kane's arrival had marked his attitude toward him. Kane found it pleasant to talk of this past— which lay beyond the time of his calamity; and all the more so, since he had such listeners. For he had not only Gwyn, but Bessie also; and she, too, showed something of the same feelings which Gwyn evinced—the same attitude of eager attention, the same look of intense interest, of utter and complete self-absorption in the narrative of the speaker. She had shown all this on the previous day; and now she showed it still more strongly.

In the morning they strolled about the grounds, and, after this, went out for a drive. Kane sat with Bessie in the back-seat, Gwyn in the front-seat. As they had found in the house and about the park many objects which called up old associations in Kane's mind, so did they also find, beyond the grounds, places that lived in his recollection, and which were associated with the events of that halcyon time when he made his boyish visit to Ruthven Towers.

Beyond the limits of the park the country became hilly, and among these eminences was one which was very conspicuous from the road as they drove along. It was a precipice about two hundred and fifty feet high, whose dark, rocky sides presented a gloomy contrast to the rich vegetation all around, and the waving trees and grassy slopes beyond this. The moment Kane caught sight of this he seemed unusually excited.

"There," said he, "is a place where I did one of the pluckiest things I ever did in my life."

"Oh, do, dear brother Kane, tell us all about it, if you please, brother Kane. I do so love to hear about these adventures of yours, so I do. Do, please—won't you, brother Kane?"

Kane looked with a smile at the beautiful face, whose eyes were fixed on his with an expression of the most anxious entreaty, and whose tone was one of the most coaxing and irresistible.

"Well, really, Bessie," said he, "it seems absurd for me to be talking so much about myself."

"Oh, but you know we do so love to hear all about what you used to be, and to do!—don't we, Gwynnie darling?—and we haven't seen you all these years—now, have we, Gwynnie darling?"

Gwyn lent his solicitations to those of Bessie, and Kane went on to tell about a boyish exploit, which was really very creditable.

"You still call that place the 'Witch's Rock?'" said Kane, inquiringly.

"Yes," said Gwyn.

"Well," said Kane, "when I was here, I no sooner heard that name than I was wild to visit it, and to hear the story, if there was

11

any story, that was connected with so strange a name. It was some story about a witch that lived in a cave on the side of that cliff ever so long ago, and kept the whole country at defiance, though they all turned out to hunt her. No one could get at her, though, and she remained there. How she lived, no one knew; but the legend had it that she never died, but was living there yet. Now, you see, that was just the thing to set me wild with curiosity. In the first place, the existence of a cave in the face of the cliff was a temptation in itself; and then, again, the idea that the witch might be living there yet was a still stronger one. I didn't believe in the witch, but I did believe in the cave, and, as no one had ever got into it, I thought I'd try for myself. Well, I got some ropes, and, without saying a word to any one, went to the place, and let myself down from the top. It was about the most risky thing I ever tried. The cave was sunk in, and it wasn't possible to get a foothold in it at all, without swinging backward and forward. However, I succeeded in the attempt, and actually penetrated into it. It was not much of a place. It was about ten feet wide inside, and twenty deep, and I dare say had often sheltered fugitives in the stormy times of the past. I cut my name there, and, I remember now, I forgot my knife, which is there yet, unless some one has visited the place and picked it up."

"By Jove!" said Gwyn, "I don't believe I should have the nerve for that sort of thing, old boy. I shouldn't mind so much lowering myself down, but it's the swinging part of the business that would upset me."

"Yes, that was the hardest part of it," said Kane.

"But, oh, how perfectly awful!" cried Bessie. "Why, it makes me positively dizzy even to think of it, so it does. And how you ever dared to do such a thing I can't imagine at all, at all.—Now, can you, Gwynnie dear?"

"I wonder whether I could do such a thing as that now?" said Kane, gazing thoughtfully at the precipice. The carriage had stopped. They all looked there.

"Why, what a perfectly horrible idea!" cried Bessie. "Why, I'm sure you'd be dashed to pieces, so you would."

"Oh, no," said Kane, with a smile, "there's no danger of that. The only question is, whether I could do the swinging part of it."

"Oh, how awfully funny!" said Bessie. "Sure but I almost wish you would, Kane dear."

"By Jove!" said Kane, "I feel very much like it. I'd like to try whether a man's nerves are as steady as those of a boy."

"And then there's your knife," said Bessie. "Oh, but wouldn't it be the fine thing entirely if you should get in there again, and find that nobody had ever been there since yourself, at all at all, and wouldn't you be the proud man!"

"The knife?" said Kane. "By Jove! wouldn't I like to get that knife again! The knife? why it would be like getting back part of my boyhood. I should take it as an omen, if I found it—an omen for good in the future—that things are going to turn out for me all right in the end."

"Sure but you never could get down there," said Bessie; "never at all at all. Oh, no, you wouldn't have the nerve now. It's too terrible. Why, really it makes me quite dizzy to think of it.—Doesn't it make you dizzy, Gwynnie dear?"

"Dizzy? pooh!" said Kane, whose eyes were fixed upon the cliff, as if by some strong fascination. "Dizzy? why, no man that has a man's head on his shoulders need think any thing of that. I could easily go down and back again, but I might not be so agile as I then was, and might not be able to get a foothold."

"But, oh, what a triumph it would be! and, oh, but it's the proud man you'd be if you were to find the knife!"

"Look here, Bessie," said Gwyn, suddenly, "'pon my word, this is hardly the thing, you know; you seem to be actually tempting Kane to a dangerous adventure, when you ought to be trying to prevent him."

"Me tempt him?" said Bessie, reproachfully. "Me? sure it's only encouraging him that I was, and I'm really frightened out of my wits at the very idea, and I'm sure I don't believe that he'd dare to do it, and that's the only comfort I have, so it is."

"Dare? That's the wrong word to use, Bessie. You'll only make Kane the more determined."

Kane laughed merrily. In his laugh there was a ring and a gusto that had not been known in any laugh of his for years. He was for the moment like a boy again. The prospect of renewing his old enterprise and re-

peating his boyish feat, of itself seemed to have rejuvenated him.

"Dare? ha, ha!" he said. "When a lady dares a man to do any thing, there's nothing left but to do it. But, at any rate, I feel confoundedly like going; and, by Jove! I will go."

Bessie smiled radiantly at him, and threw, immediately afterward, a deprecatory glance at Gwyn.

"Nonsense, Kane! don't think of such a thing; it's dangerous."

"Dangerous? pooh!" said Kane. "I tell you the sight of this rock has made me a boy again. I want to find my knife. Gwyn, my boy, you don't know how I cling to that glorious boyhood, and you'll never know till you've had a manhood like mine, and from that may Heaven preserve you!"

These last few words were spoken with sad and solemn intonations. These words Gwyn had occasion afterward to recall—afterward, when they seemed to him to have a prophetic meaning.

For the present, at any rate, Kane had made up his mind, and for the rest of the day was full of this new idea. His old grimness departed utterly, and a boyish enthusiasm about his coming attempt took the place of it. Gwyn made a few feeble attempts to dissuade him from it. He felt some strange, indefinable presentiments of evil, but did not know how to express these in words, and so his attempts to dissuade Kane were only laughed at. But Bessie cheered him on. Bessie talked about it incessantly. Bessie laughed about it, and made merry about it; and even if Kane had been inclined to give it up, he could scarcely have done so under such circumstances. But Kane was not inclined to give it up. The idea had taken complete possession of him, and nothing now could have prevented his putting it into execution. He spent some time that day in making preparations for his adventure. These preparations were not at all elaborate. They consisted simply in procuring a rope of sufficient length and strength, and tying a series of alternate knots and loops. This was the mode which he had adopted when a boy, and its complete success at that time recommended it as the best thing which he could do now; besides, in this recent revival of boyish feeling, any thing that could connect him more closely with those early days was welcome, and nothing seemed pleasanter to him than to repeat, even to the minutest details, the plan which had formerly been so successful.

Another evening came—the second evening at Ruthven Towers for Kane. By this time he and Bessie were on terms that were most cordial, most fraternal, and most confidential. He had thus far refrained from mentioning the real object of his journey here, from the fear that the mention of this might mar the joy of this intercourse. Yet through this day he had thought much of this, and the more he thought of it the more absurd did such hesitation seem. Here was this noblehearted brother and this gentle and loving wife—his brother and sister—why should he hesitate any longer to tell them what he wished to tell? Not the story of Clara—that was too sad, too tragic, too terrible, for such innocent ears as Bessie's to hear—but rather the story of Inez. Was not Bessie the friend of Inez? Did not Inez still love her and trust in her? Why delay to make known to the only friend that Inez had the terrible loneliness of her position? What could be better for the poor, lonely girl than to be able to join her friend once more? Once together, all could be explained; or even if any mystery remained they could wait, secure in one another's love, until light should be thrown upon it.

Kane's confidence in Bessie was complete. It had grown rapidly, but he had come to her as a brother, and she had met him as a sister. Under these circumstances there had been none of that reserve which otherwise might have existed.

Accordingly, that evening he told them about Inez. He told the story to both of them, for they were both one now, and he never dreamed of telling Bessie any thing which Gwyn might not also hear. It was his confidence in Bessie's gentle and noble character, her loyalty, and her innate worth, that led him to this. He did not tell, however, the whole story as Inez had told it to him. The perplexing mystery of her claim to be the daughter of Bernal Mordaunt, when Bessie had been acknowledged as that very daughter, prevented him from touching upon the subject, and from even mentioning the name. He merely mentioned that Inez had received a letter from one who professed to have been appointed by her father as her

guardian; that Inez had believed the letter, and, with the utmost recklessness, had complied with his request to come to him at Paris. When there she had found out that this man was not what he professed to be, and that, for some unknown reason, he wished to keep her in his power. She was subjected to restraint for a time, but managed finally to escape. She had written twice to Bessie, but had received no answer.

In this guarded way Kane told the story of Inez, and in this way he avoided altogether that painful and distressing confusion of names, claims, and rights, which the full statement of the truth would have brought forward. He did not mention even the name of Kevin Magrath for fear of distressing Bessie, but contented himself with the name of Gounod. It was enough for him just then to reveal the condition of Inez, and he was willing to leave all the rest to the future. He thought that the best thing for him to do would be to bring Inez and Bessie together on the old footing; and then Inez might tell, of her own accord, as much or as little as she chose about her story. He could not help feeling that much had yet to be discovered before the conflicting claims of these two, who were so innocent and so dear, could in any way be harmonized.

If there had remained in the mind of Kane any vestige of a doubt in Bessie, her reception of his story would have removed it. Astonishment, grief, sympathy, joy, all seemed to struggle together in the expression of Bessie's face and in the tones of her voice. The start of horror at the wickedness of those who made this plot; the cry of fear at the danger of Inez; the exclamation of joy at her escape and safety; of all that in look, or word, or tone, or gesture, could indicate the deepest and sincerest sympathy, not one thing was wanting.

"Oh, but isn't this the blessed day," she exclaimed, at last; "and oh, but wasn't I the heart-broken girl! For, you see, Kane dear, it was the death of her poor papa—poor, dear, old Guardy Wyverne—that upset her altogether. And not one word, good or bad, would she speak to me, and me fretting my heart out, and trying to get from her even a look. It's mad she was entirely. Insane, and out of her head, and no mistake. And me that used to lie awake all night long crying my eyes out about her. I was looking forward to her coming here with me to Mordaunt Manor, where she'd get over her grief. But never a word could I get from her. Oh, it's mad she was—mad, and nothing else, from grief and trouble. There's a vein of madness in the Wyverne family, Kane dear, and she's got a touch of the family complaint, and that's all about it, and there you have it. And that's how it was with poor, dear, old Guardy Wyverne, that for the last two or three months of his life was positively out of his mind all the time. It was really awful. And only think, at the last, he really mistook poor, dear, darling Inez for me, and told her she wasn't his daughter, and that excited the poor darling so that her own mind gave way. Oh, I saw it. I often thought about that. But I thought the best way was to leave her alone, and not worry her, or bother her, and all that, and she'd soon come around. Oh, why couldn't she have been more frank with me? If she had only shown me that letter! And who is this Gounod? What an awful name! And only think of her running away on a wild errand after a perfect stranger who writes her a crazy letter! Oh, sure but it's mad she was—poor, dear, darling, old Inez. Really it makes me shudder when I think of it. To run away so, you know, I was frightened out of my wits all the time, and I should have gone all the way there with her, but I went as far as Southampton, and my courage failed. She was so perfectly awful, you know, Kane dear; and do you know, Kane dear, she didn't speak a word all the way there, and seemed really angry that I'd come?

" And then, you know, Kane dear, I went back—and oh, but it was me that had the sore heart, and then I had to go to Mordaunt Manor at once, for they were doing something about poor, dear Guardy Wyverne's estate, and they said they'd have to shut up his house and sell every thing. So I had to come here to Mordaunt Manor, and then came poor, dear, darling papa—and oh, he was so very, very ill! and—and you know what happened."

Here Bessie's emotion made her break down ; and, burying her face in her hands, she sobbed piteously. It was very sad, and Kane's eyes moistened as he saw the beautiful golden head bowed down, and the slender frame shaken by sobs. Gwyn, too, was overcome, and in his despair tried all the caresses of which he was capable to soothe Bessie's agitated feelings.

At length she revived and raised her head, but kept her eyes fixed mournfully on the floor.

"It's easy to see how her letters missed me," said she, sadly. "She had directed them to London, and they never reached me. I left no directions about forwarding letters, for I never expected to get any, and didn't give it a thought. Its heart-broke I was about dear, darling Inez, and I never thought of any thing. How could her letters ever get to me? And so there she was, and there she is now—and oh, my darling, darling Iny! my sweet, sweet sister ! what a power of suffering you've had to bear !"

Kane's eyes now overflowed. He was a brave, strong, resolute man, but he was very tender-hearted, and the sight of Bessie's grief was too much. Gwyn, also, was overcome.

"And oh, Kane dear, why didn't you tell me last night? I'll go to her at once. We must all go."

At this Kane smiled. It was just what he most longed for.

"But I'll write her too," said Bessie, "first of all, in case of any delay on our part. I'll write her this night, for I can't leave at once, not for a day or two, and if she only gets a letter to know I'm coming, it'll cheer her a little, and she'll wait patiently, the poor, sweet darling ! So you'll give me her address now, Kane dear."

As Bessie said this she drew a tablet from her pocket, and, taking out the pencil, handed it to Kane.

Kane took the pencil and tablet, and wrote the address of Inez.

Then they talked long and tenderly of their absent friend, and when at last the time came for Bessie to retire, she held her cheek for Kane to kiss, and said :

" Good-night, Kane dear, and pleasant dreams to you ! "

CHAPTER XXXIX.

THE TEMPTER.

KANE was joyous over the prospect of Bessie's journey to Inez, and still more so at her eagerness and her promptness. On the following day, Bessie informed him that she had written and sent her letter, and that she would not be able to set out herself for two or three days yet. Such a delay did not seem long to Kane, who now, that the future of Inez seemed secure, felt less haste to see her again. He could well afford to stay here a little longer, where all was so pleasant; and now that this troublesome matter had been arranged, the enjoyment which he found in his visit was more pure and unalloyed than it had thus far been. Gwyn seconded Bessie's proposal with the earnestness that might have been expected of him, and it was arranged that in three days they should all set out together. In the mean time, the active nature of Kane required employment, and the Witch's Rock once more recurred to his mind more attractively than ever. Bessie was the first to mention it. She did it, in a laughing way, by asking him if he still intended to get his knife before he left. The question was met by an eager declaration, on Kane's part, that he would make an attempt on the cliff that very day. His simple preparations had already been made, and it only remained to set forth for the scene of action.

On the way there, Bessie was more lively, more radiant, and more charming, than ever. With Kane, who was full of his enterprise, she kept up an incessant conversation of the most animated character, principally about the Witch's Rock. She made him tell the story of his old exploit all over. She was particular as to the shape and size of the cave, and the way in which he had swung himself backward and forward. And, as she listened, she laughed and shuddered by turns, till, in her excitement, she seemed almost hysterical. Kane was too much engrossed with his plan and purpose, and, as yet, too little acquainted with her, to notice any thing unusual in her manner, but Gwyn was very forcibly impressed by it. Gwyn, indeed, was himself unusually silent, and seemed somewhat depressed. This may have been on account of some forebodings of indefinable calamity in his own mind; or it may have been anxiety on account of the unusual and unhealthy excitement of Bessie; or it may have been, after all, merely the natural silence and obscurity which befalls one who makes a third party where the other two are uncommonly talkative and lively.

In this way they reached the place. The cliff was on the side of a hill, which was easily climbed by a moderate acclivity about half a mile off. By ascending this they were able to reach the edge of the cliff without difficulty, and here Kane flung down his rope and began to make the necessary preparations for his descent.

The hill was a long one, of moderate elevation, being a spur thrown out from Skiddaw; and the cliff was formed by its abrupt termination on one side. It was, as has been said, about two hundred and fifty feet in height. The top overhung slightly, and at the bottom was a wilderness of sharp rocks, the *débris* of the cliff, which had been dislodged in the course of centuries by frost and storm, and had fallen here.

The changes which had taken place here since Kane was a boy were not very extensive. On looking about him, he recognized several landmarks without difficulty. In particular, he noticed a large oak-tree, around whose trunk he had then fastened his line; and around the same tree he proposed to fasten it again. This tree, fortunately, stood over the very place where the cavern was, and consequently was by far the best point from which to start on an attempt of this nature.

Kane bound his rope about this tree with a security and a dexterity which indicated a practised hand. After this he flung the remainder of the rope over the cliff, and looked over to see how far it reached. It went down more than half the way. Then he took a carriage-rug, which he had brought with him, and put it under the rope where it ran over the edge of the cliff, so as to prevent any danger that might arise from the grinding of the rope against the rock.

As he made these preparations, he kept up an incessant flow of lively and joyous remarks; and jested about the witch, who, according to tradition, ought still to be there, and who, he maintained, was bound to punish him in some way for his former intrusion into her abode. With this Bessie chimed in, and was very merry over an absurd picture which she suggested of a fight between Kane and the witch in mid-air, the one swinging from a rope, and the other flying on her broomstick.

This conversation, absurd though it might be, was yet destined to be memorable to one of these two speakers.

It was in the midst of this laughter and merriment, that Kane advanced to the edge of the cliff, and prepared to descend.

"Good-by, Kane dear, and take care of yourself," said Bessie, with a smile.

"Good-by," said Kane; "never fear. I'll get that knife."

The next moment he had descended over the edge, and was out of sight.

All this time Gwyn had said not a word. He stood with a clouded brow, and looked on abstractedly. There was trouble in his mind. Kane, however, had not noticed this; for his attention was altogether engrossed by his preparations, and by Bessie. Thus Gwyn had watched Kane in silence while he bound the rope about the tree, while he wrapped the carriage-rug around it, and while he went over the edge of the cliff. Then he walked slowly forward and knelt down.

He looked over.

The knotted rope hung far down, and there below him was Kane clinging to it with his muscular gripe, and letting himself down farther and farther. As he went farther down, and increased the distance between himself and the top of the cliff, there began a vibration of the rope, and Gwyn could see his brother slowly swinging to and fro with a movement that increased as he descended. The sight had something in it which to Gwyn was intolerable, and, turning away, he stood up.

As he did so, he felt a slight touch on his arm. He turned with a sharp and sudden movement. There seemed something in that touch which was strangely startling to him. Yet, when he turned, he saw only Bessie. Unusual, indeed, was it for the touch of the gentle hand of this young wife to give such a shock to so loving a husband. But Gwyn had not been himself all this day. There had been something on his mind; and this something had transformed him.

So now he turned, and saw Bessie. Her face was perfectly calm and placid, and her large, soft, deep-blue eyes were fixed upon his with that open, childlike gaze which formed the sweetest and most attractive peculiarity of Bessie's face. For, when Bessie looked full upon any other person, there always seemed in her face such a suggestion of youth and innocence that the one who encountered it never failed to feel attracted. Never before had Gwyn failed to be affected by her sweet glance, but now, as he encountered it, there was no response on his part; nor did his brow relax in the slightest degree from that gloom into which it had settled.

But Gwyn's look produced no effect whatever upon Bessie. Whether she noticed it or not, did not appear. Perhaps she did observe it, but attached no importance to it; or perhaps she was too much taken up with her own thoughts to regard any thing external. She, therefore, looked at him with her usual expression, and with that same good-natured and fascinating smile upon her lips which she always wore, and, with a tender, confiding gesture, she stole her little hand toward that of Gwyn.

As her hand touched that of her husband, he shrank back and turned away his head. This movement was too apparent to be unnoticed, and Bessie stood with her hand still stretched out, looking at her husband in silence for a few moments. The smile did not pass from her face, nor did she appear to be in the least degree offended or hurt. On the contrary, after a slight hesitation, she renewed her advances in such a way that they admitted of no rejection, for she stepped toward him and quietly took his arm.

"Sure, Gwynnie dear," said she, "you're not yourself at all at all this day. Not one word have you spoken, good or bad, since last night. And I'm sure I think you're really unkind. Haven't you ever a word at all at all to throw to a poor little girl that's fairly heart-broken with such coldness and neglect?"

Bessie, as she said this, leaned tenderly, lovingly, and confidingly, upon her husband's arm, and looked up into his face with her sunniest smile. But Gwyn stood with his face averted, and his eyes looking far off at vacancy, and the cloud, still dark and gloomy, over his brow. The broad, serene tranquillity that once had reigned there—the frank, open, boyish look that had once distinguished him was gone, and in its place there had come the shadow of some stern, dark, unhallowed thought, such as had never before been known to his honest soul. And it was the spell of this thought that at this moment held him bound, so that he remained inaccessible to Bessie's witchery, to her smile of sweetness, her glance of tenderness, and her words of love. There was a change in him beyond a doubt, and, whether that change should be transient or permanent, depended very much upon the issues of this hour.

After waiting patiently for some time, Bessie found that Gwyn would not look at her; so, with a little sigh, she looked away, and at the same time nestled more closely to him, clasping his arm in both of hers.

"Sure and he must have the steady nerves, so he must—mustn't he, Gwynnie dear?"

To this Gwyn murmured something which was apparently intended for a reply, but was quite unintelligible. It seemed to encourage Bessie, however. She pressed his arm closer, and one of her hands sought out his, and this time succeeded in finding a place where it lay nestling.

"And he must be down an awful distance, so he must—mustn't he, Gwynnie dear?" continued Bessie, after a few moments, making another venture to mollify Gwyn, and draw him into a conversation.

To this Gwyn once more replied as before, in an inarticulate, unintelligible way.

"And oh, but it's the heavy man he must be, and a heavy weight on the end of that bit of string," continued Bessie, who seemed to be cautiously feeling her way onward into a conversation about whose reception she felt doubtful.

Gwyn drew a long breath, and said nothing.

Bessie stole a look up at his face. It was still averted. It was averted purposely. He was forcing himself to look away for some reason or other, and this Bessie could easily see.

"It's awfully dangerous, so it is—isn't it, then, Gwynnie darling?" said she again, in a low voice. Gwyn said nothing.

"Gwynnie," said Bessie, pressing his arm —"Gwynnie, why won't you speak?"

Gwyn drew a long breath.

"I think," said he, "we are standing too near the edge."

"Sure and what danger is there?" said Bessie. "It's like a rock you are, so it is, Gwynnie dear, and, when you are with me, never a fear have I."

She said these words tenderly and lovingly, and pressed his arm again. For a moment the cloud on Gwyn's brow seemed to be dispelled at the softer emotion which Bessie's caress had caused, but, in another moment, the tenderness had passed, and the stern look came back.

"We must not stand so near it," said he, in a harsh voice. "It's too dangerous."

With these words he stepped back about half a dozen paces, while Bessie accompanied him, still clinging to his arm. Here they both stood in the same attitude in which they had been before, Bessie still clasping his arm. A short silence followed. Bessie looked at the ground; Gwyn, as before, stood looking far away at vacancy.

All around them lay a beautiful scene; beneath the brow of the cliff was the valley, and beyond rose wooded heights. The passing breeze sighed and murmured through the trees, and the twitter of sparrows arose through the air. But nothing in this scene was perceived by Gwyn, in that deep abstraction of soul into which he had been plunged. But Bessie's eyes rested upon the rope which ran along the ground before her, holding suspended in mid-air the precious burden of a human life.

"It would be a shocking thing, so it would," said she, at length, "if any thing were to happen to him, and it's not unlikely. Stranger things than that have happened, and it's a highly-dangerous venture."

At these words Gwyn frowned more darkly, and, with a quick gesture, withdrew his arm from Bessie's clasp, and, stepping away a foot or two, he stood in gloomy silence.

"What made you let him go down, Gwynnie dear?" asked Bessie, in a low voice, after watching him in silence for a few moments.

Gwyn made no reply.

"It's a small, thin rope, and might grind itself away easy enough, so it might," continued Bessie, who, as she spoke, watched Gwyn's face closely, as though wishing to see in what way her remarks would be received; "and sure," she continued, after a pause, "if it wasn't for the bit of a rug that's under it, the rope would have ground itself out by this time. And oh, but wouldn't it be the strange thing, Gwynnie dear, if any thing should happen, and him coming here on such an errand? It would be so very—very—sad, wouldn't it, Gwynnie darling?"

Bessie did not seem now to expect any reply to her remarks in words, but contented herself with watching Gwyn's face. That face changed not, except, if possible, to grow more and more stern and dark at every new word of hers. Was there a struggle going on within him at that hour? Was his evil genius struggling with his better self? He said nothing, nor did he try to distract his thoughts by any converse with the bright and pleasant being at his side, who still showed the same sunlight in her eyes, and the same smile on her face.

"It's so very, very small a thing," she continued, "that saves him. It's the bit of a rug, so it is—nothing more. It's the rug that—that keeps dear darling Kane from—from being taken from us, isn't it, Gwynnie darling?"

"I wonder how far he is down," she continued; "sure, but wasn't it mad in him to go, and the rope so thin? Sure, and if it wasn't for the bit of a rug, where'd he be now? So thin it is, and so small, and so easily cut—"

As Bessie said this, Gwyn turned his face and looked at her with a terrible glance. His face was ghastly pale, and big drops of perspiration covered his brow. Bessie looked at him with her usual calm, clear gaze, and with the same pleasant smile.

"I wish you wouldn't look at me so, Gwynnie dearest," said she, at length; "you really make me feel quite nervous. Come and let us take a peep down and see where poor, dear Kane is. Come."

She started off toward the edge of the cliff where the rope went over. For a moment Gwyn gasped for breath. Then he said, in a harsh, hoarse voice:

"Don't go!"

"Oh, but I just will then," said Bessie, with a laugh. "Sure, I'm not a bit afraid, though you seem to be. Do you know, Gwynnie dear, I begin to think you're a sad coward, so I do?"

With these words she tripped lightly toward the rope.

"Bessie, come back!" cried Gwyn, sternly.

"Sure, I'll go back to you in a minute, so I will. I just want to take one peep, and I'll show that I'm braver than you, so I will."

With these words she stooped down, and knelt by the rope, just at the edge of the cliff, and bent her head down low. Her left hand rested on the rug, her right on the rock.

Gwyn stood like one paralyzed; there was a terrible thought in his mind; he looked at her with a wild, glassy stare of horror.

After a few moments Bessie drew back her head, and turned and looked at Gwyn with a bright smile. Then, still holding her left hand on the rug, she put her right hand into her pocket, as though she intended to draw out something.

What that something might be had in an instant suggested itself to Gwyn's wild fancy. A groan burst from him.

He sprang toward her, and, before she could be aware of his intention, before she could even shrink back, there was a wild and terrible cry in her ears. She felt herself seized in a fierce and resistless grasp, and torn from the ground. It was Gwyn's hand, the hand which never before had touched her save in love and tenderness, that now grasped her with the fury of despair. He seized her in his arms. For a moment he held her uplifted from the ground, and Bessie could see his face, and she saw in it that which made her think that he was about to fling her over the precipice. For a moment he held her there, and a shriek burst from her which was wrung out by pain and by terror. For a moment he held her—one single moment—and then he hurled her violently away from him.

She fell to the ground headlong and heavily. She lay senseless.

Her beautiful face, marble white, lay with her cheek on the hard ground; and her little hand, the right hand, which she had inserted in her pocket, still held in its grasp a simple handkerchief.

For a moment Gwyn stood horror-struck, then he staggered toward her and raised her up. The handkerchief in her hand had in it something piteous; he had imagined something else there. He had imagined horrors unspeakable. And this was all. Trembling from head to foot, he gently laid her down again, and kissed her pale face fondly, and tenderly examined her to see if she had received any injury. But, even at that dread moment, there was in his mind the presence of the evil thought which all day long had darkened his soul; and, obeying a sudden impulse, he rushed once more to the edge of the cliff and looked down.

———◆———

CHAPTER XL.

[RENEWING HIS YOUTH.

MEANWHILE Kane had gone steadily down on his adventurous descent. The rope had been formed on the model of the one which he had used when a boy, and was very well adapted for such a purpose. The knots and loops which occurred at intervals enabled him to maintain a firmer hold than would otherwise have been possible, and to secure an occasional rest even for his feet. Gradually, as he went down, he became aware of one circumstance which troubled him not a little. This was the vibration of the rope. With his weight at the end, he found himself vibrating to and fro like the pendulum of a clock, and the farther he descended the longer did these vibrations grow. But he was not one who could easily give up any undertaking upon which he had once fairly entered, and so, in spite of this, he still continued to descend. Fortunate was it for him that he had guarded against the twisting or untwisting of the rope, by which a rotatory motion might have been given to him, in which case he could scarcely have saved himself from dizziness, but this he had contrived to prevent by doubling and knotting the rope.

He continued, therefore, without stopping, though, at length, the long vibrations of the rope grew somewhat troublesome. At first, these oscillations had taken place in a line which was parallel to the face of the cliff, but, as he went farther down, this line of motion gradually changed to one which drew in more toward the cliff; and finally, as he swung in, his feet touched the rock. An oscillation in this direction favored his purpose, and he sought to preserve it for the remainder of the way. He continued descending, therefore, until at length he found himself opposite the famous place known as the Witch's Hole.

This place was very peculiarly situated. It was a recess in the face of the cliff, to which there was no access whatever except in some such way as this. The sides receded all around the cave for some eight or ten feet, and there was no foothold except on the floor of the cave at its mouth. This was only a small space about six feet wide, and was so difficult of access that one single occupant could easily have defended himself against any number of assailants. As Kane reached a point opposite this place, the vibrations of the line backward and forward brought him alternately to and from the cave. This oscillation he increased by working his body in that fashion which is used on a swing, and thus he swung himself nearer and nearer. At length his feet touched the rock on one side, and he was able to kick himself off in such a way as to direct the next movement toward the cave. In this he was successful, and the

next inward swing brought his feet to the cave floor. Still this was not enough, for the impetus had not been sufficient to give him a foothold. He therefore kicked himself off once more with all his strength. He swung far out, and then, as he swung back again, he watched closely, and held himself all gathered up to take advantage of any opportunity of landing on the floor of the cave. This time he was swung inside, within reach of a rough rock on one side of the mouth of the cave. This rock he caught at with his feet. For a moment he held himself there, and then gradually let himself down, until at length he reached the floor of the cave. He then carefully pulled in the rope, and fastened it about this very rock.

He had reached it at last, but the effort had been an exhaustive one, especially these last exertions in swinging himself into the cave. He sat down for a short time and rested, and looked all around.

The cave was not large. In fact it was rather a recess than a cave, and was merely a fissure in the cliff, the bottom of which had filled up with rubbish sufficient to form a floor. Above, its sides ran up till they met one another at a sharp angle. The depth of the fissure was about twenty-five or thirty feet, and its width some eight or ten feet. There was nothing more to see than this, and it was hardly worth the risk of a life.

Perhaps, if the history of this cave could have been told, the story would have been one quite as interesting as any of the legends about the witch which had grown up around it. Its very inaccessibility had probably caused it to be the lurking-place of fugitives in ages of the past. It required only the resolution to descend as Kane had done, and then they were safe. Still better would it have been for any fugitive here to keep a rope hanging down to the ground below, and come and go in that way. It was not impossible, therefore, or even unlikely, that this cave had been the scene of extraordinary events in the past, and that this floor, if it were dug up, might disclose articles of human workmanship—arrow-heads, stone weapons, earthen pottery—or any other things which may be left to mark the place where man has once been. Celts may have fled here from Saxons, Saxons from Normans. This may have been the refuge of fugitives in the Wars of the Roses, or in the wars of the Parliament.

Protestant or Catholic might have found here a safe hiding-place from religious persecution; here the hermit of the middle ages, the witch of the Stuart period, and the outlaw of a later age, may all have succeeded to one another.

Kane, however, had not come as an explorer, nor as an archæologist. He had not come even out of bravado, though it might have seemed so. He had come to reach out a hand to his lost boyhood; to bring back a vanished past. He had come to renew his youth, to repeat his boyish exploit—above all, to get his knife, left here long years before. He did not allow himself much time for resting. A few minutes sufficed, after which he rose and walked farther in.

He went to the farthest end of the cave, and then scanned the rocky wall carefully. He was anxious to see whether that memorial of his former visit which he had left here was still visible. His curiosity was rewarded. There on the dark rock, cut in large, bold letters, he read that memorial—his own name:

"KANE RUTHVEN."

He stood looking at it for some time with varying emotions, while all that past came back before him—that bright past, which Bessie had been assisting him, or rather encouraging him, to recall. The sight of this name suggested that other object of his search—the knife. He looked down. For some time he saw no signs of any thing; but, at length, an object met his sight, lying close against the rock, and looking like a stone. He picked this up.

It was his knife.

Dust and mud had caked about it, and the blades and springs were all rusted together; but, nevertheless, it was his own knife—the very knife which he had carried down here as a boy, and with which he had carved that name. He looked at it with a pensive gaze, and then slowly returned to the mouth of the cave. Here he sat for some time, looking out. But it was not the scene outside, magnificent though it was, which met his eyes. His gaze was fixed upon vacancy, and, if he saw any thing, it was the forms and scenes of the past which his memory brought up before him.

At length, he started up. There was nothing more to be done here, or to be seen.

He had exhausted the possibilities of the place, and had gained the object of his daring exploit. Nothing remained now but to return. This was far less difficult than the descent. He had no trouble now about directing his course. At first, as he let himself out, the long swing of the rope was troublesome, and its return swing threatened to drive him with somewhat too great force against the rocks; but this he guarded against, and, as he steadily ascended, the oscillations grew gradually less.

At length, he reached the top of the cliff.

As his head rose above it, he expected to see Gwyn and Bessie; he expected to feel their eager hands pulling at him to help him; to hear their words of encouragement, of wonder, of congratulation; to see their faces full of sympathy and delight, Bessie with her gentle and merry glance, Gwyn with his broad, frank face and hearty, loving ways. All this he expected to see.

But there was no voice sent down as he neared the summit; no hands were outstretched; no faces full of welcome smiles were there. There was silence, and it was not until he had clambered up and looked around that he saw what scene had been awaiting him here on the top of the cliff.

This is what he saw:

A prostrate female form, and, kneeling by her side, a man with a ghastly face and a look of horror. Kane saw that this man was Gwyn; yet so appalling was the change which had taken place in him that he stood dumb with amazement. For Gwyn seemed ten years, or twenty years, older than when Kane had left him. To his fresh, boyish look had succeeded a grim, austere face—a face that had a grayish tinge over its pallor; and over it there was spread an expression that was not like any thing which Kane had ever before seen in any human face. And, as he looked, there came across him, like a sudden flash, the thought that it looked like the face of a man who had been tempted of the devil, and had seen him face to face.

Thus, then, it was that Kane came back to Gwyn and Bessie.

Kane walked slowly toward his brother. Thus far Gwyn had stared at him with a dazed look; but now, as he approached, he jumped up hastily from Bessie's side, and hurried to meet him. There was a piteous

" A prostrate female form, and kneeling by her side, a man."—Page 206.

expression now on his face—one of eager welcome that seemed struggling to surmount his despair. He grasped Kane's hand convulsively in both of his, and gazed at him with an indescribable look. Kane felt bewildered. All this was incomprehensible. He could only see that some disaster had happened. The prostrate form of Bessie showed that she was concerned in this, and the anguish of Gwyn was intelligible enough on that ground; yet he could not help feeling astonished that Gwyn could have the heart, under such circumstances, to think of him, much less to come and welcome him back so eagerly. He could not possibly know what had occurred, nor could he even conjecture the inconceivable importance which his reappearance had in Gwyn's eyes.

"Heavens!" cried Kane. "What's all this? What has happened to her?"

He thought only of Bessie now. With this thought, he wondered at Gwyn's apparent forgetfulness of her; and so he tore his hand from his brother's grasp, somewhat impatiently, and hurried over to the prostrate form.

Bessie was lying on her back, with her face upturned. Her eyes were closed; her lips were slightly parted; the roseate hue of her cheeks had given place to a waxen pallor; and her waving hair flowed like a flood of golden glory about her forehead and neck and shoulders. She was motionless; she was senseless. It was a piteous spectacle.

Piteous, indeed, it seemed to Kane, who bent over her with his mind full of remembrances of her last appearance, and thoughts of the contrast between that and this—the glow of health, the blue eyes fixed on him in their mirthful innocence, the red lips curved into merry smiles, the dimpled, rosy cheeks, the laughter, the jestings—above all, the tender, loving way of referring all her thoughts and all her joys to that husband whom she loved so devotedly. And here she was now! What was the meaning of it? Here was Gwyn, crushed. Well he might be. Yet, what did it all mean?

These thoughts filled his mind as he knelt by Bessie's side and chafed her hands. But, though Gwyn also united his efforts with those of Kane, there did not appear any signs of returning animation; and, at length, Kane advised an immediate return to Ruthven Towers, carrying her with them as best they could; for there restoratives could be obtained which were not to be found elsewhere. To this Gwyn at once acceded. Kane was about to help him carry Bessie down to the carriage; but this Gwyn would not allow. The proposal seemed to excite in him a repugnance so strong that it amounted to nothing less than horror; and Kane, who could not help noticing it, was filled with new astonishment. Gwyn, however, said nothing; and, indeed, he had not spoken a word all this time. Stolidly and silently he bent down, and, encircling the slender form of his senseless wife in his strong arms, lifted her lightly and easily, and then carried her to the carriage at the foot of the hill.

Ruthven Towers was not very far away, and the carriage drove there rapidly. Gwyn held Bessie in his arms all the way, and looked at her with a mixture of helplessness and agony. On reaching their destination he carried her himself up to her own room, and committed her to the care of her attendants. A doctor was hastily sent for, and Gwyn waited in despair for the result.

Meanwhile, Kane was waiting below in a state of the deepest anxiety and suspense. Dinner came and went, and Kane was alone at that repast. Not long after, Gwyn made his appearance. He informed Kane gravely that the doctor had come and had found Bessie recovered from her swoon; he had given her a sleeping-draught, and she had been sleeping ever since. The doctor did not anticipate any serious results, and hoped that in two or three days she would be herself again.

To Kane's anxious inquiries as to the cause of the accident, Gwyn replied in somewhat vague and incoherent terms, for he was very awkward at evading the truth, and unskilled in deceit of any kind. From what he did say, however, Kane gathered the information that she had stumbled somehow against the rope, and in falling had struck her head. Of the part that Gwyn had taken in this affair he had not the remotest idea.

All that night Gwyn remained awake, hovering about in the neighborhood of Bessie's room, and anxiously watching the progress of affairs. Every thing went on well. Bessie slept soundly. Her face had regained its usual color, and she showed no trace of injury. At length he felt so hopeful about her that he went to bed. It was about dawn when he retired, and he slept until late in the following day. His first thoughts were about Bessie, and, hastily dressing, he hurried at once to her room.

But there awaited him a great surprise. On reaching the room the house-keeper met him and handed him a note. At the same time she informed him that Lady Ruthven had passed a very comfortable night, and had awakened early, feeling so well that she had gone out for a drive, and had not returned.

Gwyn was completely overwhelmed by this intelligence. He took the letter, and, looking at his watch, found that it was two o'clock. On inquiring about the time when Bessie had left, he learned that it was about six o'clock in the morning. So long an absence, under such circumstances, excited his worst fears, and the despairing thought arose that Bessie had punished him for his violence by deserting him forever. He hurried to his room with the letter, and for some time was afraid to open it, for fear that he should read his doom. At length he could no longer endure the suspense, and, tearing it open, he read the following:

"I'm quite myself again, Gwynnie dearest, so there's no use in life for you to be worrying about me. I'm going out for a drive, and may not be back for a few days. The fact is, after what has happened, I have come to the conclusion that a short separation will be best for both of us. Do you know, Gwynnie darling, I really think you must have been insane, and your head was full of horrid fancies. You had some awful idea about me which I do not like to think of. It was a terrible mistake, so it was. I hope that, if you are by yourself for a little while, you will see how very, very wrong you were, and how fearfully you have misunderstood your poor Bessie. Adieu, then, Gwynnie dearest, and au revoir. I forgive all, and love you with all my heart, dear. Don't forget,
　　　　"Your own loving
　　　　　　　　"BESSIE."

This letter drove away the worst part of Gwyn's distress, but still there remained the deepest longing to see her, and the strongest anxiety about her health. The very forgiveness which she granted him increased these desires after her, and he hurried at once to the stables. Here, to his intense joy, he found that the carriage had returned in which

Bessie had gone, and that it had only taken her to Mordaunt Manor, whereupon he mounted a horse and rode there with the utmost speed.

On reaching Mordaunt Manor the porter handed him a letter, and informed him that Lady Ruthven had gone away along with Mrs. Lugrin, leaving this for him. It was only with a violent effort that Gwyn concealed the emotion which he felt at this intelligence, and, taking the letter in silence, he turned away, full of wonder and apprehension. He had come, full of love and longing, to hear Bessie's words of forgiveness, and to bring her back. But she was gone, and he turned away with an appalling sense of desolation. What did this mean? Had she gone back from her word? Had Mrs. Lugrin persuaded her to retract her forgiveness and punish him more severely? This looked like it.

But speculation was idle. Here was her letter in his hand, and she herself spoke there.

He tore it open and read:

"GWYNNIE DARLING: When you get this I shall be on my way to Paris. Do not be at all uneasy about me, darling, for I assure you I am quite myself again. If you had been awake this morning I would have explained, but you were asleep, and I kissed you for good-by, dearest.

"You see, I feel awfully uneasy about poor, dear, darling Inez, and I am frantic to see her; and, when I came here, I found Mrs. Lugrin willing to accompany me, so I decided to go. You and dear Kane will come on immediately, of course, for I know, Gwynnie dearest, you will be quite unable to live more than two or three days without me; so, when you come, you will find me with my mamma's papa, dear Grandpa Magrath, at the Hôtel Gascoigne, 125 Rue de la Ferronière. And now, once more, good-by, darling, and don't forget,　　　　Your own loving
　　　　　　　　"BESSIE.

"P. S.—You may as well show this to dear old Kane, Gwynnie darling, for it will explain my somewhat abrupt departure. Once more, good-by.　　　　　　　"BESSIE."

CHAPTER XLI.

REPENTANCE.

On turning away from Mordaunt Manor, Gwyn was quite unconscious of the way in which he was going; and, if his horse directed his steps homeward, it was more from his own inclination than from any direction of his rider. As for Gwyn, his thoughts were busy with the events and experiences of the previous day. He went over all that he had thought, and said, and done; he recalled all Bessie's words, and acts, and looks; he arraigned himself and her before the bar of his conscience, and passed every thing in review up to that culminating scene on the precipice.

A dark thought had been suggested to him. It had come first from Bessie, when she lamented the prospect that was now before them, when she recoiled from the thought of poverty, and preferred that evil should happen to Kane rather than to them. This thought had passed into Gwyn's mind, and had taken root there. Thus far he had been an honorable gentleman, with an upright and loyal soul; but all men have their peculiar temptations, and this proved to be the very one which was most dangerous to him. It came so insidiously, it came from her whom he adored and idolized, it was enforced by her grief, her tears, and her loving caresses. In the midst of their happiness one had come who was to expel them from their paradise, and Bessie's nature could not endure the thought. So this temptation had come most insidiously, most powerfully; and, having once entered into his mind, it had taken root, and grown, strengthened, and fostered, and developed, by events and by words in which both Kane and Bessie had borne a part.

Thus the thought, "If he had never come," became a wish: "Oh, that he had never come!" "Oh, that he had been dead when we supposed him to be!" "Oh, that he were dead now!" It thus grew and enlarged itself, until Gwyn found himself at last wishing for the death of that very brother over whose return he had but lately rejoiced with sincere and enthusiastic joy.

It was Bessie who shaped his thoughts to this; it was Bessie who was the cause of this wish, who alone gave it any point or meaning. He could not bear to see her tears. He could not bear the thought of any misfortune befalling her. He had brought her here to a home which she loved, and he could not bear to see her expelled.

Then came circumstances which changed the secret wish into a temptation to act. There was, above all, the proposal to go over the cliff. Had it not been for this, Gwyn's wish might have eventually died a natural death from lack of opportunity. But the temptation came as it comes to many a man, and, following close upon the temptation, there came also the opportunity.

That opportunity reached its height on the top of the cliff when Kane's head disappeared from view as he descended on his perilous journey. As Gwyn stood there in gloomy silence, he was wrestling with the Tempter, who now, in his utmost power, was urging him to act. This was the conflict in which he was engaged, and at this moment it was Bessie herself who interposed and lent her aid, not to the tempted, but to the Tempter.

It had been her misfortune all along to aid the Tempter and to weaken her husband. She it was who earnestly urged Kane to his adventure when she should have dissuaded him; she it was who encouraged him, and jested with him up to the last moment, all unmindful of her husband's anguish; and she it was who now, at this supreme moment, came forth to deal a final blow upon his fainting resolution. It was as though the Tempter had suddenly assumed form; as though the devil had appeared in the shape of an angel; and not only an angel, but more, the one whom he loved better than life, and better than his own soul—his beautiful young bride.

What was it that she had said? She had said all that was worst at such a moment. Every word that she uttered was a suggestion of this opportunity; every word was an expression of that dark temptation whose accomplishment was now so easy. Each word that she spoke was worse than its predecessor; and, finally, at the close of this great agony of soul, the climax was reached, when she stepped to the rope with the intention, as he thought, of doing the deed herself. She called him "coward" as she turned away. and, as she stooped to the rope, it seemed to him that her gentle smile concealed a terrible purpose, and that her hand sought her pocket to draw forth a knife. Then it was that the spell was broken, the temptation passed, and he tore her from the place and flung her headlong.

Such was the history of this temptation. And what then ? Was this so ? Was Bessie indeed a Lady Macbeth of more delicate mould, leading on her husband to crime? Was all this gentle grace, and light-hearted mirthfulness, and childlike innocence, but a mask ? Heaven seemed to have poured its own sunlight over her brow, and into her eyes, and through her heart; was all this but a mockery ?

No—a thousand times no ! The moment that this thought presented itself, that moment it was cast out utterly. It was not worth reasoning about. Even if his love had not assured him of her innocence and truth, he could find countless ways of assuring himself of this, and of explaining all.

She guilty? As well call Kane himself guilty. Her first words, which had suggested the dark temptation, he now considered the thoughtless and natural utterances of a nature too innocent to conceal any feeling which it has. She recoiled, as was natural, from so great a sacrifice. She was mournful, pettish, unreasonable, like a child in the presence of some task too hard for its accomplishment. She had no concealment of any thing from her husband, and these transient feelings were thus disclosed in the fond intimacy of love. They passed away, for on the next day there was not a cloud on her brow, and her manner toward Kane was as frank and cordial as before. If the effect on him was more permanent, it was not her fault.

Then came Kane's proposal to scale the cliff, which Bessie warmly encouraged. But this was Kane's doing principally, and, if Bessie favored the plan, it could hardly be considered as a sign of a guilty purpose. So, too, when Kane went down the cliff, Bessie remained and indulged in remarks which Gwyn now considered to have been thoughtless and random, without the slightest idea of any deeper meaning. She was playful and quiet all the time ; and, if any doubt remained as to her own utter freedom from guilt, it existed in that final proof which showed itself before his eyes so piteously when Bessie lay senseless on the rock, and the deadly knife, which he believed to be in her hand, turned out to be nothing more than a handkerchief.

Between the deadly knife and that soft, white, harmless handkerchief, Gwyn now saw a difference corresponding with that which existed between the tempting devil of his fancy and the soft, innocent being whom he had so terribly wronged.

Bessie guilty? What madness! Then, Kane was guilty too. Kane had as much guilt as Bessie. The suggestion had come, and the opportunity, from both; but both were innocent, nor could they be blamed if his own mind had developed these things into criminal thoughts.

Consequent upon such thoughts as these came endless self-reproach, which had never ceased to torment him since he had hurled Bessie senseless to the rock. He shuddered now at his own madness. A thrill of horror passed through every nerve as he thought how narrowly he had escaped being the murderer, not of Kane, but of Bessie herself. There lived in his memory a terrible picture—that scene on the top of the cliff, where Bessie lay, pallid as death, her beautiful face on the hard ground, her lifeless hand outstretched and displaying in mute appeal that white kerchief—fit emblem of her innocence—a piteous sight, a sight of infinite pathos, one which could never be forgotten.

Thoughts like these were terrible, but Gwyn could not banish them. All his blame was for himself; all his love, and pity, and fond excuses, were for his injured wife. He could not blame her for her departure. She had wished it. Let it be. He would submit. He read her letter over and over. It was a sweet consolation to his bleeding heart that she had given him that kiss of farewell. It was sweet, also, that she looked forward to his joining her at once. This now was his one hope, and he could scarcely control the impatient desire which he had to follow her. His feelings prompted him to set out for Paris at once, but a moment's reflection showed that he could not leave Kane so abruptly ; so he had reluctantly to continue on the course which his horse had already taken for him to Ruthven Towers.

He now began to feel embarrassed about meeting with Kane, for an explanation of some kind would be necessary in order to account for the utter abruptness of Bessie's departure; and he did not at first see how such an explanation could be given without disclosing things that he very much preferred to keep secret. But, at length, a very natural way suggested itself, by which he might account for it all; and this was Bessie's own letter to himself. In this last letter she had not referred in the faintest way to the affair on the cliff, nor had she again said any thing about forgiveness. It was a letter full of loving words, ascribing her departure solely to her anxiety about Inez, and her eager desire to see her. Most keenly was Gwyn conscious of the delicacy of feeling which had inspired this; for, though he was convinced that the real cause of her departure lay in his own treatment of her, yet he perceived that she had adopted this affection of hers for Inez as the real pretext; and as her affection for Inez was undoubted, and Inez was in a position of actual peril, the pretext was every way plausible. He therefore concluded to show the letter to Kane, and add any further explanation which might be needed, in accordance with its tone. It was evident to him that Bessie had this in her mind, and had written this second letter, not only to console him, but also to smooth his path toward explaining it to Kane. By the time that he had reached the gates of Ruthven Towers, Gwyn had settled this in his mind, and was therefore in a position to meet Kane without embarrassment.

Meanwhile, Kane had found himself in a most perplexing situation. On waking in the morning, he had inquired after Lady Ruthven's health, and had been informed that she was quite well again. Several hours passed, and he learned that Sir Gwyn was still sleeping. Upon this, he went off on a long stroll, from which he did not return till about four. On coming back to the house, there was a general air of confusion, which excited his attention. On inquiring whether Sir Gwyn was up, the servant whom he asked informed him that Sir Gwyn had gone hurriedly to Mordaunt Manor. The manner of the servant was so singular that Kane asked some more questions, and at length learned the astonishing news, which was now whispered all through the house, that Lady Ruthven had gone away at daybreak, very hurriedly, and that her husband, on hearing about it, had set out in pursuit of her in the greatest possible haste. All this was to Kane utterly unintelligible, and, though the servants' gossip gave this story the very worst coloring possible, he refused to believe it. Still the fact remained that

both had gone away most abruptly, without a word to him; and this was the thing that perplexed him.

The return of Gwyn put an end to this. Kane walked down to meet him, as he saw him come up, and could not help noticing the great change that had come over his brother's face. At first, he felt shocked, and anticipated the worst; but, as soon as Gwyn saw him, he put all these feelings to flight by the first words that he uttered.

"Well, Kane," said he, with an attempt, that was not altogether successful, at his old ease and cordiality of manner, "you must have felt awfully puzzled at our disappearance in this fashion. But the fact is, Bessie was so wild to see Inez that she couldn't wait for us, and so she has gone off to Paris. She was all right this morning, just as well as ever; and as I had been up all night, and wasn't awake, she quietly trotted off by herself, went to Mordaunt Manor, took Mrs. Lugrin, and is now *en route* for Paris. See—here is her letter. I went off after her, but was too late. We'll have to set out at once."

As Gwyn said this, he dismounted, and produced a letter from his pocket. What he had said was spoken, not only for Kane's benefit, but also for the benefit of the servants, some of whom were within hearing. He wished to give to Bessie's departure a matter-of-fact character, so as to prevent any scandal. In this he succeeded perfectly, for those who heard it understood by his words that Lady Ruthven's departure was quite natural, and that her husband was going to join her at once. So this much of Gwyn's purpose was accomplished.

To Kane, however, these words only afforded fresh perplexity. When he had seen Bessie last, she was senseless; and now he learned that she was on her way to Paris. So sudden a recovery, combined with so sudden a departure, was to him unaccountable. Why could she not have waited? He said nothing—he was too bewildered—but waited to hear Gwyn's further explanations.

Gwyn now led the way into the house.

"I'll show you her letter," he said. "It explains all. It was a sudden whim, or some sudden fear about Inez, you know; and she was awfully fond of her, you know; they were like sisters, and all that—couldn't wait for us—had to go the first moment she felt strong enough. Tell you what—we had better start off at once."

With remarks like these, of a decidedly jerky character, Gwyn accompanied his brother into the house, and then showed him Bessie's letter. Kane read it all through most carefully. To him it seemed evident that Bessie's whole motive for this sudden departure was her uneasiness about Inez, and her longing desire to see her. Her departure was sudden, yet the motive that had prompted it seemed to Kane only an additional proof of the noble, the loyal, the affectionate, and the self-sacrificing friendship of Bessie for Inez. And this only heightened the warm admiration which he already felt for Bessie. He could not help feeling touched by this sudden impulse, in obedience to which she had hurried off to seek and to save her friend.

But with the admiration which he felt for Bessie's loyal affection for Inez, there was mingled another and a very different feeling, excited by the mention of one name in her letter. This was the name of the man to whom she was going—him whom she claimed as a loved relative—Kevin Magrath.

Now to Kane Ruthven this man had already appeared in a twofold and altogether contradictory character—first, as a sort of accusing witness; secondly, as a remorseless villain. Latterly he had adopted that view of the man which he had received from Inez, whose whole story he had heard, and whose sentiments toward Kevin Magrath he had embraced. He now thought of him as the confederate of the guilty Wyverne, as the instigator of dark crimes, as the plotter against Inez. Yet it was to this very man that Bessie was now going. She would tell him, in her innocence and her unsuspecting trust, about Inez. She, out of her very love, might thus prove the worst enemy that Inez could have, and would, perhaps, be the means of bringing the helpless fugitive once more under the power of her remorseless persecutor.

Such thoughts and fears as these filled Kane's whole mind, to the exclusion of every thing else. It was a new and most unexpected change in the current of affairs—a change for which he was altogether unprepared, and which he hardly knew how to meet. In Bessie he believed implicitly as he believed in Inez. One of these regarded Kevin Magrath as her dearest friend, while the other regarded him as her worst enemy. Of his cruel treatment of Inez there could be no doubt. She had been enticed into his power by the most shameful deceit; she had been allured to what she supposed to be her father's bedside, and had been cajoled with a story of his death, and misled by forged letters. After this she had been kept in strict imprisonment. Of all this there was no doubt, and all this had been the work of Kevin Magrath. Yet this was the man whom Bessie loved, and under whose power she was about to bring Inez once more.

Kane read this letter in silence, and was absorbed in such thoughts as these. Gwyn had expected a severe course of questioning, and had tried to prepare himself for it, but, to his great relief, no questions were asked. Kane had too much to think of. In addition to the thoughts just narrated, he had others of equal importance, and prominent among these was the question whether he ought or ought not to tell Gwyn the whole truth about Kevin Magrath. Thus far, for reasons already mentioned, he had not divulged that name. But now circumstances had changed. There was danger ahead, and Gwyn ought to know what that danger was. Perhaps Bessie, as well as Inez, might fall into the hands of this unscrupulous villain, and the measure that he had already meted to the one he might deal out to the other also.

The question was a difficult one, and at length Kane decided to allow things to remain as they were, and not to mention to Gwyn any thing about what he conceived to be the true character of Kevin Magrath but only to suggest, in a general way, his apprehensions of danger.

"I don't like this," said he, at length. "I don't like it at all."

"Oh," said Gwyn, with an attempt at indifference, "she was so awfully fond of Inez you know, she had to go."

"Oh, I know all that," said Kane, "and I admire her for such a generous impulse; but, at the same time, it would have been a great deal better if she had waited. We ought to have gone together. There is too much danger—"

"Danger?"

"Yes, danger, for her and for Inez. You see, Inez has powerful enemies, and they are, no doubt, on the lookout for her. If Bessie's movements should be made known to them—a very possible thing—they might track her, and get her into their power as well as Inez. It seems to me that the enemies of one are the enemies of the other, and that the danger that threatens one may threaten both."

This suggestion of possible danger to Bessie at once roused a new feeling in Gwyn's heart. Already he longed to fly to her, out of his deep, yearning love; but now the possibility of danger formed a new motive, and one, too, which urged instant and immediate departure.

"Do you really think so?" he asked, anxiously.

"I do," said Kane, seriously.

"Then we had better go at once. If this is so, I cannot stay here another hour. I shall have to go, and you will have to excuse me, Kane."

"Excuse you, dear boy? I'll do nothing of the kind, for I will go myself. I only came here for the sake of Inez, and I am anxious, above all things, for Bessie to find her. Since Bessie has gone, I will go too."

That very evening Kane and Gwyn left Ruthven Towers. They might just as well have remained all night, for they gained nothing, and had to wait at Keswick; yet still they both felt less impatience and more satisfaction in doing so, since it seemed to them that they were at least on the way to their destination. They were as much as twenty-four hours behind Bessie, but they both hoped that this might make no material difference.

———

CHAPTER XLII.

THE TWO FRIENDS.

Bessie's accident appeared to have left no evil results behind, for she found herself well enough on the following morning to form the resolution of going to Paris, and to carry it out successfully. On the morning after she reached her destination, and drove at once to the Hôtel Gascoigne, where she remained a few hours. She then took a cab to the address of Inez, which had been given her by Kane Ruthven.

She found the place without much difficulty, and, telling the cabman to wait, she entered and asked for Inez. She did not have

12

to wait long. A hurried step, a cry of joy, and Inez flung herself into Bessie's arms, and the two friends embraced one another long and fervently. In the first delight of that meeting but little was said on either side, and it was a long time before either appeared to be able to make any coherent remark of any kind whatever.

"I knew you would come," cried Inez, as soon as she could speak. "I knew you would come as soon as you heard. I knew you would come, you darling—you darling! And did you see Kane? and did he tell you all? Oh, I think my heart will almost break with utter joy!"

"Sure but it's the cruel girl you were to me, and it's the sore heart I had," cried Bessie, reproachfully. "Wasn't I hoping to hear from you day after day, until at last I came to the conclusion that you'd given me up for good and all."

"But I couldn't—I couldn't, dear. Didn't Kane tell you about me?"

"Sure and he did—the whole story, entirely—and, of course, darling, I was able to account for what had seemed your very mysterous silence. Oh, my own poor, dear, darling Inez! how my heart bled for yours!—and I couldn't wait one single moment longer; but, as soon as I heard about you, I left every thing—yes, every thing—and hurried here."

At this proof of Bessie's loyalty and truth, Inez was affected to tears. She could not say any thing, but once more pressed her friend in her arms.

"But how did it happen, Bessie dearest," asked Inez, after a time, "that my letters never reached you?"

"Oh, sure but that's very easily explained, Inez darling," said Bessie. "You see, I had to leave poor papa's house—they were going to sell every thing; and, as you had left me, there was no help for it but for me to go, too. So I went away to my own home in Cumberland; and, by the same token, my other guardian came to take me away at that same time, having heard, you know, about poor, dear Guardy Wyverne's death. So you know, Inez dearest, you addressed your letters to me at London, I suppose, while I was away in Cumberland all the time; so, of course, I never received them."

This explanation fully accounted for what had seemed like Bessie's neglect, and vindicated her faithful friendship. Bessie's allusion to Mr. Wyverne as her "papa" struck Inez rather unpleasantly, and she now thought that between her and Bessie there was still that terrible secret which had already been so disastrous to her. That secret put her in opposition to Bessie — it gave her claims which were antagonistic to claims of Bessie's; and, if Bessie were to know of it, Inez saw that she would lose that sweet friendship which was now her dearest consolation. At this very first meeting with Bessie, therefore, she saw the necessity of being on her guard, and maintaining as much reserve as possible about the mystery of Bernal Mordaunt. The great difficulty here, however, was her ignorance as to how much Kane may have told Bessie.

While she was trying to think of some way by which she might find this out, Bessie herself volunteered to give her the information.

"Oh, my own darling!" exclaimed Bessie, "how very, very rash it was in you, you know, so it was! And I'm sure I don't see why you couldn't have sent some agent on to this fearful place, instead of coming yourself. Your poor, dear papa's business couldn't have been so very, very pressing. And then think of the suffering you have caused me."

"I was very rash," said Inez, "very rash indeed."

"And you must never do so again," said Bessie, earnestly; "now promise."

"No, never," said Inez.

"Promise that you will never run off this way without telling me."

"I do promise," said Inez. "I do, dear Bessie. I shall not leave you till you wish me to."

Bessie laughed joyously.

"Then that means forever, so it does!" she cried; "and sure it's myself that'll keep you with me as long as I live, so I will."

"Did Kane come with you?" asked Inez, after a pause.

"No," said Bessie; "sure I just ran away, leaving them by themselves. And I suppose they'll be coming in in hot haste after me. They'll both be here by to-morrow."

"Both?" repeated Inez. "Both who? Is there any other but Kane? Do you mean your guardian!"

"Well, yes; that's what he just is," said Bessie, with a merry smile. "He's my guardian."

"What's his name?"

"His name is Sir Gwyn Ruthven. He is Kane's brother, you know."

At this astounding intelligence Inez started back, and, for a few moments, stared at Bessie in the deepest astonishment. Kane had told her his true name, but she was not aware that any brother of his was alive; and, though she was acquainted with Sir Gwyn Ruthven, yet she did not imagine for a moment that he was Kane's brother.

"Sure and I've got another surprise for you," said Bessie, regarding Inez with a sly and mischievous smile.

"Another surprise?" repeated Inez. "This is surprise enough for one day. Oh, how glad I am—how glad I am! Kane is reunited with his friends, then?"

"I should think he is," said Bessie. "Sir Gwyn is Sir Gwyn no longer. It is Sir Kane Ruthven now, and Ruthven Towers goes to him also. But that isn't the surprise I mean for you, at all at all. It's about myself, so it is, Inez darling."

"Yourself, Bessie? what is it?" asked Inez, full of interest.

"Well, you know, dear, I said that Sir Gwyn Ruthven, or Mr. Gwyn Ruthven, is my guardian."

"Yes—how strange, too! I never knew that before."

"No—no more you did. He hasn't filled that office long. It's a very peculiar sort of guardianship, too."

"But isn't he rather young and inexperienced for so important and responsible a position?" asked Inez, in a solemn tone.

Bessie laughed gayly.

"Oh, sure," said she, "this is a kind of guardianship, Inez darling, that makes youth all the more appropriate. It's guardian of me for life that he is."

And Bessie looked with such a peculiar smile at Inez, that the latter began to catch her meaning at last.

"Why, Bessie," she exclaimed, in amazement, "you look as though you mean that—"

"That he's my husband," said Bessie, triumphantly, "and I'm Mrs. Ruthven, so I am —a bride of a few weeks' standing, that hasn't ceased to be a friend either, so I haven't; for didn't I run away from my own

husband to come to the help of my darling
Inez?"

With those words Bessie flung her arms
around Inez, and kissed her fondly; while
Inez, who was perfectly thunderstruck at the
news of Bessie's marriage, and did not know
what to say, was so affected by this additional
proof of Bessie's love for her that she could
only murmur a few incoherent words of affection and gratitude.

"You see, Inez dearest," continued Bessie, "Gwyn and I had an understanding in
London, though nobody knew it, and, when I
went home, he came after me, and he was so
urgent, and I was so lonely, and he loved me
so, that—that, in fact, I hadn't one single
reason for refusing him, and a great many for
accepting him, and there you have it. But
oh, it's the loving heart and the noble nature
he has, so it is, and you know you always
liked him yourself—now didn't you, Inez darling?"

"It's enough for me," said Inez, "that he
is Kane's brother. I consider Kane one of
the most noble-hearted men I ever saw."

"True for you," said Bessie, "and, as for
Gwyn, why, sure it's enough to say that he's
Kane's own brother. And oh, but it was the
beautiful sight to see the meeting between
the two of them. They went on to make
idols of one another, so they did. I didn't
like to interfere with their enjoyment, and I
was crazy to see you, and so I thought I'd
satisfy myself, and you, and Gwyn, and Kane,
and everybody, by slipping away, and leaving
them to come after me. And they'll be coming along at once, and'll be here to-morrow,
no doubt."

It was with very diversified feelings that
Inez listened to Bessie as she communicated
this information. She felt sincere and unfeigned joy that her true friend had won a
man whom she loved, and a man, too, who
was so worthy of her; but yet it jarred
somewhat upon her to hear Bessie speak of
Kane in this way, and to think that Kane was
her brother-in-law. It had come to this, now
that Kane was brother-in-law to each of them.
Now, there was nothing in this fact itself for
Inez to object to, but the thing that excited a
sense of unpleasantness, or uneasiness, was
the additional closeness with which Bessie's
fortunes were interweaving themselves with
her own. Already there was the mystery of
Bessie's name and claim, conflicting so utterly

with her own. This of itself brought about
between them a conflict of interests, about
which Inez did not like to think; but now this
new relationship to Kane promised to bring
forward new antagonisms, and seemed to be-
token evil in the future. There were a thousand things which she wished to ask Bessie,
but dared not touch upon. Bessie still regarded her as Inez Wyverne; Bessie regarded
herself as the daughter of Bernal Mordaunt;
she must also regard Kane Ruthven as the
man who married Clara Mordaunt, whom she
believed to be her own elder sister. All
these things constituted elements of disturb-
ance, and made Inez watchful and cautious in
her words. Upon these subjects it would not
do to venture. To do so would be to endanger this sweet friendship which had come
like a gleam of sunshine into the darkness
of her life. She did not even venture to ask
after Bernal Mordaunt, for fear lest this
might bring forward the dreaded subject.
But her desire to enjoy Bessie's love was
stronger than her curiosity about her own
circumstances, or even than her filial anxiety
about Bernal Mordaunt; and, therefore, she
willingly put away for the present every
thought about these forbidden matters.

As for Bessie, she was perfectly unembarrassed, and showed all that warm-hearted and
demonstrative affection, all that frank cordiality and playful drollery which constituted
so great a charm in her manner. She made
no allusion whatever to the return of Bernal
Mordaunt, to his fondness for Gwyn, and to
his death. Whether this arose from any suspicion of the belief that Inez had in her relation to him, and from a desire to avoid
what would necessarily be a painful subject;
or, on the other hand, whether she avoided
this subject simply from an unwillingness to
touch upon a matter which was so sad to
herself, did not appear.

After a prolonged conversation, Bessie at
length proposed that Inez should go with her
at once. Inez was not at all unwilling; and,
as her luggage was slender, indeed, no great
time was taken up in making preparations.
But Inez could not leave without acquainting
the kind landlady and her family with her
good fortune, and bidding them good-by. The
good people rejoiced with unfeigned joy, and
exhibited a delight at the changed fortunes
of Inez which was extremely touching;
while, by the admiring glances which they

turned upon Bessie, they evidently thought that the lovely English girl was being restored to friends who were worthy of her. After an affectionate farewell, and amid fervent good wishes for her future happiness, Inez took her departure, and drove off with Bessie to the Hôtel Gascoigne.

Here Inez was delighted to find that the loving forethought of Bessie had caused all necessary preparations to be made for her comfort. There was a suite of rooms for the two friends, and Inez had a room to herself, with a dressing-room adjoining. In addition to this, Bessie had contrived to bring on luggage enough to supply all the wants of Inez in the way of apparel. In fact, there was nothing wanting of all that careful forethought and considerate affection could suggest. Here Inez, for the first time in many weeks, felt that perfect peace and comfort which arises from the sense of safety, and protection, and the neighborhood of loving friends. All this was given to her by these surroundings, and by Bessie's presence.

Yet out of this sweet security and perfect peace Inez had a sudden and most unpleasant start, which occurred just at the beginning of this new enjoyment, and for a time seemed to her to threaten the ruin of every hope. It was caused by a casual remark of Bessie's, made in all innocence, and in perfect unconsciousness of the effect which it was to produce.

"And now, Inez darling," said she, after the close of a prolonged conversation about Kane and Gwyn—"and now I have one of my very dearest friends here, and, if it hadn't been for him, I couldn't have come on so quick, darling—it's me dear mamma's papa—and you must see him this day. You'll love him as I do, I know."

Bessie suddenly stopped, astonished at the change which came over Inez. For, no sooner had Inez heard these words, and this allusion to Bessie's "mamma's papa," than she turned as pale as death, and started to her feet with an expression of deadly fear.

"What's all this?" cried Bessie; "what's the matter, Inez? Inez darling!"

"Is that man—here?" gasped Inez.

"That man! What man?" cried Bessie.

"Kevin Magrath," said Inez, in a scarce audible voice.

"Kevin Magrath," said Bessie; "why, that's my mamma's papa. Why, wasn't I saying that he is here, but—"

"I'll go away," said Inez, with a terrified look. "Let me go, Bessie dearest. Let me go!"

"What! Is it mad ye are?" cried Bessie, clinging to Inez. "What in the wide world has come over ye then? Sure, I don't understand this, at all, at all! Is it my grandpa that you're afraid of? Sure, and it looks like it, so it does!"

"I'll go. I will not stay. Bessie, if you love me, don't stop me. Bessie, dearest Bessie, let me go. O Bessie! that man, that man—Kevin Magrath—he is the one that has caused all my sufferings. Bessie, darling friend, let me go. If he gets me in his power again, I shall die."

And Inez tore herself away, and hurried to her room, where she began to put on her hat. Bessie hastened after her.

"Inez!" she cried, vehemently. "Inez, darling Inez, will ye trust me then? Am I nothing to you? Is it nothing for me to have done what I did, and quit my own husband to see you? Will you run away from me for a wild, fantastic freak? Is it mad ye are, then? Oh, my poor, darling Inez! how very, very cruel this is of you!"

"O Bessie!" said Inez, mournfully, "you do not know what I have suffered, and that man is the cause, Bessie. Let me go now, dear, or—"

"No," said Bessie, firmly, coming up and taking Inez in her arms. "No, dear, I will not let you go—never—or, if you do go, I will go with you. I will not leave you. I have found you, and I will follow you. But, listen to reason for a moment, will you? Inez darling, there's some mystery about you that I don't understand at all, at all—and Kane didn't explain much after all—perhaps because he didn't understand any more'n I do—and for my part I don't want to think of it at all, for it makes my poor little head ache —and I don't want to talk about it, for it's painful, so it is, both to me and to you. Don't I know it? Am I an owl? Not me, Inez darling. Let's bury it all out of sight. Let's forget all about it, dear, and be our own selves again, such as we used to be before your poor, dear papa died. But, as to my mamma's papa, if it's him you're afraid of, I tell you it's all a mistake you're under. It must be, so it must. He harm you! He imprison you! Why, it's mad you are to think of such a thing. There never breathed a nobler, truer, more tender-hearted man than that same Kevin Magrath. Don't I know him? Me own grandpa, too, the darling! Sure I do. It's all a mistake, whatever it is —a mistake, Inez darling, no matter what it is—and there you have it."

Bessie's vehemence impressed Inez in spite of herself, and she found her terrors fading away in the presence of such assertions as these. She could not help thinking that the man whom Bessie so loved, and in whom she so thoroughly believed, could not be altogether the villain that she had supposed him to be.

"Have you ever seen him, Inez darling?" continued Bessie. "Tell me, have you ever seen him then, or have you ever spoken with him?"

"Never," said Inez, hesitatingly.

It was a fact. She had never actually seen him.

"Sure, then, it's a mad fancy of yours, so it is. Won't you believe me when I tell you that he's one of the best and noblest of men, and, if you were only to see him and know him, you'd feel toward him as I do, so you would? Sure, how do I know, Inez darling, what wild fancy you've got into your head? but it is a wild, mad fancy; of that I'm sure, so I am. So come, sit down again. Sure, you haven't any cause to fear while you're with me, and where in the wide world can you go to?"

This was a question which Inez could not answer. Where, indeed, could she go now? To find Bessie had for a long time been the chief desire of her heart. How could she now fly from her?

Besides, here was Bessie urging her most vehemently to dismiss those suspicions which she had been entertaining about Kevin Magrath. Bessie trusted in him. Bessie loved him. Might not Bessie's trust and love be justifiable? After all, she had never seen him. She had judged from circumstantial evidence. Might not all this be explained away? Was she so sure that she was right, that she could put her opinion against that of Bessie?

But more than this—here was Bessie, and what harm could now befall her? Could she dread imprisonment now—with Bessie? That would be absurd. Besides, in the space of

one more day, Kane would be here, and with him his brother Gwyn, who was also Bessie's husband. There would then be three upon whom she could rely. Even if Kevin Magrath should be all that she had believed him to be, what could he do when she had the support of Bessie and her husband and Kane?

Finally, in spite of all that Inez had suffered, she found herself in a strange state of doubt as to the truth of her own belief about Kevin Magrath. Here was Bessie who assured her that this belief was false. Kane also, who had just been with Bessie, and had talked with her about these matters, might possibly have learned enough about him to change the opinion that he had formed; and, indeed, it seemed as though it must be so, since Bessie had left her husband, and Kane also, with the express purpose of going on to join Kevin Magrath, and find herself. Kevin Magrath, then, seemed to Inez to lose his terrors, since Kane had allowed Bessie to go forward on this errand.

She therefore allowed herself to be persuaded and soothed and quieted by Bessie's words, and, at length, not only gave up all thoughts of flight, but allowed herself to consent to an interview with this once-dreaded Kevin Magrath that very evening.

———

CHAPTER XLIII.

A REVELATION.

THE apprehension with which Inez looked forward to a meeting with Kevin Magrath did not last over the first few moments of that interview. He was dressed in black, rather after the fashion in vogue among English priests, than among those on the Continent. As he looked at Inez, there was on his face something so mild and paternal that her fears departed, and she began to think that she had been mistaken in him all along. He addressed to her a few affectionate words, mingled with playful allusions to Bessie's running away from her husband for her sake, and then proceeded to express the deepest sympathy for her, and the strongest condemnation of Gounod. He declared that it was all a most lamentable mistake, arising from the miserable stupidity of "that old fool, Gounod." He had directed him merely to take the greatest possible care of her, which direction he had understood, or mis-understood, so as to conceive his duties to be those of a jailer. He alluded, in touching language, to his own deep grief when he learned that she had gone, and to his fear even to search after her, lest she might sup-pose that she was pursued.

After these preliminaries, he went on to say that the time had now come, which he had so long wished to see, when he could explain every thing to her, and to Bessie also.

"I mean both of you," said he, "for you're both involved in this, and oh, but it's the shupreme momint of my life, so it is. Gyerruls—Inez Mordaunt, Bessie Mordaunt—listen to me. Ye both love one another like sisters, so ye do. Inez darlin', haven't ye ever suspected what's mint by Bessie's name? Bessie jool, don't ye suspect some-thin' when ye hear me callin' her Inez Mor-daunt?"

And with these words Kevin Magrath looked first at one and then at the other with a beaming smile of joyous expectation.

At such a singular address as this both Inez and Bessie looked puzzled. Inez looked at the speaker with earnest, solemn scrutiny; while Bessie looked first at Inez and then at him, and then back again at Inez.

"Ye love one another like sisters," con-tinued Kevin Magrath—"ye love one an-other like sisters, and why? Why is it? Why? Have ye niver suspected? Listen, then, I'll tell ye's both why it is.—It's be-cause ye are sisters!"

"Sisters!" exclaimed Inez, in utter bewil-derment. "Sisters! What do you mean?" And she turned and looked inquiringly at Bessie, who took her hand in one of hers, and, twining her other lovingly around her shoulder, looked eagerly at Kevin Magrath, and said:

"Sure an' it must be one of your jokes, grandpa darling, so it must. Inez Mordaunt, is it, and sisters, is it? How very, very fun-ny, and sure it's me that don't understand it at all at all—now do you, Inez darling?"

"Be the powers! but it would be strange if ye did until I've explained myself some-what. You, Bessie jool, have always known that yer father was Bernal Mordaunt; and you, Inez, only knowed it after the rivilation of the late Henniger Wyverne—peace be to his sowl!"

At this Bessie clasped Inez closer in her arms, and murmured:

"O Inez! darling, darling Inez, is this really so?"

"I'll explain it all," continued Kevin Ma-grath, while Inez said not a word, but stood motionless from astonishment, with all her gaze fastened upon his face, as though to read there the truth or the falsity of these astounding statements.

"Bernal Mordaunt, thin, the father of both of ye's, had two daughters—one named Clara, now in glory, the other named Inez, now in this room. Now, whin this Inez was a little over two years old, Mrs. Mor-daunt had a third daughter, who is this very Bessie, now likewise in this room."

"And is Inez really my sister, then?" cried Bessie, with irrepressible enthusiasm, "and older than me, and me always loved her so!—O Inez! dear, sweet sister! O Inez! sure but it's heart-broke with joy I fairly am, and there you have it!"

With these words Bessie pressed Inez again and again in her arms; and Inez, who was still puzzled by various thoughts, which still stood in the way of her full reception of this announcement, was nevertheless so over-whelmed by Bessie's love that she yielded to it utterly, and, returning her embraces and kisses, burst into tears, and wept in her arms.

"Ye're not the same age, thin," said Kevin Magrath, "for you, Inez, are one year older than ye've been believing; and you, Bessie, are one year younger. Sure an' there's been oninding schayming about ye's, and ye've been the jupes of it. But I'm not going now to purshue that same into all its multichudinous rameefeecations. I'm only intinding to mintion a few plain facts. Well, thin, your poor mother, Bessie, died in giving birth to you. With that death died out all the happiness of Bernal Mordaunt. Sorry am I to say, also, that you, the innocent child, were regarded by the widowed husband with coldness, if not aversion, for that you were the cause, innocent though you were, of the death of his wife, whom he adored. His other children he had always loved, but you he niver mintioned, nor would he hear about you after the death of his wife. So Bessie, poor child, you were at the very out-set of life worse thin orphined."

"I'm sure it—it wasn't my fault; and

I'm sure I—I think it was a great shame so it was," said Bessie, sobbing as she spoke; and, drawing herself away from Inez, she buried her face in her hands.

"Well, thin, Bernal Mordaunt, weary of the wurruld as he was, determined to quit it, and spind the remainder of his life in the services of religion. So he wint away and intered the Church, and became a priest. Before taking this step he committed his children to the gyarjianship of Hennigar Wyverne, whose wife was the dear friend and rilative of the deceased Mrs. Mordaunt. Now, here was the injustice which he did, poor man. His children, in his eyes, were only Clara and Inez; the young infant he would not acknowledge; he virtually disouned his own child by neglecting it, by ignoring it. Here it was when I interposed. I remonstrated with him, but he listened with cold impatience. 'Do as you please with her, Kevin,' says he to me, 'but don't talk about her to me; but for her my wife would never have died.' Those were his own words, so they were. Cruel they were, and bitter, and most unjust, but he couldn't be moved from them, and he wint away to the far East, to spind the remainder of his life as a missionary priest.

"I was saying that I interposed here. Alreddy this neglicted child had been kept by a nurse, and was now nearly a year old. I came with me sister, and I took the poor disouned child, and I had her well brought up, and I have sustained meself for years with the hope that Bernal Mordaunt might yet return to receive his injured daughter from my hands."

"O darling grandpa—then you are not my real grandpa, after all?" said Bessie, drawing nearer to Kevin Magrath, and taking his hands fondly in hers; "but, at any rate, I owe you, and you only, a daughter's love and duty, so I do."

"Sure to glory, thin, Bessie, don't I know it, and isn't it me that's always loved ye as a father, so it was?"

"And sure, then," said Bessie, holding Kevin Magrath's hand in one of hers, and reaching out the other to take that of Inez; "you, Inez darling, won't disown your sister, even if my cruel father did so turn away, will you, darling?"

Inez pressed her hand warmly. Bessie's sad fate touched her heart keenly, and this new-found sister came to her surrounded with a new and pathetic interest—that sister, cast out so long since, and now so strangely restored.

"Well, well," said Kevin Magrath, "sure it's best to let by-gones be by-gones. As I was saying, thin, Bessie was taken by me, and Clara and Inez were handed over to Hennigar Wyverne, who was to be their gyarjian. In a short time a difficulty arose. Hennigar Wyverne sent away Clara to a school in France, and changed the name of Inez Mordaunt to Inez Wyverne. The fact is, he had a scheme of getting possession of the Mordaunt property. His wife discovered this, and remonstrated. They quarrelled bitterly, and the end of it was that Mrs. Wyverne left her husband. Sure it was a hard position for an honest woman to be put in, but she couldn't stand by and see this thing done under her very nose, so she left her husband; and, for my part, I honor her for doing so, so I do. It was from her that I heard of Hennigar Wyverne's baseness, and I wint and remonstrated with him, and tried all I could to bring him back to the path of juty. I couldn't do much with him. I couldn't find out where he had sint Clara; and, whin he found that I was growing troublesome, he sint you away, too, Inez darling. Well, years passed, and at length I heard from him that Clara was dead. I heard that she had married, in Paris, some adventurer, and was dead and buried. Well, not long after that, you were brought home by him, and were known as Inez Wyverne. I now determined to bring things to a close. I had heard that poor Bernal Mordaunt was dead, and I was determined that whin you came of age, Inez, you should have your name and your rights. In order to do this, I had to go and talk plainly to him. I found that he had forgotten about Bessie, and he saw that all his fine schemes were broken up, and that I had him in my power. He had squandered so much of the Mordaunt property that he could never repay. He also had suffered much in his conscience, for he had one, the poor creature, and was a broken-down man. He at length promised to do all that was right, but begged me to give him time. He had come to love you, Inez dear; and he felt a deep repugnance to develop his crimes to you; he couldn't endure the thought of confessing to you the wrongs he had done. Well, I pitied him, for we were old frinds—and, for that matter, Bernal Mordaunt was also—and, in spite of his roguery, I couldn't help feeling sorry for him. So I gave him time, and, at the same time, declared that I would hold him to his word. Well, thin it was that I sint Bessie to live with him, or rather with you, Inez darling, for I wanted the two of ye's to love one another like sisters, and I couldn't wait for Wyverne to make his confession. 'They'll love one another at first sight,' I thought, 'and whin they find out the blessed truth, they'll love one another all the better, so they will;' and that's what I see fulfilled this day, and sure to glory, but it's mesilf that's the happy man for being spared to see it."

And Kevin Magrath regarded them both for a few moments with a radiant face, and a benevolent, paternal smile.

"At lingth," he continued, "poor Wyverne's health grew steadily worse. It was remorse that was killing him, so it was, neither more nor less; and the dread of having to tell the truth to you, Inez darling. So he wint once to the Continint, and ye both wint with him, and ye finally brought up at Villeneuve. All this time we corresponded, and I was able to follow his track, either fortunately or unfortunately, I hardly know which. Now, ye know, Rome was, as a gineral thing, the place that was more like home to me thin any other, especially since I had turruned over Bessie to poor Wyverne, or rather to you, Inez darling. Well, one day I was overwhellumned at hearing that Bernal Mordaunt had returruned from the East. I rushed to greet him, and for a time, in the joy I felt at meeting my old frind, I forgot all about the villany of another old frind. At lingth, when he infarrumed me that he was going to London as soon as possible, I became filled with anxiety. Circumstances were not in a proper position. Such an arrival would have forced on a sudden disclosure, and I knew that in Wyverne's weak state the excitement and shame would kill him. So I did the best I could. I wrote to him that Bernal Mordaunt had come, and advised him to fly for his life, or even to get up a pretended death. I towld him to get rid of the gyerruls, particularly Inez—that's you, darling—for I thought I'd give him a chance to escape, and thin come after ye, and tell ye both the whole story. I made a few further remarks, blaming him for entangling himsilf with a young doctor—a good enough young

fellow, but a great check on his movements—and thin I mailed the letter, and tried to hope for the best. I felt afraid, though, in spite of all; and whin, a few days afterward, Bernal Mordaunt left, I wint as far as Milan with him, and bade him good-by with my heart full of a chumult of continding emotions.

"Howandiver, there was nothing more for me to do, so I wint to Churin, and thin *via* Genoa and Marseilles to Paris. I hadn't been there long before I learrened the worst. I learrened this from the lips of Bernal Mordaunt, who had come to Paris straight from Villeneuve, and was intinding to go to England as soon as possible. Some ecclesiastical juties, however, compelled him to remain for a time in Paris. He it was who infarrumed me about the occurrinces at Villeneuve; and he towld me a thrilling story about being sint for to go to a dying man, and finding this dying man to be Hennigar Wyverne. I had alriddy felt it my juty, as an old frind, to infarrum Bernal Mordaunt to some ixtint about Wyverne's defalcations, telling him at the same time about his remorse and determination to make amends. I did not tell him where he was, though, and tried to dissuade him from crossing the Alps by the Simplon road. But he wanted to go that way to see some people at Geneva, and I couldn't privint him. He had no idea that you gyerruls were there, as I had refrained from telling him, for reasons which you understand. Wyverne was almost gone, and but a few words passed between thim. But yer father told me that he forgave him ivery thing, and told him so to his face."

"I did not know that any words passed between them," said Inez, mournfully, remembering Blake's account of this scene.

"'Deed and there did, just as I'm telling ye. Who towld you that no words passed?"

"The—the doctor"—said Inez.

"Dr. Blake, is it? Well, there's some misunderstanding. He couldn't have known, or he couldn't have meant it. I had it from Bernal Mordaunt himself; and, of course, there couldn't have been any mistake. And, besides, I'm sure ye must have misunderstood him, for we've talked of that same several times since—over and over, so we have."

Inez was struck by this allusion to Dr. Blake, and could not help trying to find out more about him.

"I dare say," said she, "that there may

have been some misunderstanding on my part, but I certainly have a distinct remembrance of the meaning that I' gathered from his words, and that was, that Mr. Wyverne died without exchanging a word with him."

Kevin Magrath smiled blandly.

"Quite the contrary," said he, mournfully; "it's as I have said, and Blake has mintioned it to me over and over. Do you see, Inez darling, it must be as I have said."

"I suppose it must," said Inez, "but it is very singular. Is it long since you have seen the doctor?"

"Not very long."

"Is he here yet?" she asked, making a further effort to learn something about him.

"Oh, no—he left here some time ago."

"Ah!" said Inez. She did not like to exhibit too much curiosity, especially before Bessie, and at such a time as this, when the tremendous mysteries that had surrounded their past lives were being slowly unfolded. Bessie, however, did not appear to take the smallest interest in this. She was looking pensively at the floor, with a grave expression that was very unusual with her.

"He left here some time ago," said Kevin Magrath, pursuing the subject which Inez had started. "He was a fine young fellow, full of life and energy, and I don't wonder that poor Wyverne took a fancy to him; though I thought at the time that, under the circumstances, he was embarrassing his movements. The flight that I intimeeted would have been difficult, with Blake as his medical adviser and general director. Well, well, it's all the same, for Blake knows all about it now, so he does."

"Where did he go to?" asked Inez, abruptly, unable to control her curiosity.

"Well—he left here—on an adventure, and he wint to Italy, so he did—to Rome, in fact."

"To Rome?" repeated Inez, in the tone of one who wished to learn more.

"Yis—to Rome—and in Rome he stayed."

"How odd!" said Inez. "Is Rome a good place for a doctor?"

"Sure, it's as good as any place. Why not? Anyhow, there he stayed, and there he is now."

Inez made no further remark. Rome seemed a strange place for a doctor to go to, yet so it was, and the fact set her thinking.

"He's settled there," continued Kevin Magrath after a pause. "He's settled there, and for good."

This was not very pleasant, on the whole, to Inez. It looked like neglect and forgetfulness on Blake's part, and she had expected something different. A sigh escaped her in spite of herself. But then she reflected upon her own sudden disappearance, and thought that Blake might have made unsuccessful efforts to find her, and have given it up at last in despair.

"Yis," said Kevin Magrath once more, "he's settled there; and there's no injucement that I know of that'd draw him away."

"Well, grandpa darling," said Bessie at last, "we don't care about this. We want to know more about ourselves, and our poor, dear papa, so we do. You said that he came as far as Paris. Now, what happened immediately after that? Did you tell him then about it all, and about our darling, precious Inez, my own sweet sister—or did you postpone it —or—?"

"I'll tell ye all about it, Bessie darling, and you too, Inez, my jool, but not now, not just now. What comes after this is a mournful story; and Bessie, me darling, I hardly know how I'm iver to tell it to you at all at all."

"To me!" exclaimed Bessie, in wonder; "and sure, and why not, thin?"

"Well, thin, it's jist because it makes me feel badly. There's things to say that I don't l'ke to say to ye, face to face. I'll tell it all to Inez some time, and she can be after telling it to you. In this way, I'll allow the story to filter, as it were, through her to you."

"Well, I'm sure, I think it's very strange, so I do, grandpa darling; but you're the best judge, and, if it is so awfully sad, you know, why, perhaps, I'd better hear it from Inez, or, perhaps, I'd better not hear it at all—that is, if it is really too very awfully sad—for, sure, I was niver the one that was inclined to listen to bad news, unless it was necessary."

"It depinds on what ye call nicissary. Howandiver, ye can judge for yerself afterward."

CHAPTER XLIV.

ALL THE PAST EXPLAINED.

THIS was the happiest day by far that Inez had known for a long time. The advent of Bessie, the restoration to her proper position in life, the society of friends, all these were unspeakably sweet to one who had suffered as she had. But, above all, the discovery that Bessie was her own sister formed the climax of all these joys; and Inez, after the first natural bewilderment had passed, gave herself up to the delight of this new relationship. As for Bessie, she was, if possible, still more excited. Naturally of a more demonstrative disposition than Inez, she surpassed her in her exhibitions of affection and delight, and overwhelmed her with caresses. Such a revelation as this gave them material for endless conversations, exclamations, and explanations. Each one had to tell all about her life and her past reminiscences; each one had to give a minute account of the state of her affections with regard to the other; and all the past was thus opened up by the two in so far as it might afford interest to one another. Each one, however, instinctively avoided the more mournful periods in that past; and, as Inez said nothing of her imprisonment, so Bessie said nothing of the mournful events at Mordaunt Manor.

As to the sufferings through which Inez had gone—her journey to Paris, the discovery of her father's death, her imprisonment, the examination of the letters, her suspicions, her fears, her flight, her illness, and her misery, all these constituted a part of her life upon which no light had yet been thrown. Yet Kevin Magrath had shown all the impressions which she had formed about him from his letter to Wyvorne to be erroneous; and, from what she had seen of him, she did not doubt that he would account for every other difficulty, and prove to her that she had been in every respect deceived in the opinions which she had formed about him. The remainder of his story now would be as clear, as open, and as natural, as the first part had been; and he himself would stand completely vindicated.

On the following morning Kevin Magrath came to breakfast with them, and, after breakfast, Bessie withdrew.

"I know, grandpa dear," said she, "that you'd rather not have me just now, so I'll go, and I'll hear it from Inez, if she chooses to tell me; and, if she does not choose to tell, why, I'd very much rather not hear. And, what's more, I won't even think about it. Good-by, you two dear jools of life."

With these words Bessie retired, and Inez waited for the remainder of Kevin Magrath's story.

He regarded her for a few moments in silence, with an expression on his face that was at once affectionate and paternal, and with a gentle smile on his lips.

"Inez, me darling," said he, "ye've suffered from me more than I dare to think of, but ye'll see that I wasn't to blame, and that I've really suffered as much as you have out of pure sympathy and vixation. But I'll go on in order, and jist tell a plain, consicutive story.

"Well, thin, your poor father, Bernal Mordaunt, came here to Paris, as I said, and here I found him. It was from me that he first heard that one of his daughters was dead. This was his eldest, Clara, his favorite. Whin I say she was his favorite, ye'll onderstand me. Ye see, you were only a little thing—a baby, in fact—barely able to prattle, while Clara was many years older, and had been thus the love and joy of her father years before you were born. Ye'll not be pained whin I say that he could better have spared you than her. Anyhow, so it was, and, consequintly, when he heard that Clara was dead, it was a worse blow to him than if a man had knocked him down sinsless. It took all the life and soul out of him. For he had been broken down out in China, or Japan, or Injia, by overwork, and, whin he turruned his steps homeward, it was his children that he thought of most; and by his children he meant, most of all, Clara. So, whin he heard that she was dead, it was with him for a time as though he had lost the last tie that bound him to this wurruld; and he couldn't think of any thing but her. He brooded over this. We wint out to her grave in Père-la-Chaise, and thin he forrumed the design of conveying her remains away, and depositing thim by the side of the remains of his wife. Now she—your poor mother, Inez darling—was buried at Rome."

"Rome!" exclaimed Inez, in wonder.

"Yis, at Rome, and to that place your father determined to convey the remains of

Clara. He had gone after your mother's death to Rome to prepare for the priesthood, and his love for his lost wife had injuced him to bring her body there. So now he resolved to take Clara's body. Besides, he had to go back to Rome once more, though he would have had time to go for you before returning there ; and it's a thousand pities he didn't ; and it was meself that was niver tired of urging him to do that same ; but no, he was brooding all the time over his lost daughter, the child of his best love, and had thin no thought of you—and oh, but it's the pity he didn't go for you, Inez darling !

"Well, I kept with him. We had the remains of Clara ixhumed, and took thim to Rome, and placed thim by the side of her mother's body. Well, after this, I tried to turrun his thoughts to you—to wean him from these dead loves, and bring to his heart the warmth of a living love. I told him of you, and I told him of Bessie. Of Bessie he would hear nothing. There was the same coldness and avirsion which I had noticed years before, and I could do nothing with him. He had niver loved her, so I had nothing to work on there ; but with you it was different, for he recollected his little baby Inez, named after his wife. He had her portrait once with the portraits of the others, and spoke of this with much emotion. At lingth his love for you grew strong enough to draw him away from the dead, and, finally, the thought of you filled all his mind.

"So, you see, we set out for England. We reached Marseilles and proceeded to Paris. The journey, however, was very fatiguing to him, and by the time we reached here he was unable to go one step farther. He took to his bed, and out of that bed he niver rose. He had overtaxed his strength, and the sorrow which he had enjured had greatly prostrated him. For a time he hoped against hope. He would not sind for you, though I urged him, because he wished to have the pleasure of going on to you, and was afraid of frightening you. But it was not to be ; he grew worse and worse, and at last, whin it was almost over, whin he could not write, he sint for you.

"Even then he tried to ease the blow—poor man—though he only made it worse. He did not wish the letter to come from a stranger. He dictated it to me—but did not wish it to seem dictated, for fear of frighten-

ing you. 'Kevin,' says he—'she'll be frightened,' says he—'just write it as if I was writing it,' says he—'let her think it's from me own hand, and don't say a word about it's being dictated—just take it from me own lips.' That's what he said, and that's just what I did—and, for that matter, I don't suppose' ye ever thought otherwise than that poor Bernal wrote it with his own hand ; but I mintion it now so as to show ye, Inez darling, that yer poor father was very far gone when that letter was written.

"So far gone was he, indeed, that on the next day all was over. Early that morning he implored me once more to write to you. 'Kevin lad,' says he, 'let her think it's from me own hand. It'll comfort her more—if she loves me—to think she has something from me. Kevin, I was to blame for not going to her first.' Then he hurried me on, and I wrote word for word just as he spoke—with all his incoherence and disconnected words—and I was pleased with his allusions to myself—for sure I was the only one left for ye to look to after he had gone. And I tell you this now about this letter. The letter itself won't perhaps be so pricious in your eyes, Inez darling—but the love of that father ought to be still more pricious, who died while lavishing upon you the last treasures of his love.

"Well," continued Kevin Magrath, after a thoughtful pause, "at that hour there was one to whom he ought to have given a thought—yis—one to whom he ought to have given many thoughts—one who should have had at least a share—yis, equal shares with you, Inez —in his love. I mean my poor Bessie. Niver did I cease to try to bring before him that disowned, that injured child—his own child—cast out from the moment of her birth—ignored—disliked—hated. Oh, sure, but it was meself that was heart-broken about that same ; and me trying all the time to injuce him to show her, if not affection, at least common justice. But my efforts were all in vain. I could not get him to feel the slightest interest in her. There was coldness, and even aversion, in his manner wheniver I introjuced that subject. When I spoke about her, he would be at first fretful ; then, overcoming this, he would take up an attichude of patient enjurance, like one who was putting a great constraint upon himself. And oh ! but my heart bled for the poor child. I knew what she was. I felt that, if he could but see her, he must love her—yet here he was, turning himself away, without one word to send her, even from his death-bed And, Inez darling, I, who know Bessie, I, who know her tender, gentle, loving heart, her susceptible nature, her sweet, innocent, childlike ways—I know this, that, if she was aware of the aversion of her father for her, her heart would break, so it would—she would die, so she would. Poor, poor, darling Bessie! disowned and outcast from her father's heart, from her birth till his death!

"And this," continued Kevin Magrath, with manifest emotion, "this is what I can never tell her, never. I don't even know how to begin to tell her. I can't begin to mintion it. And therefore, me child, I tell it to you, hoping that you may find some gentle way of letting her know all about it. You may succeed where I would fail."

"Oh, no," said Inez, mournfully. "Oh, no, I could never, never tell it. There is no way by which such a thing could be told. I could not have the heart to hint at it. I could not even begin to tell her about that last scene, for fear she would ask me what message he had left for her. And oh! how sad not to be able to give any message, however formal or commonplace! Oh, how cruel it was—how cruel! And, poor, tender-hearted Bessie, with her affectionate nature and her heart of love!"

Kevin Magrath wiped his eyes.

"We can't iver mintion it," said he, "as far as I can see. It can't be done, unless you may find some way some day, and that I doubt, so I do. We'll have to smother it up, and avoid the subject. But oh! it was a sin, so it was, to pass out of the worruld in such a way. And ye don't think, thin, me child, that ye could find any way to break it to her?"

"No," said Inez; "impossible. I shall never be able to speak of this subject at all, or to allow her to speak of it. It seems to me that, while she was hearing of his love for Clara and for me, she would feel an intolerable pang at finding herself cast out. No, she ought never to know—never!"

Kevin Magrath sighed.

"Well," continued he, "that letter was the last act of your poor father, for he died not long after; and, for my part, I was overwhellumed. I knew that you might be coming, me child, and I was afraid to meet you—afraid to stay and be the witness of your grief. Now, your poor father had made me promise that I would have him buried by the side of his wife and child, in Rome; and so, when he was removed from the house, I at once went to fulfil my promise, and started for Rome with his remains, afraid to wait and meet you, and leaving to others the task of breaking to you the awful news. The worst of it was, it was your poor father himself who had put me in such a position, by obstinately refusing to write, or to let me write, until it was too late. . . . So, me child, I took away the mortal remains of my frind, and of your father, and I conveyed thim to Rome—and there I buried thim, by the side of his wife and his child, your sister Clara, and there they all are now side by side."

There was a long silence now.

"Is there a cemetery, or are they buried in some church?" asked Inez, in a low voice.

"There is a cimetery in Rome," said Kevin Magrath, slowly and solemnly, "the likes of which doesn't exist in all the wide wurruld—a cimetery, eighteen hundred years old, filled with the mowldering rimnants of apostles, and saints, and martyrs, and confissors—a cimetery, to lie in which robs death of half its terrors, and there now repose all that is mortal of your father, your mother, and your sister."

"Oh!" cried Inez, "what place can that be? Is there such a cemetery? What is its name? I have never heard of it."

"The cimetery that I speak of," said Kevin Magrath, solemnly, "is known as—the Roman Catacombs."

"The Roman Catacombs!" repeated Inez, in a voice full of awe.

"The Roman Catacombs," said Kevin Magrath. "There they lie, side by side—they who loved one another on earth, who are thus joined in death, awaiting the resurrection morn."

Inez made no remark, and a long silence followed. Kevin Magrath was the first to break it, and he went on to continue his story:

"Whin I left," said he, "I told Gounod that you were coming, and I told him what to do. I told him about the sorrow you'd be in, and urged him to attind upon you, and do all that he could for you. I knew he could do nothing to alleviate such sorrow as you would have; so I laid great stress upon his keeping watch over you, so as to find out your wants. In fact, I overwhelumed him with dirictions. Well, I wint away, and I stayed away for weeks, waiting impatiently till the time whin I might suppose your grief to be moderated; and thin I came back; and I assure ye, me child, I was fairly trembling with agitation at the thought of meeting you in your bereavemint. And what do you think awaited me? What! Sure, you may imagine. Gounod, with his bewildermint, and the owld hag Briset, both voluble and eloquint about your iscape. Iscape! As if I iver mint any thing else! Iscape! Why, it was as if it had been a prison they had made for you—and so it was, and nothing else in the wide worruld. The fool! the beast! the idiot! he had utterly misunderstood me; I had enjoined upon him to watch you like a servant, and he had watched you like a jailer. I understood well how your nature must have chafed against restraint and surveillance; and thin, whin I thought of you, all alone after your maid had gone, me heart fairly ached for you, so it did. My very desire to spare you pain had caused fresh pain to you, Inez darling; and you were lost to me, for I dared not search for you. I was afraid that, if I did, you would misunderstand it all, and be all the more terrified; and what's more, even if I had found you, I should not have been able to look you in the face. I couldn't have spoken one word. I wrote frantic letters to Bessie, and she wrote back letters full of anxiety, telling me that she had heard nothing about you, and knew nothing. I declare to you, me child, those days were the worst I iver knew in all my life. And so it wint on, and I was in helplessniss and dispair until this blessed time, until yesterday, when Bessie hersilf came with the glad news about you; and I hurried her away to meet you, and waited here, with me old heart throbbing chumultuously while she was gone. But at last she returruned, and you with her; and thin I had a chance to explain, in a gradual way, and at least to let you know that, if you had suffered, I, at least, was innocent. And sure to glory, but it's meself that was the happy man last night."

So ended Kevin Magrath's story, and that story had sunk deep into the soul of Inez.

Many conclusions had she gathered from that story; and, as she listened to its details, one by one the frightful dangers that seemed to have hovered about her past, or appeared to impend over her present, were dispelled. At length, they all seemed no more than the creations of her own fancy.

The letter to Wyverne, which had been the first of these troubles, was fully explained. Wyverne's emotion at its reception, his terror of Bernal Mordaunt, his dying declaration—all these were made plain, all except his assertion that Dr. Blake was his son, and on this she laid but little stress now, since she thought that she could ask about that at any other time. With these were also explained the similarity in the handwriting of the different letters, the mystery that had overwhelmed her in her prison-house, the absence of Kevin Magrath, the espionage and strict guardianship of Gounod—all these were explained, and the terrors that they had excited vanished like so many dreams. Out of all this there remained prominent several things:

First. Kevin Magrath was a high-minded, noble-hearted man—the friend of her father, of Bessie, and of herself.

Secondly. Bessie was her own sister.

Thirdly. Her father, her mother, and her sister Clara, were all buried at Rome.

Fourthly. Dr. Blake was also at Rome—"settled there," as Kevin Magrath had expressed it.

"Inez darling, me child," said Kevin Magrath, after a long silence, "I am very anxious to go to Rome, and, if ye would like to go to see the graves of yer father, yer mother, and yer sister, I should like to show them to ye; but, at the same time, if ye feel reluctant about going, it's no matter. Bessie is anxious to go and fulfil a daughter's juty to those who niver perforrumed a parent's part to her; and I thought that you, the dear child of their care and their love, might have the same feelings."

At this proposal Inez at once thought of the far-off graves of those dear ones whom she had lost, and there arose a sudden longing to visit in death those whom she had failed to meet in life. With these came other thoughts, less holy, yet equally strong—she thought of Blake. Yes, Rome was a place which presented stronger attractions to her than any other.

"Rome!" said she. "Oh, how I long to

go there! And will you really take me?"

"I should be glad beyond all things if you would come with us," said Kevin Magrath.

CHAPTER XLV.

THE TENDERNESS OF BESSIE.

KANE and Gwyn hurried on to Paris as soon as possible, and were not more than twenty-four hours behind Bessie. On the following day they arrived there, and drove first to Kane's lodgings. Then they went to the place where Inez had been, and learned that Bessie had taken her away, and that they had gone to the Hôtel Gascoigne. This news did not in any way lessen the anxiety that Kane had felt; for it seemed to him that this movement might carry both of them into the very hands of their worst enemy. It seemed to him that there could be no certainty of their safety until he could see Inez herself, and find out what her circumstances were; when, if there was really any appearance of danger, he might warn her, or confront Magrath himself. So great were his fears now, that he hardly expected to find either of the ladies, but was rather inclined to fear that Kevin Magrath, the moment that he found them both in his power, had contrived some specious pretext for conveying them to some other place, where they would be out of reach. It was with the dread of this at his heart, that he accompanied Gwyn to the Hôtel Gascoigne.

But the first thing that they heard on asking after the ladies drove away all fear. They were both there, and Kevin Magrath was there also. Kane was hardly prepared for such good news; and for a moment did not know what there was for him to do. He had come here in all haste as the champion of the oppressed, but the comfortable surroundings of Inez put the idea of any very imminent danger out of his head. She had Bessie with her, and here was Gwyn, who could be an additional protector.

Gwyn hurried up after the garçon to the apartments where his wife was, followed by Kane. On reaching the landing, there was a sudden cry of joy, and a beautiful being, all in the glory of golden hair and azure eyes, flung herself into Gwyn's arms.

"Sure, didn't I know you'd be here this blessed morning, Gwynnie darling?" cried Bessie; "didn't I say you couldn't stay more than a day without me and be alive? and so I've been waiting here in the hall for hours and hours, so I have. But you're here at last, and that's all I want. And oh, ain't you very, very much fatigued, darling? and were you ever quite so happy in your life?"

To this torrent of loving words Gwyn said nothing. Such a reception overwhelmed him. He had expected some coldness—some hanging back. He had prepared himself for some humiliation on his own part. But this was the reality that awaited him—the utter forgetfulness of every thing but her love—this perfect forgiveness that did not leave room for any attempt at explanations. He could not utter a word, but pressed her, in silence and with moistened eyes, to his heart.

"And Kane, too!" cried Bessie, as soon as she could free herself from Gwyn's arms; "sure, but you're welcome, Kane dear, and it's great news that I've got to tell. Inez is here, safe and happy, and you'll want to see her."

She held out her little hand with a beaming smile, and Kane pressed it tenderly.

"You'll want to see Inez," said Bessie, as Kane hesitated.

By this time Kane had felt himself somewhat de trop. The exceeding and unexpected warmth of this greeting between husband and wife did not seem warranted by so short a separation, even on the grounds of their being yet hardly out of their honey-moon; but still, there it was, and he saw the intense agitation of Gwyn, and suspected that something had taken place before Bessie's flight from Ruthven Towers which had caused that flight and Gwyn's present emotion. He saw that some explanations or other were probably required by these two, and therefore concluded to retire for the present.

"Well," said he, at length, "I think I'll look in again. She is well, you say?"

"Better than I ever knew her. But you'd better come in and see her. She'll be awfully disappointed."

"Oh, I'll come again some time to-day," said Kane; "it's—it's—a little inconvenient just now—ah, under the circumstances—so I'll only ask you to remember me very kindly to her, and tell her that I hope to see her this evening."

Bessie urged him a little longer, though rather more faintly, but Kane persisted in his refusal, and at length retreated, leaving the husband and wife to themselves.

All this had taken place on the landing of the stairway. As soon as Kane retired, Bessie took Gwyn's arm fondly and led him to her rooms. Inez was not there, and Gwyn was better pleased to be alone with his wife.

Here they sat down side by side, quite lover-fashion, while Gwyn was so overcome by his unexpected happiness that he had not yet found words, but sat devouring her with his eyes. Bessie looked tenderly at him, and, with one of her characteristic smiles, exclaimed:

"Sure, I oughtn't to be so forgiving, so I oughtn't, and there you have it. But oh, I was so awfully glad to see you, you know, Gwynnie dear."

"And—do—do you really for—forgive me?" faltered Gwyn.

"Oh, come now, we won't talk about it, sure actions speak louder than words, and my actions have spoken very, very loudly, Gwynnie darling, so they have."

"O darling, I shall never be able to forgive myself."

"Oh, come, Gwynnie, sure we won't talk about it at all, at all. It was only a miserable fancy of yours, so it was, a wild deludering notion, but, tell me, sure you didn't go and tell Kane about it then?"

"Tell Kane! Of course not, darling. How could I?"

"Of course not. How could you? Surely not."

"I dare say he's noticed trouble on my face and in my manner."

"Like enough, for it was very, very sad, and is one of those things, Gwynnie darling, that one really can't think about. Its positively too heart-breaking. And I won't say I didn't feel cut up myself, for I did, but you know I couldn't bring myself to have a scene with you about it, and I thought, Gwynnie, that the best way to do was to leave you to yourself, when you'd find out your mistake the sooner, so you would; and my first intention was only to go to Mordaunt Manor; but, on my way there, I thought of poor, dear, darling Inez, and decided that it would be very much nicer and better for her, and for you, and for myself, to come here and see her. And that's just the very thing I did,

you know, and so you see, Gwynnie darling, it's my opinion that we had better not mention it again, for really you know, darling, it isn't a thing that one can very well say much about. Besides, I'm so bursting with the wonderful discovery I've made. And oh, what in the wide world will dear Kane say and think? and oh, Gwynnie darling, how I do wish he had stayed and seen her! For she's here, you know; I found her and brought her here, and she's here now, so she is, the jool of life!"

"You mean Inez?" asked Gwyn, with a sigh.

"Inez? Of course. Who else? And what do you think? Oh, you would never guess—never, never! Oh, it's the very strangest thing and the gladdest thing, so it is!"

"What is it?" asked Gwyn, who wondered what that could be which was able to excite Bessie at such a moment as this. For his own part, all the rest of the world seemed then a matter of indifference.

"You'd never guess, so you wouldn't—never—and so I'll have to tell you," said Bessie, "though I don't think you will really believe it, at all at all, that is, not just at first, you know, for it's so awfully funny, Gwynnie dear. It's this: You know my darling Inez, how I love her, and all that sort of thing, and we've always been just like sisters, too, you know—oh, she's such a darling!—well, do you know, Gwynnie dear, I've just found out that she really is my very own sister."

"Your what? Your sister? Why, what do you mean? How can that be?" asked Gwyn, in great amazement, and thoroughly roused now by this startling intelligence.

"Sure I mean what I say; things have come to light that I never knew before, and there isn't the least doubt in life but it's all gospel truth, so it is; and only think of my own darling Inez being my own sister!"

"What! is her name *Inez Mordaunt?*" asked Gwyn, in amazement.

"Sure and it is, and I got things all mixed up in my mind, so I did. I was told my name was Inez, though they always called me Bessie, but it's my other sister that owned the name, after all; and don't you think it's all awfully funny, Gwynnie darling?"

"Why, I don't know what to think, for I

don't understand it at all ; but I'm very glad, indeed, darling Bessie, if you are. I care for no one but you."

"And sure and I don't care much for anybody but you, Gwynnie, if it comes to that," said Bessie, giving him a look of touching fondness, and trustful, innocent affection, that sent a thrill of rapture through Gwyn's heart. The consequences that might ensue from her thus finding another sister did not occur to him. He did not think of asking whether this sister was older or younger. The heritage of Mordaunt Manor was at that moment of no interest to him. The presence of Bessie was enough, and the certainty that she loved him still prevented him from feeling any uneasiness about the future. It was from her, or rather for her sake, that the temptation had come to him on the top of the hill; and now, for her sake, he had become for the time indifferent to wealth, to rank, to title, to every thing, except the love that he felt for her.

Bessie went on to tell him all that she knew about it—her narrative comprising that which Kevin Magrath had told her and Inez while they were together—but of course not touching upon those disclosures which he had made to Inez alone.

"So you see, Gwynnie dearest," said she, as she concluded, "Mordaunt Manor isn't mine now, at all at all, so it isn't, no more than Ruthven Towers is yours, not a bit; and the long and the short of it is, Gwynnie, that you and I are two beggars, and don't you call that awfully funny, now ?"

Gwyn looked at her with moist eyes, and, drawing her closer to his heart, he kissed her fair brow.

"Darling !" said he, fervently, " I never valued your love so much before, and it is so precious to me that, if I lost all the rest that I have in the world, I should not care. Let Ruthven Towers go. Let Mordaunt Manor go. It will be strange if I cannot take care of you still. As long as I have you I am content."

"And O Gwynnie," continued Bessie, "wasn't it the wonderful thing that I said— you remember, of course—it was, maybe my sister might be alive and come forward. I meant my sister Clara, for I thought I was Inez, but Clara, poor darling, is dead, glory be with her, and so it's not Clara, but Inez, that has appeared ; and do you know, Gwyn-

nie dear, the more I think of all this the funnier it seems—now, doesn't it ? And then, again, it does seem so awfully funny, you know, for you to give up your title, and for me to give up mine, and for both of us to be plain Mr. and Mrs., and that, too, after all our splendor, and all the congratulations of the county, and to have to work for our living. Really, Gwynnie dear, it makes me laugh."

Gwyn smiled, out of pure delight, to see Bessie taking this approach of adversity so pleasantly.

"And I thought, so I did," continued Bessie, "that poor, darling Clara was alive, perhaps, after all ; but no, it seems she is really dead, for do you know, Gwynnie dear, poor, dear papa, before he came to Mordaunt Manor, visited her grave here, and then he and dear grandpa Magrath—who really isn't my grandpa, you know, after all, but I must call him so still—well, those two had the remains of poor, dear Clara exhumed and taken to Rome, where they buried her again by the side of poor, dear mamma, who, it seems, is buried there also. And oh, it's very sad, so it is, to find out, after all, that really she is so very, very dead, you know !

"And you know, Gwynnie dear," continued Bessie, after a few moments of mournful thought, "dear Inez is going to Rome, for she remembers dear Clara, and, having lost her in life, she longs to go, as she says, and pray over her grave. For dear grandpa says that poor, dear Clara was not well treated, at all at all, and there was sadness and sorrow about her death.

"And then, again," resumed Bessie, "there's another reason why dear Inez is willing to go, for there's a great friend of hers—and of dear Kane's, too, and of mine, too, for that matter—Dr. Blake, the one that attended poor, dear Guardy Wyverne ; well, dear grandpa says that Dr. Blake is in Rome ; that 'he's settled down' there, and is likely to remain ; and I think dear Inez is rather in hopes of seeing him somewhere about Rome, and so you see, Gwynnie dear, she has two very strong reasons for going, and dear grandpa is going to take her."

"Does she know of her father's death ?" asked Gwyn.

"Sure and she must. Grandpa had a long talk alone with her, and told her all about every thing, and things, too, that he didn't want me to hear, about my infancy, I believe, for fear it would make me too sad; and, after it all was over, she looked at me— O Gwynnie! such a look—so awfully sad and sorrowful! And oh, but I had the sore heart for her, poor darling! and I didn't dare to say a word, for sure it seemed to me just as though I'd been serving her as Jacob did Esau—just for all the wide world as though I had taken her name and place—for poor, darling papa took me for Inez, and died blessing me as Inez. But really, Gwynnie darling, it wasn't my fault, so it wasn't—for didn't I think I was Inez? Sure I did. Still, that doesn't change matters for her, and, however innocent I was about it, the fact remains— and oh, but it must be the sore fact for her! But, if any one's to blame, it's poor Guardy Wyverne, who went and changed her name. And oh, but it was hard on her, so it was, for she's suffered more than her share on account of it. And I can't help feeling that I've had a share in the wrong, and that I've been happy at her expense. And I'm anxious to make some amends, and I won't be able to be happy, at all at all, unless I do something to console her. I'm her chief consolation now —and oh, but it's the blessed thing that I hurried on as I did!"

Bessie stopped, and looked with an expression of anxious inquiry at her husband.

"Gwynnie dearest," said she, in her most winning tone.

"Well, darling?"

"I'm going to tell you something now that you won't like; but it must be done, and I won't keep you in suspense about it. I have told Inez that I would devote myself to her for a short time, and that we would be just as we used to be. She objected, poor darling, and said that she would not like to take me from you; but I laughed, and said that you would not object if I wanted it, and that you would be willing to do any little thing you could if it would be for her good. And so you will, Gwynnie dear, for here is my dear sister Inez, the one that I've wronged so much without knowing it, and she's suffered awfully, and she needs loving care and attention, and I am the only living being that can give her this. So please, Gwynnie dear, don't be after looking so dismal, for there are duties that I have in the world besides those I owe to you, and I'm not the one to stand by and see my darling Inez—my new-found sis-

13

ter—after suffering so much, left alone without any congenial friends. Of course, dear grandpa would do every thing in the wide world for her, so he would; but he is not what she wants, at all at all, nor is Mrs. Lugrin. She wants an old friend—an equal— her sister—myself—and it's myself that's the only one she can get comfort from. And so, Gwynnie, as I know you have a tender heart, and are not selfish, why, sure you'll quietly let me go for a while, and devote myself to my sweet sister."

This proposal threw great gloom over Gwyn. Yet the recollection of his own deep offence, and the total and complete reconciliation with Bessie, and her sweet and graceful forgiveness, all made it impossible for him to oppose her wishes, especially when expressed for such a purpose.

"And must I go home?" he asked, dismally.

"Go home, is it? Not you. You must come to Rome. Go home! Why, what an awful idea, Gwynnie darling! Oh, no. You must come on to Rome, and perhaps dear Kane may come, too. Bring him; you'll both be the happier for it, and we'll see one another all the time. When I said I was going to devote myself to Inez, I didn't mean that I was going away from you altogether. I want to have you near, Gwynnie darling, and see you every day."

Gwyn gave a sigh of relief.

"I'll pretend that I'm a lover again, Bessie darling," said he, sadly.

"Oh, yes, do—do, dear, darling Gwynnie; it will be so awfully nice, and funny, and all that. And you must bring Kane to Rome for company. He'll want, perhaps, to come with the rest of us, and join in our prayers over dear Clara's grave. Oh, how awfully nice! Only think—that is, I don't exactly mean nice—but you understand, dear. I want to ask himself, if I only can. But he'll be here this evening; he must come to see dear Inez; she talks so much about him. Besides, he'll be glad to know that every thing is explained."

———◆———

CHAPTER XLVI.

BEFORE HIS JUDGE.

On returning to Kane's apartments, Gwyn told him all that he had heard from Bessie, to which Kane listened in the utmost amazement. Many circumstances were explained, yet many more were inexplicable to him as yet. Above all, he could not understand how it was, if Bernal Mordaunt had died at Mordaunt Manor, that he could have written from his death-bed in Paris. These two things seemed irreconcilable, nor could Gwyn give him any satisfaction. Soon, however, there were other things mentioned which drew all Kane's thoughts away from the affairs of Inez. This was the statement that the remains of Clara had been exhumed, and had been taken to Rome for burial; and also the announcement that Blake had gone to Rome, and had "settled down in that place for good."

Both of these facts were to him of overwhelming importance. In his friendship for Blake he rejoiced to learn that he was well, though he could not help wondering why he had remained so silent. But this was of comparative unimportance in view of the astounding news about the remains of Clara.

Kane's feelings about his lost wife have been sufficiently described. It was to be near her loved remains that he had come to Paris —it was for this sake only that he lived here. Other places would have been preferable to him, but the presence here of Clara's remains gave to Paris an interest that no other place could have. It had been his habit to pray at stated times over her grave, and the anniversary of that awful day when they were separated was always observed by him with fasting and prayer. He had not been near her grave since that night of the "apparition" at Père-la-Chaise; but the anniversary was not far distant, and he would have to go there, no matter what might be his feelings, and observe the usual solemnities.

Now he learned to his amazement what had happened. This fact at once broke into all the even tenor of his life, and made it necessary for him to make some change. The removal of those precious relics destroyed all motives for remaining here. Where those remains were, there he must go. The state of his feelings was such that life was only tolerable near all that was mortal of her whom he loved, and the first thought that he had when Rome was mentioned was that he must leave Paris and go there. The information that Kevin Magrath, and Inez, and Bessie, were all going there to "pray over that grave," only intensified his desires to do the same, and all other thoughts became indifferent to him.

What he should do first was now the question. He was anxious to see Kevin Magrath. This man's character had undergone a fresh revolution in his mind. When he had first seen him, he had formed of him such an opinion that he seemed a sort of accusing witness, an avenger of blood, a relentless Nemesis. After hearing the story of Inez, he had been changed into a remorseless villain, a dark schemer and intriguer. Now, however, he appeared once more in the former light. Whatever might be the mystery that remained, it seemed evident to Kane, from Bessie's words, and the acts of herself and Inez, that the last judgment about Kevin Magrath was wrong. It seemed now as though he must have been the faithful friend of Bernal Mordaunt and his children; a just man; a tender-hearted guardian; a loyal friend; one who had been the champion of unprotected innocence, and one, too, who had felt merciful even to the guilty, whose former guilt he had resisted and denounced.

Yet the prospect of meeting with this man had in it something so terrible for Kane that he shrunk from it. For Kevin Magrath once more seemed to be the avenger of the injured Clara. He could not help recalling his look, his attitude, and his words, during that memorable evening in London—those awful words, every one of which had pierced like a stab to his heart. To go now to this man would be to expose himself to a repetition of this painful scene, to receive fresh wounds, and encounter fresh sufferings. Yet to do so was necessary. This man had assisted in the removal of Clara. He himself must have touched the casket that held that precious treasure, and from that touch the man himself seemed now to Kane's imagination to have acquired a kind of awful sanctity. To meet him would be more painful than ever, but it was necessary in order to obtain accurate information about the place in which they had laid the remains of his lost darling.

Kane therefore yielded to this necessity, and that evening called at the hotel along with Gwyn. Inez and Bessie were both in the room waiting for them. Kane greeted Inez with affectionate cordiality, and congratulated her most sincerely upon the favorable change in her affairs. But his thoughts were so occupied with the chief purpose of this visit that he did not question her very particularly, and the conversation took a general turn, which was at length interrupted by the entrance of Kevin Magrath.

He looked around with a ·beaming smile, which was at once benevolent and paternal. Bessie introduced him to Gwyn. He shook hands with him cordially with some warm words of welcome, and then, catching sight of Kane, advanced toward him.

"Mr. Hellville—ah—Hellmuth, sure it's glad I am to see ye here! It's sorry I was the last time I saw ye that ye had to make yer ajieus before the evening had begun. I hope we may be able to-night to pass the time in a more shuitable manner."

Saying this, he shook hands with Kane very warmly, and went on to chat with Gwyn, and Bessie, and Inez, one by one, in the easiest and pleasantest way in the world.

"There's no one going that knows Rome better than I do," said he, in reply to some remark of Bessie's about their journey. "Don't I know it? Haven't I lived there, off and on, for years? Meself has. There isn't a cyardinal of the holy conclave that I don't know, in and out. And they're a fine body of min intirely, so they are, but it's a pity they're so many of thim Italians. In a constichutional kingdom, as Italy now is, there's a wonderful chance for the holy father, if he only knowed how to avail himself of it. If they only wint to work the way they do in Ireland and America, they could howld the distinies of Italy and of the wurruld in the hollows of their hands. But they don't comprihind, and they won't, till another gineration comes along that grows into the new order of things. Ye see, what I always tell them is this: Ye must conforrum more to the spirit of the age. It's a liberal age and a constichutional age. Ye must be liberal and constichutional. It's no use excommunicating kings and imperors, and prime ministers and sinators. Look at the way they do in America. They take possession of the ballot-box, and thus become shupreme. Go, says I, into politics, bald-headed! Direct the votes of the people. They're all yours. Out of twinty

millions of Italians how many d'ye think ye have on yer own side? There's tin million famales. Out of the other tin million min five million are boys who are all under the control of their mothers. Out of the remaining five million adult min four million are adult pisints, altogether under the control of the priesthood, and riddy to vote as they suggist. It is a great allowance to suppose a single million as belonging to the Antipapal or Liberal party. If ye wint among these, ye'd find numerous ways of gaining control of three-quarters of thim. Me own opinion is that, out of the twinty millions of Italians, there's only two hundred thousand min who can be called Liberals. And what could they do? Got universal suffrage and the ballot-box, and ye'd swamp thim, so ye would. Ye howld the distinies of the country in yer power, and all ye've got to do is, like children of Israel at the Red Sea, whin Moses came to thim as I do to you and said, as I now say, 'Go forward;' or, like the same, when Joshua the son of Nun said to them, 'Behold the promised land! Go ye up and possess it!'"

From such high themes as these the conversation gradually faded away—Gwyn absorbing Bessie, and Kevin Magrath alternately addressing Inez and Kane. But Inez evidently took no interest in what she considered politics, and thus Kane was left as the only collocutor or listener or whatever else he may have been. Collocutor he certainly was not, however, for he simply listened, not attending particularly to Kevin Magrath's remarks, but rather thinking about the best way of seeing him alone, so as to ask him about those things which now were uppermost in his mind. At length Inez left the room. Gwyn and Bessie were taken up with each other, and then it was that Kane made known his feelings.

"I should like very much," said he, "to ask you about some things that are of importance to me. Can I see you alone for a few moments?"

Kevin Magrath smiled graciously.

"With the greatest plisure in life," said he. "Come along with me to me own room, and we'll make a night of it."

With these words he rose and led the way along the corridor to a room at the end of it. Entering this, Kane found himself in a large and elegantly-furnished apartment, opening into a bedroom. On a sideboard were bottles, decanters, and tobacco-boxes. On the table was a meerschaum-pipe, a box of cigars, and the latest *Galignani*.

Kevin Magrath rolled up an easy-chair beside the table.

"Make yerself comfortable," said he, cheerily. "Ye'll take something warrum, won't ye—and a pipe or so? I've whiskey here by me, Scotch or Irish—'Cœlum non animum mutant,' ye know; 'qui trans mare currunt;' and, for my part, I carry a bottle of Irish whiskey with me wherever I go—and Scotch too, for that matter; though, on the whole, I object to Scotch whiskey, for it savors somewhat of Calvinism. Howandiver, ye'll take one or the other."

Kane mildly suggested Irish.

Kevin Magrath smiled.

"It's charrumed I am with yer taste, and I take it as a complimint to me country," and he poured out a wineglassful, which he handed to Kane, after which he poured out another for himself. "Here," said he, "lifting it to his lips, "here is a libation which I've powered out in honor of old Ireland, let's drink to the first flower of the earth and first gim of the sea."

They both drank solemnly.

"And now," said Kevin Magrath, "having performed the first jutics of hospitality, I'm altogether at your service. But won't ye take a pipe or a cigar?"

Kane declined.

"The fact is," said he, drawing a long breath, "my name is not Hellmuth."

"The divil it isn't!" said Kevin Magrath.

"Circumstances," said Kane, "made it necessary for me on my former visit to take that name. At present there is no such necessity. I have dropped it, and have taken my own again."

"'Deed, thin," said Kevin Magrath, "I hope that yer circumstances, whativer they are, have changed for the better."

Kane sighed, and regarded the other gloomily and fixedly.

"My name," said he, is a familiar one to you. It is Kane Ruthven. I am the man that married Clara Mordaunt, and caused her death. I wish to talk to you about her. I wish also to show you that, for any evil which I did to her whom I loved, I have atoned for by life-long remorse."

At the first mention of this name a sudden and astonishing change came over Kevin Magrath. His easy, placid smile passed away a dark frown came over his brows, he pushed his chair back and started to his feet, and regarded Kane with a black, scowling face.

"You!" he cried.

"Yes," said Kane.

Kevin Magrath looked at him for some time with the same expression, but gradually the severity of his features began to relax.

"I've prayed," said he, slowly, "and I've longed for the time to come whin I could see ye face to face; and thin again I've longed and I've prayed that I might never see ye. I've prayed to see ye that I might have vengince for Clara's bitter wrongs, for her betrayal, for her broken heart, for her death, for the dishonor of a noble name, and the shame of a lofty lineage; and I've prayed not to see ye, so that I might niver have another man's blood on my hands, for I felt sure that, if I ever did see ye, that momint I'd have yer heart's-blood. But, somehow," continued he, after a moment's pause, "somehow—now that I do see ye face to face—sure, I don't know how it is at all at all, but the desire for bloody vingince has gone out of me; and ye seem to have the face of a man that's paid the full penalty already of any wrong ye've iver done, so ye do. And whither it is this that's the matther, or whither it is that I can't rise against the man that's drunk with me—but sure to glory I'm changed—and so I say to you, Kane Ruthven, in the name of God, what is it that ye seek me for, and have ye any thing to say for yerself in regyard to yur dealings with the young gyerrul that ye—destroyed?"

Kevin Magrath's manner was most impressive. It was that of a lofty, rigid, impartial judge, who will exact strict justice, yet is not altogether disinclined to mercy. Kane sustained his gaze with tranquillity, and looked at him with a solemn, sombre brow. When he had finished, he said:

"You are mistaken about me in many ways, and, when you hear what I have to say, you will have a less harsh opinion of me than the one you expressed in London."

"Go on, then; let me hear what you have to say, for it's meself that would be the proud man if ye could clear yerself of any of the guilt that's seemed to be attached to ye."

Kane now proceeded to tell his whole story. He told it frankly and fully, heaping blame upon himself lavishly, yet clearing himself of all those worse charges which Magrath had uttered against him.

After it was over, Magrath remained musing for a long time.

"Sure," said he, at last, "there was villany, though not with you. Your brother was hard, but it was my poor frind Hennigar Wyverne that was the arch-traitor and rogue. But how in the worruld did it happen that Clara did not know herself that she was the daughter of Bernal Mordaunt, and heiress of Mordaunt Manor?"

"I can't account for it at all."

"I've heard it stated on iminint authority," said Magrath, "that a boy who leaves his home, or is taken from his home, at the age of tin, and is thrown into a foreign land among strangers, will in five years forget his own name, his father's name, and his native language. I nivir believed it before, but now this looks like it. Clara lost her home and her father at tin; she had not lived regularly at Mordaunt Manor either, and was sent into France; and thus it has happened that she forgot in a few years the most important things."

"It must have been so," said Kane. "She knew her name, but had no recollection of Mordaunt Manor—at least she said nothing about it—and she certainly had no idea that she was an heiress."

Another long silence followed.

"Kane Ruthven," said Magrath, at last—"or perhaps I ought to say Sir Kane—what you have said clears you completely and utterly from the suspicions which I had forrumed about you. You have not been guilty, as I now see, of any thing worse than carelessness, or thoughtlessness. For that you have suffered enough. I must say that me conscience condimns shuicide, and in that act ye were clearly wrong; it was unnecessary; she would have drifted home or into my hands, for I was close upon her track at that very time. Howandiver, what's done can't be undone, and, as ye're an innocint and a suffering man, why—there's my hand."

With this he reached out his hand. Kane took it, and Magrath shook it heartily.

"I have understood," said Kane, anxiously and hesitatingly, "that—that she—she was removed from the cemetery."

"It was her father's wish," said Magrath, "that she should be buried beside her mother in Rome."

"She is now in Rome, then?"

"Yes, with her mother; and the other two daughters, Inez and Bessie, are going to pray over the graves for the repose of the souls of their mother and their sister."

"I should think that they would have been taken rather to Mordaunt Manor."

"It was Bernal Mordaunt's doing," said Magrath. "But they are all united, for Bessie's filial piety has accomplished one of the last wishes of her father; and, while she was living at Ruthven Towers, her father's remains were exhumed and taken to Rome."

Kane hardly heard these last words. His mind was occupied exclusively with thoughts of Clara. Magrath's information was conclusive. It was what he had wished to know, and there was nothing more to be learned. About the affairs of Inez he thought no more. She was safe now with loving friends; the mysterious circumstances about her late imprisonment were no doubt satisfactorily explained, and he himself had no further interest in the matter.

It was with a feeling of satisfaction, however, that Kane reflected on the formal acquittal which Magrath had given him of evil acts. For Magrath was now to him a stern, a just, and a wise judge, from whom a declaration of this sort was valuable, indeed. There was at the conclusion of this interview a deeper solemnity than usual in the manner of each of them, and Magrath did not press him to stay, or ask him again to take a drink.

That night Gwyn bade Bessie farewell. She was to start with Inez early on the following morning for Rome.

"You'll come on soon, Gwynnie darling," said she, tenderly.

"Immediately, of course, Bessie dearest."

"And you'll bring dear Kane?"

"Of course."

Bessie looked at him earnestly.

"We're beggars now, so we are, Gwynnie dear, but I love you, and we can be as happy in our poverty as ever we were in our wealth, so we can."

Gwyn pressed her to his heart and left.

As he walked away, his heart was full of bitterness. Kane and Inez seemed now like interlopers, who had come between him and his darling, casting her down from the wealth and luxury with which he had thought he had endowed her. Kane again had been the innocent cause of this foul wrong which he had

trace his steps, but rather to go on till he should find signs of some way of escape.

And now his active mind busied itself, as he went on, in the endeavor to discover what direction might give the best promise of escape. In spite of his conviction that the whole of O'Rourke's story was a fiction, he still thought that some portions of it might give him information; and, as his description of portions of the paths had been true, so also might his assertions about the general direction of this path on which he was going. O'Rourke's assertion had been that it ran toward the Palatine Hill, and the whole point of his narrative had consisted in the theory that it actually passed under the Palatine, and was possibly connected with some of the ancient vaults. If this were so, it seemed to Blake that an opening might be found through these vaults, and that thus his escape could be made.

With this in his mind, Blake concluded to go on as rapidly as possible along that very path by which O'Rourke had tried to lead him to destruction. In a short time he came to that place which O'Rourke had called the Painted Chamber, and, hurrying on quickly, yet cautiously, he soon reached the opening into the lower passage-way. Down this he descended, and, as he passed down, his eyes caught sight of those holes in the wall which he had so laboriously made. But it was not a time to yield to emotions of any sort, or to feed his melancholy in any way.

He now walked on very cautiously, for he was afraid of openings in the floor, and it was necessary to look well to his path. He expected before long to reach some larger chamber, which might mark the neighborhood of the Palatine Hill. For O'Rourke's story had still so strong a hold of his mind that he fully expected to see that place which had been called the "Treasure Chamber," though of course he had not the slightest expectation of finding any treasure, nor was there any possibility that one in his desperate circumstances should feel the slightest wish to find it.

As he went on, he found that the cross-passages were much less numerous than they had been. The path also along which he went had but a slight deflection from a straight course—so slight, indeed, that it was the same to Blake as a straight line. No pitfalls lay in his way, and it seemed to him that he had reached the lowest level on which the Catacombs had been made.

At length he had walked on so far that he began to hesitate. It was time for him to have reached that chamber under the Palatine, but he had found nothing in his way which, by any stretch of fancy, could be called a chamber. It had been a narrow passage-way, preserving the same dimensions all along, and the characteristic features which distinguished all the passages here. He seemed to be wandering on interminably, and at length the vague hope which thus far had encouraged him, or at least led him on, now faded away altogether, and he walked on slowly, merely because it seemed better than standing still.

There was no treasure, that he already knew; but he had now found out that there was no chamber either, no connection with any ancient vaults, and possibly no approach to the neighborhood of the Palatine. That part of O'Rourke's statements seemed now evidently thrown in to stimulate the fancy by giving plausible grounds to his theory of the treasure of the Cæsars. And where, now, should he go? In what direction should he turn? Might he not be wandering farther and farther away from the path of safety?

With such thoughts as these, amid which not one ray of hope presented itself, Blake wandered on more and more slowly. At length he reached a cross-passage, and here he came to a full stop. To go on any farther along this passage-way seemed useless. Here, too, his hesitation was succeeded by a discovery that promised the very worst. Already he had noticed that the lamp had become dimmer, but he had refused to believe it, and had tried to think that it was the hardening of the wick, but now the fact could no longer be concealed. Even as he stood here for a few moments, that light—which to him was symbolical of the light of life—faded more and more. With a despairing hand he opened the lantern, and picked off the top of the wick that had caked over, feeling all the while the utter hopelessness of such an act, for how could that prolong in any degree the life of the dying flame? It did not prolong it; the flame died down lower and lower.

Upon this, Blake, actuated by a sudden impulse, blew it out. He thought that the small quantity of oil yet remaining might better be preserved for some extreme me-

ment of his life, when a ray of light for but a minute might be of far more value than now. So he extinguished it for the present, and preserved the minute or so of light that might yet be given for future need.

All was now darkness, dense, impenetrable, appalling. His long search had resulted in absolutely nothing, and he began to think that it would have been better for him at this moment if he had never set out upon it. It seemed now as though he might have effected something, had he devoted all this time toward the task of moving away some portion of the stony barrier which O'Rourke had set up. A little reflection, however, showed him that this would have been impossible. He recollected the immense masses that closed up the opening, and considered that behind these were other masses. No; escape by that way was impossible.

He was at the intersection of two paths, and he had no idea now in what direction it might be best to go. The darkness was tremendous. The silence, also, that reigned all around, was almost equally impressive. Now, as he listened, that silence was broken by sounds which to him were more terrible even than the silence. They showed the presence of those ravenous foes who had held aloof during his progress with the light, but who now, while he stood in darkness, prepared to attack him. It was their hour, and they seemed to know it. From afar came the sound of their advance, the movement of rapid, pattering feet, the hurry of abominable things past him, the touch of horrible objects that sent a shudder through him. Since he had descended to this lower level, he had seen nothing of them, and in his other cares had forgotten them. Now they made their presence felt and feared. They came up from the passage-way on his right. He could tell by the sounds that they were very numerous; he could feel that they were very bold.

To stand still there was impossible; to do so would simply be to make an attack certain. Once he struck a match, and the flash of the light revealed a sight so abhorrent that he was glad to have the darkness shut it out again—a multitude of eager, hungry eyes, from the ravenous little monsters that shrunk back at the sudden blaze, but were ready at any moment to spring.

He must move, for movement was his only safety. The narrowness of the passage fa-

vored him, for he could not be surrounded; he might possibly drive them before him. To move along this passage, by which they were advancing upon him, was necessary. Perhaps, also, it might be best. These animals must have some communication with the outer world, and it might possibly be found in this direction. This way, then, seemed to him to be by far the most promising, or, rather, to be the one which had less of despair. He could not help wondering why the rats had not appeared when O'Rourke was with him. Could it have been the greater light or noise that deterred them, or the sound of human voices?

No sooner had Blake thought of this than he resolved to break the silence himself, and to use his own voice against them, hoping that the unusual sound might alarm them. Already they were leaping up his legs. He swung his ladder around, and advanced, pushing it before him, and wriggling it backward and forward. This was partly to drive the rats before him, and partly to feel his pathway, so as to guard against openings. Thus he set forth, and resumed his journey in the dark.

But not in silence. He was to try the effect of a human voice over his assailants. But with what words should he speak, what cry should he give there, commensurate with that appalling gloom, that terrible silence, these abhorrent enemies? No common words, no words of every-day speech, were possible. Where should he find words which might at once be a weapon against the enemy and at the same time be concordant with the anguish of his soul? No words of his could do this. He would have to make use of other words. Back went his thoughts to words heard in years past—the solemn and sublime words of the services of his Church, heard in childhood and boyhood, and remembered, though of late neglected and despised. In his anguish his soul caught up a cry of anguish—the cry of despairing souls in all ages, which never sounded forth from a more despairing soul, and never amid more terrific surroundings, than when Blake, wandering wildly on, burst forth:

"*De profundis clamavi ad te, Domine ; Domine, exaudi vocem meam.*

"*Fiant aures tuœ intendentes in vocem deprecationis meœ.*"

Nor was this the first time that this cry

had gone forth, in Latin, in Greek, or in Hebrew, from despairing souls in the Catacombs of Rome.

CHAPTER XLVIII.

BACK TO LIFE.

THE loud and prolonged cries of Blake proved more efficacious than any active efforts. There seemed something in the sound of this human voice which struck terror to the fierce assailants by whom he was threatened; and though but a short time before they had been swarming near and leaping up against him, yet no sooner had the first words of his cry pealed forth, than they started back as though terrified, and finally retreated far away. There was a mournful satisfaction in having been so far successful, but none the less there remained in his soul a feeling which was now one of unalterable despair. Though for the present his enemies had fled, yet he did not cease his cries utterly, but from time to time gave utterance to them, so that whatever power they had might be made use of.

He still walked on, pushing his ladder along the floor before him, and moving it as he pushed it so as to test the floor, and guard against the danger of openings into lower regions. He still carried the lantern which contained its few drops of oil as a last resort when some supreme crisis should arrive and light be needed. Thus he went on, nor did he forget that faint encouragement which he had gathered before he began this last march, by the fact that the rats had emerged from this direction, and might possibly have some communication here with the outer world. There was now nothing better for him than to move on, and he was resolved to move on till he died.

He had not gone far, after all. It was not long since he had left the place where his lamp had failed him; he had walked very slowly and very cautiously, for in that darkness any rapid progress was utterly out of the question. He had to step slowly and cautiously, feeling his way most carefully, first with the ladder, then with his foot, testing the ground before him, first with his toe before daring to plant himself firmly, and advancing only a few inches at a time. In this way he accomplished about twenty or thirty yards,

when all of a sudden he became aware of something which was so amazing that he stood still as though paralyzed, with his eyes fastened upon that something before him.

That something had no very definable shape or form, yet the very fact that there was something before him, upon which his eyes could fix themselves, was of itself sufficient to account for the great rush of contending emotions which now succeeded to his despair, and overwhelmed him. There was before him—before his eyes—a visible something; dim, obscure, yet appreciable to the sense of vision, and it was not far away. It was a dull and barely perceptible light—so dim that it could scarce be called light, and yet it was light, light positive and unmistakable—light, too, from no lamp, but from the great external ocean of light which he had so yearned to reach, and which now seemed to send forth this faint stream to beckon him onward, and to inspire him with hope and joy and life.

As he stood there motionless for a time, of which he took no account, that light grew perceptibly brighter, and every moment brought a fresher and a sweeter assurance to his soul that there was no mistake, that his wanderings had led him in the right direction; that there was some opening here through which came the light of the external world—the world of life. At length the assurance grew so strong that it broke down his inaction, and he started forward to reach it, still moving cautiously, and feeling his way as before. He saw as he slowly advanced an irregular aperture gradually taking form, and through this penetrated that dim yet ever-increasing light which had met his eyes. Every minute that outline became more clearly defined, until at length there was more than an outline. He saw light and shade, and the rough surface of stone, and a lighter space beyond the opening. The intense darkness from which he had just emerged had given to his eyes a greater power than usual of discerning objects illumined by this faint light; and, faint though it was, it brightened more and more, just as though the external source of this light was itself increasing in brightness. To Blake it seemed as if the sun was, or might be, rising, in that outer world; and the increasing light which he saw might be the sign of that gathering dawn.

At length he reached the place, and **stood**

for a moment scarcely able to believe in the reality of his good fortune. It was an opening into a space beyond, about three feet long and two feet high, formed by the removal of some blocks of stone. The space beyond was an arched passage-way constructed of enormous blocks of stone, about six feet in height, and much wider than the passages of the Catacombs. At the bottom water was flowing along. Thrusting his head farther through, he looked up and down. In the one direction all was dark, but in the other, at no very great distance, there appeared the glad outer world, over which was brightening the morning sky, with fields and houses reddening under the flush of dawn.

He remained here some time, drinking in great waves of this ever-increasing light with something like adoration, quaffing it like one intoxicated, hardly able to satisfy himself, but giving himself up altogether to the ecstasy of the moment. And what was this place, he wondered, upon which he had thus so strangely stumbled? What was this archway of Cyclopean stones, hoar with age, with its floor filled with rubbish, and running water passing on? A broken fragment of one of the massive rocks composing its sides had been removed, and formed the opening which had given him life once more. Doubtless this fragment had been removed in past ages by fugitives who thus were able to escape pursuit by plunging into the Catacombs. Perhaps those who removed the broken fragment cut the passage-way along to those farther in; or perhaps it was the work of some of the early Christians in the ages of persecution, and this may have been one of the secret and unsuspected entrances to the subterranean hiding-places. But what was this ancient arch itself? No place of graves—no passage-way among many others like it, was this. It was unique. It stood alone; and Blake, though a stranger in Rome, had sufficient knowledge of its most remarkable monuments to feel sure that this place upon which he had so strangely come was no other than the most venerable, the most ancient, and in many respects the most wonderful, of all the works of ancient Rome—the Cloaca Maxima.

But this was not a time for wonder, or for curiosity, or for antiquarian researches. Death lay behind him. Light and life lay before him. The horrors through which he had passed had produced their natural effect in extreme prostration of mind and body. Some rest, some breathing-space, was required; but, after that, if he would save himself, if he would not perish within the very reach of safety, he must hurry on.

He crawled through and stood in the Cloaca Maxima. It ran before him, leading him to the outer world, giving him light and life. The treasure of the Roman emperors, which he had dreamed of finding, had been missed; but he had found the work of the Roman kings, which to him, in his despair, was worth infinitely more. He stood in ooze and slime, over which passed running water, which flowed to the Tiber. Blake did not wait, but hurried onward as fast as he could. The brightening scene, visible in the distance, and growing more brilliant every moment, drew him onward, and the terrors behind him drove him forward; so that this combined attraction and repulsion gave him additional strength and speed. He hurried on, and still on, and at length reached the mouth of the arched passage. Here he saw sloping banks on either side; and, clambering up the bank on the right, he stood for a moment to rest himself.

In that brief period of rest he had no eyes and no thoughts for the scene around, though for some that scene would have possessed a charm greater than any other that may be met with in all the world. He did not notice the Aventine, the Capitoline, the Janiculum, in the distance, and the yellow Tiber that flowed between. He was thinking only of rest, of refuge. He longed for some sort of home, some place where he might lie down and sleep. He only noticed that it was the morning of a new day, and consequently perceived that he must have spent a whole night in the Catacombs.

In that night what horrors had he not endured! As he stood there panting for breath, the recollection came over him of all that he had passed through. He thought of that first moment when he discovered that he was alone; that the ladder and the clew were gone; that he had been betrayed. He thought of his despair, followed by his efforts to escape; his long labor at the walls of stone; his ascent to the upper floor and pursuit of O'Rourke; his arrival at the opening, and his discovery that it was walled up. Then he heard the rattle of stones, and the voice of his betrayer, saying, "*Blake Wyverne, fare-*

well forever !" He recalled his fainting-fit, his recovery, and his renewal of his efforts to escape; and then followed that long horror, that night of agony, in which he had wandered along that terrific pathway, with its appalling surroundings. In such a situation a man might well have died through utter fright, or have sunk down to death through despair, or have wandered aimlessly till all strength had failed him. It was to Blake's credit that, even in his despair, he had preserved some sort of presence of mind, and had not been without a method in his movements. Yet the suffering had been terrible; and the anguish of soul that he had endured intensified his bodily fatigues, so that now, in the very moment of safety, he found himself unable to obtain the benefits of that safety; and so extreme was his prostration and so utter his weakness that it was only with difficulty that he kept himself from sinking down into senselessness on the spot.

This would not do. He must obtain some sort of a home, some kind of a lodging-place, where he might rest and receive attention. His strong and resolute nature still asserted itself in spite of the weakness of the flesh, and he dragged himself onward, unwilling to give up, unable to surrender himself too easily to the frailty of his physical nature. The instinct of self-preservation also warned him to seek some shelter, where he might be concealed from the discovery of O'Rourke; for, even in the weakness of that hour and in the confusion of his mind, he had a keen sense of impending danger, together with a desire to maintain the secret of his escape. Animated by this, he went on, but by what ways and under what circumstances he was never afterward able to remember.

Afterward he had only a vague recollection of streets and houses. Few people were to be seen. The streets were narrow, the houses lofty and gloomy. It was the older, the meaner, and the most densely-peopled part of the city. The early morning prevented many from being abroad. He watched the windows of the houses with close and eager scrutiny, so as to discover some place where he might rest. At length he found a place where there was a notice in the window for lodgers. He knew enough Italian to understand it, and entered by the door, which happened to be open. An old woman was standing there, and a young girl was coming toward

her from an inner room. Blake accosted her in broken Italian, and had just managed to make her understand that he wished to engage lodgings, when his exhausted strength gave way utterly, and he sank, with a groan, to the floor at her feet.

It was fortunate for Blake that he had encountered those who possessed common feelings of humanity, and were not merely mercenary and calculating people, who would have turned away from their doors those who promised to bring more trouble than profit. It is probable that this old woman would have been quite ready to overreach, or, in fact, to cheat any stranger who came to her in an ordinary way; and yet this same old woman was overcome by the sincerest compassion at the sight of this stranger who had fallen at her feet. Such apparent contradictions are not rare, for in Italy there is more tendency among the common people to swindle strangers than there is in our own country; and yet, at the same time, there is undeniably more kindliness of nature, more tenderness of sympathy, more readiness of pity, more willingness to help the needy, than may be found among our harder and sterner natures. So this old woman, though a possible cheat and swindler, no sooner saw this stranger lying prostrate and senseless, than, without a thought for her own interests, and without any other feeling or motive than pure and disinterested pity and warm human sympathy, she flew to his assistance. She summoned the servants, she sent for a doctor, and in a short time Blake was lying on a soft bed in a comfortable room, watched over most anxiously by perfect strangers, who, however, had been made friends by his affliction, and who now hung over him, and tended him, and cared for him, as though he had been one of their own, instead of a stranger and a foreigner.

Blake was in a high fever—a brain-fever —accompanied with delirium. A long illness followed. He lay utterly unconscious; his mind was occupied with the scenes through which he had passed of late; and all his wandering thoughts turned to the terrible experience of that night of horror. During all this time he was tended most carefully and vigilantly by the kind-hearted old woman and her daughter, who were filled with pity and sympathy. Not one word did they understand of all his delirious ravings, nor did

"And he sank with a groan to the ground at her feet."—Page 200.

they know even what language it was. It might be German, or Russian, or Bohemian, or Turkish, or English, but this made no difference to them. They maintained the part of the good Samaritan, and denied themselves every comfort for the sake of their afflicted lodger.

At length the crisis of the disease was successfully surmounted, and Blake began to recover. In course of time he regained consciousness, and began to understand the situation in which he was. His gratitude to these kind-hearted people knew no bounds, and his earnest expressions of his feelings had to be checked by his careful attendants. These good people had grown to regard him as some one who was dear to them, and to watch for his recovery as for something of the utmost importance. But Blake's prostration had been extreme, and his recovery was very slow. There was also something on his mind. This was a desire to communicate with his mother. But he was unable to write himself, and these good people, though most anxious to serve him in every possible way, were quite unable to write a letter in English at his dictation. So Blake was forced to wait.

At length Blake gained sufficient strength to write what he wished. It was a feeble scrawl, and the handwriting itself expressed the whole of his weakness; but Blake, from a motive of pious deceit, tried to conceal the full extent of his illness. He wrote something about his journey to Rome on "business" (a very convenient term), and about his contracting an illness from the unhealthy climate. He assured her, however, that he was better, urged her not to be at all anxious, and entreated her to come on at once and join him. This letter he directed, and the good people of the house mailed it for him, after which they waited with hardly less anxiety than that which was felt by Blake himself for the result.

That result soon took place. In about ten days an elderly lady came to the house, and inquired, in a tremulous voice, for Dr. Blake. She was a woman of medium stature, slender figure, hair plentifully sprinkled with gray, and a face of gentleness and refinement mingled with firmness and dignity, which also bore evident marks of sorrow. She was unmistakably a lady, and she also had undoubtedly experienced her full share

of those ills to which all flesh is heir. The moment that she appeared, the good people of the house recognized her as the mother of their lodger; and, while some went to announce her arrival so as to spare Blake the excitement of a sudden surprise, others endeavored to soothe her evident anxiety by lively descriptions of the great improvement which had taken place in the health of the invalid.

In this manner a way was prepared for a meeting between these two, and mother and son were soon in one another's arms.

At first that mother had nothing to do but to nurse that son, to soothe him, and to prohibit him from mentioning any exciting circumstances. But the son had a strong constitution, which had favored his recovery, and that recovery was now materially hastened by the arrival of that mother whom he tenderly loved; whose presence at his bedside acted like a healing balm, and whose very words seemed to have some soothing, some vivifying power. After her arrival, his recovery grew more rapid, and at length he was strong enough to give to her a full and complete account of his whole history, without excepting any thing whatever. In that history she found many things to question him about. She asked very particularly about Inez and Bessie. She interrogated him very closely about the scene at the death-bed of Hennigar Wyverne, and also asked him many questions about his friend Kane Hellmuth. She was struck by the fact that Hellmuth was an assumed name; made Blake describe his personal appearance; learned from him the history of his marriage with Clara Mordaunt; and was anxious to know whether Blake had not found out his real name. But her chief interest was evinced in O'Rourke, about whom she questioned Blake over and over again, seeking to know all about his personal appearance, his age, his height, his gestures, his accent, his idioms, his peculiarities of every sort. The conclusion of all this was that she at length, with a solemn look at Blake, exclaimed: "This O'Rourke has been deceiving you, and under an assumed name. His real name is Kevin Magrath. It is impossible that these names can belong to any other except one man."

"Kevin Magrath!" exclaimed Blake. "I never heard the name before."

"I suppose not, dear," said his mother; "and so, as you are now strong enough, I will tell you all about him. You will be able to understand what his designs were about you."

CHAPTER XLIX.

MRS. WYVERNE.

BLAKE'S mother regarded him very earnestly for a few moments, and then said, in a low voice:

"You remember well, dear, every incident at the death-bed of Mr. Wyverne; you have not told me, however, all, I am sure."

Blake looked hastily at his mother. It was true, he had not told her all. The dying man had claimed him as his son; this he had not mentioned to her—how could he?

But now, as he looked at her, he saw an expression in her face which showed him that she had divined his secret, and had suspected that Mr. Wyverne had said more. The look which she gave him invited further disclosure, without keeping any thing back. Yet, still, Blake hesitated.

"When he said that Inez was not his daughter, had he nothing to say to you?" she asked. "He must. He did. I see it in your face. You are keeping it back. Don't be afraid; I am going to tell you all, and there is nothing in this that should make you hesitate about telling me."

Upon this Blake hesitated no longer, but told her all the particulars of the last scene in which he and Inez took part—he being owned as a son, and Inez rejected as a daughter.

His mother listened attentively to it all, without any comment whatever. After he had ended, she said:

"I should have explained it all at once if I had only seen you, dear, but we have never had an opportunity since then. There was no reason for reticence on your part, and there is nothing in it that is to be dreaded either by you or by me. In the first place, then, Basil dear, I may say that Mr. Wyverne's dying declaration is true. You are his son, Basil Blake Wyverne, and I am Mrs. Hennigar Wyverne, your mother and his wife."

For the latter part of this declaration Blake was utterly unprepared. In his former speculations as to the probability of Mr. Wyverne's statement, he had never thought of his mother as having lived under an assumed name. He had only thought of her as Mrs. Blake, and from this point of view the question was one which he did not care to open up. Now, however, by this simple statement, his mother had cleared up the apparent mystery. Still, another wonder remained, and that was the very fact that she had stated. If she had been Mrs. Wyverne, why had she left her husband? Why had she lived in seclusion under an assumed name? why had she kept her secret so carefully, and brought him up in such total ignorance of his parentage? Together with these, many other questions occurred to his mind which only served to bewilder him.

But now all bewilderment was to end. His mother held the clew by which he could pass to the innermost centre of this tortuous labyrinth of plot, and counterplot, and mystery, and disguise.

"You must know all, Basil dear," said she. "I will therefore begin at the beginning and tell you the whole story."

Basil made no reply, but the eager look of his face showed how great was his desire to hear that story.

"My dear papa," said Mrs. Blake, "was a doctor in London. He was engaged in a large practice, but the style in which he found it necessary to live consumed all his income. When he died there was nothing left but a life-assurance policy of five thousand pounds, which was settled on me, and has been my support in late years. Some time before his death, however, I married Mr. Wyverne, and you were born, and we lived very happily until the death of Bernal Mordaunt, and the arrival of this Kevin Magrath upon the scene.

"Your papa and Bernal Mordaunt were relatives, first or second cousins, I am not sure which, and had always been bosom friends. This Kevin Magrath was some relative of Mr. Wyverne's, not very near, though, and Mr. Wyverne's father had helped him on in life very greatly. He sent him to college at Maynooth to study for the priesthood; but Magrath got into difficulties there, and had to leave. He afterward explained the affair in a way very satisfactorily to the elder Mr. Wyverne, who received him again into favor. This Mr. Wyverne was a solicitor—I mean your papa's father—and admitted Magrath into his office, with the intention of making him partner, I believe. His own son, my husband, had disliked law, and was engaged in the banking business. The elder Mr. Wyverne, however, died before Magrath had gained the full benefit of this connection, so that he had once more to look about in search of an occupation. Your papa now assisted him, and Magrath soon acquired an immense ascendency over him. He was apparently the soul of frankness and honor, and with this there was a vein of quiet humor about the man that was very much in his favor; but, after all, he was wily, selfish, unscrupulous, and, in short, all that you, my poor, dear boy have found him to be.

"I did not see very much of him until after the death of poor Bernal Mordaunt's wife. We used to see the Mordaunts—and the children were great pets of mine—Clara and Inez. Mrs. Mordaunt and I also were very tenderly attached, and I nursed her during her last illness. Poor Bernal was utterly prostrated by the blow, and for a time it was feared that he would either die or go mad. At length he went to the Continent, leaving the children under my care. The next we heard of him was that he was going to become a priest, and go to Asia or Africa. After about a year's absence, this news was confirmed by himself. He visited us to see his children for the last time, and to make arrangements for their future welfare.

"These arrangements were simple enough. He left the children with me, for they loved me like a mother, and appointed your papa their guardian. He then left, and in about a year we heard that he had died of the plague in Alexandria.

"Now was the time that my troubles commenced. Your papa began to drop mysterious hints about the children. He talked about sending Clara away to France, and then he wished to adopt Inez as his child, and call her Inez Wyverne. At first these proposals seemed merely foolish and unmeaning, and I laughed at them as preposterous. Gradually, however, he dwelt upon it so incessantly that I saw that he was in earnest about it; and I found that I should have to enter upon an actual course of opposition. I found the children threatened by my own husband, and myself placed in the painful position of defender of those poor orphans against the evil designs of a man who was bound, by every tie of duty, honor, and affection, to guard them.

"This discovery was soon followed by another. It was not your papa himself who had originated this. I hope and believe that he was incapable of it. Kevin Magrath was the real originator, and he had gradually insinuated it into your papa's mind until he had familiarized his thoughts with it. I have said already that Magrath had gained a strange ascendency over him. In this case he stood behind your papa like some tempter, some Mephistopheles, insidiously whispering his evil and cruel schemes into his ear.

"If it had been my husband only, dear Basil, I am certain I could have defended those poor lambs successfully; but, unfortunately, Kevin Magrath was always behind him, and whenever my remonstrances or my appeals to his better nature produced any little effect, it was sure to pass away in a short time through Magrath's evil ascendency. And so I found that my own influence was growing less and less, your papa was becoming alienated from me, and I was very miserable. I had no friends to whom I could go, and my only relatives were very distant ones whom I had never seen. About a year passed, and your papa finally grew impatient to carry out his measures, so one day he took Clara away, during my absence from the house. When I came home I found poor little Inez sobbing in a most heart-broken manner, and I learned the truth. Then all my indignation burst forth. Your papa and I quarrelled. I denounced him in the strongest language. I was wild with indignation, and the opinion that I had of the man Magrath made me certain that poor little Clara's life was in danger. Your papa stormed at me—declared that Clara was safe—that she had gone to a convent-school in Paris, and would receive a good education. I threatened to inform against him, but he sneeringly asked what charge I could bring. At this I was silenced; for in the first place, as a wife, I could hardly bring my husband into the public gaze as a criminal; and, again, the charge which I had to make could not be sustained.

"I still tried to protect the remaining child from their machinations. Your papa was bent on carrying out his design of changing her name. What that design really aimed at I did not then know, but I fully believed that the intention was to deal dishonestly and foully by both Inez and Clara. Under these circumstances your papa and I grew more and more estranged, more and more hostile, until at last his dislike or even hatred toward me became evident to all. He wished to get rid of me on any terms—he wished to put Inez under other influences, so as to bring her up, no doubt, in ignorance of her real name and real rights, and I stood in the way. It became more and more an object with him to get rid of me. At length, one day, Inez was taken, and sent away I knew not where. Upon this I grew quite wild in my despair—once more there was a furious scene, in which I threatened to denounce him in the face of the world. Once again he laughed at my threats, and told me that, on removing the children from my care, he had only sought their own good, because I was not a fit person to take care of them—that he could produce them at any moment, if they were needed, and silence easily any silly clamor that I might raise. In fact, once more I perceived that I was powerless.

"But your papa had designs, and my presence, together with my suspicions, was very unwelcome. He became eager to get rid of me, no matter how. At length he himself proposed this. He said that, if I would go, he would allow me to take you; but, if I refused, he would find a way to make me. I then dreaded that he might deprive me of you also, and this last fear was too much. Besides, living there under the baleful influence of Kevin Magrath was intolerable, and so, at length, I accepted this offer.

"That is the reason why I separated from your papa, Basil dear. It was not my act—it was his. Fortunately, I was quite independent of him. He had stipulated to give me an allowance, and I pretended to assent to this; but, the moment I had got safely away with you, I resolved to put myself out of his reach altogether. With this intention I changed my name, and went to live in a little village in Wales, near Conway—the place, in fact, which you knew as your home; and for years neither your papa nor Kevin Magrath had the faintest idea where I was, or whether we were alive or dead.

"The opinion which I formed then as to the plot of this Kevin Magrath—the plot which he induced your father to try to carry into accomplishment—I have never changed since; but, on the contrary, subsequent events have all tended to confirm that opinion only too painfully. I thought that he was trying no

less a thing than to get control of the great Mordaunt inheritance. I am not sure, but I think, that your papa was next of kin to Bernal Mordaunt, after his own children; and, consequently, if these children should by any means be put out of the way—if it could be made to appear that they were dead—why, then, your papa would gain the great Mordaunt inheritance, and possibly Kevin Magrath would himself obtain such a share of the prize as might be commensurate with his own services. Now, I saw Clara taken away to a foreign country, and never expected to see her again. This I considered the beginning of that policy which was to make the children as good as dead, so as to clear the way for the next of kin. When Inez followed, then I felt sure that she was the next victim.

"It appears, however, that Kevin Magrath did not intend to lay violent hands on them. His purpose, no doubt, was to get them out of the way, and either make up a plausible story of their death, accompanied, of course, by the necessary proofs, or else bring forward creatures of their own as substitutes. Who this Bessie Mordaunt can be, of whom you speak, I cannot imagine. There are no relatives named Mordaunt. Your papa was the next of kin, and it looks as if this Bessie may be some one used by these arch-plotters as a means of gaining the estate. I cannot imagine where your papa could have obtained her, but I take it for granted, of course, that she is some creature of Kevin Magrath's. He had a little family, I remember—a wife and daughter—but that is out of the question, of course.

"Well, I may as well go on with my story. After I had left your papa, I was not idle. I put you at a boarding-school, and spent three months in Paris searching after Clara Mordaunt. I succeeded in finding her at last. She was quite happy, and I did not like to distress her by telling her what was going on. I therefore did not speak to her at all about any of her family affairs, but was satisfied to find that she remembered me and loved me. She, of course, knew me by my true name. She called Mr. Wyverne her guardian, and had no suspicion of any evil on his part. She had never seen him since she left our house. She thought my visit was known to him. After this I kept watch over her. I could find out nothing about Inez, however, for some time. At length, to my horror, Clara disappeared

They told me at the school about a runaway-match, and I found out that it was only too true. She had married some adventurer, they said. I learned that his name was Ruthven. He belonged to a good family."

"Ruthven!" exclaimed Blake.

"Yes," said Mrs. Wyverne, not noticing the astonishment that was visible in the face of her son as he said this—"yes, a Mr. Ruthven, younger son of a great family, but a *roué* and a man of bad reputation. He had run away with her, they said, and, in short, it was the old, old story. For my part, Basil dear, at that time I had no doubt that this was the doing of Magrath; that this Ruthven was his emissary, and that this had been done to remove Clara Mordaunt out of his way. It is the peculiarity of this man's nature always to avoid crime himself, and to carry out his purposes by what I may call natural means; thus, instead of doing any act of violence himself against those who might be in his way, he chose rather to effect their removal in such a way as should prevent any guilt from attaching to him. He would not injure Clara directly, but he caused her to be utterly ruined by means of this emissary, who was only too successful in his purpose.

"Well, you may imagine my despair when I learned this, and when, after all my efforts, I could find no trace of her. I returned home, and wondered how all this would end, and chafed all the time against my own weakness and helplessness. For I could do nothing. I knew that, in the eyes of Heaven, crimes had been committed by these men, yet I could prove no crimes. Through the craft of Magrath they had kept themselves out of the reach of human law.

"In the midst of my unhappiness about Clara, I received a letter from her. I had told her once before where I lived, allowing her to suppose that Mr. Wyverne lived there too, trusting her with my secret, because I knew that she would not be in a position to divulge it, since she never saw your papa. So she wrote to me, addressing the letter to Mrs. Wyverne. I had to make up some plausible story to the post-woman, who kept the little shop where the post-office was, so as to get that letter, pretending to her that Wyverne was an assumed name, and making up a story to suit the occasion, and thus I was able to get it. It was a heart-rending letter. She spoke of poverty, danger, de-

spair, and death, and entreated me to hasten on and do something to save her. It was vaguely expressed, but I saw that she was in great danger. She signed herself Clara Ruthven, by which I saw that she was married, or at least supposed herself to be. I hastened on. I hurried to the house which she mentioned as her lodgings, and arrived there only to find her in a raging fever. The people of the house told me that she had only been there a few days; that she had come in a great state of excitement, and, after sending off a letter which they supposed was to me, she had been seized with illness, which had grown worse and worse. She was delirious for a long time, but eventually recovered. I remained with her and nursed her, as I had nursed her mother; but she, more fortunate, yet·perhaps, after all, less fortunate, was saved from her mother's fate, and was restored eventually to life and health.

"I found her grateful beyond all power of language to express—most touchingly so—yet there was over her a profound and invincible sadness, which bordered on despair. On the events which had occurred since her elopement she would not speak. She made no reference whatever to her letter. She preserved a most obstinate silence about all these things, and I know no more of them now than you do. Something terrible, however, had happened. Her husband — for I will call him this—had either died or had forsaken her. I do not know which; and, whichever it was that had taken place, the effect was to crush out in her young heart all joy and hope forever.

"I tried to induce her to return to England and live with me, but she refused. I then told her the truth about her life. She was actually ignorant that she was the heiress of Mordaunt Manor. She did not remember much about her youth. She had lived so long amid foreign scenes, that this remembrance had died out. Besides, she had not lived very constantly at Mordaunt Manor, but had lived in Italy for several years with her mother, who was an invalid. But, when I told her the truth, it had no effect whatever. I told her about her sister Inez, but she was indifferent. She would not leave Paris. There was some mournful attraction about the place which kept her there. She only longed to find some home there, where she might live in peace and seclusion. At length she conceived

14

a strong desire to become a Sister of Charity. She thought that such a life would give her the seclusion and peace which she longed for, and, at the same time, that she would have sufficient occupation to distract her thoughts and save her from despair.

"From that resolve I found it impossible to move her. Every thing that I mentioned was received with indifference, and at length I found it necessary to desist and to yield to her desires. She found a sisterhood at last, and entered upon her novitiate. Then I left her, and have never seen her since, though we have exchanged letters every year."

CHAPTER L.

A MOTHER'S PLOT.

BLAKE had listened thus far almost in silence, but these last revelations about Clara filled him with the strongest emotion. He had already heard from Kane the story of Clara's marriage, and the tragic termination of that married life; but his mother's story furnished an appendix, or rather a sequel, to that story scarcely less tragic than that which Kane had told of. Yet Kane's perfect belief in her death, his vigils over her grave, in Père-la-Chaise, were so well known to Blake that they had inspired him with the same belief, and now he could hardly credit his mother's revelations.

"Do you really mean to say," he exclaimed at last, as she paused in her narrative, "that Clara Mordaunt, after all, is not dead?"

"She certainly is not dead," said his mother, placidly. "Have I not been telling all about her life?"

"She is alive now—really and truly?"

"Really and truly. But it seems to me that you show a very strange kind of feeling about it. How agitated you are, Basil dear!"

"Alive!" repeated Blake, musingly; "alive—and a Sister of Charity? That is—a nun—a nun in black—"

"What is all that?" asked his mother. "What are you saying about nuns, and things?"

"Oh, nothing," said Blake; "only, its confoundedly strange. But I'll tell you all about it."

Upon this Blake proceeded to tell her about Kane, and Kane's account of his marriage, and Kane's fancy about apparitions. To all of this his mother listened in evident surprise, and with much emotion.

"Wonders will never cease," she exclaimed. "Who could have imagined this? So your friend Kane Hellmuth must be Kane Ruthven—and so he is not an emissary of Magrath's, but an honest man."

"An honest man!" cried Blake. "I tell you, mother dear, he is one of the noblest fellows that I ever saw. There was no humbug there, I can tell you. No man ever loved a woman better than he did Clara Mordaunt. Why, only think of him now, with his blighted life, and his misery and remorse!"

"So—that was it," continued Mrs. Wyverne; "and that accounts for poor Clara's despair. She escaped death, and he died—or she thought he did. But how strange, in such a solemn and really awful attempt at suicide, that both should escape, and each go into despair about the other."

"Why, they must have met over and over. These meetings have seemed to Kane to be apparitions. I wonder if they have seemed so to her? Oh, why didn't she speak? Why didn't she explain, instead of giving him silent, despairing looks?"

Mrs. Wyverne sighed.

"I can understand," said she. "It's all over with them—she is dead to him."

"Dead to him?"

"Yes; she is a Sister of Charity. She has taken the vows, and so she is dead to poor Kane—and that, no doubt, is the reason why she has looked at him so—in dumb despair. I can understand it all. She thought him dead. His absence for years confirmed that belief. These meetings must have affected her as they affected him. She is, at least, as superstitious as he is. But, in any case, it is just as well, since they never can belong to one another again."

At this sad thought Blake was silent. His first feeling had been one of joy. He thought of flying at once to tell Kane the news, but now he saw that such news as this had better not be told to his friend.

"But I must go on," continued Mrs. Wyverne, "and tell you something about my share in these later events of your life, Basil dear. Well, then, for years I had no communication with your father, and preserved my *incognito* and my seclusion most carefully. I heard, however, from time to time, that he was alive, though he never could have heard any thing about me. At length you had finished your education, and you got that situation in Paris, and it seemed to me that you ought to know something about your past, yet I did not know exactly how to tell you, for it seemed to me to be a terrible thing to tell a son about a father's guilt. Then, again, I thought that, if your father could only see you, he might feel some emotion of affection; and possibly, if he were brought into connection with you in any way, you might gain an influence over his better nature, by means of which the fatal ascendency of Magrath might be destroyed.

"With these hopes I made a journey to London very secretly, and succeeded in finding out all about your papa's circumstances. I learned that he was in very feeble health. I learned that he had a family consisting of two young ladies, one of whom was named Inez Wyverne, and the other, Bessie Mordaunt. Who Bessie Mordaunt was I did not know, nor do I now know; but, as to Inez Wyverne, there could be no doubt. I saw at once that he had carried his old plan—or rather Magrath's old plan—into execution, and that my poor darling Inez had been brought up in the belief that her name was Wyverne, and that she was his daughter. Yet even this discovery of his unfaltering pursuit of his purpose did not destroy the hope which I had formed of working on him through you.

"Circumstances favored my wish. I learned that he was going to the Continent for his health, and that St. Malo was his destination. And now, Basil dear, you understand why I wrote you so earnestly about your health; why I insisted so strongly upon your having some recreation; why, above all, I almost ordered you to go to St. Malo. You must have wondered at what you considered a woman's whim; but it was not that, Basil dear; it was something far deeper. And I insisted on your going there solely because I hoped that you might meet with your own father. But I did not trust to accident. I made sure of a meeting between you. I wrote him a letter, and reminded him of all the past; of that better past, the past of innocence, of love, and of domestic joy. I reminded him of the child whom he once loved

before his soul had become darkened and his heart hardened through the wiles of the Tempter. I told him that his son—our son —the associate of his better past, and of the days of his innocence, was now a man—an honorable gentleman; and that this son would be at St. Malo's, ready there to become his better angel, and lead him back to virtue and peace. I told him how you had been brought up, Basil dear; how ignorant you were of all his faults; how ignorant you were of the fact that he had any connection with the name of Wyverne. I told him that I had heard of his proposed journey to St. Malo's, and had made you promise to go there, with the hope that the guilty father might meet with the innocent son, and might be moved to repentance through a father's love.

"And, O Basil dear, how can I tell you the feelings that I had as I received your letters—those letters which showed me that he had yet lingering in his heart the feelings of a father? He had not forgotten the child whom he once loved. Avarice had hardened his heart, but sickness and weakness had softened it again, and the sight of you awakened a deep yearning within him. Now you know all. Now you understand why it was that the poor invalid clung to you, why he yielded to you, why he threw at you those looks of deep affection, why he loved to see you with the injured Inez. He had repented. He was longing to make amends. He could not tell you all that was in his heart to say. He could not reveal to you the truth about his past life, for fear that you would scorn him. He had my address, and wrote me one or two letters, full of repentance for his past. He implored my forgiveness. He promised to make amends. He spoke of his deep love for you. He entreated me to find some way of making known these things to you without exciting your detestation. He wished me to come on at once, and join him, and tell all to you in such a way that you might own him for your father. He spoke of your regard for Inez, and expressed the hope that a union between you two might be brought about; for somehow he seemed to consider this the best sort of atonement that he could make.

"I was overcome. I was not very well just then, and could not travel. Besides, I thought it best to wait, leaving you two to know one another better. The profound reverence which you expressed for him touched me, and I wished this reverence to deepen into affection; and then I thought I would join you, and my work of reconciliation would be made easier. Oh, if I had but gone on then! How much suffering would have been prevented for all of us! But I acted for the best.

"Well, dear Basil, you know the rest. You went away to Switzerland, and there your poor papa died. That letter which you spoke of struck him down. I don't know what was in it, but it was undoubtedly some communication from Kevin Magrath—some threat—some terror. At any rate, he sunk down to death, and strove vainly, at the last, to make some feeble amends by expressions of remorse, by a declaration of the truth. O Basil! that father's heart yearned over you then, as Death stood near; and I believe—I know—that his repentance was sincere. Pray, Basil dear—pray for your father; pray for the repose of the soul of the repentant Hennigar Wyverne!"

Mrs. Wyverne stopped, overcome by deep emotion. Blake also felt himself profoundly moved. His mother's story brought up vividly before him the form of that venerable invalid who had manifested such a strong regard for him—the form of that dying man who, at the last hour of life, had claimed him as a son. It had been all a mystery, but now all was revealed. What he had considered a strange coincidence was now shown to be no coincidence at all, but the result of his mother's management, and of her desire to bring father and son together.

There was nothing which he could say on such a subject. It was a painful one from any point of view. His father's past could not be discussed, as it was a past filled with wrong-doing too late repented of. His father's death-bed was too sad a theme for conversation.

But there were other thoughts which had been suggested by these revelations, and prominent among them was his mother's conviction that O'Rourke was no other than Kevin Magrath. O'Rourke, he well knew, must have some motive. Down in the gloom of the Catacombs, at that first appalling moment of desertion, he had fancied for a time that his betrayer must be a madman; but after he had heard those words stealing through the piled-up stones to his ears, "*Blake Wyverne, farewell forever!*" he saw

that this treachery must have been premeditated, and that it must have arisen out of his relation to Hennigar Wyverne. Now, when that relation was assured, it became a more certain cause than ever for O'Rourke's treachery. Yet why it should be a cause, and what benefit O'Rourke could hope to gain, remained as much a mystery as ever.

"It may be true, mother dear," said he, "that O'Rourke is only your Kevin Magrath under an assumed name. I don't deny it, since you are so sure about it; but I confess it is a puzzle to me why O'Rourke, or Magrath, or whoever he is, should take the trouble to elaborate so intricate a plot against such an insignificant personage as I am. What am I, that he should labor so secretly, so persistently, and for so long a time, to compass my destruction? What benefit could he get by it? I must say, it seems to me, in the hackneyed French phrase, "the play isn't worth the candle."

Mrs. Wyverne looked gravely up.

"You speak now," said she, "as Basil Blake, not as Basil Wyverne. You forget that, though Basil Blake is insignificant, Basil Wyverne is very much the contrary. He is the son and heir of Hennigar Wyverne, a well-known London banker of great wealth. What he had of his own was immense; what he has appropriated from the Mordaunt property I cannot tell; but certain it is that you, his son, are the heir of a vast fortune. This of itself would be a prize sufficient to induce Kevin Magrath to get you removed. Supposing that you were removed, I do not see exactly how he could enter upon the possession of the estate of your papa, but I have no doubt that he would manage to do it. At any rate, you may be sure that this was his motive. He went to the Catacombs with you, as he said, for a great treasure—not, however, for his pretended treasure of the Cæsars, but for the sake of the more commonplace treasure of the Wyvernes. Such a treasure was worthy, in his estimation, of such a deed. And you see, Basil dear, his hand. You see how cautiously, how elaborately, he has worked. He has tried to remove you from the world, so that you should leave no trace whatever. If you had not escaped, there would not have been even the faintest indication which might have disclosed your fate. You would have vanished from the scene utterly. Your incoherent letter to me told nothing at all, and I imagine the letter that you wrote to your friend Kane must have been equally unintelligible. When I received your letter, I had just recovered from a severe illness, and the fears which it created almost sent me back again."

"Illness, mother dear?" said Blake, anxiously. "You never mentioned that before."

"Illness? O my boy!" said Mrs. Wyverne. "It is not worth speaking of, since it is past; but, while it lasted, I was as near to death as you were in the Catacombs. It was the news of the death of your poor papa that struck me down. It came so sudden, and at the very time, too, when I was indulging in such bright hopes. I was preparing to join you, and to perform the part of general reconciler. I hoped to be joined at last to the husband of my youth, with whom I had lived in the happiest part of my life. O Basil! dear boy, you do not know, you cannot imagine how strongly I had set my heart on this reunion, on this reconciliation. But suddenly the news came, and all these hopes were dashed to the ground. The blow was a terrible one, and for a time all hope died out, and all desire for life. I was utterly prostrated, and remained so for weeks. During all that time I heard nothing from you, and a great anxiety came over me. This made it worse. Your incoherent and unintelligible letter gave me nothing but uneasiness, and, as nothing followed it, I sank into despair. At length I recovered my bodily strength, and was able to move about; but still, dear boy, I could never find any respite whatever from the dreadful suspense and anxiety in which I was about you. At last your letter came, telling me that you had been ill, and wanted me. Such a letter at ordinary times would have been sad indeed, but to me, under those circumstances, it was like a resurrection from despair. I found new life and strength, and hurried on to you at once. But, apart from my own misfortunes, what you told me about yours, Basil dear, makes me feel certain that your Dr. O'Rourke is no other than Kevin Magrath. He's no more a doctor than I am. He played the part of one merely for the purpose of making your acquaintance. He is no more a doctor than he is a priest."

"It was as a priest that Kane saw him," said Blake, who then went on to tell about Kane's journey to London.

"Yes, yes, oh, yes," said Mrs. Wyverne, as he ended. "Every thing that you tell me only shows more and more plainly the unmistakable marks of Kevin Magrath. Now, not one word of all that he told Kane was true. Inez was not the daughter of Hennigar Wyverne, and he knew it. Hennigar Wyverne did not die poor, for he left an immense property, which perhaps Magrath is now trying to gain for himself. Above all, Clara is not dead, and he could not have known any thing about her."

"But, mother dear, if this terrible Kevin Magrath is so anxious to get the Wyverne property, what will he do about you?"

"About me? Well, I don't know. I have taken care to keep out of his reach. He is not the man to overlook me, however insignificant I may be. No doubt he has his designs with regard to me. I dare say he has formed some plan, if he can find me, to work upon my love for you, to invent some story about your going to America, and entice me away, where I shall never trouble him again. That is his mode of action. If you, dear, had not written to me, he might have done this, for I would have gone to the north-pole after you, even on the strength of a forged letter or a trumped-up story; but now, Basil boy, since I have you, there is no need for us to conjecture any thing as to what Kevin Magrath might have done."

"Did you stop in London on your way here?" asked Blake, after a moment's pause.

"Stop in London, dear Basil? Of course not."

"You did not hear any thing, then, about Inez?"

"Oh, no. I was too anxious about you, dear."

Blake sighed.

"I did not know," said he, "but that you might have heard something about them."

"No, Basil dear, not a word. You see, I came on at once, almost from a bed of illness, to you, for your sake, dear boy."

Basil was silent. He was longing to hear something about Inez.

"I shall be able to travel, dear mother," said he, after a time, "in a day or two, and Rome is horrible to me, after what has happened. I should like to go to England at once—to London—but I suppose on our way we ought to stop at Paris. I want to see Kane, to tell him what you have told me; or, at any rate, to see him, whether I tell him that or not."

"Yes," said Mrs. Wyverne, "that is no more than right. I also wish to go to Paris, for I should like very much to see poor, dear Clara."

"I do not know whether I ought to tell Kane about her or not," said Blake, doubtfully.

"Well, I'm sure I don't," said his mother; "and it seems to me that you'll have to be guided by circumstances. At any rate, I shall see her, and I think it probable that I shall tell her all that I've heard from you about poor Kane. For, dear Basil, I have come to pity that poor man, with his undeserved remorse, and his ruined life; and my sympathy with you makes me look upon him with something of your feelings, Basil dear."

"Kane is the noblest man I have ever met with," said Blake.

"Poor fellow!" sighed Mrs. Wyverne. "And only think that, while poor Clara is, after all, really alive, she is the same as dead to him."

"Well," said Blake, "the more I think of it, the more I feel that Kane ought to know it. At the worst, it cannot be so bad as his present belief. He thinks now that he is little better than a murderer; if he were to know that she did not die, he might have more peace of mind, even though she could never be his."

"I am quite of your opinion, Basil dear, quite," said Mrs. Wyverne.

They now went on to talk of many things, and more particularly about this *Bessie Mordaunt*, whose exact position amid all these affairs Mrs. Wyverne was anxious to ascertain. She therefore made very particular inquiries about her personal appearance, manner, tone, accent, etc., and gradually a light began to dawn on her mind.

CHAPTER LI.

A DISCOVERY.

BLAKE had reasons of his own for keeping his escape a secret. He therefore did not go out of the house, even though he needed exercise, but quietly waited till he was strong enough to travel. He did not know but that O'Rourke, or rather Kevin Magrath, as he now

believed him to be, might still be in the city; nor did he know but that he might have emissaries abroad. For many reasons he did not wish Magrath to know that he was alive; and accordingly he determined to travel in disguise, so as to guard against the possibility of discovery. This disguise was very easily procured—a false beard, spectacles, and a priest's dress, being sufficient to make him unrecognizable by his own mother. In a few days they set out, and reached Paris without any further incident.

Blake remained in his room that day. Mrs. Wyverne rested a few hours, and then, in the afternoon, went out with the intention of finding Clara. Toward evening Blake left the hotel, and went to visit Kane Ruthven.

Kane was alone. In answer to the knock at the door he roared, "Come in!" The door opened, and a man entered in a priest's dress, for Blake's caution would not allow him as yet to drop his disguise. Kane rose, and looked inquiringly at his visitor, but without the slightest sign of recognition. Upon this Blake removed his beard and spectacles, and revealed to Kane the pale face of his friend, upon which were still visible the marks of the sufferings through which he had passed.

"Good Lord!" cried Kane Ruthven, springing forward and grasping Blake's hands in both of his. "Blake, old fellow, is it really you? Why, how pale you are!"

He stopped abruptly, and looked anxiously at Blake, still holding his hands.

"I've had a hard time of it, old fellow," said Blake; "been sick, and am hardly well yet."

"Ah, that accounts for your strange silence. Why, I've been at my wit's ends about you. You decamped suddenly, leaving a crazy, unintelligible letter, and vanished into midnight darkness. Sick, ah! So that's it—but where?"

"You've just said it," said Blake, solemnly. "I vanished into midnight darkness."

"I don't understand you."

"Well, perhaps I'd better tell you all about myself, for I want to get your assistance, old boy. You're the very man I need now, and you're the only man."

"You may rely upon me to no end of an extent, my boy," said Kane, earnestly. "But come, sit down now. We've given queer confidences to one another in this room, and

It looks as though this would be the queerest. But you'll take something, won't you?"

"Thanks—no."

"What—not even ale?"

"Well, perhaps a glass of ale wouldn't be unwelcome," said Blake, taking his seat on the sofa. Kane at once poured out the draught, and Blake slowly drank it. Thereupon Kane offered a pipe, which, however, Blake refused.

Kane now sat down, and Blake told him the whole story. He listened in a state of mind which was made up of astonishment and horror, and said not a single word.

After this, Blake proceeded to give him the outlines of his mother's story, without hinting, however, at the fact of Clara's flight and subsequent life. This he did not feel prepared as yet to divulge. He merely wished Kane to understand what he had learned about his own birth, and about that of Inez; to explain the character of Kevin Magrath, and try identifying him with O'Rourke, to disclose the motive which had animated his betrayer.

The effect of all this upon Kane was tremendous. The last phase which his opinion about Magrath had undergone was one of reverence. He had sought him out as a culprit; he had pleaded his own cause before him as before a judge; he had humbly and most gratefully listened to his acquittal, and had received the grasp of his hand as a symbol of the forgiveness of some superior being. Now, in the light of Blake's story, Kevin Magrath stood at last revealed in his own true character—a villain, cold-blooded, remorseless, terrible!

But with this discovery there came a throng of thoughts so painful that he hardly dared to entertain them. At once he thought of Inez—of Bessie—now in the power of this man, who could take them where he wished, since they had been formally intrusted to him by their best friends — by Kane and Gwyn—the husband, the brother; thus handing them both over unsuspectingly into his keeping. The terror of this thought was too much.

Blake saw the horror of Kane's soul, and understood at once that his story had served to arouse within his friend feelings and troubles that were connected with himself, and that some new grief had arisen before Kane out of the light of this revelation. What it

was he could not conjecture. He thought at first that Kane's troubles perhaps referred to Clara; and then he thought that they might be connected with Inez. For already Blake's speculation upon Magrath's course had made him think that his next victim might be Inez. And now the sight of Kane's agitation made him feel so sure at last that Inez was really involved, that he was afraid to ask, for fear that he might learn the truth that he dreaded to hear.

There was now a long silence. Each had much to say, but did not know how to say it. In the mind of each there was that which he dreaded to make known to the other. Kane was the first to break the silence.

"Settled in Rome! for good—for good!" he repeated, recalling the statement of Magrath—"settled in Rome for good!"

"What do you mean by that?" asked Blake, in surprise.

"It was what I heard about you."

"About me?" cried Blake. "Who said it?"

"What horrible irony! What cold-blooded, remorseless humor—for he had a sense of humor—the humor of a demon; and I can imagine him enjoying this, all by himself—'settled down—yes, down—in Rome—and for good!'"

"There's only one man that could have said that of me. What do you mean? Have you seen him?"

Blake trembled from head to foot. The danger was growing greater, and drawing nearer to Inez.

"Only one man—yes," said Kane. "Of course; you are right. Your O'Rourke must be Kevin Magrath, and he was the man that said that of you."

Blake started to his feet.

"Have you seen him?"

"Yes," said Kane, solemnly.

"You know something, that you're holding back," said Blake, in feverish excitement. "Magrath has been doing something more, which you know of; and now, since I have told you his true character, you are horrified. There is danger abroad, to which friends of mine are exposed—are they friends of mine, too?"

Before Kane could answer, there was a knock at the door. Blake looked impatiently around. It was Gwyn. Kane introduced them to one another, and explained Gwyn's position as the husband of the young lady whom he had known as Bessie Mordaunt.

"Before I answer your last question, Blake," said Kane, "let me explain all this horrible business to my brother here, for I assure you he is as deeply concerned in what you ask about as you yourself are—perhaps more so."

At this Blake regarded Gwyn with sad curiosity. Kane's words meant that he was implicated, probably as Bessie's husband, and that if there was danger to Inez, Bessie was also involved. He was now content to explain all to Gwyn, so as to have his coöperation in any duty that might now arise before them, and also to get the benefit of any advice which one so deeply interested might be able to give.

Gwyn had never experienced any of those alternations of opinion about Kevin Magrath which had been felt by Kane; indeed, he had not thought much about him, inasmuch as he had only known him for the last few days. During that time he had thought of him as rather an eccentric, but still a good man, and had only objected to him on the ground that he formed one of those who were taking Bessie from him. But now, as he learned the truth about this man, and reflected that he had allowed Bessie to go with him—thinking also that Bessie, as one of the Mordaunts, might be implicated in the fate of those whom he yet believed to be her sisters—a great fear arose in his heart, and he sat looking at the others in mute horror.

"He—he—could not harm her—he—loves her—she always called him her dear grandpa, you know," faltered Gwyn, at last.

"Is your wife with him?" asked Blake, rightly interpreting the meaning of those words.

"Yes," said Kane, "and Inez, too."

At this, Blake said not a word. He had dreaded it; he had expected it; but was none the less overwhelmed when he actually heard it.

"It's a mixed-up story, and the devil himself couldn't have worked with more patient, cold-blooded craft," said Kane. "I didn't like to tell you, and I don't like to now, but Inez has had a hard time of it."

"Go on," said Blake, in a whisper.

Upon this, Kane told Blake the whole story of Inez—her imprisonment, her escape, his meeting with her, his journey to Ruthven,

and Bessie's departure to meet her friend, followed by himself and Gwyn. Some of this was news to Gwyn, for he had not known before the name of the man who had entrapped Inez. It only added to his terrors about Bessie. To Blake this was all too fearfully intelligible. The long, deep, patient plot was characteristic of Kevin Magrath. He chose to lead his victims to destruction, as his mother had said, by a purely natural process, by their own act and consent, so that he should be himself free from danger. What more? Had Inez and Bessie now gone with him voluntarily to destruction? He trembled to hear.

The rest was soon told. The story of Clara's grave in Rome, of the removal of her remains—all was horrible. He knew well how false it was. He could not tell Kane even then the truth about Clara, so as to show Kane and Gwyn its complete untruth. He could scarcely use his faculties, and it seemed as though his strength of mind and body, which had been so severely tried of late, was about to give way utterly under this new blow.

"They're lost!" he cried at last. "There's no such grave—in all—Rome."

Kane looked at him as though he would read his soul.

"Her father," said he, in a voice which was tremulous with agitation at a frightful suspicion which came to him—"her father—had her—her remains buried—by the side of her mother—in the Catacombs."

"The Catacombs!" groaned Blake. "O God! The Catacombs! O Heavens! don't you know what that means?"

At this both Kane and Gwyn shuddered.

"Stop!" said Kane, in a hoarse voice, "don't be too fast—you don't know—she was taken away from Père-la Chaise."

"She was not," cried Blake, who could not say any more.

"What do you mean?" asked Kane.

"Go and ask the keeper—go to the cemetery now—ask him if any such removal has taken place," gasped Blake.

"By Heavens, I will!" cried Kane. "He had *persuaded me.* I too was going to the Catacombs, to pray at her grave. I will go this very instant and see—" He hurried out of the room, and banged the door after him, in the middle of his sentence.

Blake and Gwyn sat there in silence, overwhelmed by the anguish of the new fear that had arisen in their minds. Of the two, Blake was in the deeper despair, for he knew all. Gwyn's knowledge was imperfect, and he could not help consoling himself by the belief which he had in Magrath's affection for Bessie. She had always spoken of him in fondest language. She rested in his affection now with the undoubting confidence of a child. Inez showed nothing of such a sentiment. Bessie seemed to appropriate Magrath as her own—as if he was her father. Moreover, once before, when he had been able to injure Bessie, he had spared her, and it was for Inez alone that he had spread his snares. Out of all this he could not help reaching the conclusion that Bessie was perfectly safe, and Inez alone in peril.

That Inez was in peril he had no doubt. What then? What part was Bessie destined to play? Was her presence any protection to Inez? If so, why should Magrath allow her to go? Perhaps Magrath was making use of Bessie to work out his will on Inez the more surely. Perhaps he was using Bessie as a decoy. Perhaps—the thoughts that came to him now were such as filled him with horror. Once more the terrible recollection came of Ruthven Towers, of Bessie with her frightful suggestions, of that appalling moment when she stood before him on the top of the cliff and seemed a beautiful demon—the Tempter in the form of an angel —in the form of one whom he loved dearer than life. The remembrance was anguish; and once more there went on within him a struggle of soul something like that which had torn him as he fought down the temptation. But the evil thought once indulged could not easily be dismissed, nor could the one of whom he had once formed suspicions become ever again altogether free from their recurrence. The thought which had once made him strike her senseless was not to be destroyed, nor could Bessie ever be immaculate again. Circumstances suggested themselves to his mind, and tormented him by the horrible coloring which they gave to her actions: her flight from Ruthven Towers; her bringing Inez once more into Magrath's power; her refusal to return to her husband; her departure with Inez and Magrath, and to Rome, and to the Catacombs; her last words reminding him that he must bring Kane too. Was it only to draw Kane to Rome that she wished him to come? Was she trying to make a decoy of *him?* and, since she had failed in

her first temptation, had she resorted to one which was more insidious? And why? Destroy Kane, and Ruthven Towers would be his; destroy Inez, and Mordaunt Manor would be hers!—A groan burst from him in his agony; he started to his feet, and paced the room unconscious of the presence of Blake.

But Blake himself had too much to think of to give any attention to his companion. Kane had gone, and he knew what news he would bring back. What then? He must act. How? When? How long was it since they had started for Rome? Could he overtake them?

Clara's grave! The Catacombs! Abhorrent, appalling thought! The Catacombs! And Kevin Magrath was now leading Inez to that place of horror—the place to which he had been led. And Inez was going of her own free will, as he had gone; drawn there as he had been drawn, by an overpowering motive. Avarice had drawn him; Love was drawing her. He had gone to find the treasure of the Cæsars; she was going to pray at a sister's grave. What damnable art was it that enabled this man to destroy the just suspicions of others?—and, after all that he had done to Inez, to win her confidence, and even that of a world-worn man like Kane? Was he, too, intending to go down into the Catacombs with Kevin Magrath? Would not he, too, wish *to pray at Clara's grave?* And Gwyn Ruthven! Was he, too, doomed? What part had his wife in all this? Why did she leave her young husband who loved her? What had she to do with the Mordaunts? What connection was there between her and Magrath? His mother knew that she was not a Mordaunt, or at least not of the family of Bernal Mordaunt. Was she true, and deceived; or a deceiver, false like Magrath? Or was she a decoy used by Magrath, though innocent herself?

Blake's thoughts about Bessie were bitter; and present circumstances, combined with what he had heard from Gwyn and Kane about her, had already created suspicions in his mind which he had not cared or dared to express. In his own thoughts he doubted her; he feared the worst about her. Thus, in this present terrible moment, it was Bessie's hard fortune to be the subject of the gravest and darkest suspicion, not only in the mind of Blake, but even in that of her husband.

At length, after a long absence, Kane roturned. His face wore a very strange expression.

"Well?" cried Blake.

"It is gone," said Kane, slowly.

"What!"

"It is true. Her — remains — were exhumed—and taken away. I saw the keeper, who showed me the books of record—and I —visited the grave."

He flung himself into a chair by the table and buried his head in his hands.

Blake was bewildered, but a moment's reflection explained all.

"It is part of that villain's consummate and most painstaking style of action. He always works in what he would call a scientific or artistic manner. Yes, he has certainly exhumed—something—and—"

Kane started up and stared.

"This is the second time," he said, with deep agitation, "that you have spoken about —about her — in that tone. In Heaven's name, Blake, what is it? What am I to understand?"

"Tone?" said Blake, confusedly. "I was not conscious of speaking in any particular tone."

With a disappointed look, Kane sat down again.

"We must act, or I must, and at once," cried Blake. "Tell me—have I time?"

Gwyn and Kane looked at one another.

"I tell you his removal of—of that—is only to make his work more thorough. He will have something to show them."

Kane looked up.

"*That* is what I mean by your tone. I can't understand you, but I see how agitated you are. I'll talk about it to-morrow. But if you are going to do any thing, Gwyn and I will help you. Magrath left for Rome yesterday morning only, with Inez and Bessie. Gwyn wanted me to leave with him to-morrow, but I was going to remain a week or two. Still, as things are now, we ought all of us to leave by the very next train."

"Will you go?—that's right," said Blake. "Yesterday morning!—and Magrath is prompt in his acts always; but this time he may be more leisurely about it, he may not suspect pursuit. He knows nothing of my escape. No—no—I think he will go about this work .cisurely, and assist those of you who wish to —descend into the Catacombs—and *pray at Clara's tomb.*—When does the next train go,

to-night? Can't we start at once? I will go now. I'll only stop a minute to write a few lines to my mother."

"Wait, Blake, boy," said Kane, as Blake, after these incoherent words, arose and walked to the door. "There's no train till morning. We had better all leave at the same time. You can write your letter here, or you'll have time to go and see your mother yourself.""

"No; I won't go and see her," said Blake. "She would make objections, and all that, or insist on coming with me. No. I'll write her, and if you can find some one to take it to her address, I'll be obliged."

Kane now offered Blake some writing-materials, and he wrote very hurriedly the following letter:

"DEAR MOTHER: I have heard the very worst. Inez has fallen into the hands of Kevin Magrath, who has taken her to Rome. You know what that means. I am going back there by the first train to-morrow morning, in the faint hope of being able to save her. If you have any news about Clara, you had better come on also. Kane Ruthven and his brother Gwyn are going to accompany me. I have said nothing to Kane about Clara.

"If you come to Rome you will find me, or hear of me at the old lodgings.

"Your affectionate son,

"BASIL."

———

CHAPTER LII.

CLARA MORDAUNT.

MRS. WYVERNE had gone out for the purpose of finding Clara, and went at once to the place which had been her last address. It was an ordinary house, which was occupied by some Sisters of Charity, among whom Clara had cast in her lot. She hoped to find her here yet; and, on asking for her, she found, to her great relief, that she was within.

Mrs. Wyverne's story to Blake has already shown that Clara was not dead, as Kane had supposed. To Kane the thought of her being actually alive was not admissible. The memory of that one great tragedy obscured all else, and he was incapable of seriously considering that theory which Blake had suggested, namely, that Clara had escaped as he himself had. But, to Mrs. Wyverne, the living Clara was the most familiar thought in the world; and, what to Kane was supernatural, to her was in the highest degree natural.

She was at once admitted, and in a few moments Clara herself made her appearance, and with a cry of joy caught her in her arms, and kissed her again and again, uttering at the same time many exclamations of affection, of gratitude, and of delight. Mrs. Wyverne herself was moved by such emotion on the part of Clara, and was rejoiced to perceive these signs of a warm human sympathy and a tender loving nature in one who might have been expected to have grown indifferent to worldly ties.

Clara took her to her own chamber, informing her that in this house they were less strict in their regulations than in other places, and that various privileges were allowed of intimate association with friends or relatives. It was a plainly-furnished room, with a single window looking out upon the street. Here they were alone together, and could say what they wished without interruption.

Clara was dressed as a Sister of Charity, and the simple costume served in her case to give an additional charm to her graceful figure, and to the beautiful and still youthful face. She had an extraordinary resemblance to Inez, having generally the same features and the same family peculiarity. But, with Clara, there was a deeper melancholy visible; in her eyes and in her face there wore the manifest traces of long and severe suffering. Inez, after her escape from prison, and while just arising from a bed of sickness, thin and pale from suffering, had seemed to him the counterpart of his lost Clara; but the real Clara had in her face a sadness such as Inez had never shown, for her sufferings had been deeper, and more intense, and more prolonged.

At first the conversation was taken up with anxious inquiries about one another's health, and questions about what each had been doing since their last meeting. Clara professed to have lived her usual life, but Mrs. Wyverne was more frank; and, beginning with the recital of her own troubles, she at length went on by degrees to unfold all that series of events which had been going on, and with which Clara herself was so intimately connected. Mrs. Wyverne did this cautiously and gradually, and now for the first time Clara learned the full measure of her own rights, the extent of her wrongs, the sufferings of those near relatives of hers whom she had not seen since childhood, but whose names and fortunes now awakened an intense interest; and,-finally, the machinations of Magrath, which had first been directed against herself, and of late had turned against her sister Inez. All this awakened deep emotion within her, but this was surpassed by the feelings that were aroused when Mrs. Wyverne brought forward the mention of Kane Ruthven. Kane Ruthven was the intimate friend of Mrs. Wyverne's son. That son, just escaping from unparalleled dangers, was even now about to visit Kane Ruthven. This Kane Ruthven, also, her husband, had been subject to remorse for years on her account, and was still mourning over her as dead. All this came out, and Clara listened with intense emotion, pouring forth a torrent of eager questions, and, forgetting every thing else, evinced an insatiable longing to know every thing that Mrs. Wyverne could tell about him.

On former interviews Clara had been merely a despairing mourner, weary of the world, seeking solace only in the life which she had adopted, reticent about her past, shunning every allusion to it. Now, the revelations which Mrs. Wyverne brought her broke down all her reticence, and poured over her soul a flood of memories which overwhelmed her. It was not the fact that Kane Ruthven was alive, not the fact that he was living in Paris that impressed her, but rather the fact that he was suffering, and for her; that he was bearing this load of remorse, and enduring these stings of conscience, on her account; the fact that he so clung to his memories of her, that he was, even now, living a life which was arranged with reference to her, and that he was associating her in all his thoughts with the angels of heaven.

All her reserve broke down, and she was now eager to tell Mrs. Wyverne her own story, eager to ask Mrs. Wyverne's advice about what she ought to do. The story which she had to tell referred to that event already narrated to Blake by Kane, but, as it regarded it from her point of view, it may be repeated here.

She began by describing her earliest recollections, which were vague reminiscences of splendid homes in England and in Italy.

Then came the death of her mother and the loss of her father; then a home among strangers, ending with her departure to Paris, and her entrance into a boarding-school. Here she was allowed unusual liberties, became acquainted with various people, and at length fell in with Kane Ruthven, and consented to marry him.

"But oh! dear Mrs. Wyverne," she continued, "you may imagine what a child I was, what a poor little child, when I tell you that, in packing up my small valise to fly, I actually put in a doll—I was passionately fond of dolls —and a multitude of little scraps of silk, and odds and ends of colored ribbons. Oh, dear Mrs. Wyverne, I could cry over the remembrance of my utter childishness and innocence, if it were not that I have other memories that are too deep for tears.

"Well, we were married, and then we travelled everywhere. We went to Italy, and finally came back to Paris through Germany. We had been gone about three months, I think. Those three months were perfect happiness. Kane was passionately fond of me, and I was far happier than ever I had been in all my life. His love was perfect adoration. He seemed not to have one single thought that was not about me; and, as for myself, I idolized him.

"Well, we came back to Paris, and lived there for several months. We enjoyed life to the very uttermost. Day followed day, and week followed week, and month followed month, so rapidly that I was amazed at the quick flight of time.

"Well, one day, there came a break in all this. I learned that my guardian had cast me off. I did not know any thing about my inheritance. I only thought it was a very, very cruel thing for him to do. He wrote Kane a terrible letter, and Kane felt cut to the heart, though he tried as hard as he could to hide from me how he felt it, but I could easily perceive it. I knew by that time every varying expression of his noble and lordly face, and every intonation of his voice so well, that any change was at once perceptible. However, he had great power over himself, and in a short time he succeeded in regaining his former flow of spirits.

"At last there came one memorable day. He had gone out early in the morning. He came back at about ten o'clock—we then breakfasted. I noticed a certain trouble in his face, which he was trying to hide by assumed gayety. I tried to quell my anxiety, but at length could restrain myself no longer, and I went over to him, and put my arms around him. He pressed me close to his heart in silence.

"'Oh, my dear love!' I asked, 'what is it?'

"'Nothing,' said he.

"I then implored him to tell me, but, instead of doing so, he gently withdrew himself, and went away, and sat down by a window in silence. At such apparent coldness as this, I was quite overcome. 'O Kane!' I cried, 'has it come to this!—has it come to this!' At this he started, and leaving his seat he came over to me, and stood looking at me with a mild, sweet, loving, and compassionate smile—looking like some protecting divinity; yet still, behind all this, I could not help seeing that lurking expression of trouble.

"'Not love you!' he said—'love!' and then he gave a little laugh. 'My darling!' he continued, in a tremulous voice, 'I do not believe that there are any other men in the world just now who know what it is to love, as I know it.'

"At this, I rose, and threw myself in his arms, and cried. Tears were in his eyes, too —and those tears made me cry all the more. But at last he regained his composure, and began to talk to me again. He then told me all—the whole truth. He informed me that, when we married, he had a certain amount of money—that his love was so great that he determined to make my life nothing but happiness. How well he had done that, I have told you. But, in doing this, he had spent every thing—and on that morning he was destitute. Besides this, he was in debt. Creditors were persecuting him—even the landlord joined with them, and had threatened to turn us out. We were to be turned out into the streets—or, rather, I was to be turned out alone, for he was in danger of arrest and imprisonment.

"Upon this, I was eager to know what he proposed to do, and in an anguish of fear I asked him if he was thinking of leaving me.

"'Never, never! Leave you, darling?— never, never!' he cried, with wild impetuosity. 'Never—it all depends upon you—if you will come with me where I go.'

"'Oh!' I cried, 'why do you talk so?—

as if I wouldn't go all over the world with you.'

"At this, he looked at me with so strange an expression that I actually felt frightened. For a long time he regarded me in silence—I was bewildered and terrified, and didn't know what to think.

"'Over the world,' he said, in a whisper, bending down lower, and still holding me in his arms—'over the world?—O my darling! —I know you would do that—but would you do more than that?'

"'Do more than that?' I faltered.

"'Would you—would you?' he said; and then he hesitated.

"'Would I what?' I asked, breathlessly.

"He bent his head down lower yet, and whispered in my ear:

"'*Darling! would you go with me out of the world?*'

"O dear Mrs. Wyverne! how can I tell you the unutterable horror that there was in that question? The whisper hissed itself through me; and every nerve and every fibre tingled and thrilled at its awful meaning. I felt paralyzed. I did not say one single word. He, on his part, went talking on in a strange, wild way, and was too intent on framing some argument for persuading me to notice the perfect agony of fear that this proposal had given me.—To die! Oh! to die! and I so young! and when I had been so happy! This was my only thought. Remember what a child I was. And to die! and so suddenly! Oh, horror of horrors! And worse, to administer death to myself! O dear, dear Mrs. Wyverne! how can I possibly tell you the utter anguish of such a thought?—Well, he went on speaking more, but I didn't hear a word, or, at least, I didn't understand, you know, for I was really quite stupefied. But I gathered, in a vague way, from what he said, that he had all along been looking forward to this, and that he had decided what to do. For himself, he was calm; but he felt uncertain about me, and had not dared to mention it before. He had gone out that morning to buy the drug that would furnish the deadly draught. This he showed me. The sight of it had the same effect on me which the sight of the gallows may have on the condemned criminal. But he was too much taken up with his own thoughts to notice my horror; and so he went on, working himself up into an eloquent rhapsody—in which he described

the joys of the spiritual state, and of the world beyond the grave. But oh! his words fell only upon the dull, dead ears of a terrified and panic-stricken girl.

"At length he made a proposal that each should pour it out for the other, or I made it in my despair—I forget which. He himself was in a very peculiar mood by this time; he was at once so absorbed in the purpose over which he had brooded so long, and at the same time so taken up with his own thoughts, that I saw the utter uselessness of any thing like remonstrance. I only thought of evasion —not of resistance; so I caught at once at the plan of pouring out a draught for myself, and in this way I hoped to escape this terrible fate which he was meditating for me. So I got up, and stammered something about getting the glasses. He smiled, and said nothing, but threw himself back in his chair. His face was turned from me. With a trembling hand I poured out some wine in a glass, and, taking this in one hand, I took two empty glasses in the other, and then went back very softly; stooping down, I put the glass of wine under the place where I had been sitting on the sofa. Then I handed him the empty glasses; he took them with an abstracted air and an enthusiastic smile. Then he made me sit down.

"Then he poured out the draught in each glass, and handed one to me. I took it—my hand trembling so that I could scarcely hold it, and looked at him as he sat there with his eyes turned toward me; but his eyes seemed fixed on vacancy, with that same excited and abstracted look which I have already mentioned.

"'Now,' said he, after some silence— 'now—my own darling—we both hold in our hands the means of escape from the darkness of poverty and the sorrow of life! Come, let us both drink together, and so pass away. When I raise my glass, do you raise yours, and thus we shall drink together, and —die!'

"At this a fresh anguish of despair rushed through me. I was filled with horror, and in that last moment of agony a sudden thought came to me.

"'What is the matter, my darling?' he asked, noticing my agitation.

"'Oh, hark! oh, listen!' I cried. 'There is some one at the door.'

"He started, and rose and went to the door. The moment his back was turned, I hastily changed the glass of poison for that of wine which was under me. By the time that I had done this, he had come back.

"'You are excited,' he said. 'There is no one there.'

"With those words he resumed his seat. On his noble face I saw a glow of lofty enthusiasm, and, as he fastened his eyes on me, they glowed with unutterable tenderness. There was also the moisture of tears in his eyes, and there was a smile on his lips. He held his glass in his left hand, while his right hand took mine. I noticed at that awful moment how warm his hand was, and how steady. It was the warmth and steadiness of perfect coolness and perfect health; but my hand was as cold as ice, and clammy, and tremulous, for I was shuddering and shivering in excitement and fear. We sat in this way for a moment or two, and then he said:

"'Now!'

"He raised the glass to his lips. I did the same. We both drank at the same time. Each of us drank, and oh, how different in each case! Then we put down the glasses, and still sat there in the same position. How long we sat I cannot tell, for my brain was in a whirl, and a dark horror was over me. I had escaped death, but I was losing him who was dearer than life. With my woman's love and yearning over him, there was a child's panic fear of death and its accompaniments. At length his grasp began to relax. He fell forward against me. I gave a shriek. I had a wild idea of going for help, and a wilder idea of flight; and so, with my mind almost in a state of delirium, I rushed from the room, and fled I hardly knew where.

"I remember getting lodgings, and writing to you, the only friend I had in all the world, and you came, and you nursed me, but I have never told you this till now."

Clara paused here for some time, and at length resumed:

"Well, dear, you know how I was. Thinking only of Kane's death, I gave myself up to despair. Life had lost all its value, and I only wished to find some occupation where I might also have the consolations of religion. This I found among those dear Sisters among whom I came to live and to work.

"Well, now, dear, I must mention a discovery that I made. It was about a year after this event. I was nursing at a hospital, and by the merest accident I heard of the case of a man who had been poisoned and sent here. The poison was too weak, or the amount was too small, and the work was not done. I was struck by this very forcibly, and on inquiry found out the date and the place. It was the date of our tragedy, and the place, too. They had not found out his name, but I knew that this patient could be no other than Kane. He had recovered! He had gone away! He had not died! He was alive! I cannot possibly convey to you, dear, the slightest idea of my feelings at such an astonishing discovery.

"After that I was in a constant state of watchfulness. I was on the lookout for him everywhere. Years passed, however, and I never saw him. At last I gave him up, and concluded that he had gone away, though, after all, I could not help indulging the hope of meeting him again. You have mentioned his strange fancies about me, dear. You now understand, and I can understand; we met by chance. He had come back here. The first time was at Notre-Dame, the next in the rail-cars, the next on the street. On each of those occasions I was as much affected as he was. The first meeting showed me that he was alive, though I knew not where to find him. This thought filled my mind to the exclusion of every thing else. The second meeting only confirmed this thought, and made me think also that he knew of my escape from the fate that he had prepared for me.

"But oh! I cannot tell you what I suffered. I had grown reconciled to this life. The discovery that he was alive destroyed all my peace of mind. It brought back all my past. Above all, I was filled with shame at the thought of the deceit of which I had been guilty. I had saved my life by a cowardly trick. He had gone, in good faith, to death, as he supposed; and had thought that I loved him well enough to go with him. But I did not. I was a coward, and in my terror I had deceived him. I dared not meet him. I was terrified at the sight of him, even though I longed to tell him all. One evening I saw him seated in the street in front of a *café*, and I caught his look. It seemed to me that he was regarding me with a stern, reproachful glance. I almost fainted in utter anguish; but I managed to reach my home. At another time I saw him at a distance. I followed him, with a vague idea of accosting him. I followed him to the cemetery of

Père-la-Chaise, and watched him for hours. I saw him kneeling before a tomb. I wondered very much, and looked at him for a long time from a hiding-place. At last I ventured forth a little, and he looked up and saw me. I shrank back again, and was so terrified that I remained there all night long. This explains to you all about our meetings, which he, poor fellow! thought were supernatural; and you see, too, dear, and you can understand, the reason why I was too frightened to make myself known to him.

"But oh! if it had not been for my own sense of dishonor—if it had not been for the feeling which I had that I had deceived him, and that he would never forgive it, how gladly I would have told him all! But I dared not. I was afraid. I knew so well his lofty nature, and remembered so well his proud confidence in me. And now, even now, O dear Mrs. Wyverne!—even now—even now—how can I even now let him know? Will he not utterly despise me? He feels remorse now for an imaginary crime, and I long to save him from this; but how can I, when to do so will only change his feelings from remorse to contempt? Oh, how I wish that I knew what to do!"

Mrs. Wyverne wondered very much at Clara's language, not so much, indeed, at the feelings which she expressed about what she called her cowardice as at the evident longings which she possessed after a husband from whom her vows must have separated her. Nor, indeed, could she help mentioning it.

"Ah, Mrs. Wyverne," said Clara, "there is something yet to be told. I am not altogether a Sister. I found out that he had not died in less than a year after I had joined them, and this always influenced my position here. For a married woman cannot become a Sister without the formal consent of her husband, and in my case this was out of the question. Besides, my case was so very peculiar, you know. I entered their house with the full intention of becoming a Sister, for I thought he was dead, but the discovery that he was not prevented my taking the vows. But the Sisters knew that I had come with the intention of doing so, under the impression that I was a widow. They knew my circumstances, they all pitied me, and so they have made allowances for me, and permitted me to remain."

This information set Mrs. Wyverne thinking.

CHAPTER LIII.

GOING TO PRAY AT CLARA'S GRAVE.

BESSIE and Inez were in a comfortable apartment in an ancient house in Rome. The ancient house was that one which had been described to Blake as having been recently obtained; but the appearance of the interior gave indications of a long occupation. The room in which they were was filled with antique furniture, and looked out upon a courtyard, surrounded by venerable walls, with a grotesque fountain in the midst.

"What a very particularly quaint old house this is, Inez darling, isn't it? and did you ever see such a dear old place—so ancient—so stately—such massive walls? And sure there's a kind of solemnity about it that's fairly delightful, so it is."

"Yes," said Inez; "I really never saw such a perfect reproduction of the romance of the middle ages."

"Sure, but it isn't romance, then, that I'm thinking of, at all at all, Inez darling; but it's religion, so it is. I don't feel like being in a feudal castle; but much more like being in some sweet, placid convent, where I'm settled for the rest of my days. And sure and it wouldn't take much to make me now consent to be made a nun of, and take the veil on the spot, so it wouldn't."

"That would be rather too rash a thing, Bessie dear," said Inez, with a smile, "for a bride hardly out of her honey-moon."

"Sure, and didn't I run away from poor old Gwynnie for the sake of friendship? and mightn't I run away from him again for the sake of religion?"

"Not very likely, I fancy, dear," said Inez, who was much amused at such an idea entering the head of so loving a wife as Bessie.

Bessie was silent and pensive for some time. Her glorious blue eyes were veiled by their heavy lashes, and were downcast and sad, while over the youthful beauty of her face there was a gentle melancholy, which threw around her a touching grace and charm.

"And O Inez darling!" said she, at length, in a low voice, "doesn't it seem sweet, then, to you, to think of those dear ones reposing in that holy place that dear grandpa has told us so much about?"

"It does seem sweet," said Inez. "I had heard in a vague way of the Roman Catacombs, but never knew what they really were. I had an idea that they were dangerous and dreadful."

"Sure, that's from the silly romances that we've read. But dear grandpa has known them all his life, so he has; and oh, but it's the holy man that he is himself, with his long life of fasting and devotion; and it's the great friend he was of our dear papa, Inez dear!"

"Yes," said Inez; "they must have been congenial spirits. I only wish I had known him before. What a beautiful enthusiasm he has for the saintly type of human character—the monks of the middle ages; and how he manages to kindle the same feelings in another! I feel it, and I know you do too, Bessie dear, for that was what made you make your remark just now about wishing to take the veil."

"Sure and I don't deny, then, that it was just that same, Inez dear; and really it would be so charming, you know; but then, poor dear Gwynnie would go on so, and be so sad, that I'm afraid I should not have the courage to do it."

"I should think not," said Inez.

"Well," said Bessie, "it must be the prospect of going to that sacred place that gives me these feelings. I've been fasting all day, and preparing myself. I could not go there as I would go to a picture-gallery. I go to the graves of my nearest and dearest ones, so I do; and sure I hope that we may be buried there some day, Inez darling—don't you, dear?"

"Yes, dear; I can think of no sweeter burial-place."

At this instant Kevin Magrath entered the room, and Inez and Bessie both rose with pleasant smiles to meet him. He regarded them both with that genial smile of his, which was benignant, tender, and paternal.

"Well, my dear gyerruls," said he, in a tone of gentle melancholy, "you may get ready now, and don't forget to put on something warrum, for I wouldn't like ye's to catch cold. In the hot summer even, whin people go down to saunter about for the afternoon, ye'll see thim all dressed like Russians, so ye will."

"Oh, you have warned us enough, grand-pa dearest," said Bessie. "We'll be careful, never fear."

Leaving the room, they completed their preparations, and soon returned. Kevin Magrath then led the way, and they followed him. Reaching the lower floor, he lighted three lanterns, each of which gave a most brilliant glow, and then descended into the cellar, followed by the two. Not the slightest hesitation was shown by either of them. The lustre of the lamps illumined the cellar most brilliantly, and the look which they cast about the place showed nothing more than curiosity and interest. The opening into the place was very much larger than it had been at Blake's visit, for the lower tombs had been knocked away, and it was thus large enough for Inez or Bessie to enter with only a slight inclination of their heads. There was also a small door, with a lock, with which the opening could be closed. The door was very massive, and so was the frame.

Kevin Magrath stopped for a short time, and looked at Inez and Bessie.

"Ye're about to inter a holy place," said he. "It's a place that will not inspire alarrum after what I've told ye's; but it will surely give ye's a sintimint of solimn awe—from the sacred, the rivirintial, and the vinirible associations around. Ye'll see numerous passages; but ye can't lose yer way with me; and, as to the solichude, why, it's only apparint, for there's plenty here moving about, and ye'll meet hundreds, so ye will, before ye get out."

With these words he passed through the opening, and Bessie and Inez came after him.

"There's nothing more ilivating in life," said Magrath, standing still and looking around, "thin a visit to this sanctified spot. There's a certain divine charrum here that imprissis ivery mind. I've alriddy told ye the whole history of this place, its nature, uses, offices, ixtint—so I need say no more on that. But now, dear gyorruls, before we go further, let us pause and indivor to achune our minds to the grandeur of the place; let us feel that we are surrounded on ivery side by a great cloud of witnisses."

After waiting a little while, he proceeded at a slow pace, and Inez and Bessie followed. Their eyes rested on those same scenes which Blake had viewed before, in this same company. The lights shone bright, but died away in the gloom before and behind. After a while Magrath walked closer to them, and made remarks from time to time in accordance with the nature of the surrounding scene. "It's a holy place," said he. "Even the very dust is holy, so it is. These passageways were ixcavated by the hands, worrun by the feet, and hallowed by the blissid rilics of apostles, saints, martyrs, confissors, virgins, and holy innocints; yes, here we have, in very deed around us, the goodly fcllowship of the saints, the glorious company of the apostles, and the white-robed army of martyrs; here, too, above all, we shall see the last ristingplace of those who were so dear to us.

"See there," said he, pointing to a small tablet; "it's a cnild-martyr, and sure, but it's a touching tuing intirely to think of these child-martyrs—buried here—but ye'll be having plinty of opporchunities to see thim all yit, Inez darling, so ye will—so we won't stop now."

In this way they went on till they reached the first cross-passage.

"Now," said he, "ye observe what I told ye—regyard this passage-way—it's a cross-street, as it were; the right hand brings ye to the crypt of the *Chiese di San Pietro in carcere*, while the left one runs to *Chiese di Gesu*. This is the true holy city—this subterranean Rome; this is the tirristrial Jerusalem, with its population of martyrs—the true Zion that I love. And here come all thim that pray for the peace of Jerusalem; here resort thim that are weary of the vanities of the upper wurruld, to hold commune with the spirits of the departed. All these paths lead to churches, or sometimes to houses that have easy connection with the streets above, so that ye can start in hot weather and visit a friend by taking one of these underground strects. Ye'll yet see these passages thronged, so ye will—yis, with busy life too. I've seen hundreds here—yis, thousands, so I have."

At length they reached that place which Blake had known as the Painted Chamber.

"Here," said Magrath, "is one of the cintral points from which sanctity seems to be irradiated all around. We are not far from our distination, so let us wait here for a momint, to prepare our minds for the last. There's a solimnity about this place that niver fails to impriss me—an awe I always feel—and never have I felt it stronger than now.

15

Look, Inez darling; look, Bessie jool, at thim painted walls. These walls speak, and see what a past they tell about."

Inez and Bessie looked around, and gazed with deep interest upon the objects visible there, and listened to the explanations of their guide. As for Magrath, he seemed to lose himself in his lofty theme, and rose every moment to a higher strain of eloquent rhapsodizing.

"Ye must contimplate the Christian worruld in the times of persecution," said he. "In those times the Catacombs opened before them as a city of rifuge. Here lay the bones of their fathers who, from gineration to gineration, had fought and died for the truth. Here they brought their rilitives as one by one they died. Here the son had borrun the body of his aged parint, and the parint had seen his child committed to the tomb. Here they had carried the mangled remains of those who had been torn by the wild beasts of the arena, the blackened corpses of those that had been committed to the flames, or the wasted forrums of those most miscrable, who had sighed out their lives amid the lingering agonies of crucifixion. The place was hallowed, and it was no wonder that they should seek for refuge here.

"Here, thin, the persecuted Christians turruned, and they peopled these paths and grottoes—by day assimbling to exchange words of cheer and comfort, or to bewail the death of some new martyr; by night sinding forth like a forlorrun hope, to learrun tidings of the upper worruld, or to bring down the blood-stained bodies of some new victim. So they saved thimsilves, but at what a cost!

"Yis, at what a cost—living here amid the damp vapors and the dinse smoke of their torches! Sure to glory, but to me the Roman spirit that enjured all this towers up to grander proportions than were ever attained in the days of the republic. The fortichude of Regulus, the devotion of Curtius, the constancy of Brutus, were here surpassed, not by the strong man, but by the tindir virgin and the weak child. And thus, scorruning to yield to the fiercest powers of persecution, these min went forth, the good, the pure in heart, the great, the brave. For thim, death had no terrors, nor that appalling life in death which they had to enjure here in this subterrancan worruld.

"Look around ye's now. What is it that ye see? Ye behold the tokins, the imblims, of the thoughts and feelings that animated thim, and the constant efforts which they made to console their minds by rifirince to shupernatural truths. In that ancient worruld, ye'll remimber, art was cultivated and cherished more ginerally than in the modern worruld. Wherever any number of min and women gathered together, an imminse proportion had the taste and the talint for art. Whin the Christians peopled the Catacombs, the artist was here too, and his art was not unimployed. These chambers were to the Christian population like squares amid the narrow streets around; and here it was that they made efforts for addorunmint. So, ye see, they covered the walls with white stucco, and they painted on thim pictures of the saints and martyrs, the apostles and prophets, the confissors and witnesses for the truth. If, in the hour of bitter anguish, they sought for scenes or for thoughts that might relieve their souls and projuce fresh strength within thim, they could have found no other objects to look upon, so strong to encourage, so mighty to console.

"Yis, in these graves around me," he continued, rising to a higher strain of enthusiasm, "I behold the remains of those who illivated humanity; of whom the worruld was not worthy. They lived at a time whin, to be a Christian, was to risk one's life. They did not shrink, but boldly proclaimed their faith, and acciptid the consequinces. They drew a broad line between thimsilves and the heathin, and stood manfully on their own side. To utter a few words, to perforrum a simple act, could always save from impinding death; but the tongue refused to speak the formula, and the stubborn hand refused to power the libation. They took up the cross, and bore the reproach. That cross was not a figure of speech, as it now is in these days of emasculated Christianity. Witness these names of martyrs—these words of anguish! These walls have carried down to us, through the ages, the words of grief, of lamentation, of ever-changing feeling, which were marked upon them by those who once sought rifuge here. They tell their mourrunful story to us in these latter days, and raise up before our imagination the forrums, the feelings, and the acts of those who were imprisoned here. And, just as the forrums of life are taken up-

on the plates of the camera, so has the great voice, once forced out by suffering from the very soul of the martyr, become stamped upon these walls all around us wheriver we turrun our eyes."

He paused for a moment, and then, clasping his hands, looked with a rapt gaze at vacancy, and burst forth:

"Yis, ye humble witnisses of the truth, poor, despised, forlorrun, and forsaken, in vain your calls for mercy wint forth to the ears of man: they were stifled in the blood of the slaughter and in the smoke of the sacrifice! Yet, where your own race only answered your cry of despair with fresh torramints, these rocky walls proved more merciful; they heard your cries, they took thim to their bosoms, and so your words of suffering live here, trisured up and graven in the rock foriver!

"Ah, my childrin! ah, Inez darling! Bessie jool! let your imagination have full swing, and try to bring before yer mind's eyes the truth of these surroundings. Contimplate thim as they once were. Ye'll see these passages not left to the silent slumber of the dead, but filled with thousands of the living. Wan, and pale, and sad, and oppressed, they find, even amid this darkness, a better fate than that which awaits them in the worruld above-ground. Busy life animates the haunts of the dead; these pathways ring to the sound of human voices. The light of truth and virtue, banished from the upper air, burruns anew with a purer rajiance in this subterranean gloom! The tender greetings of affliction, of frindship, of kinship, and of love, arise amid the mowldering remains of the departed. Here the tear of grief bejews the blood of the martyr, and the hand of affliction wraps his pale limbs in the shroud. Here in these grottoes the heroic soul rises up shuperior to sorrow. Hope and faith smile exultingly, and the voice of praise breathes itsilf forth from the lips of the mourrunor!"

He stopped abruptly, and was silent for some time.

"Sure but it's rhapsodical I am intirely, dear gyerruls," said he, at last, "but I can't help it. Whiniver I get upon these themes I am carried away beyond mysilf. I ought to have held me tongue, and given meself up to contimplation. But it's difficult to be calm amid such scenes as these."

But Inez assured him that she loved to hear him talk in this way in such a place, and that she could have listened far longer with delight and with instruction.

"Well, well," said he, "it's very kind for you to say that, so it is, and I know how amiable ye are intirely, but—I'm thinking I wint a little beyond ye; howandiver, we needn't be losing time, so let's go on now, in the hope that our minds'll be in fitting trim for the sacred juties and holy contimplations that lie befower us. Come on, dear gyerruls—come on, Inez darling—come on, Bessie jool. Follow me, children dear, for we're close by the spot, so we are."

With these words he turned, and, followed by Inez and Bessie, walked out of the Painted Chamber.

Inez followed first along the passage-way which lay between the Painted Chamber and that opening in the floor into the realms below. She was perfectly and utterly fearless. Of the gloom and the terrors around her she had not the faintest idea. She walked there as fearlessly as though she was walking along the Corso, as though she was passing up the nave of St. Peter's, but only with a deeper solemnity, and a holier calm, and a profounder awe

This may easily be explained. Once she had entertained the common opinion about the Roman Catacombs. She did not know any thing very particular about them. She had read about them in a general way, and in the course of her reading she had encountered terrible tales of people who had been lost in these endless labyrinths. But all these had been dismissed. Kevin Magrath had given her a different opinion about them.

From him she learned that they were not dangerous at all, but were a common resort of devotees; that, instead of being a series of labyrinthine passages without end, they were in reality connected in countless places with the houses above; and that the difficulty was not how to avoid being lost, but rather how to find some passage-way which would not lead into the cellar of a house, or the crypt of some church. Thus Inez believed herself to be in a place which was a common resort, a place where in every direction there were passages leading straight to the upper world. With this belief fear was impossible.

But she had stronger feelings than this

belief—the feeling of religious ardor evoked by the enthusiastic declamation of Magrath, who, from being earnest, had grown rhapsodical. She felt her soul kindling at his vehement words; she felt her most intense religious fervor evoked by the thoughts which he had called up of that sublime past, when this was a city, not of the dead, but of the living; when the faithful sought refuge here from persecution; and where, amid the relics of dead saints, there stood those living saints who themselves were destined to swell the ranks of the "white-robed army of martyrs."

Beneath all this was her solemn purpose for which she had come—the end of her pilgrimage to Rome—the graves of her father, her mother, and her sister. For this she had prepared herself, and this lay before her. For this the scenes thus far had only served to prepare her soul, and the words which she had heard seemed a fitting prelude to the solemn devotions before her.

Kevin Magrath stopped.

Inez looked around.

At her feet she saw a step-ladder. A little in front she saw an opening in the path, black, yawning!

"It's an opening into a passage below like this," said Kevin Magrath. "It's down there that we're going; there, Inez darling, they lie—the loved ones—waiting for you and for us. I brought the ladder here this morning. It's only a short distance, and I'll help ye's both down easy enough. Ye'll find it just the same down there as it is up here."

The sight of this pit at first startled Inez, but Magrath's words reassured her.

"It looks dangerous," said he, "but people always carry lights, and so there's niver any accidint. Besides, it's only in out-of-the way places that we find these lower stories. It's only a few feet, too."

Saying this, he pushed the step-ladder down into the opening. It touched the floor below, and rested there, with the top of it projecting a short distance above.

"It's a mighty convanient thing intirely," said he, "and I'll help ye's both down. *You* may come down first after me, Inez darling—and thin, Bessie jool, I'll fetch *you.*"

With these words he descended, and soon reached the place below. He placed his lantern on the floor, and the bright gleam illuminated the passage-way, showing that it was the counterpart of the one above. Kevin Magrath stood and looked up. There was a gentle smile on his face, and with this there was an expression of solemn awe which was in keeping with the scene around.

"Here," said he, "not far away, is the risting-place of the loved ones; here your father and I with our own hands, Inez darling, bore the precious rilies of poor Clara; and here afterward it was me own mourrunful privilege to—but wait till I help ye, dear; give me yer hand thin."

While he was speaking Inez had begun to descend, and Magrath stopped short in his remarks, to help her. He stood on the lower step of the ladder, and reached out his hand. Then, not satisfied with that, he went up a few steps, holding her so as to help her down. At length Inez reached the floor below.

The lamp was burning then brightly. Inez, full of the solemn purpose before her, and roused up to a high enthusiasm by the scene around, and by the events that had thus far occurred, cast one look up the pathway, and another look down, and then stood waiting for Bessie, with her eyes downcast, and her mind preparing itself for what was before her. So, in deep abstraction, stood Inez.

Bessie was on the floor above, at the head of the ladder. Kevin Magrath was on the floor below, at the foot of the ladder. He looked up and looked nothing. Bessie looked down. Their eyes met.

"It makes me so dizzy, grandpa dear," said Bessie. "It always makes me dizzy to climb ladders, or to look down places, so it does. Inez was always awfully brave."

"Dizzy is it? Sure to glory but its the big coward ye are thin," said Kevin Magrath. "Sure if ye're afraid, I'll go up and carry ye down in me arrums, so I will."

Inez was standing there. She held in her hands the lantern which she had carried. She heard these words. At the same time her eyes were struck by a flash of light in the passage at some distance. There was also the sound of hurrying footsteps, as of some one advancing. She could not help feeling some curiosity. That some one should be advancing was not at all surprising to her, for Kevin Magrath had given her to understand that the Catacombs were visited and traversed by people at all hours of the day and night. These perhaps, she thought, might be like herself, mourners, visitors to the graves of departed friends. So she stood looking.

Kevin Magrath was looking up, his back being turned, and his attention absorbed with Bessie and with his own thoughts. He had not seen that gleam of light, nor had he heard the footsteps. He was so absorbed in his own purposes.

"Inez darling," said he, not turning to face her, not choosing now to look at her, "I'll have to go up to carry Bessie down. Sure but it's the big coward she is thin!— Bessie, jool, if ye won't come down, or if ye can't, why ye needn't. Wait a momiut, and I'll bring ye in me own arrums.—Wait a momint, Inez darling. It's only a minute I'll be, ye know, and then we'll rezhume our wanderings—to the holy graves—and—we'll perforrum the last mourrunful rites, so we will."

He had spoken slowly. He seemed to think that Inez would be afraid to have him go up even for a minute, and so tried to reassure her and to strengthen her by reminding her of the purpose before her. There was, in reality, no need of this, since Inez did not have the slightest suspicion, and, from perfect ignorance, was perfectly fearless.

At this moment also, and while he was speaking, her eyes were fixed on an advancing figure hastening along. A strange thrill came over her. It seemed incredible. She could scarcely stand. The figure came nearer, nearer, nearer. It was a man, who was hurrying at a rapid run; he had a lantern, which revealed his form and face.

The noise of those advancing footsteps could now not fail to force itself through Kevin Magrath's abstraction of soul, into which he had fallen from the pressure of his own purpose. Already he had one foot on the lowest step of the ladder, and his left hand had grasped it so as to ascend, when that strange and startling noise came to his ears.

He stopped and turned.

And then, full before him, and rushing toward him, he saw It. Rushing toward him with impetuous haste, with a face ghastly white, with fierce, eager eyes, with one hand holding a lantern, and the other hand outstretched as if to strike; wild, terrible, menacing, he saw It! What? The tremendous apparition of the man whom he had led down here, and left to die in this very place; from

" it was Basil Wyverne, the man whom he knew to be dead."—Page 226.

whom he had fled up this very opening; the form of the dead; the apparition of horror! It was Basil Wyverne; the man whom he knew to be dead, but whom he saw to be living—living in this drear home of death; a spectacle of anguish unutterable; a figure appalling and abhorrent; a sight and a thought that man might not face; before which Reason trembled and vanished; and the strong, remorseless nature, hardened to acts of crime, shuddered and sank away.

"Why, Dr. Blake!"

It was the voice of Inez.

It was followed by a gasp and a groan; then the sound of rushing footsteps in panic flight, and Kevin Magrath disappeared, swallowed up in thick darkness, while the sound of those footsteps came up from afar, lessening gradually till all was still, from that passage up which the fabulous Onofrio had fled.

At the same moment a piercing cry came from Bessie in the passage-way above. For she had been stooping down low, and, startled by the movement of Kevin Magrath, she knelt down and put her head lower still, so as to see what it was that caused this agitation. And in that one instance she saw it all.

The sudden arrival of Blake upon the scene can be accounted for in the most natural manner. He had hurried to Rome with Kane and Gwyn, full of anxiety. He had found the Via dei Conti, and had recognized that gloomy building which had been pointed out by Kevin Magrath as the Monastery of San Antonio. Turning down the street at the corner, he went on until he had reached and fully recognized the house to which he had been taken by his betrayer. He could find out nothing about it now. People said that it was uninhabited, and its aspect seemed to confirm the statement.

Kevin Magrath had informed Gwyn that he would stop at the Hôtel dell' Europe, but, on inquiring there, they could learn nothing whatever about him. This made Blake feel certain that he had taken Inez at once to that house. At first he thought of communicating with the police; but the fever of his impatience made him resolve to act for himself. He could not get admittance to the house by the door, but he remembered that he could penetrate into that prison through the Catacombs. Iron crow-bars and the stout arms of his friends could soon break through into the cellars, and Inez could be reached and rescued in this way far sooner than by the movements of the police.

The emergency of the case, and his new anxiety, dispelled the terrors of the Catacombs, and Kane and Gwyn were willing to accompany him. They took all the materials that were requisite for their purpose, and hurried to the mouth of the Cloaca Maxima. Their movements excited no attention, for they looked like one of those exploring parties which may often be met with in Rome.

In due time they came to the broken stone, and passed through. After this, they had to move more carefully. But at length Blake discovered, lying on the floor, something which gave him an unmistakable clew to the path which he should take. It was that burnt match which he had lighted while standing at the intersection of the two paths, when the light had revealed the horrible spectacle of his assailants. Here lay the match, at the intersection of the two paths, and he was able at once to take up the course which was to lead him back over the scene of his wanderings.

Here the course was perfectly straight, and they at length reached the opening above. Up this Blake climbed by means of those very holes which he had cut before, when his ear caught the sound of voices, and, as his head arose above the opening, he saw a glow of light before him. He hung there listening.

It was Kevin Magrath's voice, speaking in a high key, in the Painted Chamber; and Blake heard nearly all. He now knew that he had not been a moment too soon, and that Inez was already descending to her living tomb. As Kevin Magrath ceased, he let himself down again, and they hurriedly deliberated about what they should do next. It was agreed to retreat, lower their lamps, and watch from a convenient distance. This they did, and from the gloom around them they saw all. They saw the ladder come down. They saw Inez descend first. They saw Kevin Magrath go away. They heard all that passed between him and Bessie. They heard his last words, and saw him prepare to ascend.

Then they could wait no longer, and Blake sprang forward upon his horror-stricken enemy.

———————

CHAPTER LIV.

CONCLUSION.

THE perfect fearlessness of Inez in this terrible situation, and her utter unconsciousness of danger, have already been explained. Nor did the appearance of Blake seem to her very extraordinary. Kevin Magrath had given her to understand that the Catacombs were a place of common resort, easily accessible, and, in some parts, actually used as a thoroughfare in hot weather. That Blake should be here was not unaccountable. In a moment she accounted for it, and thought that Magrath must have told him of her presence in Rome, and of her intended visit to this place. The incongruity of a lover's visit, with this sacred purpose before her, was certainly evident; yet she was conscious of no vexation; nor did she feel any other emotion than sincere joy. Thus she saw his appearance with the same quiet pleasure with which she would have greeted it in the Corso or on the Pincian Hill.

This was but for a moment or so, when she first saw who it was. A few moments more, and these feelings were succeeded by others of a more violent character.

It was indeed Blake, and he was advancing at a headlong speed, his pallid face showing an agony of anxiety and eagerness. To rescue Inez, and to avenge his own injuries, had brought him here; and, as he saw her before him, standing there, yet safe, he at first was only conscious of her; nor did the other figure, with its white face of horror and staring eyes, attract his regards. His only impulse was to seize Inez in his arms—to clasp her to his heart. His only thought was of that fate which had been prepared for her—the terrific, the appalling, the living grave, with its awful accompaniments! Even here, already in that grave, she was standing; and here he had found her! He could not know what there was in her mind, nor could he understand her ignorance of danger; but he could see in her face her innocent fearlessness and the bright welcome of her glance. It was infinitely touching.

With an inarticulate cry he caught the astounded Inez in his arms, and pressed her to his heart again and again. She—overwhelmed with amazement at such unexpected passion and vehemence; bewildered at such treatment from a man whom she certainly knew as her lover, but who yet had never declared his love; half terrified, yet not altogether displeased—at first tried to shrink away, and then yielded helplessly. But, from his broken words and exclamations, she was not long in gathering suggestions of something of that terrible doom which had just now been awaiting her here. A vague horror came over her, but in her ignorance and bewilderment that horror took no definite shape.

Though Blake had thus yielded so utterly to the rapture of his soul at finding Inez, he did not long remain forgetful of his other purpose. Lights and footsteps came up from behind him, and in a few minutes two others had reached the spot, whom Inez in her amazement recognized as Kane and Gwyn. In the faces of both there was an expression so awful that new fears were awakened in Inez; while Blake, roused by their approach, turned away from Inez to look for his enemy.

He had seen him but a short time before, standing at the foot of the ladder, staring at him. As he now looked that figure was gone, but in place of it there was another.

It was Bessie.

Her face was of a waxen hue, her lips bloodless; she looked like a marble statue, except for the bright blue of her glorious eyes, which now were fixed upon the party before her, wide open, with an expression of childish wonder.

"How very, very funny!" she said, at last.

All the others looked at her in silence. There was perplexity in the minds of Kane and Blake and Gwyn; nor could they as yet decide what her part had been. Gwyn's long agony of soul about her had gone on increasing, and finding her here now seemed a confirmation of his worst suspicions. For he had seen her coming down the ladder, and knew that she had allowed Inez to be taken down first. That one thing filled his mind with anguish.

"Sure but this is an unexpected meeting entirely," said Bessie, in a simple, unaffected manner; "but what in the wide world has happened to poor, dear grandpapa?"

At this Inez, with a start, perceived that Magrath had disappeared.

"He was here but a few moments ago," said she.

"He has gone," said Blake, in a solemn

voice, "to his own place!" A shudder passed through him, and he paused, for he thought of the fabled Onofrio, and remembered that the scene of his flight had been laid in this very place. "Inez," he continued, looking upon her with a gaze of unspeakable tenderness and compassion— "Inez! O Inez! you little know what you have escaped. It is something so appalling that I cannot bear to tell. I should prefer to put it off to some time when our surroundings might not be so fearful, but I see that it must not be put off. I must tell it now, for we are all here, and she is here"—indicating Bessie—"who is so deeply implicated, and others are here whose whole life now depends upon the answer she may give. Prepare yourself, Inez. Try to bear what is coming. In the first place, answer me this: What was it that brought you here?"

Inez looked with awe at the solemn face of the speaker. Her voice was tremulous as she replied to his question:

"I came down here to pray at the grave of my dear papa, and—"

"Your father!" interrupted Blake— "Your father! Do you mean Bernal Mordaunt?"

"Yes."

"And have you not heard the truth about him from her?" he exclaimed.

"Truth? what truth?" asked Inez, full of agitation.

A silence followed. Bessie stood looking at them as before, but none of them looked at her. They averted their eyes, for this answer of Inez opened up endless suspicions.

Blake, after a time, went on, and told Inez the whole truth about her father's return and death, of Bessie's taking her place, and receiving her father's blessing.

As the truth began to dawn on her, Inez fixed her eyes upon Bessie with a look of indescribable wonder and reproach, while Bessie looked at her with unalterable placidity. As soon as Blake had ended, Inez asked her:

"O Bessie! is this all true?"

"Sure and it is, then, Inez darling, every word of it, and I'm glad it's out, for it's been a sore load on my heart all the time, so it has."

"But why didn't you tell me?"

"Sure it's because I couldn't bear to, Inez darling. You'd have thought of me as a deceiver—as a supplanting Jacob—when all the time I was as innocent as a child. Really, Inez darling, I could not bring myself to tell it, and I was so troubled about it, too, all the time."

"But why did you always talk as though he were buried here, and come with me to pray over his grave?"

"Because, Inez darling, he is buried here, with dear mamma and poor, dear Clara. His remains were brought here from Mordaunt Manor by poor, dear grandpa; and oh! but it's myself that's fairly heart-broken with anxiety about him this blessed moment, so it is."

"He was never brought here," said Blake, sadly; "none of those graves are here. Do you want to know why you were brought here? I'll tell you—I must—though it is torment even to think of it."

And now Inez had to listen to the story of Blake. Under any circumstances such a story would have been awful, indeed; but now, in this place, to hear this was more than she could bear. Blake did not dwell much upon his sufferings, but she could imagine them. Now, too, she first learned the true nature of the Catacombs, and how terribly she had been deceived. Even though that danger had passed away, yet the very thought of it was so terrible that her fainting limbs sank under her, and she would have fallen had not Blake supported her.

But the terror which the thought of this recent danger, and the discovery that she had been the intended victim of Magrath, had given to Inez did not seem to be felt by Bessie. She stood there, pale as before, yet with an unchanged face, listening to Blake's story, and exhibiting nothing stronger than a very deep interest in his narrative. Inez marked her calmness, and she wondered to herself what part Bessie had taken in all this, and turned her sad eyes over in that direction. She remembered those letters to Bessie which had never been answered. She recalled her former feelings about Magrath, and recollected, too, how Bessie had brought her back into his power. What did all this mean? Yet the suspicion that rushed into her mind was intolerable, nor could she bring herself to put any question to one whom she even yet believed to be her sister.

It was Blake who put the question for her. Turning to Bessie, he regarded her for a few moments in silence, and then said:

"As I came up I saw Inez standing here, Kevin Magrath at the foot of the ladder, about to go up, while you were at the top watching. Magrath was going up, and you were up there, and he was going to draw up that ladder, leaving Inez here as he left me."

"Sure he never could have done it at all at all," cried Bessie. "I would never have let him. I think it is too bad, and you are very, very unkind to say such a thing, and it's too bad, so it is. And I'll never believe, so I won't, that it really was my poor, dear grandpa that betrayed you, for there isn't the least harm in life in him."

"What made him go away when he saw me come?"

Bessie clasped her hands, with a look of sudden pain.

"Oh, it's lost he is! Oh, the bitter, bitter blow!—O grandpa darling! where are you, then?—Oh, won't some of you try to save him? Gwynnie dearest—"

She stopped short and looked earnestly at Gwyn. But Gwyn averted his eyes.

Blake's last words had strengthened the suspicions which Inez had begun to feel. Her heart became hardened to Bessie. Her attitude, described by Blake, gave rise to a belief in the very worst; nor was it hard to see that the one who had supplanted her at Mordaunt Manor might have betrayed her in the Catacombs.

"Bessie," said she, and, as she spoke, her voice grew cold and hard, while the indignant feeling that arose within her drove away her weakness—"Bessie, what makes you anxious about this Magrath? He is no relation to you, and you have always believed that the Catacombs were as safe as the upper streets."

"Oh, sure, Inez dear, but how can I believe they're safe now, after that awful story? It's fairly heart-broken I am with the terror of it. And oh! if he isn't my dear grandpapa, he is my best and kindest friend and guardian, so he is."

"What made you give that shriek? You must then have been afraid about him." This question was put by Blake, in whose ears that shriek had rung as he caught Inez in his arms.

"Sure and I was afraid he'd be lost," said Bessie, "for he went off in the dark, without his lantern."

"Then you knew that the Catacombs were a dangerous place before you heard Dr. Blake's story," said Inez. "Yet you always spoke as though they were a common thoroughfare."

"Not these lowest stories, Inez darling," said Bessie. "Poor, dear grandpa—for I really must call him so—always made me understand that they were very, very dangerous, and really scarcely ever used. And I didn't tell you, because I didn't wish to make you feel badly, so I didn't, Inez darling."

"O Bessie!" said Inez, "I would give all I have if I could feel toward you as I used to. But I remember a thousand little things which show that you have never been candid. Why did you take the name of Inez when my poor papa came home?"

"Ah! sure, Inez darling, it was that very thing that always made me have the sore heart, and I couldn't bear to tell you; but I knew how he hated me, and I longed for his love, and so I met him, not as his hated daughter Bessie, but as his loved daughter Inez."

Inez turned away. She felt bewildered, and did not know what to say. She trusted Bessie no longer; yet Bessie thus far had triumphantly maintained her innocence.

"His daughter!" said Blake. "Inez, that is all a fabrication of our enemy Magrath. My mother has told me all. She was with your mother when she died. There never was any other child but yourself and Clara. And, as to the one who has taken your place, do not let any sisterly feelings shield her from your suspicions, for, by minute inquiries about her, my mother feels certain that she is Bessie Magrath, the daughter of Kevin Magrath. It was for her that he labored. She thus personated you, took your name, welcomed your father, who died believing in her. She is the one who has defrauded you out of your father's home, and your father's heart."

At this Inez was so astounded that she had not one word to say. This disclosure completed the revolution of feeling that had been going on in her; the strange suspicions of her Paris prison were turned from Saunders to Bessie; and it seemed now to her that the minute knowledge which Magrath had possessed of her life and feelings had not been communicated to him by her servant, but rather by her friend and confidante. Perhaps it was her assistance that had put her first in Magrath's power. Having learned the truth about her father, she was now able to estimate that Paris plot to its full extent, and the confederate whom Magrath must have had seemed to be Bessie. And yet—and yet —Bessie's innocent face, her winning ways, her loving words!—but then, had she not defrauded her of her dearest and holiest treasure—a father's dying blessing?

Bessie heard Blake without interrupting him, and with a childlike wonder.

"Well, Dr. Blake," said she, "I'm sure I don't really see how your mamma can know all about that, and know better than my dear grandpa. I'm sure I've always believed that I was Inez Elizabeth Mordaunt, and that Mordaunt Manor was mine. I'm sure dear grandpa wouldn't deceive me so, and tell such wicked, wicked stories, so he wouldn't; and I'm sure I shouldn't be sorry at all at all, so I wouldn't, if it were to be really as you say, and if dear grandpa was to turn out to be my own papa, for really I love him like a papa; and oh, where is he now? and why, oh, why won't some one go after him? Gwynnie dear! Oh, my dear darling own Gwynnie!"

They all stood looking at her: Blake cold and utterly unbelieving in her; Inez alienated and indignant; Kane stern and austere and solemn as Fate. But Bessie regarded only Gwyn.

He had seen her as he came up to this place, but had averted his eyes; nor had he given her one look since. He had heard every word. Dark recollections and suspicions had arisen in the mind of Inez, but these were as nothing when compared with those that arose within his mind. He had come and found her here, and the sight of her had been enough. Not one word of excuse or of exculpation or of explanation that she had uttered, not the white innocence of her face, nor the childlike wonder of her expression, nor the steadfast and open gaze of her glorious eyes, nor the unembarrassed ease of her manner, could shake in the slightest degree the conclusion to which he had come. As he stood there the breach that already existed between him and her widened every moment with every new thought of his mind, until at last it had grown to be a great gulf fixed between them—impassable forever!

These thoughts were terrible. The centre of them all was that scene, known only to her self and him, on the top of the cliff, where Kane hung suspended. The dread suspicion that

then had flashed across his mind and caused him to strike her down, now revived in all its force; from these his mind recurred to other recollections, all of which assumed a new meaning. Every act of her life—her sudden arrival at Mordaunt Manor—her attitude toward her supposed father—her flight from himself—her proposal to protract the separation so as to be with Inez—her request that he should bring Kane to Rome—all rose before him full of appalling meaning. Why did she remain with Inez?—to bring her here! Why did she wish him to bring Kane to Rome?— to use him as a decoy in completing the work in which she had failed on the cliff! Upon these conclusions his mind grew fixed; nor could the recollection of her love and gentleness and tenderness shake him from them.

So that now, when Bessie turned from the others to him, and made this direct appeal in her own old tone of love and confidence, he raised his head and turned his eyes upon her. The face which he thus turned showed all the anguish which he was suffering; his brow was dark with fixed and unalterable gloom; and, in the stony look which met her eyes, might be seen despair. It was but for a moment that he looked at her, and then he was about to say something, but he was interrupted by Kane.

"Well," said he, "after all, he is a fellow-creature; and, for my part, I don't want him to perish here. We've come prepared for emergencies—so, Gwyn, what do you say? Let's unroll our string, and explore. You take the ladder, and I'll take the clew. But hadn't you better all go up first?"

"Me go up!" exclaimed Bessie. "And poor dear grandpa as good as lost, and me the heart-broken girl that I am! What a very, very strange proposal! It's myself that would far rather go with you, so I would, and oh, I do so wish that you would let me."

"No," said Kane; "you would be an incumbrance. We must go alone."

Blake would have been glad to get Inez into the upper world, but Bessie was firm in her decision; and, as they could not leave her here, nor let her embarrass Kane's movements, they had to wait with her. So Kane took the clew and lamp, and walked on, unrolling the string as he went, while Gwyn followed, with his lamp and the ladder. He passed Bessie without a word, nor did he look at her, though she was standing close by the ladder as he took it down. Bessie watched the two as they went far up the passage-way until they disappeared in the distance.

Then she turned around with a little sigh. "I'm sure," said she, "one would think that poor dear Gwynnie had got over all affection for me."

After this she relapsed into silence, and stood there, her face turned in the direction where Kane and Gwyn had gone. Basil and Inez occasionally conversed in low whispers, but they addressed no remark to Bessie. So these three remained for nearly an hour, until at length a light appeared far up the passage-way, and Bessie advanced a few steps in eager anxiety. After a time an exclamation of disappointment escaped her.

There were only two figures !

Soon Kane and Gwyn reached the spot, Gwyn standing aloof.

"We have found nothing," said Kane, "and have come back to make preparations for a more thorough search. I propose now that we go up, and let the ladies find some place of safety. We can then find others to come down and help us here. Meanwhile, I have left the clew, as far as it ran, on the floor. We can also leave the ladder here, and some lanterns with matches."

This proposal was agreed to at once, and they all ascended. Blake led the way to the well-remembered opening. Inez walked by his side. Bessie followed, silent and pensive. Then came Kane. Last of all, Gwyn. On reaching the house, they went to the upper rooms, where Blake perceived, to his surprise, the signs of long occupation.

To his offer that the ladies should leave, Bessie gave a positive refusal.

"Leave, is it?" said she; "and me expecting my dear grandpa every minute? Why, really, how very, very absurd! And you, Inez; why, what can you possibly be thinking of? You won't leave me this way, will you, darling? It'll be so very, very lonely, and so awfully sad to have nobody but poor, dear old Mrs. Hicks Lugrin."

Inez said but little. Blake had told her of lodgings where she would be safe; he had also told her of the letter that he had written to his mother, and his expectation that she would come to Rome. He also found time to tell her about Clara. So that, even if there had been no other feeling, the excitement of Inez about this long-lost sister, and

her intense desire to see her, would of itself have drawn her away. But, apart from this, it was impossible now that she should ever again consent to live under the same roof with Bessie. Inez, therefore, went with Basil to the lodging-house already mentioned, where he left her.

They then communicated with the police, and a detachment of men was furnished, competent for the purpose, who accompanied them to the Catacombs. Here a long, painful, and most exhaustive search was made.

But of the fugitive they found not a trace.

The mournful news was communicated to Bessie by Kane. Gwyn still held aloof. Bessie's face wore a look of the deepest possible distress, and she was silent for a long time.

"Sure," said she, with a little sigh, "it's myself that's got the sore heart, and I cannot help feeling very, very uneasy; and it's really awful, you know, dear Kane; but, after all, poor, dear grandpa is so awfully clever that he'll find his way out of it yet. So, I'll wait here, and try to hope for the best. But, do you know, Kane dear, it's awfully lonely here, with only poor, dear old Mrs. Hicks Lugrin; and I'm awfully sorry that dear, darling Inez took such a dislike to the house, and I do wish she would come and see me, so I do; or tell me where she is. And oh, how good it is for you and dear, darling Gwynnie to take such pains about poor, dear grandpa! And tell dear, darling Gwynnie that my poor little brains have been so upset by all these long stories that I don't know hardly where I am. I'm not papa's daughter, it seems, and I'm no relation to my darling sister; and sure, I'm beginning to expect to hear next that I'm not dear old Gwynnie's wife. And that would be so very, very sad!"

Bessie ended this in a plaintive voice, and looked mournfully at Kane with her large blue eyes. They were full of pathos, and Kane felt very much perplexed and puzzled, after all, about Bessie.

Kane went away, with his mind full of speculations about Bessie, recalling her as he had known her at Ruthven Towers, and trying in vain to find some way by which she could be reconciled with her husband. But these thoughts were all driven out by new ones, which were suggested by certain information which he received from Blake.

For Blake, on leaving the Catacombs, after this last vain search after the missing man, had gone to the lodgings where Inez now was, to inquire after her welfare; and, on arriving there, had to his amazement found his mother. With her was Clara, who had already made herself known to Inez, and, at the very time of his arrival, the two sisters were explaining to one another all about their respective past. Clara was not a Sister, after all. She had never taken the vows, and, no sooner had Mrs. Wyverne heard this, than she resolved to effect a reunion between those two who had been so strangely divided, and who still felt such undying love. To do this in the shortest and best way, she concluded to persuade Clara to accompany her to her own lodgings. This Clara did, after a brief explanation to the good "Sisters." On arriving there, Mrs. Wyverne had found her son's letter. She had not been able to leave immediately, but had remained behind, persuading Clara to accompany her to Rome. To this Clara at length consented, and, with her desire to meet her husband, was mingled anxiety about her sister. The sister had been found, but the meeting with the husband had yet to be.

Mrs. Wyverne told Blake every thing, and urged him to prepare Kane for the meeting in whatever way he might think best. Blake, after some consideration, judged, from his knowledge of Kane's character and feelings, that the best way to prepare him would be to tell him the simple truth. This he decided to do; and thus, on seeing Kane, this was the information which he gave, and which put a complete stop for the time to the speculations of the latter about Bessie.

Over that meeting between these two, who had loved so well and suffered so much, it is best to draw a veil. Clara's self-reproaches, about what she considered her cowardice and treachery, were not justified by the opinion of the one who was most concerned; and her fears about Kane's indignation proved unfounded. It was much for Kane to be freed from the remorse which for years had blighted his life; it was far more to receive as rising from the dead one over whose memory he had wept, and over whose supposed grave he had mourned. In the interchange of confidence and the recital of their mutual experiences much had to be explained; and among these explanations was that grave itself; but this was at last accounted for, satisfactorily

enough to their minds, by the peculiar character of Kevin Magrath, who always did his work thoroughly, and who, if he wished the death of Clara to be believed in, would at once find some means to procure a grave which might pass for hers. Kane thus found that he had been mourning and praying over the grave of a stranger, or perhaps over a box of stones, at the very time when the one whom he mourned had over and over again crossed his path—and at the very time, indeed, when she herself stood before him.

No sooner did Mrs. Wyverne hear about Bessie, and Kane's report of the last interview with her, than she determined to see for herself this young girl whose real character still remained so great a puzzle. She therefore went there with Blake. Bessie was mournful, yet amiable, and received her visitors with sad politeness. She questioned Blake closely about his search, and still evinced a confidence in the return of her "dear grandpa." Mrs. Wyverne expressed a wish to see Mrs. Lugrin, whereupon Bessie at once summoned her.

Mrs. Lugrin appeared, showing no change from what she had been at Mordaunt Manor. She entered the room placidly, and looked around, when her eyes rested on Mrs. Wyverne. Perhaps Bessie had not understood Mrs. Wyverne's true name and position; perhaps she had not given the right name to Mrs. Lugrin; at any rate, Mrs. Lugrin was evidently much agitated at the sight of her. She stood for a moment staring, and then sank into a chair.

Mrs. Wyverne was quite self-possessed. She surveyed Mrs. Lugrin placidly, and then said, in a quiet voice:

"I am very sorry to meet you under such painful circumstances."

She would have said more, but Mrs. Lugrin gave her no chance, for, rising suddenly, and without a word, she abruptly quitted the room, while Bessie looked on in evident wonderment. After this Mrs. Wyverne and Blake soon retired.

"It is as I thought," said she to Blake. "This Mrs. Lugrin is Mrs. Kevin Magrath. I remember her perfectly, and she remembers me. Your Bessie is her daughter—Bessie Magrath!"

"I wonder how much she herself has known of all this?"

"That," said Mrs. Wyverne, "is to me a

perfect puzzle. Your account of her makes her seem guilty; but her own face and manner make her seem innocent. I cannot decide, and it will always remain a mystery to me whether she is innocent or guilty. For she may have been brought up in the belief that she was Bernal Mordaunt's daughter, and may have acted throughout in perfect good faith."

Blake said nothing. His own opinion about Bessie was most decided and most hostile; yet so plausible had been Bessie's own vindication of herself that he hardly knew what to say.

Two days after this Gwyn received a note. It was from Bessie, and ran as follows:

"I have been hoping against hope, Gwynnie darling, about poor dear grandpa, but I'm afraid I must give him up. It's awfully sad, so it is, and I'm quite heart-broken, so I am. I cannot bear to stay here any longer, so do not think it strange, dear, if I tell you that I am going away. I am going with dear old Mrs. Lugrin to her home. It is in Ballyshannon, near Limerick. We are poor now, you and I, Gwynnie darling, and dear Kane is the baronet and the owner of Ruthven Towers, where we were so happy; and dear Inez has Mordaunt Manor, where dear papa died. It is all so very, very strange, and so awfully sad, that it seems like a dream. But you, Gwynnie darling, love me still, I know well, and this is the only thing in life that comforts me. You'll have to get your own living, dear, and I will be patient, and wait till you find something to do, and can make a home for your poor Bessie. And I shall always be looking forward to the time when you will come for me, Gwynnie darling, and I will be content and happy wherever you may take me. I feel very sad, dear, and it seems to me that you have not been quite so kind of late as you used to be, but I know you love me, and you have all the love of your poor little girl. Give my love to darling Inez. I should like to see her, but am too sad. Give my love to dear Kane also, and tell him I shall never forget his kindness about poor dear grandpa. You will let me hear from you soon, Gwynnie darling, and come soon to your poor little loving

"BESSIE."

It was a very sad letter. There were also blots on it that seemed like tears. Gwyn was

moved most deeply, and never showed it to any one; yet he did not do as he once would have done—he did not hasten away after the beautiful young bride who had sent him so mournful and so loving an appeal. No; the decision to which he had come in the Catacombs was unalterable, and he prepared with stern intensity of purpose to carry it into execution.

This decision he announced to Kane. It was to go to America, where he proposed to work out his own fortune in any way which circumstances might present. Kane tried to dissuade him, but in vain. Gwyn was not to be moved.

"It's no use," said he. "It's all up between her and me. I've got nothing to live for. Ruthven Towers is yours, and you're the baronet. I'm an outcast now. You don't know all that's taken place between her and me, you know. We shall never meet again; and still I love her as well as ever. I can't help that. Don't try to persuade me. It's no use. As to money, there's enough for me in a little property of mother's that I found out only last year. I'll take that, and it'll be enough for me to grub along with."

In fact, Gwyn showed himself beyond the reach of argument, and Kane could only conclude to yield to him for the present, and hope for better things in the future. So he made Gwyn promise to write him at times to let him know his movements.

Gwyn left Rome on the following day, and went to America.

In a few days the rest of them returned to England.

Sir Kane and Lady Ruthven went to Ruthven Towers.

Basil Wyverne was married to Inez Mordaunt, and lived at Mordaunt Manor. His mother lived with them. He found that Hennigar Wyverne's estate was immense. How much of this had been gained from the Mordaunt property he could never find out; but his marriage with Inez prevented him from feeling any uneasiness on this score. Clara had superior claims to Mordaunt Manor, but to these she, as well as her husband, was utterly indifferent, and insisted on transferring them to Inez. By this arrangement the two sisters were able to be near one another, and their husbands were also able to perpetuate the warm friendship which they had first formed in Paris.

Out of all these events there remained two things which never ceased to be a puzzle to Kane Ruthven.

One of these was the character of Bessie. His last interview with her had produced a profound impression on him, and her gentle manner, her innocent words, and her sweet expression, had revived for a time those sentiments of affectionate admiration which he had conceived toward her at Ruthven Towers. Her own exculpation of herself seemed to him to be more just than the others supposed, and he could not help clinging to the thought that she had been deceived rather than deceiving.

The other puzzle was the disappearance of Kevin Magrath. The most thorough search had revealed no trace of him. To Kane's mind this disappearance was too utter. Had he perished, he thought that some trace of his remains would have been found. He could not help believing that he had recovered from his first panic, and had found some mode of effecting his escape; he reflected that he was possibly as familiar with these passages as he had pretended to be, and that so cool and keen a spirit was not likely to yield permanently to a shock of terror. Consequently Kane held the theory of Bessie's innocence and of Kevin Magrath's escape. Moreover, he believed that they were both living very comfortably together as father and daughter with Mrs. Kevin Magrath, the wife and mother, somewhere in Ireland—in Ballyshannon, or some other place.

This opinion Clara shared with him.

But all the others believed implicitly in the guilt of Bessie and in the death of Kevin Magrath.

For my own part, if I may offer an opinion before retiring from the scene, I would simply remark that it is *an open question*.

THE END.

BOOKS RECENTLY PUBLISHED BY D. APPLETON & CO.

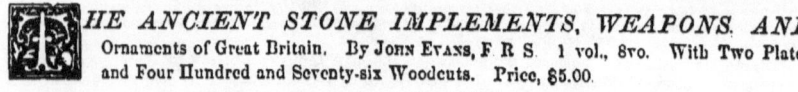

HE ANCIENT STONE IMPLEMENTS, WEAPONS, AND Ornaments of Great Britain. By John Evans, F R S. 1 vol., 8vo. With Two Plates and Four Hundred and Seventy-six Woodcuts. Price, $5.00.

HAND-BOOK OF CHEMICAL TECHNOLOGY. By Rudolf Wagner, Ph. D., Professor of Chemical Technology in the University of Wurtzburg. Translated from the sixth German edition, with extensive Additions, by Wm. Brookes, F. L. S With 336 Illustrations. 1 vol. 8vo. 761 pages. Cloth. Price, $5.00.

THE VEGETABLE WORLD: being a History of Plants, with their Structure and Peculiar Properties. Adapted from the work of Louis Figuier. With a Glossary of Botanical Terms. New and revised edition. With 473 Illustrations. Price, $3.50.

This is one of the series of Popular Books by Louis Figuier, of which "The World before the Deluge" and "The Insect World" have just been published, to be followed by "The Ocean World" and "Reptiles and Birds." They are sold at the low price of $3.50, printed in a compact form, forming, when complete, an Illustrated Library of Popular Science of unequalled cheapness.

BESSIE. A Novel. By Julia Kavanagh, author of "Nathalie," "Adele," "Silvia," "Queen Mab," "Dora," "Madeline," etc 1 vol., 8vo Paper covers. Price, 75 cts.

"There is a quiet power in the writings of this gifted author, which is as far removed from the sensational school as any of the modern novels can be."

MAJOR JONES'S COURTSHIP, detailed, with other Scenes, Incidents, and Adventures, in a Series of Letters by Himself. Revised and enlarged To which are added Thirteen Humorous Sketches. With Illustrations by Cary. 1 vol., 12mo · Cloth

This humorous volume is now reproduced with additions and new illustrations. Over 200,000 copies have been sold since its first issue, and the new generation of readers which have sprung up since will undoubtedly add their favorable testimony to the wit and humor which fill its pages.

LIFE AND LETTERS OF CAPTAIN MARRYAT, R. N., author of "Peter Simple," "Japhet in Search of a Father," etc. By his Daughter, Florence Marryat (Mrs. Ross Church). 2 vols., 12mo Cloth Price. $4.00.

NATURAL PHILOSOPHY: An Elementary Treatise. By Prof. Deschanel, of Paris Translated and edited, with extensive Additions, by J D. Everett, D. C. L., F. R. S., Professor of Natural Philosophy in the Queen's College. Belfast. Part IV Sound and Light. With 187 Engravings Price $2.00.

This work is used as a text-book in the Oxford and Cambridge Universities, and in the chief Colleges and Science Classes in the United Kingdom; while in France it has been adopted by the Minister of Instruction as the text-book for Government Schools.

RADIANT HEAT. A Series of Memoirs published in the "Philosophical Transactions' and "Philosophical Magazine," with Additions. By John Tyndall, LL. D., F. R. S., Professor of Natural Philosophy in the Royal Institution.

THE DOCTOR'S DILEMMA.. A Novel. By Hesba Stretton. 1 vol., 8vo. Paper covers. With Illustrations. Price, 75 cents.

OVARIAN TUMORS: their Pathology, Diagnosis, and Treatment, especially by Ovariotomy. By E. Randolph Peaslee, M. D., LL. D., Professor of Gynæcology in the Medical Department of Dartmouth College; Attending Surgeon of the New York State Woman's Hospital; Consulting Physician to the Strangers' Hospital; Corresponding Fellow of the Obstetrical Society of Berlin, and of the Gynæcological Society of Boston; Honorary Member of the Louisville Obstetrical Society; President of the New York Academy of Medicine, etc., etc. With 56 Illustrations on Wood. 1 vol., 8vo. 551 pages

FORMS OF WATER, in Clouds, Rain, Rivers, Ice, and Glaciers. By Prof. John Tyndall, LL. D.. F I. S. 1 vol. Cloth Price, $1.50.

www.ingramcontent.com/pod-product-compliance
Lightning Source LLC
Chambersburg PA
CBHW030633030726
47497CB00006B/1767